The Wizardess

Jenny Ealey

Eskuzor Publishing

Eskuzor Publishing

1 Monash St,
Melton South,
Victoria, Australia 3338

www.jennyealey.com

Published by Eskuzor Publishing 2016

ISBN 978-0-9876017-7-3

Printed and bound by Ingram Sparks

Acknowledgements
I would like to thank my sister Wendy Ealey who
produced the cover design and interior typesetting, and
Burnham Arlidge who painted the eagle flying over the
plains on the cover.
I would also like to thank and remember my mother
and grammarian extraordinaire, Paddy Mary Stentiford
(now deceased) who, from the other side of the world,
painstakingly edited my novels with me through all
their myriad drafts.

DEDICATION

I would like to dedicate this book to those who fear their partners and are striving to protect themselves and their children.

THE SORCERER'S OATH SERIES

Bronze Magic
Wizard's Curse
The Lost Forest
The Wizardess

West Sea
Encampment
Infestation Damage
Forestals
Dark Beech Forest
GREAT WEST R
Valley of the
Dry Mile
Lord Tolmad's Estate
Grasslands
Mountain Folk
Night in Trees
Western Forest
Hails Cliffs
Top of Range
Black Lion Cave
Lake
Montraya Castle
Falling Rain's Swamp

Wood Nearing
Wooding Deep
Tormadell Castle
Wolves Burial
First Firesite
Borovan's Ride
Ancient Elm's Firesite
Eagle Cliffs
GREAT WEST ROAD
Second Firesite
N
Not to scale

Characters

Sorcerers

Tamadil Royal Family:
King Markazon (deceased)
Queen, Markazon's wife
King Kosar, eldest son of King Markazon
Prince Jarand, second son of King Markazon
Prince Tarkyn, third son of King Markazon

Courtiers:
Danton Patronell, Lord of Sachmore, (aka Dale) Tarkyn's friend from childhood
Andoran and Sargon, friends of Tarkyn at court.
Stormaway Treemaster, wizard for Prince Tarkyn and King Markazon
Journeyman Cloudmaker, Prince Jarand's wizard

Thieving Family:
Old Ma
Gillis, Old Ma's son
Tomas, Old Ma's son
Morayne, daughter of Tomas
Charkon, son of Tomas

Grasslands:
Tolward, Lord of Middle Grasslands
Juniper, his wife
Eidelweiss, his daughter
Winguard, his son
Karlian, his healer

Trappers:
String and Bean
Pipeless, wizard and trapper (deceased)
Horse and Cart

Harkell's family:
Captain Harkell (aka Hill)
Kayama, Harkell's wife
Sorrell, Harkell's son
Marema, Harkell's daughter
Sorath, Harkell's father
Thraya, Harkell's mother
Drakell, Harkell's brother
Elena, Drakell's wife
Rena, Drakell's wife's sister

Other sorcerers:
Saker and Biggins, two soldiers from Harkell's company
Sergeant Torrigan
Colonel Argyle, Kosar's army
Captain Harman, Kosar's army
Farow, Kosar's manservant
Colonel Charford, Jarand's army
Captain Guerion, Jarand's army
Davorad, Lord of Stansbeck, financier of Jarand's encampment
Greyskies Swampwatcher, independent wizard
Orolan, chief of bandits

People of Lost Forest:
Singing Bird, woodfolk
Borovar, sorcerer
Stillwaters Pathfinder (Navira), wizardess
Caroman, wizard

WOODFOLK

Wanderers:
Waterstone
Sparrow, Waterstone's daughter
Autumn Leaves
Thunder Storm
Creaking Bough, Thunder Storm's wife
Rain on Water, Thunder Storm's son
Rustling Leaves
Grass Wind
Lapping Water
Summer Rain, healer
Falling Rain, Summer Rain's exiled
    brother
Golden Toad
Rushwind
Ibis Wings
Autumn Storm, Autumn Leaves and
    Thunder Storm's grandfather
Twig Snap
Leaf Fall

Forestals:
Raging water
Falling Branch, his son
Sun Shower, Falling Branch's wife
Rainstorm, Falling Branch's son

Gatherers:
Ancient Oak
Tree Wind
North Wind
Running feet

Mountainfolk:
Ancient Elm
Blizzard
Cavern
Dripping Rock
Melting Snow
Hail
Midnight, Hail's son, Tarkyn's ward

Wood folk near Tormadell:
Dry Berry
Leaf Fall
Twig Snap

The story so far...

BOOK ONE: BRONZE MAGIC

In Eskuzor, land of sorcerers, nineteen year old Prince Tarkyn is brought up on unjust charges by his twin brothers, the king and Prince Jarand. He throws up a magical shield and escapes, inadvertently leaving a trail of death and destruction. A family of thieves tries to rob him but then help him to flee the city of Tormadell.

After days on the run, Tarkyn wanders into the woodlands in the company of an old wizard, Stormaway Treemaster, only to find himself unable to leave. Woodfolk attack him and he retaliates with threatening displays of magic. But Tarkyn is then horrified to discover that he is the unwelcome, bitterly resented liege lord to these elusive people who fear sorcerers and whose oath to him has been spellbound to the welfare of their forest.

Before the woodfolk can take adequate measures to protect him, bounty hunters capture Tarkyn. In the chaos of his escape, the prince is severely injured. While Tarkyn lies unconscious, Stormaway, disguised as the prince, leads the bounty hunters far from the forest.

For more than a week, the prince lies unconscious, while one woodman, Waterstone, stays by his side talking quietly to him and bringing him back to an awareness of his surroundings. As he recovers, Tarkyn, raw from his brothers' betrayal and wary of the woodfolk's resentment, gradually develops an uneasy friendship with Waterstone.

Woodfolk can hold conversations and send images mentally to each other, an ability not shared by sorcerers and wizards. Gradually, Tarkyn discovers that he can receive and send images and feelings, but not words. In fact, sometimes Tarkyn's strong feelings transmit to other people without his knowledge or control.

When a hunting party of the king and Prince Jarand enters the woods, Tarkyn's reaction to seeing his brothers overwhelms Waterstone's daughter, Sparrow, and she blacks out. Waterstone is furious, hurling threats at the prince and trying to attack him. His behaviour breaches the oath, causing an area of forest to be seriously damaged before Tarkyn curtails the destruction by giving Waterstone permission to attack him.

Tarkyn discovers that Summer Rain's brother, Falling Rain, was exiled twelve years ago for revealing the woodfolks' presence to the king. Some woodfolk wish him to return. Some don't. Struggling with the politics surrounding the prince and the potential damage his own anger could cause, Waterstone almost abandons his friendship with Tarkyn

Tarkyn offers to help repair the forest, by holding up branches while woodfolk bind them, amazing Waterstone that sorcery has more than martial uses. Stormaway returns and rails at the prince for not behaving in a manner due to his station, until Tarkyn treats him to a dose of royal hauteur. Later that evening, Stormaway informs the prince that the bounty hunters who had captured him were Andoran and Sargon, Tarkyn's erstwhile friends. As Tarkyn wanders down near the river thinking about this further betrayal, an attacking wolf is stopped by Waterstone's arrow. Then, from a viewpoint above him in the trees, Tarkyn sees another wolf approaching behind the woodman. Tarkyn shouts a warning and uses shafts of magic to kill the wolf.

Because Tarkyn's ability to trust has been damaged by betrayal, Waterstone allows Tarkyn free access to his memories to establish his own trustworthiness. However, Tarkyn delves too deep and when Waterstone has fled, finds himself confronted by Autumn Leaves who intervenes angrily on his friend's behalf.

When Stormaway shows Tarkyn a little experiment that blows up, the woodfolk surround Tarkyn, arrows drawn to protect him, even though clearly resentful. Stormaway lets slip that seven years before, he had used mind power on Falling Rain when the woodman was held captive by the king. This knowledge expiates Falling Rain's guilt and revokes his exile. As reparation for the wrong done by sorcerers, Tarkyn resolves to trek across the mountains to find Falling Rain and bring him back to the fold.

Tarkyn discovers that, unlike the woodfolk, he can also share images and emotions with birds and animals, and uses this discovery as a reason to approach Waterstone and repair the rift between them. As he talks with Waterstone and Autumn Leaves, it becomes increasingly obvious to Tarkyn that the egalitarian woodfolk have a very different concept of service from him and that he must work out how much to modify his expectations.

While he is mulling this over, an eagle shares with him its view over the forest of an impending, large-scale wolf attack. Tarkyn warns the woodfolk and allows them the use of his powers.

Soon after the wolf attack has been averted, Stormaway notices green shoots appearing on Tarkyn's walking staff and upon investigation, finds that the trees Tarkyn helped to repair have recovered unnaturally fast. Much to his embarrassment, Tarkyn learns that his newly discovered powers of healing and communing with animals define him as a legend in the woodfolk lore; the guardian of the forest, who appears among the woodfolk to aid them in times of great strife.

Celebrations of the advent of the Forest Guardian go late into the night.

The next morning, Tarkyn and the woodfolk come back to the reality of considering where the source of the danger might be. The survival of the woodfolk depends on their ability to stay hidden. They realise that a hunting party will be coming to find the wolves they killed but instead, will find dismembered, cleaned wolf carcases that will betray the woodfolk's existence.

As they prepare to face this threat, Waterstone's resentment of the oath surges up, leading to a fight between Tarkyn and himself. As a result, one of Tarkyn's broken ribs punctures his lung and only his healing powers as Guardian of the Forest, supplemented by the life force of the woodfolk, save him. Through this experience, Tarkyn discovers that he can also draw on the power of the forest itself through the trees to heal himself.

Having helped the woodfolk avoid the hunting party, Tarkyn becomes aware that his group of woodfolk has been concealing the existence of woodfolk who had not sworn the oath. He feels betrayed especially by Waterstone and using an owl as a guide, leaves them to find his way to a community of oathless woodfolk.

He offers this community of woodfolk, the forestals, the opportunity to kill him to release their kin from the oath and to ensure that oathbound woodfolk do not have to fight oathless woodfolk to protect him. Despite their initial hostility, the forestals decide it would be dishonourable to help their kin betray their oath, so they cannot kill the prince. During this confrontation, Tarkyn finds a feisty ally in a rebellious young woodman, Rainstorm.

Autumn Leaves trudges into the forestal's firesite and with Rainstorm's help, faces a resistant Tarkyn. When Autumn Leaves explains that all woodfolk are sworn to conceal their kin, Tarkyn concedes the need for their duplicity, but is left feeling separate from them.

Unwittingly, Tarkyn's resigned acceptance of his isolation rolls around the woodfolk camp, causing the forestals to reconsider their attitude to him. During the following week, woodfolk gather from all parts of the forest to discuss the unknown threat. In recognition of his demonstrated commitment to them, the woodfolk decide to induct Tarkyn as a member of the woodfolk nation in a ceremony during which, by sharing blood with him through a long cut on his arm, Tarkyn becomes Waterstone's blood brother and by association, Ancient Oak's brother and Sparrow's uncle.

During the ensuing celebrations, Stormaway arrives among the oathless woodfolk and Tarkyn rebukes him when he expresses his displeasure at the risks Tarkyn has taken. Lapping Water is surprisingly accepting when she catches Tarkyn retying the bandage on his arm, having rubbed dirt into the cut to make sure he bears a scar. They return to the firesite to find that Tarkyn's unreserved acceptance by the woodfolk is short lived. As they discuss ways to meet the impending threat, including the woodfolk ability to 'flick' into hiding, resentment against the prince resurges and the opinions of the group who stayed with him, the 'home guard,' are not respected. When Tarkyn absents himself from the critical crowd, Ancient Oak follows him and gets to know him and a squirrel better in an old oak. Elsewhere, Waterstone is attacked by two mountain folk who are disgusted that he has befriended a sorcerer. Eventually, Tarkyn decides to assert his authority temporarily, but unequivocally, in the interests of protecting the woodfolk in the face of the impending threat, reasoning that he intends to leave the next day anyway so it won't matter if he upsets a few people.

However, when morning breaks, an enormous magic-driven storm threatens to cause widespread flooding and to force the woodfolk onto open higher ground. Tarkyn harnesses the power of the forest to channel magic into Stormaway who orchestrates the dissipation of the storm. When his sodden bandage is replaced by Summer Rain, Tarkyn finds that his arm has healed with a long bright green scar. However his suspicions are aroused when Waterstone refuses to have his bandage changed and he discovers that Waterstone, too, has rubbed dirt in his cut to ensure he has a souvenir of their new relationship.

In the wake of Tarkyn's suggestion of a stock take of people's whereabouts, woodfolk establish that three of their kin are missing and are possibly being held by sorcerers. A power play amongst rival factions leads to decisions being made more on the basis of whether they support Tarkyn rather than on the issues themselves. Tarkyn confronts the worst of the factions and neutralises their antagonism.

Once the course of action had been decided, Tarkyn links his mind with a field mouse to reconnoitre the sorcerer's encampment. The woodfolk are gravely shaken when he discovers that the woodfolk are indeed being held at the encampment and at least some people from outside the forest know of their existence.

With the aid of an eagle owl, Tarkyn spots a shadowy figure skulking in the nearby woods. The woodfolk capture the intruder, who turns out to be Danton, an elite palace guard and Tarkyn's childhood friend. But having been betrayed before, the prince is wary of trusting him. Only after testing Danton's loyalty to the prince, do the woodfolk allow him to stay in the woods with them. But Danton brings the expectations of the Royal Court with him, leading to disputes between several woodfolk and himself, and making Tarkyn re-evaluate his relationships with the woodfolk.

When the prince stops a fight between Danton and Rainstorm, the young woodman turns his attack on Tarkyn. The wind thrashing through the trees makes Tarkyn realise that Rainstorm and the oathless woodfolk have somehow become subject to the sorcerer's oath. Despite their friendship with the prince, Rainstorm and Waterstone are horrified when they discover that the oath has spread and it is decided to keep it from the others until after the rescue of the imprisoned woodfolk.

The woodfolk all insist that Tarkyn should not take part in the rescue because they must ensure they protect him. Because Tarkyn has also vowed to protect the forest, he cannot risk them refusing his orders and destroying the forest. So he does not insist on going with them but reluctantly takes part from a distance.

As woodfolk flit through the trees reconnoitring the encampment Tarkyn, from a distance, playfully sends them helpful but unnerving images, which causes Tree Wind to concede finally that the woodfolk will be all right under his dominion.

Danton and Stormaway infiltrate the sorcerers' camp, in preparation for the woodfolk mounting a rescue. They run into Sargon and Andoran, forcing Danton to assume the appearance of disloyalty to Tarkyn to conceal his role in the rescue plot. Once Stormaway is reassured that Danton is merely playing a role, the wizard and Danton concoct a series of unpleasant revenges on Sargon and Andoran, involving hallucinogens, itching powders and slow working non-lethal poisons.

Meanwhile Tarkyn discovers that Waterstone's objections to using horses for the impending raid stems from his fear of them. In the ensuing conversation, Waterstone becomes aware that Tarkyn is distressed by Danton's possible betrayal and the accumulation of people's horrified reactions to the oath. He reassures Tarkyn of his enduring commitment to him, as both friend and brother, and Rainstorm bravely goes swimming in an icy creek with the prince to cheer him up.

Once the campsite has settled for the night, the woodfolk use their deadly hunting skills to knock out the boundary guards and throw the chained woodfolk onto horses, which are being remotely guided by Tarkyn. As the horses carry them safely into the woods, a strong, fear-filled image that makes Tarkyn realise that Autumn Leaves has been captured by Andoran and Sargon. Tarkyn translocates into the sorcerers' encampment and rescues him. On his return, angry woodfolk confront him for putting himself at risk but he asserts that he will no longer allow them to dictate to him.

Danton's association with Andoran and Sargon causes Tarkyn and the woodfolk to lose faith in him and take him captive. Danton refuses to defend himself and insists they trust him. When Tarkyn relents, Danton then avers that Tarkyn is the only true hope for the future of Eskuzor, a sentiment that Stormaway reinforces saying:

"Your destiny is written in the stars and lives deep within the trees of the forest. It has been clear from the day of your birth for all to see who have knowledge of such things. Your father and I always knew. That's why you had to be protected. You are not only the guardian of the forest. You are the one true hope for the future."

BOOK 2: WIZARD'S CURSE

In the face of Stormaway's avowal, Tarkyn declares he has no wish to be king; to drag Eskuzor into civil war. Stormaway tells him that there are already rumours of civil war brewing between his brothers and that the encampment is a recruiting station for vigilantes wishing to fight the lawlessness created by King Kosar's incompetent rule, funded by Lord Davorad, one of Jarand's cronies.

To the woodfolks' relief, only a few sorcerers have seen the captured woodfolk but one of them is Stormaway's erstwhile apprentice, Journeyman Cloudmaker, now Prince Jarand's wizard. Woodfolk want Tarkyn to protect them against whoever is hunting them; Danton and Stormaway want him to protect sorcerers against his brothers. Tarkyn decides to prioritise finding Falling Rain and protecting the woodfolk before addressing the wider issues of the sorcerers.

Using his powers as forest guardian, Tarkyn tries to heal the rescued woodfolk's mindtalking ability, an effort that goes disastrously wrong; destroying a swathe of forest and nearly killing him before he uses rage-driven power to burn out the infection. Tarkyn repels a squadron of soldiers by sending mental images of attack to their horses and subjugating the leader of the wolf pack that runs with them. But his use of power threatens to distance him from his woodfolk companions and Waterstone accuses him of breaking the wolf's spirit.

Tarkyn wakes despondent about the damage to the forest and at the reactions of the woodfolk to his magic. However, the woodfolk recognise the extreme efforts he made to save the forest and celebrate with him. He discovers Tree Wind's ongoing antagonism has stemmed from the fact that she had intended to wed Falling Rain who was exiled as a result of King Markazon discovering the existence of woodfolk. Waterstone takes issue with Danton over the fact that Danton used to report Tarkyn's actions to the king, angering him so much that Danton hits him. Sorcerer protocol demands that Tarkyn preside over a trial for Danton attacking Waterstone, now a member of the royal family. Waterstone is horrified. Tarkyn discovers he is sovereign lord of the forests, according to Stormaway, and as such, is able to commute the usual death penalty for such a crime to a lesser punishment.

As the woodfolk prepare to cross the Great West Road, a family travelling along the road is attacked by brigands. Tarkyn uses his magic to burn the arrows and place a shield around the family to protect them. The family is fearful of him at first, since he has been branded a rogue sorcerer by his brother. At Tarkyn's request, they tie up the brigands and continue on their way as soldiers crest the rise and Tarkyn disappears back into the forest. The soldiers recognise the brigands as fellow soldiers. Stormaway breaks cover and acts as witness that Tarkyn protected the family. He then challenges the King's version of events at the tournament asking how Tarkyn could have won a tournament he was supposed to have destroyed.

Tarkyn realises that Falling Branch is the only one among them who is unknowingly affected by the spread of the sorcerous oath. He sees him privately to tell him, endures his reaction and discovers he is Rainstorm's father. Falling Branch goes off to talk to his woodfolk friends while sending Tarkyn off to talk to Danton. Tarkyn clarifies his expectations of Danton, as a sorcerer living among woodfolk.

When Tarkyn explains the spread of the oath and the concept of mutual obligations to the rest of his home guard, they offer to support him when they encounter the mountainfolk.

They travel across the open grasslands by night, with Tarkyn using his mind link to quieten the guard dogs. When two riders thunder through the night to arrive in haste at a homestead, Danton investigates and sees two young sorcerers lying mortally wounded, surrounded by parents and farm hands. Against opposition from the woodfolk, he enlists Tarkyn's assistance. Tarkyn and he enter the sorcerers' house and Tarkyn heals the children amidst a mix of suspicion, because he has been declared a rogue sorcerer, and obeisance, because he is a prince. Lord Tolward tells Tarkyn that lawlessness is rife, that bloodhounds are now being recruited at the encampment and there is talk of a secret army. Tarkyn promises to return to them in the spring and leaves, feeling even more torn between woodfolk and sorcerers.

The mountainfolk appear friendly but drug Tarkyn's companions before tying Tarkyn's hands behind him. In order to check whether the mountainfolk are subject to the sorcerous oath, two thugs hit Tarkyn but continue to belt him once they can see their blows are not causinh damage to the forest, despite Dry Berry's efforts to stop them. Tarkyn sends out a mental scream for help to which firstly a mountain eagle, then other birds of prey respond by fighting off the thugs and keeping the mountainfolk at bay until his home guard recovers. He then orders Danton to kill the two assailants. Remorseful, the mountainfolk offer to take the oath, but Tarkyn says he does not want them as liegefolk and would not entrust the forest's welfare to their honour. With help from Autumn Leaves and Rainstorm, Tarkyn bathes in an icy stream to clean his bloodied hair and talks to the woodfolk about his decision to execute the thugs.

Danton, Summer Rain and Rainstorm are then taken hostage by the mountainfolk and Tarkyn must use shields and eagles to protect his home guard and coerce the mountainfolk into returning his friends. Eventually, a compromise is reached and the mountain folk swear allegiance to Tarkyn without any sorcerous sting to the oath. However, Tarkyn still does not trust them and is unable to sleep. He gets up in the middle of the night only to find Waterstone and Autumn Leaves keeping watch over him. In the morning Rainstorm tries to teach Danton how to be less lethal with his magic and Thunder Storm demonstrates his mastery with a slingshot by making a line of different sized rocks gently sway. Eventually Waterstone helps Tarkyn deal with the intrusive images of the attack so that he can concentrate on healing himself.

Tarkyn joins the target practice and makes the rocks sway by hitting the stump underneath them. The mountainfolk take Tarkyn and a few friends for a tour of their cellars. In the caves, they find a little neglected boy who is despised by the mountainfolk. The Mountainman, Blizzard, holds the boy down by putting his foot on his chest and does not release him at Tarkyn's request. Tarkyn bellows at Blizzard who explains that he thought he was supposed to protect the prince. Tarkyn takes the tatty little boy, Midnight, under his wing and Midnight swears allegiance to him. Midnight is deaf and mute but can exchange images and emotions only with Tarkyn. Midnight is mistrusting of people, continually tests Tarkyn's commitment and is ready to run at the slightest provocation.

Word comes through that bloodhounds are tracking Tarkyn from the encampment and his tracks will lead them to Lord Tolward's house and then to the mountainfolk camp. After various suggestions and tensions, Tarkyn agrees to contact the lead wolf only if Waterstone is linked in to check that he doesn't damage the wolf's spirit.

The woodfolk cover their tracks, travel south and spend the night high in trees. Tarkyn has trouble sleeping until Waterstone ties him to the trunk. Midnight realises he has left a bracelet he made for Tarkyn in the clearing and rushes back to find it, with the hunting party less than an hour away. Tarkyn and Danton translocate to the clearing, find Midnight and ensconce him high in a tree before outfacing the hunting party using Tarkyn's ability to fire through his own shield as he clings to Danton's back in mid-air. Journeyman Cloudmaker, the hunting party's leader, realizes that Tarkyn is not a rogue sorcerer and says "This changes everything," but does not explain why. Midnight is so upset that he refuses to come out of the tree. So Tarkyn levitates to grab Midnight from behind and carry him safely to the ground.

Tarkyn, Danton and a few woodfolk find shelter from a storm in a shallow cave. They decide to operate on Autumn Leaves' injured nose but when Thunder Storm uses his slingshot to knock him out, Midnight attacks him, thinking he is trying to hurt Autumn Leaves. When Midnight realises his mistake, he cowers into the corner clearly waiting to be beaten. Thunder Storm reassures him while Summer Rain and Tarkyn continue the operation on Autumn Leaves' nose. They debate whether there might be some sort of evil loose among the mountainfolk for someone to have mistreated Midnight so badly.

The woodfolk flick into hiding, instructing Tarkyn and Danton to raise their shields as two scruffy old trappers enter the cave. String and Bean are laconic, clever and love guessing games. Because Tarkyn says firesite and is dressed in woodfolk garb, they know that Tarkyn knows about woodfolk. So they eventually admit that they do too. Three woodfolk return to speak to them. When Midnight returns with some others, he does a double take and greets the trappers effusively. Bean tells them that Midnight's mother Hail was caught in a landslide eight years ago and Pipeless, a wizard, rescued her. He fell in love with her but, frustrated by her not returning his affection, raped her. When String and Bean rescued her, she threw a knife at Pipeless, fatally wounding him. As the wizard died, he muttered an incantation that Bean carefully remembered. Hail always hated Midnight and was frustrated because he couldn't hear. Since she wouldn't allow String and Bean to adopt him, they talked her into giving Midnight to the mountainfolk but they too neglected him. String and Bean were the only people he ever saw who were kind to him.

After a mental debate with all other woodfolk, a faction wants to kill Midnight saying he is an abomination. Tarkyn says they are under oath and must protect Midnight. The woodfolk then agree to allow the trappers to live, as long as they reside with them for six months as surety.

Stormaway returns and explains that his care for Tarkyn comes before his care for Eskuzor. Meanwhile Waterstone and Danton lead a group of woodfolk in tracking down two members of the hunting party who are sneaking through the woods looking for Tarkyn. When they are captured, Tarkyn is not pleased that he was not informed of the threat earlier. He sends Journeyman's sorcerers on their two day journey back to the encampment on foot, with their hands tied behind them, but exacts no other punishment.

Midnight is missing. Stormaway says that Pipeless' last words are a curse: *Midnight will breed resentment in his mother's people and this resentment will slowly corrupt them all.* He leaves to consult his books, admonishing them not to interfere without his direction. Tarkyn is worried that Midnight's death may be needed to release the curse. A mental cry for help is received from Blizzard. When they arrive, they find an unconscious Midnight tied to a sapling with half the mountainfolk trying to attack him and the other half trying to prevent them from attacking. Hail arrives, then verbally and mentally abuses the crowd. A brawl breaks out but Tarkyn merely stands watching them with arms crossed. Gradually they settle, stand straighter and look towards Tarkyn who has been sending waves of faith in their integrity. Tarkyn immobilises Hail who blocks his way with knives. He uses his power to heal Midnight, who vomits all over him as he regains consciousness. Stormaway says if Tarkyn had rescued Midnight, it would have further undermined the mountainfolk's belief in their integrity but now they are temporarily better able to fight the curse. He adds that if Midnight had died, the curse would have been irreversible and eventually all woodfolk would become corrupted by the curse. The curse can only be lifted in the place it was created by the curser or his direct descendant, Midnight.

High on the mountain, Hail and all her kin, the mountainfolk and woodfolk trappers, gather to have the curse lifted. Tarkyn must ask Midnight, with no compulsion, to help the mountainfolk who have reviled and maltreated him all his life. Midnight misunderstands and thinks that Tarkyn has faith in the mountainfolk and therefore not in him. He runs off and it takes the combined efforts of Tarkyn and Ancient Oak to resettle him. Midnight refuses to help but when, true to his word, Tarkyn remains his friend, he changes his mind and agrees to assist.

Stormaway realises that although Midnight can lift the curse from the mountainfolk, he first must be free of the curse. However, he cannot lift the curse from himself. They need Pipeless who is dead, to do that. Stormaway tells them that a forest guardian once drew the parts of a dead person back into one place and resurrected that person but many onlookers were killed. Tarkyn is both horrified and fearful at the prospect but agrees to try, provided there are precautions.

With everyone else safely within Stormaway and Danton's shields, Tarkyn reaches his power deep into the forest and draws together the remains of Pipeless. He thrusts his hands before him and Pipeless, ten feet tall because he is not fully concentrated into one spot, towers above him and still as angry as he was at the moment of his death, sends forth a destructive power ray. Tarkyn just manages to raise his shield in time then demands that Pipeless acknowledge his authority as prince. Pipeless, bewildered by the sudden change in his circumstances, calms down and rues having created the curse. He meets Midnight, his son, and raises the curse from him. Then Midnight sends forth all his memories of his treatment by the mountainfolk and, as a cloud of Pipeless's blue magic swirls over the mountainfolk, the warped memories are challenged and dispelled. Just before he dissipates back into the earth, Pipeless says that it was too soon for Hail and him. Then, glancing at Lapping Water, the nearest woodwoman, he suggests that Tarkyn may do better in the future.

A wild wind swirls up the valley and the earth reverberates as the Mountainfolk's oath is tied to the welfare of the forest. Tarkyn waits tensely for their reaction but their gratitude overrides any resentment.

Next morning, Midnight emerges to find an array of special foods, especially laid out for him by the mountainfolk, and each of them pats or touches him to welcome him back into the fold. He then plays with the other children using his magical shield. Sparrow discovers that now the curse is no longer isolating him, he can use mind images, although still no words, to communicate with her.

Ancient Oak talks to Tarkyn while Rainstorm talks to Lapping Water, as part of an ongoing plan to get Lapping Water and Tarkyn together. They also remonstrate with Tarkyn about being too controlling when Waterstone and Danton had overseen the hunt for Journeyman's sorcerers.

Meanwhile Danton tells the woodfolk that he had served as Tarkyn's whipping boy from the age of eight and that Tarkyn, as a six year old, had become distraught whenever Danton was punished, forcing members of the Royal Family to be summoned to override him. Eventually, on an occasion that King Markazon had been summoned, Tarkyn threw up his shield and cut his arm until the king ordered the flogging stopped, earning Danton's lifelong devotion.

When Tarkyn joins the others, he has to apologize all over again and walks off, annoyed. Because he is still very tired, he stumbles over a small cliff and knocks himself out. He follows a silver fox who leads him down the mountain to a group of sorcerers who are escaping from Jarand's press gangs. To Tarkyn's surprise they are honoured, rather than frightened, to meet him and he discovers that Stormaway's machinations have turned public opinion in Tarkyn's favour. However, Tarkyn makes it clear that he does not wish to become king.

With the help of a crow, his woodfolk find him. Tarkyn writes a letter of introduction for Trey and his family to go to Lord Tolward before he leaves them. A celebration for his efforts with Pipeless awaits Tarkyn on his return.

Waterstone asks Tarkyn why he doubted Danton's loyalty after having saved him from being a whipping boy when he was little. Tarkyn can't see why Danton should be grateful for facing only consequences of his own actions like everyone else. He adds that when they were older, their first loyalty was to the king. So when the king turned on Tarkyn, he couldn't assume where Danton's loyalties lay. Remembering how much Danton loved the glitter of court, he revokes his requirement that Danton wear woodfolk garb. Danton is moved by his acknowledgement but does not revert to his own clothes

At the end of the evening, Midnight comes to sit on Tarkyn's lap, sad that his mother has still avoided him even after the lifting of the curse. He tries to get away to lick his wounds in private but Tarkyn holds him close even while he thrashes about, kicking and punching, in his distress. When he has settled, Tarkyn sends out a query about Hail's whereabouts. Just as he is discussing it with woodfolk trappers, he receives a strong feeling of desperation and determination; Hail is at the edge of a nearby cliff about to throw herself off. Tarkyn sends her a command to wait before running with several others to try to stop her.

As they come into sight, she lets herself drop off the cliff but Tarkyn sends out a shaft of magic and pulls her back onto safe ground. Between them, they talk Hail into living with how she had treated Midnight under the curse.

Next day, as they continue their journey across the mountain, Waterstone is angry, thinking that Tarkyn risked the woodfolk and forests by commanding Hail when she was so emotionally unstable. Tarkyn reminds Waterstone that he refused one of Tarkyn's commands with a minimal consequence of wind through the trees. However, Tarkyn points out that nearby trees are turning mouldy because everyone has been doubting Tarkyn's competence behind his back.

Realizing that Stormaway lied when he said that he would refuse a direct order to defuse the oath, Tarkyn quietly commands the wizard to retract the sorcery in the oath. Stormaway bows and obeys. He had promised Markazon to maintain the sorcery in the oath but had failed to mention that this was only until directly ordered to release it by Tarkyn.

The woodfolk are so relieved their forest is now safe, many are in tears. Ancient Oak pulls Tarkyn into the family celebratory hug and reconciles him with Waterstone. Tarkyn remonstrates with woodfolk about talking about dissatisfaction behind his back instead of to his face. They tell him, not unkindly, that he is irritable, autocratic and intimidating so that they hesitate to bring issues up with him. Hail stands up for him and is thankful that he is so interfering.

Looking out over the plains to the distant walled city of Montraya, Jarand's seat, Danton betrays his disdain after he has to explain to Rainstorm what a ball is. Danton is surprised Rainstorm isn't offended but the woodman says that disdain and amusement are both ways of reacting to seeing another person's culture through their own values, which makes Danton realise that he has underestimated Rainstorm.

As they descend the mountain, snow starts to fall. String and Bean lead Tarkyn's home guard, which is double the size it was at the beginning, to a cave on the lower plateau. The trappers express concern that a mountain lion has been in the cave recently.

Suddenly a deep throated roar and two streaks of gold resolve themselves into a huge mountain lion leaping at the children playing in the back of the cave. Midnight throws his dark green shield over the children and himself and backs away from the lion until Tarkyn places his shield over the lion. While the other children run crying to their parents, Midnight walks quietly over to Tarkyn who realizes the little boy is shaking with fright.

Tarkyn uses his forest guardian powers to create a standoff with the mountain lion but rather than subjugating it, he uses images of wolves to show that his woodfolk are lethal to mountain lions in a pack, just as wolves are.

They discuss how to locate and talk to Falling Rain, knowing that Falling Rain will not reveal himself to any sorcerers because of the woodfolk's bond of secrecy and won't reveal himself to any of woodfolk because he has been exiled. Ancient Oak and Rainstorm have manoeuvred Tarkyn and Lapping Water to sit next to each other but Tarkyn and Lapping Water are both assiduously trying to act casually.

The home guard works out that Falling Rain will have to be in an area that is inhospitable to sorcerers. String and Bean think of the swamp. With the search area specific, Running Feet guides Tarkyn until he connects with an egret to look for Falling Rain. At first the bird is protective of Falling Rain but eventually takes Tarkyn on a mind journey to Falling Rain's hideout halfway up a tree in the middle of the swamp.

The woodfolk travel the rest of the way down the mountain and set up camp on the banks of the lake, less than a mile from Falling Rain's hideout. Summer Rain climbs onto Stormaway's back, Tree Wind onto Danton's and Waterstone onto Tarkyn's. They levitate their way through the swamp. As a warning, an egret flies straight at Tarkyn's head, rising just high enough to miss him, at the last minute.

As they come into Falling Rain's view, Tarkyn uses his *Shturrum* spell to immobilize the exiled woodman before dropping Waterstone off next to him and then retreating to sit among the egrets in a nearby tree. Once Summer Rain and Running Feet have been dropped off too, Tarkyn replaces the *Shturrum* spell with his shield, which prevents Falling Rain from flicking into hiding. Once Falling Rain is reconciled to them, the four woodfolk head off through the trees to explore Falling Rain's domain.

The sorcerers are left behind and eddies of discontent and the odd ripple of anger whirl through these flooded forests, signalling that Tarkyn is offended at not being introduced. The woodfolk return and once they have repaired their omission, Tarkyn unbends and feeds Falling Rain's pet egret mentally asking her to accompany Falling Rain when they leave.

Falling Rain is shocked by the changes of twelve years. In a confrontation with Stormaway, it becomes clear that other sorcerers knew of Falling Rain's presence when he was held captive by King Markazon. Falling Rain only agrees to share his memories with Tarkyn so that he can identify these other sorcerers, on the condition that Tarkyn share painful memories with him. Amid protests from his woodfolk, Tarkyn agrees.

Falling Rain and Tarkyn engage in a furious mind duel, during which Falling Rain realizes that Tarkyn is not like his father. Tarkyn shows Falling Rain the scene after young Tarkyn stood up to his father to stop Danton being flogged: Markazon hugs Tarkyn as he cries himself out, then says, "You are the best of us but you will suffer for it. And in the end, you must be the one to bring hope to our nation and save us from ourselves."

To everyone's amazement, they return as friends. The woodfolk are horrified to learn that it was Kosar, Jarand and Journeyman who had discovered Falling Rain's existence, and thus the existence of woodfolk and the oath. Having experienced Tarkyn's memories, Falling Rain tells them that Tarkyn will not be able to stand by and watch sorcerers suffer under Kosar's reign. The woodfolk agree that he has earned their support to help sorcerers.

Book 3: The Lost Forest

Greyskies Swampwatcher, a little wizard living near the swamp, is brought in to report a strange sight of people floating through the swamp to Prince Jarand who then accompanies a search party of eighty men, led by Captain Harkell, to find them hoping that one of them is Tarkyn.

Alerted by Falling Rain's egret, Tarkyn's home guard immobilises the search party and Tarkyn invites Jarand to a clearing to talk with him alone. Since he knows of woodfolk, Tarkyn's woodfolk family and Rainstorm appear before him. Tarkyn's, Sparrow's and Rainstorm's behaviour outrages Jarand and he decides that woodfolk are unimpressive and would not make the secret army he was hoping to use them as. Tarkyn tells Jarand that his vigilante recruitment drives are making him unpopular.

Once Jarand has left the forest with his troop, he orders Captain Harkell to be brutally flogged by his two strongest, most loyal men. Then the company ride back to Tormadell, leaving Captain Harkell hanging from a tree by his hands.

When Tarkyn feels the captain's anguish from within the forest, Rainstorm braves the unaccustomed exposure of open ground to accompany Danton to rescue Harkell. Tarkyn heals Harkell's back and once Harkell realises that he has been left for dead by Prince Jarand, he decides to swear fealty to Tarkyn and joins the home guard.

The home guard travel up the mountain to return to the cave. Harkell watches their casual attitude to the prince but still feels wary of him. As Tarkyn once more confronts the mountain lion, Harkell's rushing to help him when he hears the lion roar makes the lion angrier but once Tarkyn has used images of the home guard being a wolf pack, it allows them to stay in its cave again. The home guard, cold and tired, make no effort to include Harkell when they bed down so he goes outside to sleep. Rainstorm, on guard duty, talks to him, tells him about 'flicking' and mind talking, while Harkell tells Rainstorm he is a blacksmith's son and can sharpen tools with magic but that he can't use magical shields well. Rainstorm brings him back inside at the end of his shift.

The next morning, Tarkyn sends a parchment via Rainstorm's egret to Harkell's wife Kayama, to tell her that Harkell is not dead. Because Stormaway's eyes are green and Jarand had said there are no green eyed sorcerers, they realise that Stormaway is half woodfolk. He tells the romantic but sad story of his parents and is formally recognized as the uncle of Autumn Leaves and Thunder Storm. Waterstone asks why, if he was half woodman, did he help to impose the oath to which Stormaway replies that it was to give them Tarkyn. Tarkyn's anger shakes the cave and he becomes withdrawn until Waterstone is able to sort him out.

Danton tells Harkell of Jarand's efforts to undermine Kosar. In return, Harkell reports that Jarand is ordering troop training more suited to war than dealing with civic unrest and that the manufacture of weapons has increased. When Tarkyn explains that he is acting to protect sorcerers, not to gain the throne, Harkell says he has found himself a truly great lord to follow and is surprised that the woodfolk don't acknowledge it too. They explain their original antipathy towards Tarkyn but concede that he is fast turning into legend. Harkell shows them how he can sharpen knives and discovers that many of them have blades made by his father and brother.

Next morning, as the woodfolk dig themselves out of their snow covered shelters, Lapping Water and Melting Snow land unexpectedly in Tarkyn's shelter and have a tug of war with Midnight to make him leave the warmth of his spot next to Tarkyn.

As they are crossing an open area, a blizzard strikes and not all of them make the cover of trees. Many of them, including Tarkyn, lose their way and are claimed by the Lost Forest.

When Running Feet falls and slides down a snow covered slope, Tarkyn and Midnight throw themselves after him. Tarkyn grabs Midnight and levitates himself and his charge. Then, just as Running Feet reaches the edge of the precipice, Tarkyn shouts, "*Ka Liefka*" and levitates him up and round, depositing him back on the path. By the time they have splinted Running Feet's broken ankle, they have lost sight of the treeline and the others.

They follow a silver fox but as they approach the treeline, the air thrums and the forest they enter is not the pine forest they expect but an ancient forest of twisted gnarled trees, a thick canopy of bared branches making it impervious to the raging storm. Melting Snow, one of the mountainfolk, is worried saying that a silver fox can lead you to destruction or salvation and that they are now within the Lost Forest where a person must face their deepest fears and the way they deal with them will determine whether they leave weaker or stronger.

The silver fox leads them to a clearing where food, wine and firewood have been left for them. Four Forest Guardians of the Past appear before them and welcome Tarkyn to their number. Each of them gives knowledge to help him in his life and in his quest to prevent civil war. Windchange tells him that he can trust Stormaway and Danton, Nightwind says he must risk pain to have a chance at happiness, Grasswind tells the woodfolk that they must be prepared to break beyond the forest's boundaries to support Tarkyn whose cause is their cause and finally, Moridan proclaims that Tarkyn is Guardian of Eskuzor not just of her forests. They say that Harkell is the wild card in the pack and that, if he proves to be true to Tarkyn, their chances of success will be greater.

Next morning the woodfolk see Tarkyn walking outside the forest unaware that he is being pursued by two figures, swords drawn. Just as the woodoflk brave coming out into the open to his rescue, the sun rises and they instinctively flick back into the forest. Overcoming their fear, they try again but when they kill the would-be assailants, they discover that the whole scenario was an illusion set up by Grasswind to test them.

Meanwhile, Harkell tells Tarkyn that he has always been ambitious, more for influence than power or wealth, and points out that he holds a high rank for a blacksmith's son. Tarkyn pleases Harkell by assuring him that he will listen to Harkell's ideas as much as he does to those of the woodfolk.

Tarkyn and Midnight chase a butterfly through the woods and get lost. Lapping Water, who has been guarding from afar, catches up with them and Tarkyn takes the opportunity of being away from the main group to awkwardly propose marriage to her. She accepts and they return to celebrate with the others.

Meanwhile the rest of the home guard are fearful about the fate of those who have disappeared into the Lost Forest. Sparrow is particularly sad because she has lost her whole family to the Lost Forest, while Danton is driving everyone crazy with his distress over losing his liege. Stormaway discovers a reference to the Lost Forest in his books although it is called the Forest of Yesterday, Today and Tomorrow by sorcerers, but as he points out, 'One mystical forest is unlikely enough. Two would beggar belief.' Just as he has worked out how to transport them into the Lost Forest, they hear a deep rumbling and look out of the cave they are sheltering in, to discover they have been claimed by the Lost Forest.

They don't know how to find their comrades but decide to use Tarkyn's technique of following the road with heart, each time they reach an intersection. This works until late afternoon, when they no longer agree. String works out that it is because some are thinking of Tarkyn and Midnight while others are thinking of particular woodfolk, which means that Tarkyn and Midnight have separated from the others. After a heated debate, they decide to go after Tarkyn, figuring he is more likely to get lost and that they are under oath to protect him.

They arrive in the middle of the celebrations of Tarkyn and Lapping Water's marriage announcement. Waterstone reassures Danton that Tarkyn will still fight for the sorcerers, not only for woodfolk.

XXIII

When Danton heads off next morning to check out the surroundings, he finds a hidden path that leads to a circular pool where he meets a lovely young woman with long strawberry blonde hair and kingfisher blue eyes that match her gown. Danton finds the Wizardess of the Lost Forest, who currently calls herself Stillwaters Pathfinder, both irritating and intriguing. She is interested in Tarkyn and his companions, and says she will only choose to meet Tarkyn at a time in the future when he has done all he can to prevent his brother's feud, but will not explain why.

When Danton returns, Tarkyn yells at him for staying away so long, but his anger springs from fear for Danton's safety because he can feel a great power close by. Stormaway realizes he knows who the wizardess truly is but won't say. Danton expresses his reservations about Harkell, who he fears is getting close to Tarkyn for his own ends.

The sorcerers and woodfolk of the Lost Forest, weapons drawn and led by Boravar, a large burly, bearded sorcerer, surround the home guard. The home guard shelter within the protection of Danton, Stormaway and Tarkyn's aqua, green and bronze translucent domed shields. Boravar introduces his companions as the Lost and says that they will simply wait until the sorcerers tire of holding up their shields, then those of the home guard who cannot face their fears will have to join them. Tarkyn contends that each member of the home guard has already faced their worst fears but Boravar says it is not up to the prince to decide that. In response to an idea from Harkell, Tarkyn tells them that, as the current Guardian, he no longer accepts the premise that the Lost Forest can indefinitely hold people who cannot face their fears.

To reignite the Lost's pride in themselves, Tarkyn grants each of them a short audience with him, and with Waterstone as his brother. When every one of them has been individually presented and the Lost have left, Waterstone rounds on Tarkyn, livid that he has had to endure the obsequiousness of the Lost when he believes in the equality of all. Tarkyn says that regardless of what he believes, they believe it is an honour to meet him. When Waterstone asks whether Tarkyn believes it, the prince grins and says 'I'm afraid I do,' at which point Waterstone attacks him and they fight while the woodfolk have to hold down Harkell who wants to rush to Tarkyn's rescue. The woodfolk explain that the two are fighting because they want to, since Waterstone could easily flick into hiding and Tarkyn could raise his shield but they are choosing not to.

Just as they roll into the stream and wade out dripping wet and laughing, the four Guardians of the Past reappear. Moridan Tamadil is censorious, which annoys Tarkyn who says that, beset on all sides with criticism, he can only follow his own path. He asks to speak privately with them then raises the issue of the Lost Forest and gains their agreement to reduce the maximum time trapped in the forest to two full moons. Nightwind applauds his ability to rule and, at the same time, maintain friendships with the woodfolk. When he leaves them, Tarkyn discovers that he has been sitting trance-like in the midst of the home guard who had not been able to see the guardians nor hear their conversation and had become anxious, especially Midnight, at Tarkyn's immobility.

As the Lost begin to leave the Lost Forest, the woodfolk attack the exiting sorcerers to stop them from spreading knowledge of woodfolk's existence. The woodfolk of his homeguard are upset that Tarkyn had done nothing to protect the secrecy of the existence of woodfolk while Tarkyn is angry that they have not raised the problem with him before it became a public issue. Tarkyn allows only Stormaway and Midnight to accompany him to confront the angry sorcerers.

Tarkyn outfaces an angry mob of sorcerers and persuades the Lost woodfolk to negotiate with them. Eventually they agree to allow the sorcerers to leave if they swear an oath to Tarkyn to keep the presence of woodfolk secret.

Tarkyn does not want to go back to his woodfolk, so sends for the sorcerers of the home guard to join him elsewhere. They spend an evening drinking and deriding the woodfolk, having being meticulously politically correct for months. The home guard woodfolk, confined by Tarkyn's orders to the clearing, similarly spend the evening deriding sorcerers, although Ancient Oak staunchly supports Tarkyn.

The next morning Tarkyn takes the Lost sorcerers' oaths in front of his home guard then retreats to the other side of the stream with his sorcerers. Rainstorm and North Wind eventually brave the icy stream to join them but when Rainstorm confesses that even he was nervous at the thought of sitting around with a group of angry sorcerers, Tarkyn relents and returns to his woodfolk. He gives them an apology but maintains that they were unkind not to warn him of his oversight. Waterstone braves feeding a horse to begin the repair of their friendship. Tree Wind, then Lapping Water join Tarkyn at the stream to talk about what has happened. When Tree Wind leaves, Lapping Water tells Tarkyn that she is struggling to know how to act with him in front of the other woodfolk, but still loves him. Rainstorm brings a group to join them, in a successful bid to make them less self-conscious about being together in front of others.

The next morning, Danton sets out to find the wizardess again and becomes aware that Harkell is following him. Danton explains his concerns about sorcerers using Tarkyn and begins to trust Harkell. Danton can't find the entrance to the hidden path, but when he returns alone later in the day, it has reappeared. This time he is greeted by Caroman, a sorcerer serving the wizardess. Danton shares a beautifully prepared luncheon with Pathfinder whose eyes this time are ice blue, again matching her dress. She says that she could not let Harkell see her because he notices too much and that Danton has not yet seen her in her true form. Despite a couple of spats, they part on good terms, with Danton saying he cares for her, although making it clear he is not proposing marriage, and will come if she needs him.

The next day, just as the home guard are leaving the Lost Forest, Moridan appears and warns Waterstone and Tarkyn not to test the bonds of their friendship too far.

Boravar thunders into the forests on a stolen war horse then allows himself to be captured by woodfolk to warn them that King Kosar intends to send in hundreds of sorcerers secretly, ahead of an official hunting party in an attempt to catch Tarkyn.

Harkell tells the woodfolk that they don't realise how generous Tarkyn is with them and they shouldn't have set him up, as a nineteen-year-old, to face such a public outcry in the Lost Forest. The woodfolk realise that the Lost Forest has tainted their actions and apologize. They also discover that the Lost sorcerers have been singing Tarkyn's praise, unaware that he has been exiled.

An elite guard, Petrand Closkaril, finds Boravar, and to ensure his cooperation, poisons him, saying he will give him the antidote once Boravar has shown him where Tarkyn came out of the Lost Forest. When he realises Boravar is trying to lead him astray, Pertrand throws his dagger at him, but Leaf Fall deflects the blade with an arrow, so that it only enters Boravar's shoulder while his sister, Twig Snap, kills the elite guard. They heave the big sorcerer onto the warhorse, then Twig Snap knocks him out to stop from singing drunkenly from the poison. They lead him all night through the woodlands until they reach Tarkyn and Stormaway. Unlike the home guard, they have never met sorcerers and are fearful of them. Long before Stormaway can prepare the antidote, Boravar goes into cardiac arrest. So Tarkyn joins his own life rhythms to Boravar's to keep his body going. Twig Snap watches over him, despite being afraid of the sorcerers and falls in love with him. Boravar, when he recovers, realises he loves her even though she has been rough with him.

Rainstorm discovers that it was Boravar's fear of hurting someone inadvertently when he became angry that had kept him in the Lost Forest for one hundred and twenty years. Rainstorm is praised for brazenly broaching issues other won't. Then Midnight trots up to Boravar, checks that he shouldn't aim at people, then instead raises his shield and sends a shaft of power across the clearing, smashing a rock. Harkell points out that Midnight has been learning from copying Tarkyn and mistakenly thinks he has to raise his shield to send a power ray. Shortly afterwards, using Danton and Stormaway as models, Harkell demonstrates how two sorcerers could combined their domed shields to capture Tarkyn in the middle, without being in danger themselves. Harkell then acts as though he will betray Tarkyn, which causes Tarkyn's anger to shake the ground and disrupt the shield being held around him. Harkell drops his pretence at betrayal then tells Tarkyn that his feelings, if managed, can become a weapon and can get him out of an impasse. Tarkyn takes persuasion and evidence before he becomes reconciled to Harkell.

Leaf Fall and Twig Snap have been frightened off by the sorcerers' displays of magic. Boravar is in despair. Once Tarkyn has located them by sensing their fear, a small contingent of woodfolk and sorcerers seek them out and dispel Twig Snap's objections. Then Tarkyn and Boravar carefully show them displays of magic.

A week later, the king rides into the forest accompanied by a small retinue of fellow hunters and attendants. While Stormaway, disguised as Tarkyn, leads most of his soldiers away on a diversion, the woodfolk knock out those attendants that remain with Kosar. Then Tarkyn appears in his shield to talk to his brother. An eagle helps him demonstrate his powers as a forest guardian but Kosar is scathing about Tarkyn, particularly about his claim that he is Guardian of Eskuzor. Nevertheless, Tarkyn warns him about Jarand's activities, saying it is not for his sake that he warns him, but for the welfare of the people who might be hurt by civil war. Kosar knows Tarkyn has dominion over the forest of Eskuzor and knows of the woodfolk but has no interest in them. After Tarkyn has left, the soldiers return to report that the 'Tarkyn' they had been following had disappeared and that the woods were full of Kosar's secretly deployed troops, all unconscious. Kosar orders their return to Tormadell, saying Tarkyn is not evil but is deluded and so is still a rogue sorcerer.

Jarand and Kosar share their anger at the way Tarkyn had treated them in their separate encounters with him. To protect himself, Jarand says that Tarkyn had no doubt spoken disparagingly about each of them to the other. Kosar determines to visit Jarand's encampment, ostensibly in recognition of his support but also to check out his recruitment drive.

The next morning, watching their armsmen train in the courtyard below, Kosar points out to Jarand the level of skill required by Tarkyn's men to reliably knock out his troops without killing them. Their flighty mother joins them and asks after Tarkyn's welfare. She allows them to see how distressed she is underneath that they would hang Tarkyn if they captured him. Jarand and Kosar come up with the idea of taking some of the Lost sorcerers hostage to bring Tarkyn to heel.

Meanwhile Waterstone, worried about preserving his friendship with Tarkyn, asks him to accompany him to the river so that he can tell Tarkyn how much he thinks of him and his achievements. Tarkyn shares his memory of his life as a prince among sorcerers. Watching the way Tarkyn is treated, even at an early age by sorcerers, helps Waterstone to understand Tarkyn's attitudes better. Tarkyn shows another memory of his father where Markazon intervenes when Jarand and Kosar are teasing and tells them not to send this one the way of the other, a phrase Tarkyn has never understood. In return, Waterstone shares memories of his parents, mentioning that there had been a couple of miscarriages between Ancient Oak and himself that had caused the sadness on his parents' faces.

Meanwhile, Twig Snap, Boravar and Autumn Leaves discover that Falling Rain is still feeling alienated from his people, even though he originally agreed with their judgement of exiling him. He does not know whether he or Tree Wind has changed too much to continue their betrothal. Autumn Leaves wants to tell everyone so they can help but Falling Rain forbids him to and agrees instead to talk to Tarkyn.

Thunder Storm sends an arrow up between an attacking hawk and a messenger pigeon at someone's mind-spoken request. When Stormaway relieves the pigeon of a note, they realise that it was he who sent a mind message. Falling Rain jumps to the incorrect conclusion that Stormaway had always been able to mind talk and therefore would have known about Falling Rain's unjust exile but done nothing about it. Enraged, Falling Rain grabs his bow and sends an arrow at Stormaway. Four people intervene to protect the wizard but then Falling Rain must face trial for attempted murder. Falling Rain says that no matter how short the exile, he will never return. The sentence is set at six years but considered to have already been served because of the time he has already spent in unjust exile. Falling Rain breaks down and is finally able to become one with his kin again. Two weeks later, Boravar, as the oldest among them presides over the wedding of Falling Rain and Tree Wind.

The pigeon's message alerts them to Kosar and Jarand's plan to take Lost sorcerers hostage. Stormaway and Boravar are charged with locating and assisting these sorcerers into hiding before they can be taken. It transpires that Stormaway has been using the funds he makes with trading goods for the woodfolk, to maintain his intelligence network for the future of Tarkyn and Eskuzor.

When Hail decides to leave, Midnight runs away, mistakenly thinking Tarkyn will let her take him. On the way back from retrieving Midnight from inside a thicket of spiny hawthorn, Tarkyn sits on a cairn which triggers a magical ward that entraps him in an aqua net. He is soon surrounded by a bandit gang led by the swaggering Orolan who plans to take the prince in for the reward or to hold him for ransom. The tables are turned when woodfolk slingshots knock out bandits and sorcerer's rays turn the earth beneath the bandits into quicksand. Tarkyn sends away the bandits before branding Orolan on his side as retribution for intending to turn him in for the reward. Because Tarkyn is relatively merciful, Orolan willingly swears his allegiance to him. Orolan tells them that some of Jarand's soldiers, disguised as brigands, rob and kill the women of travelling families, then return as soldiers to recruit the bereft men. They suspect Andoran and Sargon are running the operation but are unsure how far up the conspiracy goes.

Danton, Twig Snap, Waterstone and ten others will go ahead of the home guard to destroy this nefarious practice, provided they make sure that evidence of it is provided to the encampment, while Tarkyn and the rest focus on locating the Lost sorcerers and writing to Jarand to apprise him of his soldiers' behaviour. Both of his brothers send Tarkyn a letter to say that they are holding a Lost sorcerer as hostage to Tarkyn's support. Following Bean's advice, he sends each brother's letter to the other so they know each is working against the other.

The woodfolk, working with Danton, kill all but Andoran, Sargon and one other of the renegade soldiers at a house where they have taken their booty. As Danton leads them towards the encampment, he has to resist efforts by Andoran and Sargon to talk him into betraying Tarkyn. Then, as Sargon sways in the saddle, Andoran spears Danton with a deadly sorcerer's power ray. Danton manages to pull Sargon between them, which only slightly deflects the shaft. Danton falls to the ground, unconscious, with Sargon landing on top of him breaking his wrist. Immediately the hidden woodfolk knock out the attacking sorcerers but Danton has stopped breathing. The woodfolk send a message across miles, asking for help from Stormaway and Summer Rain, their healers, who instruct them on how to maintain Danton's breathing and heartbeat while Tarkyn contacts his mind. Then, following Midnight's suggestion, Tarkyn sends his power through the vast network of the forest to reach Danton through a tree. Danton slowly turns green and after an hour, is able to breathe independently. Tarkyn has almost lost himself to the forest but is slowly called back by Midnight, Sparrow and others and is ordered to bed by Stormaway to close his boundaries against the forest.

Andoran and Sargon recover consciousness to find themselves tied to the encampment gate with a bag of booty next to them. They are taken into custody by Sergeant Torgan. Captain Guerion discovers twenty men are missing and instigates a search which finds the dead men outside the house which is filled with bandit outfits, soldiers' uniforms and ill-gotten gains. Colonel Chaford is horrified by Sargon and Andoran's activities and determines to have them hanged and to cleanse the encampment. Lord Davorad, the financier of the encampment arrives, and while pretending to interrogate Andoran and Sargon, gives them a small knife so that they can escape.

While they wait for Danton to recover consciousness, the woodfolk with him realise how much he has done for them and decide they should work towards granting him woodfolk status. When Danton awakes, he has lost his memory, although he tries to cover it up. When he is told that the power of the forest saved him, Danton places his hand on a tree and can tell, through that link, that a storm is approaching, although no one believes him. A chance question by Danton makes his companions realize that he thinks he is a woodman and that he doesn't know who Tarkyn is.

When Tarkyn arrives, Danton fears him because he is a sorcerer and blacks out when Tarkyn says he is his lifelong friend. They realize the extent of Danton's memory loss and gradually introduce him to the fact that he is a sorcerer. Danton, who thinks Tarkyn is only a healer, treats him with casual friendliness that disconcerts him. Tarkyn decides to spend time with Danton while he doesn't remember that he is royal so that they can put their friendship on a more equal basis. Tarkyn teaches Danton how to use his sorcerer powers; chasing each other in the air and hitting stones with power rays. To Tarkyn's consternation, when he eventually tells Danton who he is, Danton's attitude to him remains casual, but they work out terms of engagement that will suffice until Danton regains his memory.

Kosar and Jarand each receive letters from Tarkyn, saying he won't rescue any Lost sorcerers held by either of them but would be happy to work with both of them. Jarand tells Kosar about the bandit soldiers which makes him realise that lawlessness must be widespread, just as Tarkyn had said.

Andoran and Sargon escape from the encampment but are followed by Charford, Guerion, Torgan and some soldiers, who witness the eerie voices of Thunder Storm and Grass Wind telling the two escapees that they cannot escape, while stones from woodfolk slingshots fly seemingly from nowhere to injure Andoran and Sargon's noses and ribs as they have injured others'. They are told that they have been administered elite guard poison and they carry their death within them. Given permission by the eerie voices, Charford takes the miscreants back into custody, with assurances that Andoran and Sargon will hang at dawn.

The rest of the home guard arrive to join the group with Tarkyn and Danton. Danton's new attitude to Tarkyn is immediately apparent. Stormaway uses scents to evoke Danton's memories. With his memory but not his previous attitude restored, Danton tells Tarkyn that he has always insulated himself against Tarkyn's angry outbursts and learnt how to manage him. Tarkyn is chagrined by this but comes to realise that Danton only did it to serve Tarkyn's interests. Danton is unusually volatile but he and Tarkyn succeed in strengthening their friendship.

Rainstorm asks Danton to become his woodbrother but Danton refuses at first, fearing that he is only being asked to save him from the embarrassing mistake he had made in assuming he was woodfolk. After reassurances, he is delighted to once more have a family and to be formally accepted as a woodman. Within a clearing in the woods, a young, blonde, passionate sorcerer had come into his own.

Part 1: The Warning

CHAPTER 1

Stormaway Treemaster extracted a small message from the leg of his favourite wood pigeon. He gave her a few grass seeds and tickled the back of her neck before turning his attention to the tiny parchment held between his forefinger and thumb. Stormaway, part woodman, part sorcerer, was an experienced wizard and needed little concentration to murmur the words that would reconstitute the parchment to its original size. As he waited for the parchment to stabilise, he gazed abstractedly at the sorcerer prince who was now generally accepted as liege, albeit with a sense of wry bemusement, by the egalitarian woodfolk.

Tarkyn was sitting under a tree on the edge of a clearing, his long black hair partly obscuring his face as he bent forward, deep in conversation with Harkell, ex-Captain of Prince Jarand's Royal Guard. Over the past months, Stormaway had watched his young liege mature from a meticulously courteous, aloof youth into a self-assured leader, friendly and more relaxed in the company of the straightforward woodfolk than he could ever have been amid the sophisticated guile of the Court sorcerers. The old wizard felt a pang of regret as a fleeting expression on Tarkyn's face reminded him of his old friend, King Markazon, who had died so many years before. Stormaway sighed. The prince looked so much like his father had at that age. Tarkyn was a fine young man, a liege to be proud of, but he was not Stormaway's contemporary. Feeling the wizard's eyes upon him, Tarkyn looked up, his eyes brilliant amber just like his father's, and sent him a warm, understanding smile.

Blast the boy! grumped Stormaway to himself. *Too knowing by half.*

Seeing the wizard's frown, Tarkyn's smile faded. "I could feel your regret and caught a brief image of my father," he said by way of explanation. "I am sorry, Stormaway, if I remind you of my father but am not the man himself. I hope I do not disappoint you too much."

Stormaway was so flustered by this remark that he dropped the parchment and had to chase after it as the breeze caught it and threatened to send it up into the trees. As soon as he had snatched the parchment back into his safekeeping and had drawn breath, he gasped, "No sire! You do not disappoint me. You have misconstrued my feelings entirely. I merely regret the loss of your father's company."

Tarkyn cocked his head and waited, knowing that some of the regret had been directed at him.

"All right. I do regret a little that you are not he, because we were such close friends and you remind me of him so much." He waved his hand. "Mind you, we argued all the time and I usually lost because he held the balance of power. But we plotted the future of Eskuzor together, and together we planned for your safe passage through the foreshadowed power struggle of your brothers. But despite all of that, we found time to drink and laugh and…He was never as reserved as you were… Not that you are so much now, but you were." Suddenly he frowned and wagged a finger at the young prince. "But don't you think for a second that I am disappointed in you. You are every bit as fine a man as your father, quite possibly even finer. You're just not him, that's all."

"Besides, you must be such a youngster in Stormaway's eyes," said Harkell, softening his unnerving acuity with a disarming smile.

Tarkyn watched the betraying flush mount Stormaway's cheeks. "I see… " Suddenly he smiled at his wizard. "Well, I can't do much about that, can I? But perhaps you can console yourself with the knowledge that your accumulated years and wisdom provide me with a much needed mentor. You link me with my heritage and guide me in the ways of magic…. And although it will always be different, I think, I *hope* that we are developing our own friendship between us."

Stormaway smiled fondly at his young charge. "Yes, Sire. We are."

Faced with the depth of feeling in his usually stoic wizard's eyes, Tarkyn covered his embarrassment by letting his eyes wander down to the piece of parchment waiting disregarded in Stormaway's hands and raising his eyebrows.

With a jolt, Stormaway remembered what he was holding. He scanned it briefly before saying to the prince. "They're on their way, Sire. The king and his brother have left Tormadell and are heading towards the encampment."

Harkell nodded in grim satisfaction. "And so the game begins."

"Indeed it does. We still have about a week until they reach the encampment. Their travel will be slow with so many people."

"And the important question; how many men have my brothers decided to bring with them?" asked Tarkyn.

Stormaway consulted the parchment. "The king has two hundred and forty armed men with him plus retainers. Jarand has only eighty of his men with him since half of his entourage are still at the encampment after dealing with Andoran and Sargon."

Tarkyn frowned. "And are we sure that Jarand is not gathering his forces around the encampment?"

"There are no reports of it from the woodfolk in the area." Harkell shrugged. "He would be mad to, Tarkyn. He knows you are a wildcard within the woodlands. He can't afford to risk showing his hand and then being stymied by you. The king would have no choice but to haul him up for treason if he tried and failed.... even though I gather he doesn't really want to."

Tarkyn gave a quietly derisive grunt. "No. Kosar will think twice before besmirching the reputation of *everyone* in our family. He doesn't want the dirt to rub off on him." He shrugged, "Besides, he always was closer to Jarand than to me. I was much more expendable."

"Twins are always closer, Tarkyn," said Harkell gently.

The side of Tarkyn's mouth lifted in wry acknowledgement as he turned his attention to Stormaway, who was saying, "So, what do you think? Can we just leave them to their own devices?"

"I would not presume to dictate to you two," replied Tarkyn, "who are so much better versed in intrigue than I, but I would suggest that if our presence is all that is holding Jarand's intentions at bay, we need to make sure our presence is felt."

A blond sorcerer bounced into the middle of the conversation. "I couldn't agree more," Danton turned to the young woodman at his side. "What do you think, little brother?"

Rainstorm frowned. "I am not little. I am seventeen now, you know." Faced with Danton's unrepentant grin, he rolled his eyes and prepared to take issue.

But before he could say anything further, Tarkyn clapped him on the back and gave a short laugh. "Welcome to the club, Rainstorm. Ancient Oak calls me little brother all the time." He shrugged, smiling, "There's nothing we can do about it. No matter how old or tall we grow, neither of us will ever be older than they are."

Rainstorm glanced at him then broke into a smile. "Yeah, true." For a moment he looked quite cocky, pleased with the link between himself and Tarkyn, "But we younger brothers are still a force to be reckoned with, aren't we?"

"…which is why I asked your opinion," put in Danton placatingly, before a sense of mischief prompted him to add, "…even though you are just out of nappies."

"That's it! You've had it!" bellowed Rainstorm, laughing as he launched himself at Danton.

A little off to one side, standing beneath the overhanging branches of a pair of huge sycamore trees, Falling Branch and Waterstone watched as the two of them rolled in the dust at everyone's feet. Falling Branch shook his head, smiling "This used to be such a quiet family."

Waterstone gave a short laugh. "No it didn't. You and Rainstorm were always fighting with each other. Just be glad that he now has someone other than his father to draw his fire."

Falling Branch chuckled. "Oh I am." He glanced at Waterstone. "It's rather nice having a sorcerer in the family."

Waterstone smiled. "Yes, it is, isn't it?"

When the two newly-linked bloodbrothers had played themselves out, stood up and dusted themselves down, Stormaway remarked dryly, "Just as well Kosar's men aren't bearing down on us as we speak."

"Wouldn't have done it, if they were," said Rainstorm firmly. "We have a week to sort them out, as I understand it… plenty of time to knock my cocky older brother into shape before they arrive." He chortled and ducked as Danton swung a casual fist at him. "Anyway," he continued, in belated answer to Danton's question, "I think Tarkyn is right. We don't have to be aggressive or embarrassing, but Tarkyn does need to let them know he is still watching them."

Falling Branch sent a dry mind message to Waterstone. "Never did I think to see such tact in my son."

Waterstone let out an audible grunt of laughter that made everyone look around. He waved his hand. "Sorry. Private joke. Not to anyone's detriment, I assure you." He hastily moved the conversation on, "So shall we make our presence felt on the road through the forest, or wait until they reach the encampment?"

"I think we need to do it before they reach the encampment," replied Harkell. As they conferred, he was working his way diligently through a pile of arrows that needed sharpening. While someone else was talking, he would run his fingers gently along each edge of an arrow tip, murmuring "*Feeyen*", and sending a small spray of purple sparks along the edges, honing them. "They will be more vulnerable in the woodlands. Once they reach the encampment, the gap between them and the treeline will make them more difficult to deal with."

"And how do we know that this Lord Davorad won't take things into his own hands and launch an ambush on the king?" asked Waterstone.

"No one would follow Lord Davorad. He depends on his association with Prince Jarand for his influence," explained Danton. "If he acted without Jarand's agreement, or attacked the king when Jarand was in the possible firing line, Jarand would foreswear him and leave him isolated."

Stormaway nodded. "Lord Davorad does not have enough firepower on his own to subdue the kingdom, even if he were more popular. He depends on his alliance with Prince Jarand. He will do as the prince tells him to."

"So ideally, we need some way of alerting the royal twins to our presence without letting their men know, don't we?" asked Rainstorm. He thought for a moment, "You could use your power with animals, Tarkyn, but I'm not sure that Jarand would recognise it for what it was."

"No, Jarand didn't realise, and neither did I for that matter," said Harkell, "that you took over control of our horses when you ambushed us."

Tarkyn gave a wry smile. "And I am not sure that I convinced Kosar either. He may have believed it for a while but I suspect he has convinced himself by now that the eagle's movements were coincidental. After all, he didn't really accept the fact that I am Guardian of the Forest....let alone of Eskuzor."

"Do you want to visit them again?" asked Waterstone, carefully neutral, not wishing Tarkyn to endanger himself but also not wishing to make an issue of it unnecessarily.

"No, I have nothing else to say to them at the moment. It would be taking an unnecessary risk for little point." Tarkyn smiled at the look of satisfaction that crossed Waterstone's face.

"I could send a message on your behalf via one of my pigeons," suggested Stormaway.

Tarkyn shook his head. "No. As Orolan, our brigand friend, put it, I want to flex my muscles, that is, *our* muscles, to make sure they stay aware that I can do something about it, if they decide to ignore my wishes."

Harkell chuckled, as he raised an arrow tip to eye level to check its acuity. "In all my wildest dreams, never did I contemplate being a party to ensuring Prince Jarand's compliance, let alone that of the king."

Tarkyn raised his eye brows and said disdainfully, "They are merely men, after all. You, with your outlook, should know that, as well as anyone."

Harkell lowered the arrow and raised his soft brown eyes to meet Tarkyn's "Perhaps. But saying that, they are very powerful men with many people at their command."

"Tarkyn!" exclaimed Waterstone, his eyes gleaming with laughter, "I never thought I would hear you speak so disparagingly about members of your precious Royal Family."

"Hmph. If you remember, I said that I no longer acknowledge any allegiance to either of them. And I do not feel very kindly towards them. They may outrank all of you, but I respect all of you more than I respect them."

"Thanks," said Waterstone with a lurking smile. "And even though they outrank you, we respect you, and each other, more than we respect them."

"Huh." The prince folded his arms, "Well, for your information, I think you will find that at least Rainstorm and Danton feel that, as Guardian of the Forest, I outrank my sorcerer brothers."

Waterstone gave a short laugh. "And I think you will find that I couldn't care less who outranks whom."

Tarkyn unfolded his arms and chuckled, "So, nothing new there, then."

"Come on you two. What are we going to do to flex our muscles?" asked Danton impatiently.

Tarkyn shook his head, "Danton, Danton. Be calm. After all, we have all just waited patiently for you two to pick yourselves up out of the dirt."

"Whatever we do," said Rainstorm, ignoring this little jibe, "I think we should show them that we can penetrate their defences."

Harkell nodded his approval, "Yes, I agree. In fact, that's pretty much all you need to do to make them feel vulnerable."

"I think we should do something nice for them," said Danton slowly. A slow smile spread across his face as everyone stopped and stared at him. "Tarkyn, I have never seen you more menacing than when you were treacly urbane to those two bounty hunters we captured – you know, the two who had been part of Journeyman's posse. Being kind to someone when they know you have them at your mercy can be very unnerving."

Tarkyn narrowed his eyes, "Hmmm. You may be bombastic with your magic, Danton, but the subtle way you manipulate people is quite worrying, particularly now I know that I myself have been a victim."

Danton gave a little bow. "Sire, it is merely your own strategy that I am suggesting." He straightened up with laughter in his eyes.

Tarkyn put his hands on his hips and frowned, "Does no one take me seriously these days?"

There was no answer to this, since reassuring him was likely to sound either patronising or sycophantic. So instead, the prince found himself surrounded by grinning faces. He threw up his hands, "Fine then. As long as we know where we stand."

"Why don't we place a basket, full of fruits and flowers, in the king's tent beside his bed while he is sleeping?" suggested Lapping Water, calming down the air of hilarity that was threatening to hijack the discussion.

"With a note," added Rainstorm with relish.

"We could say, 'Welcome to the woodlands'," suggested Lapping Water.

"They are not welcome," said Tarkyn flatly.

"'With best wishes'?" suggested Rainstorm.

"I don't wish them well."

"'With kind regards'?" suggested Danton.

Tarkyn shook his head, "No. I don't feel kindly towards them."

"So, 'As a token of my esteem' probably won't do either then?" said Rainstorm.

"No."

"You could take it as read that the note is sarcastic," suggested Autumn Leaves, strolling into the middle of this.

"Perhaps. But some people miss sarcasm even when they have the tone of voice to listen to, let alone with just words on paper. No. I think I would prefer to be clear in my statement. I would not like either of them to think that I am trying to curry favour with them."

Waterstone regarded the prince with his head slightly to one side, "You're still angry, aren't you?"

Tarkyn turned to stare at him. After a moment, he asked, "And why shouldn't I be, after what they did to me?"

"Because, my liege," said Danton gently, "we are playing a strategic game here."

A tinge of colour crept into Tarkyn's face. There was a noticeable pause before he said stiffly, "I beg your pardon. I would not wish my personal feelings to jeopardise any of you, or our efforts to protect Eskuzor." He thought for a moment, "However, I do not accept that I have to lie to play this game of yours."

The man who had followed Tarkyn since childhood smiled warmly at him, "....which is why manoeuvring within the machinations of intrigue with you has been so much more of a challenge than it would have been with other members of the Royal Family."

Tarkyn let out a breath and grinned, "Poor Danton. What a trial I have been to you! But since you have always managed to find ways through, even with the hindrance of a naive, inconveniently honest liege, I am sure you will continue to do so." He directed a wry smile at Autumn Leaves, knowing that he too struggled at times with the prince's level of integrity. "I still want something in that note that is a genuine reflection of my sentiments."

"Why don't you write, 'As a token of our shared commitment to Eskuzor's future'?" suggested Stormaway, lifting his head from studying the piece of parchment he held in his hands. "It might not be a completely accurate reflection of their feelings, but it is of yours."

Tarkyn nodded slowly, "Yes. That will do nicely."

"I'm glad we have the weighty issue of the note's contents sorted out," remarked Harkell dryly. "Now all we have to do is figure out the minor detail of how we are going to get a basket of fruit and flowers into the king's tent through a barricade of armed guards."

"Spoken like a true soldier," said Tarkyn. "I'm pleased someone here is focusing on the practicalities."

"I think we should have String and Bean here if we are trying to solve a puzzle," said Lapping Water firmly.

"Good idea. I'll go and find them," said Tarkyn, rather to everyone's surprise. He threw a smile over his shoulder as he strode away, "Back shortly. See what you can come up with while I'm gone."

A few moments later he heard the sound of pattering feet coming up behind him, "Hello, Lapping Water," he said without turning around, knowing her footfall when she chose to let it be heard, "I should have asked if you wanted to come with me, shouldn't I?"

"No, not necessarily. But I thought you might like some help in interpreting the lookout's directions." The woodwoman's green eyes twinkled up into the prince's.

Tarkyn chuckled, "I'm not that bad at directions, especially if I can recognise the whereabouts of the images."

"Oh. I'll go then, shall I?"

Tarkyn wrapped an arm firmly around her waist, "No. You don't have to be useful, for me to want you with me.... just as you decided that Danton could stay with you all, regardless of his future usefulness." He smiled down at her. "I'm so glad that you asked Danton to be a woodman. I have never seen him so happy." He sighed, "He's had a very hard life, you know."

"But at least he had you."

Tarkyn grimaced, "There are two sides to that coin. I always turned myself inside out to behave well so that Danton was not punished on my behalf, but on the other hand, I ordered him around without a second thought, any time of the night or day, as it suited me. And, as you may have gathered, unknowingly placed him in difficult, dangerous situations through my unwillingness to prevaricate."

"Ever since he was eight." When Tarkyn nodded confirmation, she continued, "You can't have been too bad. After all, he followed you into exile to have more of the same dished up to him."

"Hmm, perhaps. Or perhaps he just didn't know how to live without me, after all those years of having his world revolve around my every move."

Lapping Water shook her head firmly, "No. He was prepared to move on, when he saw your suspicion of him when he first arrived. He didn't intend to stay and talk you around. And he did the elite guard training away from you, I gather."

Tarkyn looked sideways at her and smiled, "Your first point is justified but Danton completed the elite guard training in order to serve me better, not to become more independent. That was merely Andoran's interpretation of it."

"Oh." There was a pause while Lapping Water digested this. Then she said, with a martial gleam in her eye, "Well, if I do any training, it will be purely for my own development."

Tarkyn's eyes gleamed with amusement, "I'm sure it will be. *I* think you're perfect, just as you are."

"Oh." She leaned her head against his shoulder as they walked, "That was a nice thing to say."

Tarkyn gave her a squeeze, relieved that he had neatly sidestepped her first assault on his authority. Although the woodwoman had said she could accept the inequality in their relationship, Tarkyn knew that the practice would be harder than the theory, and expected rocky times ahead.

Just as he was congratulating himself on his adeptness, Lapping Water glanced up at him and said with a disarming smile, "Don't think I don't know what you're up to. But I will accept your compliment for what it is, because I know you wouldn't have said it if you didn't mean it."

For a moment, Tarkyn looked disconcerted. Then he smiled, "Absolutely true. Shall we ask the lookouts where String and Bean are?"

Lapping Water gave a low gurgle of laughter. "I know where they are. But if you want practice at following the lookouts' directions, you can ask them."

"No thanks. I'm not *that* bad. I do have some sense of direction, you know."

The woodwoman laughed, "I am glad you think so. Just promise me you won't depend on it too much."

"Oh, very funny." Lapping Water's laughing face drew a reluctant smile from Tarkyn. He sighed, "I can't help it if I was brought up among parallel lines and right angles. All these curves and bends are disconcertingly irregular."

Lapping Water spluttered with laughter, "I bet you were hopeless amongst your parallel lines and right angles anyway."

"Hmph. Might have been." The prince grinned, "In actual fact, I never had to find my way anywhere. My retainers always did it for me."

"And is that why you are hopeless at directions, or did they always do it for you because you couldn't? "

"My retainers would always have organised my movements, regardless of my prowess." Tarkyn smiled down at her, "But I suspect that my lack of practice has merely exacerbated my complete and utter lack of talent in that area."

Lapping Water laughed, "So now, luckily for you, you have a whole new host of people who can show you where to go, and find you when you are lost....What would you have done without us?"

"I don't know." Tarkyn shrugged, "What I had done up until then, I suppose. Stop at each cross road and follow the road with heart."

"Guess, you mean?"

Tarkyn shook his head sadly, "Lapping Water, I don't think you have a romantic bone in your body. I'll have you know Stormaway and company used my marvellous technique to find us in the Lost Forest."

Lapping Water chuckled, "All right. I concede. After all, your technique also led you to us, didn't it?"

Tarkyn looked much struck, "So it did. Maybe I should test it out sometime."

The sorcerer prince and the woodwoman he was to marry, pushed aside long swaying branches to make their way into the canopy of a huge willow. Above them, sturdy branches petered into long fine cords studded with bright green new leaves that trailed to the ground in a curtain around them.

"Perhaps if you don't panic trying to figure out which way to go, and let your natural instincts take over instead," said Tarkyn's practical love, "you may actually have a sense of direction after all." Tarkyn sent her a speaking look that made her gurgle with laughter. "No. Perhaps not."

As they emerged from the other side, the river came into view. At this point in the forest, it was fast flowing and recent rains had swollen the waters. A background roar spoke of rapids further downstream and the surface of the water was dinted with eddies. Small twigs and branches ducked and swirled as they were pushed along by the waters and occasionally a larger log would float purposefully by.

String and Bean were kneeling over a large deer skin that they had laid out on the bank of the river, rubbing it down with rough stones to remove the last of the flesh and fat, while Boravar and Twig Snap sat leaning against a nearby willow watching the proceedings, little Twig Snap's hand engulfed in that of the big burly sorcerer.

Tarkyn and Lapping Water made themselves comfortable against a large rock since there was no real urgency, knowing that String and Bean wouldn't want to leave their task half finished.

"Look, Tarkyn," beamed Twig Snap, "I hope you're impressed. Here I am, one woodwoman with *three* sorcerers, all by myself. Very brave, don't you think?"

"Oh, very brave," Tarkyn replied with heavy irony, "especially when you know all three of them would protect you with their lives, if you needed them to."

"Would they? I mean, I know Boravar would, but I don't know that I would expect it of String and Bean."

Tarkyn smiled, "Don't doubt it for a second. Beneath those scruffy exteriors beat hearts of pure gold. They are two of the kindest, most gallant men you would ever want to meet."

Twig Snap's eyes grew round and although the two trappers bent lower over their task, she could see the heightened colour in their faces.

"Aw, settle down Tarkyn," muttered Bean through his beard. "You're embarrassing us."

Tarkyn chuckled quietly but didn't let up, "Twig Snap, String and Bean rescued Hail from the wizard Pipeless and then spent months braving the real risk of Hail's knives to look after her, both before and after Midnight was born. In fact, they even helped Hail to give birth to Midnight."

As Twig Snap's eyes grew rounder still, String cleared his throat and asked, without looking up, "So, did you two come down here for a particular reason or simply to torment us?"

"We have a conundrum for you."

At that, two shaggy heads lifted, eyes alight with interest.

"Go on," prompted String.

"How do we get a basket of flowers and fruits, unseen, into the heavily guarded tent of the king?"

String and Bean looked at each other. "Well, I can see why you would want to," said String casually, "But it is certainly a tricky problem."

Tarkyn smiled, "That's what I like about you two. You can fast track though several minutes of conversation by working out what must have been said."

Bean frowned at him, "Why are we in your good books all of a sudden? You've done nothing but praise us ever since you got here."

The prince waved his hand. "You two are always in my good books. I wouldn't have my little Midnight without you. He probably wouldn't have even survived the pregnancy. And you two were the only kindness Midnight knew in the first seven years of his life."

"You had to ask, didn't you?" growled String to his fellow trapper.

"Yeah. Error. I can see that now," grumbled Bean back. "So, moving right along, what do we know about the defences around the king's tent?"

Tarkyn shrugged. "Nothing beyond surmise at the moment. Presumably there will be guards around the perimeter of their campsite and at least one, maybe two guards stationed outside the king's tent."

"Magical wards? Shields?" asked String.

"Possible entry through the rear of the tent?" asked Bean.

"We will need detailed information to finalise any plan but we can think about it in the meantime." While he was talking, String was running eyes over the deer skin, gauging its readiness for the next part of the process. "How many nights will they spend in the forest, do you think?"

"It depends on what time of day they get to the eastern edge, but I would say only two, possibly three, nights before they reach the encampment," replied Lapping Water. She threw a pebble into the river. "My guess is that they will want to spend a minimum amount of time in the forest after their recent encounters with us, but with so many men, horses and equipment to organise, they will need at least three days."

Boravar gave his deep chuckle, "Besides, they will have to appear unhurried. They have no reason to rush and they won't want their people to think that they are scared."

"True," String looked thoughtful. "So they won't be able to have an excessive number of guards in that case either, or have magical wards if it is not their usual practice."

"Unless they appear to keep things as normal but surreptitiously increase their guards," suggested Bean.

"No," Tarkyn shook his head. "Kosar and Jarand will know that guards talk among themselves. If they decide to keep up a front of unconcern, they will not be able to use their men for extra insurance. Otherwise the very men they are trying to deceive would be party to the deception."

"Unless of course they just blatantly admit that they are nervous of what you might do," said Lapping Water. "After all, their public position is that you are a rogue sorcerer loose in the forest somewhere. It would be reasonable to take extra precautions against that."

"Hmm. I don't know," pondered Tarkyn. "In both encounters with them, we made it clear that we wouldn't hurt them..."

"I'm not sure about that," objected Bean. "You said to Jarand, 'Not at this time and in this place.' You didn't give him an unequivocal assurance."

"True, but presumably they realise I wouldn't hurt them gratuitously. Otherwise we could have killed them at the time, not to mention killing their men wholesale, instead of just knocking them out."

String scratched his beard. "You do realise that, with the two of them in one place, you could wipe out both barriers at once that stand between you and the throne, if you were so inclined. Presumably they are aware of that too."

"Bound to be, I'd say," said Bean. "So there are three possibilities as I see it; either they have taken you at your word that you do not desire the throne, or will appear to have taken you at your word but be intent on trapping you, or they will be bristling with guards."

Boravar grunted, "Regardless of the apparent number of guards, I think we would be safer to assume that they will have put in place more precautions than meet the eye."

"Very wise, Boravar." The rock Bean had been using had become slick with fat. So he threw it into the deep waters of the river with a satisfactory plop and wandered down to the water's edge to find a new rougher rock. "That will save us from having to second guess what the royal two are thinking. We'll just assume the worst and make allowances for it."

"We will need a discussion with Stormaway if there are magical wards involved," said String. "I don't know enough about them to know how to get around them."

"Well, I think we should ask the woodfolk near the edge of the forest to observe the camp's arrangements and let us know in time for us to be in position for Kosar and Jarand's second night in the forest," said Twig Snap firmly. "Ancient Elm and the others would be happy to help out."

"That would be helpful, certainly," agreed Tarkyn, "But they won't be able to report on the presence of magical wards, if there are any. You can't see them until you trigger them...unless you do a revealing spell as Stormaway did in the encampment."

CHAPTER 2

Much the same discussion was taking place between the king and his twin as they rode south through fields and villages towards the Great West Road that would take them through the forest.

Making sure they were out of earshot of their followers, Kosar said, "So how are we going to play this? Do we set up our campsite surrounded by guards, making it clear that we consider Tarkyn a public menace? Or do we give a semblance of nonchalance and provide ourselves the same level of protection that we have always done during visits to the woodlands?"

Jarand shrugged, "I see little point in deploying more men. We have far less men between us this time than last time you entered the forest. You were easily bested with six hundred men....as was I with my eighty men," he added hastily when he saw the beginnings of a frown on Kosar's face. "You know the only sure defence against Tarkyn and his woodland army will be magical shields."

"Yes, I suppose so." The king sighed. "It is so inconvenient though.... particularly when I am inclined to think that they will be an unnecessary precaution. And there are so few people these days who can maintain shields for a reasonable length of time. You and I can, but we don't want to be concentrating on maintaining shields. Your wizard, Journeyman, can. However, my wizard, Bookbinder Stargazer, may be a wealth of portents and information, but is not a practical fellow. I have eight handpicked elite guards who will be able to assist us but it will be a nuisance having shields over us the whole time."

"On the other hand, the two of us together make such a prime target for a possible pretender to the throne, Kosar. Despite his protestations, it is hard to imagine that Tarkyn could resist the opportunity."

The brothers were a striking pair, their travelling clothes richly embroidered and studded with small jewels; Kosar wearing black with blue and silver embroidery, Jarand in gunmetal grey embroidered in gold. Wavy auburn hair and piercing grey eyes set in a chiselled handsome face made each of them impressive in their own right, but the two of them together more than doubled the impact. As always, the king wore a thin band of gold, interwoven with filigree silver around his head to differentiate him from his twin.

Kosar waved his hand languidly at villagers who had gathered by the side of the road to watch them pass, knowing full well how the two of them, mounted on fine chargers at the head of a large column of men, would strike them. "Yes, I know you think it unwise for us to travel together and you are probably right. But this is my kingdom and I refuse to be cowed into changing my intentions in fear of my renegade brother. I intend to proceed through the forest at my own choice of pace….but I concede that we must put up with the inconvenience of shields." What he didn't say was that he considered Jarand a far greater threat than Tarkyn, and it was more against his twin that he might need the protection of a shield as he slept.

Chapter 3

"Blast them!" exclaimed Tarkyn, in response to a report back from the woodfolk near the edge of the forest. "Now we'll have to start our planning all over again. How can we penetrate their shields? We can't."

"Never mind," said Stormaway. "I'm not sure the idea of me disguising myself as one of the brothers and slipping into the king's tent would have been all that safe. What if one of them had decided to go back to the tent himself or someone who had just seen the two of them together, had walked into me?"

"Well, if you had wanted to place the basket of fruit and flowers while the king was sleeping, you couldn't have disguised yourself as the king anyway. People would know he was already inside the tent," protested Rainstorm. "And it wouldn't be half so scary for him to discover that someone had been in his tent in his absence. It is much better if he thinks someone has entered the tent and stood over him while he slept."

"And the idea about you or Danton translocating into the tent and leaving the basket there won't work either, will it Tarkyn, if they have a shield up?" When the prince shook his head, Harkell added, "Not that I liked that idea. I have reservations about either of you placing yourself at risk, just to deliver a basket of fruit and flowers." He waved his hand to preclude a barrage of protests, "I *know* it's more than just a basket of flowers but still..."

"Besides," added Danton, "we would be disoriented and nauseated for several seconds after we arrive by translocation, which would be very risky."

"Hmm," Bean stroked his beard, deep in thought, "Now, if I remember correctly, the only way to get through a shield that is over someone, is to come up from underneath."

"Yes, Bean," replied Tarkyn dryly, "But if you are thinking that I could send a mole or rabbit to tunnel up into Kosar's tent carrying a basket of flowers, you need your head read. Not only would it be impossible for any animal to do that, but it would be obvious how they had got in. They would leave a mound of disturbed dirt, wouldn't they?"

Bean waved away Tarkyn's objection. "I wasn't thinking of that." He gave a slight, distracted smile. "Not even with a single flower rather than a basket. No. I think we have to abandon the idea of leaving something in the king's tent while he is in there, if he is shielded." He glanced sideways with a complicit smile at String, "No. What we will have to do is to *appear* to leave something in the king's tent while he is in there."

String slapped his knee in appreciation, "Good idea, Bean."

As one, the two scruffy trappers turned to the wizard, who raised his eyebrows in query.

"Now, Stormaway," said String. "Firstly, we will have to be slightly less ambitious with our gesture of shared commitment to Eskuzor's future. Secondly, we need the combined talents of you and you," here he transferred his gaze to Tarkyn, "our forest guardian. There will be no risk to either of you."

"And thirdly, we need something that will expand overnight," added Bean. He looked around him, "Any ideas?"

"I can use a minimising spell on the note," said Stormaway, "as I do when I send notes by pigeon. But I could make this one a decaying spell so that it wears off before morning."

"Good. What about flowers and fruit? Will it work on them?"

The wizard shook his head. "Doesn't work very well on living matter. Too juicy. Tends to turn them to mush and then they don't reconstitute properly." He shrugged. "Besides, it's a common spell. Their wizards will realize the note was there all along. In fact, their wizards are likely to recognise any magical trick I come up with."

"Hmph." Bean scratched his fingers through his hair before pulling out a spiky twig that had been caught in it. "We're a bit stuck, aren't we?"

"Perhaps Tarkyn could use his power as forest guardian to grow a vine under the side of the tent during the night," suggested Lapping Water.

"I couldn't make a vine penetrate a shield and I couldn't give a vine, or any other plant for that matter, power to grow that it could use later, even if we found a way to place it inside the tent before the shield was raised."

"Excuse me, Tarkyn," came a timid, tinkling voice. As Tarkyn swung around to face her, Melting Snow started like a scared rabbit but held her ground. "A nightflower might work." When Tarkyn nodded encouragement, she continued, "Nightflowers grow in only a few shaded dells deep within the forest. I wouldn't think that any sorcerers had ever seen one." A general murmur among both woodfolk and sorcerers confirmed this opinion. "They are called nightflowers because their buds unfurl overnight to produce large purple flowers before daybreak."

"This sounds promising… But do they close up during the day and open again the next night? Kosar and Jarand might then realise how they had been tricked."

"No," replied Ancient Oak, coming to her aid, "Once opened, the nightflower blooms night and day for about a week before wilting and dying." The woodman smiled warmly at her. "Good idea, Melting Snow."

Tarkyn caught his woodbrother's eye and gave a knowing little smile. Ancient Oak coloured slightly and sent back a repressive frown. Sadly for Ancient Oak's future peace, this did not go unnoticed by Rainstorm.

"I hope these flowers don't all bloom at once," said String. "Because the chance of that occurring on the day we want them is pretty slim."

"About one in three hundred and sixty five, String," said Bean prosaically.

Lapping Water smiled. "We may just be in luck. By the most amazing stroke of good fortune, the nightflowers are due to bloom in three days' time, on the night of the first full moon of summer."

Tarkyn and Boravar looked suitably impressed but String and Bean exchanged glances then looked at Lapping Water.

"What a coincidence," said String dryly.

"Lapping Water?" queried Bean even more dryly.

The woodwoman chuckled, "All right. Nightflowers blossom at various times from the end of Autumn into the first months of summer… and you can tell when each flower is about to bloom because purple streaks appear along the sides of its green bud."

"So what do we think? Will these flowers suffice?' asked Tarkyn, conscientiously negotiating. "And is there time for someone to travel to and from one of these dells to collect some of these flowers?"

As various woodfolk nodded, Stormaway said, "At the very least, it will make your brothers uncertain, especially if you can introduce the nightflowers into Kosar's tent while it is guarded."

"It will do," said Harkell decisively.

Chapter 4

"**R**eady, Running Feet," said Tarkyn briskly two days later, as the last of the sun's rays winked out between the trees. "Let's go."

The pair of them walked away from the firesite into the gloom of the overhanging trees. Despite the difference in height and power, Running Feet no longer felt the slightest anxiety in Tarkyn's presence. He and the Forest Guardian had become a firm team that formed naturally any time that Tarkyn needed directional assistance in linking with an animal. When they were well away from the sound of voices, they found themselves a comfortable, mossy spot where they could sit with their backs against a fallen birch log.

"So the first step, as I understand it," said Tarkyn, "is to reconnoitre inside Kosar's tent while he is seated with Jarand and their retainers around their campfire. So it looks like I will need to elicit the help of another little fieldmouse, doesn't it?"

Running Feet nodded, "I would say so. Anything much larger might attract attention....and may not be able to squeeze under the wall of the tent."

Tarkyn gave a grunt of laughter, "Let's just hope this one doesn't find any horse dung to eat." He was rewarded by a flash of white in the darkness as Running Feet smiled in response. "Now, how far away and in which direction have they set up camp?"

"Judging by information sent to us by various woodfolk, I would say they are about four miles away in a south easterly direction."

"Which is...?"

A more protracted flash of white showed that Running Feet was grinning. "Don't worry, Tarkyn. Just tune in and I will take your mind there."

"And do you know of a good rendezvous point to which I can direct this little mouse after we have finished our investigation?"

"Just a minute. I will ask the closer woodfolk." After a few minutes of silence, Running Feet said, "There is a dead, hollow oak about two hundred yards from the camp's perimeter. Autumn Leaves and Lapping Water are taking some strong smelling cheese with them to the rendezvous to aid our mouse's sense of direction."

Tarkyn chuckled, "Well, I hope *I* like the taste… though it would have to be better than horse dung."

By mutual consent, they stopped talking as Tarkyn tuned into Running Feet's mind and was taken on a mental journey along a narrow path through dense foliage, out across a gorse-strewn heath, over the Great West Road, back into a great beech forest on its southern side and over a small stream.

"The royal campsite is around here somewhere," said Running feet. "Over to you."

Tarkyn let his mind wander across the forest floor looking for a little rodent mind. After several sweeps of the area, he found what he was looking for and, with a little nudge, connected with a small animal.

As he made his presence felt and requested the animal to head towards the campsite, Tarkyn began to realise that there was a different quality about this rodent from the little field mouse he had connected with previously. This little character was brasher and less timid than the last. Far from being fearful about the prospect of entering the campsite, this animal was inquisitive and relished the possibility of an adventure.

"You've found yourself a water rat, Tarkyn," murmured Running Feet quietly. "She probably lives in the bank of that stream we just passed. A better choice, all things considered. She is quite a bit bigger and stronger. She will be a little easier to spot, but I expect she is practised at avoiding detection."

When Tarqun had first connected with animals, he hadn't been able to talk to Running Feet until he had pulled out of the animal's mind but as he become more adept, as long as he was careful to keep his focus, he could now do both at once.

"Let's hope so. I think she's a bit of a risk taker. I'll have to keep her in check, I suspect. Let's go."

Even as Tarkyn spoke, his little co-conspirator scuttled towards the campsite. The water rat spotted the guards on the perimeter and sped straight towards one. At the last moment, just as Tarkyn was about to intervene, the cheeky rodent ducked into the shadow of a small shrub and watched until the guard came to the limit of his patrol and turned to walk the other way. As soon as the guard's back was turned, the water rat sped in between the tents and headed straight towards the light of the fire.

"What's she think she's doing?" demanded Tarkyn. "She's going to be in amongst all the people in a minute."

Sure enough, the doughty water rat scampered right to the edges of the firelight, so close that Tarkyn could depict what his brothers were eating for dinner. There was no coincidence in this, as what was being had for dinner was foremost in the water rat's mind. An attempt by Tarkyn to redirect the rat's attention was met with a clear retort that food came before action.

Since Kosar, Jarand, a couple of servants, Journeyman the shield wielder, and another thin-faced ferrety looking wizard were encased within a bluey grey haze, the water rat had to look elsewhere for falling titbits. She snuffled her way around the outside of the firelight until she had manoeuvred herself into the shadows close to a group of officers who were jettisoning bones and scraps of pie crust and bread into the darkness behind them.

"Oh good!" murmured Tarkyn. "Just what I feel like. Table scraps!"

Suddenly Tarqun's mind came face to face with another rat. For several fraught moments, a pair of beady brown eyes glared at him before a particularly large chunk of pastry landed between the two rats and they realised that there was plenty for both of them.

While the water rat was having her snack, Tarkyn was able to scan the surrounding area through her eyes. Kosar and Jarand's tents were close behind them, clearly differentiated by their coloured canvas and the coat of arms over the doorway of each. There were guards standing on either side of each doorway and guards patrolling along the sides of the tents even though the securely pegged canvas walls would normally be sufficient defence against infiltration. After all, no man could crawl beneath the canvas wall, stretched tightly as it was between heavy pegs driven into the ground every three feet around the base of the tent. It might even be a tight squeeze for a rat. As the rat's head came up from nibbling at another morsel of pastry, Tarkyn spotted another guard passing through the view between the two tents. So the rear of the tents was also patrolled.

Tarkyn's patience had run out. He gently increased his insistence in the water rat's mind, pointing out that she could return later for a second course. As Tarkyn felt the rat giving this point her due consideration, he threw into the mix the thought of the smelly cheese that Lapping Water and Autumn Leaves were bringing. Immediately the little rat's nose came up, twitching in anticipation.

Tarkyn chuckled, "Greedy little bugger, isn't she?"

"Maybe she has a family waiting for her in the banks of the stream?" suggested Running Feet.

When Tarkyn put this suggestion to her, he received back an image of tiny ones in her stomach.

"Oh no! We can't use her to do this!" exclaimed Tarkyn. "She's pregnant! No wonder she's so hungry."

Running Feet shrugged phlegmatically. "Show her what you're asking her to do and give her the choice. If you ask me, I think she'll go for the adventure and the cheese."

As indeed turned out to be the case. Following Tarkyn's direction, the little rat scuttled around the perimeter of the firelight and, as soon as she spotted an opportunity when all heads were turned the other way, sped across a patch of open ground into the shadow of a tent peg.

"Do we need her to go into Kosar's tent now? Or should we just leave it until she has the gift to deliver?" asked Tarkyn.

"If we have time, I think it would be better if she went in now, to make sure she can get under the canvas wall and to see where she can put it. It will be safer for her if she has had a chance to stake out the territory first."

Tarkyn nodded and conveyed their decision to the water rat. After a quick look around, the water rat nudged her way along the bottom of the tent wall until she reached the place midpoint between pegs, where there was the most give in the canvas. Here she pushed her way determinedly beneath the tent wall, flattening herself and scrabbling to get through.

As she paused to get her breath, Tarkyn sent a wave of concern for her and her babies but received back an airy reassurance. Already, she was surveying the inside of the tent, her nose twitching as she smelled the aromas of scent, leather and men. It was dark in the tent and she could only see the bulk of large objects at first. She snuffled her way up a wooden pole and onto the king's bed. She clambered over the pillow and then started with fright as she sank into the sumptuous eiderdown covering. Once she realised that she wasn't going to keep sinking, she jumped about and rolled over on it, enjoying the sensation of her landings being cushioned. After a few moments, she shook herself, sent a cheery little exclamation and headed off to explore the large travelling chest on the other side of the tent.

She climbed up a chair leg and from there jumped the short gap onto the top of the chest. She sniffed her way around a hairbrush, a closed razor and a china mug with a shaving brush placed neatly inside it. Then she came face to face with another rat in the gloom and squeaked with fright. She glared fiercely at the other rat who glared straight back at her.

"How do I tell her it's a mirror?" asked Tarkyn quietly.

"Send her an image of her looking into the stream. She will have seen herself when she is drinking," suggested the woodman.

"Good idea."

When the rat received the image, she checked by weaving back and forth. Then she sniffed at the mirror with interest before turning away from it and ignoring it. From there, she climbed down onto the floor and scuttled over to inspect the row of boots against the back wall of the tent that stood beneath a rack of clothing. There were several knee length pairs of boots and a couple of pairs of ankle boots and three pairs of court shoes.

"Wolves' teeth!" exclaimed Running Feet. "What does one man want with all those shoes?"

Tarkyn chuckled, "Oh. Those are not all his shoes. That is merely a small selection he has brought with him on the journey. In fact, I would say he is travelling quite light." The prince grinned, knowing Running Feet would be oscillating between astonishment and censure. "Now you begin to see what I left behind me."

"And here I was, thinking you were a sensible person," said the woodman trenchantly.

"Sadly, no. And I have only changed from necessity not particularly from choice."

And yet Running Feet knew that the necessity the prince was talking about was his decision to absolve the woodfolk from the level of service he had received previously from sorcerers.

The woodman grunted, "Hmm. Perhaps I am right, after all. You are sensible. You have placed our welfare above your material desires."

"Hmph. Well, I think dragging a travelling trunk and a large wardrobe of clothes through the treetops and the deep woodlands might have been a bit much to expect." But saying that, they both knew he could have. "Anyway, back to the task at hand. I think the shaving mug will be the best place. We just have to make sure the stems of the nightflowers stand no higher than the rim. I'll send Lapping Water an image of the shaving mug with the water rat standing beside it so she can tell to what height to trim the bud's stems."

The little water rat had finished her inspection of the footwear and sent through an impatient query. In response, Tarkyn returned a wave of gratitude and directed her towards the hollow oak a little way from the campsite, where Lapping Water and Autumn Leaves waited with smelly cheese, a neatly tied package of nightflower buds and a tiny minimised parchment.

Chapter 5

The sun had not yet risen when Farlowe, Kosar's manservant rose from his pallet at the foot of the king's bed to prepare for the day. He grunted as he straightened from his hard bed. He was getting older and it was becoming more difficult to keep up with the requirements of his master. But he would never risk losing his place at the king's side by making any mention of his discomfort. As was his wont, he moved quietly to the dresser with the intention of pouring water into the shaving mug to soften the brush before he used it on the Royal throat and chin. The sight that met him in the dim light stopped him in his tracks.

Three purple fluted flowers, each the size of a man's hand, greeted him from the shaving mug. A tantalizingly sweet perfume drifted through the air towards him. His first instinct was to remove the flowers and carry on with his usual morning routine. But after a few minutes of uncertain vacillation he decided that it would be foolhardy to interfere with something that was clearly a gift for His Majesty.

Independent thought was not a prized attribute of His Majesty's servants. So it took another few minutes for the realisation to dawn that the existence of those flowers within the king's tent was a logistical impossibility. Once the implication of their presence had dawned on him, he found himself in a quandary as to whether the king's ire would be greater if he woke him or left him to sleep. In the end, he compromised by tut-tutting under his breath as he went about his tasks. Several minutes later, as the king began to stir, Farlowe immediately decided that he should have woken him earlier.

Kosar awoke with a frown on his face, "Farlowe. Be silent. You are making the most irritating noise. I do not expect to be woken by the clucking of my manservant." He glared at Farlowe before rolling over to face the tent wall, pulling the eiderdown more firmly up under his chin and closing his eyes again.

Having got this far, Farlowe screwed up his courage. "Ahem. Excuse me Sire. I am loath to disturb you but I think I should inform you that a gift has arrived for you."

"Farlowe," growled the king, "you are trying my patience. A gift is no rare thing. I really think it can wait upon my rising."

Farlowe bowed, even though the king wasn't looking at him. "Very well, Your Majesty. It awaits you on your dressing table when you are ready."

Kosar's drowsy mind, intent on falling back to sleep, took a minute to digest this. Suddenly, his eyes flew open and he surged upright, scattering the bedcovers.

"*Where* did you say it was?" he demanded.

His manservant swept his arm to indicate the nightflowers as though performing some grand introduction.

"When did they arrive?"

"I do not know, Sire. It must have been some time during the night. They were not there when I went to bed last night but were already in place when I awoke."

"Give me my robe. Send in my shieldwielders."

In very short order, two shieldwielders stood before the king, still gathering their wits from being woken so abruptly with the third standing just outside the door so that he could continue to maintain the shield over the tent.

"Explain this!" snapped Kosar, waving at the purple flowers. "They were not here last night."

"Sire, one of our shields has been over you and your tent at all times since you retired. We began the night with the other two shieldwielders outside the shield. I had the first shift. When my shift finished, Syros placed his shield over my shield before I extinguished mine. The same procedure occurred when Calson took over. At no time has your tent been unshielded, Sire."

"I repeat, explain this!"

The three shieldwielders looked at each other and shook their heads.

"Your pardon Sire, but we cannot."

"Remove your shield. It is clearly pointless. I want the guards doubled around my tent. Send me the captain of the guard and request my brother to attend me. Now! Out, the three of you! " Kosar turned away without waiting for a response and gave his attention to the exotic bouquet on his dressing table. It was then he noticed the small parchment lying beside the shaving mug. He unfurled it and read,

Kosar and Jarand,

Please accept this gift as a token of our shared commitment to Eskuzor's future.

Tarkyn

The hairs on the back of Kosar's neck lifted and he repressed an instinctive reaction to look behind him. His heart thumped loudly in his ears as it became borne in on him that neither guards nor shields had succeeded in keeping Tarkyn at bay. After a moment of pure fear, reason reasserted itself. He took a long slow breath before turning to his manservant.

"Farlowe, find also Bookbinder Stargazer and Journeyman Cloudmaker and bring them here." Kosar was pleased that his voice betrayed no sign of his perturbation.

Minutes later, Jarand appeared in the doorway, wrapped in a long, finely embroidered, deep blue velvet dressing gown, his hair hastily brushed, clearly disgruntled at being called for so early in the morning. He gave a shallow bow, "You requested my presence, Sire."

"Come in, Jarand." Kosar thrust the parchment towards him, "Here. Read this."

As soon as Jarand's eyes lifted in enquiry, Kosar indicated the nightflowers. "They were placed on my dressing table sometime during the night." Before Jarand could respond, he added, "I have already questioned the shieldwielders. A shield was in place at all times since I retired."

As Jarand gazed at the flowers, his eyes narrowed, "Insolent young pup! His temerity knows no bounds, apparently."

"Nor his power."

After a few moments, Jarand turned to face his brother, "It does not mean that he came here himself."

"No. But one of his followers must have been here… Perhaps these woodmen of his can penetrate shields."

"I doubt it. Perhaps it is some sort of ruse…"

"Such as? People cannot levitate objects through shields, Jarand. Neither can they translocate through them." He waved his hand to forestall Jarand's objection. "Anyway, I have called for the wizards and the Captain of the Guard. If it is a ruse, we will uncover its working."

Jarand raised his eyebrows disdainfully, "Whether it was a ruse or not, at the very least, someone found a way into your closely guarded tent without raising the alarm." A thin smile stretched his lips. "Perhaps these flowers are, after all, merely a gesture of goodwill."

Kosar snorted. "Do not try my patience, Jarand. You know perfectly well that a true gesture of goodwill could have been delivered to us by carrier pigeon while we sat around the campfire." He snatched the parchment from his brother. "No, mark my words. This is a warning. A show of strength beyond anything he has done before. He is making it blindingly clear that we are vulnerable to his attack, no matter what precautions we put in place." Kosar paced up and down the confines of the tent in agitation. "And he doesn't bother to threaten our men. He strikes directly at us."

"He has not actually caused any harm, you know," said Jarand mildly. "In fact, I begin to think you must be right in saying that he does not want the throne." He shrugged. "After all, if he can penetrate our defences like this, he could have killed both of us in our beds if that had been his goal." He paused for a moment to check that no one was in earshot before continuing, "Despite the deaths he caused in his escape, surely he must know that the people of Eskuzor would crown him king if he were the last Tamadil left alive."

Kosar almost snarled, "Many would flout my rule to call him king now. Make no mistake, Jarand. He is more powerful, possibly more popular now, than he was when we took steps to remove him." The king stopped pacing and slapped his thigh in irritation. "Blast him, Jarand. I will not allow Tarkyn to think he can dictate to me. I will find a way to make him rue this night's work."

Chapter 6

Further discussion was forestalled by the arrival of Farlowe who bowed and presented the wizards and Captain Lomas.

When the three of them had filed in and arranged themselves to stand stiffly within the cramped quarters of the tent, the king spoke, "Gentlemen, I have a mystery here that requires a solution. This morning when I awoke, secure, as I thought, within a magical shield, I found that I had been honoured by a gift of flowers with an accompanying parchment. All three shieldwielders, Farlowe and I were within the shield. No one else could have come or gone through the shield. And when I retired, there were no flowers and no note." The king turned his gaze on his Captain of the Guard. "Before that, the tent was closely guarded whether I was within it or not. Is that not so, Lomas?"

"Yes, Your Majesty. All sides of your tent were patrolled regularly, in addition to which, guards are posted at regular intervals around the perimeter of the campsite."

"And yet these flowers and the note have appeared beside me as I slept." The king glowered at them. "Someone gained access to my tent. I had expected better protection of my person." He let the implications of this statement sink in before saying shortly, "I want an explanation… We will begin with the wizards. Is there any way you know of, no matter how unlikely, that a magical shield can be penetrated?"

Bookbinder and Journeyman looked at each other for ideas. Bookbinder shook his head. "No Sire. Nothing can pass through a magical shield either from without or within."

"Straight away, you are wrong!" snapped the king. "My brother Tarkyn can send a shaft of power from within his own shield. I have seen it myself."

"Yes Sire," said Journeyman hurriedly. "And indeed I too have seen it. But Prince Tarkyn told me himself that he could not penetrate another's shield."

"And you believed him, a rogue sorcerer?" It was no part of Kosar's plan to let any of his subjects know that he had come, reluctantly, to trust Tarkyn's veracity.

Journeyman reflected carefully before replying, "I did not at first believe anything he said… but he demonstrated the skills he claimed to have mastered… And I think he would have penetrated our shield if he had been able to, since he could have defeated us more easily that way."

Kosar nodded curtly. "Your reasoning is sound but perhaps out of date. He may have developed more skills since our recent encounters with him." He handed the piece of parchment to Bookbinder Stargazer.

Bookbinder studied it carefully on both sides, running his hand over it and raising it to his eyes. Finally, he said, "This could have been minimised and restored to its original size using a spell that decays over time but if so, there is no trace left of the spell. A trace will only last for two or three hours, you know. It is therefore possible that this parchment was a very small item when it was introduced into your tent. Hmm..." He frowned heavily, his beetling brows almost meeting in the middle. "The flowers, however, present us with a different problem altogether." He gave a superior little cough. "Obviously, one is unable to minimise flowers." He turned to Farlowe. "When did you first discover them?"

"Just before dawn this morning. It took me a little while to notice them in the gloom."

"Hmm... Sire, some flowers close at dusk and re-open as the sunlight strengthens. Some flowers, once open, bloom continuously night and day until they wither. But all flowers, when they first open, do so in response to the sun's rays."

"So what are you telling us?" demanded Jarand, who was irked by Bookbinder's didactic manner.

"These flowers were introduced into His Majesty's tent as you see them now, in full bloom and quite remarkably large." The ferrety wizard steepled his fingers before him, "I think the solution is quite simple, after all, Your Majesty... Other than yourself, only one person had unquestioned access to your tent at any time of the day or night. He brings in hampers if Your Majesty desires refreshment, large jugs filled with water for your ablutions...What could be easier than to smuggle these flowers into your tent in one such container and then to secrete them until Your Majesty was asleep?" He gazed dispassionately at the man he had effectively condemned to death. "Without a doubt, this could not have been accomplished without a traitor in our midst and that traitor could only be Farlowe, your manservant." He gave a little bow, indicating that his performance was over.

The colour drained from Farlowe's face. He fell to his knees, his hands clasped before him. "No, Sire, no! It is not true. I have always served you faithfully. Don't believe him, Sire. He is wrong. I am true to you. Please Sire."

But his pleas fell on deaf ears. Kosar did not even look at him. He crooked his finger at Farlowe and then towards the doorway as he addressed Captain Lomas, "Take this man outside and string him up by the hands ten feet above the ground. Then order your men to pack up and be ready to move out in two hours' time. Just before we leave, you may use this traitor as target practice. Begin at the feet and work your way slowly upward. Thank you for your assistance, gentlemen. You may now leave us."

Once the brothers were alone, Kosar heaved a great sigh of satisfaction. "We are becoming fanciful fools, Jarand. Night terrors about our brother's mystical powers when all along, a simple explanation was staring us in the face."

Jarand smiled, "Yes, it is indeed a relief. A little concerning that one so trusted has been found to be false," He shrugged, "But straightforward treachery is so much easier to deal with than the thought that Tarkyn could penetrate our defences."

"Yes, a pathetic effort by Tarkyn at trying to unsettle us, when all is said and done. And now that Tarkyn's agent has been uncovered, we will have less need for precautions. I knew all along there must be a simple explanation. That's why I called in the wizards and the Captain of the Guard."

"Just so, Sire," said Jarand, manfully keeping any hint of dryness out of his voice.

CHAPTER 7

High in an overhanging oak tree, Falling Rain and Tree Wind watched with interest as firstly Jarand and the shieldwielders were called into the tent followed, a little later, by the Captain of the Guard and the wizards.

"Interesting. Kosar is not keeping our little surprise from his closest advisors, only from the bulk of his men. But these learned wizards of his will never figure it out," chuckled Falling Rain. "Even if Kosar remembers Tarkyn's connection with the eagle, it will never occur to them that he might work with a small animal like a water rat."

After a period of inactivity, Tree Wind leaned forward. "Look. Something is happening."

Far below them, Captain Lomas thrust Farlowe out of the tent to send him sprawling onto his face in the dirt. The poor manservant made no attempt to move, knowing his case to be hopeless.

As Lomas signalled to a couple of his men, his voice drifted up to them, "This man is an agent of the Rogue Prince. String him up by his wrists."

The Captain watched as two men guarded the prisoner while others procured coils of rope. The soldiers dragged him roughly to his feet and secured a length of rope around each wrist. The Captain then pointed up into the very tree from which Tree Wind and Falling Rain were watching.

Two lengths of rope snaked up through the air to loop themselves over separate branches lower down in the tree. The soldiers grabbed the loose ends and hauled downward on them with no attempt at finesse. Farlowe was yanked into the air, his arms dragged in two directions. He shrieked with pain as his arms were stretched beyond their normal limits.

The woodfolk heard the Captain's voice saying sharply, "Enough. Slacken those ropes off a bit. He may be a traitor but we don't want to have to endure his yelling while we're getting ready to leave. Just tie the ends firmly and get back to your packing. Once we're packed, we will finish the job. We leave in two hours."

Falling Rain and Tree Wind looked at each other aghast.

"This is a disaster," breathed Falling Rain. "This poor man is being blamed for our trick. Tarkyn will be horrified."

Even as he spoke, Tree Wind was transmitting the images of events to the woodfolk further afield.

Four miles away, the main body of Tarkyn's home guard, the group of sorcerers and woodfolk who usually accompanied him, had lit a fire and were preparing breakfast ready to pack up and shadow Kosar's troops.

Since it was still not long after dawn Tarkyn, not a natural early riser either by nature or upbringing, was not yet among them. There was an air of anticipation as the people seated around the firesite waited to find out Kosar's reaction to their ruse.

"Ah, water has boiled," said Autumn Leaves, lumbering to his feet to make the tea. He lifted the great kettle from the fire and added the aromatic leaves. He stood patiently waiting for it to brew, occasionally giving it a stir with a stick. When he judged it was ready, he nodded and moved around the firesite, filling each person's cup. In the middle of pouring a cup for Danton, he went still as Tree Wind's mind message and images came through. So great was his consternation, that he forgot what he was doing and kept pouring after the cup was full.

"Ow!" yelped Danton, dropping his cup as scalding water spilled onto his hand. "What are you doing, Autumn Leaves?"

"Blast! Sorry!" exclaimed the heavy woodman, hurriedly putting down the kettle. "Sorry Danton."

All around him, woodfolk had stopped what they were doing, with looks ranging from distress to horror on their faces.

"What is it? What's going on?" demanded Danton between sucking his burnt hand, unnerved by the reaction around him but unable to sense mind talk as woodfolk could, to understand the cause.

"Waterstone, you wake Tarkyn while I explain to the sorcerers," said Autumn Leaves.

Without any of the hesitation Farlowe had felt about waking Kosar, Waterstone thrust aside the tangle of brush that hid the door to Tarkyn's shelter, ducked in through the entrance and shook the prince by the shoulder.

"Come on Lazy Bones. Wake up. Things have gone badly wrong."

The urgency in his woodbrother's voice snapped Tarkyn into immediate wakefulness, his stomach turning over in dread. "What's happened?"

"Your brother the king is stringing up some poor hapless sorcerer for colluding with you. Somehow, they've decided that this poor character planted the note and flowers."

Tarkyn wasted no time on expressing his reaction, "Show me."

Waterstone transmitted the images to Tarkyn. Even though Tarkyn was unable to hear sound in images, he could see clearly what was happening.

He met his woodbrother's eyes. "Whatever it takes, I can't allow this to happen. You know that, don't you?"

"Yes, Tarkyn. We all know that. None of us wants someone punished unjustly."

Minutes later, as Tarkyn emerged from his shelter, String and Bean hurried to meet him. "Sire, we have been trying to figure out why they have blamed this fellow. They must have decided that the shield could not be violated and that therefore only someone within the shield could have placed the flowers next to Kosar's bed," said Bean.

Tarkyn nodded, "Undoubtedly. That man is Farlowe, Kosar's personal manservant, loyal to him since he was a lad. It is unthinkable that he would betray his master....and even more unthinkable that he should be punished for disloyalty. He would have been the only person whom guards would let into the tent without question… precisely because he is so trustworthy."

"What can we do?" asked Harkell. "He will not want to come with us, even if we can find a way to rescue him."

"And we don't have long," said Waterstone. "The Captain said that they would finish the job, whatever that means, when they were ready to move out. He gave his men two hours to pack up. So, I would say we have a little over an hour and three quarters left at this stage."

"I must get a message to Kosar, denying any connection with Farlowe," said Tarkyn decisively.

"But why should he believe you?" String paced up and down wringing his hands. "It would be in your own best interests to ensure the release of your own agent back into a position of trust in the king's household."

"True… in which case we need to provide some proof if we can." Tarkyn forgot all about negotiating with his liegemen. "I need parchment and pen, Stormaway to minimise the message, and a carrier pigeon."

"No Tarkyn. A carrier pigeon will return the message to the palace, not to Kosar in the middle of the forest," said Stormaway.

Tarkyn waved his hand in irritation. "Very well. I will guide the pigeon to the king…with Running Feet's help."

"Why don't you use a different bird that will make Kosar realise that you are controlling it?" suggested Rainstorm.

"And why don't you people figure out the logistics of delivering the message, proving Farlowe's innocence and stalling for time, if we need to, while I concentrate on drafting the message with Danton and Stormaway?" Tarkyn snapped back, clearly rattled by the unfortunate turn of events.

Rainstorm, not at all chastened, grinned. "Fine. As long as you're happy to follow our suggestions."

Tarkyn threw him one last speaking look before turning his attention to the blank parchment that had just been delivered to him.

An hour later, Tarkyn frowned with the effort of concentration. "So, let me see if I have this straight. Water rat, first. Then prepare our defence against them raising a shield. Once everything else is in place, I contact Elsie. Are you sure Falling Rain is willing to risk his pet egret?"

Waterstone nodded. "Yes. We think the risk is minimal."

"And woodfolk are deployed in the trees surrounding the king's camp to prevent Farlowe from being attacked?"

"Yes. But it is up to you, Prince," said Rainstorm, his eyes shining with excitement, "to counteract the possibility of a shield."

"They can't shield Farlowe as long as he is in contact with rope and trees. Sorcerers have to have a clear space around themselves or the person they are shielding. But once they take him down from the tree, they will be able to encase Farlowe and themselves within a shield and we won't be able to protect him. So, paradoxically, he will be in greater danger when and if they release him… I will have to intervene the moment he touches the ground before his connection with the trees is severed." With a wry glance at Rainstorm, Tarkyn added, "Well, we can only try. This is a mad idea of yours, Rainstorm. But no one has thought of anything better." He waved his hand to shoo them all off. "Go on. Leave me with Running Feet to get started." He looked down at Midnight who was snuggled up next to him within the circle of his arm. "Do you want to stay, little one?" he asked, matching images to words.

The little boy smiled up at him, bright green eyes gleaming beneath his thatch of dark brown hair, and nodded.

As soon as they were alone, Tarkyn addressed the woodman, "So woodfolk near the king's camp have spotted a flock of birds, have they?"

Running Feet smiled sympathetically, "Yes, a large flock of starlings."

"*Starlings*?" Tarkyn wrinkled his nose in distaste. "Why not an exotic flock of parrots, or beautiful white egrets or pink flamingos?"

Running Feet laughed. "I do beg your pardon, Your Highness, for asking you to commune with commoners but this is the only flock of birds in the vicinity at the moment." As Tarkyn smiled reluctantly, the woodman added, "Most people feel the same way about starlings as you. They have a reputation for being riddled with lice." He grinned, "However, that will make the king all the more eager to get rid of them."

Tarkyn's smile broadened. "Good point!"

The forest guardian took a deep breath, closed his eyes and connected his mind to Running Feet's and Midnight's. Running Feet directed them to a stand of trees three miles to the south east that was alive with speckled black, chattering birds. Tarkyn simply watched them at first while he contemplated how to tackle them. There seemed to be no clear leader so eventually he targeted one bird who at least seemed to be winning the arguments in his immediate vicinity.

Tarkyn nudged at the little bird's mind until it became aware of his presence. Immediately, the bird's mind connected Tarkyn with the consciousness of the whole flock. Tarkyn could feel them marvelling at being contacted by the forest guardian, rippling with excitement and anticipation.

Perhaps the excitement relayed itself beyond Tarkyn because suddenly Midnight was connected directly to the flock. Midnight's youthful exuberance dovetailed with the energy of the starlings and he crowed with delight as they swept his mind with them as they rose in a cloud above the trees, flowing and weaving as they waited eagerly for Tarkyn to direct their energy.

In response to Midnight's appreciation the starlings, usually so unpopular, flew in a joyous upward spiral then soared vertically before falling in a sickening dive towards the forest's canopy. At the last possible moment, they swung into a horizontal plane skimming the top of the trees. Tarkyn and Running Feet laughed at the unbridled joy of Midnight and the starlings, before Tarkyn reluctantly imposed a sense of purpose on the starlings' movements. Without the slightest hesitation, the starling flock threw themselves into the forest guardian's intentions with Midnight's mind sweeping along with them. Within minutes they had settled into the trees around the king's camp, twittering excitedly in anticipation of further instructions.

Chapter 8

Kosar sat at a carefully laid table, Jarand on his right hand, facing away from the sight of his suffering manservant. He was in a very bad mood causing both Jarand and the king's retainers to be more than usually circumspect around him. Although Kosar professed to be satisfied with the straightforward outcome of the investigation, he would not admit, even to himself, that a part of him was bitterly disappointed that the man who had worked most closely with him since his father's death, had turned out to be false. Consequently, anyone who came within his orbit risked his ire.

The chill of the morning air irked him and he had muttered obscenities at the shrillness of the dawn chorus which seemed to have increased in volume and intensity. He had even considered ordering the guards to shoot at the irritating birds to scare them away.

Kosar had just finished complaining about the coffee's poor quality and lack of heat when a white egret circled down out of the sky, unremarked by the guards, dropped a rolled parchment onto the table in front of him and veered off to rise slowly into the air and out of sight behind the trees before anyone could react.

Kosar stared in bemusement at the parchment, his heart sinking as he worked out the implication of the mode of delivery. After a few moments he gave his head a little shake and said to Jarand, "I didn't tell you about the eagle, did I?" When Jarand shook his head, Kosar continued, "When I met up with Tarkyn, he professed to be able to communicate with animals. Needless to say, I dismissed his claim, even though a huge eagle did appear to cooperate with his wishes; it landed on top of my shield, right above my head and then flew to the roof of my tent." He frowned, "But now, unless I'm much mistaken, we have just had a parchment delivered by a wild egret… and I will lay any money that this missive is from Tarkyn."

It took Jarand considerable restraint to refrain from urging Kosar to open it. He had already been snapped at a couple of times and was hoping to avoid a third occurrence.

Slowly Kosar undid the thin leather thonging and smoothed the parchment out on the table. He nodded morosely in confirmation as he saw Tarkyn's signature at the bottom of the page. Kosar looked up at Jarand, "Not only has he been able to draft the services of a wild bird, but Tarkyn already knows of Farlowe's fate, less than two hours after we ourselves decided it."

Together the brothers perused the words on the sheet;

Kosar,

Judging by your actions, your advisors have jumped to an obvious but incorrect interpretation of last night's events. On my word as a Tamadil, I can assure you that none of your servants, soldiers or retainers was in any way responsible for the placement of my gift to you and Jarand in your tent last night. I did not intend my gesture of goodwill to jeopardise anyone's welfare.

I know you would not wish for an inadvertent miscarriage of justice, especially against one who, as far as I know, has served you faithfully.

Hopefully this matter is now resolved and you may continue your journey to the encampment in peace.

Tarkyn.

Jarand lifted his head to look at Kosar. "Is that a veiled threat at the end, do you think?"

"Without a doubt."

"Surely you can't allow him to threaten you like that?"

The king shrugged, "I could call his bluff and see what happens, but I suspect we will find ourselves surrounded by unconscious retainers if I do."

"So what are you going to do? Release your prisoner on the word of the very outlaw with whom he is suspected of colluding?"

"Hmm. It is an interesting dilemma." Kosar sipped his coffee, having quite forgotten his previous objections to it. Slowly, he smiled, "I have a mind to play with my young brother. Let us just tease him a little and see what he does." He beckoned to the Captain Lomas and spoke in a carrying voice, "Captain, I have just received new evidence that absolves Farlowe from involvement in any subterfuge. However, as a warning to other would-be conspirators, I want you to fire one arrow into his leg so that his limping gait reminds others of the fate of traitors. As an added bonus, if it should chance that this new evidence is false, he will find it difficult to run from us."

Captain Lomas bowed, "As you wish, Sire."

Kosar and Jarand swung round so that they had a good view as Captain Lomas drew back his bow and took careful aim. Just as the Captain was about to release the arrow, he gave a grunt of pain as his right hand flinched, causing the arrow to go wide.

As he stood there rubbing and shaking his hand, the king raised his eyebrows, "Captain, your aim is not as good as I remember it."

With heightened colour, the Captain gave an apologetic bow. "I beg your pardon, Sire. Something stung my hand just as I fired."

"Interesting. When you feel ready, perhaps you could have another try."

"Certainly, Sire."

Once more the Captain took aim. This time, before he had even fully drawn back his bow, a sharp thwack was heard and the bow fell from his nerveless left hand.

"Lomas, ask your men to bring Farlowe down. Then I want a magical shield placed around Farlowe, Jarand, myself and you. Once it is in place, if your hands are too painful to aim truly, request the services of another marksman to stand within the shield and complete your task." Kosar leaned back, put his hands behind his head and said with great satisfaction, "And now we will see whether they can really penetrate a shield. Little by little we will learn their capacity and when we know it, we will know how to retaliate." He watched expressionlessly, as his manservant was lowered to the ground to collapse in a frightened, aching heap on the ground before him.

But even as a shieldwielder was being summoned, pandemonium broke out. A low-flying flock of starlings swept in, frightening the tethered horses, setting them rearing and plunging against their ropes. The starlings swirled around the campsite before streaming in to settle themselves on the king's table, on the backs of chairs, and on the ground around Farlowe. The air was filled with their raucous chattering as the last birds to arrive flew back and forth, arguing amongst themselves as they jostled for positions. One audacious bird even hopped onto the king's shoulder and pecked experimentally at his hair. Kosar swatted it away, but it simply flew in a small circle to land on his shoulder once more. When Kosar tried to raise his voice above the din to demand that Captain Lomas continue his preparations, vast numbers of the birds rose into the air, screeching and swarming around his head.

But amongst the chaos, the original bird stayed in place on his shoulder. As Kosar swatted away the other starlings that were swooping around him and dive-bombing him but never actually hurting him, he gradually became aware that this one starling was watching his face intently. With a surge of anger, he realised what it was waiting for.

Although his voice could not be heard above the din, the king said slowly and clearly, "I concede."

Immediately the birds fell silent and returned to their perches on table, chairs and ground. The sudden silence felt uncanny.

The king glanced wryly at his brother, "I think I have tested Tarkyn's limits far enough. Unless I am much mistaken, his patience has run out."

He turned to Captain Lomas who was standing uncertainly before him awaiting further instructions. "Now that I see my manservant on the ground, I believe your men have already been too rough with him. He has clearly suffered enough. If he is indeed innocent, he should not be subjected to any further discomfort. Have him carried into my tent and place him on his pallet. Ensure that he has good food and water."

Kosar eyed the little bird that was still perched on his shoulder, wondering whether there would be any point in making a sudden grab for it. As though reading his thoughts, it took off suddenly. As quickly as they had come, the flock of starlings rose with a whirr of small wings and flowed as one, up and out of the campsite.

Jarand and Kosar were still watching the birds disappear into the foliage of nearby trees when a soldier walked from Kosar's tent, holding a small rolled parchment. He bowed stiffly and proffered it to the king.

"How was this delivered?" demanded Kosar.

"I do not know, Your Majesty, but it was found on your bed when we took Farlowe into your tent."

Kosar eyed it distastefully and took hold of it between forefinger and thumb. "Thank you. Leave us and go about your duties." He threw it down on the table. "Here," he said to Jarand. "You open it."

Kosar and Jarand,

Since I cannot expect you to take the word of a hunted felon, I provide proof that a message can be delivered into your tent without Farlowe's agency.

Tarkyn.

Despite his best efforts to appear dispassionate, Tarkyn's anger at the need to write this missive could be felt through his words.

Jarand gave a grunt of mirth, "So our little brother didn't like me calling him a hunted felon then."

"Apparently not," Kosar sipped his coffee while he thought. "So Jarand, what are your thoughts? Should we continue to raise shields against Tarkyn? Frankly it seems a bit pointless to me."

"I agree. If we have survived breakfast unshielded, we will survive the rest of the journey." Jarand peered into his cup and signalled for a servant to refill it. "He is a strange one though. Fancy going to all that effort to save a fellow who is loyal to his enemy."

"Yes. That, more than anything, convinces me that he won't hurt anyone unless we drive him to it." Kosar shrugged. "However, he has also shown that he will act if he feels the need."

Jarand glanced around at the surrounding trees. "And just think of all those birds that are perched in all those trees throughout the forest. There must be thousands of them. If Tarkyn can control them…" He gave a slight shudder.

Part 2: The King at the Encampment

CHAPTER 9

Jarand's encampment was now well enough established to attract merchants and tinkers. Even reclusive trappers, hoping to sell their furs without venturing into a big city, could be found dotted around the campfires. And with the added clientele, came purveyors of hard drink, food and entertainment. The dining tent catered for the troops and for those travellers who had been set upon by bandits and had little or no money at their disposal. But some of the tents had become eating places that provided a wider choice of dishes for those who could afford it, while others had set up as brothels or taverns. Singers, jugglers and acrobats strolled from fire to fire, entertaining soldiers and civilians in exchange for a few tossed silver coins.

Tonight there was a buzz of excitement in the conversations around the evening campfires. The king and Prince Jarand were due to arrive tomorrow. Word was that the king's visit to the encampment was a gesture of gratitude for his brother's support in aiding those who had fallen victim to banditry. The soldiers polished their kit as they chatted and everywhere people were discussing plans to tidy up and hang garlands and streamers to welcome the royal brothers.

The mood was not so joyous in the officer's mess. Jarand's higher ranked officers were uneasily aware of the encampment's ulterior purpose; providing soldiers for the prince's massing army in the south of Eskuzor near his seat of Montraya. They hoped desperately that the king would accept at face value the encampment's ostensible purpose as a marshalling point for victims of banditry. The officers had been at some pains to ensure that any squads of half trained recruits had been already shipped out to Montraya. Any recently-rescued potential recruits would not be approached to join the ranks of Jarand's 'fight against lawlessness' until the king had returned to Tormadell.

Travellers, merchants and other civilians sat around the many campfires that were dotted around the encampment, gossiping, laughing at the odd joke and transacting business deals. Six scruffy trappers huddled in a corner of one such campfire, talking quietly among themselves. They hunched into their motley fur coats against the chill of the evening, their hair draggling down over their shoulders and their faces obscured by long, shaggy beards.

A dark haired trapper with a broken front tooth and a crooked nose, who went by the name of Horse, picked a bit of meat out of his teeth before growling, "So String, where have you two been since the start of winter? I thought you were coming down to Montraya again. We had such a hoot last year. Stirred a bit of life into those taverns, so we did. They would have had a very dull winter without us." He grunted with satisfaction as he worked the piece of meat loose. "Hmph. This year wasn't much fun. Couldn't move for soldiers. I'm sure there are more of them around than last year. Cart and I left early. We're on our way back into the mountains in a week or so."

String gave an artistic shrug. "We were heading down the mountain with our furs when Bean pulled up crook. Not like him. Usually strong as an ox. Still, there we are. Holed up in a cave for six weeks." He shivered. "Bloody cold up in those mountains in the middle of winter. Luckily we had enough time to stockpile wood and supplies before the snow set in. But not something I'd want to do too often. Even with Bean's sharp mind, it was a bit dull for all that time." He took a draught of rough mountain whiskey that would have slain a lesser man. "Saw a lovely silver snow fox," he added casually.

"Did you get it?" asked Cart, his unexpectedly high voice emanating from his large body.

"Na. Too far away."

"Just as well. Bad luck, those silver foxes," said Horse gloomily. "You're best off to leave them alone. I've known of a few blokes who hurt themselves trying to trap them; the trap's snapped, branch fell on them…. one was caught in a small avalanche and swept down a few hundred yards. Happened too many times to be a co-incidence."

Bean shook his head "They're not natural. But I reckon they won't hurt you if you don't try to hurt them. The one we saw led us to the cave. I'm sure of it. Then it vanished into the swirling snow and we didn't see it again the whole time we were there."

A trapper with dirty blonde hair kept his purple eyes trained on String and Bean and, as he listened with amazement to their artful story-telling, it dawned on him that many of the tall tales and legends of the mountains had originated in the inventive minds of bored trappers.

"And what about you two?" asked Horse. "Haven't seen you around before. What's yer names?"

The blonde trapper flicked a thumb at his companion. "He's Hill and I'm Dale. We usually work further east and sell our furs in Tormadell." He glanced at String, "Is this bloke always so nosey?"

"Aw, sorry," said Horse gruffly. "Can't help meself. Love to find out about people… but I don't take any offence if people don't want to tell me. It's up to them."

"Dale, yer mate looks pretty nosey himself," piped up Cart. "His eyes never stop moving."

Hill brought his soft brown eyes to bear on the speaker's face and smiled, "Yes. I'm pretty curious. Such a lot to see when you've been away from people for a while."

"Ain't that the truth?" Horse nodded at a green clad merchant who was sitting across from them, clearly in the middle of negotiating a price on a case of wine. "Now, see that bloke over there? He's an interesting character. Rumour has it that a long time ago he used to live in Tormadell and was thick as thieves with the old king. But after Markazon died, he fell on hard times. Left the capital and turned up from time to time selling all sorts of unusual wares; wines, wood and leathercraft, sauces, pickles, jams…"

"They don't sound unusual," objected Hill, watching Stormaway finally reach an agreed price. "They sound pretty run-of-the-mill to me."

Horse frowned as he tried to figure out how to explain, "Nah. It's the quality of them, Hill. The foods have different herbs and flavourings in them. The wines are brilliant, I hear, but I've never been able to afford any." He guffawed, "Actually if I had that much money, I'd spend it on something stronger. But anyway, the wines also have their own particular flavour." He leant in closer. "They say he has managed to get a contact among one of the Island colonies. But here's the thing; No one ever sees him bringing the goods into port!" He leant back with a knowing smile on his face.

The scruffy blonde trapper raised his eye brows. "So…? So what are you saying?" he asked, not wanting to put ideas into the man's head that may not have already been there.

"Smugglers," pronounced Horse in a triumphant whisper, leaning in closer again. "He must be using smugglers… and avoiding the king's excises."

Hill cast a worried glance at Stormaway before asking the trapper, "And is that common knowledge? Are the king's men after him?"

Horse shrugged. "Not that I know of. Figured it out meself. And I'm not about to dob him in. I don't hold no truck with authority. That's why I stay in the mountains most of the time. Less complicated."

"Bit like you two," said Dale with a grin.

"Bit like all of us trappers, *Dale*," returned String with a warning scowl. "And now there's bloody royalty turning up here tomorrow. Talk about awful timing."

"And soldiers everywhere. There are too many of them around here already," said Bean dolefully. Then he gave Hill a cheeky grin, "Can't get a decent pub brawl going in this atmosphere,"

String smiled, "Never mind Bean. We'll be leaving in a couple of days. As soon as the weather clears on the mountain."

Cart shook his head, "No sign of it yet. Still blowing blizzards up there, last I heard. Shockingly cold winter this year. Yer better off keeping your nose clean and staying here for a bit."

A group of soldiers strolled past, casually surveying people as they passed. Hill drew himself further down into his shapeless coat and stared steadfastly at the ground. Dale kept his eyes firmly on the fire even though the last soldier gave him a half-hearted kick in the ribs on the way past.

"You fellas watch yourself," admonished the soldier, a youngster strutting his stuff. "We don't want any trouble with the king coming tomorrow."

"We ain't planning any," growled Horse. Once the young soldier's back was turned, he waved in his direction and muttered, "Off you go to bed, you little whippersnapper. Mummy'll be wondering where you are."

Although he didn't hear this remark, the ensuing chuckles made the soldier's ears turn pink. Hill shook his head, "You have to be careful with the newies. They can be a lot more dangerous than the older ones. They get vindictive if they feel slighted."

"I knew it. See. I told you, Cart. This bloke's got his eyes on everything."

"Yer didn't tell me. I told *you*, Horse."

"Yeah but I was thinking it anyway. Knows a bit about soldiers too, I reckon." Horse frowned, "Where'd you say you met these blokes, Bean?"

"I didn't, Horse, and I'm not going to, either. Don't need to justify myself or my friends to you. You got a problem… go somewhere else."

Surprisingly, Horse chuckled, "Yeah, well said, Bean. Trapper's code: A man's business is his own unless he chooses to share it. Sorry."

"I was in the army once," said Hill suddenly. "Didn't mind it for a while. Commanding officer was a thug though. So I left." He took a long pull on his wine and shuddered at some memory. "A life away from soldiering suits me better."

"Didn't desert, did yer?" asked Cart quietly, looking around surreptitiously.

"*Cart*, yer not supposed to ask. Remember?"

"I can ask. He just doesn't have to answer."

"No. I didn't desert. More like I was kicked out," answered Hill tightly.

"Actually, flogged half to death and left to die," said Dale, who then encountered a scathing glance from his friend. "That commander was a bastard, I can tell you."

"Knew him yerself, did you?"

"Met him once or twice. Definitely someone to be wary of."

"I suppose there aren't too many like that, are there?" said Horse, hoping this would lead to the commanding officer's name.

Dale laughed, "Jarand's army is riddled with them." He waited long enough to receive another glare from his friend before adding, "And the king's men are not much better."

"They're not all bad," said Hill sullenly.

"I know, my friend," Dale, having been a king's man himself, patted his knee. "I know."

Shortly after this, Horse and Cart wandered off to settle down for the night in their own tent that they had pitched in a quiet corner near the boundary. As soon as they were out of earshot, Danton turned on Harkell, "What on earth were you doing, telling them you'd been a soldier?"

"There are thousands of soldiers. It doesn't pinpoint who I am…. Unlike what you said. Why did you tell them about the flogging? I don't want to advertise that for my pride's sake anyway. But more than that, it narrows down the possibilities of who I am." Harkell frowned, "I thought you were good at this undercover stuff."

"I told them that to get them back onside, after you had worried them by telling them that you'd been a soldier." Danton gave a rueful grin. "I didn't realise you'd be sensitive about being flogged. I was publicly flogged so many times, mainly as Tarkyn's whipping boy but occasionally for my own misdemeanours, that I lost all embarrassment about it." His grin widened, "And if I, a lord, am not embarrassed, you could hardly expect me to anticipate that a mere blacksmith-captain would be." He chuckled and dodged as Harkell swung a half-hearted fist at him.

"*Will* you two stop it?" hissed Bean. "Do you want to bring the guards down on us?"

"Yeah," chimed in String. "Tarkyn helped you grow those beards and long hair to disguise you, not to make you a target. But you have to realise that most soldiers have an aversion to them."

Bean shrugged philosophically, "Just natural, really. Soldiers like authority. Trappers hate it, and soldiers know they do. So watch out."

Danton smiled, "Just acting as they'd expect." He leaned in and said quietly, "I've seen a couple of King Kosar's agents already, no doubt checking things out before he arrives. We'll have to be careful. They are not dressed as soldiers… and there will certainly be others whom I may not know." He jerked his head slightly to the right. "They're back behind me with that group of travellers… the man with the yellow jerkin and his companion with the drooping moustache. Do you see them?"

In the next couple of minutes, String, Bean and Harkell managed to gaze around themselves and spot them without being obvious.

"Stars above, Danton!" exclaimed Harkell quietly. "Does Stormaway realise?"

"Won't matter if he doesn't. He's in full swing in his alter ego as the merchant who is so well known that even Horse recognises him. But we'll tell him if we get the chance." Danton shrugged. "Anyway, I'm the only one in any real danger. Our royal twins will know that I am in league with Tarkyn because Jarand recognised the colour of my shield when I used it against him. They may suspect Stormaway but they have no real evidence and are more likely to tail him in the hope that he may lead them to Tarkyn."

"Wouldn't they simply tail you too, if they worked out who you are?" asked Bean.

"Unlikely, I think," said Harkell, answering for him. "Jarand will be out for revenge if he can get it. Don't forget, Danton's shield was instrumental in Tarkyn besting Jarand in front of his men. I suspect he would rather torture Tarkyn's whereabouts out of Danton, if he caught him."

String shook his head. "It's bloody risky, all of this. I can see why you needed to come; Danton with your knowledge of the king's men and Harkell with your knowledge of Jarand's. But it's still risky. And what would happen if any of Jarand's men spotted you, Harkell?"

Harkell grimaced and stared into the fire. "They may feel a little sorry for me, and they might even exchange a few words with me out of sympathy. But I think they would not want to be tarnished by my disgrace and would then give me a wide berth."

Danton's hand came down on his shoulder "Sorry Harkell. I didn't really understand how hard this is for you. I suppose I became a bit blasé about being flogged to keep myself insulated from it. But it never spelt the end of my career, nor was it so severe or humiliating as the flogging you endured in front of your men."

"No. Nor did it lose you the respect and comradeship of your fellow officers; respect that I had spent years earning." Harkell glanced up and managed a wry smile, "I suppose I had conveniently forgotten all that I had lost until now, when I find myself surrounded by my previous companions and in dread of watching spurious sympathy light their faces if they realise who I am."

"Or even worse, disdain," said Danton.

"At least that would make me angry, rather than squirm with embarrassment."

"Just remember," growled Bean. "It was that bastard's cruelty that led to this. Under any fair commander, you would have had a chance to redeem yourself by now."

"Yeah, and it wasn't your incompetence in the first place. It was Tarkyn's uncanny power that led to your defeat." String gave a little chuckle. "It led to his own downfall, for that matter. That's why the twins exiled him; they knew he was too strong." Suddenly his eyes narrowed and he pointed across the fire towards a small scruffy figure in grey robes who was sliding along the side of a tent, dodging out of the way of passers-by. "Isn't that the weasly little wizard who betrayed Tarkyn's presence in the swamp to Jarand?"

Harkell squinted in the direction of String's finger for a few moments before replying, "Yes, that's him. Don't be too hard on him though. He didn't even know it was Tarkyn he had seen and he had no idea that his information was important. He was as unenthusiastic as he could safely be, about being dragged along for the ride with Jarand." The ex-captain chuckled. "Poor fellow had never been on a horse before. I had to catch him to stop him falling, when he dismounted."

At that moment, the little wizard looked around and met Harkell's eyes across the clearing. After a shocked moment, his face was transformed by a huge smile and after glancing to his right and left, he threaded his way across the thoroughfare and scurried around the fire straight up to Harkell to grasp his hand with both of his.

"Captain Harkell, I am so pleased to see you. Are you well? I feared most grievously for you. I came back to find you as quickly as I could, but I couldn't get away from Prince Jarand until the next day and by the time I arrived back at that dreadful tree, you were gone." He glanced at Harkell's companions. "How do you do? I hope you are taking good care of my friend here. If it is you who rescued him, you have my heartfelt thanks."

"Rescued him from what?" asked String, not wishing at this stage to betray that he had been anywhere near the meeting between Jarand and Tarkyn.

Greyskies Swampwater gave an apologetic little smile, "If you don't know, then I don't think it is up to me to tell you."

Harkell couldn't help glancing at Danton and was amused to see heightened colour in his face. "Thank you for your discretion, Greyskies" he said, "but they do know. Dale here cut me down and String and Bean," Harkell gestured introductions as he spoke, "were among those who looked after me while I recovered. And if you don't mind, Greyskies, I am going by the name of Hill at the moment since I am unsure of my welcome among Prince Jarand's men."

Greyskies huffed, "Understandable, dear boy. Terrible business, it was." He looked at the others, "I was forced to stand by and watch, unable to do anything to intervene." An expression of uncertainty crossed his face, "I suppose you think a wizard should have been able to do something? I have thought and thought but I could only have created a temporary disturbance. I don't have the knowledge, power or inclination to have killed all those men… and anything less would have meant the certain death of both Captain Harkell and myself. Besides, Prince Jarand is a very powerful sorcerer, even if he doesn't have any wizard training." He sighed unhappily. "I was always more inclined towards herbs and medicines than warfare."

Danton studied him through narrowed eyes. "And what of your loyalty to His Highness, Prince Jarand?"

Panic swept over the little wizard's face and he looked for the all the world like a frightened grey rabbit. "I did not mean… I would not, could not…Oh dear. I thought you trappers weren't concerned with that sort of thing." He wrung his hands, glancing fearfully over one shoulder after the other. "Oh dear. I think I'd better be going."

Before he could move, Danton's hand shot out and grabbed Greyskies' arm in a firm grip, but Danton's voice was gentle as he said, "No, Greyskies, please don't go. Your words are safe with us. I beg your pardon for alarming you."

Greyskies looked pointedly down at Danton's hand gripping his grey sleeve. Danton's hand began to feel very warm but although he loosened his grip, Danton did not let go altogether. Ignoring the increasing heat, he smiled, "Will you stay if we offer you a cup of tea, with some raspberry and almond cake?" Then, in his own time, he let go of Greyskies' sleeve.

Greyskies brushed down his sleeve and considered them all carefully before, with a curt nod, sitting down suddenly in their midst, "I would kill for a cup of tea at the moment. I only arrived a little while ago. I missed dinner and there are so many people everywhere."

"Why have you come here?" asked Harkell. "I thought you usually stayed close to your beloved swamp."

"I do, most of the time. But sometimes I get a bit restless living down there on my own, and the spirit of adventure grabs me, so away I go." He accepted a cup of tea from String and took a sip. "Hmm, lovely. If you want to know the truth, I thought the spectacle of the king and prince riding in together might be worth a look. And there is some interesting merchandise passing through here. It's become quite a trading post, I gather." He dropped his voice, "And to be honest, after being dragged up before Prince Jarand and forced to ride a horse for miles and then being forced to watch that act of pure barbarism against the one person who had been kind to me…Well! I've been giving Montraya a wide berth since then… But I need supplies, especially some of the more exotic herbs I use. So here I am." He sipped his tea. "I may be going to enjoy the spectacle but I'm going to make sure I keep well out of Prince Jarand's way… and the king's for that matter."

As the evening wore on, it became borne upon the others that Greyskies had indeed spent too long on his own and as a consequence, was all too ready to talk the night away. It took considerable tact to bring the evening to a close but this was not achieved before they had agreed to share sleeping accommodation and to accompany him on a tour of the encampment on the morrow. The little wizard finally snuggled down into his sleeping bag, blissfully unaware that he had talked the ears off his companions.

Chapter 10

anton woke suddenly. His heart leapt in fear at the sound of heavily shod feet and raised voices just outside their tent. But as a soldier thrust his head through the doorway and bellowed at them, Danton breathed a sigh of relief. It was only a military patrol moving methodically through the encampment, making sure that everyone was up betimes, in preparation for the royal brothers' arrival. Tarkyn's little band of agents was no more their focus than anyone else.

"Bloody soldiers! So officious," grumbled String. "It will take us all of ten minutes to pack up, and the king isn't due here for another four hours."

Nevertheless, he and Bean did not delay in tying their belongings into neat bedrolls and stowing them in their backpacks beside the others' in the corner of the tent. The five of them repaired to the central mess tent for breakfast, before setting off on a tour of the encampment to get their bearings.

One hundred feet of cleared ground separated the outer perimeter of the encampment from the forest edge. Despite their best efforts which were somewhat hampered by the presence of Greyskies, none of Tarkyn's sorcerers could see any sign of the woodfolk from within the encampment.

Danton suppressed a sigh of frustration. He knew Rainstorm, his new woodbrother, would be watching him and yet he could make no gesture to acknowledge him nor communicate with him in any way. He turned away from scanning the trees to find Greyskies watching him. The little wizard made no remark so that Danton felt unable to explain his behaviour without being obviously defensive.

But a little while later Greyskies observed, "For those of us used to living in the forest, the forest almost calls to us when we are not there. I see the trees beyond the perimeter and I know how the light looks as it shines through their leaves, how the wind sighs through the branches, how the leaves and twigs crackle underfoot as I walk. I know the birdsongs and the sounds of deer rutting, the scream of a rabbit that has been taken by a fox, the call of egrets as they settle at dusk… and it is all there waiting for me to return home."

A smile spread over Danton's face. "It is beautiful, isn't it? You know, I once lived in Tormadell and I loved the flamboyance and the ever-changing ebb and flow of crowds all around me. It took me some time to appreciate the quietness of the forest." His mouth quirked, "Saying that, you still run into a few people in the woodlands. People like String and Bean, for instance. But not in the vast numbers you meet in the city."

Greyskies gave a little smile, "You don't run into many in the swamp lands where I live. I have to go to the nearest village if I want to hear the sound of a human voice." He looked as though he might have said more but instead swept his eyes around the sea of tents and asked, "Now where do you think I might find a herb trader?"

"Let's try this row," suggested String.

The little group wandered down a narrow lane between two rows of tents. They passed a clothing stall; a shop displaying rolls of dyed silks, wool and cotton; another selling breads and sweets; two small eating houses and a makeshift tavern.

As they passed a blacksmith's stall, Danton asked Harkell, "Do you know him? Not a relative of yours, is it?"

"Do you *know* how many blacksmiths there are in Eskuzor?"

Danton grinned, "I'll take that as a no then, shall I?"

Harkell shook his head, smiling.

They were just about to turn into another alleyway when Bean spotted Stormaway coming out of a stall further down the row they were in. "Hang on, Greyskies. Why don't you ask Stormaway Treemaster? He's bound to know where you can procure rare herbs. He may even have some to sell himself."

Greyskies immediately became flustered and turned away so that he was hidden with their group. "Oh no, I don't think so. Oh no, I couldn't do that."

"Why ever not?" demanded Bean. "He is a merchant like any other, keen to sell his wares for the right price."

"Oh no, no, no," fussed Greyskies. "He is a lot more than that. Stormaway Treemaster is one of the Masters of our craft. He is possibly the greatest wizard in the land. I can't just go up to him and start a conversation with him. Oh dear me, no."

"Yes you can," said String, grinning. "He is a friend of ours. Come on. Bean and I will introduce you." Knowing it would be unwise for Danton to be seen with Stormaway, he added, "Dale and Hill can head off and find us something for lunch before the stalls get too crowded. We'll meet up back at our tent."

The little grey robed wizard scurried along behind String and Bean, and hung back as they neared Stormaway.

"Stormaway," said Bean, dragging Greyskies firmly to the fore, "I'd like you to meet a new acquaintance of ours, Greyskies Swampwatcher, who hails from the Southern Swamp."

Greyskies tripped as he was hustled forward but when he had gathered himself together, he bowed low saying, "My Lord, Wizard Treemaster, it is a great honour to meet you."

String raised his eyebrows. "Unusual for you to be receiving such obeisance, Stormaway."

Tarkyn's wizard glanced at him scathingly, "Not beyond the forest. As Greyskies understands, I have a reputation in the sorcerer world both for my trading and wizardry." He turned to the little wizard. "Ignore these ignorant louts. It is a pleasure to meet you." Just as Greyskies beamed in response, Stormaway added politely, "I believe you are acquainted with Prince Jarand," which immediately sent him into a fluster again.

"Oh. No. I mean, yes. I mean, not really." Greyskies took a deep breath and started again. "Yes. I am acquainted with him but no more than that." As a couple of Jarand's soldiers glanced idly at him as they sauntered by, he said hurriedly, "Of course, it was a great honour to meet him and to be able to assist him."

"I'm sure it was," said Stormaway soothingly. "And have you come here in the hope of renewing your acquaintance with His Highness?"

"Oh no, not at all. I have come to procure certain herbs that do not grow in the area I live... and to watch the arrival of the royal twins." He leaned in towards Stormaway and confessed, "In fact, I found proximity to His Highness to be rather too overpowering for me."

"Indeed? As you may know, I have had some experience of the royal family and I agree that one must tread warily around them. They wield so much power, don't they? … some less discriminately than others."

"I do not know enough of them to compare them but I do believe it is a brave, or perhaps a foolish, man who chooses to live at a royal court."

"Wizard Swampwater, you are quick to trust a new acquaintance with remarks that could bring you to the censorious notice of the royal twins."

The hunted look returned to Greyskies' eyes. "Ooh dear. I thought you no longer had any dealings with the royal family. I did not mean to imply that I am disloyal, merely that I found Prince Jarand … frightening."

"And you'll be interested to know, Stormaway," intervened Bean, "that Greyskies is a friend of Hill's."

"Will I?" asked Stormaway vaguely. "Do I know this Hill?"

"Yes, you met him the other night. You know, he was with Dale."

"Oh yes, the trappers from the east of the mountains. I remember now. How interesting," said Stormaway, with patent disinterest.

Greyskies glanced at Bean, before addressing Stormaway with unexpected dignity, "Wizard Treemaster, it was a pleasure to meet you but I won't take up any more of your time. I beg your pardon for holding you up."

Stormaway raised his eyebrows, "So there is some strength beneath that fluster, after all."

For the second time in twelve hours, Greyskies found his arm gripped to keep him from leaving. This time, however, he did not apply heat to the hand that held him.

"Do not be so quick to leave, Greyskies. My lack of interest in your friend Hill does not extend to you." Stormaway released his hold on Greyskies' arm. "If you could spare the time, I would be most interested to hear about the herbs you use down in the south and would be happy to assist you in procuring those herbs that you seek."

Greyskies stared at him for several seconds in silence but then, having apparently decided that Stormaway's words were genuine, relaxed into a broad smile, "I would be delighted to share my knowledge with a worthy colleague."

When String and Bean left, the two wizards were deep in conversation and their departure was barely noticed.

Chapter 11

Thus released from Greyskies' presence, Harkell and Danton were able to carry out a more thorough reconnoitre of the encampment, noting the location of the officers' tents, and where the king's and prince's tents were being set up, close to that of Lord Davorad, the financier of the encampment. Danton was able to discern a few more of the king's agents while Harkell pointed out which of Jarand's officers were most likely to be privy to the Prince's plans.

"Have you seen any of Jarand's agents?" asked Danton.

Harkell lifted the side of his mouth in wry self-deprecation. "I was never privy to that level of information. I was a straightforward Captain of the Guard. I never had anything to do with espionage or subterfuge."

"Well, if you spot anyone here that you saw coming and going from Jarand's castle from time to time, let me know." When Harkell glanced at Danton but said nothing, Danton gave a grunt of laughter. "Sorry. You knew that, of course."

"It had occurred to me," said Harkell with a faint smile.

"You realise that Greyskies' testimony to your character was the first verification we have had that you were not one of Jarand's thugs."

Harkell's face tightened. "Did you need it?"

Danton smiled and slapped his companion on the back, "No, not after spending the last few months with you. In fact, I didn't even think of it at the time."

Harkell grunted. "I'm pleased to hear it." After a moment, he added with a little grin, "I would not like to think you had so little judgement of your own."

As they walked between the rows of tents, Danton noticed many changes since his visit to the encampment with Stormaway four months ago when they had been preparing for the rescue of Golden Toad and his family. The encampment had increased substantially in size and was developing a look of permanency from people's efforts to make themselves feel at home. There were not yet any wooden structures but people had planted out flowers and herbs around many of the tents and the pathways were now well defined, several of them strewn with gravel and sawdust against the mud of winter.

As the morning progressed, people finished their preparations and began to gather near the gateway. Some had already been standing patiently for hours before the expected arrival, to procure the best view. Smartly turned-out soldiers stood guard in front of them, keeping a passage clear for the royal party.

Finally, a trumpet sounded and the crowd cheered as King Kosar and Prince Jarand came into view between the trees at the head of a column of soldiers and retainers. The rich embroidery and bright colours of Kosar and Jarand's clothing and pennants, the livery of their retainers and the vibrant reds and blues of their soldiers' uniforms cast the makeshift decorations of the encampment into shade. The royal brothers waved in acknowledgement of the crowd's welcome, Jarand half a horse length behind and one degree more restrained in his salutation. As the brothers approached, each section of the crowd bowed until they had passed. Harkell knew the woodfolk would be watching and hoped that this spectacle would press home to them the generosity of Prince Tarkyn's lack of formality with them.

All too quickly, Kosar and Jarand had ridden past, to dismount and disappear into Lord Davorad's tent for refreshments and discussions. After the long wait, it felt like an anti-climax, but word soon spread that the king intended to conduct a tour of inspection later in the day.

"We'll have to make sure you're not inspected, Danton," said Bean.

Danton grinned, "Nothing easier. We'll follow the rear of the inspection party."

In the event, the tour of the encampment went without a hitch. It had been a clever political ploy of Kosar's to take such an interest in the plight of the victims of banditry and to lavish praise on the efforts of Lord Davorad, Prince Jarand, and his officers and soldiers. Everywhere the king walked, people were eager to tell him of their experiences and to thank him for coming. The king's soldiers spread throughout the camp but blended in rather than taking over, making no obvious attempts to enquire into the running of the encampment, so that Jarand's senior officers breathed a communal sigh of relief.

By the end of the day, Danton, Harkell and Stormaway were ready to say that Tarkyn's warning has been heeded and that a truce of sorts seemed to have developed between the brothers. Although they did not meet to confer, the three of them sent messages to each other through String and Bean so that their joint impressions formed the basis of the information to be sent to Tarkyn.

As the sun set, a black crow left its perch on the ridge of the king's tent and flapped its way over the white canvas roofs until it landed on the ground near Stormaway. It ruffled its feathers and pecked at some meaty bits the wizard had strewn on the ground for it. Stormaway had chosen clean tasty pieces of bacon for the crow, knowing that Tarkyn would taste them as he became one with the crow to direct its movements. He smiled at the bird as it pecked at its snack, and through it, at Tarkyn. Slowly, careful not to startle it, Stormaway grasped the crow and clamped a small ring around its leg. He stroked its head for a few moments, checking that no one was watching him, before forcing a small twist of parchment through the ring on the bird's leg. Then he fed it a particularly tasty piece of cheese he had found in one of the stalls before releasing it.

The crow eyed him for a moment before taking off and flapping into the darkening sky.

CHAPTER 12

inutes later, the crow landed in an old oak close to the forest edge and sidled along the branch, cocking its eye at Rainstorm who had, this time, been trusted to stay in the front line of action. The young woodman kept very still until the crow had looked him up and down. Then he smiled and slowly held out his arm. The crow ruffled its feathers uncertainly but after a moment, hopped up onto his arm and allowed him to remove the twist of paper from the ring on its leg.

Rainstorm gently released the crow and waited until it had shuffled away along the branch before untwisting the little piece of parchment. He found it very strange dealing with the crow. Although on the one hand, it was being directed and reassured from afar and Tarkyn could see him through its eyes; on the other hand, it was still a nervous wild bird and needed to be treated with care.

The woodman watched the parchment expand as Stormaway's minimising spell deteriorated. When the size of the parchment had stabilised, Rainstorm connected with Tarkyn and scanned the symbols on the parchment. Because he couldn't read, the symbols meant nothing to him and the images he sent to Tarkyn lacked the detail needed to distinguish one letter from the next.

At a firesite a safer five miles deeper into the forest, Tarkyn grimaced at Waterstone. "I'm not sure that this plan is going to work. We might have done better to wait for the crow to fly straight here with the message." He sighed, "I wish I could transmit words as you do. Could you please ask Rainstorm to focus on one letter at a time? I can then write them down as he sends me the image of each letter. It will be slow but it should work."

A minute later, Waterstone came back into focus, biting his lip to stop from smiling. "Rainstorm asks whether there is a gap between each letter."

"Yes, there should be."

In response to this, Tarkyn received an image that could have been the wandering path of a snail. He frowned with concentration but could make nothing of it. "Blast Stormaway! He's written the message in cursive. There are no gaps between the letters, only between the words. So Rainstorm is sending me the first word and, because he doesn't understand their significance, he isn't noticing all the tiny strokes and differences in height that would tell me what combination of letters I'm looking at."

Waterstone thought for a minute before mind talking to the young woodman waiting with the parchment in his hand, anxious to get it right but not knowing how. "Rainstorm, think about a flock of sparrows… they all look alike from a distance, don't they? But when they come closer, you can see differences between them. You can tell which are males because their colouring is darker and if you concentrate even harder, you can begin to recognise individual birds."

"Isn't it clear enough for Tarkyn?" asked Rainstorm, cutting to the chase of Waterstone's carefully worded criticism. He frowned down at the parchment in his hand. "Just a minute then. Let me try again."

Gradually, as Rainstorm ran his eye meticulously along the scrawled line Tarkyn could at last recognise the letters but realised two things; firstly, that Rainstorm had not begun scanning at the beginning but was actually focussing on some word at the centre of the parchment, and secondly, that he was carefully following the line of writing in the word from right to left. Tarkyn sent him a wave of encouragement before breaking contact once to speak to Waterstone, "I discover that I have made a few assumptions. Could you ask Rainstorm to start at the top left hand side and to follow the writing from left to right along the top line and then to move down to the next line and scan from left to right again?"

Waterstone raised his eyebrows. "This is more of your straight lines and right angles, isn't it?"

Tarkyn smiled. "I suppose it is, although Stormaway's writing is not angular. But I must admit the base of each word follows a straight line from left to right across the page at a right angle to the side of the page."

"Hmm. And do you vary which way the line goes for different meanings or to different people?"

"No, we do not. But there are other languages, I believe, whose writing follows a different direction on the page."

Waterstone shook his head. "All these complications, simply because you sorcerers can't mind talk. And poor old Danton and the others can't talk to any of us from the encampment, except through this cumbersome method."

Once Waterstone had relayed Tarkyn's further instructions to Rainstorm, the prince was finally able to decipher his wizard's report. When he was clear on its contents, he relayed them to the woodfolk around him, "Both soldiers and rescued civilians have been regaling Kosar with tales of brigand attacks, so he now has verification of the spread of lawlessness that I mentioned to him at our meeting. He is being publicly gracious to Jarand for his efforts, and Jarand is being equally courteous in return. So far, so good. It seems that there is no longer any evidence of rescued travellers being recruited to Jarand's forces. So that may cast doubt on what I told Kosar… although I suppose that it is possible that Jarand has indeed suspended that practice."

Autumn Leaves snorted. "I doubt it. Only until the king leaves the encampment, I would say."

"Hmph," Tarkyn looked pained. "Having Kosar's public recognition of his contribution to Eskuzor's security may mellow Jarand, you never know." The woodfolk around the prince exchanged glances, drawing a wry smile from him. "I can see you think I am being overly optimistic, but it would be better for all of us if I were right."

Waterstone laughed, "That does not, however, increase the chance of it."

"True." The prince picked up a dry stick and began to break pieces off it as he talked, "There are two other items of interest. That grey-robed wizard from the Southern Swamp has turned up and recognised Harkell. He was pleased to see him still in one piece. He seems well-meaning enough apparently, but is a bit of a chatterbox. Not much else on him. The other important piece of information is that the encampment is beginning to become a permanent colony." The guardian of the forest threw away the last of his stick and looked around at the sea of green eyes watching him. "That's not very good news for the forest, is it?"

Chapter 13

The arrival of the royal party had swollen the numbers around campfires. The taverns, market stalls and eating houses were packed. The six trappers were back in the corner of the campfire they preferred, keeping their heads down and out of trouble while elsewhere Stormaway was dropping a judicious word here, closing an astute deal there, and sometimes making contact with the people in his wide-reaching insidious spy network. Even Danton and Harkell did not know who Stormaway's agents were. It occurred to Danton that if anything happened to Stormaway, his whole organisation would fall apart, since only he held the knowledge of its workings.

Danton took a pull on the flagon of mountain whiskey and grimaced as it burned its way down his throat. He shook his head and shuddered, "Dog's teeth, String! I don't know how you can guzzle this stuff."

"Years of practice, Dale." The skinny old trapper grinned as he received the flagon into his waiting hands. He was just raising it to his lips when he saw Greyskies approaching them with two large, tough-looking soldiers in tow. He lowered the flagon untouched and murmured, "Watch out. Looks like we may have trouble."

As Harkell looked around, his whole face stiffened with shock. It was only for an instant, before his features were schooled into an expressionless mask. "Get Danton out of here now. He mustn't be seen with me," he muttered in an urgent undertone.

Sting peered artistically into the flagon and dragged Danton to his feet, hissing in his ear, "Put your hood up." Aloud, he said, "You've drunk the last of it. Come on. Your turn to buy another one."

The last thing Danton wanted to do was abandon his friend but he trusted Harkell's judgement and knew that he could intervene from a distance if needed, with an attacking power ray. Surrounded as they were by soldiers, an attack from any distance would be extremely unwise, so he supposed that it made little difference. He allowed String to drag him away but refused to go further than the shadows of a nearby tent where he and String could watch events unfold.

By now the two soldiers had reached Harkell and were lowering over him where he sat cross-legged on the ground. Cart and Horse had drawn away, leaving Harkell alone with the wizard and the two soldiers, but Bean lingered inconspicuously nearby.

Suddenly the soldiers snapped to attention and saluted. "Captain Harkell," they said in disciplined unison.

For a full minute, Harkell did not react. Then slowly, he stood up and despite his scruffy appearance and his shaggy hair and beard, drew himself to his full height which was still less than theirs, and saluted in return. He nodded stiffly to each in turn, "Saker, Biggin. You may stand at ease."

"Thank you, sir."

An awkward silence ensued. The two soldiers glanced at each other then back at Harkell but said nothing. Finally Greyskies huffed and said apologetically, "I had to tell them I had found you safe and well. I knew how much it mattered to them."

Harkell stared at the two men who had flogged him almost to death. He could still remember the power and pain of each stroke as the brass buckles on the ends of their belts had bitten into his back. He knew they had not held back when Prince Jarand had ordered his flogging.

But he also knew that the Prince would have noticed if they had, and it was not they who had chosen to use the buckle end of their belts on him. And he also knew that he himself had nominated these men when Prince Jarand had asked for his strongest, most loyal soldiers. Neither he nor the soldiers who now stood before him had known then what Prince Jarand would order them to do. But even if they had refused the Prince's order, they could not have saved him nor would they have impressed the Prince with their loyalty towards him. Instead, they would have shamed him as a poor disciplinarian.

He remembered back to times before that dreadful day when they had worked together with him quelling pub brawls, restoring order, presenting themselves meticulously on parade, always respectful and always proud to be under his command. They were tough and strong but they had never been reprimanded for brutality as some others in his command had been. With a slight shock, he realised that they were hoping he could forgive them. And he was even more surprised to find it in himself to do more than that.

"Saker, Biggin, I am proud of you for carrying out unpleasant orders under difficult circumstances. By doing so, you proved your loyalty both to your prince and to me."

"Sir, if we could have… "

Harkell held up his hand to forestall him, "I know, Saker. You do not have to tell me. I have always admired the way both you and Biggin used the least force possible when dealing with wayward citizens. You have my heartfelt thanks for holding to your duty."

The two men before him sagged with relief. Then they pulled themselves upright and saluted smartly. "Thank you, sir."

Harkell managed a smile, "Are you two on duty now or would you like to share a drink with me?"

"We have just come off duty, sir. Hence the uniforms. It would be a privilege to join you," said Saker.

As they sat down, Harkell said, "I'm afraid we only have raw mountain whiskey to offer you."

"We brought some wine ourselves in the faint hope that you might be prepared to endure our company," Biggin nodded to Greyskies who produced two flagons of southern wine from somewhere within his robes. The soldier glanced at Bean and frowned, "Your face looks a little familiar. Do I know you?"

"Sorry boys. Let me introduce you. Saker, Biggin…. Bean." Harkell gave a little grin. "You may have seen Bean down in Montraya last winter. He stayed up in the mountains this year so I expect it has been quieter in Montraya this winter."

Bean scowled, but Harkell's soft twinkling eyes eventually drew a reluctant smile from him.

Saker paused in uncorking a flagon to think for a moment. "Didn't you have an offsider with you? Now, wait a minute, let me see if I can remember… Bean and... Mmm. Something and Bean?... I've got it! String and Bean. Where's String then?"

Bean waved his hand airily. "Somewhere about. I think he went off to get more whiskey."

Saker laughed, "If I remember him correctly, he probably went off in one of his panics when he saw us approaching."

"Yep. That's String. I expect he'll be back in a while when he sees you aren't going to drag us off." Bean took a pull on the flagon of whiskey and waited until the accompanying shudder passed before asking, "You were in Harkell's patrol, weren't you. I remember. You only had to walk in the door of the tavern and everything would go quiet."

Biggin gave a slow smile, "Yeah. That's usually all we have to do. Advantage of being built big."

"Hmm. And since you know Greyskies, I presume you accompanied Prince Jarand and Captain Harkell on the quest to find the Rogue Prince that ended so unfortunately?" Just as the two soldiers were tensing up, Bean smiled, "No wonder you were so anxious about Harkell's welfare if you were forced to watch him undergo such dire punishment."

Biggin and Saker looked at each other. "It was worse than that…" began Saker.

"Yes, I suppose it was," said Bean conversationally, not realising the enormity of their involvement. "Anxious is too mild a word. You must have been beside yourselves, wondering whether your captain would survive."

"We were," whispered Biggin. "It was nearly midnight by the time we got back to Montraya. We were dog tired. We'd been riding since mid-morning. But as soon as we were dismissed, we procured fresh mounts and rode straight back out there."

Saker turned to Harkell and gave a wan smile, "But you weren't there, sir. We did try, but you weren't there."

Harkell smiled warmly, "Thank you. I'm sorry I wasn't there after all your efforts… and yours, Greyskies."

Bean grunted, "Just as well he wasn't. He wouldn't have survived that long and crows were already gathering when we cut him down."

"Did you rescue him?" asked Saker.

Bean waved a self-deprecatory hand. "Well, me and some others."

"Do you think we could talk about something else?" asked Harkell, sounding strained but actually concerned that they were heading towards the dangerous territory of Bean's companions.

Biggin bobbed his head. "Sorry sir. We should have thought." He handed one of the flagons of wine around. "So what will you do now that you have recovered?"

With a shock, Harkell realised that without Tarkyn's intervention, even now months later, his damaged back muscles would still have been stiff, even if infection had not killed him first. He gave his head a little shake at the thought. "I do not know. I think I will probably continue to throw in my lot with the trappers. After all, my days as a soldier are over."

"I suppose so, sir," said Saker doubtfully. "But it's such a waste. You're the best officer we ever had… You know, Prince Jarand did send a patrol back out two days later. Perhaps he meant to bring you back in himself, sir."

"Perhaps." Harkell did not sound convinced. Suddenly, he jabbed at the fire with a stick and sent sparks spiralling upward, "But more likely, he was just intending to retrieve the body to put on display somewhere, as a warning to others who failed to protect him."

To cover the awkwardness that followed Harkell's outburst, Bean thrust his flagon towards Biggin. "Here. Try this. Let's see how you handle our mountain brew."

Biggin peered into the flagon and gave it a shake to assess how much was left in it. It was half full. "Mind if I have the rest?" he asked with his slow smile.

"Help yourself," said Bean, his eyes gleaming in anticipation.

Biggin upended the flagon and slowly and deliberately drank down the half flagon of fiery mountain whiskey. When he had finished, he lowered the flask and wiped his hand across his mouth. Then he smiled benignly at Bean. "Very strong, but smoother than most. You must have had a good season to pay for whiskey of this calibre."

Bean goggled at him. "Fiery going down, was it?" he asked hopefully.

"Lovely," responded Biggin.

"Well! That was a bloody waste of half a flagon," exclaimed Bean in disgust.

Harkell chuckled. "You won't catch these two out so easily. They were always the strongest and most loyal of all my men."

Something clicked in Bean's brain as he remembered conversations he had had with Harkell about the terrible flogging he had endured. His gaze travelled from Saker to Biggin before coming to rest on Harkell, "These two?" he said slowly. "These two were your most loyal men? The men you recommended to Prince Jarand?"

"Yes, Bean, they are," said Harkell gently.

For once, Bean was at a complete loss. He had heard Harkell say he was proud of them for carrying out difficult orders but he had not realised what orders. Some of the revulsion he felt must have shown on his face because when he looked again at Saker and Biggin, their faces had become shuttered and tense. He knew he could not afford to antagonise two of Jarand's soldiers so he made an effort to neutralise his expression.

"Don't bother hiding how you feel," said Biggin morosely. "It couldn't be any worse than how we feel about it. And we have been facing that look from our fellow soldiers ever since."

"I hope they have not been ostracizing you," said Harkell sharply.

"That's the least of it. Straps cut, thorns under the saddle, sand in our sleeping bags…"

"Spiders once," added Saker.

"Hmph. Much as I appreciate their sentiments, they are not very clear sighted in their reactions," said Harkell. He turned to Bean, "If there had been the slightest hesitation on the part of these two to do Jarand's bidding, or the slightest indication that their loyalty to me might override their loyalty to Jarand, not only would I have been summarily executed, but so too would they. And the rest of my troops would also have been punished. Prince Jarand may have been angered by my ineffectiveness at protecting him but at least, thanks to these two, he was left in no doubt that the discipline among my men was exemplary."

Bean grunted, "Cold comfort, I would have thought."

"But all I had left."

Bean met Harkell's eyes and for a moment glimpsed the depths that Harkell had plumbed. Then he remembered that Tarkyn had almost failed in healing Harkell because for a while, Harkell had lost the will to live. Bean drew a breath and turned to Saker and Biggin, "In that case, I suppose you did the best by my friend that you could."

Biggin raised his eyebrows in surprise but Saker grunted, "I told you not to underestimate these two. Come on, Bean. Where's String? I promise we won't eat him."

"I'll get him," offered Harkell. "Back in a minute." He wandered over to the shadows of the tent where he could see Danton and String waiting. When he reached them, he jerked a thumb over his shoulder, "All you need to know at the moment, String, is that those two men were under my command and remember you, quite fondly, amazingly enough, from Montraya last year. Saker assumes you have gone off in a panic and has requested the pleasure of your company, promising he won't eat you." He turned his attention to Danton, "And what you need to know is that they are loyal as the day is long to Prince Jarand and if you, with your blonde hair and purple eyes, are on a wanted notice anywhere, they'll turn you in, quick as look at you."

"Yes sir," responded Danton smartly, with a grin. "I'll go for a wander then, shall I?"

Harkell smiled, "If you don't mind. Come on String. Come and say hello."

String rolled his eyes, "Oh my word! Horse and Cart will probably never talk to us again after this."

"No great loss there," murmured Danton as a parting shot.

CHAPTER 14

It was an intended act of kindness that caused the trouble.

After seeing their captain alive and in one piece, Saker and Biggin were determined, unbeknownst to Harkell, to see what they could do to restore his fortunes. They tried to open the conversation with their present captain, a stolid, unimaginative young aristocrat who could see no advantage in risking his career to champion his disgraced predecessor. And they were stonewalled by every other officer they approached. No one wished to be associated with someone who had fallen from the prince's grace.

Eventually, they changed tack and watched the prince's tent until they were able to identify one of his advisors. A ferrety young wizard seemed to spend a great deal of time on errands for His Royal Highness. His name, they discovered, was Journeyman Cloudmaker. They waylaid him as he was leaving a tent that specialised in herbal remedies. Apparently the prince was suffering from a surfeit of spit roasted boar.

"Excuse me, Wizard Cloudmaker," Biggin bowed slightly to indicate that he offered no threat. "Could we offer you a hypothetical situation and ask your opinion?"

The wizard frowned in irritation, "If you are quick."

"If Prince Jarand ordered the flogging of an officer, what would happen to that officer once he had recovered?"

"It would depend on the severity of the offence, of course. I could hardly make that judgement. If the man survived, presumably he would either be banished or re-instated, possibly at a lower rank." His eyes narrowed, "Of whom do you speak?"

Saker and Biggin looked at each other before Saker drew a breath and said, "Captain Harkell sir."

Journeyman waved an impatient hand, "Never heard of him."

"He was in charge of the men who were immobilised by the Rogue Prince, sir."

Suddenly they had the wizard's attention. "Oh. And he has turned up, has he? Very interesting." He gave himself a little shake and produced a sympathetic smile, "I have not heard that he was banished. Hmm. Don't say anything yet, but I will see what I can do. Where is he, if I wish to contact him?"

And eager to help their captain, Saker and Biggin gave him clear directions to the trappers' campsite.

Chapter 15

It happened so quickly there was no time to run. One minute, the trappers were sitting around the campfire swapping yarns with Horse and Cart. The next, soldiers converged on them from four sides. The only luck they had was that Danton happened to be off procuring another flask of whiskey when they came.

Before anyone could speak, the officer in charge, Sergeant Torgan, snapped a salute and said, "Captain Harkell. We have orders to bring you before His Royal Highness, Prince Jarand, immediately."

Glancing neither left nor right, Harkell rose to his feet and saluted in return, Without a word, he fell in behind the sergeant, hemmed in on all sides by soldiers of the Prince, and was marched towards the royal enclosure.

Well before Harkell's escort reached their destination, they turned right and marched their charge down a dimly lit alleyway between two rows of tents.

"Where are you taking me?" Harkell's voice was sharp with alarm.

"Well sir, you won't want to appear before His Highness looking like that, now will you?"

"I can't imagine that it will matter how I look."

"Now come on sir, stop kidding around. You know it's not proper for an officer of Prince Jarand's to appear out of uniform before His Highness." He gave a friendly chuckle. "And I think your hair could do with a trim, pardon me for saying so. And you might want to lose that beard. Even an officer on trial must look his best."

"And for what am I being tried?" But even as the words left his mouth, he knew the answer.

"Desertion, sir."

With sickening certainty, Harkell realised that Prince Jarand would hang him high to exact the last possible morsel of revenge from him for having failed to stop Tarkyn from besting the prince in front of his men. From then on, Harkell maintained sullen silence, submitting to the barber and dressing in the Captain's uniform provided for him. He wondered vaguely which officer had been pressed to part with his spare uniform.

Half an hour later, a new man stood before Sergeant Torgan. The scruffy trapper had been transformed into a well groomed captain of the guard. After months of wearing loose clothing, the jacket felt stiff and constricting but Harkell stood straight, defiantly proud of the uniform that he had taken so many years to earn.

When he was escorted into the prince's tent, he was shocked to find the king seated beside his brother. Harkell bowed low and remained bent from the waist, with his hand on his heart, until the king bade him rise.

"Your name?" rapped out the king.

"Captain Harkell, Your Majesty."

"And do you know why you are here?"

"I believe I have been arraigned on a charge of desertion, Sire."

"And did you desert your post?"

"It could be construed that way, Sire."

"Yes or no," snapped the king.

"No."

"And now you are lying," Kosar stood up and walked over to stand face to face with Harkell. "Unless you prefer me to believe that my brother is lying."

Harkell looked straight into his eyes. "No Sire. I would prefer you to be able to trust Prince Jarand. It matters little to the welfare of the realm if I am found to be false. Yes, I did desert my post but unwittingly, Sire."

The king waved his hand impatiently. "You talk in riddles. I have no time for it. I leave you to my brother's judgement." With that, he walked out into the night, leaving Harkell alone with the prince.

Harkell bowed as the king left. He straightened to find Prince Jarand studying him. "Captain Harkell, I will concede that you may have been in no fit state to return to duty immediately. But months have passed and you have made no attempt to return to your command. Are these not the facts?"

"Yes, Your Highness."

"Well, man, I'm waiting. Explain yourself."

A look of surprise flitted across Harkell's face.

Prince Jarand frowned, "Why the surprise? Surely you did not expect me to hang one of my best officers without giving him a chance to explain his actions."

Since this was exactly what he did expect, it took Harkell a moment to come up with a response, "Your Highness, you left me, dying, on that tree beside the road to Montraya. So it did not occur to me that you would want me to return."

"I sent out a patrol to bring you in, but they returned empty-handed."

"So I have just heard, Sire. But had I still been there, I believe they would have been too late to recover me alive."

For a moment, the prince's eyes narrowed but he seemed determined to be conciliatory. "I was very angry, Captain Harkell, at your failure to protect me. It took me some time to cool down." Harkell nearly missed the prince's next words in his astonishment that Jarand had come so close to an apology. "I can ill afford to lose a competent officer because of one error in judgement. Besides, my brother Tarkyn has since bested the king when he had over six hundred men deployed. We only had eighty with us."

"I offer no excuses, Sire, but I believe we did not have the Rogue Prince's full measure when we set out to find him."

"We still don't," snapped Jarand. He paced over to the table and picked up a piece of parchment. "Here. These are your orders. You will resume command of your company, effective immediately. Report back here tomorrow at midday. Meanwhile, Sergeant Torgan will show you where your men are billeted."

Harkell put his hand on his heart and bowed, his head spinning with his sudden change in fortune, "Thank you Sire."

Part 3: Captain Harkell

Chapter 16

"Your mate seems to be in a bit of trouble," drawled Horse. He chewed the end of a chop bone before spitting it out on the ground. "You didn't mention he was a Captain."

"His business. Anyway, he has done nothing wrong," replied Bean stiffly.

"Yeah, but when did that ever save anyone if they decide to go for you?"

String nodded tensely, "He's right. I knew this was a bad idea. We should never have come here. Now we're all going to be arrested. Oh dear... oh dear..." Suddenly he sprang to his feet and ran headlong into Danton who was just returning with a flagon. "Did you see?" demanded String with more than a tinge of hysteria, "They've got Harkell."

"Yes, I saw," Danton thrust the flagon at the panicking trapper. "Here, have some of this and settle down. The last thing we need is you drawing attention to yourself. You'll end up getting yourself arrested too, if you're not careful." With a firm hand, Danton steered String back to the campfire and pushed him down to sit next to Bean. "So what do you think, Bean? It didn't look like a normal arrest to me. No roughhouse. No shackles. In fact, they didn't lay a finger on him."

"Nah, but I think they would have, if he'd tried to run... What are we going to do, Danton?"

Danton cast a warning glance at Cart and Horse before replying, "We find Stormaway. Then we decide. You two go one way, I'll go another. We'll meet up at our sleeping quarters in half an hour's time, with or without Stormaway."

When they reached their tent at the agreed time, they found that the wizard had arrived before them and was pacing up and down impatiently.

"Where have you lot been? I've been looking all over for you. We have to leave. Now. Harkell's been reinstated into Prince Jarand's service. It's all over the camp. Even now, they could be on their way to arrest us."

"We've heard," said Danton shortly. "Word of it is everywhere. His flogging must have been used as a cautionary tale across the whole of Prince Jarand's service, for so many people to be interested." He grabbed his bedroll and stuffed it into his back pack, "I wish I could talk to him. Gauge his intention."

"Perhaps you can come back later. But right now, we can't afford the risk of waiting around. String and Bean as well. Harkell knows we are all loyal to Tarkyn."

No one argued. They hoisted their packs onto their shoulders and with a last look to make sure they had left no identifying items behind, headed for the door. The sound of military footsteps crunching on the gravel outside the front of the tent, stopped them in their tracks.

"Quickly. Under the back wall," hissed Danton.

They sped to the back of the tent but the canvas was strung too tightly for them to get under it. Bean and Danton hauled together on the canvas until a peg came loose. As soon as Danton had yanked it out of the ground, the four of them dived through the gap, dragging their packs with them. They had not even had time to roll to their feet before they heard soldiers entering the tent. They didn't wait. Danton pointed to their left and they crept quickly down the narrow space created by the backs of two rows of tents, away from the king's enclosure and the soldier's quarters.

As they reached the first thoroughfare, they straightened up and turned to their right to walk unhurriedly past shuttered stalls. The crowds were thinning as people said their final goodnights and turned their steps towards their sleeping quarters. Danton and Stormaway were adept at disappearing into a crowd and little heed was paid to another set of travellers lugging their possessions on their backs. With the trappers in tow, they zig-zagged between rows of tents, never going for too long in one direction and matching their pace to that of the dwindling crowds. From time to time, they paused long enough to listen but their straining ears picked up no sound of pursuit.

As they neared the far edge of the encampment, Stormaway reached inside his cloak and threw small black missiles above and behind him. They shot upwards, angled back over the tents to disguise the fugitives' position. With a series of sharp reports, the missiles blossomed into a pre-arranged signal of four brightly coloured flares high in the night sky.

Deeper in the encampment, they could hear exclamations of appreciation from the crowds. Stormaway threw another ten up in quick succession, to foster the belief that it was a display in honour of the king.

And while the guards had their eyes trained on the fireworks, Stormaway, Danton and the trappers slipped between them and ran for the cover of the trees.

As they entered the forest, Rainstorm and Thunder Storm swung down from the branches where they had been poised, ready to fire on the guards if needed. Glancing to check that there were indeed four of them, the woodmen asked no questions but guided them quickly and quietly into the depths of the forest to Tarkyn. In their wake, other woodfolk removed all trace of their passage.

The location of Tarkyn's firesite had already been moved. Even though it was the middle of the night, every man, woman and child had packed up, obliterated all trace of their stay and transferred to a new site. As Stormaway, Danton and the two trappers arrived, woodfolk were still settling children back to sleep, collecting water, setting out cooking utensils and coaxing a new fire into life.

While others prepared the new firesite, Tarkyn stood at the edge of the clearing awaiting their return. He carried a very sleepy Midnight, who tended to become nervous and unsettled when the firesite was moved. The little boy was draped over Tarkyn's left shoulder but roused himself briefly to wave at the newcomers.

"Are you all right?" asked Tarkyn sharply as soon as they were within earshot. "What has happened? All we know is that four of you have had to leave suddenly. Where is Harkell?"

The four sorcerers arrayed themselves before him and bowed briefly before Danton spoke. Even if Tarkyn was prepared to forgo their obeisance they, particularly under the critical eye of Stormaway, were not. "Sire, Harkell was taken under guard to Prince Jarand. He has since been reinstated as Captain of the Guard."

The strength of Tarkyn's shock rocked everyone within a twenty-yard radius and made Midnight whimper in his arms. Those woodfolk who could leave their newly settled children, poured out of their shelters to see what was amiss.

"Sorry, little one," murmured the prince, stroking Midnight's back. When he had soothed Midnight and himself, he looked up at the four sorcerers facing him, "So, when faced with the liege lord he was born to serve, he betrayed us, did he?"

"It would appear so, Your Highness," said Stormaway as they walked over to the fire. "Even as we made our escape through the back of the tent, soldiers were approaching from the front. We only just left in time. I think we must assume the worst and prepare against it."

Tarkyn heaved a sigh, "And what is the worst, Stormaway?"

"One thing is sure. He won't know where we are, although he will know the general area," said Waterstone, who has just emerged from settling Sparrow. "We may have to consider leaving the vicinity of the encampment altogether."

"He knows the potential effect of your reactions, an effect you have just demonstrated," said Danton with a sympathetic smile.

As Lapping Water handed out freshly brewed tea, she said, "And he knows the full extent of your control over animals. He is quite likely to explain to Jarand how you overcame his company of soldiers by controlling their horses, isn't he, since that would explain his failure to protect."

"Anything else?"

"Yes, of course there is. He knows all about woodfolk and how lethal we can be," Autumn Leaves thumped Tarkyn on the back and guided him to a log that he could lower himself onto, with Midnight in his arms, "You're rattled, aren't you, by another betrayal?"

Tarkyn nodded tightly. After a minute, he raised his eyes from staring into the fire to look at the woodman, "Yes. I really like Harkell and I thought… I thought he shared our care for Eskuzor. I know he said that he's ambitious but it did seem that his ambition was to have influence over events that have real effect on Eskuzor's future." He gave a sad smile. "And I thought we were giving him that."

Bean cleared his throat, "Tarkyn, there was word in the camp that Jarand had, in fact, sent out a patrol to bring Harkell back to Montraya after the flogging…in which case Harkell's major premise for forsaking his allegiance to Jarand, that he had been left for dead, would no longer stand."

"And despite my original misgivings," said Danton, "I do believe Harkell to be an honourable man. More than that, I think his honour overrides his personal ambition. But I don't know which way his honour will take him if he now believes that Jarand did not abandon him. He was born and bred in Jarand's lands. He spent thirty-five years in loyal service to him. He gave you his oath, Tarkyn, only when he believed that Prince Jarand had deliberately left him to die. Even after that dreadful flogging, he would have remained true to Jarand, had he thought that Jarand still wanted his service."

"And what of his oath to conceal the presence of woodfolk?" demanded Autumn Leaves.

"Again, I do not know. Jarand already knows of our presence. So if the prince asks about woodfolk, will Harkell feel obliged to tell him what he knows?" Danton shook his head, "I find it hard to believe that he would turn on us after what we have been through together but on the other hand, there were definitely soldiers entering our tent as we left."

Tarkyn listened with a gathering frown, "Tell us how they came to find out that Harkell was in the encampment."

"That pesky, chatty wizard, Greyskies Swampwater, took it upon himself to tell the two men who had actually flogged Harkell," grumped String. He waved his arms in exasperation, "Because apparently those men, by Harkell's own judgement the best of his company, were feeling bad about what they had been ordered to do."

Bean cleared his throat, "In fairness, String, I would have to say that they did seem genuinely remorseful."

"So, did these men then betray Harkell? That doesn't make sense, if they were so concerned for him," objected Tarkyn.

String shrugged, "Who knows? Probably they just told someone who told someone and so on, until it came to the wrong ears."

"Might have done it deliberately, String," said Bean, scratching his beard. "Might have thought they were doing him a favour."

"And maybe they were doing him a favour if that is truly where his heart lies," said Tarkyn heavily.

"I don't think we can assume that," said Waterstone firmly, "And I don't think we should abandon him to his fate if he goes to it unwillingly. I have counted him as my friend and I will not so easily forsake him."

Waterstone's attitude lifted the whole mood of the gathering. Tarkyn sat up straighter and smiled, "Well said, Waterstone. When I last saw him, he was my liegeman and as such, I have a duty to protect him. Besides, I too count him as a friend. I think the least we should do is give him a chance to explain and check that he is not being constrained against his will."

Stormaway gave a gentle cough, "Your Highness, rumours were rife after Harkell's arrest. The earliest information suggested that he was to be tried for desertion. So it caused something of a sensation when news spread that he was to be reinstated."

Tarkyn stared at him.

"Sire, it is possible that he cut some sort of deal," finished Stormaway apologetically.

Danton also looked unhappy. "And even if we give him the chance to explain, how can we believe what he says? If he has changed his allegiance to Jarand, will he not pretend to keep faith with us so that he can gather information on Jarand's behalf?"

"If we can extricate him and he chooses to rejoin us in the woodlands, there will be little doubt that he has stayed true to Tarkyn, since he wouldn't be able to send messages from within our group to Jarand," said Lapping Water.

"I think he could. Unless we watch him minutely, he could leave a trail or set a tree aflame to betray our position at a crucial time in the future." Stormaway rubbed his chin, "I suppose he would find it hard to smuggle in carrier pigeons but they could be left at pre-arranged points within the forest for his use."

"And what if he chooses to stay with his men?" Danton kept his eyes trained on a stick he was rolling between his fingers. "Do we kill him to keep our knowledge safe or do we chance his word and keep in touch with him?"

"*I* would not want him killed," said Rainstorm firmly. "He is my friend, as he is yours and he has been through too much already. He has a wife and children back in Montraya. If he is suddenly welcomed back into Jarand's army, he may be able to see his family again. He has a lot to weigh up."

The debate raged deep into the night through several large pots of tea.

Chapter 17

Harkell left Prince Jarand in a daze, amazed that he had survived the encounter and even more amazed that he had been reinstated, particularly at his previous rank. And now that he was reinstated, the looks that he encountered from soldiers and officers may have contained sympathy but most also contained unfeigned welcome.

When he entered the section designated for his company, The Royal Montrayan Guard, the cheers were deafening and he was surrounded by smiling faces and applause. Being the good officer he was, he thrust his personal concerns to the back of his mind and responded cordially to his men's greetings.

In the midst of the noise, Sergeant Torgan leaned in and murmured, "I'll head off now. By the way, did you know Saker and Biggin risked making themselves very unpopular by pushing your cause with several officers? I don't think they had even realised they'd succeeded until you appeared just now."

Harkell turned his attention to the two big soldiers standing a little to one side. Now that he studied the position of the men around them, he could see that they were cheering and smiling with the rest of them but were not part of their company. That, at least, was a problem he could easily address. He nodded his thanks and dismissed Sergeant Torgan saying quietly, "Make sure you carry out my orders."

He gestured to the two soldiers to come forward. Immediately, an expectant hush fell over his men. "Saker and Biggin, I believe you have been lobbying on my behalf."

A derisive snort from somewhere near the back of the room made Captain Harkell look around, "The next man who interrupts when I am speaking will regret it. I have never put up with insubordination and I am disappointed to hear that in my absence, some of you have treated fellow soldiers with disrespect." He waited until he could have heard a pin drop before turning once more to Saker and Biggin to repeat publicly the gist of what he had said to them at the campfire, "You have my heartfelt thanks for carrying out such difficult orders. By doing so, you preserved the honour of our company as a disciplined, loyal unit. To have done otherwise would have brought death and dishonour to members of your company."

An uncomfortable silence was finally broken by a scar-faced old soldier called Nory, "Sir, I thought you didn't approve of brutality. We thought we were supporting you."

Harkell nodded, "You are absolutely right. I don't. So I expect you to carry out any orders you receive with the least force possible. Sometimes that still means a great deal of force is required. If you remember, Prince Jarand's orders were quite specific."

And since this was coming perilously close to saying that he didn't approve of Prince Jarand's level of brutality, Harkell quickly turned the conversation to the safer ground of catching up on events in his soldiers' lives and court life that he had missed, and from there, onto the practicalities of accommodation and duty rosters.

Only when the reunion had run its course and those not on duty had retired for the night, did Harkell have any space to think about what had happened and where he stood. Danton was right in saying that Harkell was a man of honour and he now found himself sworn to two liege lords who were in conflict with each other. Worse than that, he was sure that Jarand would suspect him because of his protracted absence while on the other hand, his reinstatement into Jarand's army would undermine Tarkyn's faith in him.

Harkell heaved a sigh in the darkness. Here he was, a man of integrity in his own mind, but doubted on all sides. And try as he might, he could see no way of proving his good faith. By the time he fell asleep, he was no closer to a solution.

So it was with a sense of inevitability that Harkell awoke in the early hours of the morning, with cold steel pressed against his throat.

"Morning Danton," he whispered, feeling the knife's pressure against the movement of his throat. "I hope you realise that my batman is asleep over there."

"Is that a warning or a threat?" murmured the elite guard in his ear.

"A warning, of course. It will do neither of us any good if you are found in my quarters. I am glad you are here. We need to talk. I will come outside where we can talk undisturbed. Can you make sure that I'm not under surveillance?"

"How do I know you won't raise the alarm, the moment I move away?"

Danton saw a flash of white in the darkness as Harkell smiled, "You will have to trust your own judgement. I have nothing else to offer you."

Danton was a little non-plussed by Harkell's casual reaction but he had not been sent to kill him, only to discover his circumstances and to determine whether he needed to be rescued or conversely, what threat he represented. After a moment's hesitation, he nodded and disappeared outside to scan the surrounding area.

Harkell grabbed his clothes and his cloak and after glancing at the suspiciously still batman, crept to the door of the tent. On second thoughts, he stole over to the sleeping figure and leant down over him, listening for sounds of breathing. Reassured, he headed once more for the door.

At a nod from Danton, he crept out of the tent and followed in the noiseless wake of the elite guard until they reached a row of closed stalls, away from any sleeping quarters.

"What stopped you from waking your batman?" asked Danton. "I saw you standing over him."

"Not the prospect of a knife in the back from you, if that's what you're thinking," replied Harkell tartly. "I was checking you hadn't already killed poor little Nyrus. He seemed too still."

"Don't worry. He'll sleep it off and never know he's been drugged… Handkerchief over the mouth impregnated with poison from an elite guard's toolkit."

"Same as the one that nearly killed Boravar?

"No. This one doesn't need an antidote."

Harkell considered Danton, "You're pretty good, aren't you? Penetrated Prince Jarand's soldiers' quarters, presumably slipped past the boundary guards… twice. And all without raising an alarm."

Danton gave a grunt of laughter, "You think that's good? Once, I actually sneaked past woodfolk lookouts, without even realising they were there."

"Very impressive. But this all goes to prove what I already know."

"Which is?"

"That I need to find a way to prove that I am still loyal to Prince Tarkyn."

"Considering you have now returned to Jarand's service, that will take some doing. You're lucky I didn't just kill you to stop you from talking to Jarand."

"I doubt it. You would already have done so, if that were what you intended." Harkell gave him a smile, full of friendship and warmth. "My liege would not so quickly abandon his liegeman, whatever the appearances of the situation, without at least giving him a chance to explain."

"It was a community decision, you know."

Harkell laughed quietly, "I'm sure it was. And I'm also sure that the prince would have overridden any decision he did not like."

Danton smiled reluctantly in return before folding his arms to keep his distance. "So go on. Convince me. You can start by telling me why you sent those soldiers after us."

"I sent a message to warn you but the note was returned to me unopened. It's in my pocket here somewhere. Just a minute," He rummaged round and produced a small twist of parchment, which he handed to Danton, "You can't read it in this light but you can keep it and read it later if you like. It says something like, '*Leave now. Thank the healer for his help and tell him that I have every faith in him and his methods.*'" He shrugged, "I know it's cryptic but I couldn't risk being more explicit in case it was intercepted."

"This does not prove your loyalty."

"No. I can think of nothing that will. I was merely answering your question."

Danton hesitated for a moment before saying, "I don't doubt your honour…"

"Thank you."

"… but I don't know which way your honour will take you." Before Harkell could say any more, Danton added, "And that doesn't mean that I will believe what you say. I myself have lied for honourable causes."

Harkell began to lose patience, "Obviously, Danton. Whoever I choose to follow, I will have to lie to the other." He flung up his hand. "Now, be quiet and listen. I will explain to you why I am and always will be Prince Tarkyn's man. It will be up to you to decide whether or not I am lying."

He sat down on an upturned crate and pulled his cloak around him. For a moment he concentrated on fiddling with the folds of the material before looking up resolutely to meet Danton's eyes. "My whole concept of honour has changed since I first struggled to abandon Jarand as my liege." He took a breath to give himself time to gather his thoughts. "All my life, I have fought against society's expectations, to rise from my beginnings as a blacksmith's son to the position of Captain of the Guard. And yet, in all that time it never occurred to me that a prince might treat me with respect or consideration." He gave a wry smile, "You have no idea what a shock it was that Prince Tarkyn considered an oath of allegiance to be a two-way contract between liege and liegeman. And when he actually avowed that I would not be held to my oath if he mistreated me, well!… It took my breath away." Harkell's voice had become husky with emotion. He had to clear his throat before continuing, "At the time, I accepted the savagery of Jarand's punishment as an inevitable consequence of my own failure, but I wouldn't again."

Danton thought carefully before he spoke, wishing to challenge Harkell but at the same time loath to make light of his display of emotion. However, he remembered that Harkell had admitted that he was a practised actor and hardened his heart, "But I have heard that Jarand sent out a party to bring you back in. So he had not abandoned you, as you thought at the time. Surely then, your premise for betraying your inherited commitment to him no longer exists." He waved his hand to indicate Harkell's military clothing, "Look at you! He has even reinstated you at your previous rank."

"And in one fell swoop, undermined my credibility with Prince Tarkyn," said Harkell bitterly.

"You have not yet answered my objection, Harkell," pressed Danton gently.

Harkell waved a hand then dropped it despondently, "There's not much point, is there? You have no reason to believe me."

"If there were no chance of believing you, I would have killed you out of hand, my friend." Danton placed his hand on Harkell's shoulder. "Give me the opportunity you said you would, to decide whether or not you are lying."

Harkell suppressed a sigh, "Very well. There are several reasons that my loyalty will not revert to Jarand. Firstly, Jarand may have sent out a patrol to save me after he left me for dead, but it was too little too late. As far as I am concerned, Prince Jarand has failed to fulfil his obligations as liege lord, not only in his harsh treatment of me but also in his ongoing lack of concern for *all* of his dependents. And secondly," here he gave a quirky little smile, "since I now find myself in the position where I will prove false no matter what I do, I am effectively free to make my own choice." He lifted his chin and looked steadily at Danton. "I have watched Prince Tarkyn working to protect Eskuzor's future while Jarand schemes only for his own self-aggrandisement. Having seen Jarand from Prince Tarkyn's viewpoint, there is no possibility of going back… My original commitment to Prince Tarkyn required a huge leap of faith, but association with him has served to strengthen my resolve to stand by the one man in Eskuzor with the integrity and power to guide Eskuzor's future." Harkell had become so impassioned as he spoke these words that he finished slightly out of breath. He gave an embarrassed smile, "So there you have it. Take it or leave it. I have no more to say. If he will accept me, Prince Tarkyn still has me wholeheartedly at his command."

Danton eyed him for a moment trying to read his expression in the darkness. "And what if Tarkyn ordered you back into the forest?"

"Danton," said Harkell gently. "You weren't listening. His will is my command."

"One thing puzzles me. Why do you now refer to your erstwhile friend Tarkyn using his title, when you used to be more informal?"

Harkell put his head on one side, "Surely you know. I would not presume a close relationship with His Highness that may no longer exist. Conversely, I do not bother with Jarand's title because he has lost my respect."

Danton seemed to reach a decision, "Tell me what happened."

As briefly as he could, Harkell described his audience with the King and then with Prince Jarand.

"Uncharacteristically generous of Jarand, wouldn't you say?" Danton mulled it over, "And he didn't even ask you where, or with whom, you had been?"

"No, but I'm sure he will. He knows I disappeared close to his encounter with Prince Tarkyn. And no matter what I say I suspect he will feed me misinformation to test me." Harkell gave a crooked smile, "So whether you trust me or not, don't trust my information."

"Do you want to stay?"

"No, but I will, unless Prince Tarkyn commands otherwise. I would much rather be at his side and with all of you but as he said, 'There are different types of service'…" Harkell pulled at his cuff for a minute before resolutely raising his eyes, "… and Danton, if I disappeared now after Jarand has made a public gesture of welcoming me back, it would embarrass him and would be an undeniable betrayal. Such a public betrayal would not go unpunished. If he couldn't reach me, my wife and children would be at risk." His voice was thick with regret. "And you cannot rescue them all. There is also my brother and my parents."

"I see… You are right, of course."

Harkell glanced at the sky. "Dawn is coming. So if you're not going to kill me, I had better get back before I am missed."

Danton gave Harkell a firm pat on the shoulder. "Good luck, my friend. We will all miss you but we will not forsake you. Keep your eye out for that crow."

So saying, he glided off, a dark movement among the shadows.

Chapter 18

"**B**ut is he safe?' demanded Tarkyn.

As instructed, Danton had woken Tarkyn to report, the moment he returned. Rainstorm had met him at the forest's edge and had stuck like glue to his side ever since.

"I would say that Harkell's position is… *difficult* if he intends to hold true to you," replied Danton. "My best guess is that King Kosar and Prince Jarand have realised that Harkell may have useful knowledge about you or may be in contact with you. It is not in Jarand's nature to be so forgiving. I suspect they will begin to question him when they think he has had time to appreciate Jarand's generosity and to consider the implications to his family. Alternatively, they will set him up and use him in an attempt to track you down."

The prince dragged his wolfskin cloak around his shoulders and, careful not to wake Midnight, emerged from his warm shelter into the dawn chill. It was an indication of his level of concern that he had risen so early.

Rainstorm took one look at his drawn face and set about getting a fire started. As he leant a handful of twigs against each other, he said, "And they know about your power with birds now Tarkyn, so that crow may be noticed if you use it to contact him."

Tarkyn waved his hand impatiently. "But I must contact him. So I will send a message into the encampment with String and Bean and find a fieldmouse to deliver it. They won't be looking for that."

"But what approach are we going to take, Sire?" asked Danton

"Worry about that later. Firstly I must get a message to him." When Danton looked as though he would ask another question, Tarkyn said tetchily, "Its contents are not to do with you or anyone else. Now, get me pen and parchment. Let String and Bean know that they are going back in. No, wait until they get up. Then tell them. And I would prefer you and Stormaway to remain with us for the time being."

Aware that Tarkyn was in an irascible mood, Danton bowed and left to do his bidding without further comment.

"It's not Danton's fault that Jarand has got hold of Harkell," observed Rainstorm mildly, in a break between blowing on the first tiny flames of his fire.

Tarkyn glared at the young woodman, who held his gaze unwaveringly, his green eyes unusually solemn. Suddenly the prince smiled. "You wouldn't be championing your brother's cause against your prince, would you?"

With a spark of defiance, Rainstorm muttered, "Could be."

Tarkyn decided that this was going nowhere useful and reverted to the original statement, "I do not hold Danton responsible. It was an unfortunate sequence of events that none of us could have foreseen. But it was I who sanctioned Harkell going into the encampment." He pulled his cloak around him, "Allow me, if you will, a little leeway to be anxious about him."

Rainstorm's face softened, "It was not your fault either."

"But unlike Danton, I am responsible for Harkell's welfare. And sooner or later he will be placed in a position where he will be unable, in all conscience, to follow Jarand's orders." Tarkyn watched Rainstorm mulling this over, "What if Jarand orders an attack on the king and Tormadell? What if he finds me or any of you, and orders Harkell to kill one of us… And that is just the sort of thing Jarand would do to test his loyalty. What will Harkell do then? He knows that if he refuses, not only he but his family will pay the price."

"His family were not threatened when he was punished last time," objected Rainstorm.

Tarkyn shook his head, "No, but then Harkell was merely punished for making a mistake. He had not deliberately defied or betrayed Jarand. These would be far more serious matters." The prince picked up a stick and started to break bits off the end of it but he was too agitated for this to calm him. He threw the stick away and jumped to his feet to pace back and forth, glancing at other woodfolk who were arriving to join them, surmising correctly that Rainstorm had summoned them, while he continued to talk, "And both Jarand and his soldiers know he disappeared close to where I was seen. There has to be a question mark in their minds hanging over Harkell's allegiance, especially since he has not been seen by anyone since then. And if Jarand is any judge of men, he will know that Harkell would lay down his life for what he believes in. So Jarand will take steps to enforce Harkell's compliance. Would Harkell be prepared to lay down his family's life to defy Jarand? I don't know. But I hope he is not placed in a position where he has to make that choice."

"He said he would return to the forest, if you commanded it, Tarkyn," said Danton, arriving with the writing materials, "knowing that would expose his family to Jarand's wrath."

Waterstone frowned, "You could not demand that, Tarkyn, if it would place his family at risk."

Tarkyn stopped his pacing and scowled at the woodman, "I do not need you to tell me that. And I am sure Harkell knew I would never force him to risk his family when he said it; make of that what you will."

"What I make of that," said Autumn Leaves mildly, "is that he trusts you to consider his welfare."

Ancient Oak smiled at his royal bloodbrother, "And that being the case, Tarkyn, you and all of us will have to find a way to extricate his family."

Tarkyn's shoulders dropped noticeably. He let his gaze encompass all the gathered woodfolk and sorcerers, "Would you be willing to do that?"

There was a fractional silence while the woodfolk conferred mentally. "Yes, Tarkyn, we would," responded Ancient Oak, reiterating what he had said, but now with the clear support of the whole group. "For you, so that you do not have to shoulder the responsibility on your own, and for Harkell."

"Where would we hide them? That would be… let me see… at least six more sorcerers. I can't keep sending sorcerers to Lord Tolward's house. He has already taken in seven refugees that I sent him. His holding will not sustain many more."

"We will accept Harkell's family to abide among us, if we must," said Tree Wind, "Harkell's unusual thinking instigated the liberation of all those woodfolk who were trapped in the Lost Forest and helped us to over-set the King's intention of trapping you. His straight talking repaired the rift between you and us that had opened in the Lost Forest and, at great risk to himself, he showed you how to protect yourself against an attack by enemy sorcerers. We cannot afford to lose such a person. If we are to protect Eskuzor, we need him on our side without fear of compromise."

CHAPTER 19

"Enter."

Captain Harkell, immaculately turned out, walked out of the early morning sunlight into the relative gloom of the prince's tent and bowed, hand on heart. No one watching him could have told that his heart was thumping within his chest or that every nerve was on edge. He straightened up and waited for the game of cat and mouse to begin.

Prince Jarand was seated on a heavy, ornately carved chair that would have required significant effort to transport for his use. His cold grey eyes surveyed the captain from head to foot, as though searching for any slight fault in his presentation. Slowly he brought his eyes up to meet Harkell's and stared at him for a full minute before speaking.

"Captain Harkell, I believe you owe me your life. Had I followed my brother's inclination, you would have been hanged for desertion."

"Sire, I have always owed you my life."

The prince nodded slowly, "That is true. All people subject to my authority live or die by my will." He studied his nails for a moment before returning his gaze to the soldier standing before him. He gave a chilly smile that sent a tingle down Harkell's backbone, "We return to Montraya in a fortnight. No doubt you are looking forward to being reunited with your family."

Since Prince Jarand had never shown any interest in the family affairs of anyone serving him, Harkell was a little disappointed at the prince's lack of subtlety. The first statement alone would have been sufficient to lay the threat of his family's welfare on the table. "Indeed Sire, I will be very glad to see them."

"Just so," Jarand indicated a straight backed chair that had been placed a little to one side. "Be seated, Captain Harkell. You and I have a lot to discuss."

Harkell could barely contain his surprise. In twenty years of service, he had never before been invited to sit in the prince's presence.

"Thank you, Sire."

He sat down stiffly, attempting to look formal, but at ease. *Overall,* he thought, *I probably just look nervous.* He tried to remember that this man was simply Tarkyn's brother and that, according to Harkell's own philosophy, all men were of equal value. And yet, he had only to look into Jarand's eyes to see the prince's certain knowledge of his own superiority and conversely, his utter disregard for the worth of those around him.

That is his belief, not mine. Tarkyn is far greater than Jarand and I can converse with him on equal terms. He smiled privately, *I may not have equal status from Tarkyn's point of view, but he definitely considers me worthy of respect.* Harkell took a deep breath and let it out slowly. He was ready.

Or thought he was. "Now Captain Harkell, tell me what it is like to live with my brother, Prince Tarkyn."

Harkell's eyes bugged out of his head. He was so shocked that he coughed and choked on his own spit. When he had recovered from his coughing fit, he found Jarand waiting patiently, a faint smile playing around his lips.

"So, Captain. Has that given you the time you needed to think?"

"No Sire. That is, I was too busy trying to get my breath to think. But I do not need time to think. That would imply that I was contriving my answers."

The prince raised his eyebrows, "Not necessarily. It might imply that you were considering how best to describe my brother's living conditions to me."

"May I ask why you think I have been in Prince Tarkyn's camp, Sire?"

"No, you may not. I have asked a simple question and I require an answer."

Harkell racked his brain trying to work out on what Jarand was basing his apparent knowledge. He hoped and suspected that it was simply surmise based on the fact that Tarkyn had been close to where Harkell had been abandoned. In the end he opted for partial honesty. Aware that he may be condemning himself, Harkell began to talk, "Conditions are primitive, my lord. Accommodation is makeshift and temporary because he must move frequently to stay ahead of his pursuers. Prince Tarkyn sleeps on the ground, or on pine needles or rushes if they are available. He eats relatively simple fare and wears basic practical clothing."

"And what of his powers?"

Harkell thought carefully, not wishing to give away any powers that Jarand was as yet unaware of. "His shield and power shafts are strong. He can produce light and fireballs… And he can direct the movements of some birds."

Prince Jarand frowned, "Not all birds?"

"I think not, Sire. I think some of the more fearsome predators will only respond to him, if they choose to." He did not add that he was fairly sure that if Tarkyn were under threat, the raptors would respond without hesitation.

"And can he penetrate another's shield?"

"I have no idea, Sire. But I believe he can penetrate his own."

"And did you speak with him yourself? Do you know his intentions?"

Harkell looked down at his hands for a moment before resolutely meeting the prince's eyes once more. *Quite artistic*, he thought. "Sire, I was semi-conscious for a lot of the time I spent in the prince's camp. I was kept in an old tent while I recovered, and saw little of His Highness during that time," he said, not wishing to describe the woodfolk's shelters too closely. "It was only when I ventured forth that the prince spoke to me but even then only in passing. I do not think he trusted me, Sire." He paused for a moment. "I did overhear some conversations though. He seemed to speak quite freely with his companions."

"And…?"

Harkell breathed a private sigh of relief that the prince did not know enough to doubt his story so far. He frowned as though puzzled, "He seemed to support you and King Kosar… although I gathered his support was conditional." He glanced at Jarand, apparently embarrassed to say more. When Jarand merely waved his hand to continue, he covered the awkwardness by saying, "To be honest Sire, I was surprised that he was not intent on retaliation."

"Were you?" Jarand's voice was icy. "And yet the king and I were the injured parties, not Tarkyn. After all, the king lost many guards and a public icon when Tarkyn fled from our *legitimate* justice."

Harkell's heart gave an unpleasant thump. He had inadvertently allowed his prejudice to show. "I beg your pardon, Sire. I did not mean to imply the fault lay with you or the king… merely that Prince Tarkyn may have taken that view."

"I do not remember saying that your opinions were of value," snapped Jarand. "Keep your comments to observations only. What is the size of his company?"

Harkell paused, knowing that this was a vital piece of information but not wanting to be so inaccurate that he might be caught out. Eventually he said, "The size of his company varies, Your Highness. At times there are less than fifty. At other times, I believe he has had over two hundred gathered together. Very few compared to Your Highness… However, I was under the impression that there might be others he could call upon."

"And who were his companions?"

Harkell bit his lip before replying, "I know Lord Danton was there… The odd trapper visited the camp from time to time… but mostly I was kept isolated." He glanced at Jarand then looked away. *Show him I have compromised loyalties…*

"Captain Harkell! You are being evasive. I know he has woodfolk with him."

...but then show my heart is really with Jarand. Harkell let out an audible sigh of apparent relief. "Yes, Sire, he does. I was sworn not to tell anyone of their existence and since they healed me, I felt obliged to keep faith with them."

Jarand frowned, "You tread a dangerous path if you place your loyalty to others above your loyalty to me."

Harkell was quite unmoved by the prince's threatening tone. After all, his words merely summed up Harkell's entire situation. "I beg your pardon, Your Highness. But it sits ill with me to break an oath."

Jarand stared at him, for the first time taking in the basic integrity of the man before him. "Tell me about them," he demanded flatly.

Harkell took a long breath as he thought furiously, trying to remember what Jarand would either know or surmise by now. "They can be recognised by their light brown hair and green eyes. They wear similar clothes to those Prince Tarkyn wore when he met you. Everything about them is designed to help them blend into the woodland."

Jarand nodded, "I met four of them when I spoke with Tarkyn. They appeared suddenly in the clearing. What do you know about their magical abilities?"

"Very little, I'm afraid. I did not notice anyone appear or disappear while I was with them. I did ask one of them, a fellow named Rainstorm..."

"Yes. I met him. Go on."

"And he said they didn't have any magical abilities. He didn't mention the appearing that you have described. Perhaps they take it for granted."

Jarand frowned, "And if they take that for granted, what else can they do that they think nothing of, I wonder?"

Harkell decided this question was rhetorical and did not answer. For several minutes, silence reigned while Jarand thought through what Harkell had told him. Suddenly he galvanised into action.

"Guardsman, in here."

Harkell's stomach turned over, leaving him feeling weak and sick, but Jarand merely ordered the guardsman to fetch wine and food. Harkell's reaction did not go unnoticed however. Jarand smiled to himself in real amusement, although Harkell could only manage a weak smile in return.

"No, my fine captain. I will not hold you responsible for being rescued by people loyal to my brother. And the information you have given me is consistent with what I know from other sources." He waited until the refreshments were brought in and placed on a side table. He waved the guardsman away, his eyes never leaving Harkell's face. "You may pour two glasses, Captain. Have one for yourself."

As Harkell murmured his thanks and rose to do Jarand's bidding, he reflected that if Jarand had extended this courtesy to him before he had met Tarkyn, he would have been overwhelmed by the honour of it. As it was, he merely recognised it as another move in Jarand's game.

The prince sipped his wine, never taking his eyes off Harkell. As the minutes lengthened, Harkell became bored with waiting for Jarand's next move and his soft brown eyes began to wander around the tent, taking in the rich tapestries, the unlit lantern hanging from the centre pole and the finely woven carpets underfoot. He noted the tension in the tent walls, the travelling wardrobe in the corner and the width of the doorway. While his eyes wandered around the interior, his ears listened to the sounds of people passing the tent and the faint click of a guard's weapon as he shifted his position.

Suddenly the prince lost patience and put his glass down abruptly. Harkell's eyes snapped to attention.

"Captain Harkell, you forget yourself. Your demeanour has changed since last I saw you. You would never before have felt at ease enough to survey my quarters right under my eye."

Despite his best intentions, Harkell's eyes twinkled ruefully at the dread prince. "Your pardon, my lord. I am afraid curiosity is my besetting sin."

Jarand was non-plussed. After a moment he ventured sarcastically, "Perhaps you have become used to the more informal style of my brother?"

"Your Highness, I would never mistake your expectations for his, despite the courtesy you have offered me."

"Hmph. You are no doubt aware that your disappearance in the vicinity of my brother followed by your protracted absence places your loyalty in question? … Particularly when you yourself acknowledge that you thought I no longer required your service."

Harkell nodded, "Yes Sire."

"So? Do you not wish to convince me of your loyalty?"

"I can think of nothing to say that would convince you. We both know that I would profess my loyalty to you whatever my true inclinations."

"Stars above, man!" exclaimed the prince springing to his feet, with Harkell hastily following suit. "Have you no sense of self-preservation? I can think of no other person from whom I would endure this level of insolence."

Harkell bowed, hand on heart. "Sire, I speak only the truth. My loyalty cannot be judged by my words."

"Get up! What are you saying? Do you want me to order you to capture or assassinate my brother? That would prove your loyalty beyond doubt, would it not?"

"If I succeeded, it would. But as things stand, neither you nor Prince Tarkyn has any faith in my loyalty. His followers would not let me near him."

"But you could find him, couldn't you?"

Harkell thought for a moment. "I believe so, but only unarmed and alone. His woodfolk would know if I were followed and would lead me astray."

Jarand nodded decisively. "It will do. You are the first clue we have had to finding him, the first link, the only source of any information about him, other than what he chooses to reveal." Suddenly he turned the full force of his glare upon Harkell. "I believe myself to be a reasonable judge of character. And so I will tell you that I believe that you are no longer wholly devoted to my cause." As Harkell went to speak he stopped him with a gesture. "Despite that, you are a useful tool. You will do as I ask because you must and, at least for the time being, I ask only that you perform your duties as Captain of the Guard and that you liaise between Tarkyn and myself."

Harkell blinked with relief.

"You must let no one in this encampment know the task I have assigned you. *No one.* Is that clear?"

"Yes Sire."

Jarand strode to his table and grabbed a rolled parchment, stuffing it into a deep blue cylinder. "Here. I want this delivered tonight. By you. In person. Directly to my younger brother. Not via some carrier pigeon or some wild egret. Clear? In person." He handed him a separate parchment. "These orders will get you past the perimeter guards. I expect a report when you return. That is all. You may leave."

For the rest of the day, Harkell went through the motions of organising his men, responding to queries and complaints, and making plans for the return to Montraya at the end of the week.

At the evening meal, a hiccough in the conversation heralded Captain Harkell's entry into the officers' mess. After a moment's hesitation, he bowed with a theatrical flourish before exclaiming, "Please don't interrupt your conversations on my account. But while I have your attention, does anyone know where I can procure a good barrel of rum? We seem to have polished ours off last night."

A roar of laughter greeted this sally and any awkwardness pertaining to Harkell's return was soon forgotten in a deluge of suggestions. Harkell felt a tinge of regret that he was no longer simply one of their number. There were many good men here. He gave a mental shrug; by supporting Tarkyn, he was not betraying them. He was working for all of Eskuzor.

He sat down to eat his dinner at one of the long trestle tables and soon realised that his ordeal with Jarand would be nothing compared to the complications of keeping his story straight against the barrage of interest, mainly friendly, that now assailed him.

"So come on Harkell, tell us where you've been," demanded Captain Guerion with a friendly slap on the shoulder, as he sat down next to him. "What have you been up to since we last saw you? Did you come across the Rogue Prince?"

Harkell laughed and shook his head, "So many questions." He looked at the ring of expectant faces and knew that he could not fob them off completely. "I have been in the mountains and in the forests closer to Tormadell. It was a long cold trek across the mountains and I spent some time in the Forest of Yesterday, Today and Tomorrow before finding my way over to the north of the ranges."

Needless to say, mention of the Lost Forest increased rather than eased their interest. He described the eeriness and quiet of the Lost Forest, how the howling gales had not penetrated its branches and spoke of the hopeless apathy of the people who had been constrained to live within its borders for decades, and in some cases centuries, simply for failing to face their fears.

"And were you there when the Rogue Prince released them from its spell?"

Harkell gave himself time by taking a mouthful of his fast cooling venison stew. Once he had decided on his approach, he took a swig of beer and gave a little grin, "There? It was I who suggested to him that he could challenge the right of the Forest of Yesterday, Today and Tomorrow to confine people."

His grin broadened as astonishment appeared on the faces of the officers around him.

"You *spoke* to the prince?" demanded Guerion. "Does Prince Jarand know this?"

"Certainly he knows. I did not speak particularly of the Forest of Yesterday, Today and Tomorrow with His Highness, but he knows I have spent some time with his brother."

"In that case, why has he not hanged you as a traitor?"

Harkell shrugged. "Why should he? Prince Tarkyn knew I was an officer in Prince Jarand's army. I did not pretend to be anything else. How could I? It was Prince Tarkyn's men who found me and looked after me until I recovered." There was no need to say from what. Every man there strove every day to avoid a similar fate.

For a moment there was silence. Then Colonel Carrioll, an old grizzled soldier from an old aristocratic family, asked slowly, "Are you telling us that the Rogue Prince allowed his men to rescue an officer of his enemy? Was their intent to torture you?"

No one watching him could mistake the surprise on Harkell's face at this suggestion. "No. Not at all. They looked after me and let me travel with them until I was well enough to leave them."

Colonel Carrioll's eyes narrowed, "And what was a prince doing listening to the likes of you?"

"By that do you mean; listening to me as his enemy's officer or as a commoner?" asked Harkell conversationally.

"Lay off him, Carrioll," growled Guerion.

Harkell raised his hand to stop interference, keeping his eyes trained on Carrioll's face as he waited politely for a reply.

"Either," snapped the colonel

Harkell smiled, "I believe the Rogue Prince has had to keep company with many low-lives since his exile," This raised a few appreciative sniggers, "and is more inclined to listen to people from all walks of life now, than he would have been within the aegis of the royal family."

Colonel Carrioll tut-tutted, "It's a bloody disgrace. No wonder he has been declared a rogue. A prince of the Tamadil line should be set apart, revered. Does he have any sense left of his heritage and what is due his station?"

Harkell grinned, "Oh, very much so, sir. He may have eschewed many of the formalities of court, but he never forgets that he is a prince of Eskuzor and woe betide the man or woman who does."

"What?" asked a young officer eagerly. "Does he kill them out of hand? He is a rogue, after all."

Harkell snorted in derision. "No. He merely gives them a dressing down… but he can be very scathing if he chooses to be."

Another young officer leant in and said in an undertone, "Well, I have heard that Prince Tarkyn is not a rogue sorcerer after all."

"Really, Hotchins?" drawled Carrioll. "In direct contradiction to His Majesty's proclamation?"

The note of warning did not escape the young officer who immediately took fright. "I did not say I believed it, sir. I simply said I had heard it spoken around the bars."

"What is your opinion, Harkell?" asked Guerion, who was not so easily intimidated. "Was it obvious to you that he was a rogue?"

"I would not like to set myself up against His Majesty's proclamation and so will say nothing."

Guerion chuckled, "Well, that's clear enough."

"You tread a very fine line, Captain Harkell," growled Colonel Carrioll, "and so I warn you."

"Yes sir, I do. But you may report everything I have said to His Highness with my blessing. He knows that I have resided with his outlawed brother and has still chosen to reinstate me… but feel free to challenge his judgement if you are so inclined."

The old colonel stared down the smothered smiles. "Cheeky young jackanapes! Hurry up and finish your dinner. We've a lot to do before we leave for Montraya." So saying he got up and stomped off, leaving Harkell surrounded by grinning faces.

Chapter 20

As soon as he could, Harkell returned to his quarters to get what sleep he could before setting out to find Tarkyn. He would have to wait until everyone around him had settled before he could leave and would need to return before dawn, just in time to start the new day. He hoped that Jarand did not send him out too often. Otherwise he was going to find his new role very taxing, working both night and day.

He sat on the bed and allowed his batman to pull off his boots. Not wishing to undress, he told Nyrus that there had been reports of bandits close by and that he would stay dressed in case he was called out during the night. Nyrus, a solemn devoted boy of fourteen gave a slight nod and said gravely, "Me mam never lets me keep me clothes on when I go to bed but I reckon sometimes it's safer." After a moment's reflection, he added, "Seems a waste of time to me, all this dressing and undressing but me mam says yer has ter."

Harkell frowned down at him, a smile lurking in the back of his eyes, "Don't let me catch you sleeping in your clothes unless I expressly order it, Nyrus. Too many nights like that and you'll stink these quarters out."

"No sir. I mean, yes sir." He lifted his eyes and a shy smile lit his face, "I'm glad you're back, sir."

Harkell gave him a warm smile, "Thank you, Nyrus. I am glad to see you again too." He lay down on the bed, "Now, either go to bed or go out for a while. I want to sleep now in case I have to go out later. Make sure you're quiet when you come in."

Nyrus bobbed his head, "Yes sir."

Not long after the young batman had left, Harkell heard quiet scrabbling and then felt something scurry up his arm. He opened his eyes to find himself face to face with a quivering little fieldmouse sitting on his chest. Knowing the mouse was frightened, Harkell restrained himself and smiled very slowly. The mouse dropped a tiny parchment on his chest and bolted. A moment later, Harkell spotted it sitting, panting with fright, on the top of his sword at the end of the bed.

Waving his hand slowly over the parchment, Harkell murmured the words he had heard Stormaway use to dissipate the minimising spell, "*Ka encreshir.*"

The little mouse started with fright as the parchment began to grow but stayed where it was, calmed by a distant mind. Very slowly, Harkell smoothed the parchment and read:

Harkell,

Your arguments for your decision were eloquent enough to convince Danton. Quite an achievement.

Harkell breathed a sigh of relief and read on:

Thank you for choosing to stay true to me. Eskuzor's future shines brighter for having you working for her.

For myself, I am glad that I have not lost someone whom I have come to regard as one of my closest friends.

I am sorry that I allowed you to be placed in such a dangerous situation. It is my will that your care for your family should be paramount in your dealings with Jarand, even if it may be at a cost to us. I know you will do your best to support us.

Finally, be assured that I will not forget the pact between us and that I will do all within my power to protect you and your family. My companions also wish you well and are at one with me in my desire to support you.

Your friend and liege,

Tarkyn.

By the time he finished reading, Harkell was grinning from ear to ear. He read and reread it several times before folding it carefully and placing it in an inner pocket. He knew that prudence dictated that he should destroy it, but it meant too much to him and he could not bring himself to do it. As a compromise, he decided that he would sew a secret pocket into the lining of his jacket to keep it safe. And since he now had no hope of going to sleep he sewed it there and then, watched by the little field mouse from the top of his sword. From time to time, Harkell would smile at the mouse, knowing that Tarkyn could see him through the mouse's eyes.

An hour later, Nyrus' lugubrious efforts to enter the tent quietly while under the influence of strong drink routed the fieldmouse, and Harkell was left to put his swaying batman to bed to prevent him from sending every item in the tent flying. Harkell forbore to lecture him, sure that tomorrow's headache would be every bit as convincing as anything he could say to him now.

Once Nyrus's snores had assured him that his batman was asleep, Harkell readied himself to leave. He pulled on his boots, flung his cloak around his shoulders and concealed the dark blue cylinder in a deep pocket within its folds. When he was ready, he poked his head out of the tent to check that all was quiet. He had his cover story ready if he needed it but he did not want some friendly officer offering to accompany him.

He stepped out and walked quietly but quite openly towards the edge of the encampment. When he reached the perimeter guards, he nodded in acknowledgement with no intention of showing them Jarand's orders unless challenged. In the event, the guard snapped to attention and bade him good evening as he passed.

Harkell walked briskly down the track that led to the Great Western Road until a curve hid him from the view of the guards.

CHAPTER 21

For good measure, he walked another ten minutes before stopping. Then he veered off to his left into the woodland and doubled back quietly along the side of the track before taking up position behind a large oak to watch the track and check that he had not been followed. He waited for a long twenty minutes and was just turning to head further down the track when a voice at his shoulder said, "Looks like you weren't followed then."

Harkell started violently and swung around to find Twig Snap standing beside him, grinning. He blew out a breath and smiled in return, "Hi Twig Snap. It's good to see you. I was hoping one of you would make contact with me."

"Have you come to see us or are you on some business of Jarand's?"

"Both."

Twig Snap put her head on one side while she considered him. "I can see why you were checking that you weren't followed then. Do you mean to tell me that Jarand knows you are coming to see Tarkyn?"

Harkell nodded. "I carry a parchment that he has ordered me to deliver into Tarkyn's hands. I told him I could only do that if I were not followed."

"Hmm. Just a minute." Harkell waited patiently while Twig Snap's eyes went out of focus as she mindspoke to other woodfolk. After some considerable time, she refocused, "Sorry about that. You've taken us a little by surprise and we needed to plan how to get you safely to Tarkyn without leaving a trail."

"Of course you must. After all, they still have those bloodhounds they used once before. The fact that Jarand has not had me followed does not mean he won't use my trail to try to reach you after I have returned. I wouldn't trust him an inch."

"Exactly," Twig Snap put her hands on her hips, "It's a pity you can't travel through the treetops. It would save us all a lot of bother."

"Sorry. We sorcerers are not as adept at climbing as you and I can't levitate as Tarkyn, Stormaway and Danton can."

Twig Snap huffed. "Pest! Never mind. Ancient Oak is bringing a horse for you. I'm afraid you will have to ride along the middle of the stream for at least a mile, which will be quite slow in the dark, and then change horses. Then we'll take your original horse back to the point where you entered and Ancient Oak will ride it straight out the other side while you ride on further up the stream. After that, Ancient Oak will cross another stream and hopefully confuse the trail there. But if they pick up that horse's trail again, it will lead them to a small troop of soldiers who are camped near the Great Western Road."

Harkell chuckled in the darkness, "Marvellous. And what about the horse that I am to ride further?"

"Boravar will bring you his great warhorse. That horse is still with us even though his prints are a nuisance to blur. We couldn't abandon him after he carried Boravar to safety." In response to an unseen signal, Twig Snap slipped her arm into Harkell's crooked elbow and drew him deeper into the forest. "Come on. We need to be further away from the road. Ancient Oak will be here in about twenty minutes."

Once over the stream, Twig Snap directed him to tether the war horse some distance away and complete the last stage of the journey by foot. So it was past midnight by the time they reached the woodfolk firesite.

Despite the lateness of the hour, he was mobbed by welcoming woodfolk the moment Twig Snap, Boravar and he broke cover. And since Twig Snap had transmitted the information that Harkell would only be able to stay a few hours, even the children had been allowed to get out of bed to greet him.

He smiled in response to their admiring comments, some teasing, some genuine, about his blue and red uniform, and reaching into his pocket, produced a handful of lollipops that he distributed to the children. Midnight pulled at his cloak until Harkell relented and lifted him up onto his hip. Among the hubbub, Harkell's eyes wandered the firesite until he spotted Tarkyn standing quietly on the other side of the fire, flanked by Danton and Stormaway, waiting for him. But anxious though he was to greet his liege, he did not risk offending the woodfolk by rushing to disengage himself from their welcome.

Gradually, as the excitement subsided, everyone became aware of the prince standing a little apart, waiting quietly. Waterstone gave his head a little shake and smiled wryly at the royal attitude of his bloodbrother that would not allow him to join the crowd's greeting of Harkell even though he had been possibly the most anxious about him.

A hush fell and Harkell let Midnight slip to the ground before walking around the fire to go down on one knee, hand on heart and head bowed, before his liege. "Your Highness, I may wear Prince Jarand's uniform but my heart is yours. I am your man, body and soul, til the day I die."

"Thank you, Harkell. I am pleased to welcome you back and wish it were not for so short a time." He touched the soldier's shoulder, "Please rise."

Harkell straightened, looked into Tarkyn's eyes and realised that the prince had withdrawn into the cool formality that characterised him when he felt unsure of his ground. Without thinking, he smiled warmly, "Sire, thank you so much for your letter. I have it here, sewn into my jacket, and will keep it with me always. It will be a constant reminder to me of the bond between us." His smile broadened, "And thank your little mouse friend too."

Suddenly Tarkyn's reserve cracked and he smiled in return, "It was the least I could do after placing you in such risk."

"Harkell, you should thank all of us too, for putting up with him," said Rainstorm, flicking a thumb in Tarkyn's direction. "He's been like a bear with a sore head, worrying about you."

"And we were all knocked sideways, literally, with Tarkyn's shock when it looked like you had betrayed him," chuckled Autumn Leaves.

Harkell gave a crack of laughter, "Sire! I can see you still need more practice at directing the energy of your feelings."

"I am working on it, Harkell. Watch."

For a moment, nothing happened. Then gradually, Tarkyn's face became rigid with anger and suddenly, the ground shook, not so much that anyone fell over but enough that everyone swayed or staggered. The sorcerer grinned, "I can do it more fiercely than that, but it takes greater and longer concentration. Besides, the little ones get frightened if it is too severe."

"Well done, Sire. You are making great progress." Harkell shook his head in amazement, "I know you don't use it much, but your power is breathtaking."

Tarkyn smiled and clapped him on the back, "Thanks. Now stop calling me Your Highness and Sire, and come and have a glass of wine while you tell us how you are managing and why Jarand has sent you."

As they arranged themselves around the fire, Harkell noticed that Danton and Stormaway stayed on either side of Tarkyn, but he did not challenge them over it, knowing that in their place, he would do the same.

When news on both sides had been exchanged, he produced the dark blue cylinder from within the folds of his cloak and held it before him, but out of Tarkyn's reach. He dodged it sideways as Stormaway made a grab for it. "Give me some credit, Stormaway. I have been charged by Jarand to deliver this directly into Tarkyn's hand but I have no intention of doing so. Naturally we will all want to ensure that it is not a trap of some kind first."

Having made his point, Harkell handed the cylinder to Stormaway who gave a slight smile, "Your pardon, Harkell." The wizard inspected the cylinder from all angles before asking, "Tell us exactly what Jarand said."

Harkell thought back, trying to recall what had passed between Jarand and him as accurately as possible, "Despite my best efforts, he decided that I was no longer completely loyal to him… " Against a murmur of consternation he continued, "but that I would have to do what he asked anyway. He wasn't explicit but he did ask me if I was looking forward to seeing my family again. He also said that at least for the time being he would only ask me to carry out my normal duties as Captain of the Guard and to liaise between Tarkyn and himself. You may imagine my relief." He shrugged and smiled wryly. "He described me as a useful tool."

Rainstorm growled. "The man has no sense of decency whatever. Tarkyn, how could someone like you have a brother like that?"

Tarkyn gave a faint smile as he waved his hand to silence Rainstorm.

"Oh. Sorry," said the feisty young woodman shortly. "Go on Harkell."

"He also said that I was the first clue they had had to finding you, Tarkyn; the only possible link, or source of any information about you." Harkell glanced at Twig Snap and Boravar. "So I am glad you went to such lengths to disguise my trail. Jarand also told me that no one in the encampment was to know that I was coming here to deliver this parchment. He said, and I quote, 'I want it delivered tonight, by you in person. Directly to my younger brother. Not via a carrier pigeon or some wild egret.' Then he re-emphasized that it had to be in person…which is why I have not handed it directly to Tarkyn."

Stormaway nodded grudgingly, "You have done well, Harkell. Now we will have to find out what Jarand is up to." The wizard turned his attention to the cylinder. "Hmm. There are three possibilities; that the cylinder itself has been imbibed with some poison or spell that will be absorbed by Tarkyn when he takes hold of it, that some essence or spell will escape to bewitch Tarkyn when he opens the cylinder or finally, that the parchment itself is impregnated with some chemical or spell." Stormaway looked across at Harkell "What do you think? Did Jarand hand you the cylinder already sealed?"

Harkell shook his head decisively, "No. I saw him place the parchment into the cylinder before sealing it… Besides, I don't think the cylinder itself can be affected because I have handled it quite a bit and feel no ill effects. But perhaps I would not notice." He looked around at the woodfolk and sorcerers, "Am I behaving any differently from usual?"

Lapping Water smiled at him, "No. Still the same old Harkell we all know and love… though perhaps just a little more earnest than usual."

Harkell gave a short humourless laugh, "That is probably because I feel that I am the bait in an unknown trap from which I am trying to protect the intended victim."

Tarkyn reached across his protectors and patted him on the knee, "At least you know that all of us understand the predicament and are working with you to manage it," He glanced at Danton who was seated between them, "including taking what I consider to be unnecessary precautions."

Harkell smiled unreservedly at Danton, "I agree wholeheartedly with those precautions, Tarkyn. You are taking enough risk in allowing me to come here at all when Jarand is so clearly up to tricks. I am not offended."

"Did you notice Jarand putting anything else into the cylinder before sealing it?" asked Stormaway.

Harkell's smile faded. "Oh, you mean the black and yellow poisonous toad that he popped in just before he gave it to me?" He glared at the wizard. "Of course I didn't see him put anything in it or I would have mentioned it. And now I am offended. Both you and Danton have a tedious tendency to underrate my intelligence."

Harkell's flash of ill humour was so unexpected that it produced a shocked silence. The tension was broken by Tarkyn who smiled and said sotto voce, "Shocking pair of snobs, aren't they? I bet they'd get on beautifully with your Colonel Carrioll."

A reluctant smile dawned on the captain's face. "Yes. In a different time and place, I believe they would." His smile widened as he thought of the comparisons before addressing Stormaway, "I'm sorry. I didn't mean to snap like that. I know your question could have triggered something subtle that I might have overlooked." He ran his hands over his face. "Go on. Ask me anything you like. Don't let my bad temper put you off. I'm just feeling a little edgy at the moment." He thought for a moment, "Anyway, Jarand could have placed something in the cylinder before I entered his tent."

"True, he could have," answered Stormaway as though the outburst had not occurred. He shook the cylinder but there was clearly nothing rattling around in it. "It could be smeared with paste of some kind, I suppose…Hmm. Doubtful, I think." He stood up and carried the cylinder to the edge of the clearing. Facing the top away from him, he carefully lifted its lid.

Nothing happened.

The wizard looked back at everyone, "Did anyone see any haze over it as I opened it… possibly dark red like Jarand's magic?"

"Or bluey grey like Journeyman's magic?" suggested Danton.

Stormaway nodded, "Yes. Could be either. No one saw anything? Well, I certainly didn't." He breathed a sigh of relief. "Good. Now that it is open, I can run a scan for any lethal substances before we remove the parchment. Summer Rain, if you would care to assist me?"

Together the wizard and the woodfolk healer blended an assortment of tinctures and placed the result in a shallow dish. Then Stormaway set the mixture alight with a flick of green magic before holding the open end of the cylinder over the fumes.

Again nothing happened.

"Hmm." Stormaway pondered for a moment. "Well, it doesn't look as though Jarand means to do Tarkyn any direct harm. So that's something at least… And now we need someone to take hold of the parchment and to take the risk of being affected by any spell that Jarand may have used on it."

Tarkyn frowned. "Now just a minute. I am not happy that someone takes the risk intended for me. Why don't I simply wear gloves as I read the parchment? Wouldn't that be sufficient protection?"

Stormaway gave a slight bow, "Yes Sire, it would protect you, but not Harkell. If we cannot surmise what mischief Jarand is intending, then we cannot act as though Harkell has obeyed Jarand's instruction to give the parchment directly into your hands."

Tarkyn threw Harkell a wry look. "You see why I would be no good as king. These peregrinations are far beyond me. I bow to a more devious mind. Carry on, Stormaway."

The wizard smiled, "I would hope that an extra fifty years would have given me a slight edge, Sire. Now, I suspect that there is some sort of marker in the parchment that will help them to locate whoever holds the parchment. Therefore I need volunteers who are able to keep ahead of pursuers."

"I'll do it," said Rainstorm without a second thought. "I can move through the treetops and I can flick out of sight."

"If I cannot immediately neutralise the spell," Stormaway warned him, "you will have to spend some time away from Tarkyn until it wears off. Once I know its effect I should be able to counteract it, but I cannot promise it."

"In that case, I'll do it too. Keep my young brother company until you sort it out," volunteered Danton. He grinned, "I can't do what he can, but I can levitate or translocate if I am pressed."

The wizard rubbed his hands together. "Excellent! Tarkyn, I suggest you put gloves on as you suggested, because no doubt you will want to read the parchment once these two have removed it from the cylinder." He glanced around. "Is everyone in agreement?" Receiving the affirmative, he continued, "And is everybody ready, because you never know, it might do something drastic, like turning them into homicidal maniacs." Although his concern was genuine, most people watching did not know how to take this last statement and so did not react. "Very well. Rainstorm and Danton, remove the parchment."

There was a resounding minute of motionless silence while yet again nothing happened.

Danton and Rainstorm grinned a little sheepishly at each other. "Not too scary so far," quipped Rainstorm.

Danton handed the parchment into Tarkyn's gloved hands. The prince glanced around the assembly before reading out aloud,

Tarkyn,

I understand that I have you and your followers to thank for the safe return of Captain Harkell. I commend him to you as a trustworthy liaison officer.

Since I last saw you, I have revised my opinion of your woodfolk friends. Obviously they are more of a force to be reckoned with, than I first realised. I believe I may have spoken hastily on the occasion of our last meeting.

"Oh," interrrupted Waterstone scathingly, "Is he referring to his statement that having met some of us and gauged our calibre, he was no longer anxious to recruit us to his cause?"

"That must have rankled, Waterstone," said Tarkyn sympathetically. "You seem to remember what he said almost word-perfectly."

The woodman huffed, "I would have loved to show him just how lethal we can be... but you were right. It was better that he was left in ignorance."

Rainstorm folded his arms. "He was quite poisonous at the time, as I recall, but at least he is able to admit his mistake. That's something, I suppose."

"Shall I keep reading?" asked Tarkyn patiently. At a nod from the two woodmen, he continued,

As you have no doubt had reported to you, my encampment has become a safe haven for all travellers of the Great Western Road. It is gratifying to see that so many people have been rescued from the malcontents who roam this area. I do thank you for informing me of the malpractice that had begun to flourish. As you know, the ringleaders were hanged and many others were found already dead at their hide out. I suspect that I have you and your redoubtable followers to thank for that also.

I begin to think that it may be to our mutual advantage to consider an alliance. As you possibly know, Kosar is making himself popular on the back of my achievements but in actuality, has taken no initiative himself

to address the problems that beset our country. This is the first time he has ventured forth in two years. I sometimes wonder if he remembers that Eskuzor exists beyond the gates of Tormadell.

Naturally under a new ruler, any past sentences could be quashed and you could return to your rightful position as a member of the ruling family. As such, you could then be granted the lands and rights due to you when you attain your majority in a few months' time, and stand by my side to bring a prosperous future to Eskuzor.

Do not feel obliged to make an immediate commitment. No doubt you will need time to give it careful thought. However, I hope you will consider my proposition favourably. There are advantages for both of us.

Your brother

Jarand.

An air of constraint had fallen on the woodfolk.

Waterstone cleared his throat, "That is quite a generous offer. You could go back to your satin sheets and embroidered clothes, your exotic meals of many courses, your sharp angled buildings…and still work for Eskuzor's future. In fact you might be in a better position to influence events than you are here."

"I could," said Tarkyn neutrally, noticing that Lapping Water was concentrating hard on placing the big kettle on the fire and would not meet his eyes.

Autumn Leaves eyed Waterstone with tolerant amusement, "And what makes you think that Tarkyn would survive, once Jarand had what he wanted?"

"I think he would," put in Danton, rather to Autumn Leaves' surprise. "After all, it was Kosar who indicted Tarkyn in the first place, not Jarand. If Jarand had stood up too firmly against Kosar, he could have been accused of treason himself."

"Tarkyn would only be safe for as long as he supports Jarand," said Harkell. "There is no room in Jarand's court for debate."

"I don't know," countered Rainstorm. "He has admitted to a change of heart in his opinion of us. He can't be all that dogmatic."

As it turned out, Tarkyn had no interest in debating Jarand's trustworthiness, "Waterstone, if I didn't know that you were trying to be generous I might be offended. I am not either of my brothers, you know, and I would not buy my comfort for the price of betraying Kosar."

"But he betrayed you," protested Rainstom hotly.

"Yes he did. But I have no intention of descending to his level."

Harkell couldn't help grinning, "You see Tarkyn? Whether you will it or not, your greatness shines through. Who else would refuse to descend to the level of a king?"

"What you really mean is that his arrogance takes your breath away," said Autumn Leaves dryly, but with a betraying twinkle in his eye.

"And furthermore," continued Tarkyn, a faint smile being the only acknowledgement of these exchanges, "I am perfectly well accustomed to my new lifestyle and hanker less for wealth and fine dining than I would hanker for your companionship if I were no longer with you." He looked at the long shining hair that was all he could see of Lapping Water's head as she kept determinedly turned away, "And I'm not sure that Lapping Water is ready for a life among sorcerers and I am certainly not leaving without her." When she still did not respond, he said softly, "Lapping Water, do you really think me so fickle?"

When she finally turned, her eyes were red and her cheeks were streaked with tears. "No. No, I don't. But if it comes to a choice between me and the future of Eskuzor, you will have to fulfil your destiny."

Tarkyn stood up and walked over to her. He pulled her away from the fire and encircled her in his arms. "Courage, my little love. We always knew this would be hard but we will find our way through." He lifted his head and addressed the entire group, "To be clear, I no longer think of myself as being exiled. My home is here in the forest among you people. I am the Forest Guardian, after all. That is far more than a title. It is a connection with the forest deeper than even you woodfolk understand."

There was an almost audible collective sigh of relief.

Tarkyn smiled and looked down at Lapping Water, "You see? Even the most amazing miracles can occur. Who would have thought, when I first arrived, that woodfolk might be relieved that I choose to stay among them."

"But even if you stay within the forest, Sire, you could still form an alliance with Jarand. He is right when he says that he is the one who is working to combat lawlessness," said Danton.

Tarkyn raised his eyebrows. "Is it possible you have forgotten that, according to Harkell's observations, Jarand is mustering and training troops at Montraya even as we speak?"

"No. But it is hardly surprising that he is losing patience if Kosar is doing nothing while Jarand can see Eskuzor's need unanswered."

Tarkyn began to look puzzled, "I thought you believed that Jarand acts only to gain power."

Danton gave a wry smile, "Perhaps I was too quick to tar both twins with the same brush. He seems quite genuine in his letter."

Tarkyn turned to his wizard, "And your opinion, Stormaway?"

A smile was playing around the wizard's usually severe mouth, "I believe Jarand to be the same untrustworthy, self-interested despot that he has always been."

"Stormaway!" exclaimed Danton angrily. "Sometimes you are too old fashioned for your own good… or for ours. You are unable to give someone the benefit of the doubt when they are making changes."

"I agree with my brother," said Rainstorm. "Jarand has been maligned. We only have Harkell's report of this massing army. For all we know, Harkell just made it up to ingratiate himself with us."

Stormaway smiled broadly, folded his arms and stated firmly, "Jarand is as much of a disgrace to the Tamadil name as Kosar is. I could think of no one less qualified to rule this country."

Danton and Rainstorm's faces suffused with anger. Before anyone knew what was happening, an aqua streak of magic speared towards Stormaway. The wizard was prepared however, and easily raised his shield in time to protect himself.

Danton threw his shield up over Rainstorm and himself. "I'm sorry Tarkyn, but if you can't see sense, it might be better if we leave. Jarand is obviously doing more to protect Eskuzor than you. We will offer him our service and work with him to protect our country."

Although Rainstorm was at one with Danton's views, a look of unease crossed his face as he realised that Danton was planning to take him out of the forest.

Glancing at Harkell and Boravar, Tarkyn said briefly, "Be ready." He focused the anger he felt at his scheming brother, letting it grow within him into a kernel of charged energy. With a sudden, downward sweep of his arms, he discharged it into earth beneath him. The ground shook violently and, as Danton lost his balance and his focus on his shield, Boravar and Harkell moved in to grab him and tie his hands behind his back while Waterstone and Autumn Leaves took hold of Rainstorm to stop him from flicking away.

Tarkyn stood looking at them ruefully. "I apologise for the indignity but I believe Stormaway has some work to do before we can release you."

Danton and Rainstorm just glared at him.

Stormaway rummaged through his cache of herbs, "Summer Rain, I believe we are dealing with a variation of a love potion. Do you happen to have any crushed violets? I seem to have run out."

Together they brought forth herbs, tinctures, and a couple of small yellow feathers which they crushed and combined into a thick paste before adding water and heating it on a small pot over the fire. As the mixture was warming, Stormaway explained, "That parchment has been saturated with a form of love potion that makes anyone who handles it become attached to the person who has set up the spell, in this case, Jarand. No doubt there was something of Jarand's, probably hair, in the mixture that was painted onto the parchment."

"Rubbish!" spat out Danton. "This is just a trick. Stormaway just wants you to believe that Jarand is bad."

The wizard swung the little pot off the fire and placed it on a stump to cool. He poured water into two glasses and carefully added a measure of the potion to each. But when he placed it against Danton's lips, Danton closed his mouth firmly and thrust forward with his shoulder so that the mixture was thrown from Stormaway's hand.

"No matter," said Stormaway, unperturbed, "I have plenty to concoct another." He glanced apologetically at Tarkyn, "I'm afraid though, that they may have to be forced to comply. I would suggest you don't command them to cooperate. It will only make them feel worse afterwards that they didn't hold true… Just a minute." He turned to Summer Rain, "Could you prepare a cloth with some of that sleeping draft you made the other day please? The poppy and valerian mixture. Not too strong. We only want them a bit dopey at the moment, not unconscious."

"Stormaway, this is very distressing. I do not like to see my friends treated so cavalierly." Tarkyn ran his hand through his hair and stood undecided for a minute. Then he took a breath, "Very well. Harkell and Boravar, Waterstone and Autumn Leaves, follow whatever instructions Stormaway gives you." He looked unhappily at Danton and Rainstorm. "Blame me when this is all over, not them."

Summer Rain chose to apply the soporific herself, pressing dampened cloths against first Danton's and then Rainstorm's face as they glowered, helpless to resist, until their eyes glazed and their heads nodded.

Under Stormaway's instructions, their mouths were forced open and his concoction was poured down their throats. They coughed feebly and gagged but they imbibed enough of the antidote to satisfy Stormaway. In response to the wizard's gesture, Summer Rain reapplied the dampened cloths until Danton and Rainstorm drifted off completely.

"Now, if you wouldn't mind carrying them into a shelter so that they can wake up in their own time without all of us staring at them. They won't be out for long. Just a few minutes, wouldn't you say, Summer Rain?"

The woodfolk healer nodded her agreement as Rainstorm and Danton were carried out of sight.

Chapter 22

The blond sorcerer and his woodfolk bloodbrother lay side by side on the dusty forest floor. Danton was the first to recover. Slowly, he opened his eyes to find himself in the gloom of a shelter. A soft yellow light issued from a lamp in the corner. He moved slightly and was surprised to find that his hands were no longer bound behind him. He raised himself onto one elbow and realised that Rainstorm was lying beside him. Danton felt rather foggy but his head was clearing fast. Memories of recent events made him wince in horror. Just as he gave Rainstorm's shoulder a shake, he noticed Falling Branch sitting quietly in a corner away from the lamp, watching him.

As soon as their eyes met, Falling Branch smiled, "How are you feeling, my heroic son?"

"Heroic?" Danton rolled onto his back and looked up at the ceiling, his hands behind his head. "I abandon my life-long friend and liege, and you call me heroic?"

Rainstorm wandered up to consciousness at this juncture. He opened his eyes, took one look at Danton and groaned, "Oh stars above. What have we done?"

Falling Branch spoke softly, pride in his voice, "You have done nothing wrong. I have two sons to be proud of." He handed them stone cups of water. "Here, have some water. It will clear your heads and make you feel better." As they drank, watching him closely over the rims of their cups, he continued, "You volunteered to take the risk of holding Jarand's parchment even though you had no idea what might happen to you. No one holds you responsible for what you did while under the influence of Jarand's spell. It became obvious to everyone but you that you were acting out of character. Neither of you has ever had a good word to say about Jarand before tonight."

"Nor will we again," growled Rainstorm. "That conniving bastard."

Danton put down his cup and rubbed his hands over his face, "Spell or no spell, I don't know how I'm going to face Tarkyn after this."

The prince's voice came from somewhere outside the shelter, "Tarkyn is wondering how he is going to face you after condoning that rough treatment of you."

Danton scrambled to his feet and rushed outside, colliding headlong with his liege. "Oh Sire, I am so sorry. You know I would never abandon you to go off with either of your brothers, don't you?"

Tarkyn grasped him firmly by both shoulders, "Danton, you have only my thanks. You do not need my forgiveness. You too, Rainstorm," he added, as the young woodman emerged. "Without your courage and assistance, we would not have found out what Jarand was up to, or how to act to protect Harkell."

Rainstorm's face relaxed into a smile, "Oh. That's all right then." He gave a cheeky grin, "And we forgive you, because you *do* need our forgiveness."

Tarkyn laughed and ruffled his hair.

As they entered the circle of firelight, Danton and Rainstorm were given a quiet round of applause. When apologies and thanks had been exchanged, Lapping Water pranced up to Rainstorm, her eyes shining with laughter. "That wasn't quite the exciting game of chasey you were both anticipating, was it?"

"No," Rainstorm smiled in return but gradually his smile faded and after a moment's hesitation, he leaned in towards her and said quietly. "No. If you really want to know, it was much more frightening. Events moved so fast, so out of control. And then when I woke up, I thought I had lost everything and everyone… It was ghastly."

"Oh Rainstorm, you poor thing." She realised suddenly that he was on the verge of tears. She put her arm around her young cousin, led him off to one side to sit with him while he recovered.

Sometime later, a firm but gentle hand came down on Rainstorm's shoulder and he felt a warm stream of energy flow into him. "Thanks Tarkyn," he said without looking around, adding glumly. "At least not all sorcery is evil."

"No, my friend, it is not," said Tarkyn sitting down beside him. "Although what I just gave you then was the power of the Forest Guardian, not sorcery."

When Rainstorm nodded without replying, Tarkyn met Lapping Water's eyes over his head. Tarkyn leant forward and said to Rainstorm, "Rainstorm, I can imagine you might feel that you threw yourself over a yawning pit but in reality, all of us were watching every move you and Danton made, waiting to catch you before you fell. That's why Stormaway could get his shield up so quickly. He knew before Danton did, that Danton was about to attack him. In fact he goaded him into it as soon as he guessed what type of spell it was." He smiled as Rainstorm looked around at him, "Just as your sudden loyalty to Jarand was an illusion, so too was your perception that you were in any danger of harm or of losing us. We may have had to be a bit rough to do it, but we all worked together to keep you both safe."

Rainstorm let out a long sigh of relief. He gave a whimsical smile, "I don't know that I'm cut out for these sorcerer games. Maybe I'm not quite as old as I thought I was."

"No, maybe you're not. But more likely, your straightforward woodfolk culture has not prepared you to deal with the concept of changing sides or the shifting sands of illusion. Danton too is rattled and he has grown up in an atmosphere of subterfuge and misused sorcery… besides being several years older than you." Tarkyn gave Rainstorm's knee a bracing pat as he stood up, "When you're ready, we would value your input into the discussion on how we are to convince Jarand that it was I, and not you, who handled the enchanted parchment."

Part 4: The Eagle

CHAPTER 23

Despite his late night, Harkell rose before his batman who was now suffering from his overindulgence the night before. Harkell may not have punished him when he came in drunk but he cut Nyrus no slack as he sat on the edge of his bed, holding his head and groaning. Suffering from lack of sleep himself, Harkell had no compunction in ordering his batman to set out his clothes and tidy up their quarters before going to breakfast.

Harkell organised rosters and inspected kit deep into the morning, running Nyrus off his feet fetching and carrying for him. Harkell was talking to Saker and Biggin when the summons came for him to attend the prince.

"You are receiving a lot of special interest since your return, sir," observed Biggin. "Maybe he realised what a good officer you are, when he had to do without you for a while."

Harkell smiled, aware that he was under strict instructions to tell no one of the nature of his errands for Prince Jarand. "Thank you, Biggin. It would be nice to think so."

He followed the messenger to Jarand's tent and waited outside while he was announced. When he entered, he discovered that Journeyman Cloudmaker was also in attendance, looking almost predatory in his anticipation. Harkell bowed and waited.

Prince Jarand continued to write at his table, ignoring the captain while he finished his missive, dusted it and handed it to Journeyman to be rolled up and sealed. Only then did he bring his gaze to bear on Harkell. "Good morning, Captain Harkell. You may speak freely in front of my wizard. I trust you slept well?"

"Thank you my lord. Well, but not long."

Jarand's eyebrows flickered at Harkell's temerity. "Captain, I find your attempts at levity unbecoming."

"I beg your pardon, Your Highness. It was not a jest; merely a statement of fact."

"Some facts are better left unstated."

"Yes, Your Highness. I will remember that." Harkell bit the inside of his lip, in an effort to make himself behave more seriously. Somehow, he seemed unable to reignite his previous awe and justified fear of the prince.

The prince cast a suspicious glance at him but chose not to take issue. "Tell me Captain Harkell, did you follow my instructions exactly?"

"Of course, Your Highness. To the letter."

"So, did my brother receive my parchment directly into his hands?"

"Yes, Sire." Harkell considered adding, '*Why would he not?*' but prudence decided him against it.

Jarand's eyes lit with anticipation, "And has he sent a response?"

Harkell hesitated, "Sire he has, but before I left, he took me aside and bade me tell you that he needed time to bend his companions to his will before he could be more definite. Even though woodfolk cannot read, there are sorcerers with him who can and Tarkyn felt that he should tread carefully to guarantee the continued support of both the woodfolk and sorcerers who accompany him."

With that, he handed Jarand a rolled parchment. Jarand almost snatched it from him, so eager was he to peruse it.

Jarand,

I thank you for your offer. It is pleasing to see that you have understood the worth of the woodfolk.

We have seen your succour of the victims of roadside banditry with our own eyes and it is my hope that our older brother will give you the recognition that you deserve and will follow your example in securing Eskuzor's future.

In view of your offer, I am led to the assumption that your part in my trial must have been forced by Kosar. As you can imagine, it would mean a great deal to me to assume my rightful lands and privileges on my twentieth birthday.

However, because of the negotiated nature of my dominion over the woodfolk, I am unable to give you the clear, immediate answer that you would wish.

Be assured that your work for Eskuzor has my full support.

Your brother,

Tarkyn.

Harkell smiled to himself as Jarand read the letter, knowing the pains it had taken to come up with something that conveyed the impression that Tarkyn had succumbed to Jarand's potion while at the same time containing no direct falsehoods. He gave a mental salute of admiration to Danton for the task he must have had over all those years of court intrigue, trying to manage such a pedantically honest liege.

Jarand handed the letter to Journeyman and waited until his wizard had read it. When he had finished, Journeyman met the prince's eyes, a complicit smile hovering around his lips.

Jarand smiled at Harkell, "You must be relieved that Tarkyn and I are developing such accord." Harkell's eyes widened in alarm before realising that Jarand was merely toying with him. The prince's smile broadened at his discomfort, "Now Captain, you seem to know these people quite well. Explain to me why, if these woodfolk are under oath, my brother cannot just command their obedience."

Harkell's mind quailed at the thought of trying to explain Tarkyn's behaviour to such an absolute autocrat. He took a deep breath, "Sire, your younger brother maintains his belief in his superior rank but has softened his expectations for a people who are fiercely independent and have had no previous experience of royalty or fealty."

"How very peculiar of him." Jarand looked down his nose at Harkell, "Perhaps we did more damage to his self-consequence by indicting him, than we thought. Surely he is aware that it is the destiny of everyman to serve us. It has been thus for a thousand years. That these woodfolk have not served us before will be to their detriment. In fact, I can attest to it. I have met four of them, you know, and they were sadly lacking in the social niceties that, I think, differentiate men from beasts."

With a supreme effort, Harkell prevented a retort from rising to his lips.

Jarand poured himself a wine from a crystal decanter but did not offer any to the other two. "Poor Tarkyn. He is so young." He sipped his wine, "It's an absolute disgrace you know, a Tamadil negotiating. It makes me feel ill just to think of it. He has obviously been bamboozled by these people... It is just as well he will have my support in the future to sort them out." He shrugged, "Still, one step at a time. Now that he has given away his absolute power, I can see that he will have to tread carefully. But we have time." He glanced at the captain, "I think we need do no more until we are ready to leave. Then I will send you to meet him again, to see whether he is any closer to accepting my offer." He waved his hand in dismissal, "You may go."

And breathing an inward sigh of relief that another tricky encounter had been successfully negotiated, Harkell bowed and left.

Chapter 24

It was a beautiful spring morning in the forest. Except for a few droplets, the dew had dried on the grasses underfoot leaving them soft and fresh while above, the newly unfurled leaves created a bright canopy against the strong blue of the sky.

Danton stood with his shoulder leaning against a tree, waiting with feigned unconcern for Tarkyn to emerge from his shelter. Stormaway gave him a casual pat on the shoulder as he wandered past.

A minute later the wizard returned, having thought twice about it, "Danton, you have nothing to fear. Have faith in your liege."

Danton gave him a wry smile, "I do have faith in him, Stormaway, but… I just can't help myself. I have to reassure myself that all is well between us."

Stormaway smiled understandingly, "You're a good boy, Danton. You always were. Without you, Tarkyn would have been entangled in countless plots at court. Tarkyn knows, and we all know, that you would cut off your right arm before you deserted him." He glanced into the trees as he heard the flurry of a pigeon landing, "Hmm. Sounds like the latest dispatch from Tormadell has arrived. They have been few and far between recently. I'm not sure why."

When the wizard returned, he held a small parchment in his hand that was gently reverting to its original size. He frowned in irritation at Tarkyn's shelter. "Come on, Sire," he murmured impatiently to the outside of the shelter, with no expectation of the prince hearing him, "We were *all* up late. Get those lazy royal bones up and out of bed so that we may peruse this document."

Danton smiled, "It's the age, Stormaway. Rainstorm's not up yet either."

"Rainstorm is a good two, nearly three years younger than Tarkyn. And you're only two years older than Tarkyn yourself, and you're always up early."

Danton dropped his gaze and gave a self–deprecating shrug. After a moment, he looked up at Stormaway, "You should know why. When I am with Tarkyn, I always rise before and retire after him, whether it goes against my nature or not. I am an elite guard and it is my duty and my wish to guard him."

"Even though we are surrounded by woodfolk who protect him?"

Danton glanced around the clearing and smiled disarmingly, "Even so. It is no reflection on them. It is purely my own wish… After all, I leave the night watch to them."

"No, you don't," chimed in Ancient Oak from a nearby tree, "You take your share with the rest of us, on top of your self-imposed vigilance."

Danton grinned up at him, "Yes, but some parts of the night I leave to your guardianship. So I must have faith in you."

A chuckle came from the direction of the shelter as Tarkyn emerged, brushing his hair back from his face and blinking at the strong spring sunlight, "Danton, my friend, how lucky for you that you have at least some faith in woodfolk. Otherwise, you would run yourself ragged." He looked his friend up and down, "And just how long have you been standing there waiting for me?"

Danton waved an airy hand, but Stormaway gave him away, "He has been here for well over an hour. Nothing would budge him."

The prince shook his head in fond amusement. Then he strode straight over to Danton and embraced him in a strong bear hug that after a moment, Danton returned. Tarkyn grasped him by the shoulders and held him away from him so that he could look him in the eyes, "Listen to my wizard, Danton. Never doubt your liege, just as I will never again doubt you. We have been friends to each other since childhood and when we are eighty, we will still be able to say the same thing." He pulled his liegeman towards him and flung his arm across his shoulder. "Come on. Let's get some breakfast while Stormaway reads us his missive."

The first truly relaxed smile bloomed on Danton's face. "If there's any left. It's almost lunchtime."

As they settled themselves at the firesite, Stormaway scanned the parchment and gave his audience the tidbits that he thought they would find interesting. "The writer of this missive is a soldier in one of Kosar's companies. He says Tormadell seems unnaturally quiet at the moment. His company is about to leave the city to go on manoeuvres just as several others have over the last few weeks," He glanced up and smiled, "Seems high society is readying itself for a wedding, Danton… between your sister, and a Lord Randulus. Do you know him?"

Danton frowned a little, "Yes, I know him. He's quite a bit older than me. He would be in his early thirties. I would say…Which sister?"

"Eraya."

"How many do you have?" Twig Snap butted in.

"Three…and a brother."

"And are you the youngest?"

Danton shook his head, "I have a younger sister, Caran, who is twenty. My brother, Rufor, is twenty-seven, and my older sisters, Eraya and Opasa, are twenty-six and twenty-four. A man in his early thirties is a fitting husband for Eraya but perhaps too old for Caran."

Twig Snap gave a little huff, "Boravar is a great deal older than me."

Danton laughed "What can I say? Because of his time in the Lost Forest, Boravar is more than hundred and twenty years older than you, but he wasn't so much older than you when he entered it."

As Twig Snap's eyes narrowed, Danton braced himself for a punch to the ribs, but the moment passed and she merely remarked, "Boravar had two older sisters and a younger brother, you know, all of them born within five years of each other. Of course, none of them is alive now because they didn't spend any time in the Lost Forest as he did. Anyway, as a woodwoman sworn to remain hidden from the outside world, I wouldn't have been able to meet them anyway." In her abrupt way, she turned suddenly to Tarkyn, "How come there's such a gap between you and your brothers? Is it a royalty thing?"

"No, it is not a royalty thing, as you call it," said Tarkyn with a slight smile, "Both of my parents had siblings close in age to them."

"So?"

Tarkyn frowned. "I don't know. Other families have gaps between siblings. Waterstone and Ancient Oak have nearly ten years separating them," he said defensively.

"The gap between Ancient Oak and Waterstone is due to two still births in between and the time it took their mother to recover from each one," rumbled Thunder Storm quietly.

Tarkyn looked a little shame-faced, "I am aware of that. I apologise if I have brought up something painful that should be left to rest."

"No. It is all right, Tarkyn. It is, after all, your family too," said Ancient Oak who had now joined them around the fire.

Tarkyn sent him a grateful smile, aware once again of the understated but strong support of his foster brother. "Perhaps the same thing happened to my mother. I don't know."

Ancient Oak looked at him a little strangely, "Why wouldn't you know? Surely it would have been spoken about in your family if a child had been lost?"

Danton replied for the prince who was looking distinctly uncomfortable, "No, Ancient Oak. Anything that might be considered a weakness would have been hushed up. Only Tarkyn's father and mother, the physician and possibly a close lady-in-waiting would have known anything about it...and possibly Stormaway, with his close relationship to Markazon and his knowledge of healing." He looked around to ask Stormaway, but realised that the wizard was no longer in the clearing. Danton shrugged, "Perhaps it simply took the queen seven years to become pregnant again." He stood up to pour himself and Tarkyn another cup of tea. He handed one to Tarkyn, choosing to remain standing. As he leant his shoulder against a nearby beech, he jumped away in consternation.

"Danton, what's wrong?" asked Ancient Oak sharply.

Danton gave his head a short shake and gingerly placed his hand against the tree. He closed his eyes and concentrated for a full minute before re-opening his eyes and replying, "You know how I said I could tell a storm was coming from touching a tree… after Tarkyn had healed me through the depths of the forest?"

All the woodfolk around the fire nodded sceptically.

"I know you didn't believe me…"

"That might have had something to do with the fact that you didn't even know who you were at that stage," grumbled Thunder Storm.

"True," Danton gave a little grin but quickly became serious again, "But nevertheless the storm came as I predicted. And then later, by touching a tree, I saw that column of soldiers turning off the Great Western Road to head towards the encampment… remember?"

"Yes," said Tarkyn, "At just the time that Jarand's soldiers were coming to hunt down Andoran and Sargon."

"Exactly," said Danton smiling his thanks for Tarkyn's support.

"So what have you seen this time?" asked Waterstone dryly.

Danton hesitated in the face of such blatant disbelief, before plunging in. He was used to being teased by them, after all. "There are soldiers coming, hundreds, maybe a thousand or more. There are so many of them that all the trees along the northern border are faintly trembling from the impact of their feet on the earth as they march past, even though they are some distance from the forest edge."

There was a stunned silence before everyone started talking at once. Tarkyn surged to his feet and waved his hand for silence. "If this is the case, why has our intelligence network not warned us? Stormaway?" The prince frowned in irritation, "Where is that pesky wizard when I need him?"

"I am here, Your Highness," said a cool voice behind him, "… and I am hardly pesky simply because I have a few bodily matters to attend to."

"I beg your pardon," Tarkyn smiled slightly as he turned to face him, "Did you hear what Danton told us?"

"I think every woodman within mindspeaking distance knows by now."

"Perhaps Tormadell is unnaturally quiet because its soldiers are on the march," suggested Rainstorm who had appeared out of nowhere.

"If that is the case, the king has been extremely cunning about it," snapped the wizard. "None of my agents have reported anything of this nature. Should we not verify this report before we become too concerned?"

Danton flushed, "Disbelieve me as you will. I know what I have seen. Besides, you have just finished telling us that you hadn't heard from your agents for some time. My guess is that the king has not allowed any carrier pigeons to accompany these troops."

"Blast him!" exclaimed Stormaway. "It is unheard of to forbid carrier pigeons." He shook his head, "No, you must be mistaken, Danton."

This statement gave rise to another bout of many voices speaking at once. Tarkyn held up his hand and everyone gradually quietened, "If you are in agreement, I will join with a bird, if I can find one, and seek confirmation of Danton's information. I hope you will not feel offended if I do this, Danton."

"Not at all. It is hardly a tried and true magical technique. None of us has heard of it before and I have only received an image through the trees three times. Although I would like to be taken seriously, I would not expect anyone to act on such sparse and uncertain knowledge."

CHAPTER 25

Having reached agreement, Tarkyn gestured to Running Feet, his traditional partner for these forays and left the clearing so that he could concentrate in peace. As he found a comfortable place to sit in the shade of a spreading beech tree, he was surprised to find that Stormaway had followed him. He raised his eye brows in query.

Unusually, Stormaway seemed flustered and a little diffident. "Sire, I was wondering whether you might permit me to join you on this mind-journey with the bird. As you know, I only began to use mindtalk recently, once everyone had become aware of the woodfolk side of my heritage. I would value the opportunity to see your forest guardian powers at work." He gave an uncertain smile, "And I may be of assistance in estimating numbers and gauging its intent if, in fact, such a large body of men is really on the march."

"Of course you may join us," Tarkyn waited until the wizard has seated himself, "But keep conversation to a minimum. It takes careful attention to stay connected from a distance." He nodded at Running Feet to indicate that he was ready, quietly marvelling that the woodman would have any idea of the direction of Danton's alleged troops.

Once linked, Running Feet guided Tarkyn's mind northward, skirting the encampment before turning slightly right to follow along the top of a ridge for several miles. As the slopes began to steepen, he slid their minds down the other side of the ridge into a heavily wooded valley to join the path of a stream which they followed as it meandered between towering sycamores, gradually deepening and widening as other streams joined it to flow eventually into a river. The ground on either side became undulating and gradually, the slopes of the valley steepened until the river was flowing between the sheer cliffs of a canyon.

"This is the Carlavon River. In another two or three miles, it flows out of the forest onto the plains," said Running Feet, speaking slowly and quietly. "Your soldiers, if they exist, will have to cross the Carlavon if they are skirting the north west of the forest."

"There is a ford about four miles from the forest's edge," offered Stormaway. "As far as I can remember, this would be the only place that it could be crossed without a boat. So they will have to cut out across the plains to ford the river there."

"Very well. Here will do," said Tarkyn shortly, intent on finding an avian mind to connect with. In company with Running Feet and Stormaway, he let his mind skim across the surface of the water and then sweep upward, scanning the steep rock faces. Perched on a narrow ledge high above the river, a huge mountain eagle, plumage the colour of charcoal streaked with gold on its back and wings, its underside cream and gold, stood surveying her territory. Suddenly she felt a nudge against her mind. Immediately she shrieked and thrust Tarkyn's mind away. Tarkyn gasped as pain shot through his forehead.

"Bloody eagles!" exclaimed Tarkyn. "So aggressive! Just a minute, I'll try again."

"Do you think you should, Sire?" asked Stormaway anxiously.

Tarkyn merely raised a finger to indicate that he wanted no interference and taking a deep breath, prepared another sortie against the eagle's mind. This time he sent forth a warm wave of greeting and reassurance, keeping his mind clear of the eagle's, but alerting her to its continued presence close by. He could see her tilting her head this way and that, looking for the source of the warmth. As she gave a puzzled squawk and ruffled her feathers uncertainly, Tarkyn realised that she was still quite young. He instilled a sense of invitation into his stream of greeting and watched with amusement while the eagle fluctuated between outrage and curiosity, shrieking at the unseen intruder but unwilling to fly to another eyrie while the puzzle remained unsolved. When her shrieks became less frequent and less strident, he nudged against her mind again, accompanied by another wave of reassurance. Cautiously, she let him in but he knew that at any moment, the connection might snap shut.

Instead of directing her as he had the egret and the fieldmouse, he let her explore his mind first, carefully removing one defence after another as he became more sure that she would not attack him. He showed her the eagles and other birds of prey protecting him against the mountainfolk in the far south, the golden eagle warning him of approaching wolves and the constant vigilance that birds of prey kept for his safety. He let her feel his connection to the forest and all those within it. Then he waited. After a slight hesitation, she showed him the nest she had recently left and her parents coming back and forth with food. She shared with him the sickening and yet exhilarating experience of the first time she had been pushed out of her eyrie, plummeting in terror before she had spread her wings and swooped out of the dive, to glide high above the path of the river before beating her wings to gain height until she had flown above the gorge and had been able to see, for the first time, the forest stretching away in every direction.

The eagle may have been young but she was intelligent. Suddenly she cocked her head and sent a query, asking what the forest guardian wanted of her, still with no guarantee that she would comply.

Tarkyn laughed quietly, "So independent. The mountainfolk once called me Lord of the Eagles. How wrong they were. The best I can do is crave a favour, or accept whatever assistance they choose to offer, whether I want it or not. Raptors stand guard over me constantly but not at my instigation and I doubt that they would desist if I asked them to."

In answer to the eagle's query, Tarkyn sent an image of her flying along the river's course until she reached the northern plains followed by an image of many men marching below with a query. She was surprised and excited by the idea that a different type of landscape existed beyond her previous experience. Without further debate, she launched herself off the cliff face, and keeping her mind open to the forest guardian, flew northward through the gorge. Her strong wings ate up the miles but as she began to tire, she looked for thermals to carry her further aloft. The sun was higher in the sky now and as she neared the plains, the heat from the open ground provided her with what she needed.

She spread her wings and let herself spiral upward on the warm air. As she rose, the northern plains came into view beyond the forest edge. At first, all they could see were miles of patchwork farmlands, dotted with trees and small farmhouses.

Then, just as Stormaway was saying, "I don't know why I let that fool of a boy inveigle me with his imaginings," they spotted a faint cloud of dust that snaked from the forests edge to the east across the plain towards the river.

Tarkyn's heart sank. He directed the eagle's attention to the dust cloud with a request to investigate. Wishing to satisfy her own curiosity, the young eagle responded with alacrity. As soon as the thermal had carried her high enough, she glided out across the plains until she reached the next thermal. In no apparent hurry, she rode its current in a slow upward spiral to a height that allowed her to glide the rest of the way to the dust cloud with minimal effort. This convoluted form of travel tried her audience's patience but despite it, she made more speed in the required direction than most other animals could have achieved.

As they drew nearer, it became clear that the dust cloud had been formed by the feet of a long column of soldiers. Tarkyn was so focused on the sea of men marching through the farmlands below him that he did not notice until too late that the eagle, following her curiosity and her newly formed desire to assist the forest guardian, had lost height and was planing in so low that the faces and even the regiments of the officers had become clearly discernible. Suddenly he realised that officers and men were looking up at the eagle flying so unusually low above them. Even as he blasted an image of, "Up! Up!" at her, he saw two officers confer hurriedly before snapping an order.

The young eagle shrieked in panic at the sudden cry in her mind and took a moment to respond. Then her mighty wings beat the air, heaving her upward. But too slowly. All along the lines below, men were unslinging their bows and notching arrows. The eagle had climbed to a hundred feet and it almost seemed that she had made it out of range, as several arrows fell short and dropped harmlessly back to earth. But as the bowmen found their range, the second flight of arrows tore through the air around her. In response to Tarkyn's directions, she angled and zigzagged, dodging between the lethal shafts. But even as she pulled up higher, a lone arrow fired by a master marksman drove upward with deadly accuracy. Only Tarkyn's screamed mental warning to pivot sideways saved her life. Her thick covering of feathers provided some protection, but even so, the arrow grazed her underbelly, leaving a deep bloody furrow across her abdomen.

The young eagle cried piteously and folded her wings in an instinctive effort to protect her stomach. Immediately she began to plummet. The archers below, sure that they had hit their target, ran to intercept her descent. Tarkyn drew on his strength, both as prince and guardian of the forest, and sent an imperious order to the stricken eagle to rise above the pain, accompanying his command with a surge of power. The injured bird shrieked in protest but in the midst of her shock, responded to the only guidance she had, in a situation far beyond her ken. She spread her wings and, striving to ignore the agony in her belly, thrust herself upward and out of reach of Kosar's soldiers. The last Tarkyn and his companions saw of the soldiers through her eyes was their upturned faces, slack with astonishment, as the wounded eagle dragged herself out of her spiralling dive and up into the clear blue sky.

Although she was safe now from the soldiers' arrows, the eagle was not yet out of danger. She was bleeding copiously and her wings, already tired from the outward journey, were losing strength. The eagle was not built to beat her wings tirelessly mile after mile as some migratory birds were. Instead she depended on short strong bursts of flight and the updraft of thermals to keep her soaring over her territory. But in her pain-affected confusion, the inexperienced young eagle could only think to beat her wings remorselessly, striving to reach the dark green line that delineated the edge of the forest and safety.

"She's failing," breathed Tarkyn. "Her strength is nearly spent. Stormaway, you know about weather and atmospheric conditions. Help me to guide her. I have no idea where the thermals will be."

Through the eagle's eyes, Stormaway scanned the plain spread out below. "Veer her to her left. Those darker fields will be radiating more heat. As soon as she is over them, ask her to spread her wings and glide so that the hot air can carry her upwards."

Tarkyn sent her the images laced with faith in her ability. He kept up a constant stream of strength, urging her to calm down and remember all she had been taught as a fledging flyer. As his power penetrated her panic, her brain began to gain ascendancy over her emotions and she obeyed him without question, realising that he was her only hope of survival.

With the last of her strength, she gained the air over dark fields and spread her quivering wings. The updraft supported her body and took the load off her fatigued muscles, lifting her gently upward in a slow lazy spiral. For nearly twenty minutes, she let herself drift in the thermal, spiralling ever higher, allowing herself time to recover enough for the journey to the forest. And all the time, the forest guardian stayed with her, calming and encouraging, praising her courage and keeping her from submerging herself in the pain of her wound.

"Running Feet," said Tarkyn, carefully maintaining his focus on the eagle, "are there woodfolk near the edge of the forest? She is losing a lot of blood and will not remain conscious for much longer. Someone needs to find her when she crashes, bind her wound and protect her. We cannot leave her to become prey to a fox or wolf while she lies unconscious after she has given such service."

The woodman did not argue, "I will attend to it, Sire. If you hold your link firm, I will relay your message now." Only once he had carried out the request, did he add, "However I doubt that she will survive anyway. Birds are highly strung and often die from infection or fretting when they have been wounded. If she finds herself immobilised and imprisoned when she awakes, she may hurt herself more, trying to escape." He shrugged, "And it is hard to tell without seeing the damage, but if the arrow has penetrated the wall of her abdomen, infection may spread through her gut…and that is more than woodfolk medicine can reliably repair."

"Then I must heal her myself," Tarkyn's listeners could hear there was no room for argument in his tone. "Ask the northern woodfolk to bring her as far south as they can. I will take the warhorse and meet them somewhere in between."

Stormaway quelled his wish to protest, knowing that part of this forest guardian's greatness lay in his determination to protect those under his care, regardless of the cost to himself. Still, he couldn't help thinking that concern for the eagle's welfare was deflecting them from the bigger picture.

Almost as though he had read the wizard's thoughts, Tarkyn added, "But before I travel north, we must consider the implications of these soldiers' presence and what we are going to do about it."

Without waiting for a reply, Tarkyn returned his full attention to the stricken eagle, noticing that her mind was becoming foggy as she grew weaker. She was so high now that from below she would be little more than a speck against the sun. He waited until her spiral brought the distant forest into view and then prompted her to veer out of the thermal into a slow glide towards the tree line.

With Stormaway and Tarkyn's help, she found one more thermal to give her the height and respite she needed to make the forest's edge. As she passed over the first of the trees, the thermals deserted her. With her strength fading, she winged her way doggedly along the river's course towards her home in the canyon. But she was never going to make it. Slowly she drifted lower and lower until at last she admitted defeat and landed high in the branches of a dead oak tree. There she hunkered down and looked downward at her stomach to inspect the damage.

The lower part of her stomach was sticky with blood and she could see a gaping, bloody slash between her feathers. Tarkyn could feel the jolt of sickened fear that ran through her. Now that she no longer had the distraction of flying, the pain seemed to intensify and she reeled as nausea swept over her. She shook her head as she realised the presence in her mind was once again demanding her attention, urging her to descend to the forest floor. Her instincts screamed against this suggestion but as she rocked on her perch, she realised that she was in danger of losing her balance. She pulled herself together with a lurch and scanned the area for a wide, horizontal platform.

She cocked her head and saw that the main trunk of the tree in which she was perched had broken off halfway up, to form a roughly flat platform spiked with splinters of broken wood. She half flew, half hopped down onto it, and nestled down gingerly amongst the jagged shafts, sending out a sharp cry as the rough surface brushed harshly against her wound. Then, knowing she had done all she could, she finally gave in to the pain and fatigue.

Chapter 26

When Tarkyn, Running Feet and Stormaway returned to the firesite, they were mobbed by Danton and the woodfolk. Feeling an aura of disapproval, Tarkyn glanced around the trees and spotted several eagles, hawks and falcons glowering down at him. He wasn't sure whether their disapproval stemmed from him using one of their number and allowing her to be injured, or from his intention of leaving the safety of the firesite.

Before he could check with them, Danton demanded, "So come and tell us all about it. Obviously there must have been at least a few soldiers for your eagle to be fired at. How many were there? Where are they now?"

"Just a minute, young man," grumped Stormaway. "We have just been through an extremely trying experience, cajoling that bird back into the forest. Give us time to make a cup of tea and sit down."

Before Stormaway knew what was happening, Tarkyn, Running Feet and he had been ushered to comfortable seats near the fire and cups of tea thrust into their hands.

Stormaway took a sip and sighed, "Very well. There is indeed a battalion moving along the northern perimeter of the forest. The front of the column has left its previous path alongside the forest to swing out across the plain to ford the Carlavon River."

"How many, Stormaway?" pressed Danton, knowing he and Borovar were the only people not to have received any images.

Stormaway grimaced, "At least a thousand, certainly more than infiltrated the forest in Kosar's last attempt to trap Tarkyn. There is no doubt that they are Kosar's soldiers. The eagle flew closely enough to see their uniforms and insignia, silly young bird."

Danton looked in distress at Tarkyn. "I thought they were listening to us, Tarkyn. What is Kosar doing?"

"We have been fools, Danton," said Tarkyn bitterly. "You do not play with kings. We thought, naively, that we were keeping Kosar and Jarand in check with subtle demonstrations of power. But Kosar has had no intention of bowing to my wishes, even if they dovetail with his own. Instead he is bringing a sizeable force *around* the forest."

"But what is he planning to do with them?" asked Rainstorm.

Tarkyn dragged his hand distractedly though his hair, "If you remember, I warned Kosar of Jarand's intentions." He let out a despairing sigh, "And now, unless I'm very much mistaken, he is planning to bring his troops into the encampment from the west and humiliate Jarand by wresting the encampment from him in full view of his supporters."

Groans of dismay issued around the firesite.

"Oh Tarkyn! This is terrible. Just when you hoped that Jarand might be mellowing under the influence of Kosar's acknowledgement," Waterstone squatted down and placed his hand on his bloodbrother's shoulder and smiled sympathetically, "You know I did not share your optimism, but I did hope you were right."

"Are you sure Kosar's men aren't going to skirt straight down the western side of the forest, south to Montraya while Jarand is away from his stronghold?" asked Autumn Leaves.

"Not enough men for that," answered Stormaway shortly.

Lapping Water said quietly, "Tarkyn, if these men of Kosar's arrive at the encampment, not only will there be a confrontation between Jarand and Kosar but it will take place in the middle of the forest. And think how many men are in the encampment already. The encampment will have to expand even further into the forest to accommodate them."

In a heartbeat, everyone's perspective of the situation shifted. Danton voiced the change, "Tarkyn, you are Lord and Protector of the Forests, decreed by your father. Jarand may not know that, but Kosar does. If he brings these men into the forest, it is a direct challenge to your sovereignty within the forest… and it will further damage the lands under your protection."

For a few moments there was the silence of mindtalking. Then Tree Wind spoke resolutely from the other side of the fire, "Tarkyn, we know you have done more for us than we could ever repay but even so, we have rarely asked for your help… But we are asking now. Please don't let these soldiers come in to fight out their battles and carve out a place for themselves within our forest. Find a way to stop them." Before Tarkyn could formulate an answer, she added, "We will help you. We will do whatever you ask to stop them."

Tarkyn raised his hands as though to ward off the pressure, "Enough." His woodfolk did not make the mistake of thinking that he was planning to refuse them and waited. "I don't think it will come to a fight, with Jarand's troops so heavily outnumbered by Kosar's incoming battalion. But the humiliation would make Jarand vindictive and even more dangerous. So I agree we must try to avert it… Just a moment, give me time to think." With everyone's eyes on him, he frowned and used his finger to draw in the air in front of him as he nutted out his plan. When he had it clear in his mind, he nodded decisively, "I think I have every angle covered. See whether you agree." He swallowed some tea and began, "I suggest that we warn Jarand of Kosar's plan and then hold up Kosar's battalion long enough for Jarand to take his troops clear of the Great Western Road and on their way to Montraya."

The prince grinned as he was deluged with objections and questions, "I thought you'd like it." After a moment, he raised his hand and waited until he could be heard, "This will remove Jarand's troops from the forest, which would be to our advantage, since he is more focused on recruitment than on protection of travellers anyway. Secondly, if Harkell bears the news to Jarand, it will support our ruse that Harkell gave Jarand's parchment directly into my hand, and thirdly, it will remove Kosar's main rationale for bringing his battalion to the encampment."

"But won't Jarand still be angry when he finds out his brother's intention?" asked Tree Wind.

"Yes, he will, but much less so than if he were faced down publicly… and Jarand's agents will find out about this battalion anyway, as soon as Kosar's troops are back in contact with the outside world. So the best we can do is give Jarand the chance to turn the tables on Kosar, by leaving before Kosar has the chance to eject him." Tarkyn shrugged, "He may even feel that he has won the round by snatching away Kosar's chance of embarrassing him."

"If we warn Jarand," objected Autmn Leaves, "couldn't he simply use his current superior numbers to get rid of Kosar?"

Danton answered, "No. Jarand only has about eighty more men than Kosar and there are three hundred civilians whose loyalty to the king would have been stirred by his visit."

Lapping Water looked puzzled, "But Tarkyn why, if your older brothers are so unscrupulous, doesn't one just quietly dispose of the other? They were willing to dispose of you." Tarkyn's face remained impassive but, as she saw his knuckles whiten in his grip around his cup, she realised she had hurt him. She walked quietly around the fire, sat down next to him and linked her arm through his. "Sorry," she said softly. "I didn't mean to be unkind."

Using his other arm, he took a slow sip of his tea. He did not return her embrace but nor did he push her away. After a moment, he glanced down at her and said, "And I did not mean to give myself away."

The wizard diverted attention from them by answering the question, "They would have to face a huge public outcry if either killed the other. So they have to be sure of their following first, especially with Tarkyn, second in line to the throne, still alive and popular. Besides, they both have guardsmen, magical wards, their own magical powers and at times, the shields they employ. They even have tasters for all their food, you know."

This last sent a ripple of astonishment through the woodfolk.

Waterstone grimaced, "Not much of a life, is it?"

Tarkyn smiled wryly at his bloodbrother and shrugged, "It is what it is. Power and position bring with them certain dangers… and many people would gladly run the gamut of the dangers to gain the privileges."

"That is why there is so much intrigue." Danton smiled, the light of many memories in his eye, "But Sire, will you ignore the king's challenge and allow him to bring so many troops into the forest, if he still insists upon it after Jarand leaves?"

"No, but we will cross that bridge if or when we come to it. Let us concentrate on delaying the king's men first."

"Hmm. So that just leaves us with one small issue to resolve," said Autumn Leaves dryly, "How are we going to delay Kosar's troops for two or three days?"

It was decided that any storms or floods that Stormaway might create would be too temporary and the idea of Tarkyn spooking their horses was also dismissed, because most of the troops were infantrymen.

During a small pause, Tarkyn looked around the circle, "You said you would do what you could to help. I think the time has come for woodfolk to venture forth from the forest." In response to exchanged glances of consternation, Tarkyn held up his hand, "Don't worry. I am not going to suggest a pitched battle. I am thinking of a raid under cover of darkness during which we find some way to disable them or reduce their potency. What do you think?"

"I am willing to do it but, if we attack them beyond the forest's edge, aren't you making an incursion into Kosar's territory?" asked Waterstone.

"Good point." Tarkyn raised his eyebrows at his wizard, "Your opinion, Storamaway?"

"It would indeed be more judicious to wait until they were within the forest." Stormaway shrugged, "But we need to prevent them from getting anywhere near the Great Western Road which is only two hours march from the encampment. So we must stop them well before they enter the forest.

Tarkyn looked around him, "Agreed?" Receiving nods, he continued, "Then let's think of what we can do to disable Kosar's battalion."

Just as this suggestion gave rise to another round of discussion, Midnight hobbled into view, crying piteously, with one of Sparrow's arm around his shoulder and her other hand propping up his elbow to keep the weight off one of his feet.

Tarkyn held out his arms, "Oh dear, little one. What have you done now? Thanks Sparrow," he added, as Midnight clambered onto his lap.

"Come on Midnight. Let me see." Although he was speaking the words, he projected everything he said in images to his little ward.

Midnight sniffed and held his foot up for inspection. A deep gash on the sole of his left foot, obscured by dirt and bits of leaves, was oozing blood.

"Oh dear. Poor little one." Tarkyn looked up, "Summer Rain, could you have a look at this and clean it up. Then I'll heal it." He returned his attention to Midnight, "Now where have you left your boots? You mustn't leave them lying around, Midnight." An image appeared in Tarkyn's mind of a small pair of boots hidden beneath a bush next to the stream. "Oh. Playing in the stream, were you? Well, at least you hid them. Sparrow..."

Sparrow rolled her eyes. "Yes, I'll go and get them."

"Thanks."

As she skipped off, Tarkyn sent a gentle blast of sorcerous wind at her retreating figure. With her hair blowing around her face, she stopped and looked back, frowning uncertainly. Tarkyn grinned and sent another barrage of air at her. She giggled, her good humour completely restored, and headed off once more in search of Midnight's shoes.

By the time Summer Rain had bathed Midnight's foot and Tarkyn had provided a stream of *esse* to repair the damage, the rest of the company had discussed and discarded many ideas for disabling Kosar's troops. Finally, inspired inadvertently by Midnight, Rainstorm came up with an idea that was breathtakingly simple and effective, but did not badly injure any of Kosar's soldiers.

Tarkyn grinned appreciatively, "Kosar may still think I'm a softy after this but he will struggle to proclaim that I have attacked his troops. Well done, Rainstorm." He stood up holding Midnight to his chest, "So we mount our attack tomorrow night? That will give us time to recruit the northern woodfolk and to prepare… And now, I will head off up north to rescue the eagle. Is the horse ready? Thunder Storm and Creaking Bough, will you mind Midnight until I get back? I won't be long."

He gave the little boy a big squeeze before setting him down and sending him a series of images to explain what was happening. With less reluctance than he would once have shown, Midnight accepted the inevitable and even managed to produce a small smile as he walked over to Thunder Storm and took his hand.

As Ancient Oak appeared from within the trees, leading the great warhorse, Waterstone and Danton approached Tarkyn with an air of resolution about them.

Tarkyn held up his hand, "You will not dissuade me. I cannot let that eagle die."

Waterstone gave a faint smile, "We know that. We wish only to do our best to ensure your safety on your journey."

Tarkyn unbent. "Very well. I'm listening."

"We have notified woodfolk all along your route to keep watch for you. But it would be better if someone were with you who could translate their mindtalking. Images can be hard to deal with," said Waterstone.

"And Sire, you cannot find your way alone. It would be safer and quicker for someone to be with you, than for you to rely continually on images from woodfolk. Besides, riding hard while exchanging images may be risky," pressed Danton.

"And," continued Waterstone in a rush before Tarkyn could get a word in, "should you need to transport this eagle of yours, another person could guide the horse while you held the bird…or vice versa. Admittedly, the extra weight may make you a little slower, but we think the advantages outweigh the disadvantages."

Tarkyn threw his hands up, "All right. I concede. I know when I'm beaten."

Waterstone and Danton both grinned.

"Good," said Ancient Oak, vaulting up onto the horse's back. "Then if you are ready to go, I will accompany you." He stretched down his arm, "Let's go."

"Oh, so you're in on this too, are you?" Tarkyn did not sound pleased as he grabbed the woodman's arm and leapt lightly onto the horse's back behind him. The great horse sidled under the extra weight but quickly steadied.

"We all are," smiled Lapping Water.

Tarkyn overcame his dislike of being managed, enough to say, "Thank you for your care. Look after Midnight for me. We'll be back in a few hours."

CHAPTER 27

As Ancient Oak guided the great horse unerringly through the dense woodland; cantering along narrow paths until they disappeared, threading between small gaps in apparently impenetrable copses, and picking his way through tall straggly bushes, it became borne upon Tarkyn that his woodfolk had been right. The advantage of a competent guide far outweighed the disadvantage of the extra weight that the horse had to carry. After half an hour he leaned forward and murmured in Ancient Oak's ear, "Once more, you have risked my ire by directing my actions… and yet I have to admit that each time, your advice has been excellent."

Tarkyn heard a quiet chuckle from his bloodbrother, "Tarkyn, you may be a prince but you are also my younger brother. I have no qualms about facing your anger." He paused while he urged the horse up a steep narrow path between some boulders to gain the top of the ridge. "Anyway, you must know by now that I have your welfare at heart and would not direct you gratuitously."

Ancient Oak could hear the smile in Tarkyn's voice, "Yes, I do know that. You, more than anyone, helps me manage Midnight when he runs away. After the mountainfolk attacked me, it seemed you were always there, quietly standing guard, either beside me or in the nearest tree. And I know you took my side unflinchingly against the views of the majority of woodfolk, including Waterstone, when we were in the Lost Forest… I value your strong, quiet support more than you could imagine."

After a noticeable pause, Ancient Oak muttered something incomprehensible that might have been, "Thanks."

Realising his brother was embarrassed, Tarkyn abruptly changed the subject, "So, how long until we get there?"

He could almost feel Ancient Oak's sigh of relief as he answered, "Not long. We will follow this ridge for another ten minutes before taking a path to our right that will lead us down onto the valley floor. The northern woodfolk will meet us there with your eagle."

Two woodmen were waiting for them in a small clearing beside a stream. They had fashioned a sling strung between two poles so that they could carry the enormous eagle with a minimum of jolting. A cloth had been draped over the bird so that, at first, Tarkyn could not see it. As soon as the warhorse came into sight, they carefully lowered their burden onto the ground and stood, a little uncertainly, as their forest guardian dismounted.

After a glance at Ancient Oak for guidance, one round faced woodman spoke to the prince in a strange, hooting voice, "How do you do? We are pleased to meet one who has done so much for our people. I am Hooting Owl."

Tarkyn inclined his head, "Thank you. It is a pleasure to meet new woodfolk, especially when we meet to assist a creature of the forest. I am Tarkyn Tamadil, Guardian of these Forests and Prince of Eskuzor. You may call me Tarkyn." His eyes strayed to the still cloth covered mound on the ground. "Does the eagle still live?"

"Yes, she is not well, but she is alive. The arrow has torn through muscles and the stomach lining has a short perforation in it. I have cleaned her wounds and rubbed them with finely ground willow bark. We have placed the cloth over her, imbued with a gentle soporific to soothe her and keep her sedated. Once we remove it, she may regain consciousness, which would place us all in danger. I am Forest Wind, healer of the northern woodfolk."

While they were talking, Ancient Oak walked the horse into the trees and tethered it just out of sight, before returning to stand beside Tarkyn.

"Hmm, I see your point," Tarkyn studied the outline of the eagle beneath the cloth as he thought. "I may need to use some sorcery." He glanced up as he heard a sudden intake of breath and smiled disarmingly, "You did know that I am a sorcerer, I presume?"

The two woodman nodded nervously.

"Be assured. I will explain anything I decide to do beforehand so that you are prepared. You will be in no danger from me or my sorcery, only from that wild bird."

Ancient Oak drew in a breath as if to speak, then clamped his mouth shut. When Tarkyn looked at him, the woodman's eyes began to twinkle and he said, "Just another suggestion I thought of giving you…"

Tarkyn gave a grunt of laughter, "Go on then."

"Perhaps you could use your *Shturrum* spell on her the instant she opens her eyes. It's just that, if you use your shield, she could thrash around inside it and hurt herself further."

"True. It depends on how far gone she is. Is she likely to open her eyes once the drug wears off or will she remain unconscious, do you think?" Tarkyn asked the northern woodmen.

Hooting Owl shrugged, "She was unconscious when we reached her in the old oak. But surely, if you heal her, she will come around at some stage."

"Hmm. This is tricky. I have not healed a wild animal before, let alone a fearsome eagle. I need to have her receptive to my power, so the less I frighten her the better." Tarkyn looked at Ancient Oak. "I may be able to create a very small shield around her so that she can't thrash about." He grinned suddenly, "You know what it is like to be on the receiving end of the *Shturrum* spell. Which would be better, do you think?"

Ancient Oak grinned back, knowing the northern woodmen would be shocked, "I think immobilising her completely would be better, if you can do it. Then you can reassure her until she is calm, without her straining against your shield."

Tarkyn nodded decisively. "Very well. I'll try using the spell straight away but I don't know whether it will work while the eagle is unconscious. Then I will place my hand on her shoulder to send my *esse* into her. While I do this, Ancient Oak, can you keep your eyes trained on the eagle's? The moment she begins to come around, tell me and I will re-apply the *Shturrum* spell, in case it hasn't worked." Remembering Twig Snap and Leaf Fall's fear when they first saw sorcery, he asked the northern woodmen. "Would you like a demonstration so that you know what to expect?" After a short silence, he realised that Ancient Oak had sent them images instead. "So, are we clear? Very well, remove the cloth."

The forest guardian found himself looking down on a still, huddled mass of dulled black and gold feathers. He mourned for the magnificent bird he had connected with. Tarkyn waved his hand and murmured, "*Shturrum*," before stroking the eagle's head and placing his hand gently on her back at the base of her neck. With a glance at Ancient Oak, he shut his eyes and sent his awareness down through his arm. Once inside the bird, he tried to orient himself but the proportions were so different from those he had encountered inside humans that he became immediately confused. He tried heading away from her neck but soon found himself at the extremity of a wing. Grimacing in irritation at himself, he decided that all he could do was flow through her body until he found the damaged area. It did not take him long. He wove his power into the torn muscles of her abdomen and brought together the edges of the perforation in her stomach. Knowing the danger of infection, he sent a short sharp blast of contrived anger into the damaged area.

Suddenly Tarkyn felt a fierce pain in his side that shattered his focus. He returned to himself to find the three woodman struggling to hold down a very angry shrieking eagle. Ignoring the pain in his side, he gave his head a quick shake to clear his mind, waved his hand and incanted, "*Shturrum*" rather more loudly than he would have liked. Immediately the eagle stilled, her baleful golden eyes glaring at him.

"You can let go now," he said quietly. Slowly he replaced his hand on her back. He could feel her quivering with fear and rage inside her stilled body. Tarkyn let his life force flow into her to replenish her blood and strength, all the while sending waves of calm and friendship, even though he was wryly aware that one did not make friends with eagles.

When he had given her enough strength and could feel that her outrage had lessened, he took his hand away and moved slowly back from her, signalling for the woodmen to do the same.

"How far are we from her eyrie? Can she fly there from here?" Tarkyn asked in a low voice.

"It is not more than eight miles," replied Forest Wind. "Under normal circumstances she could fly there easily."

"Will she know the way from here, if we let her go?"

Ancient Oak chortled, "Of course she will. All she has to do is rise high above the forest to get her bearings."

Tarkyn gave him a withering glance, "It did not help me to orient myself at all when a crow gave me a bird's eye view of the forest."

"No Tarkyn. But then, you are not an eagle." Ancient Oak grinned, stopping himself with an effort from mentioning Tarkyn's abysmal sense of direction.

"Hmph," Tarkyn returned his attention to the eagle. "Now, you three, come and stand beside me. I am going to place a shield over us before I release the eagle." Addressing the northern woodmen, he explained, "It will look like a bronze haze all around you. It won't hurt if you touch it but you will not able to go through it and the eagle will not be able to get in. Is everyone ready?"

From within the shield, Tarkyn waved his hand to release the eagle. For a moment nothing happened. Then, as the eagle realised she could move again, she surged to her feet, shook herself and shrieked her indignation. She glared at the four men before suddenly being distracted by the memory of her injury. She preened the feathers of her abdomen, making little squawks as her beak passed over the injury. After a few minutes of intense activity, she raised her head and stared directly at Tarkyn, cocking her head from side to side. In response, Tarkyn resumed his messages of reassurance.

She unfurled her great gold and charcoal wings and beat the air, testing their strength. Then giving a final shriek, she launched herself upward and rose into the air, circling once around the clearing as she gained height, before disappearing out of sight above the trees.

Unconsciously, three woodman and a sorcerer let out breaths of released tension.

As Tarkyn waved away the shield, Forest Wind grinned, "We did it. We actually did it. We healed a wild eagle… I know you did the final healing, Tarkyn, but we all played a part."

"Yes," enthused the usually quiet Ancient Oak. "Wasn't it great to see her spread her wings and take off? Listen. You can still hear her shrieks on the wind."

As a courtesy to the northern woodfolk, Tarkyn accepted the offer of warmed rolls and tea before they departed. Hooting Owl lit a small fire at the edge of the clearing and as they relaxed around it, Tarkyn broached the subject of their proposed sortie on Kosar's troops.

Forest Wind studied him over the rim of his cup. "We are not under oath to you and we have no intention of fighting for sorcerer politics. The assistance we provided with the eagle was freely given to save a creature of the forest."

"You may not be under oath but I am," said Tarkyn. "I have vowed to protect all woodfolk but more than that, as Guardian of the Forest, I am committed to the protection of the forest itself. I, also, have no intention of enmeshing myself in sorcerer politics, except to protect innocent people, woodfolk and sorcerers alike, from my brothers' machinations."

Ancient Oak came to his aid, "In the Lost Forest, four past forest guardians told us that Tarkyn's wish to prevent civil war was also our cause, to stop the incursion into our forests by hundreds or even thousands of fighting sorcerers." He waved his arm in the general direction of Kosar's battalion. "Those troops out there are on their way to Prince Jarand's encampment which, as you know, is within the forest. Even if they don't fight, they may settle within the forest if we don't stop them." He glanced at Tarkyn, "Excuse us for a few minutes. This will be much easier mindtalking."

Several minutes passed. The prince sipped his tea and waited patiently as the other three conferred in silence. When the northern woodfolk came back into focus, they were regarding him with new respect. Tarkyn shot a wry glance at his bloodbrother who gave a wicked little grin in return.

"Did you really outface a ten foot tall wizard to save future generations of woodfolk from corruption?" asked Forest Wind.

"And did you and your friend fight off nine sorcerers just to protect a little boy?" asked Hooting Owl.

Tarkyn nodded, a slight frown appearing on his forehead. "But I thought you knew of these events."

"We had heard of them," replied Forest Wind, "but not in such detail. Ancient Oak has just replayed the events for us. Hearing about them was not the same as seeing them."

Tarkyn stood up and brushed the crumbs off the front of his soft brown shirt. "I hope you realise that even though I could, I would never order the oathbound woodfolk to fight an open battle against sorcerers. Firstly, I wouldn't want woodfolk to be put at such risk. Secondly, we all have a bond of secrecy to uphold and thirdly, our strength lies in our subterfuge." He looked across at Ancient Oak and smiled, "And fourthly, we generally work by agreement, not by my decree."

"So we understand from what Ancient Oak has shown us," said Hooting Owl, rising to his feet in preparation for Tarkyn and Ancient Oak's departure. "And since it is the wish of our fellow woodfolk, we will agree to assist you."

Tarkyn frowned, "Hmm. A forest guardian may be a legend in your tales but I do not seem to be highly valued in reality."

"I have two things to say to that. Firstly, you are one of our fellow woodmen whom we have agreed to help, and secondly you do not expect even your home guard to follow your requests without debate, particularly a suggestion that will take us out of the forest."

"But Forest Wind's emphatic refusal at the outset did not sound like the beginnings of a debate."

Hooting Owl smiled, "And yet here we are, at an agreement."

"Just setting the ground rules, young man." Forest Wind gave Tarkyn a friendly pat on the arm. "You may be our forest guardian and a woodman, but you are also a prince of sorcerers. If I had not brought that consideration out into the open, we may have refused you because we were harbouring an unspoken fear that you were using us for sorcerer ends."

Tarkyn gave a slight bow, "Then I thank you for your openness." He shrugged, "I am afraid I am still not used to my word counting for so little. I am accustomed to being obeyed without question and it is a constant struggle for me to adjust."

"Yes, we gather that sorcerers have some strange attitudes," Forest Wind smiled to take any sting out of his words. "If it makes you feel any better, we did not hesitate to provide our help with your injured eagle. And we are disposed towards supporting you as our forest guardian. But you must acknowledge that leaving the forest under any circumstances, let alone to go amongst sorcerer soldiers, is an extreme request."

"Yes, I agree. It is," Tarkyn conceded. "It will take all of your expertise to pull it off safely. So I have left the planning to the home guard and those of you who accompany them. Thank you again for your help with our young eagle." He listened for a moment and smiled, "I can still hear her shrieks from time to time…"

There was an arrested silence as they realised that they should no longer be able to hear her and that, in fact, the shrieks were drawing nearer.

Suddenly something grey and red plummeted from the sky. Tarkyn looked down to find a mangled, freshly killed rabbit lying at his feet. Then the sky was obliterated by a flurry of gold and black as the eagle's spread wings blocked everything from sight. The two northern woodmen flicked into hiding but Ancient Oak stayed staunchly by Tarkyn's side. Before they knew what was happening, the eagle swooped straight at Tarkyn to land on his shoulder, making him lurch under her weight. Once she was balanced, she pulled at the hair on the back of his head, drawing the long strands gently through her beak. Then she gave a couple of comfortable little squawks before turning awkwardly to face forwards.

The three woodman, two from behind a nearby bush, watched in awe as the enormous, fearsome bird settled herself on Tarkyn's shoulder and continued to preen his hair.

A little smile began to play around Ancient Oak's mouth. "I think she likes you, Tarkyn."

Tarkyn rolled his eyes, "Oh, for heaven's sakes. She weighs a ton. Get her off me."

Ancient Oak laughed quietly, "And how, exactly, do you propose we do that?" He bent over and picked up the rabbit. "Here. I expect this is a gift. Perhaps she expects you to eat it right here and now." He stepped towards Tarkyn holding it in front of him.

The eagle snaked her neck forward and shrieked at him.

"Stop it!" snapped Tarkyn sharply to the eagle, matching images to words. The eagle shifted her weight uncertainly and ruffled her feathers but showed no inclination to take offence at his tone. Opening his mind also to Ancient Oak, Tarkyn sent her a picture of eggs in a nest from which he and Ancient Oak were emerging.

The eagle cocked her head and surveyed Ancient Oak. After a minute she sent back a querying image of a crow and a grass parrot.

Tarkyn laughed. "She is struggling with the concept that two such different looking people could be related… But I have no hope of explaining the true relationship."

Ancient Oak looked critically at his bloodbrother with the huge eagle on his left shoulder. "You know, you two suit each other. You both have golden eyes, although yours are warmer and more orangey, and you both have black plumage."

"Oh good. Just what I need. A fashion accessory that weighs a ton, obscures all my vision on the left hand side and fends off friend and foe alike." He brought his left hand up slowly and began to stroke her. "What am I going to do with you, young one? You are supposed to go back to your eyrie."

Hooting Owl and Forest Wind emerged gingerly from behind the bushes.

"Aren't you a forest guardian? Can't you just demand that she return to her eyrie?" asked Hooting Owl.

Tarkyn grimaced, "I wish I could, but eagles are no more tractable than woodfolk. It took a great deal of persuasion to get this little madam to help me and I can't risk annoying her now. She could rake my eyes out if she took offence."

"What about that shield of yours?" asked Hooting Owl.

"No," answered Ancient Oak for him. "There would have to be a gap between Tarkyn and the eagle."

"You could use your *Shturrum* spell," suggested Forest Wind.

"I could," Tarkyn conceded, "but then what? I can't keep her motionless indefinitely. And when I let her go, she would be justifiably angry. I might not want her as friendly as this, but I don't want to turn her against me. Besides, if she turns against me, so might all the raptors. That would be extremely unhelpful."

Ancient Oak chuckled, "Then I guess you are stuck with her. It should be interesting getting the two of you onto the horse."

Tarkyn heaved a sigh of exasperation, "This is ridiculous!" He eyed the eagle and found her looking at him curiously with her head cocked, as though waiting for a response. Unthinkingly, Tarkyn began to stroke her again. "Oh dear. She really is quite cute, in a fearsome sort of way." He glared at the three laughing woodmen, "It's all very well for you. You haven't got razor sharp talons digging into your shoulder… And I don't know what she did to my side but that is still hurting as well."

"Oh, don't blame the eagle for that," said Ancient Oak cheerily. "That was me kicking you in the side to get your attention. My hands were fully occupied with holding the eagle down at the time."

"Hmph." Ancient Oak could see that Tarkyn was not pleased with this abuse of his royal person but also that he understood the necessity. Ancient Oak gave a quick mind message to the northern woodfolk explaining the dire consequences for anyone attacking the prince, with the rider that he was exempt but they weren't.

The two woodmen were taken aback. "I hope there are no other quirky sorcerer ways that present a danger to us," said Forest Wind austerely.

Tarkyn glanced from Ancient Oak to Forest Wind, correctly surmising the content of the mindmessages that had passed between them, "No. Not within the forest. I have waived the necessity for formal gestures of respect." Here, Ancient Oak demonstrated what Tarkyn meant by showing them people bowing before the prince as he walked through

Tormadell, an image he had borrowed from Waterstone. "But if you ever meet my brothers, which I hope you never do, a lack of due courtesy would be most unwise."

"Strange uncivilised practices," said Forest Wind trenchantly.

"Do you know," said Tarkyn silkily, "that is almost exactly what my brother said of you woodfolk when Rainstorm failed to bow to him." The prince drew a short breath to rein in his growing irritation, "But he was wrong and so are you. The two societies are very different but each has its own strengths…and since I am the only one amongst us to have lived in both, you are not in a strong position to argue."

Forest Wind met the prince's eyes squarely, "I beg your pardon. I can see that I have offended you. I believe that discovering the dangers attached to coming into contact with you unsettled me."

Tarkyn responded in a much gentler voice. "No, you are quite safe. You have no reason to attack me and I would overlook it if you inadvertently hurt me."

The northern woodmen glanced at each other and let out a little sigh of relief.

"So how are you going to get yourself onto that horse?" asked Hooting Owl.

Accepting that the subject was closed, Tarkyn replied, "I am going to have to send images to the eagle and the horse, and reassure each of them about the other."

"Provided you can get the eagle to agree not to attack the horse," said Hooting Owl with his strange hooting laugh.

"And I don't think you can vault onto the horse as you did on the way here," Ancient Oak had retrieved the war horse and now leapt lightly onto its back. "Just wait. I'll bring the horse up against that log and you can climb aboard gently."

"Good idea. Just give me a minute or two to sort these two out."

As Tarkyn's images explained his intention, the eagle ruffled its feathers and glared at the horse, while the horse flung up its head and snorted in alarm, rolling its eyes at the eagle. Slowly, sending continuous messages of reassurance, Tarkyn inched towards the horse, with the eagle clinging determinedly to his shoulder as he moved under her. Horse and eagle kept their eyes on each other, but each endured the close presence of the other. Tarkyn lifted his leg, slid it over the horse behind Ancient Oak and gradually lowered himself onto its back. By no outward sign could anyone tell how harshly the eagle's talons dug into his shoulder.

Tarkyn let out a sigh of relief. "So far, so good," he said, raising his right hand in farewell. "Thank you for your help, past and future. We will see you again."

Ancient Oak, keenly aware of the eagle perched closely behind him, her beak only inches from the back of his head, gave a half-hearted parting waggle of his hand. Only as the horse carried its burden out of the clearing, could the northern woodmen see the spots of blood soaking through the back of Tarkyn's shirt.

Chapter 28

While Tarkyn rescued his eagle, Danton and Stormaway, deep within a group of travellers, sauntered past the guards into the encampment. Danton was once more disguised as a scruffy trapper and Stormaway was in his alter ego of well-known merchant.

Once inside the encampment, they split up, Stormaway to return to his private, comfortable quarters while Danton set off to locate String and Bean in their corner of a communal campfire. He found them deep in conversation with Cart and Horse, arguing over the relative merits of snow hare and rabbit as sources of meat.

String broke off to greet Danton, "Hello stranger. Haven't seen you for a few days. Is all well?"

Danton shrugged casually, "I've been better. Haven't seen Greyskies lately, have you? Or those two officers I saw you talking to the other night?"

Horse frowned across at him, "What do you want with soldiers? Don't tell me you're going to turn out to be a captain in disguise too, like your mate Harkell?"

Danton shook his head, smiling disarmingly, "No. I have never served in Jarand's army. No. But I do need to get in touch with Harkell. If you must know, he owes me some money. I dropped a bit in cards the other night and so now that he seems to have an income again, I could do with getting my money back."

Horse gave a deep guffaw, "Oh, is that all? Greyskies has gone to get some food. He should be back soon. Dunno about the two soldiers." He then lost interest and turned his attention to a scorched potato he was trying to flick out of the coals.

"Hungry are you, Dale?" asked Bean casually. "I could do with something myself. Tell you what. I'll take you to find Greyskies and we can get some food at the same time."

Danton nodded his agreement, threw his pack down at the edge of the firelight and wandered off with String and Bean towards the rear of the encampment where the cheap eating tents were located.

As soon as they were out of earshot String asked quietly, "What's up? How's Harkell? Have you seen him?"

"Harkell is being used by Jarand to liaise with Tarkyn. So far, he is safe enough."

Bean raised his eyebrows, "Hmm. Tricky for him. Won't stay safe for long if he is true to Tarkyn. What's so urgent that you need to see him so quickly? Couldn't Tarkyn have sent a mouse?"

"Tarkyn is busy with an eagle. Let's get hold of Harkell and I'll explain then."

They found Greyskies without any difficulty and he trotted off happily to pass on Danton's request to Saker and Biggin.

They waited for Harkell in a busy, grubby bar where the crowd noise meant that they would not be overheard. They were just ordering their second round of drinks when Harkell, smartly turned out in his red and blue uniform, walked into the bar. A few anxious glances were cast in his direction but when it became clear that he was meeting someone, people returned to their conversations.

The four of them merely exchanged nods until their drinks were ordered and they were seated around a table in a corner where they would not be overheard.

As soon as they sat down, Harkell said, "I haven't got long now, maybe half an hour. I'll have more time later. This must be important for you to come out into the open like this. What's up?"

Danton leant in closer. "Kosar is sending a battalion to take over the encampment."

Harkell swore. String and Bean sat upright with shock. String made a convulsive movement but Bean grabbed his arm firmly. "Stop it String! The last thing we need is to have to cope with you panicking. Now breathe!"

String rolled his eyes at him and heaved in a few deep breaths. After a minute, he said tightly, "It's all right. I'm all right now. Go on Danton."

Harkell's face was white, "Oh my lord! Jarand will be humiliated before four companies of his soldiers. I dread to think how he will act out his anger. Tough times ahead for all of us."

Danton put a hand on Harkell's arm, "We are taking steps to mitigate the situation. None of us wants an armed altercation within the forest. At the moment, Kosar's men are about three days away but we plan to hold them up long enough for your troops to be on your way south without crossing their path."

String gave a low whistle, "Oh my word, the ante has been well and truly upped!"

Danton nodded, "But short of killing them, we can't hold them up indefinitely. As it is, attacking them outside the forest comes close to a declaration of war. So Harkell, you will have to tell Jarand about Kosar's approaching troops and persuade him to leave before Kosar has the chance to humiliate him. And without Jarand here, Kosar will no longer have a reason to bring his troops into the forest."

Harkell drew in a breath and held it. After a few moments he said, "Bearing bad news to Jarand is a dangerous occupation."

"It is Tarkyn's wish."

Harkell scowled at him, "I did not say I wouldn't do it."

"I'm sorry you have been charged with such a difficult task but we must make sure that Jarand is brought to understand that he must leave. Time is short and an exchange of letters needed to convince him may take too long to get you away safely. We don't want a conflict of arms within the forest, or for Jarand to be so badly humiliated that he becomes completely enraged."

"Besides Harkell," said Bean, always quick on the uptake, "warning him should further convince Jarand that you are loyal and useful to him."

"… and demonstrate that Tarkyn has been affected by the potion on the parchment and is supporting him," added Danton.

String and Bean looked confused at this last rider so Danton took a minute to explain Jarand's failed plot with the love potion.

"Jarand is going to be livid with Kosar… and everyone else in the vicinity… even if I can make him see that Tarkyn is ostensibly helping him to wrong foot Kosar." Harkell lowered his head onto his hands and said gloomily, "Oh, joy for us all."

Danton grimaced, "I think this is the best we can do, Harkell. We are hoping that Jarand may derive some degree of smugness out of cheating Kosar of his intended moment of triumph and avoid the worst of his chagrin if he is not faced down in public… with the added bonus that Jarand and his troops will leave the forest where he has spent more time recruiting men for his own army than reducing the number of bandits. But if you have any better ideas, please tell us."

Harkell sighed and straightened up, "No, I think you are making the best of a nasty situation. Let's hope you are right about Jarand. What an idiot the king is! He had the people here eating out of the palm of his hand. If he had kept it up, Jarand's support would have faded slowly away. But no! He has to show up his brother and antagonise him and his followers." His brown eyes flittered around the bar, checking for unwonted interest, before he gave a little smile, "So our woodland friends must leave the safety of the trees for a while. How do they feel about that?"

Danton smiled in return, "They are understandably nervous but they offered to do whatever Tarkyn asked to prevent the invasion of over a thousand troops, bent on confrontation, into their beloved forest."

Harkell's eyes widened, "That many?" He stood up, "I must go. Interesting times ahead. I hope all goes as you plan. Wish me luck. I may not see you again."

String jumped up and wrung his hand. "No, it won't be that bad, will it? Surely he won't kill you?"

Harkell laughed. "No. I meant I mightn't see you before we return to Montraya."

"No, you may not," agreed Danton. "I think we three and Stormaway need to be safely in the forest as events here unfold. I will miss you. Good luck, my friend."

Chapter 29

Harkell gave them three hours to get well away before he sent his sergeant with a note addressed to Prince Jarand, requesting an audience. The prince sent a curt reply saying that he was not available until the following morning but would see him then. Harkell gritted his teeth as he dispatched his sergeant with another request, this time stressing the urgency. He knew that if he left the prince uninformed until tomorrow when clearly he possessed the information today, Jarand would be justifiably incensed. Better to weather his displeasure now.

Harkell had barely had time to convince himself that he was taking the right course of action when his sergeant returned, looking shaken, and snapped a salute, "Sir, Prince Jarand will see you in twenty minutes' time." He glanced at his captain and added, "And he said that he will only see you for ten minutes and you had better have a good reason. Begging your pardon, sir."

Harkell smiled sympathetically, "Gave you a hard time, did he? Thank you for delivering my message."

At the appointed time, Captain Harkell presented himself to the prince's guards and was admitted into Jarand's tent where he found Jarand conferring with his wizard.

Harkell bowed, hand on heart and was kept waiting for some moments before being permitted to straighten.

Jarand had swivelled in his chair to glare at him, "Well, Captain? This had better be important. I am due to dine with the king in an hour's time and must prepare."

Harkell glanced at Journeyman, "Sire, it is, but I must speak with you alone."

"What utter nonsense! I will choose who attends my audiences, not you. Now, out with it!"

Harkell drew in a deep breath, "Your Highness, you and I both know that it is not in my best interests to knowingly displease you and yet I have done so once this afternoon already… And I am afraid I must do so again because what I have to tell you is for your ears alone. Whom you choose to tell after that is entirely up to you."

"I find your insolence extraordinary, Captain Harkell. Since when does a mere soldier in my army set conditions on his obedience?"

"Sire, if you insist on my compliance against my advice, then I will obey you. But at the moment, only I know the nature of the information I will give you and I am risking your ire only for your best interests."

The prince scowled at him for a full minute while Harkell stared steadily back. Suddenly Jarand waved his hand, "Leave us, Journeyman, We will talk later… Now, Captain…"

Once he was sure that Journeyman was out of earshot, Harkell took a deep breath and launched in, "Sire, an opportunity has arisen for you to outmanoeuvre your brother. The king is intending to undermine you and if you act quickly, you can not only avoid his ploy but also leave him nonplussed."

"Captain Harkell, your words smack of treason. Besides," the prince shrugged disdainfully, "you are hardly a statesman. What would you know of the intricacies of power?"

"Sire, I have not suggested that you harm His Majesty. And I may not know the games of power, but Prince Tarkyn and his advisors are better versed than I."

Jarand's eyebrows snapped together, "You have spoken again to the prince without my permission."

Harkell shook his head, "No, Your Highness. He sent one of his men to see me with the information."

"I see." Jarand waved his hand, "You may continue."

"Thank you, Sire." Harkell felt that, so far, his interview was going reasonably well, and took heart. "The king has a battalion of well over a thousand men marching around the outside of the forest and Prince Tarkyn believes that Kosar intends to wrest the encampment and its operations from you, in full view of his men and yours."

Suddenly Harkell had a wildcat on his hands.

"And why did my upstart of a brother tell you this?" roared Jarand. "So that you could revel in the anticipation? I should have had you hanged as soon as I found you." The prince drew his arm across his body before swinging it in a wide arc to slam Harkell across the side of the head and send him crashing against the wall of the tent.

"Get up!" snapped the prince. As soon as the captain had staggered to his feet, Jarand swung with even greater force, the blow throwing Harkell bodily against the edge of the heavy oak table.

Harkell doubled up, winded, a sharp pain in his side suggesting a broken rib. "Sire," he gasped. "There is still time. You can avoid this."

The prince grabbed him by the front of his uniform and dragged him upright. "Look at me when you speak to me!"

"Yes Sire." Harkell was breathing hard but managed to say between gasps, "Prince Tarkyn will hold up the king's troops long enough to give you, us, time to leave." He swallowed and licked blood from his lip from where the prince's signet ring had cut him, "You can make it appear that it was your intention all along to leave. Then the king's battalion will arrive in vain."

Jarand shoved Harkell with force back into a chair behind him. "Sit there. Pull yourself together, man!"

Jarand took a few agitated turns around the inside of the tent, while Harkell wiped his bleeding lip and tried to regulate his breathing. The prince too was breathing hard and gave himself time to get his emotions under control. When he had considered all the ramifications, the prince turned on Harkell, "How far away are they?"

Harkell made to stand up but the prince pushed him back down. "About three days march, Sire. But Prince Tarkyn's forces will hold them up for another two days at least."

"Hmm. So. We had planned to leave in four days' time with only two companies and to leave the other two stationed here. However, unrest in the south will now force us to leave at dawn, in three days' time, taking the full complement of men with us." Jarand glared at Harkell, "That is the news you have just brought me. Clear? That there is unrest in the south."

"Yes Sire."

Jarand poured a glass of water and banged it down ungraciously on the table next to Harkell, "Here. Drink this. And tidy yourself up, man. You have a lot of work to do in the next sixty hours. Now, as far anyone will know, I have not yet made any decision on how I will deal with the unrest in the south. I don't want the king to know we are leaving until we are formed up and on our way out of the encampment. "

Jarand watched through narrowed eyes as Harkell pulled his uniform square and smoothed back his hair. Harkell wiped his lip again but it was still bleeding and he would not be able to disguise the damage. When he had done the best he could, he sat still and returned the prince's gaze.

Jarand grunted, "Despite your association with my renegade brother, you are serving me well. Go now and get on with preparations for departure. We leave at dawn three days from now."

Harkell stood up wooden-faced, bowed and left, knowing that the prince had come as close to an apology as he ever would. He could feel repressed fury welling up within himself at his forced helplessness. There was nothing worse for him than being attacked and having to endure it without making a defensive move in return. It felt like the ultimate in submission. He wondered whether Tarkyn had realised that setting him this task would expose him to the savagery of Jarand's reaction. Feeling sore and battered, he decided morosely that Tarkyn probably did know, and was using him just as much as Jarand was.

CHAPTER 30

The late afternoon sun was slanting in soft golden rays through the canopy above them as Ancient Oak and Tarkyn made their way down the ridge and into the forest near the home guard's firesite. Even when the great warhorse's climb up to the ridge under its double load had made them sway back and forth on his back, the eagle had merely clung tighter and stayed where she was. By the time the sun's rays had lengthened, Tarkyn's shoulder was aching badly from the constant weight on it.

The first lookout spotted them and word spread like wildfire that Tarkyn had brought the eagle back with him. As Ancient Oak and he approached the clearing, Tarkyn worked on preparing the young eagle for the sight of people, reassuring her of their good will. But as soon as the woodfolk came in to view, she gave a raucous, threatening cry and beat her wings in alarm, unheeding of the fact that she was smiting Tarkyn on the head in her panic. Worse still, her talons dug in ever deeper against the updraft of her beating wings.

As Tarkyn struggled to contain her fear, everyone but Midnight, who didn't hear her screeches, flicked back to the perimeter of the clearing. Midnight, on the other hand, bounded straight up to the horse and beamed up at Tarkyn. Surprisingly the eagle suddenly quietened and, far from being startled by the bouncy little human, actually cocked her head to get a better view of him.

Quite relaxed, the little boy bounced along beside them as Ancient Oak guided the horse over to a large fallen log. Midnight scrambled onto the log, totally unconcerned by the eagle's close proximity and placed himself so that Tarkyn could lean on him as he dismounted. The eagle suffered Midnight's presence, but drew herself up and glared fiercely at anyone else who approached, shrieking if they tried to edge closer.

Lapping Water spoke quietly from a judicious distance away, "She is beautiful, isn't she? I'm glad she's still alive." She frowned critically. "But Tarkyn, why have you brought her back with you? Is she still injured?

Ancient Oak snorted as he stood by the horse's head. "She's perfectly all right. She just has a crush on our forest guardian here, and won't leave him alone."

The forest guardian in question raised his hand slowly and stroked her, giving an apologetic smile, "She's only a baby and I think she has been frightened by the whole experience of being shot at, and injured, and manhandled. With any luck, she'll be off in one grand swoop when she's ready."

Ancient Oak pulled the battered dead rabbit out of his satchel and held it up, "Here, what do you want to do with this?"

There was a short silence while Tarkyn conferred with the eagle. "She doesn't understand why I would want the rabbit put over the fire but she will allow it, provided I am the one to eat it." He smiled, "It's a thank you present, you see."

"Tarkyn, you can't allow this eagle to dictate to you," said Waterstone with mock severity.

"Especially when you won't let any of us do it," added Rainstorm with a cheeky grin.

"I won't," Tarkyn promised, "But I have to take things slowly. I don't want to offend her. She has done us a great service, after all…and I am not in a strong position at the moment."

"What about her? Has she eaten?" asked Summer Rain. "She needs to replenish her reserves."

After a delay, Tarkyn answered, "Yes. She hunted for herself first and ate before killing that rabbit for me. Normally, she only needs one good meal a day but she is beginning to feel hungry again."

"Good," said Waterstone firmly. "Then she can go off and hunt."

Almost as though she understood Waterstone, she began to pull long strands of Tarkyn's hair gently though her beak as though cajoling Tarkyn to look after her. Tarkyn's eyes crinkled in amusement and he began to stroke her again with gentle firm movements. "No, she can't. Not at the moment. She just needs some time to recover."

Waterstone gave a short laugh. "You're as besotted as she is."

Tarkyn just grinned, "Do we have anything she can eat?"

Scraps of meat left over from the midday meal were thrown into the middle of the clearing. After swivelling her head from side to side, checking everyone's whereabouts, the eagle gave a squawk, launched herself off Tarkyn's shoulder onto the ground and began to tear at the pieces of meat.

"Ahh. That's a relief," breathed Tarkyn, straightening up. "My poor shoulder is dying."

"Stars above, Tarkyn!" exclaimed Waterstone. "Your shirt is soaked with blood."

"I know. Sharp talons."

"We need to sew leather patches onto the shoulder of your shirt, if this little lady is going to stay around for a while" said Falling Branch, "…and probably something for your arm as well. Stay in that shirt for the time being. We'll prepare you another shirt as quickly as we can and then you can swap."

Lapping Water appeared, holding his wolfskin cloak. "Here. Meanwhile, put this on. Even if you overheat, at least it will protect your shoulder."

Tarkyn smiled his thanks, donning the cloak over his blood-soaked shirt and wriggling his stiffened shoulder. "Ow. I'd better concentrate on healing this…"

He broke off as he noticed that Midnight had wandered into the middle of the clearing and had squatted down next to the eagle, watching her as she ate. The eagle eyed him but made no move to shoo him away.

"Hmm. I think everyone may be able to gradually return to the fire, as long as they move slowly. I'll reassure her as you do it," said Tarkyn. "Young Midnight seems to have some sort of affinity with her, doesn't he?"

Lapping Water nodded, "He did spend many years mostly on his own in the wild. Birds and animals must have been the only creatures he had to relate to."

Slowly life returned to normal around the firesite. The eagle kept her eye on people's movements but seemed to trust that Tarkyn would not put her in a position where she might be attacked. Tarkyn sat down near her, leaning back against the log and pulled his little Midnight onto his knee. While Midnight snuggled up to him and watched the eagle, Tarkyn focused his strength into healing the deep puncture wounds in his shoulder.

When she had finished, the eagle launched herself from the ground but landed, much to Tarkyn's relief, above his battered left shoulder on the log. He reached up to stroke her as she nestled down into a shallow depression in the log. She tweaked at a few strands of his hair - *Yuk, with her meaty beak*, thought Tarkyn - before letting her head drop between her shoulders, yielding to her fatigue.

Chapter 31

Next morning, an uproar outside his tent woke Tarkyn well before his usual leisurely hour. As he emerged, he nearly stood on a dead rabbit that had been delivered by his devoted eagle. Said eagle was strutting back and forth in her feathered pantaloons, shrieking her pride in her catch, demanding Tarkyn's attention and keeping everyone away.

"Good morning Tarkyn," said Waterstone, who was lying in wait for him at a safe distance away. "Listen my friend, you will have to do something about this. Your eagle is putting us all in danger. She is making too much noise. Sooner or later someone will come to investigate."

Stormaway added his voice to the woodman's, "Eagles don't usually make this much noise. It is rare to hear an eagle's call. She is acting very strangely."

Tarkyn ran his hands through his hair and scrubbed his face to wake himself up. Although he objected to being pressured, he knew they were right and so controlled his immediate reaction, aware that his tiredness might make him unwontedly sharp.

Instead he managed a smile and said, "And worse than all of this, she has woken me up." He transferred his attention to the eagle, just as she launched herself from the ground straight at Waterstone who had to duck, to fly in a tight circle and land on Tarkyn's left shoulder, "… and she is so heavy. At least she is not hurting me anymore. Thank Falling Branch for the leather patches for me." He put his hand up to stroke her as she began to run strands of hair through her wickedly sharp beak. "Come on, young lady. We have to talk."

The forest guardian walked off into the trees, with the eagle bobbing up and down on his shoulder in time with his stride. As he left the clearing, Midnight appeared by his side, and passed him up a cup of tea before reaching up to hold his free hand.

As Tarkyn turned his head to smile down at Midnight, Lapping Water laughed softly as she stood beside Waterstone, "Now he has two little waifs to look after. He is too kind-hearted for his own good."

"Possibly," Waterstone laughed reluctantly in return. "But it has been good for us. It was his kind heart that saved us from the worst of the oath."

"Well, if it was his kindness that gained him the friendship of woodfolk, I can only say that it benefits him as much as it does those around him," said Stormaway.

Oblivious to this conversation, Tarkyn walked through the soft morning of the woodland, looking for a large log where he could sit to concentrate, in contact with a live tree. Getting down onto the ground with a large eagle on his shoulder would be too awkward and it was too difficult to concentrate while standing. He found what he was looking for under a huge spreading oak. A tree had fallen long ago, ripping a large branch from the side of the oak and landing close to its trunk amid a sea of leaves. It had lain there for so long that it was partly rotted and covered in moss.

Perfect, thought Tarkyn.

Tarkyn sat down with his right shoulder against the tree, lifted Midnight onto his lap, and closed his eyes. He remembered the time that an owl had shown him his part in the life of the forest, scanning out from him until he could see himself surrounded by vast tracts of trees. It had helped him to understand that being forest guardian and liege lord to the woodfolk, many of whom had still been resentful of him at that time, was simply his natural role within the life of the forest. He hoped that he could steady the eagle by showing her something similar.

Sitting there with his eyes closed, he could feel the weight of the eagle on his shoulder, her talons pushing into the leather on his shirt and the softness of the feathers against his left cheek. Against his chest, Tarkyn felt little Midnight's head leaning against him, and the sharpness of his skinny shoulder. As often happened, his heart turned over at the thought of the misery that Midnight had endured, and his arms tightened around the little boy. Gently, he connected his mind to those of the eagle and Midnight, and sent both of them waves of strength and warmth. In response he felt Midnight snuggle in closer while the eagle ruffled her feathers and gave a quiet comfortable squawk.

Awareness of the forest flowed into Tarkyn from his physical connection with the oak and through him, into Midnight and the eagle. He became aware of small rodents scurrying through nearby undergrowth and had to send a quick wave of calm to quell the eagle's excitement. He showed them a small herd of deer only yards away behind a screening of brush and a pair of playful otters in a nearby stream before changing direction to move his awareness up into the oak, past bird's nests and into the higher branches where the sun and a soft breeze played on the leaves.

Suddenly, images of the forest vanished and a huge power, stern and strong, took over Tarkyn's mind. His whole being was engulfed by the alien force, but he did not feel under attack. It was more that the forest guardian had become a small part of something greater than himself. Gradually he began to discern the nature of the power and realised it was the combined minds of scores of raptors, their fierce wills focusing in on his eagle. It felt like being at the centre of a brewing storm, surrounded by louring clouds. Tarkyn could feel their strength supporting his eagle; applauding her efforts, commiserating with her hurts, and re-grounding her in her proud heritage, but always within a rigidly disciplined framework. There were no images, but Tarkyn could feel their support of him being interwoven with their support of her and understood that they were showing her both the exigencies of his situation and his value to them.

Slowly the power faded. Tarkyn opened his eyes, feeling rather shaken, fully expecting the eagle to launch herself off to join her fellow raptors somewhere in the surrounding trees. But raptors are not by nature gregarious and the only stricture they had placed on her was that she should not endanger their forest guardian. Beyond that, her own strong will was her own.

So instead, she cocked her head to meet his gaze with her own and then, in a friendly way, no longer tinged with her previous anxious need, she took strands of his long black hair between her beak and began to preen it.

Tarkyn grinned.

Half an hour later, he strode into the clearing, the eagle still on his shoulder, grinning in anticipation of Waterstone's irritation. But in this, he was disappointed.

Waterstone came to greet him with a relieved smile on his face, "So, she decided to stay, did she? I'm so glad you and Midnight are all right. We saw eagles and hawks and kites circling overhead. Then they disappeared into the trees near you… And I know that for all your strength, you don't control them so I was worried that they might attack you or your eagle or young Midnight. The lookouts said that nothing seemed to be happening to you, but we would have been hard pressed to protect you if they had mounted a concerted attack."

When he drew breath, Tarkyn clapped him on the back and walked with him to the firesite, the eagle riding Tarkyn's shoulder nonchalantly between them, "Yes, you would. They're a fearsome bloody lot. And they did not so much attack, as take over. They commandeered my mindlink with the eagle and did what I had been trying to do, much better than I ever could have. She has now regained her own strength as a wild eagle and has been shown that I must be protected, or at least not endangered." He gave a wry smile, "Phew. They have such strong minds. Midnight and I were swamped. I'm glad my actions did not anger them."

"On the contrary," said Stormaway, offering the prince a cup of tea. "I believe they appreciated and lent their strength to your efforts to heal your eagle."

"Possibly, but they were not pleased with me after she had been injured under my direction."

"Is that so?" The wizard looked thoughtful, "You do have to tread carefully then."

Tarkyn merely nodded, his attention having been distracted by the high level of activity around the firesite. He took a sip of tea as he collected his thoughts, which had been diverted for too long by the eagle's advent, "So, what time are we leaving? And what are our plans for our attack on Kosar's men?"

"We leave within the hour," said Autumn Leaves. "Everyone is coming. Otherwise too small a group would be left close to the encampment."

"And who will be part of the attack force and who will remain within the forest?" asked the prince with deceptive mildness.

"Creaking Bough and Ancient Oak will remain with the children," answered Thunder Storm. "We will need Stormaway's ability to sense other people's magic and we will use Danton for backup. Summer Rain will remain on the edge of the forest in case anyone is wounded. The rest of us will join with the northern woodfolk in the sortie."

"And what role did you envisage for me?"

Ancient Oak, Thunder Storm and Waterstone exchanged glances but didn't answer immediately. Before they could decide what to say, Rainstorm cut across them and said, "If you really want to know, opinion was divided… not that anyone was going to dare tell you what to do after last time."

Tarkyn nodded, "So, let me hear your differing opinions. I am quite willing to discuss my role in this operation." He hesitated as though he would have said more, but instead waved his hand to invite others to speak.

Autumn Leaves answered, "It was not so much that some people thought one way and some thought the other. It was more that we want to protect you and keep you away from danger but at the same time…" He looked around at everyone. "At the same time, we are scared stiff at the idea of leaving the forest and coming into close contact with so many sorcerers." He gave a slight smile, "So probably, on balance, we would like you to accompany us."

Tarkyn's face relaxed, "I would be honoured to be a part of the first woodfolk sortie out of the forest. And I undertake to work with you to ensure that the risk to me is minimal… although this time, your forests are not at risk if I should fall."

"That's not the point, Tarkyn," said Autumn Leaves gruffly.

"No. I know it is not," He gave an almost shy smile, "I know you care for me even beyond the oath and my role. But beyond these things, my safety is no more important than anyone else's. We all care for each other. However, I will undertake to carry an object I can use to translocate out of danger. I have my shield, I can make the ground shake with a bit of concentration and I have all of you. And in return, I will do everything in my power to keep all of you safe…" he grinned, "even to the extent of following someone else's orders."

Fourteen hours later, a group of nearly two hundred woodfolk, light packs on their backs, were gathered along the forest edge gazing out across two hundred yards at the darkened camp of Kosar's soldiers. Among the hundreds of tents, a dozen campfires burned low to warm those on guard and supply them with beverages to keep them awake through the hours after midnight when the pull of sleep was most potent. There seemed to be a turnover of perimeter guards as they took it in turns to go to the fire for a warm up and a cup of tea. Every two hours, half of them would retire to be replaced by an equal number.

"That gives us an hour safely, I'd say," murmured Autumn Leaves in Tarkyn's ear. "The relieved guards will need time to go to sleep and we have to be well away before the next shift comes out."

"Any wizards or powerful sorcerers among them, Stormaway?" whispered Tarkyn.

"There is a wizard in one of the tents further down the line, but as far as I can tell, she has been asleep for a couple of hours. I suspect she is only useful for healing and for dealing with any unnatural weather changes. After all, they think the only magical opposition they may strike is Jarand's wizard, Journeyman Cloudmaker." The wizard frowned as he sent his senses scanning through the camp. "I can't tell for sure, but there are bound to be a few sorcerers capable of erecting shields or loosing shafts of power…but the emanations are not strong enough to suggest that there are hordes of them."

Tarkyn nodded, "Good. Now, don't forget, Autumn Leaves. As soon as the guards are unconscious, Stormaway has to check for magical wards. Alarms will sound throughout the camp if any of you tries to enter a warded tent."

Autumn Leaves placed his hand reassuringly on Tarkyn's arm, "Don't worry. We have each step planned out in sequence. Waterstone and I will direct in concert from each end of the camp. Danton will stay close to Waterstone and you stick with me. Boravar will remain within the forest since he cannot levitate and would make too much noise. Once all the guards have been knocked out, you, Danton and Stormaway will have to levitate yourself to approach the camp… Wait for my signal."

Half an hour after the next change of guards, the woodfolk made their move.

The distance between the forest and the soldier's camp was dotted sparsely with low bushes that would not have provided sufficient cover for sorcerer soldiers to approach the campsite unseen. But, with the combination of darkness and their uncanny camouflaging skills, the woodfolk found plenty of cover in the sparse vegetation. Their most deadly marksmen and women flicked their way from one sparse shrub to the next, blending into the foliage impeccably in the near darkness. With his heart in his mouth, Tarkyn watched Lapping Water side by side with Thunder Storm, flick the last twenty yards that brought them within firing range of the guards on the perimeter. For several tense minutes, they simply hunkered down and waited as other woodfolk flicked from bushes to positions behind tents until every one of Kosar's guards, both on the perimeter and around the campfires, were within range. A silent call rang out and Waterstone, from the far end of the camp counted down from three. Then, in one concerted fluid movement, woodfolk slingshots were released in perfect synchronisation.

Not a single guard saw another one drop. For a long, painful, drawn out minute, the invaders waited to see whether the sound of crumpling guards had woken anyone. Finally, when no alarm sounded, Stormaway levitated his way to the edge of the camp to land as quietly as an old sorcerer could. He thrust three fingers outwards and muttered under his breath, "Wards, *Rayavalka!*"

Immediately, bright green flared briefly around a large tent, equidistant from each side and about a third of the way back. A prostrate guard lay on the ground on either side of its door.

"Officers' quarters," hissed Danton to Waterstone. "Just leave them alone. None of the other tents are warded. It will make no difference to our plans if only the officers are unaffected."

"I agree," Waterstone sent out the order for the next phase of the operation.

"Right," said Autumn Leaves to Tarkyn. "The coast's clear. Follow me closely." As Tarkyn floated his way towards the camp, the woodman sent him a clear image asking him to wait at the edge of the camp keeping watch in case he was needed to rescue anyone.

The prince nodded his acquiescence, knowing Danton's and his power was purely a back-up and that the woodfolk had far more subtlety than he to enter the tents of sleeping soldiers to carry out their foray undetected.

Tarkyn stationed himself where he could see as much as possible of the soldiers' camp and watched the few woodfolk who worked purposefully among the unconscious guards, as the rest of them scattered small objects on the ground throughout the campsite before slipping silently into the tents. Minutes later, with packs bulging, the woodfolk reappeared from within the tents and flicked or ran noiselessly across the two hundred yards back into the dark safety of the forest. Tarkyn, Danton and Stormaway accompanied them silently, floating a couple of feet above the ground.

Once within the forest, each woodman or woman slipped silently between the trees until they reached a large hole that had been dug beneath an old log five hundred yards from the forest edge. Here they emptied the contents of their packs. When all of the packs had been emptied, the hole was quietly filled and all traces of it obscured by a thick covering of leaves and forest debris. Satisfied with their efforts, the woodfolk returned to position themselves with the three sorcerers high in the trees along the edge of the forest, to enjoy the spectacle that they had all worked together to create.

Chapter 32

There was a noticeable delay in the next change of guards, only partly caused by the fact that the men who should have been waking the relieving guards as they retired, were not conscious. Muffled oaths within the tents were the first signs of trouble.

Shortly afterwards, harassed soldiers appeared in the doorway of their tents, some clutching a boot in one hand and all of them irritated and puzzled. So intent were they on their search for their boots that it took them a few seconds to notice the crumpled bodies of the guards lying in the semi-darkness around the campfires. Immediately, they shouted the alarm and rushed to investigate.

As they ran in bare or stockinged feet towards the quiescent guards, cries of pain rang out and the soldiers began to hobble or collapse onto the ground. Streams of soldiers poured out of the tents in the wake of their companions and the yells of pain intensified. None of them was wearing a full pair of boots; some held a single boot in one hand and a sword in the other, while very occasionally, a soldier hobbled along wearing only one boot and brandishing a weapon.

Shouting at each other and yelling in pain, some of them attempted to reach the perimeter to line up in a defensive formation against the unknown enemy. Most of them were too intent on the pain in their feet to do more than hobble in circles or sit down to ease the pain. Even then, some of them jolted as a sharp object pierced their buttocks.

In the distant trees, the watchers laughed and grinned at the chaos they had created.

Suddenly the soldiers stilled as a whistle blew and commands rang out. Four officers, fully dressed and booted, stormed into the middle of the milling men.

Colonel Argyve, down to earth and capable, took in the disorder and the unconscious guards at a glance. "Get into formation around the perimeter." As the hapless soldiers hesitated, he raised his short, thick set body to its full height and bellowed, "Now! We are under attack. Do you all want to die?" "

Groaning soldiers hobbled as fast as they could to obey his command. The results were not impressive. Luckily for Kosar's troops, mass murder was no part of the woodfolk's plan. The soldiers peered out into the darkness, taut with fear, unable to see any sign of their enemy and knowing they would be hard pressed to fight with unprotected feet on the hostile ground.

A sergeant limped up and saluted before reporting, "Sir, every guard has been shot. No one saw or heard anything. No one can find their boots and the ground has been strewn with thorns."

The colonel waved his hand, "Some of these men have boots."

The sergeant shook his head, "Some of these men have *one* boot. As far as I can work out, every left boot in the camp is missing."

The colonel was livid. "When I catch the practical joker who did this, I will string him from the highest tree I can find. What sort of idiot would pull a stunt like this? Can't he see the danger in which he has placed the whole troop?"

A captain who had just finished patrolling the camp's pitiful defences, returned in time to say, "Sir, a practical joker did not shoot the guards. From what I have heard of previous attacks, I suspect these guards have been disabled by Prince Tarkyn's elite troops. Not one of them is dead and they must have been shot simultaneously for none to warn the others or to sound the alarm. That is a feat well beyond anything we could achieve." He blew out a long breath, "Let us just hope that, had they been going to kill us, they would have done so already. It appears that they have had us completely at their mercy and have chosen merely to disable us." He grimaced, "In fact, I suspect we are still at their mercy. Perhaps they will approach us soon to discuss terms. We are in no position to fight with upward of eight hundred men crippled and unable even to see our enemy."

The colonel fumed, "This is an act of war! The Renegade Prince has attacked a battalion of His Majesty the King,"

"Yes sir," said the captain, looking away from him as a nearby guard groaned.

"Captain Harmon, what do you mean, 'Yes sir'?" demanded Argyve.

The captain brought his gaze back to rest on his colonel's face and smiled, pleased that he had an officer who responded to nuances in his subordinates' replies, "Sir, I can't help thinking that a true act of war would have been to kill us wholesale while he had the chance."

Colonel Argyve puffed out his cheeks. After a considerable pause, he glanced at the captain, wondering how far he could trust him. Then he said casually, "Perhaps he still will. He has, after all, been declared a Rogue Sorcerer."

"Yes sir."

The colonel gave a short laugh, "No. I don't think so either." He turned to the sergeant, "Tell the men to stand down. Just double the guards. Direct their efforts into clearing the ground of these thorns and finding their boots… in that order."

The sergeant saluted and headed off to disseminate the captain's orders.

"I suppose, by rights, we should mount a search party to hunt down Prince Tarkyn, if we believe him to be in the vicinity," said Captain Harmon slowly.

"Captain, do you *ever* say what you mean? You know perfectly well that mounting a hunting expedition would be an exercise in futility. We would have no hope of finding him within the forest and our men would be shot down at will by his elite forces." The colonel watched his men hobbling or crawling around, trying to feel for the thorns in the dark without being stabbed by them. "Order the other officers to set up lamps and give these men a hand to get rid of these blasted thorns. We officers are the only men who can walk unimpeded. When the lamps have been set up, report back to me."

The young officer snapped a salute and responded smartly in a very different tone of voice, "Yes sir."

The colonel chuckled as he watched the lanky young man stride off into the darkness to follow his orders. He knew the captain was cleverer than he and so did the captain. But the young officer was smart enough to know when to push the boundaries and when to fall into line without question, while the more experienced colonel was confident enough in himself to draw on his favourite captain's wit without losing face or authority. Colonel Argyve would miss Harmon when he was promoted, which inevitably he would be.

Meanwhile he had the safety of his men to think about.

"Sergeant, I want a white flag of truce mounted on a long pole. When sufficient lamps have been set up for it to be seen, I want you to hold it up and wave it on the forest side of the camp. Clear?"

An expression of shock passed over the sergeant's face.

"No, Sergeant, not surrender. Parley."

The sergeant looked at him doubtfully from beneath his heavy brows but unlike the captain, did not express his thoughts and limped off to do his colonel's bidding.

From within the forest, the perpetrators of this discomfort watched with unseemly mirth as their victims hopped and crawled and hobbled around the camp.

"That should stop them for you, Tarkyn," beamed Autumn Leaves.

The prince laughed, "It will certainly slow them down."

"I estimate that it would have taken them three days from here to reach the encampment" chimed in Danton. "Now I can't see them travelling at all today and they will take at least another five days if they try to hobble along. Plenty of time for Jarand's troops to leave the encampment, travel the Great Western Road and turn southwards to Montraya before this lot gets anywhere near them."

"And if it comes to it, it demonstrates to Kosar that I can back up a request that he keeps his troops out of my dominion, *our* forest."

"And you *still* have not killed any of his soldiers," said Twig Snap, "which, personally, I think is a pity." She grinned as a storm of protests broke over her head. "Just kidding."

"Congratulations, Rainstorm, for coming up with such a stunningly effective idea and thank you to Waterstone and Autumn Leaves for directing it, and to the northern woodfolk and the home guard for carrying it out," said Tarkyn. He looked at Falling Branch, "You see? I told you that you had a clever son."

Falling Branch smiled proudly at his awkward, rebellious Rainstorm and threw his arm around the young woodman's shoulder, "Yes, I do, don't I? Well done, my son. I am very proud of you."

For once, Rainstorm had nothing to say and turned a soft shade of pink as he stared fixedly at the ground.

"Look!" said Waterstone suddenly. "Someone is waving a white flag."

"Sire, this is unexpected," said Danton.

"Your Highness, what do you think they want?" asked Boravar. Suddenly all the sorcerers were acting formally, as a diplomatic situation developed.

Stormaway inched closer to Tarkyn along a thick lower branch. "Sire, I believe they are unsure of your intention, and realise that they are exposed to your will."

The prince looked at the men and women ranged around him, "What are your opinions? Should we respond? Do we want to reassure them or leave them feeling vulnerable?"

Lapping Water replied, "I think we have made our point. There can be no harm in talking to them and it might even improve your reputation a little."

"There can be a great deal of harm talking to them if they capture you, Tarkyn," exclaimed Waterstone hotly. "Crippled or not, there are over a thousand men out there."

Tarkyn thought for a moment, "We will send a note attached to an arrow, asking for their representatives to meet us on the forest edge, well away from the body of their troops. I will ask Danton to meet with them first. Then, depending on their attitudes and who they send, I may decide to grace them with my presence." The prince gave a slight smile as he caught Waterstone's little head shake. "Waterstone, my friend, I am what I am. And if I choose to see them, make no doubt that I will be conferring a signal honour upon them."

Rather to Tarkyn's surprise, Waterstone grinned, "Yes, *Your Highness*, having seen your early memories, I know you will be. And now that I understand how sorcerers view you, I can sit back and enjoy the spectacle of your astonishing and interesting effect on them."

Thunder Storm was accorded the honour of firing the message-bearing arrow. As he checked the wind and sighted along the arrow, he murmured, "Slight breeze. Not too much to worry about, but two hundred yards is a long range for such accuracy. I might have to hedge my bets and go for a slightly larger target, especially with the unknown effect of the parchment on the arrow's flight."

Moments later, an arrow flew through the night air to land point down in the ground between the flag bearer's feet. The flag bearer convulsed backwards in fright before gathering his wits to retrieve the arrow and carry it to Colonel Argyve.

Tarkyn frowned, "How did you hedge your bets? That seemed pretty accurate to me."

Thunder Storm gave a low chuckle, "I was originally aiming for the pole from which the flag is flying but I decided that with the slight crosswind it was too narrow a target. As it turns out, I think I would have hit it, had I decided to aim a little higher."

"Hmph. I am glad you are on my side. You have my gratitude." Unconsciously, Tarkyn too had slipped back into the formality of his role as prince.

A short time later, two figures walked towards the forest within the shimmering dome of a tan shield. When they were within fifty yards of the forest's edge, they stopped. They were not kept waiting for long. An aqua glow appeared within the trees that resolved itself into a lone blonde sorcerer within his shield. Danton stepped out into the open to greet them. When they were close enough to speak, the two soldiers gave stiff courtly bows.

"Good morning, Lord Danton," said Colonel Argyve, aware that the first tinges of orange were colouring the horizon. "I am pleased to see you looking so well."

Danton bowed in return, "Good morning, Lord Argyve." He peered through the pre-dawn greyness at the soldier's uniform, "Or should I say *Colonel Argyve*? Well done on the promotion."

A wry smile twisted the colonel's mouth, "It is likely to be a short lived promotion after this debacle. May I introduce Captain Harmon to you? Your father knows his father, I think."

Danton inclined his head, "How do you do? It is a pleasure to meet you." He returned his gaze to the colonel, "I understand you wished to speak to us?"

"Yes I do." The colonel hesitated while he considered his options. He could bluster and express outrage at the attack which indeed he felt, or he could be more diplomatic and by doing so, perhaps gain enough trust to gather some useful information. What he would do with the information would be something to consider later. "But firstly, I would like to convey my respects to His Royal Highness, Prince Tarkyn. When our business is concluded, would you pass that on to him please?"

Danton frowned, "You are making a few assumptions here. What makes you think His Highness has anything to do with this… incident?"

Argyve smiled, "You, for a start. It is well known that it was your shield that imprisoned Prince Jarand's soldiers while the two princes conferred." He shrugged, "And the modus operandi, secondly… No one but Prince Tarkyn's forces could carry out such an uncanny attack, although I must admit the forces of King Kosar had previously assumed that attacks such as these could only occur within the cover of the forest."

Danton waited in silence, forcing Argyve to make the next move.

"My lord," began Argyve, "In an effort to protect my men, I would like to know the motive behind your attack. Is Prince Tarkyn intending to make incursions across Eskuzor? And if so, why did your men not kill us rather than disable us? Surely you lose any element of surprise if we are left to spread word of your attack?" He scratched his unshaven cheek, "I own I am puzzled by your actions."

Within the trees, Tarkyn said, "I like the demeanour of this man. I will go down to talk with him."

Having previously countered any objections, he raised his shield and levitated both himself and the eagle on his shoulder out of the tree in a graceful curve to land beside Danton. The effect was all he could have hoped. Argyve and Harmon's eyes bugged out of their heads, astonished at both the spectacle of the Renegade Prince with a great mountain eagle on his shoulder and Tarkyn's simultaneous use of two spells. As shouting broke out in the camp behind them, the two officers sank to their knees, hands on hearts.

"You may rise. In fact, I think you had better do so with some speed. Your men are threatening to riot." Tarkyn didn't bother adding that they would be cut down if they tried to approach.

"I beg your pardon, Your Highness." Argyve's voice sharpened, "Captain, go back and remind those dolts of the meaning of parley. Anyone who dares to threaten His Highness while we parley will have me to answer to… and no doubt His Highness' archers?" Tarkyn gave a brief nod to verify this. "Return when you can."

The colonel dropped his shield to allow the captain to carry out his orders. He did not bother to reinstate it as he turned to face the prince. "Your Highness, it is an honour and a pleasure to see you once more. I would wish that we met under better circumstances, both for your sake and for mine." His grey eyes transferred their focus to the eagle on Tarkyn's shoulder. "That is a magnificent bird you have there, Sire. Is this the one that swooped low over our troops yesterday morning?"

Remembering that Kosar already knew of his power with birds, Tarkyn nodded, "Yes. She is young and did not realise how low she was flying. I doubt that she or I will make the same mistake again. It cost her dearly."

Colonel Argyve gave a wry smile, "Her reconnaissance cost us dearly also."

Tarkyn stroked her, "Killing her would not have suppressed the knowledge of your presence, you know. I had already seen your troops through her eyes by then."

"And may I ask, Sire, what is your intention in attacking us? As far as I know, pursuit of you was not even part of our brief."

Realising that Kosar would be most displeased if Tarkyn revealed his dominion over the forests, the prince could see a yawning chasm opening before him. After all, he was not actually angling for an out and out conflict with his older brother. He temporised, "And what is your mission, Colonel Argyve?"

The colonel's eyes narrowed as he considered his orders and the wisdom of sharing them. Eventually, he said, "We have been ordered to assist with quelling the constant banditry that has plagued the Great Western Road."

"And would that be in concert with Prince Jarand's troops or instead of?"

Colonel Argyve considered refusing to answer. He knew that his troops were supposed to take Prince Jarand's encampment by surprise and he felt that he had already said more than enough. A welcome diversion arrived in the shape of his captain who jogged up and bowed low to the prince.

Tarquin nodded for the captain to straighten. "Are your men finding themselves able to quell their bloodlust?"

Captain Harmon looked him in the eye. "Sire, many of them are in pain and all of them feel humiliated. I believe a mixture of fear, amazement and anger greeted your arrival. There was, however, no intention by any of them of breaking the truce imposed by Colonel Argyve."

Tarkyn inclined his head towards the colonel, "My felicitations on your men's discipline and my apologies for any unintended slur on their honour."

Argyve blinked, "Sire?"

Danton smiled, "It is rare, is it not, for a Tamadil to apologise?"

"I can't say I have ever heard it before, my lord."

"When you two have finished discussing me," said Tarkyn acidly, "perhaps, Argyve, you would like to answer my question." The use of the colonel's name instead of his title in this formal situation was a clear reminder that Tarkyn outranked him and was not pleased.

"I beg your pardon, Your Highness." The colonel scratched his chin, "I find myself in a quandary, Sire. While I would like to stay on terms with you cordial enough to ensure the safety of my men, I do not feel that I am at liberty to reveal His Majesty's intentions."

Suddenly Tarkyn smiled, "I do like your straight forward manner. Perhaps if I tell you the situation as I see it, you may feel more able to be open with me." He frowned, "Where to start? Hmm. You are aware, no doubt, that there is an ongoing rivalry between my brothers?" At the colonel's nod, he continued, "I don't know whether you are aware of this, but when I met with the king in the forest some months ago, I warned him of Jarand's continual efforts to undermine his rule, often under the guise of protecting victims of lawlessness."

"No Sire. I heard only that you threatened the king in some way."

"I did *not* threaten him." Tarkyn frowned in an effort of memory, "Well, I might have said that I would intervene if I thought that Eskuzor's future was in danger...."

The colonel's eyes twinkled, "I can see how a king might misconstrue that, Your Highness."

Tarkyn chuckled, "He liked it even less when I told him that I considered myself to be the Guardian of Eskuzor." He glanced hesitantly from one to the other, "I don't know whether you have ever heard of forest guardians?"

The colonel was still boggling at the prince's assertion that he believed himself to be the Guardian of Eskuzor, and was wondering whether Tarkyn was a deluded rogue sorcerer after all. But Captain Harmon replied eagerly, "Yes Sire, I have. My father's estates back onto the eastern forests and he has an extensive library of books on the forest; its history, uses, legends. He has insisted that I learn everything I can before the time comes for me to take over our ancestral home. He says that the forest can be your friend but only if you know how to deal with it." Seeing bemused looks on the faces around him, he dragged himself back to the point, "Sorry. Yes, so, forest guardians. I have read about them."

Tarkyn smiled, "Well, that's more than I have done. So please, Captain Harmon, tell us what you know."

"Umm, let me think," The young captain's eyes drifted to the eagle sitting on Tarkyn's shoulder as he thought. Suddenly his gaze shifted several times back and forth between Tarkyn and the eagle, before coming to rest finally on Tarkyn's face. "They have a strange affinity with animals, don't they?... And they can help things to grow… and to…" He frowned, "Was your eagle injured by any of those arrows that were fired at her?"

"Yes," said Tarkyn, stroking her. "Quite badly."

"Wow!" breathed Harmon. "You're a forest guardian, aren't you?"

"Harmon!" snapped the colonel. "Remember to whom you are speaking."

The prince waved away the objection and gave a slow smile, "Yes, I understand that I am. What else do you know about them?"

Harmon frowned as he tried to remember, "They have been involved in key events in turbulent times and there is some suggestion that there have been more of them than were ever recorded… possibly because they did not always become known by the general population… Oh yes. And they live for a very long time."

"Do they?" There was a queer note in Tarkyn's voice. "How long?"

Suddenly Harmon focused on Tarkyn rather than on his memories, as the import of that question dawned on him, "It is not always certain that it is the same one that appears at different events many years apart because a different historian has recorded each of the events, but in some cases the description and name match pretty well beyond question…"

"*How long?*"

Harmon almost winced, "Possibly up to three, maybe four hundred years."

The blood drained from Tarkyn's face. Everyone he knew would grow old and die around him. He glanced at Danton, remembering he had said they would still be friends at eighty. What about at ninety, one hundred, one hundred and twenty? Tarkyn took a deep breath, "Is there anything else you know about forest guardians?"

"No Sire. I could find out the specifics of the known events in which forest guardians have been involved, but I can't remember the details now."

"Thank you, Captain Harmon. Your information has been most interesting, if a little disconcerting." The prince resolutely brought his mind back to the present situation. He turned to the colonel and spread his hands, "The upshot of all this is that I am indeed Guardian of the Forest and that name was once synonymous with Guardian of Eskuzor when the forests covered all the land. One is born, not appointed to the role, but I only discovered recently that I possessed those particular powers that denote a forest guardian and what that implies." He shrugged and smiled, "But it is not synonymous with King of Eskuzor. I have no wish to be king but I do wish to see Eskuzor into a peaceful future… and perhaps above all, I am charged with the protection of the forests."

Colonel Argyve simply stared at him.

"Huh-Hmm. Colonel," said Danton, arbiter of fashion and etiquette, "you are being discourteous. Please stop staring at His Royal Highness."

Argyve shook his head and muttered an apology, "Do you know, I can't come up with a single reason why I should disbelieve you. Isn't that astonishing?" His eyebrows puckered in concern, "But you know, you're very young to have taken on such an enormous responsibility. And to be honest, I think you will have your work cut out for you if you are trying to keep peace between your brothers. An almost impossible task, I'd say." He smiled. "Pardon my abstraction Sire. That was the time it took my mind to transform my view of you from wronged, but dangerous felon running for his life to over-arching protector of Eskuzor, imbued with powers beyond the ken of normal sorcerers. It was quite a shift in perception."

Tarkyn laughed. "I have struggled with it myself."

"So now, Sire, I will answer your question, although I would appreciate it if you didn't mention the source of your information to the king." Argyve did not wait for any sign from Tarkyn before continuing, "Our mission was to completely replace Prince Jarand's troops, to take over the encampment wholesale and to send the prince packing. Personally, although I understood the need to curtail the prince's power and his apparent recruitment drive, I thought the use of such unequivocal means was bound to be inflammatory. I did try to point this out but…" He shrugged.

"Thank you," replied the prince gravely, "That confirms what we had surmised. And in return, I will explain our attack on you. Three reasons; firstly to prevent exactly that scenario that you have just described, secondly, to prevent such a conflict taking place within the forest, and thirdly to curtail the build-up of sorcerers living permanently within the forest's boundaries. While your troops are recovering, Prince Jarand will be warned by us to withdraw himself and his troops to Montraya. He will still be angry but at least he won't smart as badly as he would have by losing face before all those people at the encampment. He may even feel mildly smug that he has stolen the march on Kosar. Meanwhile, I will write to Kosar informing him that I will only allow two hundred soldiers to patrol the Great Western Road at any one time. I think the fact that I have been able to delay you will give weight to my words." Tarkyn also shrugged, "And that was the best that I could do. I am sorry that you and your men have been caught in the middle of it."

Colonel Argyve beamed at him, "Prince Tarkyn, you have no idea what a joy it is to know that someone with power, influence, intelligence and true integrity is working to protect Eskuzor from your brothers' rivalry." He gave a deep bow, "It is an honour and a privilege to be attacked for such a cause."

Tarkyn laughed. "Thank you. I cannot take all the credit, however. I have a very skilful team supporting me."

"That is widely known, Sire. I believe your warriors are the envy of both King Kosar and Prince Jarand's soldiers." The wily old colonel cocked an eyebrow at the prince. "I don't suppose we could have our boots back, by any chance?"

Tarkyn was still smiling as he replied, "Not yet. We must make sure that Jarand and his troops have time to leave the forest and turn south before you reach the Great Western Road. If I make it too easy for you, you will be obliged to do the best you can for your king. In fact, if you attempt to leave before tomorrow evening, we will strew your path with more of those nasty thorns. So, just resign yourselves to staying where you are, until your men's feet are healed. Obviously, any messenger's safety is guaranteed, provided he does not leave before your battalion moves out." He paused for a moment as he received images from Waterstone. "Once you have received word from King Kosar that you are no longer to proceed to the encampment, hopefully within the next two or three days, you will find your boots within a stone's throw of where we are now standing," he grinned, "…but they may be a bit dirty."

Chapter 33

Kosar lay in bed in that lovely twilight consciousness between sleep and wakefulness. His dreams had been filled with scenes of departure; packing, preparing his horse, inspecting his men and setting out for places unspecified in his dream world. As he moved the next step up towards consciousness, he remembered with intense satisfaction that his unexpected battalion would arrive in the afternoon to really put Jarand with his underhand scheming back in his place. He gave a small sigh of contentment and rolled over for another short snooze before rising.

It was about then that he realised that his dreams of departure had been instigated by sounds that were reaching him from outside. He frowned as he listened for a few minutes, then sat up abruptly.

"Farlowe, what on earth is going on out there?"

His manservant, whose shoulders were still sore sometimes from the wrenching they had received, bowed, "I will see what I can find out, Sire."

As he emerged from the king's tent, Farlowe almost bumped into Prince Jarand who was on his way to see Kosar.

"Ah Farlowe. Just the man. Please apologise to His Majesty for disturbing him so early in the day and request that I be permitted to speak to him on a matter of some urgency."

Farlowe glanced behind the prince at the lines of soldiers both riding and on foot that were filing past towards the front of the encampment, before ducking back into the tent.

With deep misgiving, Farlowe stood a judicious distance from the king and bowed, "Sire, it appears that many, if not all of Prince Jarand's troops are on the move. The prince himself awaits outside and has requested an urgent audience."

The violence with which Kosar flung off his bedding suggested to Farlowe that standing well away from him had been a wise move.

"Tell him to come back in twenty minutes," snapped the king. "I will see him when I am dressed. Gather as much information as you can while you organise tea for me. Then assist me to dress."

Jarand was not at all perturbed to be kept waiting. He knew Kosar would need time to wake up properly and to come to terms with Jarand's sudden departure, especially in light of his intention of ousting Jarand's troops himself. Jarand's only regret was that he could not watch the chagrin on Kosar's face, knowing the king would have himself well in hand before he faced his brother.

When he was finally admitted to the royal presence, Jarand bowed hand on heart and waited.

Kosar was dressed and sitting at a small mahogany table, sipping tea. He waved Jarand to the other chair at the table and signalled Farlowe to pour another cup.

"Good morning, Jarand. You are up early this morning. Am I to understand that you are leaving us… without our permission?"

Jarand could barely contain a smirk at this feeble attempt to belittle him, "No indeed Sire. That is why I have come to see you at such an inconvenient hour. I had no intention of leaving unless you allow it. However, matters in the south need my immediate attention. I believe some serious unrest has resulted from the over-zealousness of some of my troops to quell lawlessness. So I feel that I must take steps both to reassure the civilians and to bring my troops into line." He shrugged, "However, if you feel you cannot spare me here…"

Kosar was fully aware that insisting that Jarand stay and then ejecting him later in the day when his battalion was scheduled to arrive would simply look irrational, so he had little choice but to accede to his brother's request. Even telling Jarand that he had been intending to eject him would sound petulant. Kosar just hoped that his own troops met with Jarand's on the Great Western Road so that his twin was made to realise what a close escape he had had; to which end he set out to make Jarand's departure as protracted as possible. "No, clearly you must attend to these matters before they get out of hand. I will be out shortly to bid you a formal farewell and to inspect your troops before they depart."

He left Jarand's troops standing for two hours in tight formation under the increasingly warm sun while he finished his breakfast and wrote a couple of letters before ordering his horse and his honour guard to be made ready for him. Finally, the king appeared in full regalia, mounted on his black charger and flanked by his guard. Indicating that he required Jarand's company, he paraded the full length of Jarand's troops, inspecting the soldiers minutely before halting and speaking in a carrying voice to his brother, "Prince Jarand, your troops look well prepared for their journey. I believe your work here is finished. I wish you well in quelling any unrest while remembering that our fight against lawlessness is to protect the people of Eskuzor, not to incite them. You may move out."

Jarand gave a shallow bow from the saddle, "In return, Your Majesty, may I wish you well in your protection of travellers along the Great Western Road? Farewell."

Wishing to leave a lasting impression on Jarand's followers, King Kosar waited with his honour guard while Jarand's men rode or marched past him. Only when the last of them had left, did he dismiss his guard with an order to sort out new rosters for patrolling the Great Western Road and retired to his tent to fume in private.

Some time later, he sent for his wizard, Stargazer Bookbinder.

As the weedy old wizard entered, Kosar snapped, "Stop looking like a scared rabbit. I am not going to eat you. Sit down." Kosar waved at the tea pot, indicating that the wizard could help himself. "So much for that grand plan. A perfect opportunity to assert my authority completely thwarted."

"Yes Sire. Most unfortunate."

"The only saving grace is that he will encounter my battalion on the Great Western Road and realise how gracious I was in merely saying that his work here is finished."

"Indeed Sire."

Kosar sipped his tea and glared at the wizard over the rim, "Still, at least we can still assert our authority over Tarkyn." Kosar gave a short unpleasant laugh, "I will show him that the forests are mine to use as I please and that he remains here only at my discretion. Last time, I made the mistake of spreading my men out through the forest. But not this time. Let's see how his sneaky little followers deal with a tightly packed, disciplined battalion of crack troops."

"I cannot imagine that the troops will pose a direct threat to Prince Tarkyn himself, Your Majesty."

"Perhaps not in person, no. But I think expanding this encampment into a thriving settlement, protected by my troops, will be a thorn in Tarkyn's side; a gentle demonstration that I am ignoring the sovereignty of the forest that my father bequeathed to him."

Stargazer was the only person in Kosar's confidence regarding Tarkyn's claim to the forests. The wizard also knew of the portents telling of Tarkyn's pivotal role in Eskuzor's future but he knew better than to share these with Kosar. Instead he said mildly, "I am sure that Prince Tarkyn will recognise the statement you are making, simply by seeing the influx of a full battalion into what he considers to be his territory."

Kosar rubbed his hands together, "Good. Yes. Well, I certainly hope he does. He needs to be taken down a peg or two."

Feeling a little reconciled to his disappointment, Kosar decided to honour the encampment with a tour, to inspect the present state of settlement and to consider in which directions and in what ways it could expand. Now that the need for surprise no longer existed, he discussed with his officers the best location for the large number of troops that would shortly be arriving. With that settled, he felt once more on the offensive and was able to enjoy his lunch with good appetite.

Tarkyn's parchment was delivered to him as he sat at a table under a tree near his tent, drinking coffee with Stargazer.

"How was this delivered?" demanded Kosar.

The guardsman bowed, "A crow dropped it, Your Majesty. It is clearly addressed to you."

Kosar waved him away and unscrolled the parchment. Stargazer shifted his chair subtly further away.

Kosar,

Thank you for gracing the forest with your presence and for making sure that measures are in place for patrolling the Great Western Road. It is important for travellers to be able to traverse the forest without fear of attack.

This auspicious visit by the two of you to the encampment has temporarily swollen the population of sorcerers in this area, a tribute to your popularity. However, I am sure you will agree that two companies of men is more than adequate to maintain a watch on the Great Western Road and now that Jarand's recruitment drive is at an end, five houses for refreshments, stores and accommodation will be sufficient for the usual number of travellers who wish to break their journey.

It was encouraging to see you and Jarand working towards the common good, but unfortunate that you did not build on your acknowledgement of his protection of travellers to forge a liaison between you. If you remember, I warned you that if I felt you were acting against Eskuzor's best interests, I would intervene and, in all conscience, I could not let you humiliate Jarand so publicly. The cost of his savage revenge would have been too high.

Consequently, I have taken steps to prevent a large contingent of your men from entering the forest from the north east until Jarand and his troops are safely on their way to Montraya. No doubt, now that Jarand has left, your men can be redeployed to protect Eskuzor's rural population from those predatory sorcerers who continue to roam the countryside unimpeded.

I must warn you that the danger of Jarand's discontent still lingers, perhaps now more than ever. I can only say that it would have been worse without my intervention.

Your brother,

Tarkyn

As Stargazer watched, King Kosar's face gradually darkened until it was a deep red by the time he had finished reading. Stargazer resisted the urge to run or to raise a shield, however feeble.

Kosar slammed the parchment down on the table. Then he picked it up and screwed it up with some force before flinging it from him. Immediately he thought better of it and demanded that Stargazer pick it up and return it to him.

"Blast his impudence! If I could get my hands around his insolent little neck, I would throttle the life out of him by small degrees and delight in watching him choke. And he is just full of bluster! Thinks he can stop a large battalion? Read that nonsense," he finished, spinning the parchment across the table to Stargazer. As he watched Stargazer reading it, the uncomfortable thought assailed him that Tarkyn was *not* full of bluster.

When Stargazer had finished reading, he raised his head and looked at Kosar, not wishing to proffer an opinion unless it was requested.

Kosar waved his hand irritably, "Go on. Say what you're thinking."

"Have you had any recent reports from Colonel Argyve, Sire?"

"No. But I did not expect any. His orders were to arrive here with as little forewarning as possible. Obviously, as they enter the Great Western Road, there may be travellers who ride ahead with the news but other than that, I wanted to keep all communication to a minimum."

Almost on cue, a messenger rounded the last bend in the road to the encampment, bent low over his saddle as his horse, lathered from the hard ride, galloped the final stretch to the guards on the perimeter. Kosar, watching cynically, knew that the messenger could not possibly have maintained that frantic pace for his whole journey. He gave his head a slight shake, knowing before he read it what tidings the messenger would bring. He was almost resigned as he held out his hand to receive the message from the weary horseman.

Much to the messenger's astonishment and relief, the king merely waved him away before reading the parchment saying, "Go and get yourself a drink and something to eat. I may need to speak to you later."

With a sense of inevitability, Kosar perused Colonel Argyve's words.

Your Majesty,

Our arrival has been delayed by an unexpected attack by the forces of Prince Tarkyn. In an unprecedented move, they infiltrated our camp in open fields, well away from the forest's edge. His warriors knocked out every one of our guards so quietly that no one was roused. It is almost beyond comprehension how this could have been achieved since there were upward of sixty men on guard duty and not one made a sound. Then they removed every soldier's footwear and strew thorns throughout our campsite. It was only when the next shift of guards emerged to take their turn that anyone even knew the attack had taken place. Before we had realised the nature of the attack, well over half of the men had sustained deep puncture wounds to the soles of their feet.

Because this left us so exposed to further attack, I sent forth a flag of parley, as a result of which I actually met with Prince Tarkyn. Needless to say, I was in no position to attempt to capture him.

The prince offered me assurances that he had no intention of making further incursions across Eskuzor but merely wished to delay our arrival. I should point out, Sire, that had he chosen to, Prince Tarkyn could have wiped out my entire force. In facing him, we are dealing with forces well beyond the normal experience of fighting men. This is not an excuse, merely a statement of fact.

I do most humbly beg your pardon for my failure,

Your Loyal Servant,

Colonel Argyve.

Kosar handed the letter to Stargazer and stared unseeingly into the distance for some time. Finally, he shook himself and brought his gaze to bear on his wizard, "Tarkyn made no threat in his letter. He let his actions speak for themselves. It seems he is a formidable foe. I can only be thankful that he does not, in fact, want my crown." He took a deep breath, "I grow tired of this makeshift town and this lowering forest. Send word to Colonel Argyve that we will leave tomorrow morning to join him on the northern plains to plan our next moves."

Part 5: The Emptied Threat

CHAPTER 34

Jarand maintained his façade of calm control until he was well out of sight of his older brother, but as his troops headed south towards the Great Western Road, his irritability betrayed his hidden anger. Although he had had the satisfaction of out-manoeuvring his brother, he had still lost control of the encampment that had been providing him with a steady supply of recruits for nearly a year. He turned to Captain Harkell who, as captain of his Royal Guard, rode closely behind him. Harkell's lip was still split and his jaw on one side and cheek on the other were dappled with bruising. The prince could see a certain rigidity in the captain's posture and suspected that he was carrying an injury to his ribs from landing against the table the other night. Good, thought Jarand, Serves him right for compromising his loyalties. With a little spurt of malice, Jarand ordered Harkell to trot his horse the length of the troops to check that all was in order.

Even riding a walking horse was hurting his ribs but, keeping his face carefully neutral, Harkell complied, gritting his teeth as each jolt sent a sharp pain through his left side. After being able to express his opinions openly to Tarkyn, he was finding it increasingly difficult to hold his tongue between his teeth as he endured Jarand's deliberate mistreatment. Drawing a long breath, he resolutely conjured up the memory of his wife and children to strengthen his resolve.

Jarand watched his captain's return, noting the beads of sweat on his forehead, the only betrayal of his discomfort. "Captain Harkell, I believe you have some unfinished business."

"Your Highness?"

Prince Jarand glanced around to check that no one but Journeyman was within earshot. "I require you to make a final visit to my younger brother to determine his progress in bending his companions to his will and to my support."

Harkell suppressed the smile that threatened to split his face. "Yes Sire," he replied woodenly.

"Parchment." The wizard placed a dark blue tube in Jarand's hand, which Jarand passed on to Harkell, "Once more I rely on you to place this parchment directly into my brother's hand. Deliver it to none but my brother. Is that clear?"

"Yes Sire." Harkell accepted the cylinder and stowed it in his saddle bag, "But your Highness, I am not sure how long it will take them to contact me. I suspect they will move away from the encampment now that you and the king are no longer together."

The prince raised his eyebrows, "But surely you are in constant contact with them, even if not directly with Prince Tarkyn?"

A frisson of alarm ran through Harkell. "No, Your Highness, not at all," he replied emphatically. "They made contact with me to send you warning of the King's approaching battalion. And when I delivered your first message, I walked out of the encampment at midnight, hoping they would contact me. When I was well away, I doubled back and hid behind some bushes to check that I wasn't being followed. It was then that I suddenly found myself beside one of Prince Tarkyn's followers who took me by a very convoluted route to the prince's camp."

"Hmm. It is most irritating that we must wait upon them to make contact with you." He waved his hand dismissively, "Very well. I will give you a week. After that time, return to me even if they have not contacted you. I would not wish to lose you again to the dubious care of the woodlands." The accusation of divided loyalty hung in the air between them. Just as Harkell opened his mouth to protest, Jarand continued smoothly, "When we reach the Great Western Road, you are to head east while we turn west towards the road for Montraya. Your official task is to check along the Great Western Road for any equipment that may have been left behind by our men. I expect you to report to me three days after our return to Montraya. You never know, if the news you bring me is good, I may give you a few days off to spend with your family. No doubt they will be pleasantly surprised to see you after all this time."

Since their welfare will depend on my arrival. Harkell bowed in the saddle, "I will do my best, Sire."

Just as they finished speaking, a cloud of dust resolved itself into a horseman riding hard towards them. As he drew closer, they realised it was a king's messenger. Jarand put up his hand and the messenger dragged his horse reluctantly to a halt. Horse and rider were both strung up, the horse prancing back and forth, jabbing at the bit and tossing its head.

"You have news?" demanded Jarand.

The horseman bowed, "I most humbly beg your pardon, Your Highness, but my message is for the king alone."

"Obviously," snapped Jarand. He waved his hand, "Give the man a drink and send him on his way."

As the messenger galloped off, Jarand turned to Harkell, a gleam of amusement in his eye, "Captain Harkell, I believe my brother is about to receive some disquieting news about his approaching battalion. How unfortunate for him."

"Indeed, Sire. I fear he may be even more put out than he was by your departure."

"I must say young Tarkyn has served me well over the last few days." Suddenly Jarand's eyes bored into Harkell. "Never forget your true lord. As you must now realise, I have Tarkyn under my dominion and with his power behind me, it will be enough to tip the balance against Kosar." He gave a little smile of satisfaction, "And now, my fine captain, I think you just have time for one more inspection of the troop line before we reach the Great Western Road."

CHAPTER 35

Harkell rode slowly east along the broad road, basking in the midday sun and the solitude, after so many days of living duplicitously with his former colleagues. His encounters with Jarand had stretched his iron will to breaking point. After years of hiding his reactions, the honesty of his interactions with Jarand's younger brother had somehow undermined his ability to prevaricate so that he now found it increasingly difficult to keep a check on his temper. He knew he was walking a tightrope with Jarand and that, at any time, the prince might get sick of him and decide to hang him as a traitor. Perhaps the sheer idiocy and danger of the games of cat and mouse had given him the insouciance that Jarand had objected to in their exchanges.

He felt trapped. It crossed his mind that he could request a transfer to another regiment that served further away from the prince but as soon as he had the thought, he knew that Jarand would not grant it. Jarand was deriving too much pleasure from keeping him on tenterhooks. And now Jarand had taken it a step further and had moved from injuring him in a rage to deliberately forcing him to endure pain, purely for the entertainment of watching him suffer. Harkell had no doubt that Jarand was still angry with him for failing to return promptly after his recovery and he suspected that the prince would continue to find ways to punish him.

He turned his mind to Tarkyn, so different from his older brothers. Tarkyn had said he would do everything he could to look after him and his family but in reality, what could he do? Montraya was far from the woodlands and the woodfolk could never venture that far afield. Even if they did, they would never show themselves to sorcerers. Harkell sighed. At least he had a week's respite.

A little while later, he dismounted and sat in the shade on a rock by the side of the road to eat some bread and cheese. Almost immediately, a voice drifted down to him from the branches above. It was Rainstorm.

"Hi Harkell. I thought you'd never leave the middle of the road. Have you come to see us again or are you on a mission for Jarand?"

Harkell gave a short rather bitter laugh, "Both. Again." He looked up. "How did you know where to find me?"

Rainstorm surveyed the road in both directions before swinging down to land on the forest side of the tree, "We have kept a constant watch on you, since you and Jarand's troops left the encampment." The young woodman peered closer and frowned in concern, "Nasty bruises you've got there. What happened to you?"

"Tarkyn's stinking brother belted me around for having warned him of Kosar's approaching troops."

"Ungrateful bastard! I bet you wish you could have belted him back. It would have made me sick, not being able to hit back."

Suddenly Harkell grinned, "Ah Rainstorm, it's good to see you again. You're right. It did. I've been running around like a bear with a sore head ever since. But seeing you has cheered me up."

Rainstorm grinned and clapped him on the back, "Come on, bring that horse of yours and we'll get you to the firesite. We have heaps to tell you."

By the time they reached the woodfolk camp, Rainstorm had regaled Harkell with their attack on Kosar's troops, adding rather shyly, "And my dad was actually proud of me."

Harkell gave a warm smile, "Of course he was. I expect he always is, even if he doesn't always show it. That was a very clever ploy. Mind you, only woodfolk could have achieved it without open conflict." Harkell's eyes flickered around the firesite, "Where's Tarkyn?... and Danton?"

Rainstorm waved his hand airily, "Oh, I don't know, maybe off conferring with Orolan's bandits…" he said vaguely.

Harkell frowned. "What business would he have with them? With his penchant for honesty, I would have thought His Highness would give them a wide berth unless he had a specific reason." Any surmises he might have had about the prince's purpose were swamped at this point by the effusive greetings of woodfolk.

Summer Rain took one look at his face and disappeared, to return shortly afterwards with a small blue phial, which she held out to him, "Here, Harkell. This will help to dispel the bruising and soothe your face until it heals."

Harkell thanked her and tossed off the offered tonic. When he had stopped shuddering, he smiled ruefully, "Ooh. Your tonics are a challenge. Do you have anything for bruised or broken ribs?"

"Yes she does," came a voice from behind him, "Me."

Harkell swung around to find Tarkyn bearing down on him. The captain was restrained in his greeting. He gave a low bow which made him grunt in discomfort from his sore ribs. "Good afternoon, Your Highness. I bring you yet another missive from your brother."

"Now come on, Harkell. Stop being so formal and straighten up. You are obviously in some pain." Tarkyn's vivid eyes surveyed the damage to the soldier's face and the reserve in his expression. He smiled, not at Harkell, but at those clustered around him, "I am sorry, one and all, but I must take Harkell from you for a little while. We will return shortly."

He put his hand out to stop Danton, "No, you need not accompany me. I… We will take our chances."

When they were far enough away for the trees to screen their voices, Tarkyn sank down to sit cross-legged on soft grass under a spreading beech tree, indicating that Harkell should do the same.

"Will you allow me to heal you or would you rather talk first while you have the pain to remind you of your grievance?" When Harkell looked at him in surprise, Tarkyn continued, "My friend, I have practised aloofness for the better part of my life and I know it when I see it. And if you remember from our discussion in the Lost Forest, although I grant freedom of speech, I am less willing to grant freedom of silence."

Harkell's face became, if anything, more closed. He dropped his eyes and found a sprig of leaves that he began to twirl between his fingers. After a minute, he looked up and said, "Sire, I have no grounds for a grievance. I am sworn to you and you gave me an order which I carried out, just as any soldier would obey his officer's command."

"Even though the command exposed you to the risk of injury?"

"Of course, Sire. It is a soldier's lot to risk body and limb to fight for his lord's cause."

"And yet, Harkell, something has upset you. Did Danton follow my request and check whether you could come up with a better solution?"

Harkell heaved a sigh, "Yes, Sire. I tell you again I have no reason to be angry with you."

"Yet all is not well."

For a few long minutes, silence reigned. Tarkyn, with great forbearance, simply waited.

Finally Harkell spoke, "If you must know, I felt, I don't know… hurt? a little betrayed?.. that someone I regarded as a friend would order me into a situation where we both knew I was likely to be injured. I thought you…" He shook his head, "Oh, I don't know. I know it's not logical but I am not very clear about anything at the moment." He ran his hands through his hair before suddenly meeting Tarkyn's eyes, "Have you ever been in a position where you have been attacked but cannot fight back?"

"Yes. Twice. Once when Andoran and Sargon captured me and then when the mountainfolk systematically bashed me," answered Tarkyn dispassionately.

"But I mean when your hands are not bound; when as a strong man, you have to force yourself to submit to being beaten, as though you were weak. It is one step further along the line of humiliation."

Tarkyn took time to imagine it before saying, "Yes. I see what you mean. That would be quite dreadful. In fact, I doubt that I could do it."

Harkell gave a faint smile, "I think you would struggle more than I. After all, it is not your destiny to subvert your will to anyone. But even you could do it, if people you held dear were hostage to your behaviour."

Tarkyn picked up a stick and started drawing in a patch of dirt. After a while, he said, without looking up, "I think you would have endured worse, if Kosar had had the chance to humiliate Jarand in front of his men…and he would have partly blamed you…and me, but I wouldn't have taken the brunt…for not warning him. And even if you were hurt on the short run, one of the reasons for this whole operation was to protect you as much as we could. I will not pretend that it was the only reason, but it was one of them."

"Thank you. I shouldn't be complaining. In fact, I wouldn't be, except that you forced it out of me."

Tarkyn glanced at him and smiled, "Come on. Tell me what life has been like for you since you went back to Jarand."

"In many ways it is good. I enjoy the day to day duties as Captain of the Guard. I always have. And there are many fine honourable men, both enlisted men and officers among Jarand's troops."

Tarkyn nodded, "I know. That is why we try not to kill them."

"Some of them have been friends of mine for many years. Captain Guerion, for instance. You probably know of him. He was the officer who interrogated Sargon and Andoran when we delivered them to the encampment." Harkell gave a wry smile, "Saker and Biggin risked their careers to support me and land me in this mess. Little Nyrus, my fourteen year old batman… And it chafes constantly with me that I cannot be honest with them." He took another deep breath, wincing as his ribs moved, "And then we come to your brother." Harkell gave a wry smile, "Tarkyn, association with you has de-mystified Jarand for me. Where once I felt honoured to have risen high enough that he would throw a few words my way, now I merely tolerate his game-playing and his cruelty. Sometimes I even struggle to remain serious and once, he caught me gazing around his tent in pure curiosity."

Tarkyn chuckled, "Those restless eyes of yours." The prince's smile faded, "And now he has injured you."

Harkell nodded, "And will do so again. He slammed me into a table and knows he hurt my ribs. So he has been forcing me to trot back and forth along the troop line. He thinks my loyalty has been compromised and he will continue to punish me until he has no more use for me."

"Hmm. If Jarand wants my cooperation, and I appear to give it, I may need to make some demands of my own to give you greater protection if you must go back to him."

Harkell sighed regretfully, "If you will allow it, I must go back, for my family's sake. Jarand gave me a week. So I can stay for another four days. If I leave early on the sixth morning and ride hard, I should be able to catch him."

Tarkyn gave a non-committal half nod that Harkell interpreted as reluctant agreement.

Suddenly the soldier laughed. "Jarand has just finished telling me that he has you under his dominion. I'm so glad he's mistaken. Whatever happens to me, don't ever let it force you into submitting to him." He added sombrely, "I couldn't live with that."

"I promise you I will not. But short of that, I will do everything I can to protect you."

For a few moments there was silence, before Harkell said, "It is confusing, you know, having you as both friend and liege lord. I accepted your order without question from my liege but was upset by such an order coming from a friend."

"And yet it was as friend as much as liege lord that I sent you to face the lesser of two evils." Tarkyn found himself a stick and began to break bits off the end of it. "I hoped you would understand… and indeed you did with your head, but not with your heart." Keeping his eyes firmly on the stick he was destroying, he said, "You know, early on, Waterstone nearly abandoned our friendship because it confused him so much. But I am glad he didn't and I hope you won't… but the choice is yours."

"No, of course I won't."

Tarkyn brought his eyes up to meet Harkell's, "Then make sure you tell me when something I do upsets you. I may not always be able to avoid it but at least we can keep it out in the open. In the invidious position which you find yourself, I cannot afford even a hint of reticence between us. I trust you but I am surrounded, as you must know, by people who are not prepared to take risks with my safety. Besides, if you have been harbouring any discontent, Jarand could have seized on it and nurtured it." Tarkyn put his hand on Harkell's shoulder, "And now, are you ready to accept my healing?"

Harkell smiled, "I always was, Sire."

Just as Tarkyn sent a wave of *esse* through his hand into Harkell, a raucous cry, and a flurry of black and gold wings filled the air as Tarkyn's eagle swooped in to land with a heavy thump on his shoulder. Harkell dived backwards in alarm and rolled out of the way. When he sat up, he was met with the sight of Tarkyn irritably trying to brush the eagle's tail feathers out of his face as she turned on his shoulder.

"Blasted bird! Now I've got a mouth full of eagle down. Ptooey. Yuk!"

As she settled facing forwards, the prince pushed her sideways so that she wasn't crowding up against the side of his face. "*Will* you move over? I can't see a thing if you stick your beak in my face." As if in answer, she delicately picked up some strands of his long black and hair and began to work it gently through her beak, as though to soothe him. Tarkyn rolled his eyes in resignation and began to stroke her.

When he saw Harkell grinning broadly at him, he smiled ruefully in return, "You may laugh but her landing jolted me and I have sent too much power into you. Look at yourself. You're green."

Harkell looked at his hands, now a gentle shade of lichen green and went off into a peal of mirth. When he had recovered sufficiently, he asked, "Why didn't I turn green after you healed my back? That was a much bigger healing."

"Because I usually leave a person's body to finish off the healing. But in this case, I sent you too much life force by mistake." Tarkyn chuckled, "It won't matter. You'll just be a little boisterous for a while."

"And how did you acquire an eagle?"

When he had heard the saga of the eagle, Harkell quietly marvelled at Tarkyn being irritated by something that would leave other people lost in wonder. "So what have you named her?"

Tarkyn raised his eyebrows, "I didn't think of it. I suppose I call her Bird, if anything."

"*Tarkyn*! That's not a very respectful name for such a magnificent animal."

"Huh! You try having her weigh your shoulder down and getting in your way and fending people off and see how you'd feel. At least she's quieter than she was. But she's a big pest." Despite his words, Tarkyn smiled fondly and gave her head a scratch. "Aren't you, Bird?" Tarkyn went still for a few moments as he received images from the woodfolk, "Time to go back. Everyone is becoming impatient, waiting to chat to you. Give me a hand up, will you? It's hard getting up from cross-legged with this great lump on my shoulder."

Harkell held out a hand and hauled the prince upright, before falling in beside him to return to the firesite, the eagle nonchalantly adjusting to the sudden jolt upward and bobbing gently up and down between them in time with Tarkyn's strides.

As they neared the clearing, Harkell sighed, "I suppose we will have to go through all those shenanigans again with the parchment Jarand has sent this time. He and Journeyman are as thick as thieves. I'm sure they will have doctored it again. But I really don't want anyone to endure anything like Rainstorm and Danton did on my behalf last time."

"No, they were pretty rattled, weren't they? But now that he knows what he is looking for, Stormaway should be able to decipher whether the spell's intention is the same as before, without subjecting people to its influence. Only if it is a new spell, will we have to experiment further." He surveyed his liegeman, "Hmm, I think the green has faded already. Perhaps you needed that added boost."

When they arrived at the clearing, Harkell reached into his pack and handed Jarand's parchment to Stormaway with a stricture to take care with it. Then he turned his attention to the welcome of his friends.

Stormaway and Summer Rain took themselves apart from the others to inspect the parchment. They donned gloves before opening the cylinder and carefully drawing forth the parchment. Stormaway cut off a small corner and shredded it into a shallow dish containing a measure of the antidote they had used on Jarand's previous missive. Summer Rain stirred it carefully and waited. After a minute she peered into the mixture, frowning, before stirring it once more. Again she peered into it, clearly dissatisfied.

"Look Stormaway. Another ingredient has been added."

Tarkyn tuned into their disquiet and strolled over to join them. "What has happened?" he asked.

Stormaway looked up from his study of the dark grey liquid. "If it were the same as last time, the antidote would have become clear when we added the parchment steeped in the same solution. But look! There is definitely a residual grey."

Tarkyn peered into the dish, "Quite a bit of it, I'd say, if the strength of the colour is anything to go by... Can you discern what it is without the need to test it on someone?"

"We can try. Although the liquid is coloured, it has clarified. So that means that the last missive's intentions of making the reader well disposed towards Jarand is again sealed within this parchment. But there is something further. We will try to deduce what that might be, and use trial and error on pieces of parchment with various substances added to the last missive's antidote." Stormaway frowned with worry at Tarkyn. "Sire, whatever you do, please don't touch that parchment or allow anyone else to touch it until we know what we are dealing with."

"I wouldn't dream of it. I will leave you to your work. Let me know as soon as you have further information." As he walked away, he gave a half smile and unexpectedly swept his hand in an arc to encase Stormaway, Summer Rain and the doctored parchment within a shimmering shield of bronze. "Your wish is my command, Stormaway."

The wizard smiled, "Thank you Sire. We can concentrate unimpeded in here."

It took them most of the afternoon to discover what substance had caused the deep grey tinge. During that time, Tarkyn had talked and joked with Harkell and others of his home guard without once allowing his hold on his shield to falter.

At last, as preparations for the evening meal were already underway, Stormaway beckoned to him, "Sire, this parchment is more dangerous than the first. I think you should wear gloves when reading it and destroy it afterwards. If you wish to keep the words, I will copy them for you."

Tarkyn nodded his agreement and asked, "And what is the new ingredient and its effect?"

The wizard took a deep breath, "An extract from a dark mushroom called Velvet Claw has been added. It would compel the reader to obey the words in Jarand's missive, Sire."

Tarkyn raised his eyebrows, "So, not only would I view Jarand favourably but I would follow any instructions he has written in this parchment?"

"Yes Sire, although the impulse would not last more than a day or so."

As they talked, Stormaway crushed a small yellow berry into their concoction and gave it a final stir. "I am so concerned about this letter that I believe you should take this antidote before you come anywhere near it. It will not affect you unless it has something to counteract. It will merely strengthen your defences." He gave an apologetic smile, "You see, Sire, if something went wrong and you came into contact with the letter, I don't see how we could subdue you long enough to force you to take the antidote and I, at least, would find it very distasteful having to do so."

Tarkyn's eyes glinted, "Yes, that would be most unseemly and the consequences could be dire, both physically and legally, for those laying hands on me, if I remained under Jarand's spell. Very well. Hand me your brew but keep some in reserve in case someone else touches the parchment."

Stormaway poured a small measure into a cup and handed it to the prince who eyed them both before swallowing it in one gulp. A smile appeared on Tarkyn's face, "Amazing. That didn't taste bad at all. I could have drunk that more slowly." He donned a tatty old pair of gloves, knowing that they too would need to be destroyed. "Let's have this dread missive."

As soon as he had the parchment in his hands, woodfolk and sorcerers alike gathered to hear its contents. Tarkyn unrolled it and glanced through its contents, preparing as he had last time, to read it aloud. He frowned in consternation at one particular passage, rereading it to make sure that he hadn't misinterpreted it. Tarkyn took a deep breath and looked up at the people around him, who were waiting to hear what his brother had written.

"Before I begin, I should mention that in addition to his previous potion, Jarand has added an extract from a fungus called Velvet Claw that compels the reader to comply with the wishes expressed in the letter. We must thank Stormaway and Summer Rain for providing their expert services in thwarting Jarand's intentions." He cleared his throat and began to read,

Dear Tarkyn,

Thank you for warning me of Kosar's plan to publicly usurp my authority. I am pleased that you have seen the wisdom of supporting my cause. I am impressed that your woodfolk were able to impede an entire battalion long enough for us to retreat from the encampment, thus leaving Kosar in a delightful state of disarray.

As your older brother, I am gratified to see that you have now bent the woodfolk to your will. Never forget the heritage owed to our name. You confer an honour on them by allowing them to serve you.

Not surprisingly, snorts of derision greeted this remark. Tarkyn waited until they had subsided before reading the final, telling paragraph.

To seal our accord, I require you to give me your pledge. As guarantee of your commitment, I expect Captain Harkell to deliver your written oath of fealty to me on his return.

Your brother

Jarand

Several people made to speak but didn't, realising that any equivocal response to Jarand's letter would betray the fact that the compulsion of the Velvet Claw had been circumvented.

Finally Rainstorm said in a rush, "You will just have to tell Jarand that the letter was forced from you by Danton or someone."

But the dubious silence that greeted this suggestion showed that no one really believed that would work.

"If I must…" began Tarkyn.

"NO!" came a vehement chorus.

Tarkyn raised his eyebrows and waited for complete silence before saying, "Surely you know me better than to think I would swear fealty to anyone, let alone my conniving brother. As I was saying… if I must, I will explain to Jarand that you people became suspicious of the sudden change in my attitude after the last letter and intercepted this one before it reached me, which is true. I will stipulate that my continued support depends on Harkell's wellbeing, but that I am not yet prepared to swear fealty to him after uncovering his duplicity."

Danton glanced sympathetically at Harkell before saying, "Nice thought, Tarkyn, but your wish to protect him will not only confirm Jarand's suspicions about Harkell's loyalty, but will also give him the opportunity to turn the tables by holding Harkell as a trump card to enforce your cooperation."

Tarkyn grimaced, "There must be something more I can do…"

"Perhaps, Sire," offered Stormaway, "you could tell Jarand how offended you are by Harkell's efforts to force the tainted letter directly into your hand against the express wishes of your advisors."

"No," said Harkell firmly. "Don't try to force Tarkyn into compromising his integrity. Besides, I doubt that it will make much difference. When I return without Tarkyn's pledge, Jarand will know that either I have played him false or failed him. But at least my reappearance will save my family."

Several people glanced uncertainly at Tarkyn but when he made no further response, inevitably all eyes returned to Harkell.

Harkell, still garbed in Jarand's uniform, shrugged one shoulder, "This was always going to happen. There is no way I can stay true to you and survive for long under Jarand's aegis. I have been walking a tightrope ever since I ostensibly returned to his service." He waved his hand to encompass the whole group, "Without you all, I would have been dead already. I thank you all for giving me these extra weeks. The opportunity to work with Tarkyn and to contribute with you towards Eskuzor's future has been beyond my wildest dreams."

Again eyes turned to Tarkyn but he only gave a slight shake of his head.

If Harkell was disappointed that Tarkyn made no further effort to help him out of his predicament, he didn't show it. In fact, he preferred Tarkyn's apparent acceptance of the inevitable. Empty words would have suited neither of them.

CHAPTER 36

The dark cobbled streets were slick with rain, shining in the yellow light of the overhanging street lanterns. Four rough looking men and a couple of ragged women slunk along the shadows of the street, deviating around the circles of light cast by the lanterns. They had sought shelter in a tavern while the rain pelted down outside but only when the last of the customers had bid their farewells to the landlord, had the group of six risen from their table in the corner and nodding their thanks, headed out into the street.

As they reached a crossroads, the stocky swaggering man in the lead, his thinning grey hair pulled back into a straggly ponytail, peered down the darkened street to his left and stopped, looking for a house on the corner with an orange door. When he spotted it, he pointed at two of the men and one woman and, with a jerk of his head, indicated that they were to head off down the smaller ill-lit street. He and his two remaining companions continued straight ahead.

They passed another tavern, dark and shuttered, a fruit stall with covers thrown over it for the night and on the corner, a small grocer's shop, blinds drawn and door barred, opposite a smithy, whose huge wooden doors were pulled closed until dawn. The house they sought was next door.

The three of them stood gazing at the solid stone house, noting its heavy front door, dark windows and a path leading down the side of its small garden to the rear. The man nodded to his companions to investigate while he waited near the front door. A few minutes later, he caught the faint sound of creaking hinges as a side window was opened and soon after, the sound of a drawing bolt just before the front door was cautiously opened. As soon as his companion's face appeared around the edge of the door, the leader ran lightly up the three front steps and slipped inside the house.

Using gestures, the others indicated that two people were asleep in the room to their right and that towards the back of the house was a single room also off to the right, in which a woman slept. Opposite her room was a nursery in which two children lay snuggled under their eiderdowns.

Signalling the others to follow, their leader slipped quietly into the first room on the right. For a moment, he stood looking down at the elderly couple who lay in the bed, sleeping soundly, unknowingly beneath his gaze. Then he gave a decisive nod and the other two moved in, the woman to the woman's side and in unison, they placed one hand over the mouths of their targets, pinning them down with the other.

The old couple awoke, their eyes starting in fright. The old man was powerfully built and put up a valiant struggle before he was subdued. But the advantage of surprise and a life of violence had given the intruder the upper hand. The old man now lay glowering, unable to move with his assailant's whole weight on his chest holding him down.

The man in charge, sat on the end of the bed, put his finger to his lips and whispered, "Please. Be quiet. We mean you no harm, I promise you. We have not even come to steal anything from you. If my people release their holds on you, will you agree to listen to us?"

When the old man's eyes narrowed, the intruder added apologetically, "I'm afraid we cannot afford to risk being discovered. So, if you do shout out, we will have to knock you out, but even then we will not kill you."

The old man glanced at his wife then gave a curt nod. As his mouth was freed, he said in a furious undertone, "What do you want? What do you mean by frightening good people in their beds in the middle of the night?"

The man in charge gave a brief bow from his seated position, "I beg your pardon, Sorath, but our business is urgent and for your benefit, not ours… My name is Orolan. I and my people abide in the forests far from here near the Great Western Road. We have been sent to bring you to your son, Harkell, who has need of you."

The woman repressed a cry. "Oh no. Is he all right? Is he injured? What has happened to him?"

"It has taken us four days to reach you, but I can tell you that he was well when we left. However, his future wellbeing and yours, as I understand it, depends on his family being brought to him."

"You are speaking in riddles, man." The old man struggled to sit up. "Get this oaf off my chest!" At a nod from his leader, the assailant took his weight off Sorath but stood close by, ready to intervene if necessary. "I am not going to uproot my family and drag them on a long journey on the say-so of a bunch of thugs. Who sent you? What proof do you have of your words? And how is Harkell's wellbeing at stake?"

"I am not at liberty to say who sent me but I can tell you that he who sent me is a man of great integrity. And he has sent me, out of care for your son. I cannot prove my words but I do have a small lock of your son's hair to show you that he who sent me has been in contact with Harkell." Orolan drew a breath, "As to your last question; Harkell is presently at the beck and call of someone who is using his life and your family's safety as surety for his obedience. The man he is being forced to serve does not have the same integrity as my own lord and so Harkell may be called upon to perform deeds that will war with his conscience. And we cannot rescue him from his predicament unless we can get you and your family safely away from the reach of this man. Harkell has already said that he would not leave and risk having this man's vengeance fall on his family."

"I see…" said Sorath slowly. "And do you know who this lord is who has my son in thrall?"

Orolan nodded, "But again, I am not at liberty to say. I can tell you, however, that this man is very powerful, yet lusts for more power, and is prepared to use any means at his disposal to gain it. He is indiscriminate with his anger and doesn't care who he hurts. He has already hurt your son grievously once and is likely to do so again."

The old woman gave a whimper and clutched at her husband's sleeve.

"There, there Thraya. It's all right. At least we know he is still alive." The old man turned on Orolan. "Stop it. You are deliberately trying to frighten us," he growled.

"No, I am stating facts. But Thraya, I can assure you Harkell has fully recovered from his previous injury, thanks to the benefactor who sent me."

Thraya breathed a sigh of relief. After a moment, she said quietly, "Sorath, I think we must go with them. What do you think?"

"I think perhaps we must." Sorath scowled at Orolan, "We have Harkell's wife and children living with us here, but do you realise that there is also my other son to consider? Presumably this man, whoever he is, could come after Drakell too?"

Orolan nodded, "I think it very likely. As we speak, this same conversation is taking place in your son's house. You must wake Kayama and the children, and be ready to leave within the hour so that we can clear the city's limits before sunrise. We have horses and supplies waiting in a large barn not far from the city gates."

"I've never ridden a horse in my life," exclaimed Thraya in dismay.

Orolan smiled sympathetically, "Then I'm afraid you will be very saddle sore by the time we reach our destination."

Two blocks away, Orolan's companions were not having such an easy time of it. In a similar fashion, they woke Harkell's brother Drakell and his wife, Elena. When it was explained to them, Drakell and Elena were quick to agree to follow them to Harkell's aid but Elena's sister Rena presented an altogether different prospect.

Even though it was Elena who woke her, Rena jerked into fearful wakefulness and huddled in terror against her pillows with her quilt dragged up around her neck when she saw strange men at the door of her bedroom.

Elena threw an irritated glance over her shoulder, "I told you to wait outside," she hissed at them.

The taller, leaner of the two glared at the cowering woman in the bed, thinking that the last thing he needed was an hysterical woman to secrete out of the city. He conceded that the sister might calm her so, with a nod to his companion, sidled out of sight along the narrow corridor towards the front of the house, his heavy boots reverberating on the bare floorboards.

Rena, her eyes wide with alarm, whispered, "Did you see his eyes? He has seen murder and robbery…more than once."

"Rena, they are not here to rob us…or to harm us." When Rena simply pulled the eiderdown tighter around her, Elena continued, "Rena, they woke Drakell and me. They could easily have killed us but they didn't. They have not threatened us," she gave a slight smile, "although I admit they did frighten us, appearing out of nowhere like that."

"That man's past is violent, I tell you. I can see it. You know I can see these things."

Elena drew a patient breath. "You may be right." When Rena looked as though she would protest, her sister added hurriedly, "All right. You probably *are* right but he is not here to hurt *us*."

"How can you trust such a man?"

Elena considered, "I suppose, because they have come with such a wild story, it can only be true…and because they could have hurt us and didn't."

"You mean, haven't so far."

"Rena, stop it," said Elena sharply, losing patience. "Pull yourself together and listen." Elena told her of Harkell's plight and the need for the family to move, to protect both themselves and Harkell. "These men and the woman with them have been sent to help us get away."

The mention of a woman ignited Rena's interest. She straightened up a little and loosened her stranglehold on the eiderdown. "Where's this woman? I want to see her."

Elena called to her husband to send her in. A few moments later, a pair of heavy boots stomped down the hallway and a middle aged woman appeared around the doorway. She still wore her cloak, ready to leave and Rena could only see a little of the thick practical woollen skirt and jacket she wore beneath it.

As soon as she met Rena's eyes, Rena shuddered and pulled the eiderdown back up. "You're the same as the man, aren't you?"

"Dunno what you mean, dearie. I'm Marga and he's Karzik, me brother, and we stick together." The woman frowned at her, hands on her hips, "Now come on dearie, why don't you get your arse outta that bed and get on with it? We ain't gonna hurt you. We gone to a lot of trouble and inconvenience to get here and it ain't over yet. We still got three days' travel ahead of us to get you back to this bloody lord Orolan has gone and sworn us to."

"What lord? Why don't you tell us who he is?" demanded Rena.

"Not allowed to, see. Orolan would have me guts for garters if I let it slip." The woman grimaced, "I mighta called him a bloody lord but that's cause I'm cold and hungry and tired doin' him this favour, not cause he's a bad lad. You ain't got nowt to fear from him."

"Your brother scares me."

"Aye, he's a fine lad."

"How do I know he won't attack me?"

The woman eyes searched Rena's face. "Ah, so that's the way of it, is it? Na, don't worry your head over that. Orolan's a hard taskmaster. He won't have the lads doing more than they have to, to get what we want."

Rena's eyes grew round, "Who are you?"

The woman spat on the floor, "Now, you stick yer nose back on yer face and out of our business. All you need to know is that we're here to bloody help you and a right trial that's proving to be. So stop bleating and get outta bed afore you put us all in danger."

And much to her sister's surprise, Rena did.

CHAPTER 37

Soft rain gradually soaked through cloaks and dampened the travellers' hair until cold little rivulets found their way down their necks. With heads hung low, their horses trudged their way doggedly along the miles of muddy, gravelly road. The sky had been a heavy grey for hours but gradually even that meagre light was fading.

Orolan swung round in the saddle and surveyed the huddled group of misery behind him. "Not long now. There is a wayfarers' inn up over that next rise. It takes all travellers, no questions asked and no information passed. But I'll send Mac ahead just to check it out. Can't afford to take chances with you or us. No one must know of your flight." A flash of white in the gloom signalled his effort at an encouraging smile as one of his men detached himself from the group and urged his horse into a canter.

Half an hour later the sodden group reined up outside the inn. Orolan gestured to his people to help Harkell's family to dismount. Otherwise, he suspected, they would have Thraya and several others in collapsed heaps in the mud as their legs gave way under them. They had suffered hours in the saddle without complaint but he knew that unaccustomed legs would betray the fortitude of their spirits.

He watched silently as the men, women and children of Harkell's family stumbled towards the inn door. Suddenly, the powerfully built younger blacksmith straightened himself and turned back, shaking his head. "Don't know what I was thinking, leaving you to tend to the horses. Sorry. Where do we take them?"

Orolan waved his hand. "You can help tomorrow. Tonight, go in with your family." When Drakell hesitated, he urged, "Go on. We need you fit for another day's hard ride tomorrow."

"Thanks." Drakell gave him a wry smile as he turned stiffly back towards the inn, "But it will take more than that to get me fit for tomorrow. I can hardly walk."

Orolan smiled in sympathy, "It will get better."

"Not tomorrow it won't," growled one of his companions under his breath, "second day is always worse."

"Jakon, you go in with them and organise food and beds," ordered Orolan. "I'll help with the horses. We'll be in shortly."

They led the horses to the roomy stables behind the inn, where a couple of stable boys ran forward to offer their services. For a moment Orolan debated whether he should insist that his people look after the horses or instead, part with some of their funds to have their horses unsaddled, rubbed down and fed for them. In the end he compromised and enlisted the help of the stable boys without handing the horses over altogether. After all, they had fourteen horses to attend to and only five of them to do it.

As he brushed down his own bay mare, he thought about the man who had sent him on this wild, desperate venture. What a strange novelty to have a prince residing nearby in the woods, always elusive unless he wanted to be found but there, nevertheless. He gave his head a slight shake as he remembered his unwise brashness in challenging that prince. He had been lucky to escape with his life. And now rumours had filtered through that the prince and his unseen followers had crippled a battalion over a thousand strong. Orolan frowned as he pondered how the number of sorcerers needed for such an undertaking could remain hidden in the woods that he and his bandits knew so well.

Orolan had only met an odd assortment of five sorcerers, including Harkell, during his confrontation with Prince Tarkyn. As he recalled, Harkell had been less than sympathetic with Orolan's plight after the prince had turned the tables on him. Yet now here he was, risking his life and his followers to rescue Harkell from Jarand's clutches. He gave a little shrug. He could see why Harkell had been so passionate in defence of his lord. The loyalty clearly cut both ways if the prince would go to such lengths to protect his liegeman. He gave a little grunt of derision. Rather, the prince would order others to go to such lengths. Still, such was the way of the world.

The bandit chief thought back to his recent meeting with Prince Tarkyn and his lord companion Danton. Only extreme need ever led the prince to make contact with Orolan and his bandits. The first time had been when Prince Tarkyn borrowed a horse so that he could travel quickly to give aid to his injured liegeman. This time it was to rescue Harkell. Unintentionally, Tarkyn's distaste for the bandits' way of life had shone through in both encounters and Orolan was wryly aware that although he would earn the prince's thanks for his efforts, he would never earn his respect unless he eschewed his banditry. A spurt of anger shook him. Orolan had people to care for; people who had been hounded into the forest by the unrest in Eskuzor. It was all very well for the prince to be sanctimonious. No doubt he had resources he could call upon. Orolan and his band had nothing but their wits and daring.

Orolan's next brushstroke was so hard that his mare shifted her weight away from the pressure. "Sorry old girl," he muttered. Blast the man! For the first time, he realised how much he wanted Prince Tarkyn's respect and how little chance he had of earning it.

He was dragged from his reverie by Mac's gruff voice. "Come on, sir. You gone to sleep or what? We've all finished."

Orolan straightened stiffly and gave his mare a final pat as the stable boy entered the stall with a bag of oats.

CHAPTER 38

Drakell was sitting alone at a table in the corner, enjoying a few minutes of solitude as he finished his breakfast of grainy bread and hard cheese. He had already carried three loads of the family's baggage out to the stables and had helped Orolan's men to load the horses. His father, the women and the children had finished their breakfast and were now upstairs making final preparations for departure.

Just as Drakell washed down the last of his bread with a mouthful of tea, the door of the inn flew open. A frisson of fear ran down him as he saw a captain of the Royal Montrayan Guards stride in, flanked by four soldiers. The captain gave an appraising glance around the room and did a double take as his eyes lit upon Drakell. With a brief word to his soldiers, the officer left them standing at the bar to walk over to Drakell's table.

The big blacksmith tensed but knew he was cornered. Jarand's soldiers represented the law of the land but they could be harsh and unresponsive in their dealings with commonfolk. And while Drakell was strong, he was not a fighter and did not like his chances of breaking past five trained soldiers to gain the front door of the inn. So he simply sat still and awaited the turn of events.

As the captain approached, a jumble of thoughts cascaded through Drakell's mind. Soldiers may be unpredictable but they were not necessarily bad and Drakell had done nothing wrong. Could he perhaps recruit the soldiers' aid in rescuing Harkell from his predicament? Hard upon that thought, he considered his strange travelling companions who had gone to such trouble to fetch and accompany Harkell's family. If soldiers could help, wouldn't Orolan simply have told Harkell's family to approach the authorities? Besides, Drakell was pretty sure that Orolan and his companions would not welcome the attention of the soldiers.

Now the captain was towering over him. To Drakell's surprise, the man gave a half bow and asked in a friendly tone of voice, "Excuse me, but are you by any chance related to Captain Harkell?"

Before meeting Orolan, Drakell would have been pleased to meet an acquaintance of his brother's. Now he was more concerned that the family's whereabouts would become known. If Drakell was tense previously, his nerves positively fizzed at this question. But he knew the family resemblance was unmistakable. Drakell's face and build were broader and his eyes were light blue while Harkell's were soft brown, but other than that, the brothers were alike. Giving up to the inevitable with good grace, he replied, "Indeed I am, sir. I am his younger brother, Drakell."

Drakell's tension eased a little as the officer's face lit with a smile, "It is a pleasure to meet you. I am a friend of his, Captain Guerion. We are so pleased that he has returned to serve with us once more."

"Is he with you then?"

"Yes. He is returning with the prince and our troops to Montraya," A wave of relief washed through Drakell. Harkell must have escaped the clutches of the power-hungry lord. Now, with the family safely away, his danger would be past. Drakell's relief lasted only until the officer added, "But the prince has sent Harkell off to scour the Great Western Road for any equipment the troops may have left behind. I, on the other hand, have been sent ahead of the main party to reconnoitre. I am hoping this inn will do for the prince's luncheon."

"Oh. So Harkell is not with you at the moment?"

Captain Guerion smiled ruefully, "No. Pity isn't it? You could have met up with him. He will be a few days behind us, I think."

"Never mind," said Drakell, trying to keep any false note out of his effort to sound hearty, "I expect I'll catch up with him back in Montraya."

"Are you headed there now?"

Drakell weighed up the fact that the family might be seen heading away from Montraya before replying, "Not just yet. I have some family business to attend to first."

The captain grimaced, "I hope you were not intending to stay here today. I'm afraid I am commandeering this inn for His Highness."

Drakell rose from the table, "No. In fact it is high time I was on my way." Reading the goodwill on the captain's face, Drakell was tempted to ask him not to mention the family's presence at the inn, but restrained himself, reasoning that such a request could draw the captain's attention to something he presently considered a non-event.

The young blacksmith arrived in the stable yard to find Orolan and his crew gone, and the rest of his family already mounted, anxiously awaiting his appearance. He swung himself up into the saddle of his big roan, grunting as sore muscles protested. His father spoke not a word, merely nodding in the direction of a narrow rutted track that led off to the right between the fields of corn.

Once they were out of hearing range of the inn, Sorath said tersely, "Orolan is furious. They have gone ahead and will meet us in the shelter of that tree line you can see beyond the fields." When his son hunched down into his coat but did not reply, he relented, "But as far as I can see, it's his own fault. He was the one who decided we would stay at that inn.

Orolan's crew are a scoundrelly lot, if you ask me. Why else would they be so worried about soldiers?"

"I told you," muttered Rena. "They have violence in their pasts."

Drakell shrugged, "Well, *they* may have, but *we* do not. That Captain Guerion who came up to talk to me is a good friend of Harkell's." He filled them in on what had passed between the captain and him.

Kayama's eyes lit up. "Oh. So Harkell has returned and is back in the Prince's Guard? I wonder where he went for so long. All he said in his letter was that he was alive and well, and would not be able to return for a while. Perhaps he has been on some secret mission for the prince then."

Sorath huffed, "Perhaps. Though I don't know why they bothered spreading those rumours of his death after their run in with the Rogue Prince."

"No. I'm just thankful he was able to send word to us."

Drakell frowned as he thought about it, "Perhaps he drew the Rogue Prince's ire during the confrontation and his own troops were protecting him by saying he was dead."

"So, if Harkell is now back in the open, I don't see why we can't ask the soldiers to help us find him," said Kayama.

"No, neither do I." Drakell peered ahead through the misty rain and kicked his horse into a trot, grimacing as his sore legs complained. "I nearly asked Captain Guerion. But you know, Orolan and his little band could have told us to do that from the start and saved themselves and us all this upheaval. For some reason they are putting themselves to a lot of trouble."

They were no closer to a solution by the time Drakell and his family caught up with their strange travelling companions on the outskirts of a patch of forest that skirted the edge of the fields. Orolan was still ropable and regaled the company with a list of Drakell's inadequacies, blithely disregarding his own role in the unfortunate encounter with the military.

"Now we will have to head cross country," fumed Orolan as they turned their horses towards a narrow, rutted lane running along the edge of the copse. "It will be slower and even harder going than yesterday. I just hope we can make it in time. Those bloody troops will scour everything in their path. And you had to chat to their captain, of all people, and just let them know who you are and where you're going!"

The big smith maintained a stolid silence as Orolan's tirade raged over his head. Goaded by Drakell's apparent disregard, Orolan snapped at his followers and spurred his horse into a rash canter across the uneven ground.

A deep voice murmured "*Torish.*"

All of the horses in the party drew gently to halt. Orolan's mare would not move despite the bandit's increasingly frenzied attempts to make her.

Drakell murmured to his own horse and brought him alongside Orolan. "You and I need to talk before we go any further. "

Orolan's eyes narrowed. "I know of only one person who can bend animals to his will like that."

The smith gave a gentle snort, "Then you don't know many blacksmiths. Any good blacksmith can quieten a horse. How else could we shoe a fractious stallion?"

A tiny smile played around Orolan's mouth, his bad humour having evaporated in the novelty of the situation. "And how are you with eagles?"

"Sorry? What have eagles to do with anything?"

Orolan waved his hand, still smiling at some private joke. "Never mind." He crossed his arms, leaving his quiescent mare to her own devices. "Go on then. Say what you want to say."

Drakell tilted his head to one side as he considered the cocky powerful little man. "It is unfortunate that we ran into those soldiers but I did the best I could to follow your wishes, given the circumstances. I could not pretend to be other than who I am. Any fool can see the likeness between Harkell and me. My inclination, which I did not follow, was to ask the soldiers to assist us."

Orolan was so stunned that he was unable to produce a sound. He kept beginning to speak and then, thinking the better of whatever he was going to say, would subside into a baffled silence.

Finally his henchman, Mac, asked in a not too friendly voice, "And what stopped you?"

Drakell gave a slight smile. "Not fear of you, if that's what you're thinking." His smile broadened. "No. I suppose more than anything it was because I decided to trust you....despite that fact that I figured you must be on the wrong side of the law to be so shy of those soldiers." Just as Orolan looked like regaining the use of his vocal chords, the smith added, "But that doesn't give you a licence to treat me like the crud you dig from a horse's hoof. Apparently you are doing Harkell and us a favour, although we only have your word for it. On the other hand, we are doing you a favour by agreeing to come with you so that you can fulfil your word to this lord of yours." He shrugged, "So it seems to me, we're about even."

Drakell saw some of the bandits flinging anxious glances back in the direction of the inn. So he murmured, "*Shirot*," allowing the horses to move forward once more. As the blacksmith's roan fell into step beside Orolan's mare, Drakell continued, "Clearly you do not want Prince

Jarand's soldiers involved in this, even though it seems an obvious solution. I have trusted you enough to accept that. But I think we deserve to know why."

Orolan rode for a few moments staring between his horse's ears. Then he looked at Drakell and favoured him with a rueful smile, "Between you and that lord of mine you keep mentioning, I am learning a bit about underestimating people." He leant forward to pat his horse's neck and sent a quick glare at his followers that dared them to comment before saying gruffly, "I am sorry you caught the brunt of my anger. I was worried that my misjudgement had placed my people at risk...and all of you."

Drakell looked back towards the inn which could still be seen in the far distance between the trees. "No one seems to be coming after us and the captain seemed preoccupied with finding a place for Prince Jarand to break his journey."

"Luckily, my people were not seen. And the threat to your family will come from the wrong people finding out where you are. This captain you met will probably go back and tell his fellow officers that he met Harkell's brother...and word may pass to the wrong ears."

Drakell frowned in consternation. "Are you saying that this man who has Harkell at his beck and call has subverted an officer of Prince Jarand's Guard?"

Orolan grimaced, clearly uncomfortable with the direction of the conversation. "It is complicated and I have given my word not to tell you too much." He gave a whimsical smile, as he kicked his horse into a trot, "I am glad you trust me because for the moment, my good faith is all I can offer you by way of explanation."

CHAPTER 39

Orolan's fears proved to be justified. By late morning, small parties of troops were scouring the fields, outbuildings and houses along both sides of the main road and one group of six had returned to the inn to pick up the fugitives' trail.

The soldiers who pursued them were fit, used to riding and gaining fast. Orolan had a problem on his hands.

He reined in and turned his horse so that he could address them, "We cannot outrun them and even though we outnumber them, even we will not attack soldiers, unless we have no other choice." He flashed a cheeky grin, "Not a moral stance, you understand. More because it would redouble their efforts to capture us."

"So what do we do?" growled Sorath. "I would rather give ourselves up to the authorities than allow my family to be shot at."

Alarm flared in Orolan's eyes. "NO! You really wouldn't. It would be safer in the short run but disastrous for you later."

Sorath nodded slowly, convinced by the intensity of the bandit's reaction. "The question still remains...."

Marga, who had been conferring quietly with her brother and Mac, rode forward and said, "Orolan, let Karzik lead. He knows this area."

Orolan nodded, "Karzik, we need to delay them. Is there any place we can block the road?"

"The road steepens and narrows in about two miles. Then it winds around the side of the mountain with cliff face on one side and a steep incline on the other... I don't know how you are planning to block it but somewhere along there would be your best bet."

"Then lead on. The soldiers are gaining on us and we have novice riders amongst us." Orolan waved everyone past, urging them to make haste, before falling in behind them.

By the time Karzik reined in, the horses were blowing hard and Harkell's family felt as though every bone in their bodies had been rattled. Orolan studied the cliff face rising twenty feet to their right before walking his horse to the left hand side of the road to peer down into the straggly trees that fell away down the hillside. He swung his horse around and stood in his stirrups in an effort to see what was at the top of the cliff.

"Well, we have two options the way I see it. We could try the trick that Pr...our friends used on us where they turned the ground we stood on to quicksand..."

Dubious headshakes greeted this idea.

"I don't think any of us feels confident enough to try that, especially with limited time to get it right," said Karzik, speaking for all of them. He shrugged, "Not even sure any of us has strong enough magic either."

Orolan waved his hand impatiently, "All right, all right. Just an idea. The only other option is to find a way to move boulders or tree trunks onto the road." He scanned the cliff face, conscious all the time of the sound of approaching horses. "Not many loose boulders that I can see. There are a couple of fallen trees up above us and down the slope a bit but they are probably too heavy to lift....Any suggestions?"

Much to the bandit chief's surprise, the solution came from Sorath. "If a group of us back track a little and climb through the scrub to the top of this cliff face, I think Drakell and I can probably push a fallen tree down onto the road. We're blacksmiths and we use our power to lift heavy objects all the time. If you boys help by levering the branches up, we can do the rest."

"Karzik, is there any way down from the top of the cliff face further along this track?" asked Orolan.

Karzik nodded, "Not too far ahead."

"Good. Then *go*, all of you. The soldiers are closing in on us. They are only minutes away. Marga and Cassia, you take the horses and Harkell's family and we will meet you further up the track." A thought struck him, "Karzik, horses couldn't get through along the top of the cliff face, could they?"

"No Orolan. I would have said so, wouldn't I? A bit pointless blocking the road if they could. No, the undergrowth is far too dense and the ground is full of hidden dips and hollows. Now, can we go?"

Orolan jumped down from his mare and ran to help Sorath dismount. Mac did the same for Drakell, supporting him while his stiff legs took his weight. Then the six men ran back down the road, the blacksmiths hobbling more than running. As they pushed their way up into the undergrowth on the higher side of the road, they caught flashes of blue and red through the trees as the soldiers urged their horses around the long bend up the hill.

Fear gave the fugitives the strength to thrust and dodge their way through scratchy and thorny bushes, the bandits slashing at the foliage with their swords. The first fallen tree they came upon was too heavily grown over and would have required too much slashing and disentangling to move it. The second dead tree was closer to the cliff's edge and resting on a gravelly patch with fewer grasses and tendrils gripping it. The reason for this became evident when they came closer. The old tree had fallen across a large bull ants' nest.

"Right, you four, stand among the branches and get ready to push," ordered Sorath. "Drakell and I will lift the trunk

Mac yelped as a bull ant nipped him on the finger. Stoically, he gave his hand a quick shake and with teeth gritted against the pain, took hold of one of the larger branches. When all four men had had a good grip on a branch, Sorath and Drakell squatted down on either side of the trunk close to the cliff edge and placed their hands as far under it as they could reach. The bull ants, outraged at the invasion into their territory, bit any piece of flesh they could find.

"*Torish*," muttered Drakell without any real hope, and sure enough the bull ants, unlike horses, took no notice. He gave a little shrug as he met his father's eyes across the top of the log. "Ready?"

In unison, they chanted, "*Liefka*." Indigo magic spread from Sorath's hands and deep blue from Drakell's. Then, with muscles bulging and power streaming from their hands, the two blacksmiths strained until, inch by inch, the grasses and vines gave up their hold and the enormous tree lifted.

"Push," growled Drakell, straining for breath, forcing himself to concentrate despite the sound of soldiers, now dismounted and crashing through the undergrowth.

The four men heaved all their weight against the branches and pushed the tree forward. Sorath and Drakell, with a final effort, thrust the trunk out over the edge of the cliff. For a moment, it teetered, half hanging over the road. With a concerted roar, all six of them heaved the tree's branches upwards until the balance shifted and the huge tree slid over the edge and down, for a moment standing upright before toppling to land at right angles to the cliff face.

"Run!" ordered Orolan, giving them no time to recover. "They're right behind us."

With no time even to check whether they had succeeded in blocking the road, the blacksmiths dragged in lungsful of air, struggling to recover. Orolan waited for them, in a frenzy of impatient but not saying another word, while they gathered themselves. When they straightened, he waved them forward and as they thrust their way through the thick scrub, he kept himself between them and the fast approaching soldiers.

Minutes later, the group of six burst out of the scrub onto the road, and threw themselves, with varying degrees of expertise, onto their horses. Even as they urged their horses forward, soldiers staggered from the bushes brandishing their swords. One wild slash bit home and a red stain appeared on Orolan's shirt sleeve. He dug his heels into his mare's sides and she sprang forward, carrying him to safety. When he looked back the soldiers, unaware that the road was now impassable except to foot traffic, were running back towards their horses.

CHAPTER 40

Over the next four days, Harkell joined in with the laughter and conversation, took part in an archery competition, which he lost by a considerable margin, and discussed the alternative tactics that both Jarand and Kosar were likely to employ. Only occasionally, did his soft brown eyes become thoughtful and introspective.

Tarkyn, on the other hand, was tense and uncommunicative while the other sorcerers and the woodfolk seemed to be simmering with an unexplained excitement. Several times, Harkell caught meaningful glances passing between members of the home guard. On one occasion, Rainstorm realised that Harkell had seen the interchange and gave a wry grimace, but didn't offer to explain.

"No, you're right," said Harkell, nodding his approval, "It is better that I do not know. Then, no matter what Jarand does to me, I cannot tell him."

Rainstorm looked stricken. "Oh no, Harkell. No. Don't think that." The young woodman actually growled in frustration, "Aagh. Sometimes Tarkyn can be so annoying."

"Perhaps. But in this case, he is right."

Rainstorm gave him a strange look but with a visible effort held his peace.

The morning of Harkell's departure dawned crisp and clear. Harkell rose early, once more donning the uniform of Jarand's Royal Guard. Despite the early hour, he could hear that others were up before him. Much as he appreciated their good intentions, he repressed a sigh. As the time of his departure neared, it was becoming increasingly difficult for him to maintain his composure. It would have suited him better to mount up and ride stoically into his short future, with no more than a cursory farewell.

With a start of surprise, he found Tarkyn at his elbow as he emerged from his shelter.

"Good morning, Harkell." Tarkyn grinned. "Yes, amazing, isn't it, that I have roused myself so early?" It did not register with Harkell, preoccupied as he was with his own concerns, that Tarkyn was no longer tense and withdrawn. "I can imagine that you might have been hoping to slip away but that would have been discourteous, you know. I'm afraid you will have to maintain your remarkable fortitude long enough to endure a short ceremony."

With a sinking heart, Harkell realised that the woodfolk, Danton, Stormaway, Boravar and the trappers were standing in a formal circle that closed around him as he and Tarkyn entered the clearing.

He felt Tarkyn's hand come down on his shoulder, acknowledging the effort this was costing him, as Boravar and a woodwoman he only vaguely recognised stepped forward to address him.

"Good morning, Harkell," said Boravar in his deep voice. He indicated the woodwoman standing beside him, "You may not remember her, but this is Calling Bird from the Lost Forest."

Harkell glanced around uncertainly, his face tight with strain, before sketching a shallow bow, "How do you do? It is a pleasure to meet you again."

Calling Bird spoke in a soft musical voice, "Harkell, we are gathered today to make a presentation to you in recognition of all that you have done for the sorcerers and woodfolk who were trapped in the Lost Forest, and for Prince Tarkyn and his followers. Our forest guardian may have had the power to put an end to our imprisonment in the Lost Forest, but it was you who challenged centuries of myth and legend to conceive the idea. You were instrumental in the tactics used for Prince Tarkyn to evade the king's trap and you risked being branded a traitor to teach Prince Tarkyn how to evade enemy shields."

Boravar continued, "And when the chance arose for you to resume your previous life, you chose to stay true to Prince Tarkyn and all of us, placing yourself at risk by your determination to evade Prince Jarand's most searching questions and to stymie his most devious ploys."

Wooden-faced, Harkell nodded an acknowledgement, desperately wishing that their vote of thanks would conclude so that he could leave to lick his wounds in private. He glanced sideways and was bewildered to see Tarkyn smiling down at him while Harkell himself felt that he was listening to his own eulogy. Harkell did not even try to smile in return.

Boravar was still speaking, "When you see the gift we are presenting you with, you will understand the esteem in which you are held, for those who would honour you have argued long and hard with the whole woodfolk community to have their oath of concealment mitigated for you."

Harkell felt Tarkyn's hand lift from his shoulder as the prince left his side to retreat behind the circle into the shadows of the trees. He vaguely wondered where Tarkyn was going.

Boravar watched him leave and at the prince's nod, instructed, "Bring forth our gift."

From behind the trees on the far side of the clearing, a group of eight uncertain sorcerers of varying ages shuffled forward, glancing diffidently around themselves as they approached. The circle of woodfolk parted, giving Harkell his first clear view of them.

His eyes widened in disbelief. "No," he breathed, "It can't be."

Kayama smiled mistily as she stepped forward into his arms. "Yes, my husband, it is. Your dedicated friends have brought every member of your family out of Montraya and into these forests; your wife, your children, your parents, your brother, his wife and even your brother's sister-in-law. We are all here."

Boravar beamed at the dazed captain, "You are safe now and can stay among us."

Little six year old Sorrell and his three year old sister Marema dragged themselves free of their grandparents' hands and ran up to their father to throw their little arms around his legs.

"Dad, Dad," piped Sorrell, his dark brown eyes and hair a smaller version of Harkell's, "We've had such an adventure. We were *kidnapped!*"

Harkell smiled through tears that streamed unchecked down his face as he lowered one arm to encompass his children who were clinging to his legs while keeping his other arm firmly around his wife. "Were you, my son?" he managed thickly, "How exciting for you."

After that, he couldn't say anything for some time, as his feelings overcame him. All of his extended family crowded around him, hugging him from every direction while the sorcerers and woodfolk of Tarkyn's home guard looked on, beaming with pleasure at the success of their surprise.

Some little time later, when Harkell's attention panned out enough to remember the audience watching his family's reunion, he cleared his throat, "Thank you, my friends. I can't begin to explain how much this means to me, but…" he looked around the circle of grinning faces and smiled in return, "I think you know." Returning his attention to his family, Harkell asked, "So have you already met everyone?"

Kayama shook her head, "We have only met a group of scruffy but kind men and women who, we discovered, are bandits," adding in an undertone, "… Strange company you are keeping, Harkell." Resuming her normal volume, she continued, "They came with us as far as the trees and told us to wait for that huge man's instruction." She looked around her a little doubtfully as she took in the slighter build and different colouring of the woodfolk. "I don't know any of these people."

Harkell took in a deep breath and let it out in a rush, "Well, you have a lot of learning to do, in that case." His eyes flickered around the clearing looking for Tarkyn who, protocol dictated, should be introduced first. Unable to spot him, he frowned in query at Danton who promptly stepped forward to fill the breach.

Speaking cryptically, Danton said, "The person you seek would like your family to settle in before learning of his presence. Instead, you may introduce me and the rest of us."

Even as he began the introduction, Harkell suddenly realised that his family would be overwhelmed with the honour of meeting Danton, let alone the prince. He sent Danton a complicit little grin as he said, "This is Danton Patronell, Lord of Sachmore." Harkell watched wryly as his whole family gave a low bow.

Harkell's father, as head of the family, took over, speaking with quiet dignity, "How do you do, my lord. It is an honour and pleasure to meet you. I am impressed that my son has been keeping such high company."

In the tree above them, Tarkyn grinned at the stunned expression on Waterstone's face. "It's a nice change for Danton to receive his due. You people never realised that he too should be accorded a measure of respect, because I required him from the start to eschew those protocols."

Harkell's father continued, "My name is Sorath. This is my wife, Thraya, and Harkell's wife, Kayama." He indicated a younger version of himself, "and my younger son, Drakell."

Drakell bowed again as he was introduced and took over from his father. He indicated a rather thickset blonde woman, "This is my wife, Elena, and her younger sister, Rena."

Rena was blonde like her sister but if anything, a little gaunt. She stood behind her sister and only came to the fore when she was herded forward by her. She looked frightened and awkward as she bowed to Danton.

To put her at her ease, Danton asked her kindly, "And who are these two little people?"

Rena gave a wavering smile as she signalled the children to come to her, "These are Harkell and Kayama's children, Sorrell and Marema. Make your bow to his Lordship."

"I did already," said Sorrell, nevertheless complying.

Rena squatted down next to him, "You do it again, dear, when you are introduced."

"Oh." The little boy beamed up at Danton. "Was that all right?"

Danton grinned at him, "Very good indeed, young man." He swept his hand around the circle, "And now let me introduce you to the rest of Harkell's woodland family. These are the people who rescued him after Prin…" He encountered a significant look from Harkell that then fell to his children. "Ahem, suffice it to say that Harkell's wellbeing is very dear to everyone here…" He smiled at Harkell in a way that encompassed all their disagreements, their camaraderie and the effect that having a lord as a friend would have on his family, "…and to me. He is one of my best friends."

"So, is it to you sir, that we owe Harkell's and our family's rescue?" asked Sorath.

"No. We have all been a party to it but you have yet to meet the man who authorised your retrieval from Montraya. Now let me introduce you to the woodfolk."

As Thunder Storm came forward to stand beside Danton, Harkell's family once more bowed low.

"How do you do, my lord." said Sorath. "I presume you are the leader of your people?"

A titter of laughter ran through the woodfolk, making the old man frown.

"I beg your pardon, Sorath, for my friends' rudeness," rumbled Thunder Storm, sending a quelling glare around the circle. "But they are laughing at me because they know I will feel discomforted by having you bow to me, but I do appreciate your effort to be respectful." He smiled, "I expect you are wondering about us. We are woodfolk and there are no ranks among us. Our people have always lived in the woodlands of Eskuzor, but for centuries, we have never revealed ourselves to outsiders." The woodman glanced around the sorcerers in the circle, "But as you can see, things are beginning to change for us. Nevertheless, other than those you see here, only the sorcerers from the Lost Forest - I think you call it the Forest of Yesterday, Today and Tomorrow - and four other sorcerers know of our existence."

Tree Wind stepped forward and said in her sighing voice, "You may take it as an indication of Harkell's value to us that we have agreed to reveal ourselves to the eight of you, and to allow you to dwell with us." She smiled at Harkell before continuing, "I suspect you will take some time to get to know us and we, you. You all look alike to me but I believe we all look alike to sorcerers when you first meet us. So feel free to ask us our names again at any time."

It was only when the family had met everyone and had time to settle themselves around the fire and eat their fill of freshly baked rolls, cheese and woodfolk-made berry jam that Tarkyn made an appearance. He walked casually into the clearing and helped himself to a cup of tea. But Harkell was not deceived into thinking that anything less than a formal greeting was required.

With a wry smile, he stood up and bowed, "Good afternoon, Your Highness. May I introduce my family to you?"

The members of his family looked around in shock, their eyes dilating as they realised who was standing there. They scrambled hastily to their feet and from there, each of them sank onto one knee, hand on heart.

"You may rise." When they were facing him, Tarkyn smiled, "Let me bid you welcome. Harkell is an astute observer of human nature and he speaks very highly of all of you. So, I am pleased to meet you." He waited until Harkell had introduced everyone before saying, "And now let me introduce my family." He indicated to Waterstone, Ancient Oak and Sparrow to come and stand beside him. He frowned, "Where's Midnight?"

A rustling overhead revealed Midnight just about to jump down onto his back. "No Midnight! It's too far down," he said, matching images to words. "At least wait until I am ready." The prince held out his arms and Midnight jumped neatly into them, sending Tarkyn staggering slightly backwards.

Returning his attention to Harkell's family, Tarkyn said, with undiminished formality, "Let me introduce Waterstone and Ancient Oak who are my bloodbrothers, my niece, Sparrow and my pestilential ward, Midnight." He put up his hand as Harkell's family prepared to bow again. "No. Please stay upright. To save your confusion and their embarrassment, let me assure you that they feel the same way as Thunder Storm or any of the woodfolk do, about overt gestures of respect. Simply use their names and do not, whatever you do," Tarkyn sent a brief grin to Waterstone, "bow to them."

Tarkyn gestured to Lapping Water who came shyly to stand beside him, "And this is Lapping Water, the woman I am to marry." He smiled down at her, swung Midnight onto one hip and put his free hand around her waist. After a moment, he looked up at the sorcerers arrayed before him and addressed Sorath, "I think it will take some time for you to fully comprehend our situation and our intentions. Meanwhile, you have my permission to speak to me or to anyone you wish. If you have any queries or doubts, please talk to someone, including me, about them. In time, I will ask you to swear your allegiance to me, but not until you have had time to get to know us."

Harkell's father gave a surreptitious frown and shook his head slightly at his wife. He glanced reproachfully at his son before saying, "Your Highness, I was told that one lord was trying to rescue Harkell from the toils of another. At no time did it occur to me that Harkell was being torn from his sworn duty to his prince."

There was a fraught silence. Then Tarkyn grinned and everyone breathed a sigh of relief, "Sorath, I can see where Harkell's strong sense of honour comes from."

"Then I hope you do not expect us to go against our conscience' replied the old man sternly. "We have been Prince Jarand's people all our lives."

"No, Sorath, I do not. But Harkell is an upright honourable man who considered carefully before making his choices. Do not reproach your son until you have heard all there is to hear."

"According to Orolan, you have taken care of the boy," Sorath grunted derisively, "not that his credentials would bear much scrutiny." Before Tarkyn could interrupt, he added, "But he is true to you and despite his cockiness, always placed himself between us and danger... He has paid dearly for his courage. So, at least for his sake, I will listen."

Tarkyn frowned in consternation, "What happened? Is he dead? I have had no word of this."

Sorath shook his head, "No. Not dead. But he has lost the use of his right arm. He was slashed by a sabre as he brought up the rear, making sure we made good our escape."

"Hmm. I must go to him," Tarkyn gave his head a slight shake bringing himself back to the matter at hand, "But meanwhile there is one oath I must insist on immediately." As the men of Harkell's family scowled and opened their mouths to protest, Tarkyn's voice sharpened, "I may not have your allegiance but I *will* have your courtesy. You have been accorded a great honour by the woodfolk and must swear not to betray their presence to any sorcerer."

"I beg your pardon, Your Highness," said Sorath gruffly. "I believe we would be quite willing to do that." The old man looked around the family group for confirmation and receiving it, nodded at the prince.

"Then kneel," said Tarkyn peremptorily. "You must swear a solemn oath never to reveal the presence of woodfolk to anyone. If you foreswear this oath, your lives will be forfeit. Do you so swear?"

In a murmured jumble all of them, even the children, replied, "I do."

"Good. Now you may rise. You might like to settle yourselves in for the night ahead. If you will excuse me, I must see Orolan."

Chapter 41

Tarkyn, accompanied by Danton and following the directions of hidden woodfolk, walked just over a mile to the bandits' camp. As he approached, he was challenged by a shout of "Who goes there?" followed by the swish of wood on string as a bow was pulled taut. Without breaking stride, he continued into the campsite, hearing behind him a dull thud as the zealous sentry was hit by a woodman's slingshot.

All around him, the bandits sank onto one knee, hand on heart.

"Thank you," said Tarkyn, "You may rise."

Orolan stood up and swaggered over to the prince, "Good morning, Your Highness. I hope you have not damaged young Gundo too badly. He was merely following procedure. He is new to our group and may not have recognised you immediately."

Tarkyn gave a slight smile, "I am sure he will do better next time." He studied the bandit standing before him, noting that Orolan's right arm was bandaged and in a sling. "I have come to thank you for your efforts on my behalf."

Orolan bowed his head briefly and answered formally, "I am pleased we could be of service, Sire."

"I understand that you risked your own life and limb to protect Harkell's family. Sorath was most impressed by your sense of honour and your courage..."

Orolan glanced up at the prince's face, expecting to see cool scepticism. Instead he found Tarkyn's eyes twinkling warmly down at him.

"From the little I have seen of Sorath," said Tarkyn, "I would say that it takes a great deal to impress him. So I have two requests; firstly, that you will allow me to heal your arm and secondly, that you and those who accompanied you regale me with the events of your journey to and from Montraya."

Orolan gave a wry smile, "Thank you for your offer my lord, but we have our own healer and he tells me the tendon is cut right through and cannot be repaired. As to the second, we would be honoured."

Tarkyn put up his hand, "Not so fast. Fetch your healer. Then find a quiet place for us to work. Only once your arm is whole, will I be ready to hear your tale."

The bandit chief looked sceptical but nevertheless tweaked a finger that sent one of his cronies running. "This way, Sire." He ushered Tarkyn and Danton towards a well-worn tent. "Welcome to my humble abode."

As they entered the tent, a woman dressed in an embroidered blouse, plain woollen skirt and incongruously heavy boots, ducked away from the door way and bobbed a nervous curtsy. Her long red hair was caught up in a clip that was not succeeding in containing it.

"Lissann, His Highness, Prince Tarkyn, and Lord Danton. Prince Tarkyn, Lord Danton, my wife." As introductions went, it was not the most polished Tarkyn had heard, but there was no ill intent in it. Before he could respond, Oralan hooked his left thumb over his shoulder towards the exit. "Sorry darling. Need some quiet. We'll see you after. All right?"

Lissann nodded, dropped another quick curtsy and sidled outside.

The prince frowned, "Is she scared of you or me?" His eyebrows went up, "I hope you don't misuse her."

A look of plain surprise was replaced by an angry scowl, "Yes. Well, what would you expect of a bloody outlaw?"

Tarkyn's mouth tightened at Orolan's tone before his natural sense of justice asserted itself, "I beg your pardon. That was unworthy of either of us." He gave a small grin, "In that case, it is I who am to blame for her nervousness."

Orolan snorted, "O'course it is. Even if you weren't a prince, you're a pretty imposing figure in this little tent."

He looked past the prince at Keepsafe Stonemaster, his scruffy little wizard, who had entered the tent. The newcomer looked decidedly nervous. "Your Highness, I believe you are wishing to repair Orolan's arm but believe me, I have done all I can. It is not the bone that is broken, it is the tendon. He may regain a little use of it but certainly not all movements. Truly, I have done the best I could."

Tarkyn smiled reassuringly at him, "I'm sure you have. After all, he seems to be worth preserving. Perhaps if we sit down, I can explain. Orolan, sit next to me." When they had arranged themselves, he continued, "I am a forest guardian and have the power to heal Orolan's injuries but I need your knowledge. What am I looking for?"

"What? What do you mean?... Sire."

Patiently Tarkyn explained, "I can go inside Orolan's arm, at least my life force can..."

Keepsafe glanced at the prince, clearly resisting the urge to doubt him. He cleared his throat. "It should be straight forward enough. The blade has cut through muscle, sinew and tendons. I have brought the skin together but the likelihood of sinews and tendons rejoining well enough to repair properly is very slim. If you really can go in as you say, then align everything on either side of the gash and join the respective ends."

Although they kept poker faces, Keepsafe met Orolan's eyes in shared disbelief. Seeing this, Tarkyn and Danton met each other's in shared knowledge and smiled.

Tarkyn placed his hand on Orolan's shoulder. "Ready Orolan? Close your eyes and relax as well as you can."

Tarkyn took a deep breath, drew down into himself and brought forth his *esse*. He let himself flow down into Orolan's arm, into and around the gash. Already infection was taking hold and some of the flesh was turning putrid. He decided that he needed to clear that out first before attempting any repairs. He became aware of himself outside, enough to enunciate, "This will hurt... but must be done." Tarkyn sent a harsh wave of anger through Orolan, destroying the infection with a wave of searing heat. In the distance he heard Orolan cry out.

Tarkyn turned his attention to the two sides of the gash. Beginning at one end, he carefully aligned like with like, weaving the ends together with his *esse*. Slowly he made his way along the length of the gash until the two sides were completely rejoined. He gave a last wave of life force and travelled back up Orolan's arm and into his own body.

Tarkyn opened his eyes to find the four of them within Danton's shield. He raised his eyebrows in query.

Danton smiled, "Orolan's cry aroused a certain degree of consternation among his followers. No one has threatened you, Sire, but I think you will find a gathering of people outside the tent. So I thought I should take precautions."

"Open your eyes, Orolan," instructed the prince. "Now, gently try to move your arm. Keepsafe, you check his range of movement."

Orolan slowly bent his arm then flexed his bicep. He opened and closed his fist a few times, straightened his arm then brought it back up again. Slowly a grin spread over his face. "Sire, I don't know how to thank you. I thought I would spend the rest of my life a cripple."

Tarkyn smiled, enjoying the little wizard's expression of astonishment even as he addressed Orolan, "You do not need to thank me. I would much prefer that you did not have long lasting ill-effects from serving me so well." He paused, "Danton, would you please take Keepsafe outside. We will join you in a minute."

Once they were alone, Tarkyn said quietly, "Orolan, when I heal someone, I come to know more of them and they of me. Forgive me if I speak plainly but it will, I think, further our relationship. You have a swaggering bravado that is sometimes off-putting and your view of the world is tainted by bitterness. But beneath that, you have a passionate loyalty to your people and to me that pushes you to acts of great courage."

He smiled. "Although we do not agree on all things, I acknowledge that in your own way, your sense of honour is as strong as mine."

Orolan swallowed, "Thank you Sire." He sniffed. "Thank you very much."

Grinning, Tarkyn clapped him bracingly on his back, "And now, if you are over the shock of being whole again, perhaps we should rejoin your comrades to hear the heroic tale of your journey to Montraya."

CHAPTER 42

Tarkyn and Danton returned to the firesite in time to join Waterstone and Rainstorm's small expedition that they had organised to do some target practice, mainly in an effort to get to know Harkell's family.

The group followed a narrow path that wound its way up through tumbled granite boulders to the top of a small rise. An egret stalked around the shallows of a pool that had formed in a depression of a large piece of granite. Enough silt had gathered over the years for reeds to grow around one edge of it.

Harkell and Kayama, arm in arm, stopped to watch it.

"I can't imagine there is anything for her to catch in that little puddle," said Tarkyn dryly, from further up the track.

Almost on cue, the egret stabbed down with its long beak and caught a little silver fish.

Tarkyn gave a wry smile as Waterstone laughed at him. "Wrong again. I don't think I will ever learn enough about these forests to hold my own with you people."

Suddenly Kayama jumped in fright as Falling Rain appeared out of nowhere, grinning at Tarkyn. "You know more about the forests in other ways than we ever will. So, I wouldn't worry about it, if I were you." He turned to Kayama, "I wanted to say hello to you personally because I feel I already know you. I am Falling Rain."

"Yes. So too do I." Tarkyn smiled as Kayama looked uncertainly from one to the other. "Falling Rain and I guided that egret to visit you in Montraya. She delivered the note telling you that Harkell was safe. Do you remember?"

Kayama's eyes grew round, "Did you do that, *personally*, for Harkell, Sire?"

"Falling Rain and I did it together. And we could see you through Elsie's eyes."

Kayama blushed, "Oh no! And there I was in all my dirt doing the washing."

"Harkell," said Tarkyn with mock severity, "Kayama is just as bad as you at taking the wind out of one's sails. Here I am, expecting thanks and all I get is horror that we saw her looking unkempt."

"Oh *no*, Sire," stammered poor Kayama, now completely embarrassed. "I did not mean to be ungrateful…" She stopped when she realised that everyone was laughing at her. For a moment it looked as though she might take umbrage but then slowly her face relaxed into a broad grin. When the laughter subsided, she said calmly, "I was grateful, you know. It meant a lot to me to know Harkell was safe."

"We know," said Tarkyn mischievously. "We watched your reaction."

As they set a series of small rocks along a fallen tree, a thought occurred to Harkell and he chuckled to himself. In response to Waterstone's look of enquiry, he replied, "Now I understand the exchanged looks I caught passing between you people over the last few days. You were plotting the surprise, weren't you?"

"More or less." Waterstone grinned as he passed Sparrow a piece of granite to add to the end of the row, "Some of us were dying to tell you and release you from your sense of doom, but *His Highness* over there wouldn't allow us to."

Tarkyn smiled at Harkell, "No. I didn't want your hopes raised until I was sure your family had made it safely past Jarand's troops. And I was hoping desperately that they would arrive before the time you had stipulated for your departure."

"Is that what it was? You've been so edgy over the last few days." Harkell gave a short laugh, "And there I was, thinking that you didn't want me to be a party to anything that I might subsequently betray to your brother."

Tarkyn was shocked, "No! That didn't even cross my mind."

Harkell laughed, "I remember saying to you that your faith in me would mean more if you were better at intrigue…"

An indrawn breath from his scandalised wife interrupted him. "Harkell! You didn't!"

The soldier chuckled, "Yes. I'm afraid I did. But now I would say that, despite his naivete, Tarkyn's faith in me is beyond price."

His wife's eyebrows puckered in bewilderment.

Harkell gave his warm gentle smile, "Because then it was based on blind reliance on an oath and now it is based on his knowledge of me."

Chapter 43

The advent of Harkell's family was not untrammelled joy. They were town bred people, unused to outdoor living and overnight they had lost their homes, their livelihood and the way of life they had followed for generations. None of them was well travelled, so their knowledge and experience of different customs, attitudes and loyalties was very limited. With the exception of Harkell's children, family members were overawed by both Lord Danton and Prince Tarkyn, tending to avoid them or to become gruff or tongue tied when they were nearby. Except for Kayama who had unquestioning faith in her husband, the adults in the family were concerned to find Harkell hiding in the woods with the Renegade Prince, a motley crew of sorcerers and strange wood dwellers and worse still, in contact with a band of thieves.

At the earliest opportunity, Harkell's father and brother drew him aside. Harkell, aware of their intentions, took them out of sight and hearing of the lookouts to a quiet place beneath a weeping willow, where they could sit in privacy on the bank of a gently burbling stream.

"Come on," said Harkell. "Ask your questions and I will do my best to answer them. I have nothing to hide from you."

"Then why did you stop Lord Danton from speaking earlier?" demanded his father. "I'm not stupid, you know. I saw the look you sent him."

"Dad, I was not hiding anything from you. I just didn't want it spoken of in front of my children… It might be better if I show you." Harkell pulled his shirt over his head and turned so that they could see the striping and scarring on his back, where the belts and brass buckles had bitten into his flesh. Harkell could hear the sharp intakes of breath behind him as he pulled his shirt back on and turned around to face them.

Sorath's face was thunderous, "Who did this to you?"

"Prince Jarand ordered me to be flogged by my own men in front of my own company of soldiers."

"Why?"

 "Because Tarkyn had gained the advantage of us while I was the commanding officer." Harkell raised his eyebrows, "Perhaps you have heard of this incident?"

Sorath and Drakell nodded numbly. Drakell answered for both of them, "We had heard that Prince Tarkyn evaded capture by immobilising Prince Jarand's force but we did not know what had happened to you. You simply disappeared… There were rumours that you had died in the melee but then Kayama told us that she had received a message that you were safe."

Sorath frowned, "But why did you not return with your troops? Why didn't you come home to us? We would have accepted you back, no matter what you had done or failed to do."

Harkell gave him a warm smile, "I know you would have, Dad." His smile faded, and his voice became flat with anger, "But Prince Jarand left me behind when he returned. He left me unconscious, hanging by my tied hands from a tree on an isolated stretch of road. Had it not been for Tarkyn, Danton and these woodfolk, I would have died hanging there." He took a deep breath, "Tarkyn took it upon himself to heal the captain of his enemy's guard. Do you wonder that I hold him in high esteem?"

Sorath grunted, "Hmph. But did he then force you to serve him?"

Harkell shook his head emphatically. "No Dad. He gave me the choice. But he did say that if I wanted to stay with him, I must swear fealty to him."

"That seems like no choice at all if you were too injured to leave."

Harkell heaved a sigh, "You seem determined to think poorly of him. Prince Tarkyn had already healed me before he gave me that choice."

"Son, I cannot be happy about you associating with bandits. Does the prince condone it or is he actually a party to innocent people being victimised?"

"Neither. A few months ago, these bandits captured Prince Tarkyn and thought they would turn him in for the ransom. He warned them that he had people nearby but they persisted in their intention. By rights, when we turned the tables on them, the prince should have had the bandit leader, Orolan, executed. Instead, Tarkyn inflicted a small brand on his side. Because his life and the lives of his bandits were spared, Orolan gave Tarkyn his oath. As their new liege lord, Tarkyn swore to protect them but not from the consequences of their misdeeds." Harkell grimaced, "We come across them very rarely. In fact, I think Tarkyn has only called upon them twice. Tarkyn strives to make his brothers address the issue of lawlessness but he cannot force these bandits to stop until there is another way for them to survive. They are displaced people who have had their livelihoods destroyed and Tarkyn does not have the means to rescue every vagabond or outlaw."

Sorath grunted again, He seemed to do a lot of grunting when he was displeased. "We too have had our livelihood destroyed. Does he expect us to take to the high road to survive?"

"*No* Dad. Those bandits know nothing of the woodfolk and are not welcome to travel with us. You, my family, on the other hand, have been granted a very rare privilege." Harkell twirled a sprig of willow in his hands and watched it as he talked, "Dad, removing all of you from Prince

Jarand's sphere of influence has probably saved my life. And more than that, it has saved me from being a slave to Jarand's whims and cruelty. Jarand gave me orders that would have entrapped Tarkyn. I could not be a party to that….and he was about to find out that I had not followed his orders." Harkell looked up and met his father's eyes. "And Jarand had made it very clear to me that my family's safety would be forfeit if I failed to return to him. Dad, I could die for my principles... but how could I let my family die for them? Only Tarkyn's intercession has saved me from returning to face Jarand's retribution."

His voice died away and left a thoughtful silence in its wake.

After a while Harkell continued, "Dad, Jarand left me to die. I would not otherwise have relinquished my oath to him."

"Very well, I accept your reason for changing your allegiance. But why to this Renegade Prince?" asked Sorath.

"Please don't call him that. He does not deserve it." Harkell gave a slight smile to take any sting out of his words. "At the beginning, I took a gamble, I will admit, based on rumours I had heard of his growing popularity but more than this, on the quality of Tarkyn himself."

Drakell studied his brother, "Harkell, you have always been a sharp judge of men. So I gather your gamble paid off?"

"Yes, it did. More than I could have imagined. Tarkyn has a greatness about him that belittles his brothers. Of the three royal brothers, only Tarkyn has Eskuzor's interests at heart. The longer I know him, the more dedicated I am to his cause."

"But what of your ambitions to become a colonel or even a general?" asked Drakell. "You worked for so long to get this far. What are your chances of promotion with someone who doesn't know your past achievements?"

"I have effectively been promoted to the highest rank below royalty. All my views are sought and considered by His Highness." His father looked most impressed until Harkell grinned and added, "So too are the views of everyone you have met." Seeing his father's face settle into an expression of displeasure, Harkell became serious again, "But nevertheless, my opinion and my contribution is acknowledged and treated with respect. Not only that, but Prince Tarkyn is committed to his obligations as liege lord in a way that neither of his brothers is... Do you know what he said to me when I gave him my oath? He said that if he ever treated me as Jarand had, my oath to him would no longer bind me." He waved his hand at the other two, "And now, he has worked with the woodfolk to rescue me from Jarand's clutches by removing you beyond the reach of his revenge. You do not yet understand the enormity of woodfolk accepting sorcerers among them."

Sorath gave another of his grunts, "Well son, I will watch and try to keep an open mind. You have had hare-brained schemes in the past, which we all scoffed at… but then look what happened. You worked your way up through the ranks." He thumped his hand down on Harkell's knee. "I know there were times when you struggled and when your fellow officers set traps for you and tried to take you down. And sometimes you would come home looking haggard with care. But you kept at it, long after another would have fallen by the wayside." He stood up, the interrogation clearly at a close for the time being, "Still, saying that, son, your way has not been my way. I have always been content to follow the family trade and hold to the old traditions. So I won't be rushing into anything."

Harkell and Drakell's eyes met behind their father in common understanding.

"No, Dad, I wouldn't want you to. Just take your time and think about it."

Chapter 44

Rena had found a quiet place in a corner of the clearing to play with the three children of Harkell's extended family. Since she had come to live with her sister and brother-in-law, Elena had often left Rena to take care of Jake while she went off on business or pleasure with her husband. Rena did not mind. She needed something to fill the void left in her life.

In the few days that she had been in Tarkyn's camp, she had flinched away if any of the woodmen had brushed past her, and her waspish refusals had virtually stemmed the flow of invitations to take part in any woodfolk activities.

She looked up as two of the woodchildren walked over to stand a few yards away, watching the children's game. Rena recognised them as part of the prince's family but, remembering Tarkyn's stricture, resisted the urge to stand and bow to them. Instead she gave a slight smile and asked whether they would like to join in.

Sparrow tapped Midnight on the arm and translated Rena's offer into gestures. "He's deaf, you know," she said. She frowned forbiddingly at the little children, "But no one is allowed to tease him. He is quite fun to play with when you get to know him." She transferred her attention to their game. "Oh. Are you building a sorcerer's village? You can show us how to build an inn. I am Sparrow and this is Midnight, in case you forgot."

With the acceptance born of extreme youth, the sorcerer children moved over and began to discuss with the woodchildren whether leaves or bark would make better roofs for an inn.

But when Waterstone came over to sit on the other side of their game, Rena could not conjure up the same careless unconcern. Naturally shy, she felt nervous of a man from a culture so different from her own. Worse still, he too was related to the prince. She watched him covertly, taking in his strange green eyes and the light brown hair and skin that seemed to fade into the background if she looked away. She noted with some misgiving the firm line of his jaw, but took comfort in the laughter lines that creased the corners of his eyes.

Waterstone took no notice of her, keeping his eyes firmly fixed on the children's game with a single mindedness that those who knew him would have found unusual. After a few minutes, he leant forward to admire their little houses and to offer a few architectural suggestions to Sparrow. Rena thought that Sparrow's eyes went out of focus, just before the little girl turned to her and asked, "Excuse me Rena, are there any other buildings in sorcerer villages? I've only ever seen one from the edge of the woods, you see."

When Rena suggested a village green and a community hall, Sparrow asked whether they were made of the same materials as the houses. Sometime later, when the merits of pebbles or sticks to build the bigger buildings and whether there was likely to be a castle had been discussed at length, Waterstone finally withdrew his attention from the children's game and spoke directly to Rena, "Do you come from a little village like this?"

"No, not any more. I was born in a small village but Elena and I moved to Montraya when…" She waved her hand, "…when marauders came through and burnt it all."

Waterstone's eyes widened. "When was this? How old were you?" he asked quietly.

"Five years ago." She glanced at him then looked past the children into the trees.

"I beg your pardon. I didn't mean to force you to face memories that you may wish to forget."

"My husband was killed in that raid… and my two year old son," she said in a low voice, still staring fixedly into the trees.

"I cannot begin to imagine how bad that must feel."

Rena surprised Waterstone by turning to him and saying softly, "Yes, I think you can. You too have suffered loss, haven't you?"

Waterstone was taken aback, "Do you say that because I am looking after the children? It is our way for men and women to share that task."

"No, nor from the lack of Sparrow's mother being introduced when we arrived. She could, after all, have been elsewhere." Rena smiled, "It radiates from you."

Waterstone frowned and ran his hand through his hair, "Well, I hope I don't go around looking hangdog. I can't say I'm too pleased to find out that it's so obvious."

Rena laughed, "It's not obvious. You hide it well and it is not all that you are. I just have a feeling for these things."

"Bloody sorcerers and their magic," he growled. He glanced sideways at her, "Sorry. I shouldn't have said that when you're so new."

"Don't tar all sorcerers with the same brush. It doesn't make me very popular among sorcerers either." She stood up and brushed down her skirts. "So, having alienated the first woodman I've actually had a conversation with, I might head off and see what my sister is doing."

"No. Don't go." Waterstone reached up and grasped her arm.

In a flash, she span around, blue eyes blazing, and slapped his hand away as she dragged her arm out of his grasp, "Don't touch me." She lifted her skirts and fled into the trees.

"Oh dear," said Waterstone to himself, not for a moment thinking of himself as intimidating, "I think I know what else happened in that raid. How on earth am I going to fix this?"

He sent out a widespread mental cry of alarm, showing what had happened without going into detail. *I don't know where she's going but don't let her get too far.*

An image came back from Tarkyn that if she threatened to pass the area covered by the lookouts that she was to be knocked out and brought back. Waterstone sighed, thinking that now was not the time for Tarkyn to become peremptory.

As it turned out, Summer Rain slipped down from her lookout post in a sycamore straight into Rena's flight path and stopped the runaway in her tracks. Rena looked around wildly seeking a path of escape but the older woodwoman spoke to her calmly and firmly, "Now stay still and think, Rena. I will not hurt you. No one means you harm. You can't leave and run off into the forest. You wouldn't be safe on your own and where would you go? You don't have to come near any of us, if you are afraid of us. Just turn around and walk quietly back to your sister. We will bring her to meet you."

Summer Rain's voice washed gently over the panic-stricken sorcerer, gradually bringing her to her senses. Rena brushed her hand over her eyes, dragging in shuddering breaths as she fought to regain control of herself. She collapsed into a heap on the ground, her skirts billowing around her and, sitting with her hands over her face, mumbled, "I'm sorry. I'm sorry," over and over again.

The woodwoman sat beside her but not touching, and inevitably produced one of her tonics from the satchel she had slung across her shoulders. "Rena, if you are willing, it may help you to steady yourself if you take this. I am a healer among woodfolk. My name is Summer Rain."

Rena sniffed and raised her head. Her eyes were red-rimmed, "I am not afraid of you. A little nervous perhaps, but not afraid. If you think your tonic will help, I would be grateful for it."

Summer Rain handed her a small phial containing a lavender coloured liquid, which she sipped tentatively. Her face screwed up at the taste but, taking a deep breath, she downed the rest of it in one draught. Her whole body gave a convulsive shudder but she made no comment, not wishing to disparage the woodfolk further than she already had. She merely thanked Summer Rain as she handed back the empty phial. The woodwoman kept talking to her quietly until the tonic began to take effect and Rena could feel her breathing becoming deeper and slower as her whole body gradually relaxed.

When she was ready, Summer Rain walked with her to her sister who was waiting for her just outside the clearing. Waterstone was nowhere to be seen but the children were once more playing with their little make-believe village under the tree, now with Creaking Bough watching them. Partly from reaction and partly as a result of the tonic, Rena soon fell asleep and did not wake until a shaft of gold from the setting sun broke through the branches above to shine directly on her face.

Shortly afterwards, Ancient Oak approached her. He stood a little distance away and said formally, "My brother wishes you to know that he had no intention of hurting you and is sorry that he inadvertently frightened you."

Rena flushed with embarrassment, "No, the fault was mine. I overreacted. I do hope he can forgive me."

"I will convey your words to him." Quite unsmilingly, Ancient Oak turned and left.

As the evening wore on, it became increasingly obvious that no woodman was coming anywhere near Rena. In fact, every male beyond Harkell's family kept to the other side of the firesite and Waterstone still did not put in an appearance. Eventually, Harkell went in search of him.

"He's on lookout duty," said Ancient Oak briefly in response to a direct query.

"Where?" asked Harkell.

Ancient Oak stared at him. "In the large beech tree about two hundred yards to our left," he said at last.

Harkell did not wait for the shift to end in expectation of seeing Waterstone. He knew one shift had changed already since he last saw the woodman. He walked to the bottom of the beech tree in question and looked up into its dark branches.

"Waterstone?" he called quietly.

A resigned sigh drifted down from above and the next instant Harkell found Waterstone standing beside him.

"What about your lookout duty?" asked Harkell, always a soldier at heart. "You can't just leave this side unguarded."

Waterstone crossed his arms, "Have you come here to criticise or do you have something to say?" Before Harkell could answer, he added, "Autumn Leaves is up there. It's actually his shift, not mine. I was just keeping him company."

"Hi Harkell," came a voice from above.

"Hello Autumn Leaves," replied Harkell dryly before saying to Waterstone, "Now come on. What is going on? Why are you shunning the firesite?"

"Because…Because… Harkell, in all my thirty five years, no one has ever been afraid of me. I can be as deadly as the next man if I need to be, but I have never frightened anyone before and I have no intention of doing so again."

"But it's not your fault…" protested Harkell.

"Of course it's not my fault. Haven't I just finished saying that I've never frightened anyone in my life? But that doesn't stop her being fearful." Waterstone shrugged, "Hopefully, she will settle down soon and stop seeing us as strange, uncertain foreigners. Then I might come back and join you."

"That is very generous of you, Waterstone."

The woodman gave a wry smile. "Partly. And partly, I don't want to risk being accused of something I haven't done sometime in the future. She was frighteningly fast to jump to conclusions."

"You are safe enough, Waterstone. The firesite is full of witnesses… and you can sit on the other side just as all the other men are."

Waterstone gave a whimsical smile, "Oh dear. Are they? I suppose they too want to avoid future accusations… or frightening her."

"And Ancient Oak is clearly championing your cause. He was very formal in his delivery of your apology and is barely speaking to me."

Waterstone chuckled, "Ancient Oak has very strong family loyalties. He always has had."

"Hmm. So I've noticed. I remember him standing up to all of you in defence of Tarkyn in the Lost Forest."

"He doesn't think I should have apologised. He thinks that Rena cast a slur on my character."

"Well, if *he* thinks that, I hate to imagine how Tarkyn is reacting."

Waterstone rolled his eyes, "Oh stars! I hope he doesn't come over all royal about it."

"He was sitting quietly at the firesite when I left."

Just as Waterstone was breathing a sigh of relief, a mindmessage came through that Tarkyn had withdrawn and had sent a message via Lapping Water that Rena was to attend him.

"Oh no. Not again," exclaimed Waterstone. "You have no idea what a hideous trial we went through when Danton hit me. That's why I gave you permission to hit me when we first met… But I haven't given permission to your family because… well, because they haven't committed themselves yet and to be honest, I forgot. I'm not really in tune with all this royalty stuff and I forget about it."

"But Tarkyn doesn't."

"No, and if he has asked Rena to 'attend him', he is being formal." Waterstone slapped Harkell on the back, "Come on. We'd better go and see what we can do to protect her."

They skirted around the clearing beyond the firelight, Harkell depending on the woodman's keener night vision to find a safe path. A faint glow in the trees led them to the place where Tarkyn stood, his eagle once more riding his shoulder, a soft globe of light resting in the palm of his outstretched hand.

The prince glanced at their set faces and said "Unless I miss my mark, you two have come, set on remonstrating with me. But what I have to say will be between Rena and me, when she arrives, and will not require the presence of either of you."

Waterstone stood his ground, "But Tarkyn, she didn't attack me. She just hit my hand away in fright. Don't put her through what Danton went through. She's frightened enough without having to stand trial for laying hands on me."

"Your care for her is touching, Waterstone, but your faith in me, less so. Now, I would like you both to leave." When they hesitated, Tarkyn raised his eyebrows. "I believe I have made my wishes clear."

"Blast you, Tarkyn! You can be so *annoying* sometimes," spluttered the woodman, incensed at having to obey him. Seeing that Tarkyn had no intention of relenting, he growled, "Very well, I will leave, but *please*, do not uphold my honour as your brother at the cost of distressing me. Please don't be unkind to her." Having done all he could without betraying his oath, he strode off into the darkness.

For his part, Harkell gave a formal bow then, letting out a breath, gave Tarkyn a nod of faith before turning on his heel to follow Waterstone.

They were barely out of sight when the sound of careful footsteps over uneven ground heralded Rena's arrival. As she stepped into the corona of light, she sank down onto one knee, hand on heart and head bowed. After a notable pause, Tarkyn allowed her to rise.

When she stood before him, he asked, "Do you fear me? Your fear radiates outward like eddies in a pool."

Rena clasped her hands tightly before and whispered, "I am always afraid. I do not fear you more than any other, my lord."

"And yet, alone of all these people, no one could gainsay me if I chose to misuse you."

"I have not heard that you abuse your position or your power." Rena's voice was tight but she had herself well in hand. She glanced up at the huge raptor squatted on his shoulder, "And it takes a special person to befriend an eagle." After a moment's thought, she added, "Besides, Harkell would not abandon his inherited allegiance to give his pledge to a dishonourable lord."

Tarkyn turned and signalled for her to fall in beside him. As they walked within the corona of light through the darkness of the trees, he sent her waves of reassurance at a variance with his words, "Your actions embarrassed my brother. By rights, I should punish you for offering violence to a member of the royal family... Are you aware of that?"

"Yes...No...I'm not sure. Your family is a little confusing, Your Highness." Rena took a breath to steady herself, "But whatever Waterstone's status, I am sorry that I took his gesture of friendship amiss."

The trees provided a dark canopy overhead, with lower branches showing up pale in Tarkyn's magical light. A large white owl swooped across their path, hooting as it passed.

As Rena jumped in fright, Tarkyn laughed quietly, "No need to fear owls. They don't attack people. Besides, he is just letting me know that I am being watched." The eagle squawked softly in response then ruffled her feathers and nudged Tarkyn's head with its beak.

"Why?"

"Because I am Guardian of their Forest. All the raptors are in league to protect me." He glanced down at her, "Are you all right, walking out here in the darkness? I realise you aren't used to it."

Rena wrapped her shawl around herself and nodded. "It's a bit spooky but," she gave a little smile, "I've just realised that I feel safe with you beside me." She threw him an anxious glance, "I hope I am not being too familiar, my lord."

"No. I asked the question, after all." Tarkyn walked on for a minute before saying, "Let me tell you about Waterstone... When I first arrived in the forest, the woodfolk hated me for having dominion over them when they had never before been subject to anyone's authority. Shortly after my arrival, I was captured by bounty hunters and was grievously injured during my escape. Waterstone spent hours and days at my bedside nursing me back to health, the only woodman who stood firm to his belief in the equality of all people." Tarkyn stroked his eagle, "He is a man of strong principles and great kindness."

"Then I am even sorrier that I offended him."

"All the woodfolk of my home guard are completely trustworthy."

Rena shook her head, "I can believe you with my head, my lord, but my heart still makes me afraid."

"And yet, I cannot allow your fears to control the behaviour of my home guard. So you and I have some work to do." Tarkyn scratched his eagle on her throat then stroked her side. He smiled as she gave a comfortable little squawk. "This eagle was badly injured a few days ago by an arrow shot by King Kosar's soldiers. I healed her." He looked down on the gaunt woman whose whole angular body telegraphed tension. "If you wish to remain with us, I need to heal you too."

Rena thought of saying that her wound was not physical but she realised that the prince knew that. "Do I have a choice?"

"You always have a choice."

Suddenly Rena switched and her anger spewed forth before she could stop it. "Not true!" she spat out. "You do not always have a choice. Do you think I chose what those men did to me?"

The eagle flapped her wings threateningly as Tarkyn stilled, clearly offended by her outburst. He said coldly, "Whatever your past or your excuse, you will not speak to me in that tone."

Rena glared at him and drew a deep breath to rein in her temper before muttering a reluctant apology.

The prince gave a curt nod of acknowledgement and continued courteously as though the interchange had not occurred. "You are right, of course. You do not always have a choice. I had no choice in becoming the woodfolks' liege lord and there are times when I give the woodfolk no choice… But I am giving you the choice in this."

Rena wrapped her arms around herself, and said sullenly, "It's not much of a choice. Either I must submit to you to lose the very reactions that keep me safe, or I lose everyone I know. Either way I become even more exposed to danger."

A mossy log beneath an overhanging oak came into view on the left hand side of the path.

"Sit down, Rena," said Tarkyn. "*Sit down*," he repeated more firmly as she hesitated. He sat down beside her and said, "You are a difficult woman. Nothing comes easily to you, does it?"

She shook her hair away from her face and looked at him, "No. Sometimes I tell people things they don't want to hear and sometimes I delve too deeply too fast. I upset Waterstone, asking about his loss."

Tarkyn gave a grunt of laughter, "So I heard. And in return he grumped about sorcerers and their magic. Don't take it personally. Woodfolk find sorcerer magic very inconvenient at times, especially shields… and especially since they are vowed to protect me."

Rena sighed, "I'm afraid I did take it personally. Sorcerers often react badly to me too, you see. Besides, it doesn't take much to make me lose my temper."

"So I've noticed." After a pause, he asked, "Are you happy?"

Tears sprang to Rena's eyes. She sniffed, "No." Tarkyn waited until she continued, "No, I miss Dorstan and Durik terribly. And I am frightened all the time, scared that someone will attack me. And I snap people's heads off so often that the only true friend who can put up with me is my sister. Even her husband gives me a wide berth." She sniffed and gave a bitter laugh, "I don't blame him, really."

"Rena, are you aware that each woodwoman is as deadly and as well defended as the woodmen?"

Rena made a disparaging moue. "*None* of the woodfolk look particularly strong."

Tarkyn raised his eyebrows, "Have you heard nothing of my encounters with my brothers?"

Rena frowned, "Yes, but …everyone says you have a well-trained band of sorcerers."

"What? Danton, Stormaway, Boravar, Harkell and the trappers?"

Rena frowned even harder, "But you must have more. What about the bandits who brought us here?"

Tarkyn laughed, "No. I made an exception when I asked them to bring you and the rest of Harkell's family here but generally, I have as little to do with them as possible. We do not share the same moral code. No, there are only six sorcerers and myself. It was largely the woodfolk, men and women, who achieved such impressive victories." He smiled as he watched Rena compute this new information. "We cannot disabuse people of the impression that my elite warriors are sorcerers. We are sworn to secrecy, just as you are."

Rena thought back to Summer Rain landing in front of her, "Was Summer Rain on guard duty?"

"Yes, and even though she is a healer, she is deadly with knife, bow and arrow, and slingshot." Tarkyn looked at Rena, "The woodwomen are better defended than you, despite your constant fear and aggression. They could teach you."

"But would this training guarantee my future safety?"

"Nothing can guarantee that, including your present behaviour. But it would make a difference."

Rena sighed and smiled, "You are very patient, you know. You could simply have demanded my response to your ultimatum."

"Except that, despite your touchiness, I do not actually want you to leave."

"Oh!" Even in the soft light of Tarkyn's orb, Rena's blush was obvious.

Tarkyn grinned, "You are not that bad!.. Let me tell you about my little friend." He sent a short image and a moment later, the bushes behind

Tarkyn rustled as Midnight came into sight. Showing not a whit of surprise, Tarkyn said casually, "Unless he is asleep or has been specifically requested to stay with someone else, Midnight never lets me out of his sight." He smiled as he patted his knee and the little boy hopped onto his lap. "Do you, Mischief?"

Midnight beamed up at him and snuggled in against his chest. As Tarkyn tightened his arm around him, Midnight looked directly into Rena's face.

Rena turned pale. "Oh, the poor little boy," she breathed. "I have never felt such a deep well of self-loathing and loneliness and rejection in anyone's past before. He didn't look at me when he was playing near me earlier on. What happened to him?"

"His father cursed his mother and her people to hate Midnight, with a passion that would gradually destroy them all. There is more besides, but that will do for the moment." Tarkyn looked down at his little charge. "The curse is broken now but the scars are still healing. As soon as he thinks he has done something wrong, he tries to bolt. His mother used to beat him, you see. He was reviled by all but String and Bean who visited him briefly every couple of months. If not for them, he may have been irredeemable."

"So you have not taken away all his feelings of hurt? I thought you could heal that sort of pain."

"Anyone who knows Midnight will be able to tell you that he is a lot better than he was. I destroyed the curse and I bring him back every time he runs, or stop him from running in the first place if I'm quick enough. And I ease his fears and his sadness and his anger but I would not stop him from being who he is. His tribulations have made him into an amazingly strong, resourceful little individual." Tarkyn and Midnight smiled at each other. "So pesky, aren't you, Mischief?"

"So, you would not change who I am?"

"No, I like who you are. You just need to calm down a little. Your fears and your memories are a part of you, just as mine are a part of me."

Rena nodded, "You fear betrayal, don't you? But less than you did, I think."

"That, too, was Waterstone's doing. He worked hard to achieve that."

Rena gave a little smile, "All right. You've convinced me. What do we do?"

Tarkyn grinned, "After all this, very little. I place my hand on your shoulder, and direct power into you to take the sting out of the memories. You will still remember them and they will still hurt, but not so badly that you lose control."

Chapter 45

As time passed and Rena still did not return, Harkell's family became increasingly concerned. Harkell placed his faith in Tarkyn and did his best to allay their fears but he was not helped by Waterstone's obvious anxiety.

Eventually Sorath taxed the woodman, "Why are you so worried?" He frowned fiercely. "If Prince Tarkyn forces himself on my kin, we'll go after him, prince or no prince."

This idea was so preposterous that it surprised a smile out of Waterstone, "Oh no. Tarkyn would never behave like that."

The woodman's casual dismissal of his fear placated Sorath but when another half hour passed, he approached Waterstone again. "But you are worried, aren't you?"

"Yes, but it is Tarkyn's bloody sense of honour that worries me, not the lack of it." He grimaced, "Tarkyn may punish Rena for hitting my hand away. He is quite pedantic about some royal expectations and he insists on Ancient Oak's and my relationship with him being recognised by sorcerers. He accepts that we can't abide the etiquette, but when she hit me, it was as though she had hit a prince of the royal line." He ran his hand through his hair, "I wish he wouldn't think like that, but he does."

"Huh. Serve her right if he punishes her," retorted Sorath trenchantly. "We've had enough of her naggy temper."

"Dad, that's not kind," said Harkell. "She has been through a lot."

His father waved his hand irritably, "I know. I know. But she gets on our nerves with her constant flinching and snapping. Hard to live with, I can tell you. Shouldn't have hit you, whoever you are."

Waterstone frowned, "I do not need the protection of a sorcerer's law."

Sorath couldn't stop himself from giving Waterstone's slight form a quick survey, prompting the woodman to glance wryly at Harkell. But Waterstone had no interest in defending his fighting prowess and merely said, as he sent a mindmessage to his brother, "And we will make sure this doesn't happen again,"

As soon as Ancient Oak presented himself, the two brothers gave Harkell's family, including the absent Rena, permission to lay hands on them.

"That doesn't mean that we want you to attack us," explained Ancient Oak with a glimmer of laughter in his eye, "Just that assaulting us will now bear the same consequences as assaulting anyone else."

"We don't believe in royal protocol," added Waterstone. "We endure it because we must and where we can eschew it, we do."

Drakell raised his eyebrows, "Your prince does not seem too exacting in his requirements of protocol to me."

Harkell laughed, "No. Our woodfolk still do not comprehend the extent of Tarkyn's generosity towards them. The prince does, however, demand respect and at times, obedience."

Waterstone snorted, "Huh. And have you seen him doing any of the chores that the rest of us do?"

Movement on the other side of the firesite diverted their attention.

"Something is happening," said Sorath, his son's father, as his soft brown eyes watched Lapping Water confer with Summer Rain and Thunder Storm before leaving the clearing with a small bundle under her arm.

Not long afterwards, Waterstone and Harkell were also summoned.

Tarkyn was waiting for them, standing not far from the firesite with Midnight on one hip and Lapping Water beside him. The eagle had retired to a nearby tree.

"Since you two were so concerned for Rena's safety, it is only fair that you are the first to know the upshot of my time with her. Would you like to come forward, Rena?"

Rena stepped from behind Tarkyn, her loose blonde hair now neatly braided into one plait down her back and her billowing skirts replaced by light brown leggings and a light brown shirt and tunic, cinched at the waist with a useful corded belt. She looked nervously from one to the other for their reaction.

Waterstone frowned, "Is this punishment, just as you decreed for Danton?"

Tarkyn shook his head, "In Danton's case, it was, but on reflection, if you remember, I rescinded it. But by then he had come to like woodfolk clothing and had realised its practicality. He now wears it by choice…as does Rena."

Rena gave an uncertain smile, "I am going to learn how to defend myself and it will be easier to fight, run and hide in these clothes."

Harkell studied her face, "Are you all right? Something has changed."

Tears sprang to her eyes, "Yes, it has. I am still sad. Nothing will make me forget Dorstan and Durik, but I have let go of the worst anguish… and the worst of the rage." She sniffed, then gave a watery chuckle, "I will still get angry sometimes but with any luck it will be when someone deserves it." She gave an apologetic smile to Waterstone, "Unlike when I was rude to you…"

Waterstone waved his hand dismissively, "I am more upset that I frightened you."

Rena spoke earnestly to Waterstone, "It wasn't you who frightened me. It was the memories. I may still start with fright sometimes, but I think the blind panic has gone." She glanced at Tarkyn, "But I am still nervous. I'm very nervous about going out into that clearing and being different from what everyone expects."

Harkell stepped forward and put his arm around her reassuringly, "I can imagine you might be. Your sister will have a bit to say, for a start. Not to mention all the men in our family who expect to see women in skirts. They have been taken aback by seeing woodwomen in leggings, let alone their own women. I think you have every reason to be nervous, but they will soon get used to it and, if this is what you want, we will be with you every step of the way."

Rena smiled up at him, "Thanks Harkell."

Waterstone gave a wry smile, "And I beg your pardon, Tarkyn, for fearing your intention. I can see you have wrought another of your small miracles."

Tarkyn looked at his woodbrother, a glimmer of a smile in his eyes, "You have no need to apologise. We still have enough differences in our values that your fear was reasonable."

Suddenly Rainstorm swung down out of the oak above them into their midst. "There are soldiers coming. A patrol of king's men. Eight of them. We must go."

Lapping Water turned to Rena. "You will have to come with us. Our plan had been that your family, Boravar and the trappers would stay to face any patrols if they came near, while the rest of us guarded your safety from the surrounding trees…but you can't face sorcerers dressed like that."

"Do you think you could climb a tree?" asked Tarkyn.

Rena's eyes shone with excitement, "Depends on the tree. If the branches start low enough, I could."

"Good," said Lapping Water. "Then follow me."

In the clearing, amidst a flurry of fast but well-ordered activity, the woodfolk reduced the firesite to suit the number of sorcerers who would remain. Danton and Stormaway left the clearing and when out of sight of Harkell's family, levitated into trees, as did Tarkyn.

Tree Wind and Twig Snap briefly explained the role Harkell's family would be expected to play and the protection that would be provided.

"Where's Rena?" demanded Elena.

"She's safe," said Twig Snap. "She is with the others, safely away from here. We'll bring her back as soon as the soldiers have gone. Now, do you understand what you need to do?"

Sorath frowned, "And what would you two young ladies know of such things?" He looked past them at woodfolk moving hurriedly around the firesite, removing all traces of their presence "Where is someone who knows what he's doing?"

Tree Wind's eyes sparked with anger. "You have vowed to protect the knowledge of our presence. And now, the first time you are called upon, you waste time with trivialities. We have no time to pander to your prejudice. I will say only this; we all know as much as each other because, in the face of danger, we keep in constant mind communication."

"I don't like dissembling. I am not practised at it," grumbled Sorath.

Tree Wind shrugged, "Then perhaps before this happens again, we will think of a different ploy. But at the moment, this is the best we can do."

Sorath glared at her, "And what if we decide to tell the truth and betray your presence?"

Tree Wind put her head on one side, "I don't think you would. You are Harkell's father, after all, and he is as honourable as anyone I have ever met….But if you did, the person who betrayed us would die and so would all the poor soldiers who heard him." She gave a ferocious smile, "And for your information, Twig Snap and I would be among the first to fire the arrows. Good luck!"

Before Sorath had time to reply, Tree Wind, Twig Snap and the other woodfolk simply disappeared, leaving Harkell's family open-mouthed in amazement.

Gathering their wits, Harkell's family spread themselves around the fire with the trappers and Boravar amongst them ready to feign surprise as the patrol arrived.

Minutes later, the soldiers entered the clearing and fanned out to place themselves around the perimeter of the clearing but beyond that, they made no threatening moves. A young lieutenant surveyed the collection of sorcerers seated around the fire, who were making no attempt either to flee or to defend themselves.

"Good afternoon, gentlemen…and ladies," he said. "What brings you so far from the main road?"

"We hardly ever use the main roads, sir," said String laconically. "No trapping to be had on a main thoroughfare. Bean and I," he nodded at Bean to indicate who he meant, although this was hardly necessary since they were the only two clad in roughly sewn furs, "have just been to that encampment a few miles from here to sell some furs and to stock up for the next season."

"You're probably from there yourselves, aren't you?" asked Bean.

The lieutenant nodded but did not pursue this line of conversation and turned instead to Harkell's family. "You people do not look like trappers."

"No, we're not," replied Sorath. "We're blacksmiths. Our village was burnt out a while back, so we're on our way to Tormadell to start a new life. We're in no hurry and these kind gentlemen offered to show us a bit of trapping…Thought that might be a handy skill to have. Our supplies aren't limitless and we still have a long way to go."

The lieutenant was not a fool. He raised his eyebrows, "Unusual for trappers to be so sociable."

"You're right, lieutenant," drawled String. "We two usually travel alone. But Sorath and I got chatting one night over a few beers and when I woke the next morning I discovered I'd agreed to show this lot the ropes in exchange for a couple of new daggers and a reel of fine wire."

Sorath chuckled, "Not too good at holding his liquor."

String scowled, "I am usually. I can drink any soldier under the table with mountain whisky."

"Yeah, but you never were any good with beer, String," chimed in Bean helpfully.

The lieutenant frowned as he surveyed them and considered, "Have you seen anyone else in these woods?"

Drakell shook his head, "No. Hope we don't either. I've heard you've had trouble with bandits hereabouts."

"We have." The young officer came to a decision, "Do you mind if we check your bags?"

Sorath grunted, "Of course we *mind*, but we'll let you. No choice, as far as I can see." He shrugged, "Anyway, can't expect you to do a good job if you don't check all possibilities. So, go ahead."

As the soldiers began to riffle through their belongings, Sorath suddenly remembered that there would be one more bag than the number of people. But the woodfolk had been thorough and Rena's bag had been taken to join her in hiding. He let out a little sigh of relief, privately acknowledging the first glimmerings of respect for the woodfolks' prowess.

The soldier's inspection was little more than cursory and when they had finished, the lieutenant nodded to them all, "Thank you for your assistance."

Harkell's mother, Thraya, noticed the officer's eyes straying to their kettle hanging over the fire, "Would you like a cup of tea before you go?"

The lieutenant smiled, "Thank you, I would. But I'm afraid we must get back. Good evening to you all." He turned and his little troop fell in behind him as they headed off through the trees back towards the encampment.

There was a cautious silence as they listened to the sounds of the retreating soldiers gradually fade away. String looked around the shuttered faces of Harkell's family and said heartily, "Right. Anyone for tea?"

Before they could reply, twelve arrows speared in from all sides to land in a perfect circle around the fire, all exactly the same distance from the next. The new sorcerers convulsed in fright and again, as woodfolk appeared all around them, grinning and congratulating them on a job well done.

"What was that all about?" demanded Sorath, justifiably incensed.

Tree Wind chuckled, "Just a small demonstration to show you that you were protected…and for your information, five of those arrows were shot from the bows of woodwomen."

Sorath's eyes narrowed and his lips compressed.

Drakell thumped a big hand down on his shoulder. "Now Dad. Don't go ringing a peal over Tree Wind. Their ways are not your ways, but it doesn't make them wrong, only different." Harkell's brawny brother waited until he felt the old man's muscles relax a little under his hand, "Go on. You must admit their marksmanship is impressive, men's and women's."

"And I pride myself on my cooking," said Autumn Leaves.

"And I sewed the leather patches on Tarkyn's shirt," added Falling Branch with a grin.

"And I," rumbled Thunder Storm, "am considered to be one of our best marksmen," He also grinned, "but I spend a large part of my time minding the children."

"And *I*," said Tarkyn, walking in on the end of all this, "do absolutely nothing at all."

This was met with laughter and protests.

"What he means," explained Rainstorm, "Is that he does nothing he doesn't feel like doing."

"Is that what I mean?" asked Tarkyn, his eyes crinkling in mirth.

Rainstorm thought for a minute, "No, that's not true either. There have been some things you've done that none of us would have wanted to do; facing down that hideous spectre, enduring that vicious infestation to save the forest, facing Falling Rain's revenge to …"

"Yes, thank you Rainstorm," intervened Tarkyn dryly. "I was actually joking…more or less."

As they were talking, Elena's roving eye had spotted Rena standing amongst the woodfolk, almost blending in except for her blonde hair. She took in Rena's garb initially with shock, but then with speculation as she considered its possibilities. When she focused on Rena's face, she knew at once that although Rena appeared nervous and self-conscious, something fundamental had changed. She walked over to her and put her hand on her shoulder.

"Welcome back," said Elena, pulling her sister into a hug.

Rena's face was wet with tears when she finally pulled away. "Thank you. I'm glad to be back." She wiped the back of her hand across her cheek, and smiled at Sorath, Thraya, Drakell and Kayama, "Prince Tarkyn has helped me to recover myself." She glanced at him and smiled, "And I am going to learn how to fight and hide and defend myself."

Sorath looked her up and down and scowled, "It is a man's job to defend their women."

Rena's smile wavered, "But sometimes the man is dead… and no one else is at hand."

"If it makes you feel safer, do it," said Thraya. She sent a firm glance to her husband, "After all, if His Highness, who must have been brought up to expect only the highest standards in dress and manners, can accept women dressed in this unusual style and taking on different roles, I'm sure you should be able to loosen your stiff neck enough to accept it too."

The old man stiffened and bowed to Tarkyn, "I beg your pardon, Your Highness. I did not mean to criticise you."

"Sorath, you are not the first of us to need time to adjust to different ways. The woodfolk are constantly bemused by our customs and Harkell, Danton and I have often been taken aback by the amazing athleticism and deadly fighting power of the woodfolk, but especially by the women's, since that is so different from our own culture." Tarkyn paused. "And you are free to express your views, even if they run counter to mine. My only stipulation is that you respect not only me, but anyone you speak to."

"Thank you Your Highness," Sorath replied, feeling honoured but at the same time gently chastised. He hesitated. "Sire, might I beg the favour of a private audience with you?"

Tarkyn, suspecting that this would be an attempt to form a male alliance, nevertheless nodded graciously. "Certainly." He indicated a winding path leading from the clearing. "Perhaps you would like to accompany me on a walk?"

Waterstone noticed that Tarkyn did not say, as he sometimes did, that he would take his chances. Clearly, he was not yet prepared to let down his guard with Harkell's father. He turned to find Danton and Harkell at his elbow.

Harkell gave a wry smile, "He needn't worry. My father is strong as an ox but not a fighting man. Besides, his knees are probably weak from the honour of speaking privately with a prince."

Waterstone chuckled, "More fool he!"

Harkell and Danton both thought of saying that in the case of Tarkyn, considering it an honour was justified, but on second thoughts decided to hold their peace.

Waterstone was not deceived and gave a short laugh, "What restraint!"

Danton smiled in return, "I thought so."

The three of them were still smiling as Tarkyn and Sorath walked out of sight around the curve in the path.

"I am pleased to have this chance to talk to you, Sorath," said Tarkyn, his tone aloof but courteous. "I believe that Harkell's reinstatement into Jarand's service after such a protracted, unauthorized absence signalled the beginning of Harkell's destruction. I have seen Jarand fixate on particular men before. Over time, he has forced them into situations where, more and more, they have had to compromise their integrity until either their self-respect crumbles or they hold fast to their beliefs at the cost of being executed for disobedience. If the offender himself has absconded, Jarand's wrath has instead fallen on the man's family. I am pleased we took steps to extricate you when we did. Harkell's position had become untenable."

"My poor son. And he would have been *executed*, merely for disobedience?"

"Oh yes. After his abortive attempt to capture me, Jarand effectively executed Harkell for failure, let alone disobedience. Disobedience towards a Tamadil prince has always amounted to treason. This is based on the assumption, now questionable, that a Tamadil prince is the king's representative and liegeman." Tarkyn glanced at Sorath, "When I first came among the woodfolk, the whole forest was placed at risk if anyone disobeyed me. This was a legacy from my father; a sorcerous oath that he had forced upon the woodfolk to ensure their fealty to me."

Sorath looked thoughtful, "I always had the greatest respect for King Markazon. He was just, but ruled with a firm hand. Assuming what you say is true…"

"You may always assume that what I say is true," interrupted Tarkyn with a definite edge to his voice.

"I beg your pardon, my lord," said Sorath stiffly and lapsed into silence.

After a few moments, Tarkyn relented, "I am pleased that you approved of my father. I loved him very dearly and lost him at a young age. In general, the woodfolk do not remember him fondly. He was the first monarch to discover their existence and he forced them to bend to his authority and later, to mine."

"I do not understand the ins and outs of royal inheritance but it seems strange to me that the woodfolk's fealty should not have been passed down to the future king."

"I agree. Most strange. Stormaway tells me that my brothers' conflict was foreseen and my father wished to protect me from it. And apparently, he and Stormaway saw me as the key to Eskuzor's future."

Sorath looked at him speculatively, "So, did you engineer your exile to fulfil your father's wishes?"

Tarkyn looked startled. After a moment he shook his head, "No, the woodfolk first made their vow to me when I was a young child and I remembered little of it. No, I'm afraid my brothers took it into their heads that I might threaten the throne and so fabricated a charge that could justify the removal of my magic as punishment." The prince grimaced, "And when it came to the point, I couldn't let them do it."

Sorath looked at him, took a breath as though to speak, then looked away without a word.

"Remember, you may ask me anything you would like to," said Tarkyn quietly.

Sorath took another breath and asked resolutely, "If your father considered you the key to Eskuzor's future, do I presume you are now working to gain the throne?"

"No. I am not and was not. Kosar and Jarand made a terrible mistake. I was devoutly loyal to Kosar as my king." Tarkyn gave a sad smile, "But as their betrayal of me shows, I am not adept at court intrigue. I have never wanted it to centre on me, as it would if I were king. It was bad enough being a sideline to it." He sighed, "And now? Now I strive for Eskuzor's future by preventing the worst of my brothers' intentions towards each other and trying to get them to work together." He stopped himself from sighing again and straightened up instead, before recounting their activities of the past week, adding, "But I must admit that we seem to be avoiding disasters more than making any real progress towards reconciling my brothers."

Sorath glanced again at the tall young man beside, him, taking in his striking amber eyes and the black hair worn outlandishly long. He noted with a sense of unreality that the prince's profile was the same as that on the older coins and he nearly had to pinch himself to believe he was actually walking and talking with the old king's son. Being Harkell's father, he had noticed the repressed sigh and realised the enormity of the task that this young man had taken upon himself, both to shoulder the burdens of the nation and to accept responsibility for the welfare of his companions. Suddenly, his paternal instincts were roused and more than anything else in the world, he wanted to support the young man who now seemed, to Sorath's mind, to be King Markazon's one true son.

The old man stopped walking. When Tarkyn halted and looked around in query, Sorath went down on one knee, hand on heart and said, "Your Highness, as a civilian, I never gave my vow to Prince Jarand. It was only ever assumed. I would be honoured if you would accept my fealty."

Tarkyn frowned, surprised at the suddenness of Sorath's decision, "What have I said that has brought on your change of heart?"

Sorath's soft brown eyes twinkled kindly at him, "It was not what you said, Your Highness, but what you left unsaid. I saw the effort it took you to rise above your despondency at the hard task that faces you… And I have heard from others and seen with my own eyes the care you take of your companions, even Rena who is not yet sworn to you and that little lad who trails around behind you." He smiled. "You are so young to have so much responsibility and I would help you with it. Will you accept an oath from an old man?"

Tears sprang to Tarkyn's eyes, the kindness from Harkell's father threatening to overset his equilibrium. "Thank you. Of course I will. I would be honoured."

"Then know, Tarkyn Tamadil, son of Markazon, that henceforward I vow to serve, honour and protect you as your liegeman, body and soul, to the end of my days."

"And in return, Sorath, I give you my vow that I will protect and support you as your liege lord… Please rise."

For several moments, the two men stood looking at each other. Suddenly Tarkyn smiled, "You remind me of my father. Gruff but kind. Not quite as fearsome though. I will be very glad to have your support in the days and months ahead." After a moment he asked, "Keep walking or head back? You still have not broached whatever was on your mind when you asked to talk to me, I think."

Sorath shook his head, "I am not so sure that I want to burden you any further."

Tarkyn made the decision for them and turned to keep walking away from the firesite. He smiled, "But I now have you to help me. So the burden will be shared, just as it is with all of my liegefolk."

Sorath gave a quiet chuckle, "You do not deceive me, my lord. I know you take the ultimate responsibility."

"True, but since I do, you must humour me by telling me what worries you."

"Sire, I do not know what passed between you and Rena but I was concerned firstly, that she might believe that she should have been able to defend herself against the marauders and secondly, that she might believe that fighting skills will guarantee her future safety. I don't want her feeling guilty about her part in her past or misguided about her future."

Tarkyn gave him a friendly smile, "Young and inexperienced though I am, I believe I covered both of those exigencies."

"That's all right then," said Sorath gruffly.

"I am pleased you raised it with me though. There have been times in the past where I have overlooked vital pieces of information and I would much rather be told than make an ongoing mistake."

"There is one more issue that I wished to raise with you." Sorath frowned, "I too am a man of principles, just like my son; in fact, just like both my sons. And I don't like being put into a position where I must lie." Sorath caught sight of that profile again and added, "Begging your pardon for speaking so freely, Your Highness."

"Sorath, I fully sympathize with your distaste for prevarication. In fact, my insistence on the truth has sometimes made life difficult for those around me… I presume you are talking about the roles you had to play when the king's men visited us an hour ago."

"Yes I am, Sire. I don't know what you are planning to do with us, but if we are to travel with you and your home guard, I think we need to learn to hide too."

Tarkyn stopped and turned to retrace their steps. "Hmm. We need to discuss this with everyone. One thing I can say though. Only those sworn to me may travel with me. I will not allow people of uncertain loyalties to jeopardise me or my companions."

"That is easily fixed, my lord. I am head of the family. I will make sure everyone follows my lead."

Tarkyn shook his head, "No Sorath. You may explain your own reasons for your decision to them, but they must be allowed to choose for themselves. They must choose to follow my lead, not yours."

The old man frowned, "You did not require your bandits to swear to you individually, from what I gather. Only Orolan swore his fealty. Why is it different for my family?"

"Because Orolan's bandits are sworn to him. Your family, no matter how harmonious they are now, are not sworn to you. Many a civil war has been fought with brother against brother. Membership of the same family does not guarantee shared loyalties. They are free men and women and must make their own decisions."

They walked in silence for a few minutes before Sorath spoke again, "Very well. If I must step aside as head of my family so that you can feel confident of each family member's conviction, then I will. I would hope, however, that in all other matters, I could carry on as before with my family."

"Yes, I would hope so too, but I won't guarantee it. As your overlord, I reserve the right to intervene as I see fit." As the old man tensed beside him, Tarkyn added, "…as I already have with Rena. But you may discuss and object to my actions as you see fit, and I will listen. I may or may not change my intention, but I will listen."

Some of the tension left Sorath, "It is a different experience to have one's liege in personal contact with one."

"More intrusive, you mean?"

Sorath glanced at Tarkyn uncertainly before nodding, "Yes, more intrusive but also more supported, I suppose."

"Sorath, I have neither the time nor the inclination to run everyone's lives… but if anyone requires my help or if the welfare of my home guard is threatened, as it was by Rena's actions, I will respond."

Chapter 46

It was not until after their celebratory evening meal of roasted venison and root vegetables that Sorath's issue was addressed. He had almost decided that his new lord had forgotten about it, when Tarkyn asked, "How will we manage with so many sorcerers, next time a patrol is nearby? Sorath, understandably, does not want to spin a tale unless he has to."

"Yeah, good question" said Bean. "That story of ours was pretty thin."

"Especially the bit about me not being able to hold my beer," growled String, a wry smile belying his tone.

"What magic do you sorcerers in Harkell's family have?" asked Waterstone. "If we know that, we can look at other solutions. I know Harkell can sharpen blades and arrowheads but other than a feeble shield, not much else. What about the rest of you?"

"Naturally Dad and I can sharpen tools. Otherwise we wouldn't be in the trade. And we can also lift very heavy objects with our power. Use it in smithing all the time. Used it to block the mountain pass to stop Jarand's soldiers pursuing us," Drakell frowned, "I would have thought Harkell could, too."

Harkell looked startled, "You know, I think I can. In fact, of course I can. Haven't had much need to in soldiering and forgot all about it. Besides, lifting objects with magic is a bit of a given in our family. Probably couldn't lift as much as you two, though."

"Can you lift yourselves?" asked Danton.

"No, my lord," replied Drakell. "But we could easily lift other people."

Danton nodded, "That sounds promising. What about you, Thraya, and you, Kayama?"

Thraya spoke in a calm, self-assured voice, "I can lift objects and raise a shield for quite some time… and I can produce a power ray, but this skill tends to be frowned upon in a female."

Tarkyn could see Sorath frowning at her disapprovingly. As liege lord, could he justify interfering in the culture of Sorath's family, when he had accepted the woodfolk's culture, even though it had differed from his expectations?

"I can levitate lighter loads," offered Kayama. "I can lift both Marema and Sorrell if we need to get over a wall or a ditch when we are out walking."

"Both together, or separately?" asked Autumn Leaves.

She smiled, "Separately, of course. Two would require two spells."

"And what about Rena and Elena?" asked Autumn Leaves.

"I can feel a person's past," said Rena. "And I can sometimes tell when people are troubled and even, to some extent, what is troubling them." She sighed, "Not very useful, I'm afraid."

"I can levitate myself," said Elena in a strong, confident voice, "And I can lift other objects, not as heavy as those Drakell lifts, but enough to be useful." She glanced at her husband, "And I can send shafts of power. I broke a vase by mistake once when I was experimenting."

"Is that what happened to that vase? What were you doing, playing with magic shafts? Leave the fighting to those whose job it is," said Drakell heavily.

Elena glared at him before lowering her eyes.

Tarkyn did not like what he was seeing. It might once have been his own culture for women to take no part in fighting other than to be abused by the victors, but he had become too used to the feisty contribution of the woodwomen. Besides, he could not afford to lose the potential assistance of anyone who could give it.

Without looking at Sorath, he asked, "Kayama and Rena, have you ever tried to use shields or shafts of power?"

Kayama glanced at Harkell before looking at the prince, her turquoise eyes twinkling with mischief, "I did try once. I blasted a branch off the pear tree we had been trying to grow for ages. I got such a fright I never tried it again."

Rena shook her head, "I have never tried but I would be willing to." She frowned, "But I've been thinking… I think I can tell whether a plant is poisonous or not. It's more or less the same as knowing whether a person is troubled. I haven't really tested it though."

"You and I should get together, Rena," said Summer Rain with a smile, "You may have the makings of a good healer."

Tarkyn leaned forward and everyone fell silent. "Let us leave that for the moment. Stormaway, I believe you have been considering options for the safe future of Harkell's family."

"Yes, I have." The old wizard addressed Sorath and his family, "I believe it would be safe for you to set up a new smithy in Tormadell. Prince Jarand would not look for you so close to King Kosar's principal seat. Alternatively we may be able to procure another of the holdings in the grasslands near that of Lord Tolward. Or you could make your home deep within the forest, perhaps in the vicinity of the forestals who are the woodfolk who specialise in craftwork. They would value your skills, as you would value theirs."

Tarkyn took over, "Or you may choose to travel with my home guard and me…You may remember that I said I would ask you to swear your allegiance to me. If you choose not to, your only options will be to set up in Tormadell, or to stay deep within the forest. We would not risk the welfare of those sorcerers on the grasslands to people of uncertain allegiance. However, we will still support you financially to set up a new smithy and to find somewhere to live." He glanced at Sorath, before continuing, "Sorath and Harkell have made that commitment, but each of you must choose for yourself."

The whole family looked at Sorath in surprise, to which he responded with a private smile and a shrug. Tarkyn met his eyes and nodded, "Having heard what magic you could bring to your own protection and to our cause, I think we could work with you to keep you safe if you travelled with us, without exposing you to further patrols." He waved his hand. "However, you have heard the options. Harkell, I would like you and your family to move apart from the rest of us to consider your decision. You do not all have to make the same choice. Stormaway, who has an intimate knowledge of both woodfolk and sorcerer considerations, is at your disposal to discuss the finer details of each plan. We move out tomorrow to travel to Lord Tolward's house. So you have until the morning to make your decision."

Rainstorm met Harkell's eyes as he prepared to follow his family to a corner of the clearing, "Good luck," he murmured. "Family conferences can be murder."

Harkell gave a strong smile of friendship in return. "Yes. This could take some time. See you in a while."

CHAPTER 47

"You're a sly old dog, Dad," exclaimed Drakell, as soon as they were out of earshot. "Is that why you asked to see the prince? So you could pledge your allegiance to him?"

"No. Never had the least intention of it when I set out. Quite surprising, really."

Somehow, the fact that their serious father could do something so significant in such an inconsequential manner seemed exquisitely funny to his sons. So, it was with some surprise that the first sound the woodfolk heard issuing from Harkell's family meeting was laughter.

Harkell mopped tears of mirth from his eyes, "What were you thinking, Dad, to swear your life away on a whim?"

Sorath smiled benignly at them, "Oh, it wasn't a whim. No, that young lad is quite extraordinary. I've never met anyone like him before."

"You've never met a prince before, Dad," said Drakell, catching Harkell's eye and succumbing to another bout of mirth.

Harkell smiled in return but for him, the moment had passed and he was now more interested in what his father had to say. "Go on, Dad."

"That is true. I have never met a prince before and maybe that is what it was." Sorath gave a reminiscent smile, "That at least could account for his breath-taking arrogance in demanding that everyone's loyalty to him must supercede all their other loyalties, even those of family ties."

Thraya's eyes grew round, "And you agreed to that? You would place your loyalty to him above your loyalty to us?"

Sorath bit his lip, "Well, it's not quite as simple as that. I would hope the two loyalties would not conflict with each other."

Harkell came to his rescue, "If you are his sworn man, what matters to you, matters to him also."

"If you must know," said the old man in a rush, "I couldn't stand by and watch a young feller like that shouldering such burdens, without wanting to help him. The boy has the weight of a nation on his shoulders."

Harkell chuckled, "They're pretty broad shoulders, all the same. He has powers you haven't even begun to guess at. And he has faced down the king, Prince Jarand, a mighty ten foot high spectre, four ancient forest guardians of uncertain humour..." His tone became more serious, "But nevertheless, I agree. Tarkyn is facing a desperate challenge in trying to save our nation from civil war. I don't know how, or even whether, he will succeed...but I will give everything I have to support him."

Drakell looked from one to the other, "Your words vibrate with a passion I have rarely seen in either of you." He focused on his father, "So, as head of the family, have you committed us all to his cause?"

"No," replied Sorath shortly. "He wouldn't let me. You must make your own independent choices." He gave a wry smile, "You must commit directly to him, not to my decision."

Harkell shouted with laughter, "Oh Dad! He is most amazingly arrogant. You know, Jarand tried to tempt him into betraying Kosar by offering to reinstate him. But Tarkyn said that he wouldn't dream of descending to the king's level by doing what Kosar had done to him… And the astonishing thing is that he wouldn't."

"That's not arrogance, son. That is integrity… And with brothers like those two, is there any wonder that he's a bit edgy about trusting those around him?"

"Poor feller," said Thraya, clucking her tongue sympathetically, "Imagine being betrayed by your own brother!" She looked at Drakell, "Imagine Harkell betraying you! It doesn't bear thinking about."

Drakell gave a slow smile to his brother, "No, it doesn't, does it? And I begin to understand what you would have been prepared to endure to protect us, as I would have for you. And I begin to see how much we owe your Prince Tarkyn."

"So what are you going to do?" asked Harkell.

"About swearing allegiance, you mean?"

"No, if Tarkyn wishes your choice to be completely independent then I will not pressure you by asking that at this stage. I mean what life will you choose for yourselves?"

In the ensuing discussion, it emerged that Sorath and Drakell had been under constant pressure for months to produce as many arrow heads, daggers and swords as they could. Jarand's soldiers had visited frequently, urging them to spend longer hours at the smithy to fill the required quotas. Although Sorath had tried to explain the slow process needed to forge fine blades, the soldiers had acted as though he were making excuses and their demands had forced the two smiths to work extended days, with no rest days to recover. Sorath had been on the verge of retiring before the demands for weaponry had begun, but there had been no question of retirement with the soldiers constantly harassing them for more products.

Neither of them wanted to work a smithy again where they could be pressed into making weaponry for the impending war. So Tormadell was eliminated as a possibility.

Drakell was not yet ready to retire and Elena was pregnant. So he wanted somewhere that they could stay and build up a stable life again. Their debate was between the grasslands and the deep forest somewhere near the forestals.

Sorath was happy to retire from smithing. He didn't exactly say it, but he felt that his sons were now grown and no longer needed his guidance, and he had never been particularly good with young children, so his grandchildren did not yet intrigue him. But in Tarkyn, he had found a beleaguered young man who, he believed, could benefit from the strength and sureness that he had to offer. Thraya thought that supporting the prince would give her husband an interest outside smithing that he had, up until now, lacked. For herself, she was interested in getting to know these woodfolk and perhaps following Rena's lead in learning some of their ways.

Harkell and Rena, of course, wanted to stay with Tarkyn and his home guard, and Kayama was quite happy to fall in with her husband's wishes.

So, finally it was decided that they would all travel with Tarkyn, at least as far as the grasslands. Then Drakell and Elena would decide where they would prefer to settle.

"So I presume, since you have all decided to travel with Tarkyn for the time being, that you are willing to give him your oath?" asked Harkell.

Drakell grinned, "Your fine prince can say what he likes about us deciding independently. But if you and Dad both believe in him, who am I to gainsay you? I trust my father's and my brother's decisions and will let them guide me."

Harkell laughed, "You are deciding independently. You are simply using excellent sources of information for your decision."

The rest of the family concurred and used their stipulated independence to follow Sorath's and Harkell's lead; not because Sorath insisted they should, but because they respected his and Harkell's judgement and agreed among themselves that the family would stand more solid with a shared commitment. Nevertheless the vows they made to Tarkyn were genuine.

Chapter 48

The following morning's departure was delayed by heavy rain that washed through the forest, weighing branches down with soggy leaves and sending rivulets of water trickling along forest paths, leaving them muddy and, in places, slippery.

The woodfolk sent out messages, asking the sorcerers to stay inside as much as possible until the rain had passed and the sun had dried the ground. By mid-afternoon, the ground was still muddy, and impatience bred the suggestion that since a patrol had already seen these sorcerers at the firesite, there was really no need to hide their footprints,

Reluctantly, the woodfolk agreed and allowed the sorcerers to emerge into the dim, cold afternoon.

"As long as we don't head off," said Autumn Leaves firmly. "We don't want to have to disguise the deep muddy tracks of twelve sorcerers." He shook his head gloomily, "Too hard."

"Oh, I see," Drakell watched a group of woodfolk moving about and realised that they were leaving only the slightest marks in the muddy ground. "Can you walk over dry ground without leaving any prints at all?"

Autumn Leaves glanced down at the mud underfoot, "Easily, but we still make sure someone follows behind us constructing divergent trails, whatever the weather. And if we travelled on a day like this, we would take to the trees from time to time to make breaks in the trail, since disguising a muddy trail might leave some traces that a very experienced tracker could discern."

"Someone like me or the trappers, for instance," said Danton.

Drakell raised his eyebrows, "You, my lord? What would a lord know of tracking?"

Autumn Leaves jerked his thumb at Danton, with not a whit of respect, "He's an elite guard. Apparently they get trained in it."

"Are you, my lord? That is impressive."

Danton chuckled, "Not as impressive as being a woodman or woman. My hunting, tracking and camouflaging skills are only impressive among sorcerers."

"He's not bad, though," rumbled Thunder Storm, slapping him on the back.

"We sorcerers could help with disguising footprints, you know," suggested Drakell. "If you show us what to do, a couple of us could disguise the footprints of the first ten and then you would only have to sort out the last two sets."

Thunder Storm nodded slowly as he thought about it, "Yes, that could work. It would certainly reduce our work load." He smiled, "Thanks. You have a practical turn of mind, don't you?"

"Yep. Always did have. When we were youngsters, Harkell would figure out what we were going to do and I would figure how to do it." Drakell gave a wry smile, "Hmm. And I'd usually end up doing most of the work as well… funny about that."

"The disadvantage of being a younger brother," said Autumn Leaves, flicking a cheeky glance at Thunder Storm.

Tarkyn entered the conversation in time to hear this last remark, "I am unlucky enough to be the youngest brother in two families. There is no justice, if you ask me."

"I grant you that the brothers in your sorcerer family leave a lot to be desired," said Autumn Leaves, "But you can't complain about Waterstone and Ancient Oak. After all, they have to do what you say."

Tarkyn saw Drakell watching him and laughed, "Don't let them kid you. It is well known that Waterstone takes his role as my older brother very seriously, which includes bossing me around when he feels the need."

Drakell produced a tight smile in return but was clearly ill at ease in the prince's presence. Tarkyn caught his breath as though he were about to say something but instead, nodded at them all and left to collect Midnight and Sparrow before heading off out of the clearing.

Danton watched him go for a moment before saying jauntily, "I didn't have to deal with my older brother very much at all after I was eight which, I suspect, was a relief to both of us."

Drakell, who may not have been as sharp as his brother, but was still perceptive, dragged his eyes from Tarkyn's retreating figure to reply politely, "Is that so, my lord? I believe I have been very fortunate in mine. Each of us would do anything for the other."

"Perhaps that may have developed between us if we had had the chance to grow up together to adulthood," Danton admitted. He shrugged unhappily, "I don't really let myself think about what I may have missed by not being there."

Drakell's divided attention was captured, "If you don't mind my asking, my lord, why were you not with your family?"

"When I was eight, I was taken from my home to become playmate and whipping boy for Prince Tarkyn. I was the sacrificial lamb on my father's political altar." The woodfolk could hear the bitterness underlying his words. For a few tense moments, Danton stripped the bark off a small stick he was holding, his mouth compressed with anger. Then suddenly he said vehemently, "My family may have been willing to sacrifice me but Tarkyn wasn't. Even though he was only little, he fought against his whole family on my behalf. He screamed and yelled and struggled to intervene every time I was punished in his stead. In the end, he even defied the king to protect me."

Drakell's eyes grew round, "How old was he when he did this?"

Danton smiled in fond reminiscence, "Seven…just. He was only six when I arrived. And after he defied the king, the whippings stopped. Tarkyn's determination overturned centuries of royal custom."

Drakell looked off into the trees in the direction the prince had taken. He shook his head, "I could see that my unease sent His Highness away, for which I am sorry. But after hearing that story, I am more in awe of him than ever."

"Hmm." Danton pulled the last of the bark off his stick, as he thought about it, "You know, I remember him saying that when a prince enters a room, everyone stops talking. Tarkyn understands your unease, but he has become used to the woodfolk's graceless disregard for his rank," here he smiled disarmingly at the two woodmen, "and has withdrawn to avoid discomforting you and, I suppose, himself. He used to be constantly aloof and it has only been in the last few months under the influence of these reprobates that he has changed."

"For the better," said Autumn Leaves, "I'm sure you were hastening to add."

Danton grinned, "Yes, I admit it, for the better. He is much happier. But he is quick to revert to courteous aloofness when he does not know someone well."

"If it were anyone else, I would go after him and try to befriend him," said Drakell uncertainly, "but…"

"Just a minute," Thunder Storm went out of focus. Shortly afterwards, he reported, "Sparrow says that they are racing sticks in the stream. If you like, you could borrow Harkell's and my children and take them down to join in?"

When Drakell nodded but looked unsure, Thunder Storm smiled, "On second thoughts, I'll come down with you."

They reached the stream just as, amidst shouts of excitement, Midnight's stick overtook Sparrow's to win by half an inch. Tarkyn's stick was languishing in an eddy near the side and had not even been in the running, but he was barracking hard for Midnight's stick since Sparrow had won the previous four races. As the race finished, Sparrow and Midnight waded into the swirling stream to retrieve their sticks.

Tarkyn's stick was so close to the edge that he thought he could reach it by lying down on the bank, but just as his hand touched the stick, the bank beneath him began to crumble. Drakell, newly sworn to protect the prince, debated whether he should use his magic to save Tarkyn from falling into the shallow stream, but screams of laughter from the children stopped him. With a mighty splash, Tarkyn rolled into the water to come up grinning and spluttering, his racing stick clutched triumphantly in his hand.

He surveyed the laughing children, "There seem to be more of you, all of a sudden and just in time to see me make a fool of myself. Well, you'd better find yourselves a good stick... and one you can recognise scooting along the stream in the midst of all the others." He glanced up at the two adults and said briefly, "If you're staying, you'll need sticks too."

Tarkyn waded out of the stream and shook himself like a dog, much to the entertainment of the children. He grinned at Thunder Storm. "That doesn't work at all, you know." Something passed silently between them and Tarkyn said, "Yes please."

Tarkyn stood wringing out his long hair and sluicing himself down as the children looked for suitable sticks for the next race. He smiled his thanks as Autumn Leaves came lumbering from the firesite with a towel.

Drakell's grey eyes moved from one to the other as he surmised the mindmessages that must have been conveyed. As he looked again at the prince, he started as he realised that Tarkyn was watching him.

Tarkyn smiled as he towelled his hair, "Drakell, you have the same roving eyes as your brother. Have you found yourself a stick yet, or have you been too distracted trying to figure us all out?" Drakell flushed with embarrassment but before he could stammer out a reply, Tarkyn added kindly, "I was not being critical. I like Harkell's curiosity and I am sure I will like yours, too."

Drakell froze inside as he desperately tried to think of something to say. After a notable pause, he said in a rush, "We have it from our father, Sire. So perhaps you may like his also. H... he is very impressed by you." Then Drakell could have kicked himself for mentioning his father's reaction when he was trying to act as though the prince were just another person. Suddenly the innate honesty that also characterized Harkell came to his rescue, "Your Highness, I wish I could be as relaxed around you as everyone else seems to be and I'm sorry if my awkwardness sent you away earlier. I have not had the practice that Harkell has had in conversing with people of higher rank and I was not bred to disregard rank as the woodfolk were." Drakell looked down at his hands that still had no stick in them, before raising his eyes to meet Tarkyn's. He gave the slightest little smile that suddenly expanded into a huge grin, "And my Dad keeps pointing out that you look like the old coins."

Tarkyn exploded with laughter. Between chuckles he said, "That must be very daunting for you," and nearly set himself off again.

Drakell nodded, smiling benignly, not at all upset at being laughed at. His attention was caught by Thunder Storm who asked, "Does he? I've never really looked at coins."

"Yes. King Markazon's profile is on all the older coins and His Highness has exactly the same profile. Not on the newer ones, though. King Kosar's profile is different." Drakell smiled, "More like your mother's, I believe, Sire."

Just as Tarkyn nodded, Midnight tugged impatiently on his sodden leggings. After a brief silence, Midnight scampered off to return with a good sized stick that he presented to Drakell.

"Shall we?" invited Tarkyn.

Chapter 49

Over the ensuing days, Harkell's family was trained hard by the woodfolk to raise each other into the trees quietly on a moment's notice. They were drilled over and over again, until they were ragged with tiredness. Each time, their choice of tree and direction was discussed; the type of tree, the height and strength of the branches, which side of the tree and its distance from the firesite if they were camped or from the trail if they were moving. Then adults and children had to practise remaining motionless and silent for extended periods of time.

Without their previous defensiveness, the woodfolk demonstrated their skill with weaponry, camouflage, approaching a target undetected and flicking into hiding, while Harkell and Danton explained the tactics that had been used against Jarand and Kosar during the various interchanges.

Nevertheless, even after days of rigorous training, Waterstone approached Tarkyn to express his reservations about the feasibility of hiding so many sorcerers at short notice.

Tarkyn listened, then sent a request for Sorath to join them where they sat a little away from the others on the soft leafy ground beneath a spreading beech tree. Sorath presented himself and, as he bowed to Tarkyn, sent a nod of acknowledgement to Waterstone. Waterstone, now more conversant with sorcerers' need to show respect, thought that this was a reasonable compromise.

"Take a seat, Sorath," invited Tarkyn, indicating the ground beside them. He had been in the woodlands so long now that he did not even register the irony of the request, merely noting that the proffered patch of ground was soft without being muddy. "Your family are doing very well in developing their woodcraft skills…"

Sorath cocked his head, recognising a palliative when he heard one "But…?"

Waterstone smiled, "You are so like Harkell. Don't miss a trick. Or rather I suppose I should say Harkell is like you."

Sorath smiled politely in return and waited for them to get to the point.

"Hmm," Waterstone's brow furrowed. "This is a little awkward for us. I know you are all trying very hard and in many circumstances the skills you are beginning to master will be enough…"

"Give us a chance, sir. We haven't had much time to learn things you have been doing all your lives."

Waterstone repressed a grimace at being called sir, "I am aware of that, Sorath. That's why I said beginning to master."

"And we can do some things you can't, such as levitate each other." Sorath looked from one serious face to the other and sighed, "You know this, don't you? You know we are trying our best and I suppose by now you have a fair idea of our strengths and limitations. So, what is the problem? Have you changed your minds about allowing us to travel with you?" The old man tried to keep his voice clear of disappointment.

Tarkyn smiled to set him at ease. "No. But despite everyone's best efforts, there may be times when all you can do is face the soldiers as you did the other day and brazen it out."

"The main problem is your inability to flick out of sight as we can," explained the woodman hurriedly. "Look!" Waterstone disappeared and a moment later poked his head around a tree ten feet away. "You see? Nothing any sorcerer can do comes close to that for fast evasion." He flicked back to his previous seated position, "And if we are in an area populated only with low lying shrubs, levitation won't help you."

"I know prevarication doesn't sit well with you and we will work to minimise the times it occurs but if you wish to travel with us, there may be times when there is no alternative." The prince shrugged, "Besides, any time you are in contact with outside sorcerers, even with the bandits who brought you here, you will have to modify the truth about the members of my home guard. Even I must be less than straight forward to conceal knowledge of the woodfolk."

Suddenly Sorath's serious face broke into a smile, "Far be it from me, Sire, to set my standards above yours. By nature, I am a rigid old man, but circumstances and two feisty sons are forcing me to challenge my assumptions." He gave a little grunt, "Or rather I should say, circumstances, two feisty sons and an unusual but worthy liege. Thank you for considering my scruples."

Tarkyn inclined his head gravely, "A pleasure."

Waterstone gave his head a little shake at the formality of Tarkyn's response. Since the increase in sorcerer numbers, his bloodbrother had shown far more of the aloof, formal side of his character. He still played and relaxed, but increasingly, he seemed to mirror the new sorcerers' expectations of him as their prince and liege. Waterstone determined to have a quiet word with him before he reverted too much to his old, pre-woodfolk ways.

Then Sorath surprised them by adding, "In that case, I suppose we had better practise our cover stories. If we must lie, we should at least do it well. I'll talk to the trappers, Boravar and my family about it... But what about Rena?"

"Good point. And the other women too, if they decide to adopt woodfolk garb." said Tarkyn.

Sorath scowled. "I would hope they, at least, would have the good taste to refrain."

Neither Tarkyn nor Waterstone said a word but their silence spoke volumes.

Finally the old man growled, "I am not going to say I'm sorry if that's what you're waiting for. That's what I think and I told you I was honest."

"Sometimes honesty can be as much of a weapon as lies." There was a sharp edge to Tarkyn's voice. "And what constitutes good and bad taste is a matter of opinion or majority rule, not fact. You would do well to remember that."

Sorath glared at him, his face flushed with anger, but feeling unable to retaliate.

Tarkyn gave a sharp nod, "You may speak your mind, provided you are not discourteous to me or my family's people. I too am a woodman. When you deride them, you deride me." When Sorath did not respond immediately, Tarkyn added dryly, "You may have forgotten, but one of those women with the bad taste to wear woodfolk leggings is my intended wife."

This time Sorath's face flushed with chagrin. "I beg your pardon, Your Highness…and yours, Waterstone." After a moment he said, "Thing is, I feel that we are being forced to become something we are not… and frankly, sometimes I resent it." He heaved a quiet sigh. "After all, I have lost everything I ever worked for, you know. I don't want to lose who we are as well." The old man looked down at his hands, which were faintly trembling, and Tarkyn could see that he wished he could just get up and leave.

"Sorath, look at me," said Tarkyn gently. The old man's face was wet with tears when he raised his head. "I am sorry my brother's machinations have brought you to this. I know you have lost your neighbourhood and your house. But the greatest thing you worked towards, you still have. The reason you came was to protect your family and they are a fine testament to your life's work. We cannot give you back your neighbourhood, at least not at the moment, but we can provide you with a new house and forge if that is your desire."

"And Sorath, we do not want you to become anyone other than who you are," added Waterstone. "We are proud of being woodfolk. You are proud of being sorcerers. We each have strengths the other does not possess. In fact, the reason we woodfolk are so evasive is that we acknowledge the strength of sorcerers and have, until recently, lived in fear of them. Even now, we would not dream of venturing among sorcerers beyond the homeguard."

Sorath wiped his eyes and sniffed. "Is that so? I remember Thunder Storm saying something like that," he said thickly. "But you know, having seen your prowess, it didn't occur to me that you people would fear anyone." After another sniff and a think, he swept his arm vaguely around the clearing, "So, are we the only sorcerers you have ever spoken to?"

Waterstone's mouth set in a grim line, "Basically yes, except Prince Jarand and King Markazon, neither of whom was very encouraging."

Tarkyn leant forward, "When I first came to the forest, the only sorcerers they had ever encountered were my father who took their freedom from them, Stormaway who accompanied him, and three vicious bounty hunters who took me captive after I had arrived as their unwelcome liege lord." He glanced at his bloodbrother with a twinkle in his eyes, "They thought that all sorcerers used their powers only to attack people."

Sorath shook his head in surprise "Oh my word, Waterstone, we're not like that. And here I was thinking that you woodfolk kept yourselves aloof from us because you disdained us and that was why it was such an honour for us to be allowed to meet you."

Waterstone was so stunned he took a moment to recover, "No, Sorath. The woodfolk creed is to take every man and woman on their merits. When we agreed to abide with you, the honour we bestowed on you was trust, not condescension."

"Hmm. And you are even sharing your knowledge of the forest that keeps you safe from sorcerers. I understand now what a leap of faith that must be for you." Sorath smiled gently, "You are a very generous people… and when I consider that our family has more than doubled the number of sorcerers you associate with, I begin to understand the honour you have accorded my son."

Tarkyn smiled, "…that astute son of yours who is even now watching us from the other side of the clearing; knowing you are upset, even from the back, and wanting to join you but feeling constrained by the fact that we have clearly pulled you aside to talk to you privately… Would you like him to join us or would you rather wait?"

"If you don't mind, I would like his company." Sorath gave a rueful smile, "I can't hide much from him anyway."

At a gesture from Tarkyn, Harkell walked swiftly over and after a glance at his father, sat down beside him and placed an arm around his shoulder.

Sorath frowned at him. "Harkell, where are your manners?" he said in a furious undertone.

Harkell grinned, "I'm assuming this is not a formal occasion. Am I wrong?"

Tarkyn smiled and shook his head.

"That's all very well, Harkell, but I think you are taking advantage of the prince's good nature and being brazenly discourteous." Sorath gave vent to a short lecture on manners which left Harkell grinning and his father feeling much better.

Part 6: Stillwaters Pathfinder

CHAPTER 50

Harkell was still smiling when Stormaway and Danton approached, the wizard holding a sheaf of missives in his hand. As Stormaway gave a small bow, Sorath hissed under his breath to his son, "You see?"

Stormaway glanced briefly at Sorath but addressed himself to Tarkyn, "Sire, we are being deluged with reports from all over Eskuzor. In the northwest, Kosar's troops are hauling people in for questioning, and rounding up suspected bandits and trouble makers. Along the Great West Road, the incidence of travellers being waylaid has diminished and there have been no reported murders."

"So, Tarkyn, even if Kosar did try to trick you, perhaps he has taken your warning to heart and is finally doing something about restoring order," suggested Harkell.

Tarkyn gave a slow smile. "I hope so. Too many have been suffering from unchecked lawlessness."

He was not given long to enjoy any sense of achievement.

"That's the good news…" said Danton, begging the question.

"Oh," said Tarkyn, his voice flat with disappointment, "And…?"

"Troops are being mobilized across the country, around both Tormadell and Montraya. Countrymen are reporting to their liege lords and bands of lords' men are heading towards the two cities, or to join up with Kosar's troops in the northwest."

"Blast them!" Tarkyn's anger radiated outwards, rocking everyone backwards.

Sorath righted himself, his eyes wide with shock, "What was that?"

Harkell smiled wryly, "That, Dad, is Tarkyn's greatest weapon." When Sorath still looked puzzled, he expanded, "Tarkyn can harness the power of his emotions. You were just moved by his anger." Harkell's eyes twinkled, "Of course, at the moment it is not so much harnessed as running away with itself.

Tarkyn grunted, "Very funny." He took a deep breath, pulling himself together. "I am afraid, my friends, that all we seem to have done is postpone the inevitable."

"Yes, it would seem so. It was inevitable that Jarand would react badly to Kosar's intended slight. And it was equally inevitable that Kosar would prepare against that eventuality," said Stormaway.

Harkell grimaced, "In fact, I think our actions and your discussion with Kosar, Tarkyn, when you warned him of Jarand's manoeuvrings were catalysts. Kosar was content to carry on within the walls of Montraya in happy ignorance of his country's plight until you brought him to book."

"Are you saying that we have made it worse?" Tarkyn's tone made Sorath frown a warning at his son but Harkell carried on regardless.

"Tarkyn, it could not have continued as it was. Eskuzor was slowly bleeding to death. Jarand was undermining every aspect of Kosar's rule; justice, maintenance of public roads and buildings, law and order." Harkell shrugged, "Besides, Jarand has been preparing for war for a long time. Sorath and Drakell have been under pressure to forge large numbers of weapons for some time now and I reported to you months ago that Jarand's troops were practicing manoeuvres that had nothing to do with keeping the peace.

"We have brought the conflict to a head," Danton looked sympathetically at Tarkyn. "Had Kosar been a decent statesman or a kinder brother, he might have been able to grant Jarand enough acknowledgment and enough responsibility to appease him, but basically each would prefer to out-manoeuvre the other. You gave them every chance but their rivalry runs too deep. To them, Eskuzor and all of us are merely pawns in their grand game."

Tarkyn jumped to his feet and began to pace back and forth in agitation. Realizing that Sorath was getting himself up from the ground as quickly as his old bones would let him, the prince waved his hand at him, "No Sorath, stay seated." After a few long minutes where no one spoke, he finally came to a halt and said bitterly, "So, our only achievement is that we have moved the forthcoming battle from the gates of Tormadell to an unknown site, presumably somewhere in the west since both are now on that side of the country."

Suddenly Lapping Water and Tree Wind appeared in front of him.

"No," said Tree Wind. "You, we all managed to keep the fight out of the forest. That may not matter to sorcerers but it matters to us."

"And we stopped the Andoran and Sargon's nefarious practice of killing off the women of traveller families so that they could recruit the distraught spouses for Jarand's vigilante gangs," added Danton dryly, his tone a clear reminder that he had nearly died in that cause.

"And after your talk with him," added Stormaway, "Jarand toned down his vigilantes and their recruitment drive…not from any moral stance I grant you, merely to improve his reputation… but nevertheless there are people alive and whole today because of your intervention who would not be otherwise."

"Which is also true of the people now being protected in the northwest by Kosar's recent actions," added Waterstone.

"And so far, the men in Kosar's small army are intact except for sore feet. If the conflict between Jarand and Kosar had not been stopped, many of them would now be dead or wounded," said Rainstorm appearing out of nowhere.

With a conscious effort, Tarkyn restrained himself from saying, "Yes, but…" realizing that by doing so, he would be running roughshod over the efforts of the people around him. "That is true," he said slowly. "I suppose I keep getting lost in the bigger picture and forget that our achievements matters a great deal to those we have affected."

"Even if the people we have helped don't know who they are," said Rainstorm, grinning.

Tarkyn smiled, "Yes, even if they don't know who they are or that they have us to thank for it." He looked at Sorath, with a little smile still playing around his mouth. "You see what a fine council of advisers you are joining. Here they are, putting all their energies into cheering me up when perhaps their time would be better spent working out how to meet this new crisis."

Harkell chuckled. "The first step of planning our next move is making sure that you aren't running round like a bear with a sore head."

"And cheering *ourselves* up so that we can keep believing we can do something useful in the future, no matter how bleak it may look at present," added Lapping Water, with an understanding smile, knowing how her words would affect him.

Sure enough, the colour heightened on Tarkyn's cheeks. "Will I *ever* learn to consider the people around me? It is I who should be spurring *you* on to greater things."

"We are quite capable of spurring ourselves on, thank you," said Tree Wind acerbically. "And you too, while we're at it."

Tarkyn did not reply to this, privately believing that it was his role to provide hope for the future but aware that the woodfolk would not agree. Instead he said, "So, how far are we from Lord Tolward's holding on the grasslands? Perhaps we should speak to him and see what further information he has to offer before we start to make any plans."

"We are half a day's walk away," replied Waterstone, "but we can only approach under cover of dark. So we will have to wait until evening to leave."

Sorath shifted uncomfortably then cleared his throat, "Your Highness, does this mean that we are going to have to fight? Is this Lord Tolward organising your supporters? Perhaps you should be training us to develop our powers of attack." He looked anything but happy at this idea as he stalwartly offered his support to his new liege.

Tarkyn smiled reassuringly at the old man, "No, we are not going to line ourselves up on a battlefield to create a three way conflict. So far, we have used the woodfolk's uncanny skills, our own sorcerer powers in new ways and my abilities as a forest guardian to outmanoeuvre our opposition....plus clever planning."

"But we will be facing our greatest challenge yet, if Jarand's and Kosar's troops face each other on an open plain," said Stormaway. "The furthest we have ventured from the cover of the forest is a couple of hundred yards."

"And our greatest strengths are surprise and subterfuge," added Danton.

"And as you may have gathered, we woodfolk do not willingly leave the forest nor do we appear before sorcerers." Lapping Water walked over to Sorath and placed a friendly hand on his arm, "And that oath you swore to keep our presence secret?... Every one of us has sworn that same oath."

Tarkyn gave a wry smile, "And added to that, we have no wish to kill off the sorcerers on either side of the conflict. In fact, our wish is to preserve them."

Sorath gave whistle under his breath, "I'll say this for you all. You're amazingly ambitious." He glanced uncertainly around the gathering, "If you would value my opinion..." Receiving a nod from Tarkyn, he continued, "I think some of you should regale our family with the tales of your past achievements and show us the new ways that you sorcerers have used your powers. We may even be able to perform some of them ourselves but, at the very least, we will know what possibilities there are that can be used in future."

"Hmm, for a blacksmith, you would make a good officer," said Danton. "I can see where Harkell got his acuity from." He smiled as Sorath went pink with pleasure. "And I hear from Orolan that you and Drakell can control horses magically and used your power to lift a huge tree to block a road. Pretty useful skills to draw upon."

Sorath chuckled, "You should have seen Orolan trying to get his horse to move. Served that dunghill cock right for being so rude to Drakell... You can only push Drakell so far."

"Can you control horses like a forest guardian can?" demanded Rainstorm.

Sorath frowned at being addressed so forthrightly by such a young woodman but seeing that Tarkyn accepted it, merely replied, "Well, can't say as I know much about forest guardians, so it's hard to say. Blacksmiths can just calm horses down and stop them, that's all. Then we let them go when we've finished. We can't make them go anywhere in particular or do anything special."

"Tarkyn's a forest guardian and he can," said Rainstorm, throwing his chest out as he bragged about the prince. "That's how he got the drop on Jarand. He made Harkell's troops' horses bunch up six abreast across the road. Then Danton put his shield over the first four rows and none of the soldiers at the rear could get past to assist Jarand. Anyone who tried to leave the road would have been picked off by us in the surrounding woods."

Sorath frowned, "I thought you said you didn't wish to kill off sorcerers…?"

"We would have knocked them out using slingshots," explained Tree Wind, "Just as we knocked out the guards of Kosar's little army." She shrugged, "Two advantages to doing that instead of shooting them with arrows; firstly, we don't have to retrieve arrows that might alert people to our presence and secondly, we don't have people raining down retribution on our heads."

"In fact," said Tarkyn, "the skill evidenced by repeatedly knocking out scores of soldiers without killing them, especially when it has been done simultaneously, has shaken Kosar and Jarand more than wholesale slaughter would have."

Rainstorm grinned, "Danton can tell you how hard it is to fire gently at someone."

Watching Danton's perfunctory smile of agreement, Harkell said quietly, "You have something else on your mind too, don't you Danton?"

Danton frowned repressively, but even as Harkell gave a grimace of apology, the searchlight of Tarkyn's amber eyes came to bear on them. Surprisingly, the prince who often reiterated that he granted freedom of speech but not of silence, let his gaze move on and instead asked Waterstone, "And while we visit Lord Tolward's house, where will you woodfolk be? There is nowhere to hide during daylight hours, is there?"

"There are a few trees and shrubs but not enough cover for all of us. If you remember, Lapping Water and Summer Rain were able to hide in that large tree near the back of Lord Tolward's house. Even in daylight that would offer sufficient cover for a few of us… if you can quieten those enthusiastic watchdogs."

"And the rest of the home guard?"

Waterstone shrugged, "They can either be deployed across a few of the holdings or wait on one side of the grasslands or the other, in which case they will be at least two hours' walk from us."

"Hmm. I must admit I will feel rather exposed, after having you woodfolk and your deadly skills surrounding me all the time."

"It is definitely a risk," said Stormaway heavily, "appearing among sorcerers when there is still a price on your head. It only needs one traitor in their midst…"

Tarkyn stopped beside a small wilting bush and absent-mindedly leant over so that he could run his hands up either side of it, sending an infusion of new life into it as he talked, "And yet I have given my word that I would return to see Lord Tolward. And don't forget, I am guardian of more than the forests of Eskuzor. I must support the poor benighted sorcerers of this country."

"Sire, in the normal course of events, a delegation would precede you to ensure that accommodation and victuals were satisfactory, that people were aware of the correct protocols, that the location was secure and to determine the order of events," Stormaway gave a slight smile, "… and to add to your consequence. Perhaps that would be advisable in this instance so that we can reconnoitre the holding and scrutinise those who will be in attendance."

Tarkyn raised an eyebrow at Waterstone, knowing his bloodbrother's dislike of the prince flaunting his rank. "What do you think?"

Waterstone grinned, "I think it is an excellent idea. I would support anything that will make this venture safer. And as for your consequence? Well, after seeing the memories of your youth and watching the overawed sorcerers in the Lost Forest queue for hours to have the honour of meeting you, I think we woodfolk concede that your heritage has a strange effect on sorcerers." He shrugged, still grinning, "It is clearly ingrained both in them and you. So we might as well make use of it."

"Thank you for those heart-warming words," replied Tarkyn dryly. "I too believe that a delegation to go before me is a wise precaution. I will leave it in the hands of Stormaway, Danton and Harkell to organise."

"Pleased to," said Harkell, glancing sideways at his father who was bursting with pride that his son was being given such a commission. He was surprised to notice that Danton looked uncomfortable and nodded with reluctance.

Stormaway sketched another bow, "I am pleased that you have sufficient cognisance of your consequence to allow us to give you your due in this."

"Stop winding Waterstone up, Stormaway," said Tarkyn mildly as he stood up and brushed himself down. "You know perfectly well by now that I know what is due to me, whether I choose to enforce it or not."

"I'll vouch for that," growled Sorath under his breath. Then his ears burned with embarrassment when he realised that he had been heard.

For a long moment, Tarkyn stared at him. Then, having made clear he did not like the style of its delivery, he merely said, "Thank you for your support. And now Danton, could you accompany me please? Little Sparrow has been drawing maps of the grasslands and wanted to show you especially, since you were so impressed with her map she drew you when you first arrived all those months ago… I thought you could explain it to me at the same time so that I can understand the layout."

Danton restrained himself from rolling his eyes at Harkell as he stood up and fell into step beside his liege. Knowing he was effectively playing along with a ruse, he responded, "Good idea. Sparrow and I have been special friends ever since we lost you and the others in the Lost Forest. So I would like to see her map." He gave a little smile. "And anything that will help your sense of geography is always useful."

As they drifted out of hearing range, Tarkyn smiled down at Danton and put his arm across his shoulders, "Come on, my friend. Stop looking so worried. I'm not going to eat you. I'm not even going to insist that you tell me whatever is on your mind. I'm just giving you the chance to, if you want to."

Danton's face relaxed into a smile. "Thanks. We have all been so busy since Harkell's family has arrived. Your time has been more in demand than ever." He bounced along at Tarkyn's side, walking quickly to keep up with his friend's longer strides. "How are you finding it, having so many sorcerers around you? I notice you've withdrawn into yourself a little."

"Hmm. Perhaps I have. I suppose I have to be more formal with new people. I have to make sure that they show sufficient respect for me… and the woodfolk at the outset. Only then can I afford to reduce the protocols." He gave a wry smile, "It is becoming more difficult to be informal when there are so many sorcerers now. Until I came to these forests, there were so few people I could trust. I even had to be circumspect with you, my closest friend, because you had a higher duty to the king, just as I did. Now I have friendships with many woodfolk of course. You can't stop them treating you as a friend, even if you wanted to, and they can't even begin to comprehend that there might be a need for aloofness." He chuckled, "Did I ever tell you about the time I said to Waterstone and Autumn Leaves that I was struggling to maintain a dignified distance and they just asked in amazement, 'Why would you want to?' …That set me back on my heels. I had never questioned my role before those miscreants wandered into my life." Tarkyn frowned, "Now I've lost my train of thought… Where was I?"

"Talking about friendships with sorcerers."

"Oh yes. Well, now I have close friendships with you and Harkell, each quite different since there are twenty years of age between you and I have known you for so much longer. I have a more formal but surprisingly warm relationship with Stormaway, a casual friendship with our two trappers and a strong connection with Boravar as a result of us sharing the same body for a few hours but one that is tempered by a certain constraint that I think will always be there."

Danton smiled, "You know, your average sorcerer would just say I have six friends. But not you."

Tarkyn's eyes twinkled, "Whatever else I may be, I am not your average sorcerer. Even with woodfolk it has been complicated. I remember Waterstone pointing out that I had to work out terms of engagement with every new person I met, much more than he or anyone else did. He's right and I think it applies even more so to sorcerers."

"Hence your withdrawal in the face of an influx of new sorcerers. You need time to think through your reactions."

Tarkyn shrugged, "Partly. And partly, I naturally equate a large group of sorcerers with greater formality. In public, I have always had a formal role to fulfill… You should know that more than anyone… And as far as I'm concerned, a large group becomes a public forum."

"Waterstone is worried that soon you're going to become so formal that you will start expecting protocols from the woodfolk that they would find uncomfortable."

Tarkyn raised his eyebrows, "And he spoke to you about it, instead of to me, because…?"

Danton grinned, "Don't worry. He was getting around to mentioning it to you. He just hasn't found the right moment yet for a big brother talk."

"Hmph… You know, it is quite awkward trying to juggle different expectations for different groups of people. I don't want to befriend every sorcerer we come across. I am quite happy to be the inaccessible prince I always was, to most of them." The prince leant down and picked up a long stick. As he continued to speak, he broke bits off its end. "I like Drakell. I could see him becoming a friend… when he gets used to me looking like the profile on the old coins! Sorath is a bit rigid for me, although to give him his due, he is trying his best to accommodate my wishes. Rena is an interesting complex character. Yes, I definitely like her. And I suspect Harkell's mother, Thraya, has that down-to-earth common sense that overrides the prejudices that Sorath holds. So I think it might be worth taking some time to get to know her. Kayama is nice enough but very bound up in Harkell and her children at the moment. And Elise? No idea. I haven't got to know her at all yet." Tarkyn leant against an oak and crossed his arms. "But do you see the problem? I don't want to be casual with people who are not my close friends. I want to keep them at arm's length. But here they are, friend and acquaintance alike, in one big group. And so, I err on the side of formality."

"…especially since in your past at court, most people were getting to know you to use you somehow."

"Exactly."

Danton looked up at Tarkyn for a moment, "Come on. Let's sit down somewhere. Do you think you could ask for some wine and food to be brought? I'm starving." He gave a little grin, "I'd do it but I can't send mindmessages."

Tarkyn smiled warmly at him as he pushed himself away from the oak, thinking that he liked the change in their friendship that had occurred since Danton had lost and regained his memory. "I can do that." As he walked across to a fallen tree, looking for a soft grassy spot, Midnight appeared from the bushes behind him. Tarkyn squatted down and held Midnight's eyes for a minute as he silently gave him the errand. Smiling broadly, Midnight scampered off. Tarkyn watched him for a few moments before sitting himself on a grassy patch with his back against a sturdy branch.

Danton followed suit. When he was settled, he gave a little smile. "When you think back only a year, it would have been inconceivable that you would sit casually on the ground like this. You've made a lot of changes. But you don't have to change everything. I have always liked who you are, even at your most formal and aloof," his smile became a grin, "even when you are bawling me out!"

Tarkyn laughed, "Thanks. Amazing how you can compliment and undermine me all at once."

Danton chuckled, "Good isn't it?" Suddenly he became serious. "Tarkyn, you don't have to change everything. Part of your strength and your attraction is your aloofness. Your friends can cope with you being inaccessible at times. Just do what you did when you entered the forest. Follow your heart. Be who you are and that will be good enough."

"Thank you for your faith in me, but who I was in Tormadell was not good enough. I did not give a single thought to those beyond my immediate circle. I knew nothing about the privations caused by my brothers' feud and accepted without question the privileges of my rank without considering what I owed in return." The prince held up a hand to stall Danton's protest. "I know what you are going to say… that I was true to my role and courteous to my retainers."

At this point, Midnight appeared with a stone flagon and two glasses. A disgruntled Sparrow stomped along behind him, carrying a plate of warm rolls, dried fruits, nuts and smoked fish.

"Uh oh," murmured Tarkyn, "I can see I have been a bad uncle and forgotten to show you Sparrow's map.

"Hi Sparrow," said Danton cheerily, leaping into the breach, "We were on our way to look at your map but suddenly I was so overcome with starvation that I couldn't take another step. Thank goodness you have come to save us with all this wonderful food."

Sparrow tried to maintain a pout but failed in the face of Danton's idiocy. "Hmph." Despite her best intentions, her face split into a grin as she handed them the plate of food, "Will you come and look at it soon?" The little girl glanced at the streaky white clouds on the horizon. "There's rain coming."

Tarkyn raised his eyebrows in surprise. "Is there?"

Sparrow nodded with the certainty of someone born and bred in the woodlands. "Yes. And I will be very unhappy if you don't come in time to see the map I specially made for you of the grasslands. You have an hour at the most, I'd say."

"Yes, Ma'am," said Tarkyn meekly. He held out the plate as a peace offering, "Would you like something to eat?"

She took a handful of nuts to share between Midnight and herself. "Thanks. That will mean you have less to eat and will be quicker." She sent a cheeky grin over her shoulder as she skipped off with Midnight to share their spoils.

"I was actually going to say, Tarkyn," said Danton, continuing from where they had left off, "that you always do the best you can with the knowledge you have. When you lived in Tormadell, you were closely guarded and cossetted. It is not surprising that you knew nothing of Eskuzor's troubles." He handed Tarkyn a roll filled with smoked fish and a few dried berries, "Here. Try this combination."

Tarkyn screwed his face up at it, but took a tentative bite. "Hmm. Not bad. A bit weird, but not bad."

Danton grinned, "My latest invention… Don't worry about being more withdrawn. I didn't mean it as a criticism. Do whatever you feel comfortable with. You are, after all, the focus of everyone's attention. And everything you say, praise or criticism, carries much more weight than what anyone else says. That would make me withdraw if I were you. It just might be a good idea to reassure Waterstone that you're not planning to impose court protocols on the woodfolk… assuming that you're not."

Tarkyn snorted, "Of course I'm not. There have always been two sets of expectations; one for sorcerers and one for woodfolk. I would not dream of distressing the woodfolk by imposing behaviours that they would find humiliating." When Danton applied himself assiduously to the creation of his next roll, Tarkyn glanced at him, "Hmm. I know I have dressed you down and humiliated you in front of the woodfolk in the past. In retrospect, I am sorry for that. But it has taken me a lot longer to question the expectations of our sorcerer society when no one else is doing it." The prince gave an embarrassed shrug, "I have always had the right to treat people around me however I wish, except in a scripted formal situation. And, as you know, my brothers consider it to be a weakness to treat their liegemen with anything more than cool courtesy, if not disdain. They and my mother have a fundamental disrespect for anyone outside our family."

"And you?"

"That is where I started from. After all, my family has ruled for a thousand years and it has been drummed into me and every sorcerer that we are superior, almost a race apart." He glanced at Danton again and smiled, "But you bounced your way into my life and I could not come to know you without realizing that you too had your own worth."

Danton grinned, "Likewise, Sire. With or without your rank, you have always had your own worth far greater, in my opinion, than that of other members of your family." His smile faded, "I do have something on my mind that I have to tell you or, perhaps I should say, ask you." He drank down the last of his wine and stood up, holding out his hand in an offer of assistance. "Shall we go? I will tell you as we walk."

Tarkyn accepted his hand to pull him up, but frowned, "You are becoming very managing, Danton. I am not sure how far I would like that to go."

"I apologise, Sire." Danton gave a small bow, hand on heart, friendly and with not a whit of sarcasm in it. "I am edgy because of the need to talk to you and my reluctance to do so. So I have avoided it until now, when we have nearly run out of time."

Tarkyn gave a quizzical smile, "You are still avoiding it. Come on. Spit it out. I've already promised I won't eat you."

Danton took a deep breath and said in a rush. "Sire, Stillwaters Pathfinder, the wizardess in the Lost Forest, has sent a message via woodfolk requesting my presence."

A wave of cool air eddied out from the prince. "And you wish to go to her."

Danton glanced anxiously at him, feeling him withdraw. "Yes Sire. But I don't want to leave you just as the conflict between your brothers is coming to a head and as you are about to visit Lord Tolward. I told her I would go to her if she needed me but only if my duty to you allowed it."

They walked in silence for a long minute. Then Tarkyn took a breath. "Of course you may go. I would not bind you to me against your will. I would value your assistance at Lord Tolward's but Stormaway can stand by my side with his shield at the ready and we have all of Harkell's family to deploy if need be." He looked at his liegeman and managed a smile, "I have mastered my initial reaction now. As a friend, I urge you to go. I think you find this lady intriguing, so you should have an interesting time. Then you can come back and tell me all about it….well, perhaps not all, depending on what happens!"

Danton gave a relieved grin, "She is certainly fascinating. She is so unpredictable; one minute charming, the next a veritable wildcat. But she would not have asked for me on a whim, I think. So I am pleased that I may go to offer her my support."

"If at all possible, I would like you back by my side before my brothers meet on the battlefield, but I know the Lost Forest is fey. Time passes differently there, so I also know you will not be in full control of that intention." He shrugged, "Besides, none of us knows exactly when Kosar and Jarand will actually face each other with their armies behind them."

"So you will not try to intervene with them before it comes to that?"

Tarkyn shook his head. "No. Despite our best efforts, they have taken little more than token notice of us. It has gone too far now, with their troops mustering openly on both sides… But we will think long and hard on how we can intervene in their battle. When would you like to leave?"

"As soon as we have looked at Sparrow's map and I have shown you the layout of the grasslands. The sooner I leave, the sooner I will return… at least, that is what I hope." He scuffed the toe of his shoe along the ground as he walked. "Would you mind if Rainstorm came with me? I'm a bit nervous of the Lost Forest."

Tarkyn smiled, "I don't blame you. I wouldn't want to go back there on my own. Take Rainstorm if he's willing. He'll probably relish the adventure. Maybe you two can think about ideas for thwarting the battle, as you travel. After all, Rainstorm masterminded our last venture."

Before Danton could reply, they rounded a bend in the path and almost walked straight across Sparrow's map, which was etched into the path across its full width. Danton's eyes widened, "Wow, it's big."

Sparrow beamed up at him proudly. "Yes, isn't it? And Midnight has been helping me decorate it."

Midnight stood next to her with his hands behind his back, a hopeful little smile playing around his mouth.

When they looked closer, the two men could see that the outlines of the houses had been filled with little stones and the trees were depicted with small twigs and leaves. Outbuildings were shown with carefully laid out lines of sticks while little red flowers showed where the dogs were housed.

Tarkyn smiled broadly at the pair of them, "This is wonderful. I will understand it much better with all of these decorations. I can see why you were anxious for us to see it before it rains." He ruffled the children's hair and squatted down to have a closer look. Midnight squatted down next to him, watching Tarkyn to copy which parts he was looking at.

"You have done a great job, Sparrow… and Midnight. It looks just as I remember it," said Danton as he reached into a nearby bush and pulled off a dead branch to use as a pointer.

Suddenly, Waterstone and Ancient Oak appeared on the other two sides of the map.

Tarkyn frowned. "This is quite a family gathering. I trust you were not listening in to my conversation with Danton?"

"Give us a little credit," said Waterstone acerbically. "It was obvious he needed to talk to you or rather, you needed him to talk to you."

Tarkyn grinned. "So you won't have heard me reassure Danton that I have no intention of imposing uncomfortable protocols even if I am behaving a little more formally at the moment."

"No, but I am glad to hear it. Actually, I was more concerned for you. Once more, with each new group, it is up to you to choose the rules of engagement. That is a heavy task for one so young. Just remember, we are here if you want us. Make sure you give yourself time away from everyone to be with your family to consolidate who you are, from time to time."

Danton cleared his throat, "I had better go and get ready…"

Tarkyn put a restraining hand on his friend's shoulder, "Danton, you are as much family as the rest of us here and you have been helping me to sort out my thoughts, just as Waterstone wants me to. Please stay."

The blonde sorcerer gave a happy little smile. "Thanks."

"As his older brother and head of the family, I second that," said Waterstone firmly. "As far as I can work out, you two were foster brothers, to all intents and purposes in your sorcerer world, even if it was not acknowledged."

Tarkyn glanced at Danton, "Yes, in many ways, we were, and Danton has always been much truer to me than my own sorcerer brothers."

"Loyalty only cuts one way with your brothers, Tarkyn. They expect it but do not give it." Ancient Oak gave his warm smile, "So Danton, it seems you have done our work for us… In that case, shall we study Sparrow's magnificent map before the rain hits us?"

Over the next twenty minutes, they pointed out to Tarkyn Lord Tolward's house, the pathway across the grasslands, the distances to the neighbouring houses on the grasslands and the road that they had not yet travelled, which disappeared west to wend its way through the forest to meet the road that ran north from Montraya. By the time the first drops of rain fell, Tarkyn had a picture of the grasslands in his mind, but no one had any faith that he would keep it clear in the ensuing discussions.

"Now I really had better get ready," said Danton as they ran for cover. "Ancient Oak, do you know where Rainstorm is?"

As they dived under a temporary shelter that had been strung beneath the branches of huge pine, Ancient Oak asked casually, "So that you can say goodbye to him or take him with you?"

Tarkyn glared at him, "You told me you did not listen in on our conversation."

Ancient Oak smiled, "Who told Danton the sorceress wanted him? A woodwoman from the Lost Forest. Of course all the woodfolk know. It's just the sorcerers who don't."

"Did you notice that, Danton?" asked Tarkyn. "Beneath that mild exterior, Ancient Oak is as tough as old boots. He doesn't give a toss if I get angry with him. He gave as good as he got, right from the start."

Danton raised his eyebrows in surprise.

"And remember?" Waterstone smiled proudly, "Ancient Oak quietly stood up to all of us in the Lost Forest in support of Tarkyn."

In response to Ancient Oak's summons, Rainstorm appeared among them, "Hello all." He smiled at Danton, "Well big brother, when are you heading off? Can I come too?" He transferred his gaze to Tarkyn, "If you can manage without me for a little while, that is."

Danton laughed, "Rainstorm, I would love you to come too. I was just about to ask you. I find the Lost Forest a bit unnerving."

"Hmm. Yes. Now you mention it, it is a strange place. It will be different without everyone with us…" Rainstorm took a deep breath and squared his shoulders, "Still, what could hurt us? I didn't see any wolves, most of the people who lived there have left…"

"You have to face your innermost fear, remember. Otherwise you can't come back out for two full moons," said Tarkyn. "And I want you back sooner than that."

"When's the next full moon?" asked Danton.

Rainstorm rolled his eyes at the need for the question, "In four day's time, you city dweller."

"Oh. So at the worst, we could be stuck there for a little under five weeks." Danton looked at Tarkyn anxiously, "Is that soon enough to return, do you think?"

Tarkyn shook his head. "I have no idea. I think, out of all of us, Stormaway would be best placed to answer that question." He paused for a moment as he mentally requested his wizard's presence. "And I think perhaps another couple of people should go with you, Danton," he gave a little grin, "if for nothing else than to add to your own consequence in the face of this arrogant wizardess. But mainly to give you both greater protection."

After another short pause during which mindmessages were clearly being transmitted, Ancient Oak said, "I would be happy to accompany you, Danton."

Before Danton could reply, Tarkyn added, "And I think you need one of the mountainfolk, who own the legend of the Lost Forest, to accompany you." He let his gaze travel casually over Ancient Oak before saying with perfect seriousness, "And I think you should have a female member of your party to advise if you are dealing with a female. So I suggest that Melting Snow would be the perfect choice, if she is willing."

Ancient Oak glared at Tarkyn, his cheeks tinged with pink. Tarkyn took no notice at all, while Rainstorm, with an unusual show of tact, addressed himself purely to Tarkyn as he replied, "I agree. She seemed to have the most knowledge about the Lost Forest when we were there before."

Before Ancient Oak could think of anything to say, the sound of heavy feet splashing through puddles signalled the arrival of Stormaway with Harkell right behind him.

"News travels fast," observed Tarkyn mildly, resigned to everyone knowing almost as soon as, if not before him. Concerned that Stormaway was taking some time to catch his breath, he placed his hand casually on his old wizard's shoulder and sent a warm soothing stream of *esse* into him. When Stormaway's breathing had eased, Tarkyn asked his opinion about the forthcoming battle.

"It is hard to say, Sire. Men from the lands who are being mustered have little skill at arms. Either side would be most unwise to take them into battle untrained."

"But surely there is a requirement that all men must train once a week for half a day?" objected Tarkyn.

"That is true, Sire. But with the increasing chaos throughout the land, such practices have become haphazard."

"Besides," added Harkell, "target practice or one-to-one fighting is not at all the same as being prepared for a proper battle. These disparate groups of men must learn to work as a unit."

"But will my brothers have the patience to wait or will their antipathy for each other drive them to charge, under-prepared, into battle?"

Stormaway nodded his approval at the question, "Exactly. That is the element that makes predicting a time line so uncertain. I think we can safely say that mustering their men will take another two or three weeks, by the time people arrive from the furthest reaches of the kingdom. As far as I can ascertain, calls to arms have not even reached some holdings yet. Then the two armies will have to advance upon each other. Since there is now no element of surprise, it is unlikely that they will advance in haste to arrive with exhausted men. No. I would think that they will indulge in a game of cat and mouse; feinting their intended destinations, feeding false information to each other, sending out diversionary groups of troops... "

"And I suspect that they may need to stall for long enough to supply enough weapons to their men," said Harkell. "My father and brother have been under pressure for some time from Jarand's troops to manufacture more weapons but the demand has been far greater than the capacity of all the blacksmiths in Montraya to meet it."

"So you do not think they will rush into battle half-cocked?"

Harkell shook his head, "In my opinion, Jarand is more prepared than Kosar. But now that his challenge is out in the open, he cannot afford to fail. As indeed, neither can the king. They will play their cat and mouse games to unnerve each other and to play for time. But both know that, having come this far, there is no turning back. One of them must emerge victorious and woe betide the other. I do not think either of them will enter this battle under-prepared."

"How could it have come to this?" Tarkyn ran his hands through his hair. "Aah, never mind. Let's get Danton sorted out first and worry about the rest later."

Chapter 51

I t was early the next morning before the rain cleared. The four travellers were impatient to set out but had no hope of finding the Lost Forest unaided. They knew that either the Lost Forest would find them or they would have to rely on Stormaway's wizardry to transport them there. They sat around the firesite with the others, their packs ready, waiting while Stormaway cross-referenced between two of his tomes of wizardry, muttering under his breath.

Finally he looked up, "Very well, you four. I am ready. If you could move a little away from the fire… Good." He huffed and puffed away as he circled them, dragging a large stick that left a shallow furrow in the ground behind him. When he had finished, he gave a grunt of satisfaction. "There. Step one completed; place person (or people, at least I hope it works for more than one but I don't see why it shouldn't) inside a circle."

"You are not overwhelming me with confidence," said Danton dryly.

"Step two," said Stormway firmly, overriding him. "Fill the circle with ash, crushed bark and crushed flowers, all from the same tree… representing yesterday, today and tomorrow, you understand." He circled the four of them once more pouring the mixture from a soft leather pouch in to the furrow left by the stick. When he had finished, he tossed the pouch so that it landed beside his books and dusted off his hands. "Now, Step three; each of you must say, 'For the king's sake and in his name, I venture forth to prove my worth.'"

"I'm not saying that," exclaimed Danton.

Rainstorm folded his arms belligerently across his chest. "Neither am I."

"Nor I."

"Nor I."

Stormaway tut-tutted, "Stop being so pedantic. This was written in the time when young men went forth to prove their worth to their king by accepting the challenge of the Forest of Yesterday, Today and Tomorrow… Lost Forest to woodfolk."

"No, Stormaway, I will not say it. You will have to find another way," said Danton firmly. "I don't mind prevaricating from time to time, but there are limits. Besides, we are not out to prove our worth. We're just going to visit Stillwaters Pathfinder, at her request."

The old wizard scratched his head. He knew an impasse when he saw one. He frowned at the sight of Tarkyn grinning hugely from the other side of the firesite, but if anyone had thought about it they would have realised that the wizard should have been more upset then he was. He waved his hand irritably as he turned away to study the text again, "Stay there. Just give me a minute and I'll see what I can come up with." After what was actually several minutes, Stormaway returned, "Very well. This may work. No promises. No one has done it in quite this way before but…So, each of you says, "For the sake of the Guardian of the Forest and in his name,"

He got no further before Danton interrupted, "Hold on. I can't say it's in Tarkyn's name without asking him, and besides, it's not for his sake. It is to help Stillwaters."

Stormaway turned to Tarkyn, "Your Highness, I can assure you that I am doing this for your sake, not just for Danton's, although you do not yet understand why. And allowing them to travel in your name will provide them with added protection in the mystical land of the past forest guardians."

The prince remembered that Stormaway knew more about the wizardess than the rest of them. He thought for a moment. "Danton, you may convey my best wishes to Stillwaters and advise her that she is welcome to our protection, should she need it. Thus, you will travelling for my sake. And if using my name offers you greater protection, then by all means, say that you travel in my name."

Danton gave a shallow bow, hand on heart, "Thank you Sire." He turned to Stormaway. "Come on then. What else do we have to say?"

"For the sake of the Guardian of the Forest and in his name, I will venture forth to seek the Lady of the Lost Forest."

Danton frowned, "That is very different from the original. Are you sure it will work?"

"No, I am not sure it will work," snapped Stormaway, completely losing patience, "And it will certainly never work if you don't try it. Now, will you try it?" When all four nodded, he continued, "While you are saying that, I will be incanting a spell and bringing forth my power. So before we go any further, just in case it works, I would like to wish you a safe and successful journey. Ready? On the count of three… One, two, three."

Danton, Rainstorm, Ancient Oak and Melting Snow spoke slowly in unison, "For the sake of the Guardian of the Forest and in his name, I will venture forth to seek the Lady of the Lost Forest."

As they spoke, Stormaway murmured an incantation under his breath then thrust his hands before him. The ring of bark, ash and flowers burst into flame and the travellers were obscured by the brilliant green of his magic. For a moment, they seemed to shimmer and then, with a quiet little pop, they were gone.

There was an uneasy silence around the firesite, finally broken by Tarkyn who said, "How do you know they have gone to the Lost Forest when the words they said were so different from the original spell?"

Stormaway waved his hand airily, "Oh don't worry about that. The words they speak are only to keep their minds focused on their destination while I do the actual spell… And for show, of course. The wizards of yore were great ones for a performance."

Harkell laughed. "So why didn't you give them something more acceptable to say at the outset?"

The normally serious wizard actually grinned, "I just love watching Danton sticking up for Tarkyn. I couldn't resist it."

CHAPTER 52

Danton came to, lying on his side, feeling horribly nauseated. He rolled over groaning and saw Rainstorm lying motionless beside him, white as a sheet. When he lifted himself shakily onto one elbow he could see Ancient Oak and Melting Snow lying on the other side of Rainstorm in a similar condition. He placed his hand on Rainstorm's chest and was relieved to feel it rising and falling regularly under his hand. With another groan, he flopped back onto the ground and waited for the waves of nausea to pass.

A few minutes later, Danton had recovered enough to begin to take an interest in his surroundings. Great oaks formed a canopy overhead, blocking out most of the sunlight, but the light he could see seemed yellower. It must be closer to sunset than when they had left. He wondered how much time had passed. Two or three hours, he guessed from the change in light.

He took a deep breath and sat up. None of the woodfolk had moved. He peered at Rainstorm's pale face and checked his breathing again. Nothing had changed. Danton still felt a little shaky but was recovering fast. He needed a drink though. He had water in his backpack but didn't want to use it if there was fresh water nearby that he could use instead. He shook his foggy head. On second thoughts, if there were fresh water nearby, he could afford to use his own water and then refill his flask. Having dragged his brain through this roundabout debate, he unstrapped his flask from his pack and drank deeply, having completely overlooked the argument that if there were no fresh water nearby, he would need to conserve what he had.

This thought struck him when he had already drunk half of his flask. He gave a wry grimace, thinking he had better not do anything else until his head was a bit straighter. He sat for a few minutes, carefully revising who he was, who the woodfolk were, why he was here, what his mission was and then, when he had steadied himself, brought his mind to consideration of more pressing issues.

Immediately, Danton stood up and scanned the nearby trees, looking and listening for any other signs of life. He could see no path in any direction and he had no idea where they were, even whether they were, in fact, in the Lost Forest. The only suggestion that they might be in the Lost Forest was the age and grandeur of the oaks that spread above them. But wherever they were, he knew woodfolk could be nearby, completely undetectable by any sorcerer. He thought it unlikely that they would attack their own but nevertheless, after a moment's thought, he raised his aqua shield over the four of them, reasoning that he did not want to run any risks with his friends' lives while they were unable to defend themselves.

Danton was just wondering whether he should venture forth in search of firewood when Rainstorm groaned into consciousness. The young woodman opened green bloodshot eyes and stared up with a puzzled frown. "The lighting is very strange…" His eyes travelled in an arc until he spotted Danton sitting quietly a few feet away from him. He gave a sickly grin, "Oh. It's your shield, isn't it? Hmm. Are we under attack? I don't think I can help much if we are."

"No, little brother, we are not. I'm just making sure you're safe."

"Oh. That's all right then." He rubbed his hands over his face and sat up abruptly. What little colour had returned to his face vanished and he looked as though he was about to vomit. The moment passed and he took a long slow breath "Ooh. That was close. I nearly lost my lunch. I feel horrible." He brought his knees up and rested his head on his hands. After a minute he said, "Is this how you sorcerers feel when you translocate? It's not fun, is it? We don't feel anything at all when we flick."

"Yes, you can see why we don't translocate very often." He offered Rainstorm his flask. "Here. Have some water. It will make you feel better."

"Thanks. And thanks for the shield. I forgot to say that, didn't I?"

Danton grinned, "If you're not in a fit state to fight, you're certainly not in a fit state to be polite. Besides, doesn't being your brother mean 'that we may call upon each other's strength in times of need?'"

Rainstorm, who was clearly feeling a lot better, grinned in return, "Yes, it does but I can still thank you."

Their attention was diverted by Melting Snow who drew in a shuddering breath and passed her hand shakily across her forehead. "Ugh. I feel awful." She looked sideways and her eyes dilated with panic when she saw Ancient Oak, pale and still beside her. "Oh no. Ancient Oak." She threw her arm across his chest, grabbed him by the shoulder and shook him. "Ancient Oak. Wake up. Come on. Oh stars! He's not dead, is he? I couldn't bear it."

Rainstorm took hold of her and detached her from Ancient Oak, turning her so that he could look into her eyes. He spoke soothingly, "No, no, no. He's not dead, Melting Snow. Calm down. You looked just like that yourself a minute ago. Just be gentle with him."

Melting Snow gave a little sniff and then, rather to Rainstorm's horror, burst into tears.

"I'm sorry," she said between sniffs. "I don't know what came over me. I'm not usually so silly." As Rainstorm put an awkward arm around her, she leaned into his shoulder. "It's just….he's such a *nice* person. He's quiet and gentle and kind … a-and so rock solid underneath."

"Don't worry. He'll be all right." He just held her for a while until she was calmer. "You like him, don't you? A lot." Gone was the taunting Rainstorm who had teased Lapping Water about Tarkyn. Now his voice was gentle.

"Yes. No." Melting Snow glanced up at him, "I mean yes, but it doesn't matter because he would never look twice at me."

"What makes you say that?"

"Because I'm too shy. When I *really* care about something or someone, I just clam up. Every time I'm anywhere near him, I get so tongue-tied I can't think of anything to say. He probably thinks I'm the dullest thing on two legs. I've hardly spoken a word to him the whole time I've known him."

A faint groan from behind them alerted them to the fact that Ancient Oak was at last recovering. Quick as a flash, Rainstorm jumped up and said to Danton, "Come on. We don't need that shield now that we're awake. Let's see if there's a stream nearby to replenish your water. You and I have used up most of it already."

Danton frowned at Rainstorm's tactics but, short of increasing Melting Snow's embarrassment by objecting in front of the quickly recovering Ancient Oak, he could do nothing but fall in with the scheme of his match-making brother.

Left alone with Ancient Oak, Melting Snow sat beside him with her arms wrapped around her knees, stiff with apprehension.

As she watched him, Ancient Oak gave her a wavering smile. "Hello," he said, his creaky voice even creakier than usual, "Are you all right? I feel awful." When she nodded but said nothing further, he asked, "Any water nearby?"

"Sorry," Melting Snow blushed at her oversight and fumbled in her haste to extract her flask from the strap holding it to her pack.

Ancient Oak reached out his hand and placed it gently on her arm. "It's all right. Don't rush. I'm not dying of thirst."

"Oh," Melting Snow was so overcome at him touching her that she convulsively gripped the flask which shot from between her hands up into the air. It flew up in an arc and landed several yards away. "Oh dear," she said faintly.

She scrabbled to stand up intending to retrieve the flask, then realised that the grip on her arm had strengthened and was preventing her from moving. She looked around and found Ancient Oak grinning at her.

"Melting Snow, calm down. You'll fall over your own feet if you're not careful."

She took a deep breath and nodded, taking a moment to gather herself. When she was back beside him, Ancient Oak sat up slowly, drew his legs up and put his head between his knees, waiting until the worst of the nausea had passed before raising his head and accepting the proffered flask. "Thanks." After he had moistened his dry mouth, his brain began to work and he looked around, asking in alarm, "Where are Danton and Rainstorm? We're not the only ones to have made it through, are we? Stars! I hope they're all right."

"Don't worry. They're fine. They have just gone to get some water." Having answered his question, Melting Snow lapsed into an uneasy silence.

"So, do you think this is the Lost Forest?"

Melting Snow gave a little shiver, "It is nowhere I recognise from anywhere else and these trees are very old... don't you think?"

Ancient Oak eyed her for a moment, "Are you cold or frightened?" Before she could answer, he summoned up his courage and put his arm around her shoulder, "Whichever it is, maybe this will help."

She tensed up so much that Ancient Oak nearly took his arm away but then she heaved a sigh of relief and leaned in against his shoulder.

"That better?"

Melting Snow nodded. After a little while, she said, "It's a bit spooky not knowing where we are." Suddenly, her excitement at being held by him bubbled over. She looked up at him from where she had been assiduously studying the ground and gave him a dazzling smile, then just as quickly, resumed her study of the ground.

Ancient Oak gave her a squeeze and a puzzled smile, "What was that all about?"

"Oh, nothing," Although he couldn't see her face, he could hear the smile in her voice.

"Hmm." He pondered her behaviour and came to the unwelcome conclusion that she was laughing at him. He started to pull away, saying, "I think perhaps I had better go and find the other two."

She turned a stricken face towards him, all signs of laughter gone, "Oh no! Don't go."

The woodman frowned at her, "Melting Snow, I don't understand... or maybe you don't understand. I'm not trying to be funny. Sometimes I don't mind being laughed at, but this isn't one of those times."

"I wasn't laughing at you," said Melting Snow quietly. She took a deep breath, screwing up her courage, "I just couldn't help smiling because I was so happy that you were holding me."

"Really?"

"Really."

Ancient Oak grinned, "I see what you mean about not being able to help smiling. I've been trying to get around to this for months now. I remember telling Tarkyn how special you were, the day after the curse was broken. That's ages ago. But you never spoke to me so I thought you couldn't like me."

"I never spoke to you because I *did* like you."

"Hmm. Now I think about it, likewise. We are neither of us very forthcoming, are we?"

"Exactly," said Rainstorm with great satisfaction, appearing in front of them. "So I'm glad you have sorted it out now."

"Oh. I see. That's why you and Danton weren't here." Ancient Oak gave Melting Snow a quizzical frown, "Were you part of this plot?"

"No. Rainstorm dragged Danton off, the second you looked like coming around and left me on my own with you." She gave a little grin. "I was horrified…"

This seemed to please Ancient Oak more than offend him and he hugged her even closer, just as Danton arrived.

Danton looked from one to the other, "I see my wily younger brother has succeeded where I would not have tried." He smiled, "Well done, you two. It will make our trip a lot easier now that you two are speaking to each other."

Ancient Oak laughed as he stood up and held out his hand for Melting Snow to follow suit, "You make it sound as though we were fighting."

Danton gave the woodman a friendly slap on the back, "No, now that you are speaking to each other, that is a joy to look forward to."

Suddenly Ancient Oak stilled. "I saw a movement between the trees over there," he murmured.

"Shield?" mouthed Danton.

"You may need it," said Rainstorm quietly, "But we won't."

A shadow detached itself from the trees and scurried cautiously forward a few feet.

Melting Snow frowned. "It's a silver fox. Maybe the same one as last time. Remember? They can lead people out of trouble or to their doom. But it was kind to us last time and at least it may lead us somewhere… What do you think?"

When they made no aggressive moves, the fox slunk forward until it was within ten yards of them. Then it sat on its haunches and waited.

Danton shrugged. "We have no better ideas. We don't even know where a path is at the moment."

They bent slowly, careful not to startle the fox and picked up their packs. As Danton moved towards it, the fox turned and began to return the way it had come. But as soon as the woodfolk took a step towards it, it turned back and growled.

"Too many of us, do you think?" asked Danton.

Melting Snow shook her head. "No, it led many more of us than this, last time. No. I think it only wants you to follow it, Danton."

Danton swung his pack off his shoulder and sat down, "So what if I won't go on my own?"

Ancient Oak smiled, "I guess we will find out."

The three woodfolk sat down with Danton and waited.

The silver fox returned to its original position, sat on its haunches and watched them.

After a few minutes, Rainstorm rummaged in his pack and brought out some nuts and fruit. "So since we're here, with nothing to do, let's eat."

"We could head off in a different direction to explore," suggested Melting Snow, nevertheless accepting a handful of nuts.

Between mouthfuls, Rainstorm said "Maybe we could follow Danton if we kept our distance."

Danton heaved an exasperated sigh. "I expect it is that annoying woman dictating the rules of our encounter. Last time, she placed a glamour over the entrance to her clearing because Harkell was with me. When I returned later in the day, the entrance was easy to find because I was alone."

Melting Snow considered him a moment, "Perhaps she would feel intimidated by a group of us arriving together?"

"Huh. I don't think so. She has people working for her, you know." He screwed up his face as he thought about it. "Well, at least one person, that is." He shrugged, "Maybe she does feel a little intimidatted. She is not used to company."

Ancient Oak smiled at Danton, his smile a variation on the one Waterstone produced that gave Tarkyn so much strength at times. "Danton, she asked you to come and you said she would not do so lightly. You have responded to her request, only to stall when it cannot be exactly on your terms."

"Well, we don't know that. Danton's just guessing," said Rainstorm, rising to his bloodbrother's defence. "That fox could lead him anywhere."

Ancient Oak picked out a couple of hazelnuts and gave a sudden smile, "I remember the grove we picked these from. It was when I was travelling with the Harvesters to avoid Tarkyn… Hmm. Anyway, let's think about last time we were in the Lost Forest. The first group, which Melting

Snow, Rainstorm and I were part of, followed the fox to a beautiful little clearing with running water and food laid on. The second group, which you were in, Danton, found the first group by following Tarkyn's absurd navigational strategy of following their hearts."

"Yes. So?" demanded Rainstorm at his most belligerent.

Ancient Oak ate a hazelnut before replying, "So why don't we think about how we feel about the fox? Do we *feel* that it will be leading Danton into danger or that we will be in danger if we are left behind?"

Rainstorm snorted, "That's a bit fluffy, Ancient Oak. Are you proposing that we let Danton go off with the fox by himself if it *feels* all right?"

"Yes. I think all four of us know more than we realise about our surroundings; the risks, the time of day, the meaning of the sounds, smells, sights… And I think intuition counts even more in the Lost Forest."

There was a protracted silence as each of them considered this, then relaxed their minds and let their senses drift through the trees. Finally Rainstorm said reluctantly, "You may be right. I don't sense any danger from the fox or anywhere else… One question though. Danton, if you think Stillwaters Pathfinder is using the fox to bring you to her on your own, does that mean she has powers like Tarkyn; to communicate with animals?"

Danton thought about it, then shook his head. "I don't think so. I can't be sure but I don't think so. Probably one of the old forest guardians is helping her."

Rainstorm's brow cleared, "Oh yeah. I forgot about them. So, what do the rest of you feel or think about the fox?"

Melting Snow shrugged, "If those forest guardians are behind all this, I'd say we might as well allow them to direct us. After all, they are quite capable of creating illusions that will lead us astray if they choose to."

"I must admit I don't feel as though I am being invited into danger," said Danton with a rueful smile. "Perhaps I should just go with good grace and see you when I get back."

"I think so," said Ancient Oak. "I don't sense any malevolence. The birds are chirruping away. The fox looks relaxed, just as it did last time. Just be ready to use your shield, if need be."

Danton stood up and once more hoisted his pack onto his back. The silver fox waited until Danton was clear of the woodfolk then turned and trotted off through the trees, with Danton following at a relaxed walk. Just before he disappeared out of sight, he turned and waved at them.

"Should we follow him, do you think?" asked Rainstorm anxiously. "We could easily keep up and out of sight."

"I don't think it's as easy as that," said Melting Snow. "I think there are woodfolk in those trees and they may not like us sneaking our way through their territory without meeting them first."

"Hmm. And I remember now; mindtalking doesn't work properly here, does it?" Rainstorm sighed in frustration, "So we can't simply ask them to keep an eye on Danton for us."

Ancient Oak smiled sympathetically. "Besides, how would we know where their loyalties lie? Everything is different in the Lost Forest. Woodfolk don't just stick with woodfolk here."

"And when did we start assuming that we are actually in the Lost Forest?" grumped Rainstorm.

Melting Snow laughed, "When the silver fox appeared. Not conclusive, I know. People on the mountains have seen silver foxes outside the Lost Forest but it seems too much of a coincidence for us, don't you think?... Stormaway's spell, the ancient trees and then the fox."

The young woodman nodded in reluctant agreement. "So we wait."

Chapter 53

The silver fox led Danton into a thick forest of pine trees. The sorcerer had to bend over and push hard to force his way through the perimeter of overhanging branches to breach the pine forest's boundary. Once inside, the trees formed a dense canopy overhead with few lower branches to obstruct his course. Underfoot, the forest floor was covered with pine needles and mosses of different shades of green and yellow. Tiny brooks, no more than a foot wide, flowed along channels they had cut in the soft ground.

"This is beautiful," breathed Danton as he stopped to look around. Immediately the fox sat and waited.

Danton squatted down next to a brook and scooped handfuls of crystal clear water into his mouth. "Hmm. Cold. Can't taste any pine in it. Lovely." He shook the water off his hand and stood up. "All right then fox. Let's go."

Danton knew it was his stance more than his words that made the fox leap to its feet and turn to lead the way once more. He followed down a gentle slope through the pine forest until they reached the other side. Once more Danton had to bend over and push his way through the branches that formed the boundary of the pine forest but it was easier on the way out because the branches were growing in the direction he was travelling.

He emerged to find himself on a dirt track with wild grasslands on the other side of it. The fox was already trotting along the track to Danton's left where it followed the perimeter of the pine forest for another two hundred yards before curving right to disappear downhill into woodlands of huge beeches, oaks and sycamores.

Danton squinted at the approaching tree line, trying to work out whether this part of the forest was familiar. It was hard to tell because last time they had been here, it had been in the depths of winter and the trees had been bare. He looked behind him. He didn't remember seeing the pine forest.

As he followed the fox through the woodlands, his sense of familiarity became stronger. The branches above him were twisted and gnarled with age, just as he remembered them, even if they were now covered in foliage. Suddenly, further up the track to the left, Danton spotted an ancient tree that bore a large oval scar where a branch had fallen off at some time in the past. His heart gave a thump of excitement.

"That's it," he exclaimed. "That's the tree I noted to find the entrance to Stillwater's clearing."

Even as he spoke, the fox turned off the path to the right and disappeared into an animal track that burrowed its way through the undergrowth. Without a second's hesitation, Danton swung his pack off his back and, pushing it before him, went down on all fours to follow his guide.

Once more, the tunnel led him around a long left hand turn, down a short slope before climbing in a right hand curve. As he crested a small hill and began to crawl the final curve to the left, Danton felt his heart beating hard in anticipation. He picked up his pace for the last thirty yards as he saw the brightness that signalled the end of the brush tunnel.

As he reached the end, he stopped to take a few deep breaths to calm himself. He didn't want to appear flustered before the redoubtable wizardess. His eyes wandered around the small circular clearing, past the soft greenery and reeds to the perfectly round pool that still nestled at the bottom of a tumbled pile of boulders. But the waterfall was gone. The heat of summer must have dried it up. The clearing was still beautiful though. Sitting on a ledge overlooking the pool, was a young woodwoman, dressed in their accustomed light brown, but in a flowing skirt rather than leggings. Her long light brown hair flowed over her right shoulder. Danton frowned in surprise, until he realised that he was actually looking at Stillwaters Pathfinder, her colouring changed yet again.

He straightened up and picked his way carefully through the bushes until once more he stood at the pool looking up at her. He gave a deep bow. "I have come, my Lady Stillwaters. I am pleased to see you once more."

"Lord Danton, I am honoured that you have left your lord's side to answer my call."

Danton repressed the urge to say, "So you should be," and said instead, "I hope you are well. The brown hair and green eyes suit you."

"Thank you. Come up and sit with me. Once more Caroman has excelled himself and produced a fine repast for us." She smiled at her manservant who had appeared out of the shadows, "And at such short notice too. Most impressive."

Danton noted the change in her attitude towards Caroman and wondered at its cause. Last time she had been quite dismissive of him.

Danton climbed the path around the back of the boulders and emerged into the small space between the rocks which was still decorated with flowering vines. He suddenly realised the flowers could not have been natural last time he came, in the depth of winter. Danton stood at the small dining table that was set incongruously within the natural setting, admiring the quality of the damask table cloth, the fine china and crystal, as he waited for Stillwaters to join him.

Caroman arrived first and with a bow, presented a tall glass of white wine on a silver tray.

"Thank you," said Danton, accepting the glass. "It is also good to see you again."

The sorcerer gave a slight smile before withdrawing in one direction just as Stillwaters appeared from the other, carrying her own glass of wine.

Danton smiled her a welcome. "So, is this your true appearance? Were you hiding the fact that you are a woodwoman?"

Stillwaters raised an eyebrow. "Why would I wish to hide it? Is it so shameful to be a woodwoman?"

"Not at all. In fact, one of the greatest honours of my life was to be accepted as a member of the woodfolk… and to become a bloodbrother to Rainstorm."

"Yes, I heard that you were. You are right, it is a great honour." She raised her glass to him. "Congratulations."

"Thank you."

The wizardess studied him. "Something has changed about you. You seem…less intense, more sure of yourself… It strikes me that you may care less for other people's opinions of you than you did…?"

Danton thought for a minute. "Perhaps. I lost my memory, you know. And with it, everything and everyone I knew, even myself. When it returned, I saw everything with fresh eyes, even Tarkyn. In fact, he used my time without a memory to teach me who he was, without the veil of his royalty obscuring my perceptions."

"That was clever of him; to grasp that opportunity. And courageous. He must be feeling very sure of himself to take that chance."

"I suppose so." Danton grinned. "But I think he has had enough time with the woodfolk who do not care about his status, to know that he can be liked just for himself."

Stillwaters tilted her had sideways and smiled, "You are definitely less in awe of him than you were." She waved her hand at the table. "Shall we sit down?"

When they were both seated, she took a sip of wine and said, "I am not a woodwoman, you know. But I am pleased you would not object if I were… And I am pleased at the change in you. It is as though you have grown into yourself."

"When I could not remember who I was, I assumed I was a woodman because when I awoke, I was surrounded only by woodfolk." He paused, knowing he was about to risk her ire. "But when I remembered who I was, I was horrified at the presumption I had made in thinking myself a woodman."

Stillwaters was surprisingly mild in her response, with only a hint of acid in her voice. "You do not approve of my most recent choice of colouring?"

"On purely aesthetic grounds, I find it most becoming. But to choose such colouring if it is not your own, makes a statement… and I am not sure what you are trying to say. Do you wish you were a woodwoman? Are you making fun of them? Do you just admire their colouring?"

The wizardess gave the ghost of a laugh. "You are a brave man, Danton Patronell, to discuss a woman's appearance with her, without giving it your full approval."

Danton grinned. "I know. But you are an enigma that needs to be solved."

"You will not solve me until I choose to let you. Two things I will tell you, though. Firstly, I wore this colouring to honour your admission among woodfolk…"

"Thank you."

"And secondly, I believe woodfolk should be honoured by any desire I might have to look like them, even temporarily."

Danton snorted. "I think they are rather more self-possessed than that… unless the woodfolk of the Lost Forest have a completely different culture from those I have met."

Stillwaters smiled, "I didn't say 'would'. I said 'should'. Sadly, the Lost Forest woodfolk are just as stubbornly egalitarian as those outside."

"And is your status so great that people would wish for your approval?"

"It was once, and it will be again, possibly even greater. And even now, I am the Wizardess of the Lost Forest."

Danton sighed. "You're being deliberately provocative, aren't you? When will you show me what you really look like?" Danton nodded his thanks to Caroman but kept his eyes on Stillwater as the manservant served small pastry boats filled with mushroom, herbs and dried slivers of venison.

She laughed. "So impatient. Soon, I promise you." Her smile faded. "All too soon." She picked up a pastry boat and popped into her mouth. "My true appearance is not so different from how I look at the moment. This is my true height, my true shape. My face is similar but not exactly the same. Only my true colouring is different."

"And are you the age that you appear to be?" Danton tensed, expecting her to take exception.

Sure enough, her voice developed an edge. "And what difference would that make?"

Danton shrugged. "That would depend on the age. If you were only six years old, for instance, I would definitely have to reconsider my attitude towards you."

Stillwaters tinkled with laughter. "You are a master at getting yourself out of tight corners." She took a drink from her glass, her green eyes shining at him over its rim. "And what attitude would that be?"

Danton put his glass down. "Hmm. It is certainly not the attitude a twenty-two year old man would have towards a young girl. But more than that, I am not sure. Last time we met, you asked me not to see you again before I left, for fear that you might miss me too much when I was gone… And last time, I told you I cared for you, too much to lie to you."

"While making it clear you were not proposing marriage," she added dryly.

"But as I remember, you replied that you too wouldn't dream of marrying someone after only knowing them for a few hours. True?"

"True," she agreed reluctantly.

Caroman quietly cleared the remains of the first course and returned with baked quails covered in a citrus and plum sauce.

They ate their quails in silence, concentrating on using the small silver knives and forks to manage them, rather than resorting to the far easier use of fingers.

Finally, when Caroman had cleared away the second course, Danton said carefully, "We have still only known each other for a short time…"

"That is true." She kept her eyes on the table cloth until Caroman refilled her glass. Suddenly, she looked up at her manservant and smiled her thanks and it seemed to Danton that Caroman gave her a nod in return, not of acknowledgement but of encouragement. Stillwaters turned resolutely towards Danton, "But we talked longer that day and months have passed since we last met. A lot has happened to you during that time. Your brush with death, your memory loss, becoming a woodman…"

"Falling under Jarand's spell…" At her look of query, he gave his head a slight shake, "I'll tell you later…"

Her mouth tightened, but after a moment she continued, "And we have had time to think about one another… But now time is running out. Events outside the Forest rush towards a resolution. Even now two armies are gathering for the final showdown between the two brothers." She drew a deep breath, "And before that happens, you and I must come to an understanding, one way or the other."

Danton's hand stilled in the act of picking up his glass. After a noticeable hesitation, it continued on its way. Danton brought the glass to his lips and, after taking a slow sip, carefully set it down again. He could feel his heart thumping in his ears as he tried to work out what she meant, how he felt and what he was going to say… because he knew that at this moment, despite her spikiness, he could hurt her or drive her away irrevocably with one misplaced word. "Stillwaters, as I approached your clearing earlier today, I felt excited at the prospect of seeing you again. I have thought of you often since we last met. After our first meeting, I thought you so grand and gracious that I told Harkell that you were above my touch. By the end of our second meeting, I wondered if perhaps you were not so unassailable as I had first thought." He smiled, "I find you witty, annoying, entrancing and frustrating by turn. It is hard to extol your virtues without including your beauty and yet the beauty I have seen is an illusion."

"Calling me annoying and frustrating is hardly extolling my virtues."

Danton laughed. "No. But those qualities are part of your allure."

Stillwaters put down her glass and stood up. For a moment, as he hastily followed suit, Danton thought he must have offended her. She clasped her hands together tightly at her waist and Danton suddenly realised it was to keep them from trembling.

"Danton Patronell, Lord of Sachmore and woodman of the forest, would you do me the honour… could you find it in your heart… to marry me?"

Oh, well that's cleared up what she meant by coming to an understanding, said one idiotic part of Danton to another.

Danton gave a deep bow, "My Lady, I am honoured. I care deeply for you, more so than for any other woman I know…"

"But you refuse," she said tightly.

"No, I do not refuse. But I wish to talk to you further before I accept."

Stillwaters' tight shoulders dropped slightly. "Do you need longer to get to know me better? We have so little time."

"I admit that I would prefer not to be rushed like this, Stillwaters. You ask for my life and my loyalty without even showing me who you truly are."

"Do you not yet have the measure of me?"

Danton came around the table and took her hands in his, noticing that her eyes were almost on a level with his. "Yes. I think perhaps I do. But do you have the measure of me? Do you choose me because I am a lord? You seem to have a care for social standing. I worry that you are isolated here and have not met others to judge me against."

Stillwaters gave a little smile. "You think I have fallen for the first courtly man I have met?" She shook her head. "There have been others here, I assure you. Many courtiers chose to come to the Lost Forest to prove their worth to the King. They may be decades older than me but it does not show because no one ages in this Forest unless they are born here. I have been courted by many but have refused them all."

"Why then, do you choose me?"

She smiled warmly at him, "Because you are willing to fence with me. Because you sidestep my traps and prove yourself equal to managing me and my moods."

"I have had years of practice, coping with Tarkyn's humours. Perhaps that holds me in good stead." He frowned. "But do you wish to be managed? I would have thought you more indomitable than that."

"I don't mean that you try to control me. I mean that you stop me from becoming too angry or too hurtful. You accept who I am without diminishing who you are. I do not want someone who merely panders to me." She squeezed his hands, "You are a rare person, Danton Patronell…"

"If I accepted you, then what of Tarkyn? I do not intend to leave him, particularly now… and I will always be loyal to him. How do your wishes and intentions fit with that?"

"My…Tarkyn is a very lucky man and I envy him. But if I could lure you away from your loyalty to your sworn liege, then you would not be the person I was looking for. I intend to return with you to work by Tarkyn's side in the foreshadowed conflict." Stillwaters took her hands out of Danton's grip. She indicated the table and sat down, putting a little distance between them. "I would never work against the Guardian of Eskuzor and I expect you would never let me anyway. But I will be honest with you; if you marry me, there may be a time in the future when your ways will part." She gave a little smile, "But, from what I have heard of his interfering nature, you and I would still see him from time to time."

Danton, once more seated across from her, drank down the last of his wine. "You seem to know much of the future," he said at last, "more than you are willing to share, I suspect. I am not sure how much I relish a lifetime of being toyed with."

Caroman arrived with a baked fish, covered in herbs, accompanied by a warm loaf of soft white bread, which he proceeded to distribute onto two plates and pass to the two of them. Danton saw the old retainer tilt his head slightly when he was facing Stillwaters and she gave the faintest shrug in return. *It is a very strange marriage proposal, thought Danton, that has a third party taking an interest in its progress. And a strange marriage proposal that takes so much negotiation… almost like an arranged marriage.*

Suddenly, Danton asked, "Do you care for me or am I just a suitable match?"

Stillwaters put down her knife and fork with trembling hands. "You are more than a suitable match, Danton, much more. I love you. I think, in you, I have found my soul mate." She took a breath and drew herself up, "But if I must, I can face the future alone. I will not beg and I will not tell you any more before you decide. The time is not right… Excuse me." Before Danton could move, she fled from the table.

As she disappeared around the side of a huge boulder, Danton saw a flash of black that he couldn't understand. A slight movement made him turn to find Caroman at his elbow.

"Is the fish to your taste, my lord?" he asked urbanely.

"Yes. No. I don't know," muttered Danton, considerably flustered. "How can you talk of fish at a time like this?"

"She will return, sir, when she has composed herself."

"What are you two playing at?" demanded Danton. "I saw the signs that passed between you."

"Sir, I can assure you, this is no game. I simply care for her welfare. I beg your pardon if I have offended you."

Danton stood up abruptly, nearly knocking the chair over, "If you can keep the fish warm, do so. I am going for a walk. I need time to think."

The blonde sorcerer found his way down into the clearing. He looked up at the ledge above the pool but it was empty. Stillwaters was nowhere in sight. He moodily picked up a flat pebble and sent it skipping across the surface of the pool nearly to the other side. His mind grabbed at the chance to be diverted so he set himself the challenge of getting a pebble to skip the whole way across. After the eighth try, his pebble skipped out of the water to hit the other side with a little clatter. He gave a little grunt of satisfaction and returned his mind to Stillwaters.

It was not sorcerer custom for a woman to propose to a man. So on that front alone, he felt discomforted. The initiative, if there were to be any, should have come from him. He felt cornered, even though he believed that she felt pressured by circumstance. He remembered her tight face just before she had left the table. If this was hard for him, how much harder was it for her, a proud independent woman, to expose her feelings to an uncertain response? And how would he feel if he walked away?

He picked up a larger stone and threw it forcefully across the pool. It hit the boulder on the other side with a loud, satisfying crack. "Blast the woman! Of course I can't leave her. And I probably do love her." He heaved a sigh, "Of course I love her. She has been on my mind since the day we left this Forest. She just drives me to distraction." He smiled to himself, "But I think life might be too dull without her."

As soon as his decision was made, he realised that he had kept her in an agony of uncertainty for nearly an hour. He raced back up the path only to find the table cleared and no one in sight. He was seized with panic that Stillwaters had given up on him and left.

Before he could decide what to do next, Caroman appeared unsmilingly and said, "If you will wait a moment, My Lady Stillwaters will see you."

He withdrew and Danton waited… and waited… and waited.

A good fifteen minutes later, the wizardess glided in, dressed in a long white billowing gown, her hair ice blonde and her eyes a glittering pale blue. When she spoke, her tone was frigidly polite. "So Lord Danton, have you come to take your leave? I hope your return journey causes you less distress than your translocation into the Forest did. Accept my apologies for leaving in that discourteous manner. The moment has passed and I am quite well again." She held out her hand. "No doubt we will meet again when I come to the aid of your liege."

Danton took her hand and kissed it. "I deserve your severity. I have been most unkind to you. Please forgive me." He straightened up so that he could look her in the eye, keeping her hand in his. "Lady Stillwaters, if you will still have me, I will marry you, and love you, and be your partner for life."

The ice maiden melted. "Oh Danton, thank you." Her pale blue eyes suffused with tears, "You see? Only you could have found a way to thaw me so fast." As he pulled her into his arms, she smiled through her tears, "Oh dear. I am all undone." She clung to him. "So whether or not I am ready, you are about to see my true shape." She buried her face in his shoulder so that all he could see was the top of her head.

As he watched, her hair gradually darkened; to the strawberry blonde he had seen the first time he met her, then to the soft woodfolk brown but then darker still until he was looking down at raven black.

"Black is all right. I like black hair. It is…" The words died on his lips as she lifted her head. Amber eyes looked up at him from a face with high cheek bones, slanted eye brows and a profile that could be seen on old coins. He held her away from him staring at her face, "Who are you?"

"My birth name is Navira Tamadil. I am Tarkyn's older sister."

He shook his head in wonder and pulled her back into his arms. "Come back here. I am not going to leave you uncertain a second time. I have no idea how this could be. I have never heard of an older sister and I lived at the palace from eight years old. Oh my stars! I can't believe it. I am affianced to a member of the Royal family." He grinned, "No wonder you're so arrogant. You're just like Tarkyn!"

Navira laughed. "*I'm* arrogant? You just put a Tamadil through twenty questions before you would accept an offer of marriage. It doesn't get more arrogant than that!" She looked at him quizzically. "Aren't you the least bit curious to know how I could even exist?"

"Of course I am, but I thought I would just boggle at one thing at a time."

Navira pushed him in the chest, "You absurd man. You see? If you had seen me as I am, you would have felt constrained to keep a respectful distance."

Danton chuckled. "True. It was much easier dealing with an ice maiden."

"You have changed, you know. I expected you to go down on one knee and address me as Your Highness when you found out who I was."

Danton looked surprised at himself. "Yes, I suppose I should have, but I was more worried about making sure you knew that I accepted you, no matter what." He smiled at her, taking the sting out of his next words, "Besides, I said I would be your lifelong partner, not your liegeman."

Caroman appeared, looking unaccountably older, carrying a silver tray on which stood three tall glasses of sparkling wine. Once he had set down the tray and handed out the glasses, he smiled warmly and held out his glass in salutation, "Congratulations, Navira, my little one, and Lord Danton. You have made an old man very happy. But more than that; in time, your union will bring happiness to all of Eskuzor."

And who on earth is he to be so paternal? And what is he talking about? wondered Danton, as he smiled his thanks and drank a toast to his future bride. *Oh well. I am part of it now, for better or worse, and I will not pull back from my commitment.*

CHAPTER 54

Above the clearing, the sky had paled to a soft yellow and the first star shone near the horizon. Danton sat beside the pool, with his back against a rock and Navira within the circle of his arm.

"I am worried about my friends," he said, "because they will be worried about me," Danton smiled, "and I'm not sure how long Rainstorm can stand the uncertainty."

Navira turned her vivid amber eyes up to him, framed by her long black hair, "Through the Lost Forest woodfolk, I have provided them with a hamper of food and wine and sent a reassurance of your safety. Beyond that, I have not presumed to say when you will rejoin them."

"So you and Caroman have not yet orchestrated my entire life?"

"Don't be mean. Caroman has been with me since I left the palace when I was ten days old, a year before you were born. He will not collude with me to run your life, I promise you. He just helped me through the most difficult experience of my life, that's all."

Danton gave her an apologetic squeeze but asked, "Why then were you so disdainful of him last time we met?"

"I… We were trying to impress you. I needed to intrigue you enough that you would want to come again." She shrugged, "And he appeared younger to show you I was protected. You were not yet a friend."

Danton laughed, "Fancy a Tamadil trying to impress *me*. As I recall, you were so haughty and even unkind at times, that you nearly drove me away."

"Hmm. That was not pretence. That is how I am sometimes… and why I need you to temper me." She was drawing circles on the ground with a strand of grass. Suddenly she looked up. "Why did you believe who I was when it must seem almost impossible?"

"Stormaway says that Tarkyn's amber eyes cannot be duplicated."

"I could be a stronger wizard than he."

Danton smiled at her, "And are you?"

"Possibly. I began my apprenticeship at a younger age than he, but he has had more years of study."

"That's impressive. Stormaway is pretty good." Danton stroked her hair. "No, that wasn't the real reason. I just know when you're telling the truth. That's all."

"Is that because I am like Tarkyn?"

Danton laughed, "No, my sweet. Tarkyn doesn't lie whereas you are quite good at it. I learnt to tell truth from lies to protect Tarkyn, not to deal with him."

"Other than my appearance, am I like him?" She asked wistfully, keeping her eyes trained on the circles she was drawing in the dust. "I don't know him at all, you see....nor Jarand, nor Kosar. Only by repute and report."

Just as Danton was considering how to answer, a stone dropped into the pool from above. Navira pulled away and said urgently, "Do not fear. You are safe but I must go." She pulled a shard of rock from her pocket, muttered, "*Maya Mureva Araya*," and was gone.

Danton was left feeling once more that he was caught in the toils of events he did not understand. He glanced up and saw Caroman waiting to wave a reassurance at him before disappearing out of view.

Suddenly three woodfolk flicked into view in front of him.

Rainstorm beamed at him. "Hi Danton. Came to see what you were up to."

Danton jumped to his feet and gave his bloodbrother a big hug, "Hello, you mad snake! I knew they couldn't keep you away for long." He hugged the other two in turn. "And how is the grand romance going?"

Ancient Oak and Melting Snow glanced at each other and grinned.

Taking this as a reply, Rainstorm said, "We met some friendly woodfolk who gave us some extra food but once we knew they wouldn't be hostile, we followed your trail. They can't have been too serious about keeping us away or they would have covered your tracks."

Danton gave a dry laugh, "Perhaps they assumed you would follow their wishes. Clearly an error when dealing with you."

"Clearly," said Rainstorm unrepentantly. "So, what's up? Anything we can help with? What does the wizardess want from you?"

Danton was tempted to reply, "Me," but he had a strong feeling that Navira would want to be there when he told his friends. So instead he said, "I will tell you all about it when you have met her, which hopefully," he added, raising his voice, "will be soon."

A cool formal voice floated down from the ledge above the pool, "Ah Lord Danton, I see your friends have decided to join you."

They looked up to see Stillwaters seated on the ledge, dressed in a violet flowing dress, her long hair hanging down over her right shoulder. Danton smiled wryly as he realised that her hair and eyes were now the same colour as his. Considering her colouring, he assumed she did not yet wish her true identity to be made known.

He gave a slight bow, "Lady Stillwaters Pathfinder, may I introduce my bloodbrother, Rainstorm, Prince Tarkyn's bloodbrother Ancient Oak, and Melting Snow, a woodwoman from the mountains."

Stillwaters smiled graciously, "You keep such distinguished company, Lord Danton. I am pleased to meet you all, even though you arrive uninvited." She waved her hand in a gesture of invitation, "Perhaps you would like to join us. Caroman, despite the short notice, is even now preparing a few delicacies to welcome you."

Smothering a grin, Danton directed the three woodfolk up the path between the boulders. They emerged to find the table once more covered in the white damask cloth, thirteen candles on a silver candelabra in its centre casting light on silver cutlery set beside large white napkins. The woodfolk looked at each other and blinked, their faces a picture of astonishment and dismay.

"Wait for Lady Stillwaters to seat herself first, then follow my lead," murmured Danton.

Rainstorm frowned, "Why should we?"

"Please. This is sorcerer custom." He gave a tight smile, "We men should also wait until Melting Snow is seated."

Being referred to as a man diverted Rainstorm enough to dilute his belligerence. He shrugged, "As long as it's not a rank thing."

Ancient Oak said quietly, "I am not sure that I feel any better about treating women differently from us unless there is a practical reason, but I will not stress you, my friend, in this unusual situation. Lead on, Danton, and we will follow."

Danton's smile relaxed, "Thank you."

Caroman entered with five tall stemmed glasses on the silver tray, filled with a deep golden wine and proceeded to offer them around.

"Is Lady Stillwaters bringing her own wine?" asked Ancient Oak, as he accepted a glass from the tray. He stared up at Caroman. "How do you do? We have not been introduced. I am Ancient Oak."

And in that moment Danton realised that despite Ancient Oak's agreement to follow his lead, the woodfolk would not tolerate being served. Just as he was tensing up, Caroman smiled disarmingly at the woodman, "I am pleased to meet you. Your family has shown great courage and open-mindedness in inviting His Royal Highness, Prince Tarkyn, into your family. My name is Caroman." He took the final glass from the tray for himself and set the tray down on the table.

"I was open-minded too, you know," butted in Rainstorm. "I took Danton into my family." He grinned. "No I wasn't. He was easy to decide about. It was accepting the first sorcerer into the woodfolk that was the hard decision. Waterstone and Ancient Oak deserve your praise." He paused, "Oh. I almost forgot. I am Rainstorm."

"And I am Melting Snow."

Stillwaters glided in, glass in hand and smiled at Danton's worried face. "Do not concern yourself, Lord Danton. Caroman and I have had frequent dealings with the woodfolk of the Lost Forest and we would do nothing to discomfort our distinguished guests." She gestured at the table. "Please be seated. Danton, would you please sit beside me? Caroman will bring out the first course and then join us."

Caroman waved Ancient Oak back, as he tried to follow him. "No, please stay here. There is little space where I cook and we would fall all over each other. I would appreciate some help with clearing up afterwards though."

Once small plates of egg fried with onion and mushrooms had been served and Caroman had joined them at the table, Rainstorm said, "Lady Stillwaters, Danton told us you change your hair and eye colour. In that case, it is very complimentary of you to choose Danton's colouring. It is quite spectacular, isn't it, the purple eyes with the golden blonde hair?" He grinned cheekily at Danton's reddened face.

Stillwaters smiled at Danton and then at Rainstorm. "You are very perceptive, young man. It is indeed meant as a compliment... and as a gesture of solidarity." Under the table, she squeezed Danton's hand, "Are you ready?" she murmured. "You or me?"

Danton smiled around the table. "I am ready and I will do it."

Rainstorm's eyebrows snapped together, "What?"

Danton's smile broadened. "It is my pleasure to announce that Lady Stillwaters and I intend to marry."

"Stars above, Danton!" exclaimed Rainstorm. "I mean... Congratulations! This is amazing."

Even as Ancient Oak and Melting Snow offered their congratulations, Danton could see the questions gathering in their minds.

He held up his hand, "Don't worry, my friends. I am not deserting you. Stillwaters and I...and Caroman?" Stillwaters nodded, "and Caroman will return with you to support Tarkyn." He gave a gentle little smile, "You should know by now that I would never abandon Tarkyn."

"So is this why you asked to see Danton?" asked Rainstorm, never one for subtlety.

Stillwaters nodded, "Yes."

There was a little silence that was broken by Melting Snow, "That was very courageous of you, Stillwaters. Did you actually ask him to marry you?"

"I did." The wizardess glanced at Danton. "And, like you, he had questions that needed to be answered before he would accept a future with me. Tarkyn is so lucky to be surrounded by such dedication."

"No, he's not lucky," said Rainstorm firmly. "He worked hard to gain our respect. We didn't give it just because of the oath or his high rank. He earned it."

Stillwaters's voice developed an edge, "I beg your pardon. I meant it as a compliment." Beneath the table, her grip on Danton's hand tightened.

"Rainstorm," said Danton gently. "Remember that Stillwaters is one among many. Please be kind to her, at least until she has got to know you."

"Oh." Rainstorm's eyes twinkled. "Hey, Stillwaters, is this a sorcerer thing; to become aloof when you're not feeling sure of yourself? Tarkyn does it all the time. I should have realised from your reaction that I was making you uncomfortable. Actually, I probably would have, except Danton stepped in first. Sorry."

Ancient Oak, watching the wizardess' tense reactions, asked, "Stillwaters, have you always lived in the Lost Forest?"

"Yes, since I was a baby. Each year, I have spent one day beyond its boundaries, to make sure that I aged at the same rate as the outside world. Other than that, I have no experience of Eskuzor."

Beneath the table, she took her hand away from Danton's and withdrew into herself as she waited for their reaction.

Ancient Oak gave his strong quiet smile, "Then we will all help you learn the ways of the forest beyond, and stand by you as you meet everyone in Tarkyn's home guard."

Stillwater smiled and tears sprang to her eyes, "Thank you."

"Watch your hair," murmured Danton dryly and received a light-hearted slap on the thigh for his trouble. He noticed with trepidation that Rainstorm was frowning.

"Stillwaters," said the young woodman, "Danton would have helped you with joining the home guard, if you had asked him to. Any of us would. You don't have to marry him to get his help."

Stillwaters laughed. "Ah Danton, you have such a character of a brother. I like him a lot. Of course I don't have to marry Danton to gain his help, Rainstorm. Danton is truly chivalrous. But there is more to the future than getting to know the home guard …and Tarkyn. As events unfold, you…and he, will understand. Besides Rainstorm, I love your brother… more and more with each passing hour."

Rainstorm beamed at her. "I'm glad. I think he's pretty good too."

Ancient Oak helped Caroman to clear the table and to bring out the next course of smoked wood pidgeon, dried fruits and salad vegetables with crusty freshly baked white rolls.

Danton shook his head, "I don't know how you do it. This food is amazing."

Caroman gave a slow smile, "Years of practice, and a magical talent for cooking."

Once everyone had settled into eating the second course, the questions began again.

"Stillwaters…or Caroman," began Ancient Oak, "I don't know how much you know of events outside this Lost Forest but we want to get back as soon as we can to help Tarkyn deal with his brothers."

"We know of the coming conflict," answered the wizardess.

"So how can we return to our kin? Do we have to face our fears again?"

Stillwaters replied, "I think you and Melting Waters already have, in declaring yourselves to each other. Rainstorm faced his a long time ago when he, as a ferociously independent young man, accepted the possibility of taking orders from Tarkyn. And Danton, in accepting me on such short acquaintance, has thrown himself into the unknown… and everyone fears the unknown." She gave a mischievous grin, "But actually, you all acquitted yourselves so well last time you were here, that you are free to leave at any time."

Ancient Oak gave a grunt, "Well, that's at least one thing we don't have to worry about."

"Yes, but in which direction is the boundary, and where will the Forest land us?" asked Rainstorm, "Last time we entered the Lost Forest in the mountains and left it scores of miles away in the forest nearer Tormadell."

The wizardess glanced at Caroman before replying, "The ways of the Lost Forest are known to me, as to no other. You may choose the place of your returning and I will take you there." She hesitated, "But, would you mind staying here until tomorrow? It would help me if I had the chance to get to know you all better before I have to meet such a large group. And you could fill me in on everything you think I need to know if I am to assist you in your efforts….And I need to pack. I have lived here all my life and cannot take everything with me."

Danton and the three woodfolk exchanged glances and nodded.

"That sounds most reasonable, Stillwaters," answered Ancient Oak on their behalf. "That would still return us more quickly than we had expected… We will only have been gone for one day, won't we?"

Stillwaters nodded, "Two, by the time we reach Tarkyn."

Part 7: Brother and Sister

CHAPTER 55

As Stormaway, Harkell and Drakell stood on the front step of Lord Tolward's house, listening to heavy footsteps approaching the inside of the door, Harkell reviewed their preparations. They and a select group of woodfolk had reconnoitred the house and its immediate surroundings before the trio had risked making their presence known. After all, the future looked bleak for any of them if caught by Jarand's troops; if Stormaway's support for Tarkyn was suspected, Harkell would hang for desertion and Drakell would be either be held hostage to lure his brother back or executed for colluding with him.

This time it was Thunder Storm, not Waterstone, who stationed himself with Autumn Leaves outside the lounge room window. Grasswind and Falling Rain watched from the tree halfway up the slope, ready to come to their aid at a moment's notice. As far as they had been able to work out, most of Lord Tolward's tenants were either in their own cottages or away from the holding altogether. Harkell drew a tight breath. He still felt uneasy about breaking cover.

The heavy front door swung open and a thickset scowly farmhand glowered at them, "What do you want, knocking on the door after dark? Folks around 'ere don't go out visiting after sundown."

Stormaway raised haughty eyebrows, "And where are his lordship's house staff? Why has he had to resort to having a rough oaf like you answer his door?"

"Because all the finer gentlemen on 'is staff have gone off to fight for Prince Jarand, that's why. And if you knew anything about anything, you would'a known that."

Not a good start, thought Harkell. Aloud he said politely, in an effort to mellow the man, "Good evening. I realise it's late but could you possibly inform your master that we are here to see him?"

The farmhand sniffed and glared at Stormaway, as he jerked his thumb at Harkell, "Now that is a gentleman. Look and learn, mate." With that, he slammed the door in their faces and stomped off into the hinterlands of the house. Two minutes later he was back. He opened the door and grumped, "Master wants to know who you are."

"I am Stormaway Treemaster. These are the brothers Harkell and Drakell."

"And yer business?"

"Our business is our own, to discuss with Lord Tolward, not you."

"Snotty-nosed git. Stay there. I'll tell 'im." He slammed the door again but a couple of minutes later, he reappeared in the doorway and stood reluctantly aside, "The master will see you now...even you, you old bag of wind!"

"Thank you," said Stormaway dryly.

They were shown into the living room where Lord Tolward and Lady Juniper were seated in comfortable chairs before a raging fire.

Tarkyn's advance guard stopped inside the doorway and bowed, Stormaway less deeply than the other two.

"Your business, gentlemen?"

Stormaway glanced around and although the manservant had ostensibly disappeared, took no chances. "We have been sent by the physician who healed your children when they were grievously wounded last year. I believe he made a commitment to come this way again."

Stormaway's words galvanised Lord Tolward and his wife. They leapt from their chairs and hurried over to greet them.

"A pleasure, sirs. It all clicks into place. Stormaway Treemaster. You were King Markazon's wizard, weren't you... and now his son's, I presume?" At a tight nod from Stormaway, Lord Tolward waved his hand, "Don't worry. I trust all my staff implicitly, especially Bantram, the rough diamond who opened the door to you." He surveyed the other two. "And Harkell...That wouldn't be Captain Harkell, by any chance, would it?"

Harkell gave another small bow, "At your service, sir, although Captain no longer."

"So I gather." Lord Tolward raised his eyebrows as he looked at Drakell, "And you are obviously Harkell's brother. You do well to keep out of Montraya. Jarand's men have been scouring the countryside for you and your kin."

"Are they still, my lord? We have Pr…" he stopped and looked at the others. Receiving a nod from Stormaway, Drakell continued, "… Prince Tarkyn to thank for authorizing our rescue."

Tolward grunted, "I am pleased to hear he is still active. And is the intelligence I received correct that he and his band of followers managed to stall Kosar's army long enough for Jarand to retreat to Montraya? I thought, when I heard that, that he must now support Jarand. But if he is harbouring Captain Harkell and his brother, perhaps he doesn't."

"No, sir, he does not," replied Stormaway. "He merely manoeuvred to avoid Kosar humiliating Jarand within the forests, in the hope that their tempers would cool. However, as you may have gathered, all we have managed to do is postpone the inevitable and to move the future confrontation out of the forest. This is good for the forest but makes our continued efforts to intervene, more difficult."

Lady Juniper frowned, "Does it? Why?"

"Because ma'am," said Harkell, "Our previous successes have been predicated on subterfuge and surprise, which are more easily accomplished within the cover of the woodlands."

"Excuse me, my lord and lady," said Drakell, turning a little pink at his temerity in challenging nobility, "but might I ask how much you have committed yourselves to Prince Jarand, if you assumed that Prince Tarkyn was supporting him? Your man, Bantram, said that your house staff had left to join his army."

"Hmm. Perhaps we had better sit down before I answer that question." Tolward raised his voice, "Bantram, you old scoundrel, bring some ale in here, will you? You'd better bring the new loaf and some cold meat and cheese too."

When they had arrayed themselves on the lounge and armchairs around the fire, Lord Tolward said, "So tell me, how are things with Prince Tarkyn and what are his present intentions?"

Stormaway leant forward to help himself to a thick slice of soft bread and a slab of bacon. In no hurry, he settled himself back and replied, "I think not. We will tell you of his plans, if and only if we are sure of your own intentions."

Lord Tolward's chest swelled and his face turned red. Just as an explosion seemed imminent, Lady Juniper put her hand gently on his arm and murmured, "Now come on Tol. You know what Karlian said. Now just take a deep breath and relax. You don't want any more of those nasty pains in your chest. Karlian is our healer," she added, by way of explanation.

"I will not relax. He as good as accused me of being a turncoat."

"Well dear, they did ask first."

"I do beg your pardon for any hint of mistrust, sir," said Harkell, "But we don't want you to suit your answer to the information we give you. Our liege's safety is paramount and if you truly support him, you will understand our position."

"You have a glib tongue on you, don't you, my fine ex-captain?" Slightly mollified, Tolward looked Harkell up and down. "Hmm. But you also have a strong, straight forward manner about you." He took a long pull on his tankard of ale before putting it down. "Very well. I will play my cards first…Our holding lies within two days' ride of Montraya. Jarand has sent out a call to arms which I am bound to obey. I received my summons nearly a week ago. I stalled for five days but the day before yesterday, a squad of the prince's soldiers arrived, heavily armed and ready to take my eligible people by force, if need be. Had my people not gone with a semblance of willingness, they would be placed in the front line of the charge when the fighting starts. So I let them go, with every appearance of regret that I was too unwell to join them."

"And are you?"

Tolward glanced at his wife, "It depends on who you are speaking to. I am not beyond active duty but I would not want to push myself too hard."

"And your children?" asked Harkell.

Juniper smiled, "They are tucked up safe in bed. They are too young by just a few years."

"And what of Trey, Varga and Vaska, and the other sorcerers that Tarkyn sent to you, to avoid being conscripted into Jarand's vigilante gangs?" Stormaway frowned at Tolward. "Have they now been conscripted into the army instead?"

"No. I told you I stalled for five days. During that time, those who were not registered tenants or land holders were able to disappear into the forest. After what happened to Trey's brother, none of Trey's family wanted to fight for Jarand. Besides, they all seem to be fervently loyal to Prince Tarkyn and only his direct word would ever persuade them to support Prince Jarand. Apparently they met him up in the foothills and sat around drinking tea with him. Seems most unlikely to me, but they swear it's true."

Stormaway laughed, "Oh, it's true enough. His Highness wandered away from our camp and fell over a ledge. When he came to, he was disoriented and couldn't find his way back. Luckily, he came upon sorcerers who were sympathetic to his cause; Trey and his family. By the time we finally found him, they were sitting around a fire, drinking tea and chatting as though they had known each other for years."

"Well, what do you know, Juny?" Tolward turned to his wife chuckling, "They were telling the truth, after all. I was sure they must have been exaggerating."

Harkell watched Tolward and decided that he was hiding something. "My lord, what actions did you take when it seemed to you that Tarkyn was supporting Jarand?"

Tolward brought his gaze to bear on Harkell and frowned fiercely at him, "You speak of your betters with an unbecoming degree of familiarity."

"Possibly, sir. I will not quibble with you over that… If you wouldn't mind answering my question…?""

"Blast you, Harkell. You're like a dog with a bone." Tolward harrumphed. "I sent a few more people to fight for Jarand than I absolutely had to. I thought… I thought… Prince Tarkyn had thrown in his lot with Prince Jarand… and to tell you the truth, I was pretty heartsick about it. So, in my anger, I threw caution to the winds for a while. I must admit Jarand's recruitment drives have been less aggressive, but I still have little faith that Jarand has the people's welfare at heart. This upcoming battle is for his aggrandisement and not for the sake of the country. I'm sure of it." He took another pull on his beer, and wiped his mouth, "I am glad to hear that Jarand has not inveigled Prince Tarkyn into supporting him."

"You have Tarkyn to thank for the draw back on pressing people into vigilante gangs," said Stormaway. "Tarkyn warned Jarand that it was making him unpopular."

Tolward grunted, "That will only persuade him while he is not in power. I don't think Jarand would care about his popularity if he had indisputable control of Eskuzor."

Harkell, ever the soldier, brought the conversation back to practicalities, "So, Lord Tolward, how many of your men have we lost to Prince Jarand's army?"

"Thirty-three, all up." He gave a lop-sided smile, "But hope dies hard, you know. So, before they left, I gathered them together and told them that if there were any sign that Prince Tarkyn was under duress or needed their help, they were to give it to him. They all know he saved Eidelweiss and Winguard's lives and even though they wear Jarand's uniforms they are Prince Tarkyn's to command."

Harkell laughed. "Sounds like me. I was in that position for a while." He became serious. "And if we need their assistance, how can we let them know? Will they be in one squadron or spread through several?"

"I believe they will be placed together, the theory being that they will fight all the harder to protect the people they know."

"And can we get word to them?"

Tolward nodded. "At the moment, that is easy enough. I can send a messenger with extra food and notes from loved ones while they are training. I'm not sure how much contact they will be permitted, once the manoeuvring begins."

"Hmm. Very little, I would think, while they are trying to out-manoeuvre the king." Harkell looked at the wizard. "What are your thoughts, Stormaway?"

"Since there are few people left on the holding, perhaps Lord Tolward, you could take a short trip into the nearby forest and gather up the people who have fled there. Is your health up to that?"

Tolward waved his hand impatiently. "Yes, yes. Don't you start on me. It's bad enough with Juny on my back all the time… So if I do that, then what? I can't bring them back here or they'll be snapped up by the press gang. They are still in the area, you know."

"If you bring them to the clearing in the old beech forest where the hundred year old beech burnt down… you know the one?" When Tolward nodded, Stormaway continued, "His Highness and others of us will meet you there tomorrow to plan our next moves."

Tolward's face lit up. "I would be pleased and honoured to meet with him. He is the only person I know who could lead this country with any care for its people."

"He had been planning to visit you here, you know, but with press gangs around, and only a skeleton staff here, I do not think it will be safe enough," said Harkell, just as Bantram entered to replenish their tankards. "Besides it will not be safe for the sorcerers hidden in the woods either."

"Na, you're right," offered Bantram, quite unsolicited. "We don't want to risk 'im… or them. 'e saved our kids. So we'd fight to the death to save 'im." As he filled up their tankards from a large pewter pitcher, he said, "Eh, did I hear right? Someone said 'e appeared before Kosar's little army with an eagle on 'is shoulder. That true?"

Drakell grinned in response, finding it a relief to talk to the manservant rather than with the lord and lady. "It is. I've seen it with my own eyes. Not only that, it's one of those huge mountain eagles. It's so heavy, it weighs the prince down on one side."

"Well, what d'yer know? Wonders never cease, eh?" Bantram tidied the tray, took away a couple of pieces of cheese rind and wandered out to the kitchen again.

Juny shook her head fondly, "You just cannot teach him. Heart of gold, but no understanding of the social niceties of acting as a house servant."

Tolward gave a lop-sided smile, "She really means no interest in the social niceties. He'd understand if he wanted to."

Harkell laughed, "I know some people who completely share his values. I suppose I do myself, but I know when to flaunt them and when not to."

"Not in front of Prince Jarand, I'll be bound," said Tolward and laughed at his own wit.

"No."

"And not in front of Prince Tarkyn either, I'd expect. His Highness was quite daunting if anyone stepped out of line when he was last here."

Harkell's eyes twinkled as he remembered the time Tarkyn had dressed him down for speaking disdainfully to him, even though he had known Harkell had done it deliberately to provoke Tarkyn's power. "He can be devastating when roused, but he is aware of my opinions and yet calls himself my friend." For the life of him, Harkell could not keep the pride out of his voice. He gave a wry smile, "But as you may gather, my belief in people's equality only goes so far. I find it a breath-taking honour that Prince Tarkyn considers me his friend."

Lord Tolward chuckled, "That young man has a power that goes way beyond his magic… and his birth right."

Chapter 56

"Someone approaches," announced Waterstone in response to a mindmessage from the lookouts.

With well-rehearsed precision, the woodfolk cleared the firesite, the sorcerers of Harkell's family levitated each other into the trees while Tarkyn levitated himself. When all was ready, the woodfolk flicked out of sight and awaited events from the treetops.

Below them, Rainstorm flicked into sight and stood in the firesite. "You can come back," he said, laughing. "In fact you had better, because I need to talk to you before the rest of our party arrive." Immediately, he was surrounded by woodfolk but in response to their silent queries, he replied out loud, "Wait until Tarkyn is here. Then I will tell you who approaches."

"I am here," said Tarkyn, as he floated down from a nearby horse chestnut.

Rainstorm wasted no further time, "Ancient Oak, Melting Snow and Danton have arrived back safely from the Lost Forest but we have brought the Wizardess Stillwaters Pathfinder, and her companion, Caroman, with us. Both of them know of woodfolk and have had many dealings with them in the Lost Forest but it is not up to us to determine whether it is permissible for them to see woodfolk beyond the boundaries of the Lost Forest." Suddenly, Rainstorm's face creased with consternation, "Oh stars! I've just realised that Ancient Oak, Melting Snow and I revealed ourselves to Stillwaters and Caroman without a second thought. We have forsaken our oath of concealment. Oh no!"

Waterstone put an arm around the stricken woodman's shoulder. "Rainstorm, it's all right. The rules are different in the Lost Forest. Woodfolk and sorcerers live side by side there. And you have done well to give us the responsibility to decide whether the wizardess and her companion may be permitted to see us."

"As I recall," said Tarkyn, "it was agreed that sorcerers could leave the Lost Forest, even though they had seen woodfolk, provided they swore an oath to me that they would not reveal your existence to other sorcerers. Many of them had seen you woodfolk as well as the woodfolk of the Lost Forest."

"But the only sorcerer from the Lost Forest who has seen us after leaving the Lost Forest is Boravar," objected Tree Wind.

"True," said Autumn Leaves, "but now Harkell's family has also been granted exemption, in addition to Tarkyn, Danton, Harkell and the two trappers."

"Hmm. So, what is their intention in coming here and on what basis would we grant these two exemption?" asked Waterstone, looking at Rainstorm.

"Stillwaters and Caroman have come expressly to support Tarkyn." Rainstorm grimaced, "And I know one good reason, at least for Stillwaters to be exempted, but it is not up to me to say. Perhaps some of the sorcerers could talk to Stillwaters or Danton or Caroman while we woodfolk watch from the trees."

"Good plan," agreed Waterstone, "although you and the other two might as well stay with them too, for the time being."

"It's a pity Stormaway, Drakell and Harkell are not here," said Tarkyn, "especially since Stormaway seems to know Stillwaters. But Boravar, Sorath, and perhaps Rena, and I will meet with them. What about you two?" he asked, addressing String and Bean.

The trappers looked at each other and shook their heads. "All a bit official for us, Tarkyn," drawled Bean. "We'll sit and watch with the rest of Harkell's family, if you don't mind. But call on us if you want to talk your thoughts through with us."

Waterstone flicked to stand in front of Tarkyn, hands on hips, "Now Tarkyn, how safe is it for you to meet with sorcerers of unknown loyalties?"

Tarkyn smiled at his bloodbrother's inevitable concern, "Danton must think it is safe or he wouldn't bring them to us, and he is a fine judge of intrigue."

"True enough." Waterstone gave a wry smile in return, "I just thought I'd ask. Take care, little brother. See you soon." With that, Waterstone and the other woodfolk flicked out of sight, while the trappers and the others of Harkell's family settled themselves on the further edge of the clearing.

In response to a mindmessage from Rainstorm, Ancient Oak led Melting Snow and the three sorcerers into the clearing where Tarkyn stood waiting, flanked by Sorath, Rainstorm, Rena and Boravar.

Danton and Caroman bowed deeply, hand on heart while Stillwaters merely inclined her head. Tarkyn studied the mysterious wizardess, admiring her long strawberry blonde hair and extraordinary teal blue eyes and wondering at the reason for her minimal gesture of respect.

"Welcome to the forests of Eskuzor. I am Tarkyn Tamadil, as you are no doubt aware." The prince spoke with quiet authority, directing his attention purely to Stillwaters and Caroman. He introduced the sorcerers standing with him before saying, "I understand from Rainstorm that you have come to offer us your support."

Stillwaters replied with equal quiet authority, "Prince Tarkyn, the wages of war would bring dreadful suffering to the people of Eskuzor.

Having come this far, it will not be easy to prevent wholesale bloodshed but I am prepared to work with you to try. I am known as Stillwaters Pathfinder, as you are no doubt aware."

Tarkyn was clearly taken aback by the implicit challenge in her tone. Here was a sorcerer who considered herself his equal. He had become used to this from woodfolk but not from sorcerers, especially on first meeting. Before he could respond, the air was rent with a raucous screech and, perhaps drawn by the tone of Navira's voice, his huge mountain eagle circled in across the top of Navira and Caroman before flapping her wings in an aerial pirouette to land on Tarkyn's shoulder and glare at this perceived threat to his authority.

Quite uncowed, Navira stared at the eagle for a moment before returning her gaze to Tarkyn without comment, every line of her body suggesting that if the eagle's arrival had been an attempt to intimidate her, it had not worked.

Not wishing her to misunderstand him, Tarkyn said, "I beg your pardon for my eagle's untimely arrival. She comes and goes on her own whim, generally speaking." After a moment, he continued from where they had left off before the eagle's arrival, "Everyone who is permitted to travel with us has sworn fealty to me to protect both my companions and myself."

"A wise precaution, Prince Tarkyn," she replied neutrally.

Only his association with woodfolk prevented him from becoming angry. With an effort, he gave a half smile. "But I suspect you have no intention of doing that…"

Stillwaters gave him a brilliant smile in return, "You are astute. No. It would not be fitting for me to swear fealty to you. But I am willing to form an alliance with you and will even swear to it, if you so desire."

"And Caroman?" Interestingly, Tarkyn did not address the old sorcerer directly but asked the question of Stillwaters.

"Caroman is my liegeman and will remain so." She placed her hand on her manservant's back. "However, if I enter into an alliance with you, so too will he."

Tarkyn crossed his arms, and stared down at her, his amber eyes glinting as they caught the afternoon light. "And why should I accept an alliance rather than your fealty?"

Stillwaters tilted her chin up and spoke with a slight edge to her voice, "Because that is all I am prepared to offer you." She let her eyes rove across the people standing on either side of the prince and up into the surrounding trees. Then she brought her eyes back to bear on Tarkyn, "I would think that you would wish to protect your companions with the addition of my powers to your cause." Watching her, Danton wondered why he had never noticed how much like Tarkyn she was. Then she relented slightly, "I understand your curiosity but I prefer to explain my status when Stormaway has returned... Until then you may take me as you find me or we will leave."

Danton's heart sank. The future did not look easy, owing fealty to one and married to the other. He realised Tarkyn was speaking to him.

"Danton, out of all of us, you have had the most dealings with Lady Stillwaters. How do you advise me?" asked Tarkyn, and then wondered why Rainstorm, Melting Snow and Ancient Oak all grinned.

"Go on, Danton," urged Rainstorm. "Give him an objective opinion."

Danton glanced at Stillwaters, received a tiny nod, before speaking to Tarkyn. "Your Highness, always remember you have my undivided loyalty. Stillwaters has good reason to consider herself of elevated status and, as far as I am aware, shares your commitment to the future of Eskuzor." Then his face split with a grin, "But you must consider my opinion in the knowledge that Stillwaters and I plan to marry."

Suddenly the clearing filled with woodfolk smiling and offering congratulations. Tarkyn threw all other considerations aside and dragged Danton into a warm embrace. After a few hearty slaps on the back, he released Danton and turned to place his hands on Stillwaters' shoulders and kissed her on the cheek.

"Congratulations. Stillwaters, welcome to our company. We will sort out our differences later. You must indeed be a special person to win Danton."

Stillwaters smiled, tears in her eyes from being so close to a brother she had never known. For a moment her hair shimmered, but as Danton placed a steadying hand on her back, she took a deep breath and held to her disguise. Her throat ached at the effort of holding back tears. "Thank you. You have been very lucky in having him as your lifelong companion. I love him dearly and have chosen him in the full knowledge that he is your sworn man." Thinking she had herself back in hand, she smiled wryly at Danton, "He made that very clear."

Tarkyn chuckled, his eyes shining with mirth, "His woodfolk friends tease him all the time for his passionate loyalty."

"Oh, you really are nice. What I have missed!" Suddenly Stillwaters' eyes suffused with tears. "Oh dear. I can't do this, Danton. Bring Tarkyn and Caroman. No one else." She clutched something in her pocket, murmured, "*Maya Mureva Araya*," and was gone.

Danton was left standing amidst a stunned crowd.

Tarkyn's frown was forbidding. "Danton. What is going on here? You know more than you are saying. If you know who she is, beyond the name she has given us, I order you to tell me."

Danton hesitated. "Sire I do know… and I will tell you if you insist," he said, echoing Stormaway's words in the Lost Forest. "But please let her tell you herself. That is what she intends to do if you join her now."

"Are you disobeying a direct order, Danton? Your loyalty seems most divided to me."

Danton stared at him. After a moment, he went down on one knee, hand on heart. "Sire, slavish obedience is not necessarily the best way to serve you. I protect your welfare as much as hers by asking you to see her privately to find out who she is."

"Get up Danton," snapped Tarkyn irritably. He ran a hand through his hair and let out a long breath. "Oh blast it. I'm sorry. I should not have been so autocratic. But Stillwaters is most disconcerting. No wonder you found her frustrating. I don't understand at all why she disappeared like that." He slapped Danton bracingly on his back. "Come on. Of course I trust your judgement. I will do as you ask."

Chapter 57

Danton and Caroman led Tarkyn to a small clearing, a quarter of a mile away. On the other side of it, Tarkyn could see the blurry edge of the Lost Forest, its old gnarled trees in sharp contrast to the younger forest in which the home guard was camped, close to the edge of the grasslands. A large overhanging pine tree stood in the centre. Stillwaters was nowhere in sight.

"We're not going into the Lost Forest, are we?" asked Tarkyn, not happy with the prospect.

"No Your Highness, we are not," answered Caroman, "although Stillwaters or I could transport you there anytime you wished…and back again."

Tarkyn put up his hand, "No thanks. Not at the moment."

Caroman gave a little cough, "I should perhaps mention, Your Highness, that Stillwaters will not appear as you last saw her. Be prepared for a shock."

Tarkyn turned to Danton, "Have you seen her true guise? And had you, before you made her an offer of marriage?"

"I saw her true form only after I had accepted her offer of marriage," said Danton with a grin.

"Stars above, you are a courageous man, Danton."

"I can only say my courage was rewarded. She is every bit as beautiful as you saw her… just different."

"Hmm. So I wonder how broadminded your view of beauty has to be, to include 'just different'?"

"I think your own view of beauty would include her true form." Danton gave a little grin. "One would hope so, anyway."

"Perhaps you would like to be seated, Your Highness," suggested Caroman, "while I see whether Lady Stillwaters is ready." He disappeared from sight under the hanging branches of the lone pine, only to reappear alone a few minutes later. "Ahem. Sorry about this. Lord Danton, could you talk to her please? She is feeling very nervous. She has never met people outside the Lost Forest before and is feeling a little overwhelmed. In addition to this, Your Highness, she is very concerned about your reaction to her in her true form."

"Danton, go and talk to her if you wish, but I think perhaps I will raise my shield until you return. I can't see Waterstone being very happy with me if I stay alone, unguarded and unprotected… and I did promise not to take unnecessary risks."

Danton nodded, "Good idea. I will be back shortly."

Caroman did not follow him into the skirt of the pine but walked up to stand in front of Tarkyn. He gave a diffident bow and asked, "Would you mind if I sat down, Sire? We have come a long way today and I am getting too old for this."

"Please." Tarkyn waved at the stump beside him. "You sounded just like Stormaway for a moment there… Are you acquainted with him?"

"Yes, more than that. He and I were apprenticed to the same wizard. 'I'm getting too old for this' is a shared joke; a little phrase we both copied from our master. He used to say it all the time… I am also acquainted with your father, Sire. In the early days, Stormaway and I worked together to serve him. Well before your time, Sire. I left the palace three years before you were born, but I have always served his interests, just as Stormaway has."

"So is Stillwaters part of this tangled web that Stormaway manoeuvres, apparently all in the best interests of Eskuzor and in accord with my father's plans; me, the woodfolk, his intelligence network…?"

Caroman glanced at him in an effort to gauge his attitude to Stormaway's manoeuvrings. "Hmm. You are partly correct, Sire. But Stormaway and I are partners in crime, so to speak. We often do not see each other for many years and he did not know Stillwaters' whereabouts until Danton reported it to you in the Lost Forest three months ago. We decided that it would be better if Stormaway didn't know, so that he would be unable to tell anyone under duress, you understand."

Tarkyn raised his eyebrows, "No. I don't understand at all. And are you aware of Stormaway's heritage?"

"I am, Sire, but that was part of the equation only recently made known to me, after he had told you and his kin." The old wizard smiled, "I have known of woodfolk for twenty two years; ever since I brought Stillwaters to the Lost Forest to keep her safe. But I never told Stormaway of them, while Stormaway has, of course, known of them all his life, but has never told me. Once he arrived in the Lost Forest, we met up and were able to talk of many things that were previously forbidden by our individual wish to keep faith with the woodfolk."

"So, until then, you did not know where I was after I left Tormadell, any more than Stormaway knew where Stillwaters was? Is that correct?"

"Yes Sire."

"Interesting. So do I gather from this that my father asked you two to keep both of us safe?"

"Yes, Your Highness."

"Hmm. Stormaway came close to failing, you know. Had I accepted my brother's judgement, I would now be in a dungeon somewhere."

"Unlikely, I think, Sire. Stormaway's network is broad. He would have discovered your plight, just as he discovered you on your escape route and he, possibly with my help, would have found a way to rescue you."

Tarkyn bent over and picked up a dry stick. He began to break off pieces as he thought, "I seem to have two guardian uncles, as does this Stillwaters Pathfinder. Intriguing." He looked up and met the old wizard's eyes, "If you have been working all these years at my father's behest and for Eskuzor, then as my father's son and Guardian of Eskuzor, I thank you."

Without standing up, Caroman bowed, "Sire, it is a pleasure." As he straightened, his face relaxed into a smile, "Ah, at last."

Tarkyn looked around to see Danton, with his arm around a beautiful, black haired woman of more than average height, emerging from the pine tree's overhanging boughs. With Danton back, Tarkyn immediately waved away his shield. As they drew closer, he blinked in amazement as he saw that the woman's eyes were the same colour as his own and her features a softer version of his own. Everything Caroman had said clicked into place. But Tarkyn knew nothing of this Caroman. How could he know that what the old man said was true? Tarkyn felt the sadly familiar sensation of his world lurching beneath him.

Phrases he had heard and not understood wandered through his mind; his father saying, 'Don't let him go the way of the other one,' to his brothers and Danton saying that Stillwaters' mother would forgive Stormaway for what he had done. And there was that seven year gap between Tarkyn and his older brothers. Could this really be…?

Tarkyn frowned the question at Danton who responded with a minute nod, just as Stillwaters said quietly, "Hello Tarkyn. I am your sister. My birth name is Navira Tamadil."

She looked so nervous that Tarkyn put aside his questions and held his hands out to her. "How do you do?" he said inanely. "I must be your brother then. This is… unexpected… but nice. Very nice." He rolled his eyes. "Oh this is hopeless. I have no precedent for dealing with this. Um, should we hug, do you think?"

Navira smiled as she stepped into his arms and put her arms around him, "I would like that. I have known of you for so long and have been dying to meet you… I look like you, I have the same colouring and even my magic is the same colour as yours."

"Is it? I'm not sure that I like not being exclusive any more." When she looked up at him with a worried frown, Tarkyn smiled, "Just joking, little sister."

She smiled in return, "Actually I'm older than you by three years."

"Oh. Are you? Blast! Still the youngest in two families then. Hmm. And you are the only sister in two families."

Navira pulled out of his embrace. "I wanted to wait until Stormaway was here so that he could support my story… and see us meet as brother and sister. But I was too overcome at being close to you to maintain my equanimity… and with it, my glamour."

"You are still very glamorous. Oh, I see what you mean…" Tarkyn smiled at his mistake before saying, "Anyway, I can at least show Stormaway the images of us meeting. And we can both fill in what we said. If all Caroman says is true, Stormaway deserves to be part of this." Tarkyn indicated the log he had been sitting on and a couple of stumps, "Perhaps we should sit down. There are two questions that I need answered before we return to join the others. How did you disappear, not only from the palace but also from common knowledge? And secondly, why have you chosen now to join us?"

"I will leave Caroman to answer the first, since I was a baby when I was taken from the palace and remember none of it. When Caroman has told his tale to your satisfaction, I will answer the second."

"Before we begin, I am aware that you have just arrived and may need food and drink. Would you like me to ask Midnight to bring us some refreshments?"

Navira nodded, "That would be very welcome. I am not so worried now about another person being here. I just wanted to deal with your reaction out of public glare."

"Understandable." Tarkyn thought for a moment. "Then, perhaps Waterstone, Ancient Oak and Sparrow should also join us since this seems to be a family affair." Navira said nothing but clenched her hands together in her lap. Danton noticed and glanced at Tarkyn debating whether to say something but Tarkyn met his gaze and smiled, "Perhaps not quite yet. Let's just get Midnight for now. Plenty of time to get to know your woodfolk family later."

"I would like to meet your little ward, Tarkyn. I admire your dedication to him."

Tarkyn chuckled, "I'm not dedicated. I just love him."

A few minutes later, Midnight arrived with a backpack on his back filled with wine, cheeses, apricots and bread. The little boy shrugged it off and handed it to Tarkyn. He stared into Tarkyn's eyes for a moment, then grinned as Tarkyn laughed.

"Oh dear. Sparrow's nose is out of joint because she couldn't come too," he explained. "Don't worry. She'll survive. I'll sort it out with her later."

Midnight handed out food and drink under Tarkyn's direction. The first time Midnight focused on Navira, he did a double take and stood staring at her for a few moments before glancing back and forth between Tarkyn and Navira several times. Then he sent Tarkyn an image of Summer Rain and Falling Rain, sister and brother, with a query. Tarkyn smiled and nodded. Midnight was clearly unsettled by this new arrival in the family and as soon as he had finished his task, climbed onto Tarkyn's knee and leant into his shoulder. With Tarkyn's arm safely around him, he sat watching Navira with undiluted fascination, until Tarkyn tapped him on the nose to gain his attention and then explained with images that staring would make Navira feel uncomfortable. In response, Midnight smiled and waved at her but during the ensuing conversation, despite his best efforts to comply with Tarkyn's wishes, his eyes kept drifting back to watch her.

Tarkyn returned his attention to Navira and smiled, "Sorry about this. Anything that affects me affects him. He worries that something may take me away from him or make me send him away. He'll get used to you in a while... Now, Caroman, explain to me how I have a sister."

"As you know, Sire, the queen's pregnancy and the subsequent birth of heirs is kept a close secret until such time that her retainers are sure of the survival of the offspring. This is for two reasons: Firstly to preserve the reputation of the Tamadil line as strong and flawless, and secondly, to protect the queen, and the king, from the public glare so that they can react in private, should anything go wrong. The birth of the twins was not announced until a fortnight after their delivery. Your birth, Sire, was not announced until a month afterwards."

"I often wondered about that. Was I such a sickly baby?"

Caroman took a sip of wine and shook his head, "No Sire. You were a strong healthy baby. But the queen had two miscarriages and a child who died ten days after her birth, before she gave birth to Navira. As you are about to hear, Navira's infancy went disastrously wrong, so the queen was very circumspect about announcing your arrival into the world."

Tarkyn frowned, "But surely, if a healthy baby girl had been born, no matter what happened, news of it would have leaked out?"

"No Sire. For the last few months of her pregnancy, the queen kept only her closest lady in waiting and a midwife in attendance on her. Stormaway, as the king's counsellor and I, as the queen's counsellor, also knew and attended Her Majesty. But after her previous unhappy experiences, the queen did not take any chances and only one nursery maid joined us after the birth." He shrugged. "As you must realise, had any of these closely trusted servants spoken out, it would have been regarded as treason and dealt with accordingly."

Having been bred in the shadow of the monarchy, none of the sorcerers sitting there thought it at all strange that a person might be executed merely for gossiping. Anything related to the Tamadil family's private lives was a state secret.

"Navira was born a strong healthy baby, just as you were, Sire. She was the spitting image of her father, ju..'

"I know. Just as I am," grumbled Tarkyn. "May we leave out the comparisons for now and just get on with the story?"

Caroman gave a little cough, "My apologies, Sire. *Unlike* you, she was not only a female but her power showed very early. As you can imagine, untrained power in a baby is very dangerous. Navira would lie in her cot gurgling and as she waved her fists, streaks of bronze power would knock baubles swinging, burn wiggly lines in the wood of the cradle, set fire to blankets and on one occasion, sent a cat yowling out of the room. And that was when she was playing. When she was angry; if she was discontented because she was hungry or um, had other bodily issues, power would pour off her hands in all directions, blasting anything or anyone in its path. The only way to contain her was for Stormaway or me to place our shield over her. With a bit of practice, we refined it so that we could shield her and contain her hands while leaving free whichever end of her that needed attention."

Tarkyn gave a friendly laugh, "Feisty little thing, weren't you?"

Navira smiled wryly in return.

"Stormaway prepared a potion for her that calmed her magic enough to stop the random streaks of power," continued Caroman. "But the queen was very upset and wouldn't let the princes near her until she was contained."

"A wise precaution, I would have thought," said Tarkyn.

Caroman nodded, "True enough. But your mother was besotted by the twins. With each miscarriage and the early death of her next child, she had become more protective and obsessed with them. I think she wouldn't allow herself to become as attached to you two, in case you went the way of the sister who died. That sister also had your colouring, you see. Besides," Caroman stopped and looked as though he wished he hadn't said the last word.

"Go on, Caroman," urged Tarkyn. "You were going to say..."

"Oh dear Sire, this is all very difficult... Very well. As you must know, your mother, Queen Rimalla, hails from our neighbouring country to the south east, Asthania. The Royal Family of Asthania is not as strong in magic as the Tamadils. She herself has little power, and the twins, although powerful, do not compare with you or Navira, or even Danton here. Within your family at least, Sire, the magic genes seem to be inter-connected with your colouring. So knowing how powerful Markazon was, the queen was a little fearful of the power that Navira and you would potentially wield."

"Perhaps that in part explains why she never bothered to organise my magical training and why she made no effort to stop the twins from indicting me." To cover his feelings about his mother, Tarkyn dropped his eyes to the little boy in his arms, ruffled his hair and smiled at him when Midnight looked up.

"She may not have known of the indictment until it was too late, Sire. I understand it took place in the middle of the night."

"She was up and fully dressed when the Great Hall fell down less than twenty minutes later. No. She would not have stood up for me," said Tarkyn bitterly. "She may have worried about my welfare when she thought me alone and friendless in the forests but she would not have crossed my brothers to save me."

"I think, sadly, that you are probably right." Caroman sighed. "So you will understand what happened next. Once Stormaway's potion had taken effect, the boys were permitted to visit their new sister. She was now about ten days old. They were fascinated by her, wanted to hold her and kept trying to touch her. But under the queen's orders, no one would let them. So then the boys thought up the idea of sending gentle power rays at her from a distance. The nursery maid, Myrah, expressed her concern but the queen believed that the princes would be safe enough at a distance and wouldn't hurt their little sister. They weren't bad boys then, just indulged and they loved the way she giggled and squirmed…"

Danton butted in, "If I am more powerful that they, how come they could master small trickles of power? I find that extremely difficult."

Tarkyn laughed, "I can vouch for that. His power is as subtle as a rock."

Caroman steepled his fingers and gave an irritatingly superior smile, "Danton, your power is probably too strong for you to control with finesse without extra tutoring. But when they were young, the twins' power was so weak that they would have to work hard to produce strong bursts of power. They could do it, but a weak trickle is what came naturally to them. The queen would have been aware of that when she allowed them to play with their sister in that way."

Danton raised his eyebrows, "Oh. I see. Hey Tarkyn, maybe it wasn't their station in life that prevented them from entering tournaments when they were growing up. Maybe they would have lost dismally and didn't want to be shown up."

Tarkyn smiled, "Possibly. Now shush Danton. Let Caroman finish his story."

Caroman nodded his thanks and continued, "I'm not sure whether the twins' baser instincts took over or whether they thought that if she liked a little, a lot would be even better." He shrugged, "It might even have been a simple mistake. After all, as you say, they were young to be wielding power accurately. Whatever the motive, over the next few days, they learnt how to increase the flow of power. Myrah and I both warned the queen but she would not listen to us."

Caroman took a long draught of wine before taking the story up once more, "On the morning it happened, the midwife and the queen's lady in waiting were seated in the bay window talking to the queen about her postnatal health. I had recently arrived and was standing just inside the door watching the little ones and chatting to Myrah while I waited to speak to the queen. Myrah was once more trying to get someone to listen to her worry about the boys being permitted to use their power rays and asked me to speak to the queen on her behalf. The boys were trickling power at Navira, making her giggle. Slowly they raised the intensity until she stopped smiling and then began to whimper. Just as I stepped forward to intervene, a little bronze shield blossomed around her. Despite Stormaway's potion, the fear had spontaneously triggered her shield.

"The boys thought this was a great joke. They looked at each other, counted to three and, with fierce frowns of concentration, sent twin streaks of power at her to test her shield. But under the stress of her fear, Navira's shield had become reflective and sent the boys' power straight back at them. I don't know whether you are aware of this, Prince Tarkyn, but reflective shields can not only reflect but also concentrate or multiply the power."

Tarkyn looked sombre as he shook his head, "No. All I know about reflective shields is that mine killed one full squadron of the king's guard."

"Sire, while you remained ignorant of your ability to produce a reflective shield, you were a walking time bomb. Perhaps your brothers were too young to remember, but your mother knew of this possibility, yet did nothing to educate you." Caroman spread his hands, "At the very least, that was irresponsible. At worst, she deliberately set you up to fail."

A frown had gathered on Tarkyn's brow. He said coldly, "It is not your place to pass judgement on the queen's actions. Perhaps we could stick to the story?"

"Certainly, Sire. Both boys were badly burnt on their hands and chests. Their howls of pain brought the queen running. Needless to say, when they told her what had happened, their story lacked their part in the altercation and instead they claimed that Navira had attacked them."

"Perhaps that is what they thought really happened," said Tarkyn. "Kosar told me he had never heard of a reflective shield when I met him in the forest."

"You are generous, Sire. They may indeed have thought themselves attacked in the first instance. But I myself explained the concept of a reflective shield to the queen and princes, and still they did not give ground… So I'm afraid Kosar had definitely heard of a reflective shield by the time he met you in the forest." The old wizard sighed, "My arguments fell on deaf ears and in the end the queen couldn't see past the fact that the heir to the throne had been injured, even if by an infant. She had been frightened by Navira's power from the beginning. Unfortunately the king had left the palace shortly after the birth and was still from home when all this happened; on the other side of the kingdom, hearing complaints from tenant farmers whose crops had been poor the previous year. As you know Sire, the law is clear. If a member of the Tamadil family is attacked… "

"Especially the heir," put in Danton.

Caroman nodded in agreement, "Especially the heir, the assailant's life is forfeit, even if it is another member of the family."

"But that is outrageous," snapped Tarkyn. "Navira didn't attack them. If anything, they attacked her."

"In truth Sire, I don't think either attacked the other. The boys thought her shield would hold and were just playing."

"Nevertheless…"

"I agree Sire. Nevertheless, Navira did not attack them… But the queen would not believe any of us, only her precious boys." Caroman looked down at his hands. "While Markazon was away, she was the sovereign. She could have granted clemency. She could have ordered Navira to be held close for a number of years or she could have ordered her exile… But she chose to have her own child executed. I think the queen was frightened of what she had created, and didn't want to risk either her sons' safety, or the public embarrassment of a rogue Tamadil sorcerer. When I look back, I believe she was in the grip of a postnatal malaise which may have clouded her judgement. I suspect too, that in her effort to avoid being a weak regent for the king, she reacted too far the other way." He raised his eyes to Tarkyn and the prince could see that even now, the memories distressed him. "I hope… in fact, I am sure she later regretted her decision." The old wizard gave a wan smile, "Luckily, as her most trusted advisor, and wizard, I was given the task of killing the infant. She did demand that the child's body be brought before her so that, as acting sovereign, she could ensure that the deed had been done," he shrugged, "but any wizard worth his salt can create a temporary appearance of death in a person."

Tarkyn frowned. "And how did you know that my father would wish you to deceive the queen? He could not, after all, have anticipated the need…"

"That is not entirely true, Your Highness. If you remember, he knew of bad portents concerning the princes when he assured your future with the woodfolk… The king already knew of them by the time Navira was born and he had seen that she carried a strong mix of true Tamadil genes. He took Stormaway and me aside before he left and made us swear that we would protect the princess, no matter what."

"And when he returned, did he know what had truly happened or did he think his daughter dead?"

Tarkyn turned as Navira spoke, "Stormaway carried the official secret message of my execution together with the even more secret message of my survival to my father while Caroman fled the palace with me, never to return. That night, Stormaway and Caroman parted company for the next twenty two years but both worked in their own way for your welfare and mine. There was no pursuit, I believe. The queen thought she had broken Caroman's heart by making him kill such a young child." She looked fondly at the old wizard, "As indeed she would have, had he really done the deed." She smiled, "The wily old rogue… well he wasn't old then… managed to get a message to Myrah the nursery maid, to meet him outside the city walls." She gave a cheeky little grin, "I expect he couldn't have handled all those dirty nappies and late nights on his own… So Myrah and Caroman brought me up in the Lost Forest." Navira glanced at Danton sitting quietly beside her. He squeezed her hand and she gave him a smile before continuing, "Every year, we would travel to a prearranged rendezvous to meet up with my father." A shadow passed across her face as she looked at Tarkyn, "You are just like our father, you know, except for the length of your hair. I miss him, even now, eleven years after the last time I saw him."

"So too do I." Suddenly Tarkyn swung Midnight off his lap, leapt up, and started to pace up and down. Midnight took one look at him to check he wasn't in trouble then scampered off to climb the great pine. "But why didn't he bring you back? Why live with such an unfair judgement when he had the power to overturn it? And why did he never tell me, or Kosar, or Jarand that you lived?" He came to a halt standing over Navira, hands on his hips.

Navira met her brother's eye, but Danton could feel the tension in her body, "Because, for many years, I could not control my magic. To all intents and purposes, I was a rogue sorcerer. Our father made sure I was safe and cared for, but there was no question of me returning until I could control my magic. My return would have caused major ructions between the queen and him, and a scandal across the nation. He had to make sure I was safe… By the time I was ten, I had it nearly under control but then I moved into the teenaged years," the wizardess gave a little grin, "and I and my magic, separately and together, became a little rebellious." Her smile faded, "I don't think he would have burdened you with the knowledge of a rogue sister. He was waiting to see whether I could master my magic," her eyes filled with tears, "… and he died before I could."

Tarkyn crouched down in front of her and took both of her hands, one of them from within Danton's grasp. "He must have had faith that you would succeed. He kept coming to see you, didn't he? And, had he thought you a true rogue sorcerer, he could not have let you live, for the sake of the kingdom's safety. He was, after all, the king, and his care for the kingdom came above all else."

Navira nodded, tears spilling down her cheeks. "Yes. Yes, I know all that. Caroman has told me a hundred times. I just wish I could have shown him, that's all." She sniffed and managed a smile, "But thank you. You are such a kind brother. I wish I had grown up with you."

Tarkyn laughed, "We would have had to be much more formal in the palace… and I expect I would have been an annoying younger brother. At least now, I have grown up enough to be acceptable company for a young lady… At least, I hope I have."

"You are quite acceptable to me, little brother."

"By the way, Sire," said Caroman, "Kosar does know of the princess' existence, though I am not sure that Jarand does. Stormaway had the documentation to prove her identity, and when Kosar became king, Stormaway, as Markazon's personal advisor, briefed him on Markazon's plans and wishes regarding Navira's continued existence…"

Tarkyn grunted, "No wonder poor Stormaway was removed as court wizard, if Kosar's loyalty lay with my mother. Stormaway must be a great wizard indeed to have escaped with his life after that discussion."

Caroman smiled complacently, "Yes Sire. Stormaway, Stillwaters and I are the greatest wizards in Eskuzor and the known worlds… and with our help, you may be able to prevent the bloodshed of a full scale war."

Chapter 58

Caroman's words unsettled Tarkyn. He had become used to commanding more power than any of those around him. Even though Stormaway and Danton were strong in magic, their power had always been directly at his disposal. So he was not at all sure that he liked the advent of such a powerful, manipulating triad. Caroman and Stormaway had clearly been guiding events in Eskuzor for decades and from what he gathered, both from Danton and from Navira herself, his sister had known of him for years but had made no push to meet him until now. In fact, she had actively avoided him in the Lost Forest when they had been there three months previously. And now Danton, his closest sorcerer ally, had aligned himself with this powerful wizardess and her secrets.

Tarkyn stood up and walked away from them, using the pretext of calling Midnight down from the pine tree. When he had the little boy in his arms and had nattered to him long enough to feel more settled, he turned to face them, "If you are ready, Navira, I think it would be courteous to introduce you in your true guise to our woodfamilies; my brothers and niece, and Danton's brother and father, before meeting the others."

"You already know Ancient Oak and Rainstorm," said Danton. "The only new people would be Waterstone, Sparrow and Falling Branch."

When Navira did not respond immediately, Tarkyn thought she was going to refuse, but after a few moment's thought, she said, "Should we also include Melting Snow? After all, she too came to the Lost Forest with you, Danton, and besides," she gave a little smile at Tarkyn, "I suspect that she will soon be a member of your… *our* extended family."

Tarkyn looked in surprise at Danton, "Is that right? Has Ancient Oak finally made his move? I hadn't noticed in the excitement of receiving our wizardess here."

Danton grinned, "Yes, thanks to some very obvious manipulation by Rainstorm."

Tarkyn gave a crack of laughter. "That boy is incorrigible. What would we do without him?" Still smiling, he turned his attention inward and sent summonses to the people they had agreed upon.

In suspiciously fast time, the six woodfolk flicked into view. As he surveyed them, Tarkyn suddenly exclaimed, "Oh whoops! I forgot Lapping Water. If we include Melting Snow, I must include her." When she appeared moments later, she stood with arms crossed, looking anything but pleased. "I'm sorry," said Tarkyn contritely. "I was thinking about Danton's and my family and those who accompanied Danton to the Lost Forest."

"And of course I'm not family."

"Not yet. Nearly." He smiled placatingly, "but near enough to be included."

"As an afterthought."

Not wishing to pursue the discussion any further in public, he gave a fractional nod and turned his attention to Navira who was standing waiting, with an expression of disdain on her face which reminded Tarkyn that she had thought it presumptuous for a woodwoman to marry a Tamadil. *I will address Navira's attitude later*, thought Tarkyn, feeling beset by disgruntled women. *Now is not the time. Navira is not making a good impression though.*

He was saved by Caroman who said urbanely, "Perhaps you would like me to make the introductions, Your Highness?"

"Yes. Thank you," chorused Tarkyn and Navira. They both looked startled and then amused.

Waterstone laughed. "There goes the use of titles then. Too ambiguous. What a shame!"

Navira raised her eyebrows. "You do not seem to command much respect, Prince Tarkyn, among your companions."

"No, none at all," replied Tarkyn dolefully, refusing to be drawn.

A perplexed frown appeared on his sister's face, "From the way Danton and Rainstorm spoke of you, I had expected more."

"Ah. Did you? But then you hadn't met Waterstone, who is the head of our woodfolk family and my oldest brother. He has always taken a certain leeway with expectations."

Navira's face relaxed into a smile. "Oh well, that explains it. I am pleased to meet you, Waterstone. Your fame for unprejudiced acceptance goes before you. I am Navira Tamadil, Tarkyn's sister… and consequently yours also."

Waterstone smiled, "I beg your pardon. I forgot to introduce myself."

"You do not seem to be fazed by the fact that Tarkyn has a sister, hitherto unknown…"

Waterstone glanced at Tarkyn before addressing her, "When you disappeared from the clearing, Navira, you asked Danton to bring only Caroman and Tarkyn to see you privately, to which Tarkyn agreed… after a short altercation with Danton." He gave a little grin, "However, Tarkyn did not say, as he usually does, "I will take my chances," and none of us answers either to Danton or you. We knew from the Lost Forest that you are powerful, so since we were concerned for Tarkyn's safety, we followed."

Danton frowned angrily at Tarkyn, "Did you deliberately omit to say you would take your chances? I thought you were accompanying me in good faith."

Tarkyn threw his hands up in a gesture of surrender. "No, no, no. I didn't do it deliberately. I assumed that our intentions were obvious, as indeed they were. Waterstone interpreted my actions to suit his own wishes."

Waterstone smiled unrepentantly. "Yep. Besides, as Danton successfully argued, slavish obedience is not necessarily the best way to serve or protect you…In fact, definitely not, in my opinion."

Navira surveyed the people around Tarkyn, considering their openly expressed anger and independence. Then she raised her eyes to her brother and said coolly, "Your Highness, Rainstorm said you had earned your woodfolk's respect but I see no sign of it. I was bred to expect that a Tamadil prince, or princess, would wield absolute power and exact unquestioning respect and obedience… Perhaps your exiled state has diminished your value in the eyes of your retainers."

She was immediately surrounded by loud, indignant protests. In a move that shocked Tarkyn to the core, she reacted instantly against the barrage of noise, flicking her hand and snapping, "*Shturrum*". The woodfolk froze mid-sentence.

"How *dare* you attack my people?" Tarkyn's voice shook with anger. "Release them immediately." He nearly backed his demand with a threat but then decided that his word alone must be enough.

His unruly emotions decided otherwise.

The ground around him trembled and as he realised what was happening, Tarkyn threw his good intentions to the winds and thrust his arm downwards, finger pointing rigidly at the ground. The earth jolted beneath their feet, knocking everyone over. Navira lost her balance and with it, her hold on her spell. Tarkyn snapped Danton a quick order and when she picked herself up, Navira found herself next to Danton within his aqua shield. Tarkyn stood facing her, surrounded by woodfolk, all of them within the dome of his bronze shield. Caroman, almost forgotten, stood to one side unshielded.

Into the silence, Danton asked dryly, "So is this what you meant, Navira, when you said that you and Tarkyn would struggle to deal well together?"

Navira flashed him a look of pure venom. "So much for supporting me. You have imprisoned me at Tarkyn's command, without a word of protest."

"True, I have. But I have chosen to be within the shield with you, rather than on the outside looking in."

She gave a derisive snort, "What makes you think you can contain me? My power could knock you out and your shield would blink out in a moment."

Danton smiled. "I know that. If I really thought you would hurt me, I would have remained outside. What need have you to escape? All I am providing is a safe haven for you, while you get used to having so many people around you." Slowly, he placed his arm around her back and drew her towards him. "I don't think you expected so strong a reaction from these woodfolk, did you?" She gave the tiniest shake of her head which encouraged him to continue, "I think what you expect of people's behaviour towards the Royal Family holds true for Kosar and Jarand but not, as you have seen, for Tarkyn. But it is his expectations that are different, not the esteem in which he is held. As you must now realise, he is valued by those around him with a fierce loyalty, unparalleled by that commanded by his brothers."

Navira gently removed Danton's arm from around her and walked, head held high, to the closest point to Tarkyn and the woodfolk that she could reach within the shield. Clasping her hands tightly in front of her, she said with quiet dignity, "Your Highness, I did not intend my actions to be an act of aggression against you or your companions. I found myself in the midst of many hostile? no, *emphatic* people and felt the need to protect myself. You do not need your shield against me. I have come here to prevent harm, not to create it. If you people would prefer it, I will remain in this clearing apart from you, and Caroman will act as intermediary between us to plan our actions in the forthcoming conflict."

Tarkyn felt a nudge in his side and looked around to see Lapping Water gesturing to let her out of his shield. He raised one side of his shield only enough to allow her out. When she stood between the two shields, Danton responded to a gesture from her by raising his enough to let her in.

Lapping Water approached the wizardess and said, "In the midst of this turmoil, we have not yet been introduced. I am Lapping Water. I understand you have reservations about me marrying your brother. You share these reservations, perhaps for different reasons, with many woodfolk." She put her hand gently but firmly on Navira's arm. "Let us put our differences aside for now. Right now, I would like to welcome you to Tarkyn's home guard. It is not surprising that feelings ran high while such a momentous meeting has taken place. I think not only you and Tarkyn, but all of us, are strung up. I suspect Tarkyn felt nearly as assailed as you did." She forced a smile even though Navira's face was still rigid. "We forgot, when we jumped to Tarkyn's defence, that you are one among many. On behalf of all of us, I beg your pardon."

A little shudder went down Navira's backbone. "Thank you," she said softly. She placed her hand over Lapping Water's. "Perhaps your match with Tarkyn is not so unequal after all."

Lapping Water, who did not believe in inequality, laughed. "No perhaps it's not." She raised her voice a little, "Tarkyn and Danton, I think we could dispense with shields, if we are to have any chance of resolving this situation. Do you agree?"

Danton looked to Tarkyn who nodded. "Navira?" asked Danton. When she nodded, he said, "If at any time you feel unsafe, even if there is no genuine threat, let me know and I'll raise it again."

"I can raise my own shield, you know."

Danton grinned, "Of course you can, but that would feel more lonely, wouldn't it?"

With the shields lowered, Lapping Water turned to Caroman, "And now perhaps we should finish the introductions. Poor Navira still doesn't know who half of us are."

"Yes, she does," objected a little voice. "She only hasn't met Falling Branch and me. Hello. I'm Sparrow. You have very beautiful shiny hair. You're my aunty and I'm your niece, you know. I've never had an aunty before. How are you at reading maps? And building little village houses? And how is your sense of direction? As bad as Tarkyn's? His is awful, you know."

Tarkyn came up behind her and ruffled her hair, "Sparrow, give Navira a chance to answer. You haven't drawn breath."

Sparrow grinned up at him, "So much to find out. It's exciting, isn't it, to have a new relative. Are you excited?"

Tarkyn gave a lop-sided smile, "Yes, I suppose I am." His grin broadened. "Yes of course I am." He turned to Navira. "I am sorry that I too over-reacted. Sometimes my emotions control my magic. Is that what happens to you?"

"Yes. Only emotion can turn a shield reflective."

"That's true, isn't it? If you and Caroman would be willing, I would like to hear about your magic and tell you about mine. We need to exchange this knowledge anyway, to support each other against my… our brothers' intention to lay waste to the country."

Lapping Water drifted away with Sparrow as Waterstone approached. Tarkyn could see that the woodfolk, this time, were taking care not to crowd Navira and in line with their intentions, he also retreated to leave Navira alone with Waterstone.

"Navira, I should have said this before, but I didn't get the chance before everything went pear-shaped. Welcome to our family." After the faintest hesitation, Waterstone stepped forward boldly and gave Navira a hug which, after the faintest hesitation, she returned.

She came out of the embrace to find Ancient Oak standing beside Waterstone.

"I too welcome you," he said and embraced her.

"Thank you," said Navira. "I am sorry I rode roughshod over you. I can assure you I do not intend to bully anyone with my power."

Ancient Oak waved his hand airily. "Don't worry. Tarkyn was a little excitable with his magic when he first arrived amongst us. All of us have been subject to that *Shturrum* spell at least once." He smiled, "You will get a friendlier reception than he did, because we are not under oath to you. Tarkyn had a tough time at the beginning."

"Did he?" Navira looked thoughtful. "I didn't realise."

"Oh yes," reiterated Waterstone, "A very tough time. Like you, he was one among many but he had no Danton or Caroman to support him. Stormaway's initial role was to stand in judgement over him and although Stormaway then supported Tarkyn, he usually left him to cope on his own… And the rest of us resented Tarkyn and the oath like blazes. It took a major effort at the start even to be civil to him."

"Oh, poor Tarkyn!"

"Indeed. And all this at a time when he had just been turned on by the two brothers whom he had looked up to all his life."

Navira smiled. "I am glad you were kind to him."

Waterstone shrugged. "So am I. That way, I got to know him." He hesitated. "I won't take up too much more of your time right now, when others are waiting to talk to you but I would like to say just one thing. It seems to me that you are trying to put a theoretical knowledge of the world into practice. Would that be right?" When she nodded, he continued, "Tarkyn, on his own in our different culture, had to make his own decisions about how he was to be treated, knowing he had the power to enforce whatever he chose. You may choose to follow his example of informality, or that of your older brothers, or perhaps choose somewhere in between. But when you are making that choice, factor this in; Jarand and Kosar are discourteous, often cruel and oblivious to anyone's needs but their own. We have all seen them and some of us have met Jarand, but none of us respects either of them." He smiled at her to soften his words. "You have made a wise choice in Danton. He knows both sides of the picture. But if you need to talk, I too am always here."

"Phew! You have a power all of your own, don't you?" She blinked, trying to take in all that he had told her. "Thank you. I am beginning to realise what a privilege it is to be part of your family."

Waterstone laughed. "Coming from a Tamadil, that is high praise indeed."

CHAPTER 59

Tarkyn watched with Waterstone, as Danton detached himself from Navira, then skirted around the huge pine tree to join them. The prince smiled and shook his head as his liegeman approached, "Danton, my friend, you have given yourself a challenge. She is everything you said she was and more. Frustrating, beautiful, intriguing… and she's even more volatile than me. And now, my friend, you will become an official member of the Royal Family and my… our brother-in-law. What do you think of that?"

Danton smiled as he sat down next to Tarkyn, "Before I lost my memory and gained this new perspective, I don't think I could have dealt with it at all. I would have been overwhelmed with the honour. But now… now, I am still honoured of course; quite amazed in fact, but overwhelmed, no." He grinned, "And I suspect I will have to earn every moment of it. My beloved is temperamental and powerful, just as you were. So I am used to that. But she is also, as I am beginning to realise, dreadfully inexperienced in the ways of the real world. Caroman has taught her as well as he could, but she has only practiced at behaving as a princess should in her small, rarefied world inside the Lost Forest, not within the uncertain courts of Eskuzor. Frankly, the mind boggles at what lies ahead, should she wish or be able to return to sorcerer society."

"And what would prevent her from returning to take her place as a member of the Royal Family?" asked Waterstone.

"I would, for a start," retorted Danton. "I am known as Tarkyn's confederate and would be arrested as soon as I showed my face in court. Secondly and more importantly, I am committed to Tarkyn and all of you, to intervene between Kosar and Jarand. But apart from that, the king would have to acknowledge her identity, ratify that she is no longer a rogue sorcerer and commute the sentence passed on her by her mother."

Waterstone looked thoughtful, "She's very powerful, isn't she? If Kosar thought he could have her on his side, perhaps it might be worth his while not only to acknowledge her but also to pardon you, Danton. Then he might even gain your power too."

"What are you thinking, Waterstone?" demanded Danton angrily. "I'm not going to fight for the king after what he did to Tarkyn, even to get Navira reinstated. She has known from the beginning that my loyalty to Tarkyn overrides everything else."

"Hmm. But did you know who she was when you said that?"

"No. I had no idea. But she said that she would not be interested in me if I were someone who could betray my liege. So…"

Waterstone smiled, "I was not thinking of you betraying Tarkyn or us. I know you too well, to think you would. But have you thought that if you were with Kosar, you two would be in a strategic position to influence events in accordance with our plans?… in a much better position, in fact, than you are now?"

"My word, Waterstone," said Tarkyn in mock admiration. "I fear some of our devious sorcerer thinking is beginning to rub off on you." He considered for a minute, his eyes trained on Navira as she talked to Lapping Water and Caroman, before returning his attention to his companions, "There are problems with that suggestion. We are going to need Danton's and Navira's power overtly on our side to prevent this conflict. If we succeed in stopping this war, Kosar will still be king, but will have realised that Navira and Danton are acting against him. They would be arrested for treason; at best exiled, and at worst, imprisoned or executed, whereas, if she fights with us openly to prevent bloodshed, she will be regarded as a worthy opponent afterwards but not a turncoat. What do you think, Danton?"

"Kosar could choose not to exonerate her, to keep faith with his mother…Hmm, but if he sees an advantage in having her at court, I think he would throw that consideration aside." Danton ran his hand through his golden blonde hair, leaving bits sticking out every which way. "Oh dear. I don't want to support Kosar, even after this conflict is resolved. I don't mind the concept of living back at court, provided I could visit all of you regularly. But I could not stomach serving Kosar."

Tarkyn smiled at him, "Perhaps you two could be ambassadors from the Guardian of Eskuzor, using your power to ensure that Kosar rules more effectively and more justly. Then you would still be serving me, not him, but still be useful enough for him to reinstate Navira to her rightful position."

Danton eyed his liege, "And what if Navira gradually allies herself with Kosar? Then where will I be?"

"This is very tricky for you, isn't it, Danton?" said Waterstone sympathetically. "I don't think it was fair of her not to tell you who she was, until after you had committed yourself. In fact, you would have every right to retract your agreement honourably in these circumstances."

Danton gave a wry smile, "No, I wouldn't do that. She needs me and I love her, even with all her moods and peccadillos and complications. I just hope I can manage the balancing act between serving Tarkyn and supporting her."

"Danton," said Tarkyn, "I couldn't be happier that you are marrying my sister. In the whole kingdom, you are the most qualified person to stand by her. You know and can handle court protocol and politics, you share my wishes for the kingdom's welfare and you understand both woodman and sorcerer. It is my wish that you support her, even against me in the odd argument, provided you are straight forward about it."

"Thank you. That makes it easier."

"And if she did decide to ally herself with Kosar, provided she does not support him against me, there should be no conflict of interests. Remember, she was brought up by one who has worked for the future of Eskuzor and she has grown up with the shades of Forest Guardians. Unlike Kosar, she knows the significance of my role as Guardian of Eskuzor."

"Yes, she does. She said she would never act against the Guardian of Eskuzor and that she knew I wouldn't let her… and I can tell when she is lying."

"Not straightforward like her brother then?" asked Waterstone in surprise.

"Not like this brother." Danton chuckled. "She gets quite annoyed when I catch her out."

"You know," said Waterstone, who had been thinking it through, "she is very unlikely to forgive Kosar for letting her mother think that she had attacked him. Jarand's and his refusal to speak up would have killed her, if not for Caroman."

Danton grunted, "Maybe, but I suspect from the way that Caroman told the story that he emphasized to her that they were only little when it happened. Anyway, we are getting way ahead of ourselves. We have yet to stop this war."

"Hmm, true," said Tarkyn. "I wonder how Stormaway and company are going? They have been gone for two days. They should be back soon. It is not far from here to Tolward's holding."

"I'll send out a message and check for news of them," offered Waterstone, going briefly out of focus. After a pause he reported, "They are not far away. They should be approaching the firesite within the hour."

"Good, I'm glad they are back and safe." Tarkyn stood up and brushed his hands off. "Time for us to prepare to return to the firesite. I will enjoy this."

Chapter 60

Tarkyn's advance guard walked beneath overhanging sycamores until it joined a narrow deer track that ran through long grasses along the edge of a slope. As he walked, Harkell brooded over the thirty-three men who had already left to join Jarand's army. They might actually be in a strategic position to lend assistance when the time came. But would their training convert them to following Jarand wholeheartedly or make them wish more fervently for Tarkyn to provide an alternative? On balance, Harkell decided, they were unlikely to be faced with anything more persuasive than a reiteration that Prince Jarand was their overlord and it was their duty to fight for him. It was not Jarand's policy to reason with his officers and that attitude went down through the ranks.

As the path became steeper, Harkell gradually became aware of the sound of heavy breathing emanating from his brother. Drakell was built for blacksmithing. He was strong but his leg muscles were, as yet, unaccustomed to hours of walking. And if Drakell was tired, he would be plodding with heavy feet, making it harder for the woodfolk to disguise their trail. Harkell waited until they reached a small clearing under a tree where they would not leave a flattened swathe in the long grasses if they sat down, then called a halt.

Drakell sank down gratefully, with his back against a tree, and pulled out his waterflask.

Harkell smiled encouragingly, "Not far to go now. Then we can all rest and have a good meal."

"Sorry," mumbled Drakell. "I know I'm holding you all up."

Harkell knew his brother did not have the same confidence as he. He suspected that their father's continual criticism had eaten away at Drakell, making him unsure and quick to apologise. There was no doubt that their father loved them but he was not always wise in his approach to his sons. That had been one of the reasons that Harkell, more sure of himself, and more frequently clashing with his father, had left the smithy to seek wider horizons. He grinned at his brother. "Don't worry. You just give us an excuse to have a rest we will all enjoy. There is no deadline to meet."

Autumn Leaves, one of the heavier woodmen, sat down next to Drakell. "I'm never sorry to take a break. Anyway, Waterstone's been chatting to me and I thought you sorcerers might be interested in what he's been saying." When Drakell frowned and looked around them, Autumn Leaves added, "He's mindtalking. He's not here but he is in range for messages."

Drakell laughed, "Oh I see. I was confused for a moment and thought perhaps he had come to meet us."

Autumn Leaves grinned, "Only mentally. Anyway, Danton, Ancient Oak, Rainstorm and Melting Snow are back from the Lost Forest and not only have they brought back the wizardess and some other chap called Caroman, but Danton is going to marry her."

Amid the uproar that greeted this intelligence, Harkell remembered when Danton had angered him all those months ago in the Lost Forest when he had said that the Lady Stillwaters was above Harkell's touch. After a heated exchange, Danton had admitted that he thought the wizardess was above his own touch too, but Harkell had often wondered whether Danton had just said that to mollify him. Danton was, after all, a lord and had been clearly disdainful of Harkell at first… But perhaps she had unbent at her second meeting with Danton. Danton had not spoken much about her after that, except to say that he would respond, if he could, if she asked for him… And now he was to marry her. Harkell, as a loyal married man, was not a rival to Danton for the wizardess' interest, but Danton's words still rankled. He realised that Autumn Leaves was speaking again.

"And then suddenly, this Stillwaters lady disappeared, literally, and wanted Tarkyn and Danton to go after her to meet her privately. All very strange. Tarkyn and Danton had a stand up row about it which, I gather, Danton won by acting submissively… Cunning bugger, that Danton. So off they went to meet her, with Waterstone and Ancient Oak following surreptitiously to keep their eye on Tarkyn." Autumn Leaves drew breath, "And then, specific woodfolk were requested to join them… and now they are waiting for us to return to present a big surprise of some sort, for all of us at the firesite."

Drakell pulled himself to his feet. "You have inspired my legs into action. Let's get going so we can see this surprise of theirs."

Harkell clapped him on the back. "Not long now. Another half an hour, maybe three quarters at the outside."

Drakell smiled and rolled his eyes, "You realise before I came to these forests, the most I ever walked was a quarter of a mile to try out a different pub. Maybe a bit further once a year, to get to the fair."

Harkell laughed. "Get on with it. You've been in the forests for weeks now."

"I know. I'm getting better. It was just that hill at the end of a long day."

"I quite sympathise, young man," said Stormaway in gruff camaraderie, "Speaking for myself, I'm getting too old for this constant trekking."

Harkell looked at him in surprise and caught a twinkle in the old wizard's eye.

When they finally reached the firesite, they were greeted warmly but their return was clearly not uppermost in anyone's mind. Before they could even sit down or get themselves a drink, Waterstone and Ancient Oak stepped into the clearing from the other side. Immediately, woodfolk and sorcerers converged on them from all sides, demanding to know why Stillwaters had disappeared so abruptly, where they had been and what had happened. With some effort, Waterstone waved them to silence.

"We have a grand surprise for you all. The Lady Stillwaters will appear again shortly and all will be revealed. I urge you though, not to crowd her too closely. She has lived a reclusive life in the Lost Forest and will take time to become used to larger numbers. She will be accompanied by His Royal Highness Prince Tarkyn and Danton Patronell, Lord of Sachmore." He smiled benignly at the puzzled frowns he saw on the faces of the woodfolk who knew that he put little store by titles. Waterstone's eyes searched the assembled crowd until he found Stormaway who was standing at the rear beside Harkell. His eyes met Stormaway's and he smiled a private smile to him as he said, "Stillwaters Pathfinder is an honourific gained through years of wizardly study. I will now present her by her birth name." He lifted his arm. "I have the honour and pleasure to present to you our sister, Her Royal Highness, Princess Navira of Eskuzor."

Amid the murmurings that greeted Waterstone's introduction, a faint mist dissipated to reveal Navira, flanked by Tarkyn and Danton. All three were dressed in the sumptuous attire used only for attendance at court. Navira wore an exquisite full length gown of burnished gold, studded with tiny pearls and trimmed with white lace, a white ribbon of state across her breast bearing a bronze coat of arms. Her long black hair, held back from her face with a gold tiara, flowed down her back in shining waves. Beside her, Tarkyn wore the burnished gold surcoat and black lace that Waterstone had seen in his memory, his chest crossed by a black ribbon. Unusually, his long hair was confined by a gold band at the base of his neck. On Navira's left and one step back, Danton stood resplendent in indigo, his coat embroidered with silver filigree, and his unruly blonde hair tamed into a ponytail by a silver clasp.

The sorcerers, as one, went down on one knee, hand to heart, while the woodfolk's faces bore expressions ranging from amazement to bemusement at the magnificence of the royal party's attire. As Tarkyn took Navira's hand and led her forward towards Stormaway, the sorcerers bowed their heads as they passed. Tarkyn and Navira reached him and the old wizard also bowed his head. When he straightened, his eyes were shiny with tears.

"Stormaway," said the prince quietly, "the two charges that you and Caroman took on all those years ago have finally met. Thank you for your part in protecting my sister."

"It was an honour, Sire. You are both worth every moment of effort."

"Thank you. Please rise." Tarkyn leant down, put an arm under Stormaway's elbow and helped him up from his knees. With a little smile, he said, "You are getting too old for this." He turned and swept his arm around to encompass every sorcerer. "You may all rise." When they were standing, he continued, "And I would also like to introduce Caroman to you. He, like Stormaway, is a wizard who once worked for my family. Since then, he has been working in concert with Stormaway for the future of Eskuzor. He and his partner, Myrah, brought up my sister in the Lost Forest. So we now have three powerful wizards, Stormaway, Navira and Caroman, the most powerful in the land I'm told, to support our cause."

"More powerful than you, Tarkyn?" asked Rainstorm, picking up an undercurrent in the prince's voice.

"Certainly more knowledgeable than I, in the ways of magic."

"We three share great knowledge and power," said Navira, her voice low, melodious and authoritative, just as Danton had first heard it, "but no power is as great as that of the forests of Eskuzor and no authority higher than its Guardian. King Kosar and Prince Jarand may not acknowledge this but they, like most sorcerers, know little of forest guardians. I, on the other hand, have been raised in the Lost Forest where the Forest Guardians of the past reside. Prince Tarkyn is not my liege lord but I will always work with him for the welfare of Eskuzor."

Harkell watched the three of them, marvelling at the existence of a Tamadil sister but at the same time wondering what this presentation heralded for the future relationship between commoners like himself and them. The difference between their exquisite finery and his plain woodfolk's raiments rammed home to him the difference in rank. Even his finest dress uniform could not compare. Tarkyn and Danton had not looked at him nor at anyone other than Stormaway who was also highly ranked. Their demeanour was formal but at least not disdainful. Harkell heaved an inward sigh. He had thrown away a hard-earned captaincy for his place at Tarkyn's side and he had felt alive as never before when his opinions had been listened to by a prince of the realm. But now, faced with the aloof courtesy on the faces in front of him, he felt his privileged position slipping away.

And now Tarkyn was progressing slowly around the circle, introducing Caroman and Navira individually to every member of his home guard, giving equal attention to everyone. Harkell felt completely anonymous as, with no more or less favour, he was introduced and made his bow.

Tarkyn, Navira and Danton moved to one end of the clearing and sat on a fallen log with Stormaway and Caroman sitting on logs on either side of them. The rich court dress looked almost incongruous in the casual woodland setting, saved only by the assurance with which it was worn.

"And now," said Tarkyn, "we will hear from our intrepid advance guard, whom I wish to welcome back." He turned to his wizard, "Perhaps you would like to fill us in, Stormaway?"

Since when is Stormaway the leader of our expedition? thought Harkell angrily. *What has happened while we have been away that has changed the social order so dramatically?*

Stormaway gave a brief description of their encounter with Lord Tolward and answered questions put to him by Tarkyn, Navira and Danton. By the time Tarkyn turned to him, Harkell was seething with resentment, but he knew his place in a royal court and did his utmost to keep his feelings to himself.

"Harkell, do you have anything to add?" asked Tarkyn with courtesy but none of his previous warmth.

"No, Your Highness," Harkell replied, deciding to keep any vague ideas he might have to himself in such a formal setting. He suspected that everyone felt constrained by the atmosphere. None of the woodfolk was contributing spontaneously as they normally would. Even Rainstorm had had nothing further to say. Realising his reply sounded a little blunt, he added, "Stormaway has presented the facts quite accurately, Sire."

"But I am interested in your impressions and opinions, Harkell, not simply the facts."

Harkell blinked in surprise. "I beg your pardon, Sire. I was not sure whether you continued to value my opinion."

"And why would I not?" asked Tarkyn, raising his eyebrows.

Harkell was at a loss to reply. He could not say in this public forum, that it was because he was now being treated as prince to commoner, or because now he felt like an outsider looking in. Suddenly his temper, which he had guarded so carefully all those years in Jarand's court, got the better of him. "Because, Your Highness, so far today you have addressed yourself exclusively to those people among us who possess power and high rank. I have neither."

"Is that not the usual practice of a prince holding court, unless he is responding to submissions?" asked Tarkyn mildly, but looking so intently at him that he seemed to be trying to convey some hidden meaning.

Something clicked in Harkell's brain, driving his natural perceptiveness to overcome his envy. "It is certainly true in Prince Jarand's court, Sire. I have often noted that the ideas of many of his wisest liegemen are stifled by their fear and his disinterest. This, of course, makes the prince's ideas shine by comparison, but means that he must run his affairs without the full value of those around him."

"Have I given you any cause to fear me?"

"No, Your Highness. In your brothers' courts, the fear of punishment hangs in the background like a rancid smell. But even without that, in a formal audience such as we find ourselves, there is always the fear of overstepping the mark or making a fool of oneself by mistaking the protocols. In such circumstances, I would never presume that my opinions were of any value unless asked directly... Even then, I would expect them to carry less weight than those from higher ranks."

"And have I given you any cause to think your ideas are not valued?"

"Until now, no." Harkell hesitated. "Sire, since you did ask for my opinion, I will also say this. I had already decided not to mention any half formed ideas. In the past, many of our successes grew from a free exchange of suggestions, many of which initially sounded preposterous. However, in this present forum, I would not dream of opening myself to possible ridicule."

"If I didn't know better, I would say that you two had carefully rehearsed that interchange," snapped Navira, rising to her feet. "Very well, you have made your point, Tarkyn... or rather, your uncommonly courageous, common man has made it for you. My compliments, Harkell. You may not fear retribution, but you brave my brother's temper to state your case."

Harkell grinned and sketched a bow, "I have braved it before, my lady, and at much greater risk."

"So I understand," said Navira. "Danton has been fulsome in his praise of you."

"That is generous of him." Harkell inclined his head towards Danton, "I am honoured, my lord."

Danton looked distinctly uncomfortable and glanced a question at Tarkyn.

"I think," said the prince, "it is time to dispense with..."

Before he could finish, Navira gave a sharp little nod and waved her hand. Following her lead, Caroman waved his also. The exquisite court dress faded from sight, leaving Tarkyn, Navira and Danton dressed in the soft browns of woodfolk clothing. They stood up and dispersed to different corners of the clearing; Danton choosing a position only a few people away from Navira, while Stormaway took Caroman in hand to introduce Summer Rain to him.

"So now perhaps, we can work out what we are going to say to these sorcerers when they gather in the clearing of the old beech," said Tarkyn cheerily, blithely maintaining control while thinking that he was relinquishing it. But now, the world was back in its orbit and everyone started talking at once.

Autumn Leaves lumbered to his feet, "I don't know about you lot, but I would kill for a cup of tea right now."

"No. Sit down," urged Ancient Oak, "You've just walked a long way. Rainstorm and I will get it, won't we, Rainstorm?" He chuckled. "... Even though we have such lofty connections."

Someone threw a small pine cone at him, which he dodged with ease. His quip overcame Rainstorm's natural teenaged reluctance and the young woodman sprang up to help with good grace, happy to do anything to dispel the discomfort of the past scene.

"So Harkell," said Tarkyn, "What is your half-baked idea?"

"I have several, Sire. We need these sorcerers to assist Stormaway's intelligence system in finding out the most likely sites for the meeting of the two armies. Once these sites have been determined, we will need them to reconnoitre the area around them, to seek out nearby cover where you, Danton and your powerful wizards can conceal yourselves. Depending on the location, some woodfolk may even be able to accompany you. Thirdly, these sorcerers will be able to offer you protection as you travel from the forests."

Tarkyn glanced wryly at his sister, before replying to Harkell, "These ideas seem almost complete to me and very good. What is half-baked about them?"

"The detail, Sire. How will they assist Stormaway's network? Who would be best placed to do so? How will they protect you? What sorts of places will they be looking for? How will they get messages back to us? What will we do with the women and children?"

Waterstone gave a derisive snort, "Not to mention what the mighty five will do when they get to the battleground."

Harkell grinned, "I thought I'd leave that to them to figure out."

"And what about us?" demanded Rena. "They may be the most powerful but what about Thraya, Elena and Kayama? They can all use power rays and Thraya can also raise a shield for a reasonable length of time. Drakell, Harkell and Sorath can lift heavy loads and sharpen objects."

Tarkyn raised his hand, "Rena. I have not said only five of us will be instrumental in stopping this war. I haven't a clue how we are going to achieve it. There are few of us against two armies of several thousand. I suspect we will need all the help we can get."

"You're not using our women as soldiers," stated Sorath flatly.

Harkell saw Navira glance at Tarkyn to watch his reaction. Unaware of his sister's scrutiny, Tarkyn raised his eyebrows, and said icily "I beg your pardon?"

Harkell's father opened and shut his mouth twice before clamping it shut.

"Exactly, Sorath," said Tarkyn dryly. "You do not dictate to me, under any circumstances. I will, however, note your concern for your companions, but I will not accept that their… hmm … female status... prevents them from taking risks. And I will gladly accept whatever martial or magical abilities they are willing to offer in our cause." As Sorath went to speak, he added, "I would think carefully before you say anything further. You run the risk of casting aspersions on the actions of my sister and my betrothed, both of whom are very proper women who are willing to fight to their last breath to save Eskuzor."

Sorath shook his head and muttered quietly, "I don't know what the world's coming to. Not how it was, when I grew up."

"The world is still as it was when you grew up, Sorath, outside the forest. But it won't be for long if Kosar and Jarand lay the country to waste." Tarkyn turned to Thraya, "How long can you hold up a shield? And can you change its shape and size? What would be its greatest size, do you think?"

"I have not really experimented with it, Your Highness. It is not very useful for everyday life," Thraya avoided her husband's eye and added, "But I would be very happy to now. Perhaps one of those more experienced in magic could work with me?"

"I would be pleased to do that, Tarkyn," said Navira, leaving unsaid that Thraya might feel more comfortable working with a woman.

"Tarkyn," said a perky little voice from the side, "What about Boravar? He can make a shield. Remember? It's a beautiful peacock blue one."

Tarkyn smiled, "Thank you, Twig Snap, for reminding us." He looked at Borovar. "Well my friend? How strong and flexible is your shield? And how strong are your shafts of power?

"Sire, I have had years to develop my skills in the Lost Forest." The big sorcerer gave his quiet smile. "I am not one to push myself forward but I am at your disposal if you need me."

"You have not answered my question, Borovar."

Borovar gave a wry smile. "I can hold my shield for hours at a time and in whatever shape you like. And I can vary the strength of my power to fire ferociously like Danton or gently enough to ruffle your eagle's feathers without hurting it." As murmurs of surprise rippled through his audience, his face reddened with embarrassment, "Oh dear, and now I sound like I'm bragging. I promised myself I wouldn't do that. I am, after all, a lot older than all of you and should not need to strut my stuff in the same way you young ones do."

Tarkyn laughed, "You don't sound like you're bragging. You just sound matter-of-fact. So I gather you must have as much skill as a woodman but with magic. That's impressive. You're a dark horse, aren't you?"

"Not really, Sire. I did say that I could do nothing more scary than you, but you can be very scary so that wasn't being particularly modest." He gave his deep chuckle, "I expect you just assumed I couldn't do much because I don't come from a noble background."

"That's a reasonable assumption, let's face it," said Danton, quick to jump to Tarkyn's defence. "After all, most of the aggressive magical power does lie within the nobility."

Borovar put up a placating hand, "I agree with you, Danton, it does. I'm not saying it was a rash assumption, just wrong in this case."

"So we now have twelve sorcerers with varying degrees of useful power for the upcoming confrontation," said Waterstone, "String and Bean, what about you?" When they shook their heads, he continued, "And how many sorcerers with aggressive magic or shields will be within the ranks of the twin's armies?"

"I would say no more than ten on each side, which would include at least a couple of wizards" said Danton.

"Ten? On each side? Stars above! What hope do we have of stopping them?" demanded Autumn Leaves.

"Not to mention the thousands of soldiers," added Harkell dryly.

Tarkyn smiled, quite undaunted. "The way I see it, we have several major advantages. Firstly, we are not trying to defeat anyone. We simply wish to contain them or prevent them from hurting each other, until Kosar and Jarand agree to back down."

"That could be a long time," said Autumn Leaves.

"True. Secondly, I can create mayhem amongst the cavalry units by controlling the horses and thirdly, Navira and I can raise reflective shields."

"*And* you can summon flocks of birds, Tarkyn," suggested Rainstorm, as he handed out cups of tea.

"And can Caroman create weather like Stormaway?" asked Running Feet.

The wizard replied for himself, "Yes, but it needs planning and vast amounts of power. We can either work the power up over time or draw on the forest's power through the prince, in the way Stormaway did last time."

Waterstone frowned. "It seems to me that we're going to have a very overworked forest guardian; controlling horses, birds, reflective shields and providing power for weather. I think we had all better think of ways to stop these armies that don't rely solely on Tarkyn's power and goodwill."

Tarkyn grinned, "Spoken like a truly protective older brother."

"Which I am," said Waterstone firmly. "Someone has to pull you in before your enthusiasm and the demands of others overstretches you."

"All right. Point taken, even though I haven't agreed to anything yet. We're just looking at possibilities at the moment, you know."

Watersone met his eyes and smiled at him but said nothing more.

Navira accepted a cup of tea from Rainstorm and took a sip before asking slowly, "Shouldn't we warn Kosar and Jarand that we intend to intervene; that they run the risk of being embarrassed in front of thousands of their men?"

"Tarkyn has already warned them separately and together," answered Stormaway. "They have appeared to take heed, but in reality each of them has continued to plot against the other." He shrugged. "I suppose we should, once more, give them fair warning. But don't expect them to change their intentions."

"What's the point of that?" demanded Rainstorm. "That will just reduce any element of surprise we might have."

"It will," agreed Navira, "But it will set the terms of the engagement. They will know that we are not there to attack them."

Rainstorm snorted. "That won't stop them from attacking us if they think we are trying to interfere."

"True," Navira thought for a moment, "But it might make them cave in more quickly. After all, from what I understand, Tarkyn has always followed through on his word, hasn't he? So they must now have some trepidation about crossing him."

"Good point," said Rainstorm enthusiastically. "I think you're right." He smiled, "You're quite canny, aren't you?"

Navira inclined her head, "At times."

"So why have you joined us now?" he asked suddenly. "Tarkyn asked that question earlier and you haven't answered him yet. You could have joined us months ago when we were in the Lost Forest, close to your home."

Navira took another slow sip of her tea. "Several reasons. I wanted to meet Danton, the man who had stood by my brother through thick and thin; to gauge him, to gain a closer view of Tarkyn, to have an ally before I met you all. But more than this, I wanted Tarkyn to know that he had exhausted every avenue in his efforts to protect Eskuzor and that what will happen henceforward is inevitable."

Rainstorm frowned. "What? You mean this out and out war they are planning?"

"Yes, partly."

"What's the rest of it, then?"

Navira gave a small smile, "There are some things that only wizards are privileged to know. You will find out in the fullness of time."

Rainstorm's frown deepened, "Danton is right. You are annoying."

Rather surprisingly, she chuckled, "Does he say that to you too, does he? What you both really mean is that I am mysterious and you are frustrated."

Before Rainstorm could come up with a riposte, Waterstone cut in. "No doubt Navira will tell us when she is ready and not before. Right now we have a war to stop. So Stormaway, what will we have to deal with from the twins' wizards?"

Stormaway accepted a cup of tea from Ancient Oak with a nod of thanks. "From the information I have gathered, I would say that Kosar's wizards are not aggressive. There was one with the troops we immobilised who I think specialises in healing. The king's personal wizard, Stargazer Bookbinder is as his name suggests; full of portents and book learning, very useful for advice but not a practical wizard. He does have some shieldwielders, as we have seen before. Jarand's wizard, Journeyman Cloudmaker is a different proposition altogether. It is he who created the dangerous storm that Tarkyn and I dispelled and it is he who trained the wolves to hunt woodfolk. He was also behind the poisoned parchments. Yes, he is a force to be reckoned with."

Danton scoffed. "Huh. I'm not sure how scary he would be out in the open. Tarkyn and I outfaced him and eight sorcerers with very little difficulty."

"I doubt that he will be out in the open," replied Stormaway. After a sip of his tea, he smiled, "… especially after his encounter with you two."

A thought struck Rainstorm, "I wonder if he and Jarand poisoned the summonses they sent out, to guarantee the compliance of Jarand's lords?"

"Interesting suggestion, Rainstorm." Stormaway took another sip, beginning to relax after the trek from Lord Tolward's. "Possibly some of them may have been spiked, perhaps those destined for the less certain of his lords. But each poisoned parchment requires a little of Jarand's blood or hair and causes him discomfort as the spell takes effect. So I doubt that he would have spiked every summons."

"What about Lord Tolward? Would Jarand consider him uncertain?" pressed Rainstorm.

"Hmm," Stormaway looked across at Harkell. "Good question. What do you think?"

"Possibly. His holding is one of the furthest from Montraya. And Tolward did send off more of his people to enlist in Jarand's army than he had previously intended to."

Waterstone frowned. "More and more I dislike the thought of Tarkyn coming out into the open to meet this Lord Tolward."

"H-huh." Drakell cleared his throat and then looked as though he wished he hadn't.

"Go on Drakell," said Tarkyn, smiling encouragingly. "We would value your comments."

Drakell cleared his throat nervously again before saying, "Ahem. This poison makes the person reading the letter support Prince Jarand. Is that right?"

Stormaway nodded, "Even if he uses the Velvet Claw mushroom to force obedience, the ingredients to persuade the receiver to his cause must also be present for that to work."

Drakell took a breath and continued, "Well, Lord Tolward said that he thought Prince Jarand was fighting this war for self-aggrandisement, not to help the people of Eskuzor. That doesn't sound as though he is under a spell to like Jarand, does it?"

"Not unless he is thinking one thing and saying another," said Danton.

"Not so easy to disguise your sentiments if they have been induced magically," responded Stormaway. He smiled at Danton. "Remember? You and Rainstorm did not become devious supporters of Jarand. You stood up for him hammer and tongs when normally you would have been much more subtle in the face of a crowd of people who clearly didn't support him."

Danton grimaced, "True. So we did." He gave a little shudder. "Don't remind me. That was a hideous night."

Rainstorm watched him until Danton met his eyes, then gave a faint smile of shared memory.

"So probably Tolward just threw caution to the winds in a fit of pique when he thought Tarkyn was no longer acting independently," concluded Stormaway.

Waterstone frowned. "Fairly harsh for those extra people who were sent to war on a mere distempered whim, wouldn't you say?"

"Yes," said Danton deliberately drawing the woodman's fire away from Tarkyn. "I, who was used as a pawn to further my father's ambition, would be the first to agree with you. But it does not make all of our sorcerer society bad. And from what I have seen, I think Lord Tolward is usually a fair overlord."

Waterstone, with great resolution had just decided not to reply when a grey and white pigeon flew into sight among the trees and landed, cooing loudly, on a branch above Stormaway's head. With irritation born of tiredness, Stormaway began to haul himself to his feet to retrieve the message from the ring around the pigeon's ankle.

Tarkyn held up his hand to stop him. "Wait." After a moment's silence, the pigeon fluttered down to land on the wizard's knee.

Stormaway smiled, "Thank you, Sire." He stroked the pigeon gently and gave it a few seeds from his pocket before carefully extracting the little piece of vellum. He muttered some incomprehensible words and the vellum increased in size. He handed it to Tarkyn saying, "Sire, this bears the king's seal. There is no danger in touching it. You cannot minimise an enchanted piece of parchment or vellum. Only one spell can act on an object at any one time. So minimisation would override any previous spell."

"But you just finished saying that Velvet Claw was used in conjunction with persuasive ingredients."

"Tarkyn, a concoction smeared on a parchment, no matter how complex, is essentially a single spell. A minimisation is entirely different, requiring nothing but words and knowledge to instigate it."

"Amazing, Stormaway," Tarkyn shook his head, "You are such a wealth of knowledge."

"Hardly," said Navira disdainfully. "Such knowledge as this is known by every fledgling wizard."

"Thank you for pointing out the extent of my ignorance," said Tarkyn, with a courtly nod but tight mouth. "And perhaps in return I could point out your lack of courtesy in deriding my vote of thanks to Stormaway?"

Navira's face burned with chagrin, not as Tarkyn first supposed at her fault but at being dressed down in public. "No doubt you are used to treating people as you wish, Tarkyn, but you will not speak to me like that."

As Tarkyn drew breath for a rebuke, Ancient Oak intervened. "I think you will find, Stillwaters," he said gently, drawing Navira's and Tarkyn's fire and everyone's surprised attention, "that your brother tries to be very careful with how he treats people. And he is usually willing to respond to suggestions, but is not so responsive to demands." He smiled disarmingly at Tarkyn before adding, "But of course, sometimes his temper, like yours, gets the better of him."

For a moment the issue hung in the balance. Then Navira let out a breath, "Tarkyn, you seem to have surrounded yourself with courageous people. I am sorry I highlighted your lack of training." She smiled at Ancient Oak before saying pointedly to Tarkyn, "But in future, if you don't mind, could you address my shortcomings in private?"

Tarkyn smiled wryly, "You will be interested to know, Navira, that Sparrow thinks Ancient Oak is the steady one in our family. Waterstone and I are more emotional, apparently." His eyes dropped to the message he was holding. He unfolded the vellum and studied its contents before reading it out to his waiting audience.

Tarkyn,

When you met me in the forest, you said that if I ever needed you to help with Eskuzor's welfare, to come into the woodlands and call out. Fortunately your practical wizard has provided a more dignified method of communication.

As you are no doubt aware, Jarand is gathering his forces on the Western Plains to challenge me for the crown. I did not think he would take his resentment so far, but everything you warned me about him is true. I have no choice but to meet his challenge.

Your past actions have convinced me that you will indeed intervene if you believe I am acting against Eskuzor's best interests. So I wish to point out to you the importance of maintaining a stable monarchy. Our family has ruled for a thousand years and has kept Eskuzor safe and prosperous. Much as it pains me, I believe that I must quell Jarand's pretensions once and for all. So, for the sake of Eskuzor, I ask that if you intervene in this conflict, you do so by supporting me, the rightful king, against Jarand.

Your brother,

Kosar, King of Eskuzor.

"Oh!" exclaimed Rainstorm, "He is trying to impress you. He didn't sign himself as your brother last time nor as King of Eskuzor."

Tarkyn was thoughtful. "Hmm. So what do you all think?"

"I think he has decided you make a better friend than an enemy," said Danton, "which is perfectly true."

"However," added Bean, "he also said he had no choice and that is rarely true."

"Very rarely," agreed String. "It's usually just that the other choices are unpalatable."

Bean nodded, "Yeah. He could abdicate… not saying he should, but he could. He could negotiate… Now there's a novel idea… Open warfare is not the only choice."

The prince smiled, "Thank you for pointing that out. Unless you question that statement, his letter is quite persuasive."

"Oh, there are other holes in it, my lord," said Caroman. "Your family may have ruled for a thousand years but this is not the first conflict over which descendant should have the crown."

"And I would also dispute that Eskuzor is as safe and prosperous as she could be," added Waterstone. "Any country so torn by internal conflict must present an easy target to outside powers, and her prosperity has been damaged by lawlessness and the continual drain on her resources by the few who rule her but who do not actually produce anything themselves."

"Lucky then, that it is only a few," snapped Tarkyn.

"Their number may be small," snapped Waterstone straight back, "but their drain on resources is disproportionately large."

Tarkyn and Waterstone glared at each other, once more squaring off over their fundamental differences.

"Remember Moridan," urged Stormaway quietly. Tarkyn and Waterstone visibly relaxed, remembering the old forest guardian's caution to take care with their friendship. The wizard's mellow voice washed over them, "I think we can all agree that Kosar's letter does not bear close scrutiny."

"No, it doesn't," agreed Tarkyn, "But I must admit I found it persuasive on first reading. I am glad you are all here to guide me."

Within three hours, another pigeon arrived, this time carrying a missive signed by Jarand.

"Not so surprising," said Caroman. "They are twins. They think and do a lot alike."

"Not quite so friendly, this one," said Tarkyn as he prepared to read it out.

Tarkyn,

I am disappointed that I have not heard from you. Perhaps misfortune befell Captain Harkell and he was unable to deliver my message or your reply. Amazingly his whole family also seems to be missing. In his absence I have reverted to the use of pigeons to contact you.

As you must now realise, Kosar has no intention of allowing me to exert any authority or to take any significant role in governing Eskuzor. Yet, if we worked together, we could make this country great.

I can no longer stand by and watch Kosar run Eskuzor into the ground.

I am not sure how much use your little woodland army would be out in the open but I am still willing to accept your fealty. Otherwise, I suggest you leave us to our own affairs.

I offer you a final word of warning, brother; if you value your woodlands, do not move against me. For your delectation, I have arranged a small demonstration of the consequence you face, if you choose to defy me.

Jarand

Even as Tarkyn's last words faded away, several woodfolk jumped up in alarm in response to distant minds.

"Fire!" shouted Waterstone, so rattled that he forgot to keep his voice down. "The bastard has set the forest alight!"

Part 8: Fire

Chapter 61

Autumn Leaves' face was white with shock, "There are trees burning along a quarter mile front...and it's spreading fast."

The ground beneath them surged.

As people rocked where they sat and the large kettle fell over in the fire sending up a billow of steam, Harkell said calmly, "We're horrified too, Tarkyn, but can we keep it to one disaster at a time?"

Tarkyn glared at him, using him as a focus for the few seconds it took him to pull the most extreme of his feelings under control. As the ground quietened, Harkell nodded his approval.

Tarkyn returned his attention to Autumn Leaves, "How far away?"

"Four miles. Five at the most."

Tarkyn sprang to his feet. "Right. Danton, Borovar, and Thraya. You head off to the forest's edge and use shields to stop the fire from spreading. Caroman and Stormaway, I will stay with you to provide you a conduit for the forest's power so that you can produce some sort of weather to quench the fire. Navira, you go where you will do the most good, but don't let yourself be seen by Jarand's soldiers in your true form. Waterstone?"

"Woodfolk at the forest's edge will attack the soldiers from the cover of the trees to prevent them from lighting more trees," replied Waterstone on behalf of the woodfolk. "If our kin have to betray their presence, they will wipe out every soldier within view. Some of us will stay here to protect you and the children and to keep you informed. The rest of us will join the fight at the forest's edge."

"We will come with you," said Sorath firmly. "We can help with the fire and the fight."

"Have we covered everything?" demanded Tarkyn.

"What about the sorcerers hiding in the forests near Lord Tolward's?" suggested Harkell. "We could use them."

"Good idea, Harkell." Tarkyn drew his dagger with its royal crest on the hilt and handed it to Harkell. "Take this as a token of my authority. Tell them you are my Troop Commander. What does that make you? A colonel? A general?"

"A general," supplied Danton. Despite the gravity of the situation, he gave a little grin. "More impressive. They don't have to know how few troops we have."

Tarkyn nodded, "A general then. Organise them, Harkell, and bring them to repel Jarand's troops and help with fighting the fire if needed but I hope we power wielders should be able to handle the fire." He looked around, "Now have we covered everything?"

"The immediate issues," answered Waterstone, already moving. "Revenge will come later."

Danton commandeered the great warhorse that Borovar had brought into the forest. Three up, with Thraya sandwiched between Borovar and Danton, they rode, sometimes cantering, sometimes reduced to a walk by pressing bushes, along narrow paths towards the edge of the forest. For the first couple of miles, woodfolk hung out of the trees as they passed and directed them towards the fire. But long before they reached the flames, they could smell the smoke and soon fiery leaves were swirling through the air around them, carried on a stiffening breeze.

"The wind is picking up. It's going to fuel the fire and drive it further into the forest," shouted Danton in an effort to make himself heard by Borovar at the front.

A woodwoman he didn't know leant out of the tree above him and shouted back, "It's strange weather. No clouds. Only smoke and now a strong wind."

Danton heard a rumbling somewhere in front of him. "What?" he shouted.

Borovar raised his voice. "I think our friend Journeyman may be working up a gale to drive the fire into the forest."

"Could be." Danton looked back at the woodwoman as the horse bore them forward. "Tell Tarkyn and the wizards," he urged. He wasn't sure, but he hoped he saw the woodwoman nod before she was lost to sight as they rounded a bend.

The smoke was getting thicker and the three riders had to cover their mouths to stop from coughing. The horse, already overburdened, was beginning to snort and wheeze. Borovar pulled it to a halt and swung his leg up and over its head before sliding to the ground.

"That's it. We can't take him any closer." Once the other two had dismounted, he wrapped a rag around its nose, turned it around and patted it on the rump to send it back the way they had come. "See you, old fella…"

They jogged another hundred yards, but then had to slow to a walk for Thraya to keep up. Now they could see flickers of orange through the trees and even though they were still several hundred yards away, could feel radiant heat from the fire.

A young woodman approached them nervously, "Are you from Prince Tarkyn?"

They nodded, knowing that if they had answered in the negative, they would have been shot where they stood.

"I am Morning Breeze." His face was streaked with soot. "The fire front goes for hundreds of yards in both directions from here. We are trying to beat out the flames at the forward edge of the fire but the heat is so intense that we can only dart in and out. The fire is on the ground and up in the branches; a wall of flame fifty feet high." A hint of panic crossed the young man's face but he drew breath and kept himself together.

The three sorcerers looked at each other in dismay.

"We can't cover that distance, not fifty feet high," breathed Danton. "What do you suggest?"

An older woodwoman appeared, "The wind is driving it. Even if you can break it up, it will help. I am Swirling Wind."

"Won't that create wind tunnels between our shields?" asked Boravar.

Thraya's calm voice made itself heard above the noise of the wind. "I don't know whether I can change the shape of my shield, but you can, can't you? Can you make them a shape that will send the wind back on itself?"

"Maybe." Danton pushed his hand through his hair that was already sticky with sweat. "We can only try. Perhaps if we curve our shields on each end back towards the fire, the wind will swirl back into its own path."

"Stand between us, Thraya," said Borovar, placing his big hand reassuringly on her back. "Now put your shield up around you to shield yourself from the heat and smoke until we get into place."

They walked steadily forward, Boravar within a shimmering dome of peacock blue, Danton within aqua and Thraya within a lilac dome, squinting against the harsh glare and ducking as larger pieces of burning debris slapped the outside of their shields. The roar and crackling of the firestorm soon made speaking impossible. Following Danton's gestures, they fanned out to stand fifty yards apart. Then Danton and Borovar swung their shields from around them to create a straight translucent wall in front of themselves. They stretched their shields upward and curved them forward at either end. Following their lead, Thraya concentrated and created a wall but could not stretch it as high. Danton gestured to her to make it narrower and higher, worried that flaming branches from above could fall on her. Frowning fiercely, she changed the shape of her shield and then, with visible mental effort, achieved a curve on either end.

Thraya could feel the wind buffeting her shield but she knew that as long as she maintained concentration, she was safe. Borovar sent her a smile of encouragement and she carefully held her concentration long enough to smile back.

In front of them the fire raged. The wind that swirled off the ends of their shields interfered with the wind roaring in from the plains so that it blew the flames this way and that amongst the burning trees. Thirty yards beyond either end of their short line, the wind howled unchecked, driving the fire deeper into the forest. Suddenly, Thraya realised that the fire was passing them on either side and could swing around and join up behind them. She yelled warning and pointed, but as she focused on the impending danger, she lost her grip on her shield and it winked out of sight, leaving her exposed and far too close to the flames.

Belatedly Thraya realised her error and desperately struggled to regain her focus. With a mighty effort, she raised a quivering shield, closing her mind against her burning face and hands. Steadying her concentration, she brushed frantically at the burning twigs that had landed on her clothes, trying to get rid of them before they set her clothes alight.

Suddenly, a huge bronze shield blossomed over the top of her, engulfing both her and her shield.

"Let it go," said Navira gently. "I have you safe." Gasping with relief, Thraya dropped her shield and turned to find the wizardess standing beside her, holding out a water flask. "Here. Drink this. Splash some on your face and hands. Then I'll give you an unguent to rub on your burns until Tarkyn has time to help you."

Thraya nodded, tears in her eyes. "Thank you. Sorath is going to kill me. He didn't want me to help in the first place."

"I think he'll just be glad to have you in one piece." She waited until Thraya had applied the unguent, ignoring the fire that now raged around them on all sides. "Now I am going to walk you out to the front edge of the fire. There you may either join us again to raise your shield against the fire or raise it to protect yourself and get back to safety." Navira shrugged. "Totally up to you. You have natural talent as a shieldwielder but it depends on how much pain you are in, and only you can tell that."

They walked back, treading carefully over smouldering, blackened branches, sending little swirls of ash, some still glowing, puffing upwards from under their feet. On either side of them, Danton and Borovar had retreated but were still holding their shields before them, striving to slow the fire's progress.

Once they were back among the unburnt trees, Navira called loudly, "I need to speak to some woodfolk."

Immediately, Waterstone, Twig Snap and Rainstorm appeared.

"Thank you for coming," She indicated Borovar and Danton. "I need to be able to instruct them above the noise of the fire. "Could you please station yourselves so that you can pass our words on to each other?"

Rainstorm flicked to stand beside Danton, and Twig Snap beside Borovar.

She lifted her shield from around her and raised it into a straight sheet of shimmering bronze in front of her, then using her own shield to demonstrate, she instructed, "Ask them to think of their shields as bread dough. They can expand them slowly in every direction, making them thinner and thinner to accommodate the extra height and breadth. Their shields can become so thin that they will no longer protect against arrows or spears but they will still hold back insubstantial things such as fire, smoke and wind. As they do it, they can move further away from me so that between us, we can cover a much greater fire front." She waited until Danton and Borovar had stretched their shields to twice their previous size. "Now ask Danton to move along until he is at the right hand end of the fire front. Then he can protect us from fire passing around behind us on the side."

"I will help too," announced Thraya. She gave a wry smile. "Otherwise, I will have nothing to do but think of the pain."

Navira smiled in acknowledgement of the sorceress' courage, as Thraya resolutely raised her shield, "Then you stay here, while Borovar and I move further along to the left. That way, you will have Danton and me on either side of you. Waterstone, we will need another woodman or woman to be a contact for Thraya."

"Already done," said Waterstone, as Autumn Leaves appeared beside the old sorceress. He walked beside Navira as she edged to her left, parallel with the fire front, slowly expanding her shield. "And we'll make sure you all have water and food."

Navira nodded distractedly, keeping her mind on her task.

"I think you would do better to overlap your shields, not leave gaps," said Waterstone. "With your expanded shields, you'll be covering nearly half of the fire front. If you can contain this section of fire, our people can concentrate their efforts on the section left of Borovar and hopefully create a fire break. Once this section in front of us has burned out most of its fuel, you can all move to your left and we will mop up whatever fire is left here."

Navira considered the wisdom of Waterstone's words before giving a little smile, "Your wish is our command, sir"

Waterstone grinned, "Thanks."

Chapter 62

Once everyone knew what they were doing, Tarkyn ignored the ensuing activity and strode to a large sycamore on the edge of the clearing, assuming the wizards would follow. He walked around it until he had found a smooth section of trunk at chest height. Then he dragged off his shirt and stood with his back against the tree.

Caroman frowned, "What are you doing?"

"Last time I provided a channel for the forest's life force to Stormaway, the river of power running from one hand to the other made me feel nauseated. Perhaps if I use my back to absorb the power and use a hand on each of you, it will feel more even."

"Good idea, Tarkyn. It may work," said Stormaway, "And you'll have a larger part of yourself in contact with the tree which may increase the amount of power you can absorb."

"Come on then." Tarkyn placed a hand on the shoulder of each wizard. "Let's get on with it."

Caroman's eyes met Stormaway's and a smile passed between them.

Stormaway did not waste time telling Tarkyn to have patience. He could see that he was distressed by Jarand's perfidy and was struggling to hold his emotions in check. Instead Stormaway said, "First we must search the nearby skies for the glimmering of a storm. It is much easier to build on an existing weather pattern than to create one from scratch."

The two wizards each placed one hand on the other's shoulder and their other hand on Tarkyn's shoulder so that they formed a triangle.

"Close your eyes, Tarkyn, and join with us." Beneath his breath, Stormaway muttered a complex chant that he repeated over and over. After a few moments, Caroman began to chant with him, their voices blending and twisting in and out of harmony. Tarkyn had no idea what they were saying, so left them to their chanting. Instead, he focused on the images in their minds. At first, all he could see was an empty expanse of deep blue. Now and again he saw skerricks of wispy cloud but the sense of searching continued. Then he became aware of a shadow of darker greyer blue that gradually became more defined.

"Are we going towards it or is it coming towards us?" he asked, careful to keep focussed.

"Neither," replied Stormaway, trying to cover his irritation at being interrupted. "We are merely tuning in to it."

Soon the darker grey dominated their projected vision. It billowed and roiled around them.

"That will do, I think," said Caroman, as both he and Stormaway dropped their hands from the shoulders of the other two, leaving only Tarkyn's hands on the wizards' shoulders.

"Not sure how much moisture there is in it. We are going to need quite a bit." Stormaway's voice sounded muffled, as though he were talking from a distance. "Tarkyn, if we summon this storm, is there any chance that you could draw moisture from the forest? It will be a lot quicker than trying to draw water from the surrounding atmosphere."

For a moment Tarkyn didn't answer. Then he took a deep breath. "If I could drag the particles of Pipeless the wizard out to stand before me, then I should be able to draw out particles of moisture, shouldn't I? Wait. I will take myself down into the depths beneath the forest. Whatever happens, don't let go of me."

"You have my word," said Stormaway solemnly.

"You concentrate on bringing the storm here."

"Yes Sire." Stormaway's voice contained a distinct smile at Tarkyn giving orders when he knew so little about the technicalities of what they were doing.

Tarkyn's mouth quirked. "I heard that."

Taking a slow deep breath, the forest guardian let his mind sink down the trunk of the huge sycamore, drifting down the length of the major tap root. Sixty feet below the surface of the forest, he found the end of the great tree's roots soaking water from a fast-flowing, underground stream. He formed a clear picture in his mind of trees burning and of water surging up in a great spout that arced up and into the midst of the fire, dousing it. Then, as an experiment, he added his force to that of the trees and drew a small quantity of water up through the root system, up the trunk, along one of the lower branches and out through the leaves, in a scattering of droplets above the wizards' heads.

Tarkyn resurfaced just in time to see the two old wizards spluttering and shaking their heads as they were showered.

Confronted with Tarkyn's grinning face, Stormaway rolled his eyes at Caroman, "Did I mention that our forest guardian has an over-developed sense of fun?"

Caroman, with water streaming down his face, grinned in return, "No, but I daresay we can forgive him, since he seems to be able to draw forth water, as we requested."

"On the other hand, we have lost our focus, and with it, the storm."

Tarkyn looked a little shame-faced. "Oops."

"Ignore grumpy old men, Sire," advised Caroman. "It may have taken us an hour to find it, but we can easily pick the storm up again, now that we have located it."

"Oh good. Because I need some instruction before we go any further."

"I'll instruct," said Stormaway firmly to Caroman. "You work on bringing the storm closer."

Tarkyn realised he had just witnessed a small demarcation dispute. He grinned, "Let me guess; Navira is Caroman's protégé and I am yours, Stormaway."

"Something like that," muttered Stormaway.

Caroman laughed, "He is sharp, isn't he?" Seeing Stormaway scowl at him, he said quickly, "All right, all right. I'm going. Keep your hand on my shoulder, young fella." So saying, he closed his eyes and sent his mind flying after the storm.

Stormaway studied his protégé, standing against the sycamore with strands of his long black hair floating in the gathering wind, drawing on the might of the forest with so little effort that he was ready to listen to instruction at the same time. *He's like an enthusiastic Great Dane puppy, all strength and willingness, but so little knowledge...So little taught knowledge,* the wizard amended. *He has a great deal of instinctual knowledge. How long did it take him to work out how to draw moisture from the forest? Twenty minutes? Less. Probably most of that time was spent on actually doing it.* Despite himself, he smiled, "You did well to draw that moisture, Tarkyn. I thought it would take you longer."

Tarkyn looked startled then pleased. "Thank you."

With a touch of remorse, Stormaway realised how rarely he praised the prince; easy to take a forest guardian's powers for granted and to forget that Tarkyn was also an inexperienced young sorcerer, who had lacked parental guidance for most of his formative years. Stormaway harrumphed, bringing his attention back to more pressing matters. "Now, watch Caroman. As soon as he has relocated the storm, he will send out his magic and stroke it across the sky towards him. This will pull the air towards us, bringing the storm in its wake. You must have patience, Sire. It will take some time."

A few minutes later, Caroman gave a grunt of satisfaction and began to move his arms as though he were pulling in a kite. Streaks of black appeared above them. With each movement of his arms, the streaks became stronger and more clearly defined.

"His magic is black," exclaimed Tarkyn. "That's amazing. I've never seen that before."

"Hmm. It is rare, very strong and very dangerous. Just be glad he is on our side."

Tarkyn watched him drawing in the storm for a minute or two before asking, "But why then does he not have a double honorific as do you, Stormaway, and Stillwaters? After all, he is just as strong as you, if not more so, from what I can gather. Other wizard names have meaning. So what does Caroman mean?"

Stormaway glanced sideways at him, "Caroman's full name is Care-of-Man Throneguard."

Tarkyn gave a low whistle of consternation, then winced at Caroman's frown of distraction. He murmured quietly so as not to distract Caroman further, "If his name reflects his role in the scheme of things, then he is indeed a force to be reckoned with."

"But as you may notice, Sire," broke in Stormaway, anxious to allay any misgivings that Tarkyn might have, "Caroman's intentions dovetail with your own."

"Hmm. They do, but both of you have been highhanded in your care for Eskuzor. I would hope that you now have less need to keep your own counsel."

Stormaway met and held the prince's gaze. Both knew that Stormaway had manipulated Tarkyn as a young child into becoming the woodfolk's liege lord and had manoeuvred him in lesser ways since. What the wizard saw now in the prince's eyes made him bow and say, "I live to serve you, Your Highness."

Tarkyn inclined his head, "I do not doubt that, Stormaway. I merely doubt your faith in me. Until you are open with me, I will know that you do not trust me to make the right decisions."

Stormaway blinked in surprise at his protégé's acumen. Tarkyn watched in faint derision as a parade of thoughts crossed the wizard's face. Eventually Stormaway said, "Sire, sometimes there is no right decision; only the lesser of two evils. I trust you to strive to your last breath to protect Esuzor and I would not wish to undermine your determination by burdening you with everything I know."

"Are you saying I will fail?"

"No Sire, but you may not like how you succeed." Stormaway held up a hand to forestall Tarkyn's next question. "Tarkyn, I cannot read the future but I can see the possible futures and I can tell you there is no easy way forward. If you trust me…us, let us keep our own counsel for a while longer. In the end, it will benefit you and all of Eskuzor."

Tarkyn frowned at him, debating whether to order him to say more. Finally he shrugged, "The forest guardians of yore told me I could trust you and you have always proved to be true… even though you are devious. So, once more I will give you my faith." He drew a deep breath, resolutely turning his mind from his wizard's words, "So what happens next, Stormaway? I can draw the moisture from an underground stream that is passing beneath us up into the sycamore's leaves, but then what?"

"Normally the sun's heat draws moisture upwards into the atmosphere but that will take far too long. If you draw the water out of the forest, I will create a strong updraft that will carry the droplets up into Caramon's storm. We just have to wait for his storm to arrive."

The top edges of white cauliflower clouds were just becoming visible above the trees on the eastern side of the clearing, following the unnatural black streaks in the sky. As they watched, more and more of the billowing clouds came into view until the front edge was almost above them. The temperature had dropped and a cold wind was giving Tarkyn some regrets about his shirtless state.

"Right, Tarkyn. This is it."

Just as they were about to start, Tree Wind raced up to them. "We have received a message from the fireline. There is a wind sweeping in off the plains and they think it might be Journeyman's work." She shrugged, "I don't know whether it matters but we thought you should know."

Tarkyn grinned, "I don't know either, but thanks."

Stormaway gave a grim little smile, "Against one wizard, it would matter. Against the might of the forest guardian, Caroman and myself, it will be irrelevant. But thank you for letting us know." Turning back to Tarkyn, he said, "Now, draw as much moisture as you can up into the tree's foliage but keep your hand on my shoulder so that I can tap your power. Can you do all that?"

Tarkyn blew out a breath, "Yes, I guess I can. You start, so that I can steady myself with directing the flow of power to the two of you. Then, once that is stable, I will be able to shift my focus to the depths of the forests to start drawing up the water."

"Good lad." Tarkyn's eyebrows twitched at such an informal turn of phrase but, despite that, Stormaway suspected that the prince would quite like being the junior partner for once.

Tarkyn watched as Stormaway swept both arms upward sending green magic streaming towards the sky. Then the wizard swept up one arm after the other as he coaxed the air around them to rush towards the approaching clouds. Once Tarkyn felt a balanced draw on his power travelling from his back out along his arms and through his hands into the wizards' shoulders, he closed his eyes, and let his mind plummet down through the sycamore's tap root. Using his own power, he drew on the underground watercourse, gently at first, then slowly increasing his insistence until a steady flow of moisture rose through the tap root, up into the sycamore's veins and out onto its leaves.

Those who had stayed in the clearing watched as the whole sycamore glowed with bronze magic, while black magic streamed beneath the lowering clouds urging them westward and a green current of power flowed upward sweeping the moisture from the sycamore's leaves with it. And between the two wizards, the forest guardian stood glowing with bronze power, his black hair being drawn towards his hands by the flow of power that coursed through his arms into the wizards.

The clouds grew darker and heavier, roiling within themselves as they passed slowly overhead. For forty minutes, the storm, mightier by the moment, blocked out the sun as the three power wielders changed it nature and its course. Then a patch of blue appeared over the eastern trees as the last of the storm clouds began their journey overhead towards the western plains.

Stormaway continued with one hand, while he tapped the forest guardian on his shoulder. "Enough, Tarkyn. When you are ready, you can stop drawing on the forest for power and moisture."

Stormaway and Caroman lifted their arms and drew their power back into themselves, then dropped their arms and waited, carefully not dislodging Tarkyn's hands on their shoulders until he was ready. For a minute or two, they were deluged with water from the sycamore as the moisture continued up from the stream beneath them but without Stormaway's power to draw it upwards into the clouds.

Tarkyn opened his eyes. For a few moments, he just watched the droplets falling on the wizards and felt water trickling down the trunk of the tree onto his bare back. Then he shuddered and dropped his hands from their shoulders. "I'd move if I were you," he said with a wry smile. "That water is freezing. I did stop when I felt your hand on my shoulder, Stormaway, but a lot of moisture was already on its way up. You'll just get wetter if you stay where you are."

As they moved away, Stormaway realised that Tarkyn wasn't following them. "What about you?" he asked. "You look half frozen."

"I am, but I need a few minutes to replenish myself. I channelled the forest's esse to you two, but used my own power to draw the water out of the forest. If I move away from the tree at the moment, I think my knees may buckle."

Caroman's eyes grew round, "Are you saying that you did not draw on the forest's power to raise all those gallons of water to the surface?"

Tarkyn shook his head, "No. Too complicated to channel it to you and use it in another way at the same time."

"Very impressive, Sire. Neither of us could have done that. If not for the forest's power you gave us, it would have taken us hours to evoke that storm, let alone engorge it with water."

Too tired to answer, Tarkyn let his head drop back against the sycamore's trunk, and closed his eyes again, shivering as the icy water ran down his back. Moments later, he felt himself being himself being manhandled by many arms. His eyes snapped open to find Lapping Water, hands on hips, silently directing four woodfolk to lift him.

"What on earth are you doing?" he demanded.

"That sycamore is not the only tree in the forest, Tarkyn, just the only one shedding water. So we are moving you to a dry tree." Lapping Water met his stunned gaze, daring him to countermand her. After a moment, she laughed, "Just endure a minute of indignity in exchange for a nice dry tree, nearer the fire. When you're settled, I'll bring you a cup of tea. How's that?"

Tarkyn grinned over his shoulder as he was carted past, "Rather unexpected, I must say, but good. Thank you."

"What about us?" asked Stormaway plaintively.

"What about you?" replied Lapping Water, as she carried a towel and dry shirt over to Tarkyn. "You didn't supply the power, he did. But I'll concede you did a lot of concentrating and arm waving. I'll get you all a cup of tea and something to eat while you dry off and we wait for your storm to do its work."

CHAPTER 63

Bringing Drakell and the trappers with him openly and a few woodfolk skirting along beside them with the cover of the trees, Harkell took nearly an hour to reach the clearing of the hundred year old burnt beech tree. When they arrived, no one was in sight.

Bean looked around and shrugged, "Maybe they haven't had time to get here yet."

"Maybe they don't want to show themselves until they know who they're dealing with," said String.

Drakell moved casually back along the path a little so that he stood beside a clump of dense scrub.

"There are many sorcerers hidden in the surrounding bushland," reported Creaking Bough quietly. "They are not soldiers."

"Thanks." Drakell wandered back into the clearing to relay the message.

In response, Harkell nodded and drew forth Tarkyn's dagger. Holding it by the blade high above his head so that the crested hilt was in view, he announced in a clear, carrying voice, "I come in the name of Prince Tarkyn." He paused to let his words sink in, "If you wish to support His Royal Highness, step forward, for he has need of you."

Slowly the clearing filled with sorcerers; family groups, bands of comrades and many, including children and women, with no obvious association with anyone else. Some were well dressed, some virtually in rags, but all looked at Harkell with a mixture of hope and suspicion.

A skinny, tough-looking man near the front scowled at him. "Lord Tolward said the prince would be here himself. Who are you?"

Suppressing a self-conscious grin, Harkell replied with due gravity, "I am General Harkell, commander of Prince Tarkyn's troops. A dire emergency has arisen that requires the prince's presence. But he also requires your assistance."

"Harkell?" queried a big man to his right, folding his arms. "Ain't that the name of that captain who deserted from Prince Jarand's ranks?" When Harkell nodded, the man growled, "Risen pretty high pretty fast, haven't you?"

From zero to general in thirty seconds, as I recall. Harkell smiled. "Yes, I have. But contrary to appearances, I have been in Prince Tarkyn's service for several months now…. ever since our first encounter with him in the forests on the other side of the mountains near Montraya."

"And who are you?" asked the skinny man, rudely pointing his thumb at Drakell.

"I am General Harkell's brother, Drakell."

"And…" began the skinny man.

Harkell's voice cut in sharply. "We don't have time for this. A forest fire is raging only six miles from here. Prince Tarkyn is working with two wizards to create a storm to douse it. But that will take time. Meanwhile, we need help to fight the fire and stop Prince Jarand's men from lighting any more of the forest."

"I told you I saw smoke," said an old lady with a satisfied cackle amidst the babble of consternation that greeted this announcement.

A well-dressed man in his thirties, who still managed to look rough, sniped back, "Shut up, Old Ma. Listen to the general."

Harkell nodded his thanks as he waited for the comments to die down. When everyone was completely quiet, Harkell began. "I want all men who can fight, over on my left. Bring anything you can use as weapons. I want everyone else to gather blankets, towels, anything that can be used to smother the fire and move to my right. I realise you don't have much with you but when all this is over, we will finance replacements for your damaged belongings." He turned to his brother, "Drakell, can you organise our fire fighters while I organise our soldiers."

Drakell's eyes widened in alarm at the prospect of directing people, but he was astute enough to realise that taking issue with Harkell would jeopardise his brother's tenuous control. So he merely nodded and strode to Harkell's right with all the assurance he could muster.

As soon as he stopped, the old lady stomped up to him, "D'you want me to organise who's gonna mind the kiddies? Can't have kids fighting fires. Dangerous enough for us adults." Just as Drakell was breathing a sigh of relief, she added, "On one condition though…"

"Which is?"

"That you arrange for me to meet that prince of yours when this is over."

Drakell looked at her askance. "Hmm. I will do my best. I can promise to ask him but I cannot speak for the prince."

The old lady gave a decisive nod, "Good enough," and set about ordering children into groups, with older children minding the younger ones.

Within a few minutes, Drakell found himself surrounded by women and old men carrying blankets, old coats, and even an old moth-eaten saddle cloth.

"We can use switches of leaves or sticks too, if we douse them in water," suggested a weathered old man who looked as though he'd been a farmer. "They'll catch alight eventually, but so will blankets."

Bean nodded, "Yeah, and we can use sand or dirt.…"

"Heavy to carry, but if we had shovels..." added String hopefully.

Another flurry of activity produced a few old shovels and some bags.

"Right. Everybody ready?" asked Drakell. "Let's go. We are going to fight the fire on its southern edge while shield wielders fight it further north."

On the other side of the clearing, Harkell watched two hundred men line up with axes, staves, hammers, knives, a few bows and even fewer swords. His heart sank. Judging by the way they deported themselves, very few of these men were trained fighters. If they met Jarand's men head on, they would be slaughtered. He would have to make sure that his motley crew significantly outnumbered the opposition in every skirmish to have any hope of success.

"Does anyone here have military experience?" he asked.

A dozen men raised their hands.

"Come forward."

After a brief interrogation, Harkell worked out a line of command based on the men's previous experience that gave him four captains each with two sergeants under them, who in turn led approximately twenty five recruits each. Harkell scanned the new companies as they lined up.

"Who of you are Trey, Varga and Vaska?"

As the three brothers stepped forward, he said to them, "Prince Tarkyn has spoken of you. I want you three to be my assistants; to run errands, take messages, protect my back and other duties as I require. Are you prepared to do that?"

They straightened their shoulders and chorused, "Yes sir," but did not have the training to salute without feeling foolish.

Harkell smiled his approval. "Thank you."

"Pleased to help," added Trey, reminding Harkell that these were independent men, not the blindly obedient soldiers he was used to commanding.

"Captains," said Harkell, "the fire is burning along the western edge of the forest, a few miles northwest of here. Soldiers lighting the fires have been moving from north to south. So we will march due west to the forest's edge, and then approach the fire and any soldiers still setting the forest alight, from the south. Once the soldiers have been dealt with, we will assist with fighting the fire. Clear? Move your companies out."

Harkell's motley troops marched swiftly along larger forest tracks, eager at last to be doing something. Any semblance of lines disappeared as soon as the track narrowed and they had to fall into single file. When the track widened, they just walked in comfortable groups. Harkell manoeuvred himself so that he was walking next to an overzealous captain who was trying to force military marching style onto his company.

"I appreciate your effort but leave it," said Harkell quietly. "We can reform at the other end. Our harder task will be to keep these raw recruits alive long enough to train them."

As soon as they could see the skyline between the trees, Harkell called them into order. "Stay close, move slowly and quietly. No heroics. No one attacks until I give the order."

They could hear the fire on their right and see the fierce orange between the trees as they crept up towards the open plains. Gusts of wind brought the smell of smoke but they were two hundred yards south of the fire and the wind was mainly westerly.

But when they reached the forest's edge, an eerie sight met their eyes. Fifty dead soldiers lay, neatly lined up in a long row, out in the open but close to the southern edge of the fire. Closer inspection showed that each of them had been shot once with deadly accuracy. The arrows that had killed them had been removed, as had all of the dead soldiers' weaponry.

Harkell felt a shudder travel down his spine. He grunted, "I think some of the locals were not happy about having their forest burned."

"Bloody deadly locals," exclaimed Trey, wide-eyed with horror.

Harkell smiled wryly, "Yes they are. They work in concert with Prince Tarkyn on request. But they keep themselves to themselves. So you won't see them."

As Harkell walked along the row, inspecting the dead soldiers, he became aware that some of his recruits were not looking too well, reminding him again that he was not dealing with hardened soldiers. After a moment's thought, he called them together and said, "We will rest here briefly before joining the fire fighters. During that time, I want each of you to walk along this line and study these men's faces. You may not agree with the orders they followed but they are all men like you. This is what fighting will bring; dead men on both sides, men like you and me. So for those of you with no fighting experience, remember this. War is serious, not a grand adventure and we will avoid it where we can."

As he passed along the line of dead soldiers for the second time, he realised something else; he didn't know any of these men. That was possible, he supposed, since Prince Jarand's army was large. He walked back and studied the captain. An unknown face stared up at him. He squatted down and closed the staring eyes, shaking his head in confusion. Surely he would know the captain, at least by sight. Logging this information into the back of his mind, he stood up and directed his raggle-taggle army to join the fire-fighting efforts.

Harkell spotted Drakell, blackened with soot, deep in the midst of the fire fighters, using his blacksmith's power to throw fallen burning branches back towards the edge of the forest. After issuing orders to his captains, Harkell jogged over to join him.

"No need for our raw recruits to endanger themselves fighting soldiers. The woodfolk have killed off the entire company. No slingshots this time." As he neared the fire, he reeled back, "Whoa. This is hot. How do we get in close?"

Drakell wiped his brow, "People dart in with blankets or whatever they have, to beat at the flames, then dart out again before they get too hot. It's slow work."

"Where are the woodfolk?"

Without taking his eyes from Harkell's face, Drakell said, "All around us. But since this mob have arrived, they've retreated. They need the break. They have been fighting for hours now, both the fire and the soldiers."

"If people fill bags with sand or soil, couldn't you or I levitate them into the fire?"

"Yeah, we could but I don't have the skill to turn a bag in the air. I could only drop it... We'd run out of bags in ten minutes."

"Blast!" Harkell thought furiously for a minute. "What about lifting a log and dropping it over and over again to smother patches of fire?"

Drakell brightened, "Yes, we could do that. I wonder if anyone else has lifting power?"

"Let's you and I do it. Then if others can, they will follow."

They tied kerchiefs across their faces and laboured away until the sweat poured down their backs and obscured their vision. Every time a log landed, it dampened the fire beneath it but as soon as they lifted it, most of the fire spread back to fill the gap.

Harkell waved his hand. "Stop. This isn't working. The actual ground touched by the log is too small because the log's circular. We need something flatter."

"We could use branches with green leaves, at least until they catch alight."

"All right. Let's try it."

They pulled down on a live branch from the nearest tree, using their magical power to augment the power of their muscles. The branch came away with a loud snap sending them staggering backwards.

"One each or both together?" asked Drakell.

"One each." As he spoke, Harkell was already tugging on another heavy, leafy branch.

Drakell added his power to his brother's until the branch broke, sending them sprawling.

"This is not very dignified for a general," laughed Drakell.

Harkell rolled his eyes, "No, it's not, is it? Never mind. Let's just hope it works."

They picked themselves up and each lifted a branch and using their power, thrust it into the fire. Each of them dropped their branch on a burning patch of ground, using it as a beater. Immediately, the flames were dampened beneath the thick leafy covering. They lifted the branches again and again, sometimes dropping them onto burning shrubs and grasses, sometimes slamming them sideways into the trunks of burning trees. Before long, the leaves on their branches dried out, and began to turn brown and smoulder. They managed to smother another few patches before the leaves on their own branches ignited. The brothers pulled the burning beaters to the edge of the fire and stamped on the flames until they were out.

Then they bent over gasping to get their breath back, coughing from the dry air and smoke. To their right, they could see the blue, lilac, bronze and faintly in the distance the aqua of high translucent shields holding back the fire's progress to the north. To their left, sorcerers were darting in and out with blankets and switches of leaves beating back the fire at its edges. Further along, a few groups had followed the brothers' lead and were working together to hold large branches, some of them using magical power to lift and move them. Still the heat of the fire kept people from entering its borders. All their efforts were merely preventing the fire from spreading further into the forest, not extinguishing the areas already fully alight.

Suddenly Harkell felt a faint breeze play over him from his right; from within the forest.

He straightened and smiled to his brother, "Help is at hand." Harkell raised his voice, straining to make it heard above the roar of the fire, "Do you feel that breeze? Help is on its way. Keep going. All we have to do is contain the fire for another half an hour, maybe an hour at the outside... and we are. You are doing a great job. Keep it up. Don't let it get past us."

Slowly the breeze gained strength and within minutes, had strengthened into a stiff easterly.

Harkell and Drakell turned to drag down two new branches and found that someone had pre-empted them and a pile of large leafy branches was stacked behind them. The brothers grasped new branches and dashed forward once more, to beat out the encroaching flames using a combination of brute strength and magic. When these branches had caught alight and had been stamped out, Harkell and Drakell stopped again to rest, drinking deeply from a water flask that had appeared miraculously beside them. Harkell wiped his mouth and looked up.

Through the smoke he could see soft grey clouds scudding across the sky. As he watched, the clouds changed shape, rolling in on themselves as they blossomed into banks of dark cauliflower storm clouds. He smiled as he redirected his attention to his men, knowing that Tarkyn and the old wizards were literally cooking up a storm.

He pointed overhead, "Look. Storm's coming in from the east. Shouldn't be long now."

Even as he spoke, the first drops of rain landed with little puffs among the burning embers. Steadily, the rain increased, until the blackened ground was sodden and rivulets of water ran down the fire fighters' necks. As they retreated, the fires in the grasses and small bushes flickered out as the rain dampened their fuel. Storm-driven wind lashed water against the burning trees, sending up billowing columns of steam as flames were extinguished. For a while, all they could see were white clouds of steam masking the occasional flicker of orange flame.

Long after the fire had been reduced to a few isolated burning branches, the storm hammered down on them.

"Can't someone tell them it's enough?" asked Harkell of no one in particular, as he sheltered under a large beech tree.

"We have," came Rainstorm's voice, hard to discern against the rain of the storm, "but it has to blow itself out apparently."

"Where are Borovar and Danton and my mother?" asked Harkell. Realising that some of his troops were looking at him a little oddly from several feet away, he raised his voice, "Drakell, did you hear my question?"

Drakell smiled, having watched Harkell's interchange, "Sorry Harkell. Hard to hear above this wind. Say it again." He grinned as Harkell frowned in irritation.

Harkell had just finished repeating himself when Danton and Borovar ducked into the shelter of the beech. His eyes narrowed, "Where is my mother?" His stomach contracted, "Is she all right?"

"She got a bit close to some flames," replied Borovar in his deep soothing voice. "She has a few burns but don't worry. She is all right. She is being taken back to see Tarkyn for his assistance."

Aware of the audience of outsiders, Danton said, "She was quite heroic, General Harkell, Drakell. You should be proud of her." Danton smiled, "She kept going even after she got burnt. Stillwaters rescued her and is still with her."

The rain was easing and only a few big drops here and there were making it through the leaves of the beech.

"So who are you two then?" demanded the skinny belligerent man.

Danton raised his eyebrows in a passable imitation of Tarkyn's disdainful expression, "I beg your pardon. Who gave you the right to question your betters?"

The skinny man's mouth opened and shut several times before he subsided. Even though Danton was dressed only in woodfolk's garb, his accent and demeanour, when he chose to employ them, were unmistakable. Having made his point, he replied, "I am Lord Danton. Borovar, General Harkell's mother and I worked with the Wizardess Stillwaters to stretch our shields to their utmost limits to contain the northern end of the fire. By the time the rain came, our efforts, combined with the firefighters', had stifled more than half of the fire. Thanks to the work of you and your comrades, the fire was not able to spread too far into the forest on this southern end either. I thank you all for minimising this terrible disaster. His Royal Highness will meet with you, as promised, back at the agreed rendezvous point tomorrow. We will send word ahead when he is on his way."

"But I saw the prince's bronze magic further up the fire front," said a quieter older man whose face was streaked with blackened sweat. "Why not now?"

Harkell exchanged glances with Danton who answered, "His Highness has many calls on his time, especially in the aftermath of this emergency. He would rather meet with you when he can give you his undivided attention." When the quiet man nodded, satisfied with this response, he added, "I pass you back to General Harkell."

Harkell and Drakell spent the next few minutes issuing orders for the refugees to return to the clearing of the old fallen beech tree.

Once the refugees were on their way, Harkell turned to Danton, "Come with me. There is something I want you to see."

They emerged to find blue skies overhead, the storm completely dissipated. But blackened devastation, still steaming in places, met their eyes. No grasses or foliage was left. Only trunks and major branches, burnt bare by the raging fire, stood stark against the ruined landscape. The fire had destroyed nearly a square mile of forest.

Danton heaved a sigh, "Oh, what wanton destruction! The woodfolk will be feeling sick at the horror of it."

"*I* feel sick at the horror of it." Harkell shook his head despondently. "We sorcerers are going to be unpopular after this."

"We tried to stop it."

"Yes, but it was sorcerer affairs that caused it in the first place."

"True," said Danton, "The forest guardians of the past said the conflict might invade the woodlands... and it has."

Harkell grimaced in agreement. He took a deep breath, resolutely walking towards the area burnt by the fire. "Come on. Come and see this."

He led the way thorough the blackened area towards the edge of the forest. Their boots crunched on brittle stems and ground the charcoaled remains of small branches into dust as they picked their way between dead and dying trees. The acrid stench of wet charcoal assailed them from all sides. Harkell could have led them around the outside, but somehow he felt the need to pay homage to the death of so much, by confronting the devastation.

Once they reached the open, unburnt plain on the other side, both sorcerers breathed an unconscious sigh of relief. Without speaking, they walked the two hundred yards that brought them to the carefully laid out row of dead soldiers.

Danton glanced at them before frowning at Harkell. "What?" he demanded, not realising how unnerved he was by the strange sight. "I think it's quite reasonable that the woodfolk were less than discriminating about the number of soldiers they killed. These bastards, or at least some of them, are responsible for the death of hundreds of forest animals, scores of trees...just lucky no woodfolk were killed."

Harkell waved his hand. "Come down off your soap box. I'm not upset at the number. I'm not surprised they killed everyone in sight. Besides, they may have had to kill some because they'd seen woodfolk." Harkell walked Danton along the line of bodies, "Now. Look at these men closely. Do you know any of them?"

Danton frowned. "Why would I?"

"Because *I* don't."

An arrested expression crossed Danton's face. "You don't? Not even the Captain?"

When Harkell shook his head, Danton finally did as Harkell had asked and scanned the faces of the dead men. Five times he stopped and looked up at Harkell before continuing his examination.

"Well?"

"Four of them are elite guards and the officer is Captain Tyrus...all Kosar's men. I don't know about the others but it is a fair guess that they are too."

"Stars above! We need to see that letter again. Kosar has duped the lot of us."

Danton shook his head in admiration of Kosar's subterfuge. "No need. I know he can take off Jarand's tone of voice when he wants to; advantage of being a twin. He must have spies inside Jarand's camp to get the content so accurate... Well he would, of course. Goes without saying. We had better let Waterstone and the rest of the woodfolk know about this, before they wreak retribution on the wrong brother."

Chapter 64

Far from the firefighters, Tarkyn was sitting near the fire, dry and gradually warming up, his hands wrapped around a hot cup of tea. Because he was keeping a close guard on his outrage, a cacophony of distress beat unnoticed against his mind.

His first inkling was a gentle nudge under his arm.

He looked down to see a black nose poking up between his arm and his chest. Tarkyn raised his elbow in response to the creature's insistent nudging, revealing a young badger, its coat singed and a livid red patch along its side.

As he opened his mind, the pain and fear of hundreds of burnt and displaced animals battered him. The forest guardian reeled under the impact. At first, he simply absorbed their misery, forcing himself to fully acknowledge the damage wrought by his brother. But after a few moments, he partially closed his mind so that he could cope with the intensity.

"How could I have just sat here when animals are suffering?" He demanded of himself as he put down his tea cup and patted his lap invitingly. "Come on little one. Let me see what I can do for you."

The badger climbed trustfully up onto Tarkyn's bent legs and gave a little whimper.

"Poor one. Hold still." Tarkyn placed his hand on its back and let his *esse* flow into it.

A minute later, with the red patch now a healing pink, the badger grunted, nudged Tarkyn's chest with its nose and trundled off without a backward glance.

Immediately, a large pigeon fluttered down from his right and hovered in front of him so that Tarkyn could see that its feet were raw and blistered.

Tarkyn grimaced, "Sorry. I don't think I can heal you on the wing. You will have to land on your sore feet and stand still." Everything he said out loud, he translated into images for the pigeon.

The pigeon landed on his outstretched arm with a strangled coo of pain. Tarkyn closed his other hand over the pigeon's back and moments later, the pigeon took off, cooing joyously. It fluttered once around his head before heading off into the trees.

There followed a constant stream of mice, rabbits, hedgehogs, badgers, ferrets, a pair of pine martens, pigeons, magpies, an owl, blue jays, even an adder with a burnt underbelly. Tarkyn would have moved himself closer to the fire front so that the injured birds and animals didn't have to travel so far but he couldn't get a long enough break from healing them to move an inch, let alone four miles. Instead, he pulled off his shirt again so that he could keep contact with the tree behind him to maintain his strength and sent messages to woodfolk to collect any injured animals or people they could find and bring them to him. At the same time, he sent forth a general broadcast showing animals approaching woodfolk if they were hurt.

Occasionally, someone would give him a progress report on the fire but he had little attention to spare and could only hope that their storm and the efforts of other sorcerers and woodfolk would prevail.

Late in the afternoon, Navira arrived with Thraya. They trod their way carefully towards the forest guardian, avoiding animals that scurried across their path and trying not to scare off those that shied away from them.

"Hello," said Navira, "You have found yourself a comfortable job." It was only when Taruin looked up at her that she saw the strain in the set of his mouth and the dark smudges under his eyes. "Oh dear. You're suffering with them, aren't you?" She put her hand on his shoulder. "You created an excellent storm. The fire was virtually out by the time we left. I taught Thraya, Danton and Boravar how to thin their shields so that, between us, we covered half of the fire front." She nodded at the woman beside her, "But Thraya needs your help. She got burnt early on but despite that, stayed til the end, holding the fire at bay. She's a very courageous woman."

Tarkyn smiled, hiding his concern for her reddened weeping face. "That's most impressive. Thank you." He patted the ground beside him. "Now, sit here and I'll see what I can do."

He explained his intentions before placing his hand on her shoulder and, for perhaps the hundredth time that afternoon, drew on his *esse*. This time, he followed it into Thraya, checking the extent of the damage and staying until he had rebuilt several layers of skin on her face and hands. He persevered well beyond the time of the healing process, hoping to reduce the scarring by providing more *esse*, but he was uncomfortably aware that he had left Harkell's back scarred after its healing and was not sure how much he could achieve with the aftermath of Thraya's burns. When he returned to himself, he looked anxiously at Thraya's face and glanced at Navira for her reaction.

Navira beamed at Thraya, "What a wonderful job our forest guardian has done. I'm impressed, Tarkyn. I haven't seen the healing power of a forest guardian before."

Thraya smiled and breathed a sigh of relief. "Thank you, Sire. I felt almost nauseous with the pain and now it has gone." She put her hand to her face and asked Navira, "How does it look? Is there scarring, do you think?"

Navira put her head on one side as she considered, "The healed sections of your face, across your nose and cheeks, are definitely pinker than the rest but not too badly. I think I can concoct something that will bring them permanently back to their original colour." She smiled reassuringly, "Between us, Tarkyn and I will have you as good as new… except for the eyebrows. I'm afraid you will just have to wait for them to grow back."

CHAPTER 65

Everyone was too exhausted in the aftermath of the fire to do anything more than feed themselves and drag themselves to bed. But Tarkyn lay in the darkness of his shelter, unable to sleep. Once having tuned in to it, he could not banish the forest's distress from his mind. He was horrified at the destruction that sorcerers' antagonism had brought to the woodland and he quailed at the thought of risking it again by continuing to interfere in his brothers' rivalry. And yet, he knew that he could not stand by while thousands of sorcerers died needlessly for his brothers' whims.

He opened his eyes to see the green lanterns of Midnight's eyes staring at him from his corner of the shelter. Tarkyn smiled wryly and held out his arm and lifted his heavy wolf skin cloak invitingly. Immediately the little boy shuffled over, to snuggle within the circle of Tarkyn's arm.

Tarkyn was shocked to realise that Midnight was quivering. He looked down and locked his eyes into Midnight's. "What is it, little one?"

A jumble of images assailed Tarkyn; people hurrying off in different directions, Tarkyn surrounded by bronze light standing under the sycamore with the wizards calling up the storm, the stream of injured animals and overriding it all, distress from the people, animals and forest around him and bewilderment from Midnight.

"Oh Midnight, you poor thing. No one told you what was happening, did they? I am a terrible guardian. Sorry, little one. You shouldn't stand back. Ask me if you're worried, even if I look very busy." As he sent out images steeped in apology to match these words, Tarkyn wondered at the feelings of distress that Midnight had picked up from the animals and the forest. Surely no one but he could do that. "I will show you, little one." Tarkyn sent images of fire burning, blackened tress, people battling the flames and animals fleeing.

Midnight's eyes widened in horror. His little hand clutched at Tarkyn's arm as he sent urgent images of Tarkyn placing his hands on the surface of a charred trunk, drawing forth new leaves and repairing damaged bark and branches.

Tarkyn shook his head regretfully and, matching images to words, said, "It is not as simple as that. I cannot bring life into something that is dead. I can only help things to grow that are still alive."

Midnight sent an image of green wood with a covering of charcoal.

"You're right, little one. There may be some trees that could recover with my help," A brief spark of enthusiasm was quickly swamped, "but the area is so huge…What could I hope to achieve?"

Midnight showed him the vastness of the forest with one little blackened square on one edge.

Tarkyn lay back and thought about it for a while, all the time stroking Midnight's hair. *I can't walk to every burnt tree and shrub, test them to see whether they have any residual spark of life and then repair them. They said there's at least a square mile of burnt out forest…That's over three million square yards. It would take the rest of my life. And I would only be able to repair a few trees before I had to return to the forest to replenish my power.*

Midnight tugged at his arm. When he had Tarkyn's attention, he sent an image of tendrils growing out from the forest into the blackened area, attached to a query.

What connection was left between the woodlands and the area burnt by the fire? Tarkyn couldn't simply make vines grow outward to cover the damaged area. That would change its whole character. And even with his encouragement, the bushes and trees along the edge would not grow more than an extra few yards sideways.

Suddenly he knew; the underground river that he had tapped and the enormous root system that existed far below the surface of the forest. Perhaps he could use his power to send the forest's strength underground into the network beneath the burnt section. Midnight was right. That burnt section was just a small part of a much greater whole. His emerging plan suffered a setback when he remembered that he could only repair those trees that were still living, no matter how much power he threw at them. But the root system… Surely the fire could not have destroyed those huge root systems below the surface…maybe those of small bushes, but not those of the enormous sycamores, oaks and elms. In time the roots would die, but not yet. All he needed was some remnant of life to work with.

Tarkyn contained his excitement long enough to show Midnight his intention before he threw off the wolfskin cloak and jumped to his feet, dragging Midnight upright by the hand.

He gave Midnight a hug of excitement. "Come on, young fella. We have work to do."

Outside the shelter, the clearing was in darkness. Dying embers glowed dully in the untended fire. A quiet snore issued from a nearby shelter. Close by, an owl hooted. Tarkyn smiled wryly, knowing his presence outside the shelter had now been noted among birds of prey in the vicinity. He gazed around the nearby trees but couldn't see his eagle or where the lookouts were stationed… hardly surprising, when he usually couldn't spot them in broad daylight. He shrugged. He didn't mind who knew he was going. They could follow him or not as they wished.

For a moment, he stood frowning, remembering from which direction the firefighters had returned. "Come on, young one," he whispered, setting off into the trees. He trod carefully and quietly, not wanting to wake anyone needlessly. He did not have the uncanny night vision of the woodfolk so as soon as he was clear of the shelters, he murmured, '*Lumaya*,' raising an orb of light in the palm of his hand.

All in all his subterfuge was a pointless exercise, more a token gesture than anything else. He knew all woodfolk would have heard him leave the firesite. Sure enough, a few minutes later, a rustling beside him heralded the arrival of woodfolk. He looked around to see Rainstorm and Ancient Oak yawning and rubbing their eyes as they fell into step beside him. Midnight waved at them from Tarkyn's right hand side.

"*What* are you doing, prince?" demanded Rainstorm in hushed irritation.

Tarkyn gave a low chuckle, "Sorry I got you out of bed. You didn't have to come. I have my trusty little wood sorcerer with me. He can watch my back when I get to where I'm going."

Midnight noticeably straightened when Tarkyn conveyed the meaning of his words, even though he was not at all sure what he would be expected to do.

"Which is where?" persisted Rainstorm.

"To the site of the bushfire."

Ancient Oak ducked around behind Tarkyn so that he was walking on the other side of Midnight. He ruffled the boy's hair and produced an apricot for him to munch as they walked. "And what is so urgent that it can't wait until morning?" he asked mildly. "We haven't upset you, have we? You took a lot of finding last time we lost you."

"No. Don't worry. I'm not avoiding you or leaving you. But I am upset about the fire as, no doubt, are all of you."

"Of course we are." Ancient Oak shook his head, "It's such wanton destruction. Hmm. It must be even harder for you, tuned into all those poor animals. It's bad enough for us, just thinking about their suffering."

"So you can understand why I couldn't sleep. When I thought of something I could do, I just had to get started. Besides, time is running out, I think."

As they walked, Tarkyn explained his plan.

"It just might work," said Ancient Oak after giving it due consideration, "You know, seeds lying close to the surface may have been germinated by the fire's heat. You may be able to speed their growth too."

"I hope so." Tarkyn tuned to the younger woodman, "You're very quiet, Rainstorm. What do you think?"

Rainstorm yawned, "Sorry, prince. I've been busy letting everyone know that you are all right and what you're planning to do."

"Did I ask you to tell everyone what I have been saying?" Tarkyn's voice had developed an edge of displeasure.

Rainstorm grinned sheepishly. "No. But on the other hand I knew you wouldn't want them to be lying awake worrying. I tried just telling them that we were with you and all was well, but they wouldn't stop pestering me until they knew what you were up to."

The prince grunted, only partially placated, "You know I don't like unwittingly sharing my conversations with countless unseen others. Ask me next time."

"Yes, Your Highness," said Rainstorm with a twinkle in his eye.

Tarkyn gave a reluctant smile, "You are an out and out bounder, young Rainstorm. I can only hope you will respect my wishes."

"I do my best."

Tarkyn's smile broadened, "Yes, you do. I shouldn't have said that. You do." He clapped the young woodman on the back, "Come on my friend. Let's leave them to their beauty sleep, now that you have set their minds to rest, and concentrate on the task ahead."

When they reached the edge of the verdant forest, the hulks of burnt out trees lowered in the gloom before them like accusing ghosts. Tarkyn gave an involuntary shudder.

Two woodfolk, unknown to Tarkyn, were waiting for them. The prince raised an interrogative eyebrow at Rainstorm.

"Your Highness, Prince Tarkyn, may I present Swirling Wind and Morning Breeze? They are local woodfolk who worked with us this morning to control the blaze. Since the fire burnt out part of their home forest, they have a vested interest in your activities and in assisting you."

Tarkyn smiled his appreciation at Rainstorm's efforts at formality before turning to the new woodfolk, "I am pleased to meet you…and this is Midnight. He is my ward and a wood sorcerer who will hold a shield over me while I work."

"We too are pleased to meet you," Swirling Wind shifted uneasily, not accustomed to such close proximity with sorcerers. "And we would like to thank you for the storm you created that finally put out the fire. We were also impressed by the efforts of your fellow sorcerers with their amazing coloured shields and branch throwing abilities."

"It is the least we could do when it is my brother who is to blame for the fire's instigation."

"So we understand," said Morning Breeze noncommitally. The woodman studied Tarkyn for a long moment, "You know, I've seen your brothers in the distance once, when they were hunting. Compared to you, they look quite ordinary; shoulder length brown hair and greyish eyes… different from us, of course, but nothing like as striking as your long black hair and your eyes the colour of flame. No, if I'd had to guess, I would have said you would be the one wreaking havoc." He smiled disarmingly, "Just shows how wrong you can be." As Tarkyn blinked in surprise, the woodman asked, "So what would you like us to do?"

With an effort, Tarkyn returned himself to their purpose, "If you people could direct us to a place where Midnight's shield and my magic will be less conspicuous, we can get started. I would appreciate it if you woodfolk could stand guard in the trees so that no sorcerers approach us unexpectedly. We are close to the edge of the forest here and I don't know how far away my magic can be seen."

The woodfolk led them to an overgrown gully from whose steep sides rose grand towering oaks and beeches. Between them, tangles of vines and blackberries provided dense cover.

Tarkyn settled himself sitting cross-legged in front of a gnarled but strong old oak, his palms pressed against its trunk. For some reason he felt that he needed to be facing the oak and his connection with the forest. Midnight and Ancient Oak sat next to each other on his left. After some discussion, they had decided that it would be asking too much to expect a little boy to hold up his shield for possibly hours on end. Instead, they had stationed Ancient Oak as the link between the lookouts and Midnight, so that if any sorcerers approached, Midnight could raise his shield in response to the woodman's signal.

Tarkyn took a deep breath. "Ready?"

Ancient Oak nodded and placed a hand on Tarkyn's shoulder, providing the forest guardian with his anchor to the outside world. Tarkyn closed his eyes and let his consciousness melt into the heart of the oak. He flowed down its trunk into the oak's great tap root; down through layers of soil, through fissures in rocks, through subterranean streams, until he touched and entwined with the roots of other great trees. Oblivious to the world outside, the forest guardian followed the network of roots, gradually spreading his consciousness wider and deeper beneath the woodlands. As he flowed outward, he infused his being with Midnight's image of the vast green forest marred by a small patch of blackness. Then he created an image of water and the forest's *esse* flowing through the healthy roots of green trees into the withering roots that lay below the remains of the fire.

He took a breath and as he released it, let himself flow further and further afield. A point arrived when Tarkyn knew he had dissipated himself as far as he could. He had not connected to the furthest reaches of the forests but he had set his intention in train and hoped that, once started, it would spread beyond him. For a long time, he continued to send forth his image of the forest's power seeping into fire damaged trees. Then slowly, Tarkyn intensified his will and began to pull himself back, striving to draw some of the forest's life force with him as he went, hoping he could redirect it towards the forest's burnt edge.

At first, it felt as though the forest's power slipped through his fingers and he could gain no purchase on it. Slowly his summoning became more effective and he was able to grasp wisps of the forest's *esse*, drawing it towards the edge of the forest. Gradually the wisps became threads as the forest's life force responded to the guardian's insistence. The flow of power gained momentum until suddenly Tarkyn realised he was no longer pulling. He was being pushed.

CHAPTER 66

So exhausted were the home guard that they actually went back to sleep once they knew Tarkyn's plan. But by first light, uneasiness at the thought of Tarkyn working unsupported by them drove many from their beds.

They hunched around a freshly lit fire, waiting morosely for it to gather warmth, shivering in the chill of the early morning.

"I would like to see Tarkyn working with the forest," said Navira, pulling her cloak closer around her shoulders. "I wish he had waited."

Waterstone took a filled kettle from Autumn Leaves and positioned it on the fire. "Yes. I think all of us do, but I can see his point. The sooner he starts the more he can do before the trees are completely dead." He shook his head, "And I don't think there will be much left to save, even now."

"Perhaps we can replant the area with saplings, as we did over the wolves' remains." For the benefit of Caroman and Navira, Autumn Leaves explained, "Tarkyn can take a green stick, poke it into the ground and within minutes, create a flourishing new sapling."

"We could recruit some of our refugee sorcerers to cut thin branches and plant them within the burnt area," suggested Danton. "Then Tarkyn could make them grow."

Watestone looked dubious, "I don't know. It took us four days to repair a gale-swept circle of two hundred yards radius. This is a hundred times bigger."

"From what Rainstorm told us, I gather he is trying a different technique this time," said Stormaway. "Rather than repairing individual trees, he is trying to direct the forest's power into healing its own"

"If Tarkyn can harness the forest's power to flow into the damaged area, then its *esse* should be able to give life to green sticks, just as Tarkyn can," said Caroman. "It is worth a try."

"The task is enormous. We would need thousands of saplings," objected Autumn Leaves.

"We have over three hundred refugees, all tired but very willing to assist. If they each planted ten, that will be over three thousand…" said Harkell. "Drakell, Borovar, Danton and I will organise them. Two of us can walk straight to the site of the fire and the other two can ride to the refugee's campsite."

Lapping Water had become more and more tense as the conversation progressed. Finally she said, "You are all focussed on how you will use Tarkyn to repair the fire's damage. But have you stopped to think? Do you have any concept of the enormity of the power that Tarkyn is trying to direct? I hope he knows what he is doing."

Waterstrone grimaced, "He doesn't, of course. How could he, when he's never done it before?"

A swirl of disquiet wafted among them.

"I believe you are right to be anxious, Lapping Water," said Summer Rain quietly. "Stormaway, I think you and I should join him, in case he overtaxes himself."

"Caroman and I will go with you," offered Navira. "Our knowledge or power may be of use."

Waterstone glanced at Lapping Water for confirmation before saying, "And so will we. Autumn Leaves?"

The big woodman nodded.

Danton frowned, torn between options.

Navira decided for him. "Danton, go with Harkell and his family to organise the refugees. If Tarkyn is taking a risk, then let it produce as good an outcome as it possibly can. Help them to ready the green sticks. If Tarkyn began hours ago, I can't imagine we have much time to prepare. We will take care of him, I promise you."

In the end, none of them was still at the firesite to drink tea when the kettle boiled.

CHAPTER 67

When Stormaway and his contingent arrived in the gully, Ancient Oak still had his hand firmly on Tarkyn's shoulder with Midnight slumped asleep against his other side. Perched in a branch above them, Tarkyn's great mountain eagle flapped her wings and snaked her head forward at Stormaway's approach.

Ancient Oak tapped Midnight on the shoulder to let him know that others had arrived. The little boy sat up with a jerk and without hesitation, threw his green shield over Tarkyn, Ancient Oak and himself, wrapping it around the tree's trunk. Ancient Oak patted him on the back then pointed. With a sigh of relief, Midnight waved away his shield.

Ancient Oak smiled. "Well done, little one."

"How is Tarkyn?" asked Waterstone, ignoring the eagle and the shield.

Ancient Oak hesitated as he tried to find the words to explain, "He's… not here. He's gone. He has spread? filtered ? himself through the trees' network of roots."

Caroman's eyes widened. "How will he return? Can he return?"

"He's done something like this before, when he recalled the parts of Pipeless to remove the curse," said Stormaway. "He had to send his *esse* wandering far and wide through the forest collecting the remnants of Pipeless' body so that he could bring them back to one place before reassembling it. I'm sure you would have read about the forest guardian, Moridan Tamadil, recalling a shade in a similar fashion. Stormaway cleared his throat. "… with rather more catastrophic results."

"Ah yes, that was the forest guardian who killed off half a community of woodfolk, wasn't it?"

"That's the one. However, he was able to return to his own body and so was Tarkyn." Stormaway looked down at the inert figure of their present forest guardian, sitting cross legged, with his palms against the oak trunk and his long hair hanging down on either side of his face. The old wizard heaved a sigh, "But I do wish he would ask for advice before throwing himself impetuously into untried magic."

"And what would you know about guardian magic?" asked Rainstorm, appearing suddenly as someone finally relieved him from his guard duty. "I could kill for a cup of tea."

"I know enough about forest guardians to have identified Tarkyn as one in the first place. I guided him and the home guard to use his guardian powers to save his life when his lung was punctured… and I taught him how to recall Pipeless," replied Stormaway acerbically. "Just because I myself do not possess the powers does not mean that I have no knowledge of them."

"Yep. You're right. Silly question." Rainstorm yawned. "Sorry. I've been up for hours. Let me rephrase it: What do you know about drawing on the forest's power to undertake such a major repair to part of the forest itself?"

"Here. That may improve your temper," Stormaway pulled an apple out of his pack and handed it to him before answering, "Tarkyn has twice drawn a large quantity of power from the forest to work with me to manage the weather… but in each instance, the power has travelled through him to me or to Caroman. He has not before mobilised the forest to use its own power on itself." The old wizard shook his head frowning, "For some reason, this worries me. Hmm. In the past, he has just pulled a narrow stream of power through a specific point of contact. This time, it seems he is trying to draw power from all over the forest and direct it upwards over a huge area; the whole burnt out square mile."

"I share your concern, Stormaway," said Caroman heavily. "He is undertaking the use of power on a vastly different scale. I know of no other guardian who has done this. Even when Moridan Tamadil was faced with hundreds of diseased trees, he walked through the forests, healing them over several months. Admittedly, he tried to recall Scarecrow Treehealer to help him but when that didn't work, he just continued one by one. Perhaps it didn't occur to him."

"Or perhaps it was too dangerous…" added Navira.

"Should we try to recall him?" suggested Lapping Water. "He's been gone for over four hours now."

"We did once before," said Sparrow, "when he had stretched himself too far to reach Danton. Remember? When Danton was nearly killed by Andoran.'

"We did too," Rainstorm was suddenly full of enthusiasm. "You, me, Ancient Oak and Midnight. I think you're right. We should do it again…. What do think, Stormaway?"

The wizard nodded, "Even if it means he returns with the job only half done, I would rather have Tarkyn safely back with us. Look at his colour."

Tarkyn's hands were the green of lichen, a darker green than they had seen him before.

They needed no further prompting. Ancient Oak and Midnight stayed where they were while Rainstorm, Lapping Water, Waterstone and Sparrow seated themselves so that they could all touch him. Once in position, they began to call his name over and over, until it became a monotonous chant.

Navira looked on uncertainly, "Should I join in too?"

Caroman shook his head, "No, woodfolk will do better at this. He is somewhere, or everywhere, in the forest and their connection with the woodlands is stronger than ours.

Far below his body and his friends, Tarkyn was being swamped by the might of the forest all around him, finally galvanised into action. The feeling of incipient power was enormous. Tarkyn was no longer trying to direct it. Instead, he was scrambling to return to himself before he was subsumed by it.

Then the earth around him surged as a ponderous wave of power rolled in from deep within the forest, overtook him and swept him up, tumbling and gasping, as it flowed inexorably towards the forest's edge. Somewhere, far above him, he felt hands gripping his shoulders and faint sounds drifted down to him. He remembered what they meant but he had no way of controlling the movement of his essence within the turbulence of the forest's unleashing power. Into the roiling *esse* of the forest, Tarkyn strove to infuse his wish to return to his body. Suddenly the wave that was driving him forward heaved and a fearsome current swept him upwards, thrashing and helpless.

Outside, an hour passed but still the woodfolk kept position around Tarkyn and kept chanting his name. The air became increasingly heavy. Flocks of birds shrieked and flew out of the trees in alarm. Even Tarkyn's eagle took to the air as, far in the distance, they heard the roar of a wild wind rushing through the trees, growing louder as it neared. The ground shuddered beneath them, sending a slow ripple up the gully and out of sight beyond the ridge.

Suddenly the trunk of the oak tree bulged, thrusting Tarkyn from it with such force that he was thrown twenty feet backwards, sending woodfolk flying sideways. His body landed with a sickening thud and did not move. When they reached him, Tarkyn lay sprawled on his back, unconscious, his face and hands the dark green of pine needles.

CHAPTER 68

Danton, Borovar, Drakell and Harkell directed operations from the middle of the burnt area. Because they were far from the cover of foliage, no woodfolk were able to communicate with them, so they had no way of knowing anything of the drama that was being played out only a mile away.

The refugee sorcerers had been a little chary at first of following Harkell and Danton once more, when they had still not had their promised audience with the prince. But although they were tired, most were also bored with waiting and reasoned philosophically that they might as well be doing something useful. They did not really understand what they were hoping to achieve but, following instructions, they each had cut thin six-foot branches, as straight as they could find, as they walked towards the site of yesterday's fire. By the time they arrived, each of them had a bundle of at least ten green sticks.

Harkell and Danton led them to the centre of the burnt patch and waited until they had all gathered around close enough to hear them.

Danton swept his hand around, "Now, as you can see, there are some areas that are more badly burnt than others. If there is the faintest sign of life in a tree or a bush, do not plant your green stick too close to it. Our aim is to force your sticks to stand upright in the ground. You may need to use a dead, harder stick to force a hole first. It doesn't matter how you do it. What matters is that part of your stick is in the ground and that it is standing upright."

Harkell held up his hand as murmuring broke out, "Prince Tarkyn has a unique power; he can make plants grow. Usually he does this one plant at a time. So he would take one of your green sticks, poke it into the ground and after a few minutes, leaves and small branches would begin to appear."

"Never heard of that before. Anyway, can't do that if he's not here," objected the grumpy man from yesterday.

"Even if he was here," said Old Ma, "he can't do that to... what?... a couple of thousand sticks. Take days, weeks even. Besides, it's too close to the edge of the forest. What if one of his brothers comes past? Bad enough for us if that happens, let alone him."

"Lord Danton and Borovar will protect you with shields, should any soldiers arrive unexpectedly," replied Harkell. "However, we do have lookouts placed along the perimeter of the forest who will shoot a fiery arrow as a warning, should that occur. The prince would not wish you to be placed in danger."

Before anyone else could object, Danton cut in hurriedly, "And Prince Tarkyn has devised a plan whereby he directs the forest's growing power into this area through the root system. He has not tried it before so it may not work. But if it does, we need to have all those sticks in the ground ready to grow."

"What if it doesn't work?" Inevitably it was the scrawny whinger who asked this question.

Danton restrained himself from sighing. "If it doesn't work, the prince will have to do the best he can, moving slowly around the burnt area. Needless to say, he will not have time to do it all because, out there somewhere, his brothers are about to start a war."

"Let's get started then, shall we?" suggested Trey.

Harkell nodded and using his troop formation from the previous day, organised squads of people to head off in different directions. Those who had not been in Harkell's troops yesterday attached themselves to whichever group they preferred, mostly on the basis of friendship or kin.

Long before all the sticks were planted, the atmosphere had become leaden. Harkell and Danton urged people to greater efforts. Then they too heard the rushing of the wind in distant trees and glanced upward, looking for storm clouds. When blue sky greeted their eyes, they looked at each other, puzzled and with the beginnings of excitement stirring in their guts.

"Something strange is going on," whispered Harkell, "Maybe Tarkyn has actually succeeded."

Danton's eyes widened as he watched the trees sway wildly one rank after another. "Stars! If he has, it's something huge."

And now they could see a faint ridge in the earth moving towards them from the edge of the green forest.

"Watch out," yelled Harkell. "I don't know what it is, but it's coming this way."

As it reached the first sorcerers, the rolling ground rocked them and many of them fell over. The ridge rolled slowly past and for several minutes, an eerie silence descended. Then small green shoots began to force their way up through the ground at their feet. Burnt out trees sloughed off blackened bark as new branches began to force their way out from the burnt trunks. Even fallen trees sprouted again from their blackened stumps. Any green stick already planted sprouted branches and leaves, expanding outwards and upwards into established saplings.

The sorcerers looked around themselves in amazement, often sidestepping as insistent new seedlings pushed up under their feet. Shouts down the line of command galvanised them into action. With renewed vigour, they thrust their green sticks into any areas still bare and watched with great satisfaction as their green sticks flourished.

But the power of the forest didn't stop there. The woodfolk on lookout duty at the edges of the forest saw the crops in nearby fields grow a foot higher and any fence posts made of green wood took root and were soon thrusting leave-covered branches to the sky. Along the verges, any small sapling grew into a well-established tree while well-established trees grew stronger and broader. The wind blew seeds from the forest into neighbouring fields and out across the farmlands, way beyond the horizon. Wherever the seeds fell, they germinated and began to grow.

Surrounded by forest on all sides, the grasslands where Lord Tolward lived diminished alarmingly in size as vines, oaks, beeches, mountain ash and sycamores grew at a staggering rate around the perimeter. As the wind carried seeds across the grasslands, shrubs and young trees sprang up everywhere. Lord Tolward and his family watched in dismay from within their homestead, as their holding changed before their eyes.

Danton, Harkell, Borovar and Drakell met each other in the middle of the mayhem of the fire-affected area. They looked at each other in consternation.

"Stars above," breathed Drakell. "Look at the power around us. Is this all Tarkyn?"

Danton shook his head. "It can't be. This is the might of the forest unleashed. It's bloody scary. I think we need to check in with the woodfolk."

They jogged to the perimeter where they could stand under the trees of the undamaged forest where they knew woodfolk would be waiting. Already the distinction between burnt and unburnt areas was blurring.

A woodwoman they had not met before answered their call from high in a horse chestnut tree, telling them of the wild growth that was occurring beyond the forests' borders.

"The forest guardian has drawn forth the strength of the forest to repair its own. But while the forest guardian was only thinking of the area burnt by fire yesterday, we think the forest may be repairing some, if not all of its territories. We cannot see how far this rampant growth has spread because we can only see to the horizon. I am Running Water."

"Hmmm. Was he angry at all when he called up the forest's power?" asked Harkell, with a faint smile.

"I have no idea," replied the woodwoman. "But I do know that he is now at death's door, dark green and unconscious."

Danton's stomach turned over. "No. Oh no. He can't die… just for a square mile of burnt scrub. Can we help? Is there anything we can do?"

Running Water consulted before saying, "Your wizards are with him, a woodfolk healer and several other woodfolk. They are trying to drain off the excess power of the forest. I do not see what more you can add."

The four sorcerers stood irresolute, knowing they should return to the refugees but wanting to rush to Tarkyn's side. Finally Drakell said, "Danton and Harkell, you know him best. You go to him. Borovar and I will stay here and finish what Tarkyn has started. Are you prepared to stay, Borovar?"

The big sorcerer drew a deep breath and nodded, "Go on, you two. I know Danton will be useless if his liege is under threat and you won't be much better, Harkell. So off you go. Get out of our hair."

Danton was not deceived but was willing to accept Borovar's generosity, "Thanks Borovar, and you, Drakell. I'm sure you'll manage without us."

As soon as they were out of earshot, Borovar let out his breath, "Yeah, right. Neither of us knows the first thing about leading men. So what do you think? Should we tell them about Tarkyn?"

"No idea. Probably not at this stage, if we want them to keep working on his project." Drakell glanced up into the tree, "Running Water, if you have news, can you let loose an arrow or something to let us know. Please? This is really hard, knowing something bad is happening and having to ignore it."

"Yes, of course we will. We can fire an arrow over two hundred yards especially if we aren't trying to be too accurate. We will only fire it if something changes. If he dies, we will skewer a dead leaf onto the arrow. If he is clearly going to live, we will skewer a green leaf onto it."

"Thank you," said Drakell bleakly as he turned with Borovar to deal with the refugees.

Chapter 69

Ancient Oak lifted Tarkyn's shirt from his inert body and peered underneath. "He's dark green all over." He grimaced. "That can't be good. It's too much."

"Is he breathing?" demanded Stormaway, rushing over to kneel beside him. Ancient Oak gave way so the wizard could examine him while Lapping Water knelt on the other side holding Tarkyn's hand. A minute later, Stormaway breathed a sigh of relief. "He's breathing. His heart is beating, but too hard and fast."

"He's been suffused with too much of the forest's *esse*. It is poisoning him," exclaimed Caroman.

Lapping Water looked across Tarkyn's body at Stormaway. "Remember how he vomited after giving you power from the forest after that storm that you diverted months ago? When he drained away some of the excess power by placing his hand back on the tree, he felt better."

Stormaway considered, "Yes he did, but we can't place him against a tree at the moment. The forest's power is pushing outwards. A tree won't be able to absorb Tarkyn's excess. It will send more into him and kill him."

"When Tarkyn sends his *esse* into people, the green fades," said Waterstone. "Healing people uses up some of his reserves."

"True." Stormaway sounded dubious. "We did once send out our own *esse* into him but I doubt that we can pull it from him. I think only he can direct the flow from himself to others, just as only he can draw that power from the forest." He shrugged. "Still, it's worth a try… unless someone has a better idea."

"No. Let's do it. I don't like the sound of him; his breathing is laboured." Waterstone directed everyone into position so that they were all touching Tarkyn. "You instruct us, Stormaway."

"Very well. Not the children, I think." With some reluctance, Sparrow and Midnight drew back. "When we did this before, we visualised reaching deep inside ourselves and directing some of our *esse* to flow up and into Tarkyn. So this time, when I say, visualise drawing *esse* into your hand from wherever you are touching him and pulling it down into yourselves. There are…let me see…" He counted; Waterstone, Ancient Oak, Rainstorm, Summer Rain, Navira, Caroman and himself. "…seven of us. So the worst that can happen is that we all turn a little green or become too energetic. Hmm. Not sure about the green; might be a forest guardian trait."

"Come on, Stormaway," said Waterstone impatiently. "We are all willing to take a risk. Just get on with it."

Stormaway ignored Waterstone's outburst. "Are you all clear? Then begin now. Draw his life force in through your hands."

For several minutes, they concentrated. But all that happened was that Tarkyn's breathing gradually became more ragged and an occasional spasm ran through his body. No one turned even faintly green nor felt any sense of extra energy.

"It's not working, Stormaway," said Lapping Water tightly.

"No, it's not." A sheen of sweat glistened on the wizard's brow. "…and I don't know what else to do."

Midnight crept in next to Ancient Oak and avoiding Stormaway's gaze, squatted down and placed his hand gently on Tarkyn's forehead.

Stormaway frowned but was not about to get into a fight over the top of Tarkyn's body. He shrugged, "If it makes him feel better, he may as well. We are clearly not in danger of being deluged by Tarkyn's excess power."

Hearing this, Sparrow snuck in next to Waterstone to join Midnight.

"Shall we try once more?" asked Waterstone, giving his daughter a reassuring smile.

Flustered, Stormaway rubbed his hands together, "I, we, I don't know. We may as well, I suppose. But if it doesn't work this time, Summer Rain and I had better start trying to come up with some sort of antidote. It's straining his system. He is going downhill."

"*Now* Stormaway," urged Waterstone.

Once more they closed their eyes and tried to draw out the forest's power that was threatening Tarkyn's life. After a few minutes, Ancient Oak felt Midnight move beside him and heard the sounds of someone retching. Thinking that Tarkyn must be recovering, his eyes flew open. But it was not Tarkyn who was retching. It was Midnight. Ancient Oak dodged aside just in time to avoid a stream of vomit as Midnight lost his breakfast.

"Stars above, Midnight! You're green!" he exclaimed.

Everyone's eyes shot open and they stared in amazement at Midnight.

"Not as green as Tarkyn," observed Caroman, "but not just sickly pale either."

"He's draining Tarkyn's power and it's too much for him," exclaimed Stormaway. "Quickly! Everyone line up so that one person is touching Midnight and the rest have contact with Midnight through that person" He rubbed his forehead. "No. On second thoughts, take it in turns to take his hand. I think that may work better." Stormaway tapped Midnight's arm to get his attention and then used images and hand gestures to explain that Midnight should draw the *esse* from Tarkyn and direct it into the person touching him.

Midnight turned away to heave up once more but all the time he kept his hand on Tarkyn's forehead. He wiped his mouth on his sleeve and nodded weakly. Summer Rain brought him a drink of water and wiped his hand and mouth before taking his hand in a firm grasp. Immediately she felt a gentle warmth infusing her. When she began to feel uncomfortably warm, she yielded her place and Lapping Water took Midnight's hand, giving it a squeeze of encouragement as she did so.

Slowly, person by person, Tarkyn's colour faded until eventually he was a lighter green than Midnight. Still the little wood sorcerer persevered, fighting the nausea, until Tarkyn's colouring was pale but back to normal and his breathing was steadier.

The last person to take Midnight's hand was Stormaway. He held the grubby little hand until Midnight too was back to normal then gestured towards Tarkyn to say that Midnight could take his hand away now. Midnight shook his head and transmitted an image of Tarkyn tumbling through billowing surges of power, lost and disoriented. He gave a little smile and managed to convey that Tarkyn had always been his rock and he would be Tarkyn's.

Stormaway shook his head in wonder. He let go of Midnight's hand and ruffled his hair in appreciation as he stood up. "He's only seven. This child is wise beyond his years."

"He's not just wise, Stormaway," said Navira. "He's a forest guardian. No one else could do what he has just done… You saw for yourself. None of us could do it."

Stormaway seemed a little dazed, "But can he communicate with animals?"

"I don't know," answered Waterstone, "but he gets on awfully well with Tarkyn's eagle. And he uses images to talk to us, just as Tarkyn does…and I can think of several occasions where he responded to people's feelings when he wasn't looking at them."

"Besides, how old was Tarkyn when he began to receive images from animals?" asked Navira.

"The age he is now; nineteen," replied Stormaway, "And even then it was young for a forest guardian to be recognised for what he is."

Lapping Water sat down beside Midnight and offered him a drink. "Midnight was always going to be special; the product of a wizard and a woodwoman. That's unusual straight away. And then he has spent most of his little life isolated and abused by people. He has had a lot of time to develop a close relationship with the forest and its creatures."

She queried Midnight about Tarkyn's progress and asked what she could do to help. Midnight indicated that more than one hand might further confuse Tarkyn but that he himself would like something to eat. She smiled, "You must be feeling better then."

"It's more than the result of his early life's experience, though," said Tarkyn's sister, "He has the ability to draw and direct the forest's power." The wizardess caught Midnight's eye and smiled at him. "Does he possess other magical power?"

Waterstone studied Midnight, frowning as he sifted through his knowledge of the little boy, "You're trying to match him with the characteristics of a forest guardian, aren't you? 'A person of great power, with the ability to encourage growth and healing, and to communicate with animals.'"

As Navira nodded, Stormaway provided the answer to her question, "Midnight threw up his shield to save the children he was playing with from an attacking mountain lion. With no wizardly training, he is able to change his colouring. He can also raise a shield and fire a shaft of power at the same time. As far as I know, only Tarkyn can do two spells simultaneously…So, in answer to your question, yes. Our little fellow squatting beside Tarkyn is extremely powerful, especially for one so young."

Just then, Tarkyn groaned. After a minute, he opened his eyes and saw Midnight's face peering anxiously down at him.

"Hello, rascal," he croaked. Without rising, he reached up and took Midnight's hand from his forehead and held it for a moment. Then he gestured for Midnight to come around beside him. When he had done so, Tarkyn wrapped his arm around his little ward and closed his eyes again.

Midnight sat within the circle of Tarkyn's arm staring at his face, waiting for him to open his eyes again. After a minute, he put his arm across Tarkyn's chest and as Lapping Water watched, tears began to roll unchecked down his cheeks. He sank his head onto Tarkyn's shoulder and gave way to sobs that racked his little body from end to end. For a hideous moment, Lapping Water thought Tarkyn must have died, but Tarkyn's arm tightened around Midnight, banishing the horror of that possibility.

With what seemed to be a great effort, Tarkyn lifted his other hand and stroked the little boy's head. "It's all right, little one. I'm back. I'm just tired. That's all," he murmured. "You have been very brave and very strong, but now you can go back to being a little boy again. I'm here. Don't worry. I'm here."

Lapping Water assumed that Tarkyn was matching images to words because after a while, Midnight's sobs eased until he lay in the crook of Tarkyn's arm sniffing and hiccoughing. Lapping Water's heart was wrung. "Oh, you poor little boy. Through all of that crisis, you let no one see how distressed you were that you might lose your Tarkyn."

Navira smiled at him "He will make a fine forest guardian when he grows up."

"He already is a fine forest guardian," murmured Tarkyn. Without opening his eyes, he grinned, "We forest guardians are all very emotional, you know."

Chapter 70

"What on earth is going on?" thundered Jarand. "Where's my blasted wizard when I need him?"

He was sitting at a table within his mobile camp, attempting to eat his lunch, twenty miles from the forests' edge. At least forty tents had collapsed as plants grew inexorably up from beneath them. Several horses had pulled free from their tethers as they had backed away in alarm from bushes that had appeared in front or beside them.

Journeyman presented himself before the irate prince and bowed.

"Get up and explain this nonsense." Even as the prince spoke, a small vine wound its way up the table leg and around Jarand's fork.

The wizard was trembling. "Sire, I beg your pardon, but I do not know. I can only report that the phenomenon is widespread, although I do not yet know its extent."

"What about Montraya. That is forty miles from here. What about my castle? My lawns? My gardens? Are they affected?"

"Sire, I do not know. I will send messengers forthwith to find out."

"And how can we fight a pitched battle if plants keep popping up in front of us?" He slammed his hand down on the table and grabbed his fork out of the grasp of the vine. "This is ridiculous. It must be stopped."

Journeyman quailed, "Yes Sire."

Jarand waved his hand, "GO! Get out of here. Come back when you have something useful to report."

Ninety miles north of Jarand and thirty-five miles from the forest's edge, the king was standing on a small hill surveying the land around him. Fields planted with wheat and barley were now dotted with fully grown trees. Along one field, a whole row of pine trees had grown up from a newly raised fence. Each roadway was lined with shrubs and blackberries interspersed with larger trees. His own tent had been shoved up and sideways by a determined gorse bush. His army's tents and his horses had suffered in the same way that Jarand's had.

But Kosar was not railing like Jarand was. He knew, or thought he knew, that he was looking at revenge for the fire he had caused to be started. His heart was heavy in his chest as he surveyed the workings of power beyond anything previously imagined.

Stargazer flapped up the slope to give a brief bow and stand beside him. "Sire, I have no understanding of this. The only faint reference I can find is that of mythical beings called forest guardians who can make plants grow. But the text did not seem to suggest that they could grow things on such a grand scale as this." He gave an apologetic cough and tittered nervously, "Besides, it is only a legend as far as I am aware."

Kosar turned to him. "No. It is not a legend. It is a fact. Tarkyn is a fact. So is one of our ancestors, apparently. Tarkyn told me he was the guardian of the forest and I derided him." He swept his hand in an arc to draw Stargazer's attention to the extent of the changes. "In fact, he told me he was Guardian of Eskuzor and I effectively laughed in his face."

"Oh."

"Indeed. Oh. And now I have angered him and he has struck back tenfold. I think it might be wiser to avoid that tactic in future."

Stargazer was the only person outside the forest other than the king that Tarkyn held sovereignty of the woodlands, "It is possible, Sire, that Prince Tarkyn may have regarded the firing of his forests as an act of war."

"Well, he has certainly retaliated with an act of war. He has increased his territories without firing a shot... I do not count the company of soldiers he killed, who were, after all, an inevitable sacrifice." He glared down at the countryside below him. "Look at that! How are we going to march an army down roads that have tree roots coming up through the surface and branches hanging halfway across them?" He frowned, tapping his fingers on his arm. "Is this just aimed at my army or is it more widespread? Will Jarand be faced with the same issues, I wonder."

"It is too early to say, Sire. I have no doubt messengers will be speeding towards us with news of this, if it has occurred in other places. Perhaps we may have a better idea by this evening."

A spurt of anger shook the king. "Blast the man! At every turn, I have under-estimated Tarkyn. He could take my throne tomorrow if he chose to, so great is his power. But instead he plays this game of cat and mouse. If he doesn't want my throne, why can't he just leave me to deal with Jarand as I see fit?"

Stargazer gave a deprecatory little cough, "I have heard, Sire, that he is concerned for the common man and does not wish him to perish in a war."

Kosar waved his hand impatiently. "I know, I know. He said that to me when I met him... But as far as I'm concerned that sort of attitude is a betrayal of our heritage. I was right to brand him a rogue sorcerer, you know. He's completely delusional if he thinks Jarand and I are going to settle our differences in any way other than a pitched battle. It is a time honoured practice and I intend to uphold it." He shrugged disdainfully. "Truth to tell, I expect it gives the peasants something to get excited about."

"Indeed Sire. You are almost doing them a favour."

The king's eyebrows twitched together in suspicion but his wizard met his gaze blandly. Kosar grunted, "Hmm. Perhaps not quite that, but I am certainly providing them with a source of interest."

CHAPTER 71

"Two guardians of the forest? *Two?* It's unheard of," exclaimed Thunder Storm. "None of our legends talk about two forest guardians."

"And none of our legends talk about a *child* forest guardian," added Tree Wind whose pregnancy was beginning to show but not yet to slow her up.

"*What?* Our little Midnight? A forest guardian?" Bean beamed from ear to ear. "Always said he was a great kid. Just think, String. We have helped to bring up a forest guardian."

"Yeah, nice for Tarkyn, isn't it?" agreed String. "Means he won't have to grow old alone."

Thunder Storm frowned, "What are you talking about?"

Bean shrugged, "Just something Tarkyn mentioned to me. When he met General Argyve, the young captain told him that forest guardians live to be three or four hundred years old. A bit lonely, I would think, wouldn't you? Tarkyn was pretty disturbed about it when he found out. Don't think anyone else took much notice of that little fact at the time."

Thunder Storm thought back to the scene where Danton and Tarkyn had stood, well away from the forest's edge, talking under a flag of truce to Kosar's officers. "We didn't hear what was being said. How did you find out about it?"

"I just found Tarkyn looking pensive one day and asked him what was wrong. Don't think he's too happy at the prospect of watching everyone he knows die around him."

The woodman watched Bean chewing on a bit of grass. "I saw a fox piss on that piece of grass a little while ago."

Bean took the piece of grass out of his mouth, stared at it for a minute before putting it back in his mouth to suck on it again, "Probably every bit of greenery I eat out of the forest has been pissed on or shat on at some stage. Just have to rely on my body coping with it. Has so far. No need to suppose it will stop now… Anyway, I don't believe you."

Thunder Storm shrugged and smiled, "Worth a try." He leaned over to disentangle a new sapling from a vine, "You know, my kids will outlive nearly everyone they know at the moment, same as Tarkyn. Only when they're older, will they know people who will outlive them. It's just a matter of degree."

"Yeah true," said String, "but Tarkyn is going to have to be a whole lot older, like four hundred years older, before anyone he knows may outlive him."

"Bloody lucky, if you ask me," rumbled Thunder Storm. He looked around himself at the profusion of new growth that had sprung up out of the charred ground. Beneath their feet, the ground was still crunchy with charcoal but all around them trees, which looked as though they had been growing for several years rather than several hours, thrust branches covered in bright green leaves, towards the sky. Vines seemed to have grown particularly well and had woven themselves around bushes and up into the boughs of trees, in some cases threatening to overwhelm newly established shrubs and saplings. The woodman shook his head, "If he can do this in a morning, what will he achieve over four hundred years? The mind boggles."

Bean grunted, "This is the least of it. Have you been to the edge of the forest yet?"

Thunder Storm shook his head, "Don't like going to close to open land unless I have to."

"Strictly speaking," said String, "he isn't able to achieve this in a morning… not without killing himself." He waved his arm in a semi-circle, "Besides, this was the forest's power running rampant. It nearly killed Tarkyn and it has damaged roads, fields, walls, sheds and houses. I would hesitate to call it an achievement."

"So would I," said Tarkyn as he joined them, his eagle perched on his shoulder and Midnight holding his hand. He surveyed the part of the burnt area he could see. "I harnessed the forest's power to repair this area but I hate to think what the outcome of the forest invading Kosar's kingdom will be. Perhaps I should write to him to explain what I had intended."

"No, Tarkyn, don't lose your advantage," said Bean firmly. "You will have frightened the pants off him with this display of power. He will just assume it's retribution. If you want to keep the forests safe from a future attack, you have to stand firm."

"I couldn't agree more," said Danton, arriving in his liege's wake. "Even if he regards it as an act of war, he has no way to fight against it."

Tarkyn knelt and placed his hand on a small bush that had been trampled underfoot by sorcerers. He waited a moment until he could feel it swelling with new strength before taking his hand away. Throughout this little exercise, Midnight clung determinedly to his other hand. When Tarkyn straightened, he swung Midnight up onto his hip, understanding that Midnight was going to cling to him until he felt secure again. "I wonder what effect this will have on Kosar's plans to confront Jarand?"

Stormaway strode to join them between the shrubs, his green robe billowing behind him, "I expect he is wondering the same thing. The roads, or what is left of them, will be crowded with messengers carrying reports to Jarand, Kosar and me. Actually, most of my missives will come by pigeon but my agents will gather information from messengers on foot and on horse. Only when they and we get a full picture of the damage, can we begin to plan. Once you have met the refugee sorcerers, I will be glad of their assistance to gather intelligence on the new situation."

Tarkyn heard an embarrassed cough behind him and turned to find Drakell standing sheepishly at his elbow.

"Excuse me Sire, but I have a request I promised to convey to you… In return for looking after the children while we fought the fire, one old woman asked to be granted an audience with you. I said that I would ask, but could not guarantee your response."

The prince raised his eye brows. "Did you now?" He couldn't resist waiting a moment to watch Drakell squirm but then he clapped him on the shoulder and smiled, "You did well, but always be wary of sorcerers who use you to get close to me. Did she give a reason for her request?"

"No Sire, and in truth, I didn't think to ask. I just assumed she wanted the honour of meeting you."

Tarkyn glanced at Stormaway and Danton. "Your thoughts?"

"She could be an assassin who has infiltrated their ranks," said Danton, "or she may have a particular cause she wishes to further," he smiled, "or she may just want the honour of meeting you, as Drakell assumed."

"Hmm…" Tarkyn looked into the bright green eyes of his little Midnight. "And what do you think, young one? Even if her motive is purely to have the honour of meeting me, should I grant her that honour?" Thunder Storm rolled his eyes, just as Tarkyn looked up. The prince shook his head in mock sadness, "You see? Never will the woodfolk understand my true consequence… You may mock, Thunder Storm, but if I allow sorcerers to approach me at will, I will not be able to keep company with woodfolk, now will I?"

A slow smile appeared on Thunder Storm's face. "Very true. Perhaps we should be grateful for it, after all."

Smiling at the woodman's irony, Tarkyn turned to Drakell, "I will grant this woman an audience if it means so much to her. Warn her to keep her hands in clear view at all times. Thunder Storm, will you and other woodfolk watch from the trees for the least sign of attack? Danton and Stormaway, you may accompany me to help me determine her motives. Harkell too, if he is available."

Two hours later, Drakell reappeared and bowed, "Sire, The old woman awaits. She was most insistent that she bring four other people with her but I have insisted that they must wait in company with Boroavar and Sorath while you see her. I trust that you are happy with that?"

"Thank you Drakell. Could someone look after Midnight please?" Tarkyn nudged the eagle in the chest. "Go on, Bird. Go somewhere else for a while." Once he was clear of his two charges, he asked Drakell to present her.

Drakell crooked his finger and at his gesture, a scrawny well-dressed old woman with a weathered face and work-worn hands, hobbled down a faint path between the trees until she stood facing the prince. She struggled down onto one knee, hand on heart.

To everyone's surprise, Tarkyn leaned forward and, placing his hand under her elbow, helped the old lady to rise to her feet. They were even more surprised when he said, "Hello, Old Ma. I am so pleased to see you again."

The old lady smiled at him, pink with pleasure that he remembered her. Then she scowled at Drakell, "You see, young man? Nothing havey-cavey about me wanting to see His Highness. Who wouldn't, if they had the chance?" She returned her attention to Tarkyn and looked him up and down, "You're looking all right on it, Your Highness. I'm glad you got away safely. Me and the boys didn't hear anything about you for a while. But we decided silence must have meant you got away, because the king would have made a great fuss if he'd found you."

Tarkyn smiled. "I managed not to get caught but I'm afraid I ate all the provisions you bought me in the first two days, and every time I tried to buy more with the money from the diamond pin you sold for me, I ended up being chased. So I had become very lean and hungry, from eating only wayside berries, by the time Stormaway," Tarkyn gestured at his wizard standing beside him, "found me and shared a rabbit with me."

The old lady cackled, "Ah, a bit of hunger never hurt anybody. Ask one who knows... Just as long as you got away safe, that's the main thing."

"Where is the rest of your family? I would like to see them too."

Old Ma beamed, "They'll be right proud to hear that." She jerked her thumb over her shoulder, "They're back that away with some hulking great giant of a man and this one's father."

Once Tarkyn had nodded at Drakell to fetch them, he turned his attention to his bemused liegemen, "Stormaway and Danton, may I introduce Old Ma?" He stopped and frowned, "Actually I don't know your real name, Old Ma. Would you prefer me to use it?" he asked.

"No, almost don't remember it myself. Old Ma is who I am now."

Conversation was suspended as the four other members of Old Ma's family approached and went down on one knee, hand on heart.

"Please rise." Tarkyn smiled. "What a surprise it is to see you all again... and a pleasure. These are Dillis and Tomas, old Ma's sons, and Morayne and Charkon, her grandchildren," he said and in turn introduced his liegemen.

"You're looking good on it, Your Highness," said the taller man quietly.

"Thank you, Tomas. I see you have bought new clothes. They suit you." He grinned at Stormaway, Harkell and Danton, "You must be wondering who these people are… Old Ma and her family looked after me, the day after I fled the palace and before I had escaped from Tormadell. They sold my diamond pin for me, winding their way between proclamations of rewards for my head and evading the guards who were searching for me, to return with supplies for my journey. As guards searched the warehouses, they hid me and then guided me to the city's edge under cover of darkness." He smiled, "We only spent from dawn to midnight of one day together, but it was a pivotal day in my life."

Danton bowed. "It is a pleasure to meet people who have been of such assistance to my liege. I myself tried to find him on that fateful night but could not pick up his trail. It took me four weeks to finally track him down."

"We all decided he would be harder to track on foot than if he were mounted," said Tomas. He smiled, "Remember Sire? You had nowhere you were going to, so it didn't matter how long it was going to take to get there."

Tarkyn grimaced, "I remember. I had no future that I could imagine then. I took your advice about hiding my valuables, by the way." He gave a short laugh, "But I think I have hidden them so well that even I will struggle to retrieve them. They are hidden high up in a crevice on a cliff face behind an eagle's nest… belonging to two very aggressive eagles."

Stormaway suddenly frowned at Tomas. "*You* told him to hide his jewellery?"

Tomas scowled back at him. "Yeah. I could see him being rolled before the week was out. So I told him to hide most of his stuff."

Dillis joined his brother, "His Highness didn't have a lot of savvy. Pretty wet behind the ears, we reckoned. Don't think he'd ever been in a slum before. You should have seen him in his beautiful, embroidered cloak…. Stood out like a sore thumb. He might as well have worn a sign saying, 'Rob me.'"

Tarkyn watched this interchange without comment.

Tomas smiled at him, "You are very restrained, Sire. Dillis, as usual, is setting himself up as a complete idiot. After all, if you were so gullible, how come you got the jump on us?"

"He only did at first, if you remember," retorted Dillis. "Then we turned the tables… or we would have, if we hadn't realised about then that he was the prince."

Stormaway cut across what was fast turning into a bickering match by asking dryly, "Your Highness, did you not tell me that a thief advised you to hide your valuables? Am I to infer from this, that Tomas and this thief are one and the same?"

Tarkyn nodded. "Stop being so pompous, Stormaway. Of course they are." He received a clear image from Autumn Leaves showing himself in mock horror at Tarkyn hobnobbing with dishonesty, to which Tarkyn sent back a shrug and a grin.

Danton was frowning at Dillis, "Just how did you meet His Highness?"

Dillis put his hands on his hips in swaggering defiance, "We was trying to rob him, if you must know."

Tarkyn held his hand up, "Enough. How we met and how we continued were two very different things. I do not want these people called to account by you. They helped me and were kind to me when they could have made a lot more money by turning me in."

Old Ma hobbled up to Stormaway and shook her finger in his face, "And for your information, Prince Tarkyn trusted us to be honourable and we were. And for your further information, we ain't stealing no more. We've left Tormadell and we're looking to buy a small holding to keep the five of us, ain't we boys?"

"Really?" Tarkyn raised his eyebrows. "Will half the value of my diamond pin buy you a farm?"

Dillis guffawed. "I told you he was wet behind the ears. No Your Highness, but it set us up to make a few profitable ventures which increased our collateral, so to speak."

"Dillis," snapped Old Ma. "You mind your manners. That's enough of your cheek."

The middle aged man turned a dull red. "Sorry, Ma. Sorry, Your Highness."

Tarkyn turned to the teenage girl, "And how are you, Morayne? I hope you have not learned any more about how genuinely dangerous men behave?"

Morayne glanced at him quickly then hung her head and blushed, "Only once, Sire. We were camped alongside the Great West Road, and when I went to fetch some water, a man grabbed me and threw me to the ground." She sniffed. "I yelled as he dived on top of me and he was dragging at my bodice when Dillis and my dad arrived and dragged him off me." She sniffed again, "That was really scary…Not like you, Sire."

Danton frowned, "What does she mean; not like you? Of course that's not like you…or like most men for that matter."

Glances passed between the five thieves but they did not reply.

Tarkyn watched them and smiled, "Honour among thieves, eh?" He gave an embarrassed shrug as he answered Danton, "My friends here will not betray me so I will tell you; I held a knife to poor Morayne's throat for a good forty minutes to keep the rest of the family at bay. But afterwards, she informed me that she knew that I hadn't intended to hurt her, even though I had been trying to convince them all that I would."

Stormaway glared first at Tarkyn and then at the family, "I don't know whose behaviour shocks me more. Yours, Sire, or this thieving family's."

Dillis snorted, "Well, I don't see why you should be shocked by a thieving family thieving. Natural behaviour, if you ask me. Much less natural for us to be trying to run a farm… But I take your point about His Highness. He shocked us too, getting out of the five of us circling him with knives….But we were even more shocked when his hood fell down and we found out who he was. Could have knocked me down with a feather, you could."

"And then he decided to trust us and tell us about how he'd defied the king and wrecked that hall and killed all those guards." Old Ma cackled as Tarkyn began to protest, "All right, I know. You didn't kill them on purpose… So after him trusting us like that, we were honour bound to help him, being as he was… and still is, I suppose… on the wrong side of the law."

"Na. Be fair, Old Ma," protested Tomas. "As soon as we knew who he was, we'd have done anything for him."

"Probably. But His Highness won me over, heart and soul, when he said to us…" Here she paused for dramatic effect and placed her hand on her heart, "'*I have placed my fate in your hands and my faith in your honour.*' Old Ma heaved a deep sigh, "I have never been so honoured in all my life." She smiled her crooked-toothed smile at Tarkyn. "You have no idea how much that meant to me… to us, Your Highness. You gave us back our self-respect."

CHAPTER 72

It was not until dusk that the rest of the refugee sorcerers finally had their promised audience with Tarkyn. In the interim, reports had come in from woodfolk on all sides of the forest and Tarkyn had joined his mind with his eagle's to fly over the surrounding area to survey the effects of the forest's unleashed power, while a steady stream of pigeons had brought messages to Stormaway from further afield.

Unusually for Tarkyn, he was nervous before meeting the refugees. He had not been in the presence of so many sorcerers since his arraignment. He fussed about the fact that many of them, even the thieving family, were better dressed than he. But on the other hand, he did not want to appear other than as he truly was. He had no wish to use the wizardly glamour they had used to introduce Navira to the home guard, arguing that it had merely been a temporary contrivance to make a point. He did not know how long, or how often, he would appear before his band of loyal refugees and so did not wish to create an impression he could not sustain. Eventually, Elena, Rena and Thraya with Falling Branch's assistance, created an impressive surcoat from a green surcoat of Drakell's, recut and trimmed with materials from the women's dresses. They fashioned a sash emblazoned with Tarkyn's coat of arms; an eagle with its wings spread on the upper left quadrant, a hand with a flame in its palm in the lower right quadrant, three crowns in the upper right quadrant and an oak in the lower left quadrant. Over this splendour, Tarkyn elected to wear his wolf skin cloak, which was both dramatic and unusual for princely attire.

Danton grinned at him. "You look well dressed and striking, Sire. Your cloak bears witness to your life in the forest while your surcoat proclaims your heritage."

Tarkyn gave a tight smile in return and rubbed sweaty palms down his leggings, "Thank you Danton. Shall we proceed? Make sure you are alert for any sign of danger, however slight."

Danton's eyebrows twitched in amused understanding at the unnecessary reminder, "Of course, Your Highness."

Tarkyn pretended not to hear the laughter in his liegeman's voice and, drawing a deep breath, stepped out from behind the cover of a bank of holly and hawthorn into the view of the refugee sorcerers.

The crowd of three hundred had mysteriously swelled over the past two days. As Tarkyn appeared, a thousand sorcerers threw up their hats or their hands and cheered. Someone in the crowd yelled, "Three cheers for His Highness," which brought forth further boisterous shouts.

During all of this, Tarkyn stood silently, a faint smile of acknowledgement on his lips. As the last cheer died away and Tarkyn still stood unmoving, it was borne upon the crowd that this was not just some rebel leader. This was a prince of the Tamadil line. One thousand sorcerers sank to their knees and, with heads bowed, placed their right hands over their hearts.

For a long second, they waited.

"I thank you for your greeting," murmured Tarkyn, "You may all rise."

High in the trees at the edge of the clearing, Rainstorm shook his head and said mentally to Waterstone and Lapping Water, "What an ornery bastard he is. Didn't just accept their warm welcome. Had to have his precious formality."

Lapping Water laughed soundlessy, "You should know by now he reverts to formality whenever he is unsure of his ground."

"Besides, he will want to keep his distance from this many people," added Waterstone.

Below them, Tarkyn waited until the refugee sorcerers were again standing, with their eyes trained on him. When he next spoke, his voice was warmer, "And I also thank you for your magnificent efforts at quelling the bushfire and in helping me to replant the damaged area." He gestured to his companions, "I believe you know Lord Danton and General Harkell….and I believe you also know Drakell, and Borovar.

"I understand that I and the forest have done more than repair the damage caused by the fire. From reports coming in, it appears that new trees have appeared as far southwest as Montraya and as far northwest as Westsea. Most of the new growth is close to the forest edge but the wind that blew up early this morning has taken seeds far and wide. Most lanes and roadways now have wide verges of woodlands on either side of them and some fences have become lines of fully grown trees. We have received reports of at least five minor roadways that now have shrubs and trees growing in the middle of them and the main road south from the Great West Road to Montraya is blocked in several places by tangled vines, small trees or bushes. Although not all reports have reached us yet, it seems that most of the new growth has occurred on the western side of the forest as an extension of the healing that was performed on the burnt out area. The forest's strength was mobilised from its centre towards the west."

As murmuring broke out, Tarkyn held up his hand, "I understand your concern. If you have abandoned holdings to come here, then you may find them changed when you return. I can imagine that many fields will have to be ploughed around trees that have sprung up… and trips to market may take longer if roads are blocked."

A brawny farmer raised his hand and when acknowledged, said, "We ain't concerned, Your Highness. Well, maybe a bit, but it's not that. We're flabbergasted! How on earth can one man redesign a whole countryside in one day? It's unheard of."

While Tarkyn was warring with himself about whether to admit that the forest's power had overwhelmed his intention, Danton glanced at him for consent and took over, "I think we are all stunned by the extent of the power that was unleashed today. The fire was a deliberate attempt by King Kosar, not Prince Jarand as we first thought, to force Prince Tarkyn to stay out of the upcoming conflict between his brothers." He smiled at the crowd's angry reaction, waiting for the noise to die down before saying, "But I suspect the prince's retaliation will make them think twice before trying to force his hand again."

"And what *exactly* do you plan to do?" demanded the belligerent skinny man rudely.

Tarkyn turned his head to stare at him. As the silence lengthened, the man first struck a defiant pose then began to squirm under the prince's gaze.

"Your name?"

"M-Magadon, Your Highness."

"And are you always this offensive, Magadon?" A murmur of assent from the people around him caused Magadon to scowl and Tarkyn to raise his eyebrows, "Apparently so." The prince turned deliberately away from him and asked, "Does anyone else have any questions?"

Trey cleared his throat, "Sire, do you have any intention of usurping your brother?"

Tarkyn smiled to show his approval of the manner of delivery of the question. "No Trey, I still don't." The sorcerer coloured with gratification that Tarkyn had remembered his name. "But I have every intention of thwarting his desire to sacrifice his subjects in his battle against Jarand. We have yet to work out the finer details, but we will not allow my brothers' armies to decimate each other or the countryside."

He let his gaze travel over the whole crowd. "As you have probably realized, our efforts to persuade Jarand and Kosar to work together have merely postponed the inevitable. At this stage, we need details of possible battle sites so that we can plan our intercession. We need your local knowledge but also I would ask some of you to venture forth under Stormaway Treemaster's guidance to assist in gathering information about troop movements."

Vaska stepped forward and bowed before speaking, "Sire, we have heard wondrous tales of the feats of your private army... and yet you appear to have so few following you…?" He frowned, "Why are they not here with you?"

"They are here, Vaska. They are all around you, but they do not number the thousands of my brothers' armies. Nor would I risk them, any more than I intend to risk you or any of Eskuzor's sorcerers."

"But Sire, the country is littered with your supporters. If we gathered them together, could we not raise a challenge to the king?"

The prince smiled, "Perhaps, and I am truly grateful for your support. But I wish to find a way to secure Eskuzor's future without a bloodbath. A three way civil war would decimate the population and cause wide spread suffering on a scale far beyond the discomforts of your present dissatisfaction."

Varga stepped forward to join his twin and, like him, bowed before speaking, "Your intentions are admirable, Sire, but even if you can avert this war, what do we have to look forward to in its wake? ….More of the king neglecting his subjects while he fends off his brother's wiles?"

Tarkyn's eyes narrowed. He did not like being held to account so blatantly. It was one thing for him to choose to shoulder the nation's welfare and quite another for others to demand it of him. A tight wave of anger jabbed out from him, unbalancing the first two rows of sorcerers.

As they looked around wildly in alarm, Harkell intervened, "Be careful how you express yourself. You do not have the right to hold His Highness to account. You have just experienced some of his irritation."

Varga bowed hurriedly, "I beg your pardon, Sire. I did not mean to press you."

Tarkyn nodded an acknowledgement while Harkell continued, "You are perhaps unaware that the king has heeded Prince Tarkyn in some respects by mounting sorties against raiders in the north west of the country." He gave a smile of fellowship, "And I suspect the king will be even more willing to listen after having trees uproot his roads and overturn his tents."

Tarkyn took over. "My hope is that I can persuade them to come to some sort of written agreement. It is slow work changing their lifelong antagonism towards each other. And I think it is only just dawning on them that I can and will back my demands… *requests*. They are still testing me." Tarkyn's voice echoed with unexpressed power, "… but I am your country's guardian and I *will* not allow her to be laid to waste or her people used as pawns."

The prince's passion made his audience stir nervously. Suddenly he smiled. "I did not mean to discomfort you. I now have an announcement that will surprise you all… We thought long and hard before we decided to honour you with this information." His gaze travelled slowly around his audience, "Twenty two years ago, a daughter was born to my parents, King Markazon and Queen Ramilla."

The crowd gasped in amazement.

Tarkyn waited until they were again quiet before continuing, "As an infant, her power was unusually strong and because of her age, uncontrolled. An incident occurred where the princes provoked her, and in response, her shield activated. But, in the same way that my shield reflected back the attacking rays of the guards in the Great Hall, so did her shield reflect the princes' power. Fortunately, at the age of five, their shafts of power were not strong and they received only minor injuries."

Tarkyn had the crowd in the palm of his hand. Their silence was so complete that they could hear the faint scratching of claws on bark as a squirrel skittered its way up the trunk of a pine tree.

"Sadly, my mother felt that her daughter represented too great a risk and ordered her execution." Tarkyn nodded in agreement at the shocked intakes of breath. "Fortunately, two wizards of great power colluded to bring the infant girl out of danger and arranged for her to be raised far from Tormadell in the legendary Forest of Yesterday, Today and Tomorrow."

Tarkyn paused for a moment to give his audience time to absorb his words. "You might think, after my brothers' betrayal of me, that I would rejoice in anything that throws my family into a poor light. But this is not the case. My family has ruled Eskuzor for generations and I am proud of my heritage and the blood of my father. It pains me to discover that my mother acted so precipitously in the absence of my father. But I know she acted as she did to protect the people against what she saw as the threat of a rogue sorcerer. After all, my sister had injured the heir to the throne, however unintentionally." He drew a deep breath, "I find it ironic that I must feel grateful to two people who have obviously performed acts of treason against my family." He raised his hand and let it drop. "However, these wizards and I believe that they acted in the best interests of Eskuzor… And so, at the end of all this, let me introduce to you my sister, Navira Tamadil, Princess and Wizardess of the Forest of Yesterday, Today and Tomorrow."

The crowd erupted, cheering and whooping as Danton reappeared with Navira's hand on his arm. Head held high, she came to stand beside Tarkyn; two heads of long black hair and two sets of vibrant amber eyes. No one, looking at them, could have the slightest doubt that she was who

Tarkyn said she was. Without prompting this time, the crowd sank to their knees, hands on hearts.

"Thank you," said Navira in her deep authoritative voice. "I have long awaited my return to Eskuzor and I am moved by your welcome. Please rise."

Danton addressed the crowd, "King Kosar knows that Princess Navira lives but he does not yet know that she has grown safely into her powers nor that she has returned to Eskuzor." He smiled at her, "With civil war pending, we did not think that now was a good time to apprise him of it. But once the conflict is over, Prince Tarkyn will suggest that the king waive the sentence that was passed on Her Highness so that she may take her rightful place at court."

"And what of you, Sire?" asked Trey.

Tarkyn shook his head. "No. The king would never accept me back, but equally I would not wish to return. I will remain aloof from the machinations of court and act as watchdog on behalf of the people and forests of Eskuzor. However, we believe that Princess Navira may be able to exert some influence when she returns to court."

"Excuse me, Your Highness, but are we to keep knowledge of Princess Navira a secret?" asked a courteous voice.

Tarkyn swung his head around to find that the speaker was none other than Maragon. "A good question. No. You may spread the knowledge of my sister far and wide. We are well able to protect her, should King Kosar refuse to waive the sentence and we hope that it may force his hand if people know of her." He let his gaze travel around the crowd, "Once more I thank you for your support. If there are no more questions, I will leave you to Stormaway Treemaster and General Harkell. Good evening."

So saying, the prince and his sister withdrew.

Part 9: The Battle of the Dry Mile

CHAPTER 73

As Stormaway hurried along the path, his green robes flapping around his legs, he nearly tripped over Midnight who darted laughing from between two trees. He grabbed the boy by the shoulders to steady himself, frowning down at him in irritation. Immediately the smile was wiped from Midnight's face as he ducked his head, cowering. Stormaway's grip tightened to make sure the little boy didn't rush off distressed. Heaving a sigh at this delay in his plans, the old wizard lowered himself onto one knee and used one hand to tilt Midnight's unwilling chin up so he could look him in the eyes. He pointed to Midnight then himself and before wrapping his hands around each other in the gesture for friendship.

Midnight blinked in surprise.

Using the sign language that he had developed for the community to use with Midnight, Stormaway explained that he would never physically hurt him, and reiterated his care for him. Midnight stared at him for a few seconds then gestured an apology for startling him. Then with a shy smile, Midnight wrapped his hands round each other and pointed to Stormaway.

Stormaway smiled, and tousled the little boy's hair. "Thank you, Midnight." He thought about how little praise he had given Tarkyn and decided to make sure he didn't make the same mistake with his younger protégé. Matching words to gestures, he said softly, "You know, we are all forever in your debt for saving Tarkyn." After a moment's thought, he added, "…and for protecting the woodfolk children against the mountain lion and for reliving your memories of neglect to release the mountainfolk from the curse. You are a very brave, talented young man and a dedicated student. I am proud to know you."

Tears sprang to Midnight's eyes as he looked down at his feet, unable to manage the embarrassment of such fulsome praise after a young life filled with derision. Stormaway tapped him gently on the nose to regain his eye contact. "And you are getting much better at trusting us and not running away." He put an arm around Midnight and gave him only a brief hug, not being a demonstrative person by nature. "Now, shall we go together to find Tarkyn? I must speak with him."

Midnight nodded and with a grin, pointed in the direction from which he had erupted. A soft morning mist clung between the trees and drifted around the wizard's feet as he followed Midnight through the undergrowth and around a granite boulder to emerge in a tiny meadow, dotted with yellow and white wildflowers. Stormaway was not surprised to discover Tarkyn less than fifty yards away from where Midnight had been. He was sitting on a small rocky outcrop, surrounded by wildflowers, deep in discussion with Harkell on the possible uses of shields and other magical tactics in the upcoming confrontation.

The wizard gave a shallow bow, "Sire, I return to you one small forest guardian, in one piece and reassured, after I made the mistake of frowning at him when he ran out in front of me."

Tarkyn laughed, "Well caught, Stormaway. You have saved me the effort of chasing after him." He crooked his finger at his little charge, "Come here, little one." Once installed on the prince's knee, Midnight gave a shy smile and waved at Stormaway. Tarkyn raised his eyebrows in surprise, "Hmm. You are in favour."

"I have been worming my way into his good books by giving him some well-deserved praise."

When Tarkyn looked a query at his charge, Midnight coloured and pressed his face into Tarkyn's chest.

Stormaway smiled broadly, "He's a funny little fellow, isn't he?"

"He is… and worth his weight in gold."

"I couldn't agree more."

Tarkyn looked in some surprise at his usually taciturn wizard.

Stormaway shrugged, "If not for him, you would no longer be here. For that alone, his value is priceless."

Tarkyn gave a faint smile, "So, to what do we owe the pleasure of your company? Have you come to add your ideas to ours?"

"No Sire, at least not in the first instance." The wizard indicated a log. "May I?"

"Of course. Be seated."

Stormaway sat down and drew forth a sheaf of parchment, rags and scraps. "These and what is in my head represent the sum total of our intelligence. At last the die is cast. For the last fortnight, both Kosar and Jarand have been stymied by the changed landscape. They have spent days sending messengers far and wide to gain a revised understanding of the terrain. But now, with the combined efforts of my network and the refugee sorcerers, I am fairly sure that we know the whereabouts and the intentions of Kosar and Jarand's forces. They each know the location of the other and it seems clear that they are converging from either side on a flat valley that runs between gently sloping hills about twenty miles west of the forest's edge and about thirty-five miles southwest from here."

"That is reasonably close," mused Tarkyn. "We could be there by this evening if we pushed ourselves."

"Not with the children, Sire. That is at least twelve hours of solid walking, without breaks. I think we should take it in two stages and aim to be there by noon tomorrow. That will still give us a day to prepare."

"Hmm. I suppose if we plan before we leave here, that will be time enough. What do you think, Harkell?"

"We are lucky to have any preparation time at all. A full day is a luxury. Besides, if we need the assistance of the refugees, they are further to the east than us and will take even longer to reach this proposed battle site. If possible, it is better not to overtire people. Bad decisions are made when people are too tired."

Tarkyn nodded, "Very well. We will aim to arrive there tomorrow."

With that issue settled, Harkell returned his attention to the terrain, "This valley you're talking about, Stormaway… Surely there will be a watercourse of some sort running through it. How can they hope to attack each other across a river or stream?"

"You're right. There is a watercourse. A waterfall plunges down from a ravine at the eastern end of the valley," explained Stormaway, "to feed a stream that meanders over a rocky course along the middle of the valley. But then the stream disappears underground for a mile or more before reappearing further to the west."

Harkell thought for a moment while he visualised the valley, "So I presume Kosar is approaching from the north and Jarand from the south. Does either have an advantage? What is the vegetation like? How close can we get to this dry mile under cover?"

Stormaway held up his hand to stop the deluge of questions, "Just a moment. One of your refugees drew a map, marking in everything he thought you might find useful. Thanks to our enthusiastic forest guardian, the entire water course is bounded by shrubs, blackberries, vines and some larger trees. There are several weeping willows at places along the stream. Oaks and sycamores are scattered across the fields."

He pointed to perhaps thirty rings on the map which depicted willows. "As you can see, where the stream goes underground, there is less cover; a few bushes and trees, but substantial gaps between them." Stormaway straightened up and puffed out his cheeks. "So, in my view, I would say you could get to the eastern edge of the dry mile unseen but no further. If I were the king or Jarand, I would plan to mount my battle on the western half of the dry mile, as far from the forest's edge as possible."

"Hmph," Harkell pored over the map, his eyes following the tracks onto the hills and gauging the distances between patches of cover. "So what lies to the west? How close can we get from that side?"

Stormaway's eyes lit up. "My thought exactly! Ten miles to south west lies the village of West Wandering. It is a substantial village of some hundred cottages, two inns, a guild hall and a market place." He smiled. "All roads to and from the village are now bordered with thick shrubbery, just as all roads in the west of the kingdom are, thanks to His Highness here. The stream broadens as it meanders into the village from the valley but both sides are thick with vegetation." He gave a small grunt. "I don't know whether they were always bordered with vegetation or if this is the result of seeds washing down and being germinated by the forest's surge of power but either way, they provide cover."

Tarkyn eyes gleamed. "This seems almost ideal for our purposes. One would almost think they had forgotten my promise to intercede."

The wizard chuckled. "In fact, I think this is possibly the most barren, least vegetated area either of them could find. Their only other choice was to deviate far to the west and fight it out on the sand dunes of the coast. Your forest-driven magic, Sire, has changed the face of Western Eskuzor beyond recognition. Even crop fields have trees scattered through them."

"If I were my brothers, I would aim for the middle of the dry mile, leaving space on either side and I would station sentries on each end to give warning of our approach."

"And I would set booby traps along the sides of the stream amongst the scrub," added Harkell.

Tarkyn grimaced, "We will have to be very careful. Perhaps our trapper friends would be best able to ferret out any potential hazards. I'll talk to them about it." He looked at Stormaway. "So how long do we have before the armies are lined up facing each other?"

"From the information at hand, I would say that they will be camped opposite each other by noon at the latest, the day after tomorrow. If they have camped nearby the night before, they may move straight into battle." Stormaway shrugged, "Still, you never know, they may choose to parley."

Tarkyn nodded grimly, "They *will* choose to parley, if I have anything to say about it."

As soon as they heard the news, the home guard gathered to confer at the firesite. Now, at last, they had enough information to work with.

Stormaway glanced at Navira and Caroman before voicing their common concern. "We're strong wizards, Tarkyn, but we cannot control a full mile of battle front. We need to find a way to stop the armies from spreading over the full length of the dry mile. Even if they maintain a distance on either end from the tree lines, they will still be spread over fourteen or fifteen hundred yards.

"You can produce a widespread storm, can't you?" asked Lapping Water, as she walked into the clearing and slung two hares off her back into the waiting arms of Tree Wind and Running Feet who were organising the evening meal. "And what about your shields? There are eight of you with shields, aren't there?"

Navira's eyes narrowed as she watched Lapping Water, clearly disapproving of the down-to-earth pragmatism of the prince's future wife. She looked at Tarkyn for his reaction, only to find him giving a smiling nod of approbation. She drew a shallow breath and addressed herself resolutely to the question, "Even with thinned shields, we could each only produce a shield a little over one hundred yards in length. And those over-stretched shields would only keep out smoke and flame; not arrows, spears or swords." She shrugged, "Anyway, what is the point of creating a wall of shields between the two armies? Sooner or later, we would tire and the armies would then attack each other. We can't stand in the dry mile forever. The same applies to a storm. A storm may make it unpleasant for the soldiers for a while, but it too will blow itself out and we will still have two armies facing each other."

"Sorry I asked," said Lapping Water tartly.

Navira must have realised that some of her disapproval had leaked into her voice because she added hastily, "No, it is good that you did. It helps us to work out what will and will not work."

"Don't patronise me," snapped Lapping Water as she lifted her quiver over her head and placed it on the ground in front of her. "I'm sure you can manage perfectly well on your own."

"Perhaps they can," said Tarkyn quietly, "but I can't. I need the views of everyone, not just the wizards or the magic-wielders."

Lapping Water's antagonism melted. "Sorry. I'm just tired."

She picked up her quiver and carried it over to sit beside Tarkyn while she inspected her arrows. He gave her head a stroke but did not put his arm around her, understanding that her hunting was not complete until her equipment was back in perfect working order.

Autumn Leaves brought her a cup of berry juice and a small bowl of nuts. "Here. That should keep you going until dinner time." In response to Tarkyn's raised eyebrow, the woodman rolled his eyes and asked, "You would like some too, would you, your lordship? Anyone else?" He was promptly deluged by requests and wandered off muttering, to procure refreshments for everyone gathered around the firesite. In the way of woodfolk, Waterstone and Creaking Bough unobtrusively followed him to assist.

"So how will we narrow the battle front?" asked Tarkyn.

"You could grow a row of trees before they get here," suggested Rainstorm.

As Tarkyn looked uneasy, Stormaway cut in, "I think the forest has expended enough energy already. I suspect you will find next year's harvests sparser than usual….And I think Tarkyn would be wise to keep away from the forest's power until he is fully recovered."

Rainstorm frowned in concern. "I didn't know you were still sick, Tarkyn. I thought we, or rather Midnight, drained off all the excess life force."

"You did, but that deluge of *esse* overtaxed my body and I couldn't just attach myself to a tree as I usually do, to heal myself." Tarkyn gave an involuntary shudder, "In fact, just the thought of it makes me feel sick at the moment… Too much of a good thing has become a bad thing. Hopefully, I'll get over it." He accepted a mug of juice from Autumn Leaves with a nod of thanks. "If there is no alternative to growing trees, I will of course, but another plan would be greatly appreciated."

"So, are you still weak?" asked Rainstorm.

"No, I don't think so. Just allergic to the forest's *esse*, at the moment."

Rainstorm considered for a moment. "What about Midnight? Could he do it?"

"The forest's power is still too unstable, I think," said Stormaway, "and Midnight is not experienced in drawing upon it."

"Experience didn't do Tarkyn much good," retorted Rainstorm. He held up his hand to forestall an angry outburst from the wizard. "All right, I take your point. We need another idea."

"Why don't we use dissonant rays as we did with Orolan?" suggested Danton, helping himself to a handful of hazelnuts from a nearby bowl. "We could create a tract of destabilized earth so that men and horses would sink into it when they tried to advance."

Stormaway shook his head, "We need to reduce the battle front to less than a thousand yards. We can't destabilise the earth over six hundred yards. The widest area I have destabilized was only twenty yards wide."

"What if you were on horseback?" asked Tarkyn. "That would increase your height above the ground and mean that you could aim your magic in a wider circle."

"True, but only to about thirty yards at the outside. Still not enough."

"But…" Harkell, his soft brown eyes gleaming with ideas, jumped to his feet and using a stick, started drawing in the dirt to illustrate as he spoke, "we could destabilise a series of circles along six hundred yards. What did we work out, Tarkyn? Besides Midnight who is too young, we have eight sorcerers who can produce power rays; you, Danton, Stormaway, Caroman, Navira, Rena, Borovar and Kayama. I understand you have to work in pairs to do this, so that would be four pairs who could produce destabilized circles of earth. If each pair made three circles with a gap of twenty yards between each, they would cover one hundred and fifty yards. So, between four pairs, six hundred yards would be peppered with treacherous ground." He straightened up and smiled, "So, what do you think?"

"Men and horses could still get through the twenty-yard gaps," said Danton, "but it will take them some time to work out where the safe passages are and even then, it will severely hamper the armies' capacity to charge each other over that six hundred yards. Seems a good plan." He looked at Stormaway, "What do you think? Will that be sufficient?"

The old wizard looked to Caroman for confirmation, before saying, "It will do, I think. At worst, there will be minor skirmishes but Tarkyn, we may not be able to prevent all casualties. We will be facing the full forces of Eskuzor; nine thousand on Jarand's side and eleven thousand on the king's."

"And sworn duty will not be all that is driving these men to attack each other," added Harkell. He was diverted for a minute while his six year old son, Sorrell, wandered over and showed him a horse he had made by tying together an assortment of sticks. When he had duly admired it and suggested that the children could race their horses if they each made one, he returned to the matter at hand. "Sorry. As I was saying, many will relish the opportunity to prove themselves, to earn kudos, promotion and the bounty gleaned from corpses on the battlefield after the fighting is over." Harkell gave an understanding smile. "You may not like your brother using people as pawns, Tarkyn, but not all go to war unwillingly."

"I am aware of that, Harkell," said Tarkyn tetchily. "I did grow up among armsmen, you know. But equally, both armies have called to arms hundreds, possibly thousands of civilians who have not chosen a military life." His voice rose as his irritation gave way to his underlying passion. "I do not want the manhood of an entire generation decimated to play out my brothers' rivalry. Already great swathes of farmland have been pillaged to feed the passing armies; people's livelihoods destroyed, crops ruined. How can people re-stock and sow for the next season's harvest if all their grain has been commandeered and their livestock slaughtered to the last beast? This destruction must be stopped."

Harkell spoke quietly into the stunned silence that followed Tarkyn's impassioned outburst. "I think we are all agreed that it must stop. Of course we must strive to prevent this battle. I was merely pointing out that some soldiers, including officers, will grasp any chance to engage the enemy, no matter what obstacles we place in their path. Despite our best efforts, many may die before we can force the princes into a resolution."

Tarkyn glared at him with a severity that would have made a lesser man quail. "Soldiers are trained to follow orders. Surely even eager soldiers will not attack unless commanded to do so. We must strike before the order to attack can be issued."

Harkell may not have quailed, but he did revert to speaking formally. "That will certainly give us the best chance of preventing casualties, Sire. And we must ensure that those in command are made aware of the treacherous nature of the six hundred yards so that they do not order their men into battle across the destabilized ground although, if they scout out the terrain well, they should notice it without our intervention."

"So, now that we have a means of narrowing the battle front, what do you wizards intend to do?" Tarkyn stood up and busied himself with fetching wood from the woodpile and feeding it onto the fire as he spoke. His movements reeked of nervous energy. "How can we force Jarand and Kosar to negotiate?"

Stormaway glanced at Caroman and received a nod before answering, "If your brothers are stubborn, it may take a combination of … hmm… persuasive measures. But we have one strategy above all others that we think will persuade them without threatening or harming them in any way."

Once Stormaway had explained the wizards' strategy and had survived the barrage of questions from both woodfolk and sorcerers that followed, he added, "But it will be up to you, Tarkyn, to find a way to bring your brothers together first. And we will need everyone's help to prepare. Sequencing will be everything."

"For the first time, I think we may actually succeed in forcing my brothers to negotiate." Still unable to sit quietly, Tarkyn filled the big kettle from a hessian waterbag and balanced it on the logs he had recently placed on the fire. When he was sure it was secure, he glanced at Waterstone with a little grin, "…but I think I will have to place myself right in the thick of it to entice my brothers together. I promised you that I wouldn't place myself at risk unnecessarily but I'm afraid that this time, it may be necessary."

Waterstone looked grim. "No need to look so pleased about it."

"I'm not pleased. I am merely grinning in anticipation of your concern."

"Hmph. Just make sure you put in place every conceivable precaution."

Tarkyn laughed and stood up from where he had been squatting beside the fire. "I will, big brother. I promise you, I will."

Chapter 74

Once they had devised a workable plan, the home guard packed swiftly to begin their relocation to a firesite closer to the dry mile.

Danton and Harkell were charged with contacting Orolan to borrow a dozen horses, as various members of the home guard would need speed and manoeuvrability. Since Jarand's encampment had transferred to the control of Kosar's troops, the outlaws had moved their camp to the southern side of the Great Western Road. So, double up on Borovar's war horse, Danton and Harkell were able to reach it within a couple of hours.

As they rode into the outlaw's camp, Orolan strode over to meet them, smiling a greeting. "It never ceases to amaze me how you people can find my camp, even though it is well hidden and we move often." He glanced from one to the other, "What's up? You two look like you're on a mission." He gave a derisive grunt of amusement. "Of course you're on a mission. You don't socialise with my sort."

Harkell studied him for a few moments before giving a half smile, "We didn't start well, you and I, with you taking the prince hostage. And I'm not enamoured of the way you earn your living but… I owe you a huge debt of gratitude for rescuing my family and from what I gather, Prince Tarkyn's view of you seems to have mellowed." He let his gaze wander around the outlaw's camp, taking in the shabby dress but friendly camaraderie of its occupants before returning his focus to the outlaw leader's face. "And from what I can see, I would say there are similarities between running an outlaw band and commanding a military company that may just give us enough common ground to share a friendly wine or two. "

"But not right now," cut in Orolan, in anticipation of Harkell's next words.

Harkell laughed, "No. Not right now. Tarkyn's brothers are meeting on the battlefield in two days' time, which gives up less than forty-eight hours to stop mass bloodshed."

"Yep," said Orolan decisively, "Socialising can wait. What can we do to help?"

Having been with Tarkyn when Orolan told them of his trip from Montraya, Danton smiled, more easy with him than Harkell was. "Stop playing hard done by, Orolan. Three weeks ago, the prince and I stayed with you for hours … well beyond the time courtesy demanded…And we enjoyed your story and each other's company. Give poor Harkell a break."

Orolan grinned, "Old attitudes die hard. It took years of injustice and disregard to get that chip on my shoulder. It's going to take more than one friendly encounter to get rid of it. But I concede you've made a start." He waved a hand to dismiss the discussion. "Now, from what you say, time is short. So let's get down to business."

An hour later, they rode out of Orolan's camp, Danton mounted on the war horse and Harkell on a frisky black mare, each leading a string of horses.

Despite the assistance of various local woodfolk, it was early afternoon before they intercepted the home guard who, by then, had been travelling for over three hours. Harkell and Danton stopped only briefly to deliver the horses and reiterate plans before heading off once more, this time to find the refugee sorcerers.

"I can't stay with you and these sorcerers once we reach the battleground, you realise?" said Danton as they rode along a well beaten path through over-hanging beeches. "I will have to assist with making those dirt pits."

"I'm aware of that." A certain dryness in Harkell's tone indicated that he felt he was being underestimated again. However, he made no more issue of it than that and continued quite genially, "Thanks for coming. It will make it easier to have two of us organising them initially."

Danton gave a little laugh, "I must remember to call you General Harkell."

Harkell chuckled, "It makes me feel a bit of a fraud, but it impresses that unruly lot of refugees."

"Not only that, but if any of those refugees are spies, and let's face it, some of them almost certainly are, it will give the impression that Tarkyn is better supplied with troops than he is."

"True, although, if I were truly a general, I would be sending one of my captains to talk to the refugees." Harkell dodged under a low hanging bough and drew his horse back to a walk as the path closed in. "And I suppose sometime soon, I will be introducing you as Your Highness. How does that feel?"

Danton glanced at him then looked away. Harkell noticed a heightened colour in his cheeks. After a few moments, he said, "I too will feel a fraud being called Your Highness. It seems quite surreal, doesn't it?" He shook his head, "I had no idea who she was, you know."

"Even when you told me she was above your touch… and mine? As a lord, not too many people outstrip you. Perhaps at some level, you had an inkling, even then."

Danton steered his horse around a log that had fallen across the narrow path. "No. I wasn't thinking royalty when I said that. She was just so arrogant and disdainful when I first met her; so mystical and aloof that she seemed beyond reach… and yet she also said things that rocked me and changed the whole way I viewed myself."

"Did she? You didn't tell me that bit. As I recall, I was newly arrived and you weren't particularly friendly towards me at that stage." He grinned as he pushed his horse through interlocking branches. "Don't worry. I know it sprang from your loyalty to Tarkyn… which is so passionate that you set yourself up to be teased by woodfolk and wizard alike."

Danton frowned. "Which wizard?"

"Stormaway, when he made you say those words 'in the king's name' so that you could be translocated to the Lost Forest. He knew you'd kick up. He just wanted to watch you stick up for Tarkyn."

Danton chuckled. "Bastard!" he said, with no heat at all.

"So what did she say that impressed you about yourself so much?"

"Well, you know when I was younger, Tarkyn cut himself to stop the king from continuing my punishment? I always saw that purely as Tarkyn's nobility and courage. But Navira said that she was glad he did it and that I was worth it."

"Stars above, Danton. If that didn't tell you she liked you, I don't know what would."

Danton shook his head, laughing. "No. It wasn't like that. It was more as though she were proclaiming an indisputable truth."

"That's just because she's a Tamadil. They seem to have a natural gravitas in their tone that can make the slightest comment assume grave importance."

A few minutes later, a little smile began to play around Danton's mouth. "Now I think about it, she said she acted disdainfully towards Caroman on my second visit because she was trying to impress me." He laughed. "It doesn't get much better than that, does it? Having a Tamadil trying to impress you?"

Thinking of the hours that Tarkyn had spent trying to harness the power of his feelings to gain his own approval, Harkell smiled. "No, it doesn't."

He pulled his horse to a complete halt, long grass brushing against his thighs on either side. He turned in the saddle and looked around. "Hmm. Are we lost?"

Danton surveyed the sea of long grass ahead of them which showed no discernible track before giving way to tangled brush and trees. "Hmm. I would say yes." He slapped his thigh in frustration. "And just when we don't have time to muck around. We should have brought Waterstone or Autumn Leaves with us. We could have dropped them off just before we reached the sorcerers' camp. Too late now." He took a deep breath and yelled, "Halloo. We are on forest guardian's business. Is anyone nearby who can help us?"

A rustling in the grass near Harkell's left stirrup made his frisky black mare sidle nervously. He looked down to see three unknown woodfolk standing within three feet of them. He raised his eyebrows and asked, "Were you there all the time or did you just flick here?" After a slight hesitation, he added courteously, "I am Harkell."

"How do you do? We were just over there," replied a woman in her thirties with a baby strapped to her back, pointing to some nearby bushes, "but came to your call. I suppose you might call it flicking but that is not a term we use. I am Leaf Wind."

An older woodwoman spoke. "If you are on the forest guardian's business, then you are working for all woodfolk. How may we help you? I am Rainshower."

"Pleased to meet you. We are looking for a large camp of sorcerers. We think it is in this direction, close to the burnt out square mile... but our path seems to have deserted us. I am Danton."

A short silence of mindtalking reigned before Leaf Wind said, "Follow me," and turning on her heel, led them to the left along an almost invisible path through the long grass. Out of courtesy, Danton and Harkell dismounted to follow her and talked quietly with her as they walked. The path skirted the tangle of trees before opening out onto a broader track that showed signs of frequent use. As soon as the horses had picked their way into the open space of the track, she turned. "I will come with you no further. You will be faster on your horses. Follow this track to the right until you ford a small stream. Then turn left and follow the stream on the other side. It is impassable on this side. That will lead you into the sorcerer's campsite." Suddenly she smiled. "This has been quite an adventure for me; meeting and walking with two sorcerers. I wish you well."

They thanked her profusely and remounted. Forty minutes later, they rode into the refugees' camp.

The refugees had divided themselves on the basis of families or friendship, with a little pile of belongings marking each group's staked territory within the camp. As soon as Harkell and Danton appeared, they left their huddles and converged on the two newcomers from every side, clamouring for news.

Harkell held up his hand and waited. When it was quiet enough for him to be heard, he said, "Lord Danton and I bring you greetings from Prince Tarkyn and a request for assistance. The battle between the king and Prince Jarand is now imminent."

"I thought Prince Tarkyn was trying stop it," shouted a lanky teenager. "My brother is amongst Prince Jarand's troops. Poor bastard couldn't hit a barn door with a pitchfork and couldn't outrun a lame duck, let alone the press gang."

Harkell waited while a babble of similar protests rose then slowly subsided in the face of his stoic silence. Keeping his voice pitched low so that they would have to strain to hear it, he continued, "As you so rightly pointed out, Prince Tarkyn does intend to intervene. We now know the time and the location of their confrontation so finally, we can spring into action. The armies will be facing each other in a valley about forty miles from here that we have dubbed the Dry Mile. And from Stormaway Treemaster's information and calculations, they should be there by the day after tomorrow."

Another hubbub broke out. In an aside to Danton, Harkell muttered, "Stars above! These people are trying my patience. I'm used to addressing disciplined troops. I could have explained the whole thing and had it organised by now, if I'd been speaking to soldiers."

"Just a minute," said Trey, who was standing close enough to hear him. He turned from them and addressed the crowd in a carrying voice. "Come on, my friends. Time is short. Give them a chance to speak. We can comment and ask questions when we have heard all they have to say."

The crowd quietened almost at once.

Danton raised his eyebrows in a gesture of surprised appreciation and spoke into the silence. "We need a contingent of two hundred to help us to prepare, not to fight. If you volunteer, you must be willing to walk forty miles over the rest of today and tomorrow. If possible, we need you at the battle site by dusk tomorrow at the latest, ready to work. It would be safer for the rest of you to remain here, well away from the two armies."

Immediately they were overwhelmed with volunteers, clustering around their horses and calling out. Trey held up his hand and again they quietened. "I know we all want to help but, not only do we have children and elderly people who must stay behind, we also need people to hunt, protect and care for them. There is also honour in supporting your fellow refugees. Those wishing to volunteer, go with Vaska and Varga to stand under the spreading oak. If you are at all unsure that you can march so far so quickly, be honest with yourselves and the rest of us. Otherwise, you jeopardise our opportunity to take part. If discussion does not sort this out within twenty minutes, we will draw straws." He looked around. "Everyone happy with that?"

A few people nodded, but most acquiesced simply by following Trey's suggestions. Once they were gathered around his brothers, Trey turned back to Danton and Harkell, "General Harkell, Lord Danton, do you have time for a mug of tea and some food before you go?"

As they dismounted, Harkell nodded at the organised crowd under the oak tree. "There have been some changes since we were here last."

Trey scanned the campsite and brought his vivid blue eyes back to meet Harkell's. "Yes, sir, there have. Too many feckless people, undisciplined by routine or Eskuzor's law, becomes a dangerous proposition. Eventually I and a few others called a meeting to address it." He gave a shrug. "I was chosen to lead them and a few others of us, including my brothers, make up a small council who see that everyone is cared for, and that disputes are settled without knives or fighting. Because these people chose us, they listen to us. If anyone disputes our right to intervene, he or she is shouted down by everyone else."

A teenaged girl approached Danton and curtsied as she presented him with a cup of tea. When he had smiled and thanked her, she moved on to present Harkell with a cup of tea and a smile, but no curtsey.

"This is my daughter, Lorin," said Trey, giving her a friendly pat on the back. "Thank you. Now off you go." He gave an apologetic smile, "She is at an age where she becomes easily besotted. She spoke of nothing but Prince Tarkyn for weeks, after his brief visit with us."

Danton grinned. "I remember. She gave him a brooch to remember her by, didn't she, just as he was leaving?"

A tinge of colour crept into Trey's cheeks. "Yes. I was mortified. Had I realised what she was going to do, I would have forestalled her, I can assure you."

"Tarkyn didn't mind. He understood." As they sat down, Danton waved his hand around to encompass the campsite. "Impressive, Trey, to have gained the trust and loyalty of these people in so short a time."

"Hmm. It is not all clear sailing, I can assure you." Trey used sipping his tea as a chance to check that no one was in earshot. "It is an uncertain group… and there has been quite a bit of turnover since the fire. Some going, new ones coming in… and I am concerned that some of these transient people are reporting our activities either to the king or Prince Jarand." He lowered his voice. "If I were you, I would not tell our volunteers any more than you need to. Most of us have Prince Tarkyn and Eskuzor at heart but not all, I think. You don't want your strategies stymied by information getting into the wrong hands."

A teenaged boy came over and handed around a plate of hard, fired-baked rolls, filled with soft cheese.

"And this is Lokley, my son," said Trey with a quizzical frown. He waited until Lokley had left, before adding, "Not quite the problem that his twin sister is, but it is unusual for him to be serving food. I suspect he too wanted to meet you."

Danton laughed. "I can see you have your hands full with your family, let alone the rest of these sorcerers."

"I have the teenager era ahead of me," said Harkell with a grin. "My children are still only young." He bit into a roll and realised how hungry he was. "Thanks for the food. We have been on the move since early this morning." He lowered his voice, "… and thank you for your warning. Let us hope that once this confrontation is resolved, there will be no more need for recruitment and most of you will be able to return to your homes."

Trey grimaced. "…before we are raided by a press gang."

Danton reached over to clap him on the shoulder. "It was safer with smaller numbers, wasn't it? But now that your numbers are over a thousand, it will be impossible to conceal your existence for any length of time. At least over the next few days, the princes will be concentrating their efforts on the battle. But who knows what will happen after that? Still, you may be assured that Tarkyn is determined to force his brothers into negotiation."

Danton and Harkell gave Trey detailed directions to the rendezvous point before handing back their empty mugs and returning to their horses. As they mounted, Harkell inclined his head towards the spreading oak. "Looks like they have reached a consensus, Trey. Unfortunately, we can't stay any longer. So we will leave it to you to direct them. We have a lot to do before these armies arrive. I will arrive at the rendezvous point soon after nightfall tomorrow. Farewell."

Chapter 75

Harkell and Danton cantered back along the stream path enjoying the afternoon sun, glad to be on their way once more. White and yellow wildflowers grew along the bank of the stream between weeping willows swaying over the water. Oaks and sycamores grew to their left, their overhanging branches dappling the sunlight from time to time.

Suddenly, an arrow speared out of the trees and lodged in Harkell's saddle brow.

"Shield!" yelled Harkell. "We're under attack."

Even as he looked across, Danton toppled from his saddle, an arrow in his shoulder. For a moment, a haze of aqua flickered in the air around him but then extinguished as Danton hit the ground. Two men jumped from the trees and held him down. With no gap between the men and himself, Danton couldn't raise his shield, even if he were in any condition to do so.

"For the forest guardian's sake, help us!" shouted Harkell, hoping woodfolk were nearby.

He yanked his horse to a halt and threw himself into the fray, drawing his sword from its scabbard as he jumped. He drove the blade into the ribs of the nearest assailant then used his left hand to grab him by the hair and drag him off Danton, before stabbing the second man in the back and hauling his body to the left. Two more men appeared from the cover of the trees and began to close on him from the right. Four were coming at him from the left. They were dressed as refugees but moved with disciplined coordination.

Harkell stood over his prone friend and swept his sword in an arc, keeping them at bay. One man, more foolhardy than the rest, leapt at him. Harkell turned his wrist to intercept the man's blade. Their blades slid the length of each other until the swords were hilt to hilt. Harkell heaved sideways, quickly disengaging. Capitalizing on the sudden release of pressure against his blade, the other man swept his sword in a vicious cut aimed at Harkell's chest. Harkell ducked and drove forward and low, thrusting his blade into his assailant's stomach. Then he pushed the man away from him so that he did not land on Danton.

But now, Harkell had five men close upon him, with a ring of swords aimed at his throat. More were running up to join them from within the trees. He straightened to face them, knowing as he raised his sword, that he could not prevail against so many.

"What do you want?" he growled. He felt sure he knew, but needing to buy time, in the faint hope that there were some woodfolk nearby coming to their rescue.

Suddenly he saw a couple of the men's eyes flicker sideways. Following their line of sight, he caught a brief glimpse of a large tree branch in his peripheral vision before, in an explosion of pain, everything went black.

When he swam back to consciousness, the first thing Harkell saw was a pair of vibrant purple eyes watching him intently. At least Danton was alive, lying on the ground facing him. That was something. And someone had bandaged his shoulder. But his face was bruised and battered.

Harkell groaned. "Ugh. My head… You OK?"

Danton's eyes shifted suddenly left and then back again, which Harkell interpreted as a warning. As usual Danton was under-estimating him, he thought. If you wake to find yourself lying on your side with your hands bound behind your back and your ankles tied, you don't need to be warned to be careful with what you say. Then his groggy mind stopped being belligerent and started to work. He glanced quickly up to his right and saw a flash of light brown among the yellowy green foliage above him, before the eye movement sent a shooting pain through his head and he closed his eyes again.

After a minute or two of slow motion thought, he realised that he had seen the trees through a haze of yellow. Not good. He and Danton were being held within a sorcerer's yellow shield. Even if woodfolk were nearby, there wasn't much they could do to rescue them from within a shield.

Harkell took a couple of slow breaths and tried opening his eyes again. He brought his legs up to his chest but when he tried to sit up, his head jarred so much he was nearly sick.

As he eased back onto his side, Danton murmured, "Take it easy. Give yourself time to recover. You've been unconscious for a couple of hours. "

"YOU. Keep quiet… Awake, is he?" came a hard voice. "Let's get him upright and get started."

A rough hand dragged Harkell into a sitting position. His head swam so badly that, with a perverse sense of satisfaction, he vomited down the front of his captor. As the man sprang back in disgust, Harkell fell sideways again.

But in the short time he had been upright, he had had time to take in his surroundings. Within a yellow shield of about three yards in diameter, Danton and he were being guarded by two soldiers, one of whom was the shieldwielder. The soldiers both had knives and swords, but his own scabbard was empty; and within the shield, there were no loose rocks or stones that he could use as weapons. Outside the shield, a group of about ten men were gathered a short distance away and Harkell's frisky black mare was tethered to a nearby tree. There was no sign of the warhorse.

Harkell wondered at the other men being unshielded, but decided that either they had no other shieldwielders or at most one other, who was saving his concentration for taking over the guard duty later on. Presumably, the shieldwielder who held them captive was not powerful enough to produce a large enough shield to protect the whole troop.

When the soldier had wiped himself down, he returned and dragged Harkell upright again. Harkell's head thumped painfully but the nausea had passed. He had no intention of complying however, so allowed himself to topple in the other direction.

"Blast you, Captain!" growled the man, giving himself away as one of Jarand's soldiers, "Pull yourself together." The soldier shifted his attention to Danton and hauled him into an upright position with little effort and no care, shoving him to lean against a large rock. Danton let out a grunt of pain as his damaged shoulder was jarred. "You see?" the soldier said scathingly to Harkell. "Your friend can manage to sit upright."

"His friend hasn't been unconscious for the last two hours," said Danton acerbically. "Looks to me as though he's got concussion. I expect he can't keep his balance with his hands tied behind him."

The soldier scowled at him. "Don't think we're going to re-tie your hands in front, your lordship. Your powers as a sorcerer and elite guard are too well known." He wandered over to his companion and had a muffled discussion before approaching Harkell again. "Right. You're just a soldier, plain and simple, like the rest of us, Captain. In all your years in our prince's army, no one ever saw you use any kind of magic. So if it means you can sit up, I'll re-tie your hands in front of you. We need you to have your wits about you to answer our questions."

Keeping a wary eye on Danton, the soldier re-tied Harkell's hands and once more sat him up. This time, Harkell stayed upright, although he slumped forward to rest his head on his tied hands on his knees.

The soldier gave a snort of derision. "Don't know why we're even bothering to tie him up at all, Walkern. He's as weak as a kitten." He grabbed Harkell by the hair and pulled his head up. "You may have betrayed us, Captain, but I expected better of you than this."

"I have not betrayed you," Harkell murmured. "I am fighting to save you all."

"He's delirious, Fergan" said Walkern, still carefully holding his focus on the shield. "Get him some water. No point in belting him like you did his lordship. He'll just pass out again. Make sure those ropes are tight, though."

As Fergan yanked on the ropes around Harkell's wrists to check their pressure, Harkell croaked from a dry throat, "I don't see that there is any point in us trying to escape, with all those men waiting for us outside your shield." There was a strange emphasis on the words that made the soldier hesitate as he walked the few steps to his companion to fetch the water flask.

Then three things happened in quick succession: The ten men outside the shield dropped where they stood. With a grunt of effort, Harkell swept his bound hands from one side to the other, shouting "*Liefka*," which launched Danton on a stream of purple magic into the two soldiers at shoulder height, sending them sprawling. And in the moment that the shield winked out, woodfolk arrows speared from the branches above to fell the two soldiers before they could recover.

"*Never*," said Harkell, with grim satisfaction, "underestimate the son of a blacksmith!"

Danton rolled off the two dead men and scowled at Harkell, panting with pain. "Aagh! Blast you, Harkell! Fancy using me as a human spear when I've just had an arrow taken out of my shoulder." After taking a few moments to recover, he said grudgingly, "At least it was softer, landing on them than on the ground."

Harkell laughed. "Sorry. But you were the only thing I could use as a missile." Suddenly everything seemed to recede into the distance. Then, with detached interest, he watched the world tip sideways.

The next time he came around, Harkell found himself lying on the ground, unbound, with his cloak flung over him. Danton was sitting beside him, leaning against a rock, his left arm in a sling, his right hand wrapped around a mug of tea.

Danton leaned over him. "Back with us, are you, you mad bastard? You weren't recovered enough to pull a stunt like that." He smiled, then winced as the muscles pushed on a bruise on his cheek. "But I'm glad you did, even if it hurt. I wasn't enjoying their company…. Not one bit."

"I can see that. Did they hurt you anywhere else?"

Danton's answering shrug made him grunt with pain. "Let's just say they made good use of the arrow wound before they bound it."

"Bastards. They wouldn't have done that if they were from my company."

Danton drank from the mug and then handed it to Harkell. "Here. I'll hold you up while you drink."

This proved to be quite a challenge with only one arm in commission. In fact, Danton could do little more than lift Harkell's head while he drank. Harkell took a few sips then sank back down.

"Thanks." After a minute, Harkell frowned, "They don't seem to have persevered for long, do they? I know they hurt you... but not as much as they could have, if they were determined to make you talk… Strange."

Danton gave a little grin. "I was saved by my reputation."

"What? As an elite guard, trained to resist torture?"

Danton's grin broadened. "No. As Tarkyn's faithful follower. They made a few token gestures of belting me around and grinding the arrow tip into my shoulder but basically they knew that I would endure anything rather than betray Tarkyn."

"Hmph. Whereas I, with my uncertain loyalties, would be an easier target?"

"Yes. I think it was just as well that you were unconscious for most of the time."

For a couple of minutes, Harkell lay in silence. Then he sighed. "I have to ask this: who was it just as well for? Me or Tarkyn?"

Danton laughed, "I was wondering how long you would take. Both, if you really want to know; you, because you would have been hurt badly, Tarkyn, because he would have been distressed by you having to endure the torture." He patted Harkell's shoulder. "No, my friend, not because you might have betrayed him."

Harkell gave a little grunt. "Who's to know what a man may say under torture? I have no intention of ever succumbing, but I suspect many brave and honest men have been forced into betrayal against their intentions."

"True. On the other hand, you are a blacksmith's son…"

Harkell chuckled. "It was a bit melodramatic, wasn't it?"

"Perhaps. But it is nice to see you being proud of your heritage, when I gather you have spent a lot of your life concealing it."

"I had good reason to conceal it, but I think I may have thrown the ingot out with the dross. I stopped using those powers peculiar to blacksmiths; honing blades, lifting heavy objects and staying horses. Seeing Dad and Drakell, solid and true, hold their own with you and Tarkyn, rekindled my pride in my family."

"Hmm…My family's history goes back through generations of nobility. But it produced a man who sold his son for his own advancement. I take no pride in my family." The bleakness in Danton's voice softened as he added, "…at least, not in my sorcerer family."

"But your family also produced you, Danton," said Harkell gently. "And no one is more selfless or courageous in support of your liege and your fellow man. And from what I know of history and present day politics, Tarkyn's family is full of black sheep but no one could doubt that he is still proud of his heritage."

"Hmm. I hadn't thought of it that way." Suddenly Danton grinned, "We have come a long way, you and I, to reach the point where a blacksmith's son is trying to persuade a nobleman to be proud of his family." He gave Harkell a friendly pat on the shoulder. "I can't just switch pride back on, you know, but I will think on what you have said."

Harkell smiled, "Speaking of Tarkyn, we'd better get on with it." He raised himself carefully on one elbow and squinted around the little clearing. "Where have all Jarand's soldiers gone?"

"Hmm. Our bloodthirsty allies, not liking sorcerers at the best of times, were not impressed with the way we were treated. So they killed every one of them. They've dragged the bodies under that tree over there and covered them with branches for the time being. They want to know what, if anything, to do with them."

Harkell shrugged. "Just leave them there. Jarand's scouts will find them sooner or later."

"Will you be able to ride or should I go on ahead?"

"You can't travel alone with your arm in a sling and Jarand's soldiers in the area. And if you put your shield up, you'll be more conspicuous and it won't help you to get away from them if they surround you." Harkell took a deep breath and sat up. His head gave a huge throb and blurred his vision for a moment but then settled. "So far so good. Should be able to stay in the saddle."

Danton smiled at him. "I don't know what use you think you'll be, if we are attacked by Jarand's men."

Harkell grinned back, "Moral support." He held out his hand, "Right then. Give me a hand up." With a surge, he stood up. The treeline seemed to bulge towards him as his head throbbed with pain. He swayed on his feet, held upright only by Danton's grip on his arm. "Ooh. This is not good. I need a horse in a hurry."

An older woodman appeared out of nowhere, leading the great warhorse.

Harkell raised his eyebrows in surprise, "Where did this old fellow come from?" Seeing the woodman scowl, he clarified hurriedly, "I meant the horse. He wasn't here last time I came round. I am Harkell."

Mollified, the woodman replied, "He is an experienced campaigner. He cantered off when Danton was dragged off him, but waited nearby. When only you two were left alive in the clearing, he returned. I am Wind Gust."

The pain in Harkell's head had reduced to a steady throb but he wasn't looking forward to the jolt of getting up into the saddle. "Pleased to meet you. Do you think, if I get my left foot up into the stirrup, you and Danton could heave me up onto the horse? I'll do what I can to help."

"Just a minute," said Danton. "I have an idea. Wind Gust, could you just steady Harkell so that I can let go?"

Once Wind Gust had stepped up to Harkell and held him propped against the horse's flank, Danton waved his hand and intoned "*Ka liefka.*" The woodman started backwards, as Harkell rose into the air on the end of an aqua stream of light and was deposited effortlessly onto the warhorse's back.

"Ah. That feels better. Thanks." Harkell grimaced. "Perhaps we had better see whether some woodfolk will scout for us so that we can avoid further ambushes. I couldn't fight off a small brown rat at the moment. What do you think, Wind Gust?"

"I agree. Danton has explained the urgent need for you to return to our forest guardian's side. We will ensure your safe passage from here on."

Muttering, "*Ma Liefka,*" Danton lifted himself on to the frisky black mare who took immediate exception to such unorthodox behaviour and skittered wildly across the clearing as Danton grappled to gain control of the reins one-handed.

Harkell murmured, "*Tirosh,*" and the mare quietened, while Danton sorted himself out.

Danton smiled. "Thanks Harkell, blacksmith's son."

The sun was below the horizon as the woodfolk handed up their weapons, food and water for the journey, with assurances that they would safeguard the two sorcerers until they reached Tarkyn. When everything was stowed, Harkell released the staying spell on the frisky mare and they resumed their journey.

Chapter 76

Harkell and Danton plodded through the darkness, for hour upon hour, eating and drinking as they rode, since to dismount would have cost more energy than it was worth. At one point, an owl swooped across their path before disappearing into the trees.

"Tarkyn, do you suppose?" asked Danton, with a faint stirring of interest after hours of stolid endurance. "It would be nice to think he was looking out for us."

Harkell grunted, "It would, but he has a lot on his mind at the moment."

"How much longer, do you think? My hand is going numb holding the reins and my shoulder is getting sorer and sorer."

"We can stop again if you like. Rest your hand and the horses. Your mare is so tired now that I won't even need my little spell."

"How's your head?"

"Not too bad. Just a dull ache, unless the horse stumbles. But he's pretty sure-footed, even in the dark…I'm not sure how far the home guard were planning to travel today but I would say we have at least another hour, maybe two before we reach them."

Suddenly, in the distance, they heard the sound of several horses approaching. Soon afterwards, they could see a silvery light through the trees coming towards them around the bend in their trail.

"Stars! I hope the woodfolk are guarding us as they said they would," muttered Danton.

They pulled their horses into the shadows of the trees and picked their way through overhanging branches until they were screened from the path. But despite their efforts at concealment, the approaching horses pulled up on the track just where they had left the road. Overhead an owl screeched and moments later, Tarkyn pushed through the brush, with Midnight perched in front of him and an orb of light hovering above him.

He beamed at them. "Hello you two. I am so pleased to see you, even if you do look a sorry sight. Come on out onto the road. We can't all fit in here between the trees. A few of us are here."

Harkell and Danton smiled with relief. Harkell relaxed so much, he swayed in the saddle and had to stop himself from falling.

Once they were back on the track, Drakell and Borovar helped each of them to dismount and then almost carried them to a comfortable spot on the ground where they could lean against trees, while the others set out food and lit a fire close to them at the side of the track.

"Danton," said Tarkyn, full of energy, "Navira sends her love and is sorry she couldn't come because she has to work with Stormaway and Caroman on perfecting the spells they are going to use. And Harkell, Kayama would have come but your children were on edge so she thought she should stay with them. She too sends her love."

Harkell leant his head against the tree while he waited for the hammering to stop. "Thank you for coming. I can't tell you how glad we are to see you. It's been a long ride."

Danton smiled up at Tarkyn, "We would have made it and we still will, but it is great to see you all. How long do we have, before we have to get back on the road?"

"As long as you need. If we have to, we can stay the night here and leave in the morning. Provided we leave early, we will catch the others before they arrive at the Dry Mile. There is, however, a cost." The prince stepped aside to reveal Summer Rain coming towards them. "Summer Rain is about to ply you both with one of her tonics before examining you. And then you must endure me healing you."

Danton frowned, "But what about your own strength?" He accepted a small bottle from the woodfolk healer and screwed up his face as he gulped down an evil looking green potion. After a shudder, he continued, "You mustn't jeopardize that for us if you can't replenish it. You will need everything you have, to deal with your brothers."

"I also need you two. And you should know by now, I will not willingly let anyone suffer on my behalf." Tarkyn smiled at them. "My strength will replenish itself, just as yours will, without using a tree. Besides, would either of you stand by and let your friends suffer, if you could do something about it? I think not."

"Of course you wouldn't," said Rainstorm, handing them freshly brewed cups of tea. "And, let's face it, you can't expect Tarkyn to have a lower set of standards than you."

Harkell spluttered with laughter then wished he hadn't, as his head gave an almighty throb. He drew in a sharp breath and Rainstorm deftly caught his cup as it tipped out of his hand.

"Lie him down flat on the ground," ordered Summer Rain. "No more nonsense, Tarkyn. He is seriously injured, if he is still struggling to stay conscious after all these hours."

"I'm not," protested Harkell. "I'm just tired and my head hurts and my coordination is a bit wonky."

"And you were hit by a log the size of my leg," added Danton. "Now be quiet and let them get on with it."

"Yes sir," Harkell gave a little grin before closing his eyes.

Between them, Tarkyn and Summer Rain found a hair line fracture in Harkell's skull and an area of bruising on his brain that could have taken weeks, if not months, to fully repair without Tarkyn's intervention. He was lucky to have survived at all. Danton's injuries were less serious but his gouged shoulder wound and the bruising on his face horrified the little group gathered around him and unfortunately reinforced the woodfolks' long held belief in sorcerers' propensity for cruelty.

Tarkyn straightened up and stretched. "There, my friends. Now you can regale us with your adventures."

"Thanks." Harkell gave a quizzical little smile. "Perhaps in a while… If you look behind you, Tarkyn, you will find that you have gained quite an audience."

Tarkyn turned on his heel to find a cluster of forty or more unknown woodfolk standing in a semi-circle, watching him. Any concern he might have felt was allayed by a quick glance at Rainstorm, who was grinning hugely.

"Good evening," he said quietly to the gathered woodfolk. "I am Tarkyn."

A rather portly woodman nodded at him. "Good evening, Guardian." He waved his hand around him, "We are the woodfolk of the south west forests and we wished to thank you for repairing the fire's damage and for bringing the might of the forest to bear on the encroaching farmlands of the sorcerers. We were also interested to watch you use your healing powers on your fellow sorcerers. I am Dust Storm."

"Once the need was pointed out," said an equally portly woodwoman, whose bulk made Tarkyn wonder how such tubby woodfolk managed to move through the trees, "we protected Danton and Harkell and will keep watch for you tonight so that all of your party may sleep undisturbed. We can provide you with three good flasks of mountainfolk wine and more food as you require. I am Barking Deer."

"In return," continued Dust Storm, "we ask that we may share your firesite and get to know the legendary guardian of the forest. It would be a story we could pass down to our children."

Barking Deer glanced at the bulk of Borovar, "Of course we would like to catch up with our kin, but we would also be pleased to talk with your sorcerer companions." Suddenly a smile lit her face that made her look twenty years younger. "…and are deliciously apprehensive at the prospect."

This produced a ripple of laughter that melted the constraint of Tarkyn's companions.

"You are the first woodfolk to have actively sought the chance to talk to sorcerers. So we would be honoured to share our firesite with you, especially since it is within the area of the forest that you inhabit." Tarkyn waved a welcoming arm. "Please join us."

As the impromptu party progressed into the early hours of the morning, Danton and Harkell subsided quietly against a tree and went to sleep, happily exhausted.

Chapter 77

Tarkyn's small rescue party caught up with the bulk of the home guard at noon and by late afternoon, tired and hungry, the last of Tarkyn's home guard reached their new location, less than a mile from the eastern edge of the Dry Mile. Several had ridden Orolan's horses to arrive ahead of time so that they could prepare shelters and hunt for the evening's meal. Time was short, energy was limited and everyone knew they would have to spend many hours of the night making preparations.

By Stormaway's calculations, neither army would arrive until sometime in the morning of the following day, but the home guard needed time, under cover of darkness, to implement the first phases of their plan, without hindrance from scouts or vanguards.

The woodfolk used the cooking fire to burn branches from flowering shrubs to produce ash. As soon as dinner was over, Harkell and Drakell headed off northeast to the rendezvous point where they would meet the refugee sorcerers while woodfolk combined the ash with flowers and bark from the same shrubs and, under cover of darkness, left the mixture in small piles around the perimeter of each side of the battlefield, before withdrawing to the cover of the forest.

When the darkness had deepened, eight sorcerers rode across the exposure of the Dry Mile to reach the western side of the proposed battlefield. Eight woodfolk accompanied them so that the sorcerers could communicate with each other through the woodfolk's mindtalking. Waterstone, with his fear of horses, was not among them.

Rainstorm, forever game but unused to horses, clung like a limpet to Danton, while Ancient Oak rode with practised ease mounted in front of Navira. Up ahead of them on the great warhorse, Twig Snap held tightly to Borovar, more because she loved him than because she needed to.

The horses cantered westward along the length of the dry mile unchallenged, before finding shelter in the trees and shrubbery that grew along either side of the western part of the stream. Sorcerers and woodfolk drew up and waited for longer than Tarkyn found comfortable, to see whether any unseen patrols on either side of the valley raised the alarm.

No sudden light or sound split the night. Only the occasional rustling of nocturnal creatures disturbed the silence. Finally, the woodfolk, far more sensitive in both hearing and vision than the sorcerers, conferred and agreed that the coast as clear.

"Let's go then," murmured Rainstorm. "No unknown sorcerers within earshot."

Danton clapped him on the knee, "Thanks."

"We will leave two hundred yards at this end," said Tarkyn, "because none of the soldiers will be prepared to venture within that range of any dense foliage."

Stormaway took over, "So, we want the first pair stationed at the two hundred yard mark and then a pair at every hundred and fifty yards after that. Tarkyn and I will lead so that I can position each pair as I go."

Navira, and Danton were the first to take up position, followed soon afterwards by Caroman, with Falling Branch behind him, and Borovar. Then Stormaway waited with Kayama five hundred yards out from cover until Tarquin and Rena rode past them to their designated position. When he was sure all were ready, Stormaway murmured an instruction to Summer Rain seated behind him, who transmitted it to the other woodfolk.

Suddenly two bright streams of magic flared on the western end of their line. Navira's bronze and Danton's aqua shafts of light traced a thirty yard diameter circle on the ground, twining round and round each other as their paths crossed. Moments later, the black of Caroman's magic entwined with the peacock blue of Borovar's as they inscribed a similar circle. Closer to the east, Tarkyn's bronze magic paired up with Rena's cornflower blue while Stormaway's green magic joined with Kayama's dusky pink.

The harsh twanging of dissonant magics thrummed through the air, forcing the woodfolk to hold their ears. The intensity increased for several minutes until the ground was trembling under their feet. Then suddenly, aqua and bronze winked out, quickly followed by black and peacock blue, green and pink and lastly bronze and cornflower blue. Their ears rang so much in the aftermath that, for a while, no one could hear whether their work had drawn any unwanted attention.

When the quiet of the night returned, each pair of sorcerers moved fifty yards further out from the edge of the scrub and repeated their performance. Slowly, a huge, golden moon rose above the trees in the east, brightening the scene and sending long shadows along the Dry Mile.

"How much longer will this take?" asked Autumn Leaves from behind Tarkyn. "We could be seen out in the open like this under such a bright moon."

"Not much longer. Maybe twenty minutes, half an hour. Then we ride for home. Don't worry. No one could see enough in this light from a distance to know you weren't sorcerers, anyway."

Autumn Leaves grunted, "That's not the point."

"No. The point is that you feel exposed out in the open. I know it's hard." Tarkyn smiled over his shoulder, "Thanks for coming."

When Harkell and Drakell and their squad of two hundred refugee sorcerers emerged into the open space of the Dry Mile, they could see in the distance, the brilliant colours of sorcerer power rays on the western end of the dry mile, but not the riders.

Harkell turned to them. "See the colours? Both Prince Tarkyn and Princess Navira are working with other sorcerers to reduce the width of the battle front by making the western end untenable for an unimpeded charge."

Twice more, the night flared with colour until a length of six hundred metres had areas of loosened earth every twenty yards where men and horses would sink deeply enough to discourage their forward movement but not deeply enough to smother them.

Harkell gathered the refugee sorcerers around him to issue instructions. Much to his relief, the group of two hundred was more disciplined than the crowd had been at the campsite. "We will focus our efforts from two hundred yards from the eastern edge where we are now, across a distance of about eight hundred yards… Keep your eyes peeled. Sooner or later, advance scouts will be arriving in the area, if they are not here already. Their job is not to attack but to report. However, if you come face to face with one, he may attack to escape. So, be alert."

As Harkell explained the task, puzzled looks passed between the sorcerers but they had seen the wonder of Tarkyn's power transforming sticks into trees so they did not demur. Harkell divided them into groups, and dispersed them around the perimeter of both armies' predicted positions. He had no way of telling exactly where the armies would position themselves but he assumed that neither would concede the advantage of higher ground, which meant that the gap between them would occur along the middle of the valley. He estimated that the troops would be drawn up, ready to attack, about four hundred yards apart. For the wizards' plan to work, Tarkyn had to find a way to manoeuvre the royal brothers away from the bulk of their respective armies and into that four hundred yard gap.

Harkell directed two thirds of the refugee sorcerers to scrape shallow furrows along the perimeter while the rest gathered the mixture of bark, flowers and ash from the piles left by the woodfolk and scattered it along the shallow ditches. When they had finished, they stomped on the filled furrows and scuffed them to make them less noticeable. It was a long job, creating nearly four miles of filled furrows, but Harkell's coordination combined with the sorcerers' diligence meant that it was completed well before day break.

When they had finished, Harkell gathered them together, "Drakell and I thank you, Prince Tarkyn thanks you and with any luck, if all goes according to plan, the whole of Eskuzor will acknowledge your efforts tonight. I know it is a long walk back to your campsite but when you return, you will find food and drink waiting for you. We don't expect either army to arrive for several hours yet, so try to get some sleep. Be wary if you venture close to the battle. There will be scouts from both sides in the area. Those of us who remain here will watch your backs and ensure that no advance scouts follow you. Once again, our thanks."

"Good luck," said Trey, speaking for them all. "It is no easy task that you have set yourselves. Our hopes and the hopes of Eskuzor ride with you."

The sorcerers bid a weary farewell and trudged up the northern slope and from there, north east into the forest towards their campsite.

Chapter 78

Just after midnight, having finished their task, Tarkyn and Autumn Leaves, accompanied by the other seven horses and their riders, rode back into the trees a short distance from the firesite where String and Bean were waiting to take charge of the horses.

"Are you sure you'll be all right with these horses?" Tarkyn asked, as he dismounted.

Bean took the reins from his grasp with easy competence. "Stop worrying, Sire. String and I have led pack horses through the mountains for years… and ridden them from time to time."

"Yeah," agreed String. "Not too much we don't know about horses. You leave them to us. You have plenty else to worry about."

"Like this little nonsense," said Tarkyn lightly, scooping up Midnight who had been waiting with String and Bean for his return. "And were you good for your honorary uncles?" he asked his little ward, matching images to words.

Midnight nodded and, tapping Tarkyn on the chest to make sure he was looking, showed him yet another carved animal of indeterminate species that String had carved for him.

Tarkyn resisted the temptation to ask String what it was, but the trapper responded as though he had spoken his thoughts aloud, "It is a silver fox. Colour's wrong, of course, but the general shape is right."

Tarkyn grinned, "Yes, in a very general sort of way. Thanks. See you in the morning."

The group walked back along a circuitous route to the firesite, with the woodfolk among them making sure that their footprints were obliterated. When they reached the firesite, they found that most people had already gone to bed.

"All went well?" asked Waterstone, although he already knew through mind talking that it had.

Gradually, one by one, people wandered off to bed down for the night until only Tarkyn, Waterstone and Lapping Water were left sitting by the fire. Around them, towering oaks loomed against a star-studded sky, the fire casting long shadows of the people seated around it across the ground and up into the lower branches of the trees.

Midnight was lying in Tarkyn's lap leaning into his shoulder but his eyes were alert, watching every movement that Lapping Water and Waterstone made. Sparrow, on the other hand, was fast asleep.

Waterstone leaned forward, careful not to disturb Sparrow and pushed a log further into the fire. "I suppose we should be heading off too, young Tarkyn. It's after midnight and we have a big day ahead of us."

Tarkyn nodded but showed no inclination to move.

Lapping Water watched him for a minute. "You're worried, aren't you? Midnight can feel it. That's why he can't settle."

Tarkyn was just debating whether, as their leader, he should allow his uncertainty to show, when Waterstone cut across his thoughts. "Tarkyn, you don't have to be strong all the time, least of all with us two. Talk to us now so that you can be strong later." Waterstone's mouth quirked. "We can cope, you know. We're used to being leaders too. All woodfolk are."

Tarkyn bent over his little ward and gave him a squeeze. "You're a traitorous little ratbag, Midnight, giving me away like that." He did not translate for Midnight, who snuggled closer in response to the hug. Finally Tarkyn heaved a sigh and looked up. "Of course I'm worried. Thousands of men, armed to the teeth, converging on us from all sides. A truly bizarre plan that has never been tried before and my two brothers who, even if we do succeed in forcing them to negotiate, are just as likely to turn around and renege on any agreement in a week's time."

"And you," added Waterstone. "standing in the midst of thousands of sorcerers who, to show their loyalty to Kosar and Jarand, will be crying out for your blood,"

Tarkyn's stomach lurched even as he gave a wry smile. "It's not that I fear for my life. I just dread the moment when I walk out into that sea of derision. Some men may have mellowed but most will follow their princes' lead. I had enough jeering from the mountainfolk. I don't look forward to it from sorcerers."

Suddenly the shadows to the east wavered and reformed and a quiet voice hissed, "Remember us, Tarkyn. Keep your mind focused on all those who support you." Four translucent figures hung in the air beyond the ring of firelight. As Tarkyn made to rise, Grass Snake waved his hand, "Stay where you are. Don't disturb Midnight."

Despite Grass Snake's words, Tarkyn lifted Midnight off his knee and stood up. "Thank you, Guardians of the Past, but I prefer to stand, both to give you your due and to meet you eye to eye." He smiled, "Besides, Midnight uses my example to learn how to behave."

Midnight stood in close to Tarkyn's side and wrapped his arm so tightly around his guardian's leg that Tarkyn had to move his other foot to keep his balance. Tarkyn laughed, "Midnight, you're going to drag me over." He gently disengaged him and placed his arm across the little boy's shoulders, sending him a message that he was safe and to be brave.

Midnight glanced up at him before returning his gaze to the forest guardians of the past and giving them a solemn wave.

The four guardians did not unbend enough to wave back but they inclined their heads and smiled their acknowledgement.

"Midnight, we welcome you into our company," said Nightwind, the woodwoman guardian. "You are a true forest guardian just as Tarkyn is… and we were. You have endured more than any of us and yet you have chosen to use your strength with good will. We are honoured to have you amongst us."

Midnight's face reddened. Clearly the guardians were able to communicate with him, in the same way that Tarkyn was. The little boy dropped his eyes to his feet and busied himself with scuffing a furrow in the dirt with his toe. A squeeze on his shoulder and an instruction made him glance at Tarkyn. Then, taking a deep breath, Midnight straightened up, squared his shoulders and brought his gaze up to meet the guardians' eyes.

Suddenly the four guardians smiled.

"What did he say?" asked Waterstone.

"He thanked them, then asked how it felt to have light pouring through them".

Lapping Water grinned but said nothing. Tarkyn met her eyes and smiled, before Moridan Tamadil, Tarkyn's forest guardian ancestor, regained his attention, "Tarkyn, I am pleased to see that your friendship with Waterstone has prospered."

"And I, that your path with Lapping Water has remained steadfast," murmured Nightwind.

"We do not know why two forest guardians exist at the same time," continued Windchange Treewarden, the wizard guardian, "but the appearance of forest guardians has always been in a time of need. Eskuzor needs you, Tarkyn, and you needed a forest guardian to save you. So perhaps that may be part of the reason."

"But it is more than that. Tomorrow you strive to deal with twenty thousand men," Moridan grimaced, "and worse than that, two stubborn princes. We know you wish to protect Midnight and do not want to abuse his trust. But do not exclude him. He has proved himself more than once. Allow him to use his strength. After all, you know that in all the world, he would rather be by your side."

As Tarkyn opened his mouth to protest, Grass Snake put up a hand to forestall him. "Tomorrow, two forest guardians will serve the interests of Eskuzor better than one," he hissed. "Do not let your care for one stand in the way of your duty to all."

Tarkyn's eyes narrowed. "Do not presume to dictate my priorities. I never forget my duty. But caring for one is part of taking responsibility for all… and I will find a way to do both where I can." The prince took a deep breath to calm himself. "That said, I accept your point that Midnight should not be sidelined as I had first intended. Now that I think about it, Stormaway excluded Midnight from their attempts to heal me and only Midnight's quiet, unsupported determination saved me. He should not be forced to act alone again." Tarkyn looked down at the little boy standing as close to him as he would allow, and stroked his head. "You are right. Midnight is strong. He is easily frightened but he holds his own despite his fear. I will align Midnight's powers with mine… I can mind link through his shield as easily as through my own, so that will provide added protection and flexibility. Plus he can help me to control the horses."

Midnight raised his head and beamed at Tarkyn. Suddenly Tarkyn felt as though a great weight had shifted from his shoulders. He allowed himself to acknowledge that acting alone tomorrow would have taxed his ingenuity, strength and luck to their limits. For the first time since the plan had been devised, Tarkyn felt the muscles in his shoulders and neck relax as the first faint hope blossomed that they might actually succeed.

Tarkyn smiled back then looked up to thank the forest guardians of the past. But the words died on his lips; only the long black shadows cast by the fire greeted him. The guardians were gone.

Chapter 79

The morning of the battle dawned dull and overcast. West Wandering was full of Jarand's men. Officers had commandeered the two inns and squads of soldiers patrolled the streets, laughing and talking loudly, full of uneasy bravura in anticipation of the upcoming battle. Window boxes on the inns and cottages overflowed with a riot of colour while neat front lawns had burgeoned into tangled wildernesses of long grasses and sprawling bushes under the auspices of the forest's power.

A vanguard had worked hard to clear straying vines, unexpected bushes and one large willow tree from the road that entered the village from the southwest. The fruits of their labour were piled on either side of the road on the outskirts of the village. Even the relatively small numbers of the vanguard had churned up the mud that was a legacy of the wizards' storm. By the time the main body of the army tramped through the village in a few hours' time, the roads would be close to impassable.

The rampant growth had created corridors of bushland right across the west of Eskuzor providing cover for birds, animals and even, if they desired to travel so close to sorcerers, woodfolk.

Deep within the tangled shrubbery that marked the stream's course, six sorcerer refugees from Lord Tolward's estate watched an old couple wander up the street, nodding vaguely at passing soldiers. The old man, although strongly built, was too old to be pressed into service as a soldier but walked hunched over, apparently against the bitter wind. His wife was unremarkable except that, when she looked up, it could be seen that she had no eyebrows.

"I hope these liegemen of Lord Tolward's who've been drafted in Jarand's army can read," grumbled Sorath. "Not much point in going to all this trouble to pass them a note if they can't."

"No dear. But I believe they are a close-knit community on Lord Tolward's estate so they will all know most things about each other; certainly who does and doesn't read." She placed a reassuring hand on his arm as they stopped outside a baker's shop. "Besides, there are over thirty of them, aren't there dear? Most unlikely that there's not a reader amongst them…and whoever we hand the notes to, will at least recognise it as writing and hand it on to a friend to decipher."

"Hmph. As long as they don't hand it on to one of Jarand's captains instead."

Thraya decided that she had pandered enough to Sorath's determined pessimism, so ignored this little sally. Instead she pointed to same freshly baked rounded fruit loaves displayed in the baker's window. "These look perfect, dear. We can hand these to the soldiers as they pass with the note pinned onto the bottom of them."

Sorath glanced around nervously, "Shh. Keep your voice down."

"No one is close enough to hear but they are close enough to see you looking suspicious. So straighten up and try to look casual. In we go." So saying, Thraya opened the door of the bakery and stepped inside, firmly guiding her spouse beside her.

Three hours later, the rest of Jarand's army came into view, marching four abreast. The village's high road was lined with townsfolk waving, wishing the soldiers good health and safe return, throwing the odd flower or quickly handing them pieces of fruit or buns as they passed. A particular squad of soldiers must have been pressed from West Wandering because several villagers became teary and the incidence of passed fruit and bread increased noticeably as they passed down the road.

Sorath and Thraya took up a position closer to the south western edge of the village where the scrub along the creek came up close to the road. Hidden in the bushes, Tolward's refugees waited in silence, watching each approaching group of soldiers intently. After ten minutes, the smiles on Sorath and Thraya's faces were becoming fixed and they were becoming tired of waving. Occasionally they saw a soldier or officer they knew from association with Harkell but at these times they kept their heads down and pretended to be involved in repacking theirs bags. The danger of recognition as Harkell's hunted relatives was minimal with the soldiers now focussed on an imminent battle. Besides, the troops were tired after hours of marching and it was taking all their concentration to keep upright in the increasingly slippery mud.

Suddenly a voice from behind the bushes exclaimed, "There! That group just rounding the bend now. The first of them is young Jokan. See the skinny one with straggly brown hair. The bloke next to him is one of ours too. See him? He's got red hair and freckles."

"What about the men beside and behind them?" hissed Sorath.

"Nah. The other two in their row, I don't know…but they're all ours, right across the rows for the next five, no six… wait 'til they get clear of the bend…seven rows."

Sorath took a deep breath. "Right, thanks. Come on Thraya. This is it. Leave the first two soldiers. Then give a loaf to the nearest soldier in the next four rows."

As Tolward's soldiers came abreast of them, Sorath thrust a loaf into the hands of a soldier behind Jokan. Thraya gave one to the soldier in the next row but the second loaf was bumped out of her hand as the soldier passed. She scrabbled to pick it up and gave it a hasty wipe before thrusting it into the hands of the closest soldier in the sixth row of soldiers. She let out a relieved breath and looked at Sorath who grinned at her, empty-handed.

"Well done, my dear. You just made it," he said. "So, we have done what we could. Four loaves with the same message are now amongst Tolward's conscripts. Let us hope that they read them and follow the instruction, bizarre as it may seem to them."

Thraya nodded as she waved at a random group of soldiers who were now marching towards them. "What a rush! After all that waiting, there were only seconds to deliver the loaves as they passed."

Once clear of the village, the army broke for lunch before the final ten mile push to the battlefield. The officers had no intention of setting up their army to fight on empty stomachs, if circumstances allowed otherwise.

The men from Tolward's holding gathered in a small group to eat their field rations. They were all aware that not only did they have fruit loaf to add to their rations but that they had been contacted surreptitiously. Very casually, as they ate, the four messages passed from hand to hand. In fact, only three of the conscripts couldn't read and they were told the contents of the message orally when no other soldiers were in earshot. For each of them, the reaction was the same. The message firstly lit their eyes with hope but left them bemused by the end. It read:

When a wizardess appears over Kosar's troops encased in an aqua shield, tell everyone around you that she is the Wizardess from the Forest of Yesterday, Today and Tomorrow, otherwise known as the Lost Forest.

With thanks,

Winguard and Edelweiss's <u>independent</u> healer.

Jakon shook his head, "Is it in code or a straight message, do you think?"

Rostin a timid but clever young farmhand whose friends had protected him through the worst of their training, answered, "The signature line is more or less in code… but the rest… I don't know. It seems like a straight forward instruction to me… just weird." He shrugged, "Not too surprising it's weird, if there's a wizard involved."

"So, we take it straight?"

Rostin nodded, "I think so. Now we'd better get rid of the evidence."

A few minutes later, a patch of flame flared slightly as Jakon filled their pannikins with tea from a huge kettle on the communal fire.

CHAPTER 80

Tarkyn sat in the fork of a tree near the eastern end of the valley, wearing his green beautifully crafted surcoat, emblazoned with his coat of arms. Waterstone and Midnight sat on either side of him, beneath his eagle perched on the bough above, watching as Kosar's army topped the rise and advanced into the Valley of the Dry Mile.

The king cut a fine figure, riding at the head of his troops on a black charger, his standard waving and slapping above him in the stiff breeze. He was dressed in the same blue with red trim as his soldiers, but wore a broad sash of deeper blue across his chest, emblazoned in silver with his coat of arms. His wizard and senior officers rode one horse length behind him, but as he realised that his brother's army had not yet arrived, he allowed them to draw abreast of him.

The soldiers lined up along the full length of the Dry Mile, cavalry at the front, row upon row of foot soldiers at the rear. A few minutes later, a scout galloped in from the south west. After a short conference with the scout, officers ordered the troops to stay in position but to take their ease and to eat a modest lunch. At the rear of the field, men carried supplies from the wagons positioned out of sight behind the crest of the hill, to erect and furnish a command tent. As soon as it was ready, the king and his senior officers withdrew to confer within.

Tarkyn noted this with some misgiving. If Kosar stayed within the command tent, it would be even more difficult to force him into the no man's land between the two armies' positions.

Tarkyn watched as young cavalry officers, eager and nervous before the anticipated battle, were dispatched to explore the lower ground and the southern slopes before Jarand's troops arrived. Two young lieutenants, with more spirit than sense, raced each other ahead of the others, down the westerly end of the slope. One was mounted on a flashy young stallion that was too strong for him and strained at the bit, trying to bolt after hours of slow plodding. The other rode an older mare that was merely obeying her master as she galloped down the slope.

As they neared the bottom of the slope, the stallion surged ahead and careered headlong into one of the dirt pits, foundering up to his chest in loose soil. The stallion's rider sailed straight over his head and disappeared ignominiously into the dirt, to come up spluttering and flailing his arms. The mare, too close behind to stop, plunged into the pit, her rider hauling her sideways to save her from barrelling into the stallion. He managed to keep his seat but found himself struggling to control his frightened mare, also up to her chest in loose dirt and dangerously close to the panic-stricken stallion that was thrashing and rearing, trying to free himself from soil that pressed in on him from all sides.

Realising that the horses were in imminent danger of injuring themselves and their riders, Tarkyn sent waves of calm followed by images of how to escape from the pit. To the amazement of onlookers, the stallion gradually stopped thrashing and the mare stopped rolling her eyes and jabbing at the bit. For several moments they stood trembling, until even that subsided.

Slowly, they pushed their way through the loosened dirt until their hooves hit the firm edge of the pit. Then each of them bunched their hindquarters and reared upwards until their front hooves found purchase on firm ground. But from a standing start, it was too high for them to jump out. The mare's rider swung out of the saddle onto the solid ground and joined the willing hands that grabbed the horses' bridles, girths and saddles to pull from the front while other soldiers jumped into the pit to push from behind until finally, both horses struggled back onto firm ground and stood there panting, heads bowed.

Colonel Argyve sent Captain Harmon to give the two riders and their gathered comrades a dressing down, which resulted in a more decorous exploration of the lower reaches of the battleground. Now working methodically, they had soon mapped the extent of the destabilized areas that Tarkyn's sorcerers had created the night before.

Waterstone relayed a message that woodfolk had spotted Jarand's advance scouts observing the activities of Kosar's troops.

"So both sides will know about our dirt pits now," murmured Tarkyn. He nodded in the direction of Kosar's troops. "See? They are already contracting the bulk of their troops to this end of the Dry Mile and leaving only enough on the western end to guard their flank in the gaps between the dirt pits."

"It seems strange, doesn't it, that they just sit there waiting for the other army?"

Tarkyn shrugged. "If Kosar's troops advanced further down into the valley, they would be on lower ground and would have to fight uphill. If they advance further to the top of the southern ridge, they would be facing forest and one small road along which Jarand's troops are currently marching. This would give Kosar's troops a decided advantage, except that Jarand would simply withdraw his troops and refuse to engage…and they both now wish this confrontation to take place. So that would serve neither of their ends."

Waterstone gave a snort of disgust. "It's just a bloody game to them."

"Yes, it is. But a very serious game, especially for all those men down there who may be maimed or killed."

The arrival of a scout caused a stirring in the ranks of Kosar's men. Minutes later, the king and his officers emerged from their command post, remounted and rode to the front of the massed men, in a deliberate display of strength. Orders rippled through the army to stand ready as the first of Jarand's soldiers topped the rise.

In a remarkably short time, the two armies stood facing each other, four hundred yards apart. Although Jarand's men also wore red and blue, red was the predominant colour on their uniforms, so from a distance, it appeared that a red army was facing a blue one. At the head of his troops, Prince Jarand sat on a black charger that could have been the twin of his brother's. He too wore the uniform of his men, a deep red sash bearing his coat of arms crossing his chest.

A word of command rang through the air and slowly, in tight order, the armies began to close on each other. The troopers held their horses on tight reins and advanced carefully until only two hundred yards separated the front ranks. Neither army wished to advance more quickly than the other, since that would force them to attack uphill.

Unseen by either army, Tarkyn took a deep breath. "Time to go, I think."

Alert to his intention, his eagle swooped down from the branch above and landed firmly on his left shoulder, settling herself in by ruffling her feathers and preening a few strands of his long dark hair. Tarkyn rolled his eyes at Waterstone. "I would prefer to walk unimpeded into the breach between my brothers, but she is impervious to my will."

Despite his tension, Waterstone managed a small smile. "Never mind. She will lend you gravitas; a little quirky I will admit, but gravitas none the less…"

"Hmm… Whereas little one here will make me look like an uncle taking a stroll in a park."

Waterstone put his head on one side as he considered the trio. After a moment, he said, "Think of it as symbolic. The forest guardian accompanied by a child representing the people he protects and by an eagle representing the wilderness he protects."

Tarkyn gave a grunt of laughter. "Very good, Waterstone. That thought may actually help me to ground myself." He gave the woodman a pat on the back. "See you."

Swinging Midnight onto his right hip, Tarkyn murmured, *"Ma liefka,"* and launched himself forward into the space beneath the branches. As soon as he had drifted clear of the tree trunk, he waved his shield into place around the three of them, hoping devoutly that the eagle didn't take fright at some point and try to fly off through his shield. As he floated out beyond the cover of the trees and landed in plain view, ripples of recognition spread through both armies. Horses jabbed at their bits and stamped their hooves as their riders reacted in surprise.

Contrary to Tarkyn's fear, no one jeered. After word of his presence had rippled through the ranks, it was as though everyone waited with baited breath.

With every eye on him, Tarkyn expanded his shield forward, creating a long narrow tube down which he could walk unimpeded. Now, even if a shieldwielder placed a shield over his, he could still reach the point between his two brothers. He swung Midnight down to stand beside him and took hold of his hand. Unhurriedly, he walked down the centre of the valley between the two armies, the eagle on one shoulder and Midnight beside him; past mounted officers some of whom he had known all his life, past troopers whose eyes swivelled to follow his progress. No one spoke but Tarkyn could feel amazement, hope, relief and stunned disbelief emanating from the sea of men he walked through.

As he moved forward, he contracted his shield behind him, aware as he did so, that he appeared to be cutting off his safe passage back to the woodlands. He could use the small leaf in his pocket to translocate but not through someone else's shield if they surrounded him. Part of his mind noticed the grass on the valley floor, studded with tiny yellow flowers, and the tracks of rabbits, mice and deer criss-crossing his path. He hoped the animals had found somewhere to hide, well out of harm's way.

After what seemed an eternity, he reached the position directly between Kosar and Jarand. Now, from the more committed knot of people closer to his brothers, Tarkyn could feel disbelief, frustration and anger.

With all eyes on Tarkyn, it came as a shock when two swallows flitted in from behind each of the armies and dropped a small message in the lap of each of Tarkyn's brothers. The little birds were so fast and agile that no marksman could have a hope of hitting them as they swooped over the princes, then flew bobbing and weaving towards Tarkyn in the centre of the valley. For a few moments they spiralled over their forest guardian's head before swinging and weaving their way back into the forest.

Jarand dropped the note in alarm as it began to increase in size but gestured for Journeyman to retrieve it and read it to him. Then, with deliberate disdain, he took the note from his wizard, threw it under his horse's hooves and tugged sharply at the bit so that his horse trampled it. In his response, Kosar barely glanced at his note's contents and tossed it to Stargazer Bookbinder.

"Well, we tried," murmured Tarkyn. At a glance from Tarkyn, Midnight raised his own dark green shield and waited until Tarkyn lifted one side of his bronze shield enough to let the little boy out. Matching words to images, Tarkyn instructed, "Keep your shield touching mine. Good boy. Now you call Kosar's horse while I call Jarand's."

The two great black chargers tossed their heads, striving to free themselves of the pull of their bits. Despite the backward pressure on their mouths, they began to mince forward. Both princes threw up their dark red shields as they realised that they were being carried inexorably towards Tarkyn. The horses, now unable to receive messages from the forest guardians, took a few more steps forward before slowing. Shieldwielders from both sides were ordered forward but Journeyman arrived first, throwing his shield over Tarkyn and Midnight, enclosing their green and bronze domes within his shield of pale blue-grey.

Now Kosar and Jarand advanced willingly, sure that they had their pestilential brother trapped. The front lines of cavalry swung in on either end to form a circle around the forest guardians, so intent on capturing Tarkyn that for the moment, their enmity was put aside.

"Enough is enough, Tarkyn!" The king glared down at him from the back of his charger. "We will no longer brook your interference. It seems your own arrogance has now betrayed you." He waved his arm. "How could you hope to prevail against the assembled might of Eskuzor? Pure lunacy."

Behind the king, an ethereal ice maiden inside an aqua globe drifted from the edge of the forest and rose into the air above his troops. As Navira rose higher, she threw open her arms and announced, "I am the Wizardess of the Forest of Yesterday, Today and Tomorrow. Some people call it the Lost Forest."

Seeing Jarand's and other people's attention focussing behind him, Kosar whipped his head around before turning back to Tarkyn and demanding, "What chicanery is this?"

Tarkyn merely shrugged and kept his eyes trained on Navira.

Although she could be seen clearly right across the valley, her voice did not carry to Jarand's troops. But deep in the midst of Jarand's army, Jakon and Rostin recognized their cue and exclaimed loudly, "Look. That's the Wizardess from the Forest of Yesterday, Today and Tomorrow; the Wizardess from the Lost Forest."

The message passed like wildfire through Jarand's troops and in moments, every eye was trained on Navira, hanging within the aqua of Danton's shield in the air above them. As they watched, flames sprang up on the ground along the perimeters of two squares in which the bulk of

Jarand's and Kosar's troops were standing. The flames were not so big or fierce that men panicked but the heat made them back away.

Suddenly an enormous pulse of bright green power obscured Jarand's army while black power, dark as ink, enveloped Kosar's. The earth seemed to shrug as the air thrummed and a detonation resounded down the valley.

When the air cleared, nineteen thousand men had disappeared.

For long moments, an eerie silence hung over the Valley of the Dry Mile. Kosar and Jarand now had little more than an honour guard each; a few rows of cavalry and perhaps three companies of men further along the valley who were guarding the gaps between the dirt pits.

Kosar's face was white with shock. "Tarkyn, what have you done? You have wiped out the manhood of Eskuzor."

Tarkyn raised his eyebrows, at his supercilious best. "Wasn't that what you intended to do?" He watched as Kosar struggled to find an answer. "Now, you must negotiate…unless you intend to stage a mock battle with a handful of men?"

The disparagement in his voice made Kosar's face suffuse with anger.

"No," he roared, "Now we will see you hanged."

Tarkyn was barely listening to him. He had his attention trained on Midnight. "Are you ready?"

Midnight glanced at him and nodded, as he received a string of images reiterating their plans.

For a moment nothing happened. Tarkyn stood quietly within his bronze shield but trapped within the broader light blue dome of Journeyman's shield, as he summoned up images to fuel his anger. Faced by the vindictive rage of his older brother, it wasn't hard. He held his anger in check like floodwaters behind a barrier; powerful but controlled. Suddenly, he swept his arms downward and thrust stiffened fingers toward the ground. A shockwave of fury billowed outward, shaking the earth beneath them, sending horses plunging in fear and men sprawling. Journeyman's pale blue sheild winked out. Only Midnight and Tarkyn's shields remained intact.

Oblivious to the mayhem, Midnight focussed solely on directing the two great chargers. While other horses began to settle, the royal horses plunged and kicked, then reared so high that they threatened to topple backwards. Already shaken, the princes struggled in vain to keep their seats and were thrown into ignominious heaps on the ground.

Immediately, Tarkyn expanded his shield to create a dome over himself, Midnight in his shield and the two fallen princes. Then he created a second shield within the first that covered only Jarand and Kosar.

Tarkyn lifted the edge of his outer shield near his little helper. "Right. Out you go. Quickly, before they recover."

Midnight crawled out from under Tarkyn's shield, then increased the size of his dark green shield so that it covered Tarkyn's. As soon as it was in place, Tarkyn winked out his outer shield, which left him standing beside Midnight, outside the bronze dome that covered his brothers but inside Midnight's.

The eagle glared at Midnight who, in response, expanded his shield higher. With a shriek of discontent, Bird stretched her wings and flapped a short distance to land on the apex of Tarkyn's translucent bronze dome. From directly above Tarkyn's brothers, she cocked her head to train her unnerving gaze firstly on Kosar and then on Jarand. She shrieked her derision at them before ruffling her feathers into place and raising her head. From that point on, she disdained even to acknowledge them.

With what dignity they could muster, Kosar and Jarand picked themselves up, each flicking his own dark red shield around himself, and glowered at Tarkyn.

Tarkyn nodded amiably, "A wise precaution, but only against each other. You need no protection from me. I would already have killed you, had I intended to. And now perhaps you will negotiate. I will have chairs, a table, food and drink brought to you so that you may be at your ease."

"I will do no such thing," spluttered Kosar, almost incoherent with rage. "I am King of Eszkuzor, your liege lord. How dare you humiliate me like this in front of my men?"

Tarkyn shook his head. "You are no longer my liege lord. You sacrificed that right when you sacrificed justice. And I did warn you, Kosar... Time after time I have used the least force possible to turn events but neither you nor Jarand have heeded me. Now you have forced me to extreme measures."

"You are still surrounded, Tarkyn," said Jarand with little conviction, but unwilling to concede defeat.

"True." Even now, Tarquin was not prepared to reveal his ability to translocate unless he had to. "But with the very ground beneath your feet at my command and my hidden warriors awaiting my call, I do not feel very vulnerable. Should I choose to, I could wipe out the small forces you have left."

"But what do you hope to achieve?" objected Kosar. "I thought your whole objective was to save the common man. Instead, you have slaughtered him wholesale."

Tarkyn was distracted from his brothers by a voice behind him saying, "I doubt it, Your Majesty. You are right in your estimate of Prince Tarkyn.

He is not a wilful killer of men." Tarkyn turned to find Colonel Argyve behind him. When Tarkyn's eyes lit on him, he bowed. "Good afternoon, Your Highness. I see your eagle is still well. Once more, you and your remarkable forces have won the day against overwhelming odds. Might I ask where you have put your brothers' armies?"

Tarkyn grinned. "Well met, Colonel. As you see, I am still battling to protect Eskuzor. And as you so correctly surmise, of course I have not killed them." His grin broadened. Now that their manoeuvrings had come to a successful conclusion, he was able to relax a little. "They are in the Forest of Yesterday, Today and Tomorrow. It took an almighty feat of magic to translate them there but I have at my disposal three of the most powerful wizards known to man. An unfair advantage, I will admit."

"Indeed, Sire? I know of one of them; Stormaway Treemaster. But who are the others, if you don't mind me asking? And who is this little fellow?"

Tarkyn thought that by ignoring his king for so long, Colonel Argyve was risking the king's displeasure at the very least, but he decided that it was up to the Colonel to choose his battles so he continued to converse with him while furniture and victuals were being procured. "The other wizards are from the Forest of Yesterday, Today and Tomorrow. Their identities would provide too much of a distraction at the moment, but as soon as my brothers have reached an understanding, I will introduce them." He smiled down at Midnight and ruffled his hair while mentally praising him and adjuring him to maintain his shield. "This young scamp is my ward, Midnight. He, too, is a forest guardian."

The general smiled, "Then you will have a companion as you live out your long lifetime. I am pleased for you."

"What long life time?" demanded the king.

Colonel Argyve gave a nod of respect before saying, "Sire, Captain Harmon comes from an estate close to the forest. So his father's library contains books that make reference to guardians of the forest. Judging by the appearance of the same guardian at events across several centuries, it is surmised that they live for up to four hundred years."

"Four hundred years?" Kosar stared at Tarkyn. "You really are some sort of mythical creature, aren't you? And have you stolen the men of Eskuzor so that you can rule them in your mythical forest?"

"No. But if I must I will, while the threat of civil war lingers. At the moment, I am merely holding them hostage until you come to a resolution." Tarkyn shrugged. "After all, as things stand at the moment, you yourself have very few men left to rule."

Jarand frowned, "So, with all this power and all this advantage, with both of us at your mercy, why don't you simply take Eskuzor's throne?"

"It is not mine to take. I am Guardian of Eskuzor, not its king."

Jarand shook his head, clearly at a loss with this attitude.

Conversation was interrupted at this stage by the arrival of several soldiers carrying the items Tarkyn had requested. Tarkyn instructed them to set up the two ornately carved chairs and the cedar dining table and to lay out the food and wine, thinking as he did, that his brothers did not travel light, even to war. When everything had been arranged to his satisfaction, he ordered the soldiers away. First Midnight and then Tarkyn expanded their shields so that Kosar and Jarand had access to the table.

Tarkyn waved his hand in invitation and managed to say without a hint of mockery, "Your Majesty, Your Highness, your negotiating table awaits."

CHAPTER 81

In a field on the north eastern edge of the Lost Forest, ten thousand bewildered men looked around themselves, blinking in the sunshine that shone here today but not in the Valley of the Dry Mile. Beneath about a third of them, horses tossed or shook their heads and sidled a few steps but beyond that, seemed either oblivious or accepting of the change. All of the men felt nauseated by the effects of the translocation. Surprisingly, very few of them had lost consciousness as Danton and his party had when they had been translocated to the Lost Forest, but they had an increased sense of disorientation, since they had no idea what had just happened to them.

As they began to feel better, muttered questions wandered through their ranks:

"Where is the king? Prince Tarkyn? Prince Jarand? The other army?"

"Where are we?"

"Where are the officers?"

In actual fact, many officers were still with them sharing their predicament, but most of the senior staff had been positioned close to the king and not within the square of ash, leaves and flowers, so had been left behind.

With true heroism, the remaining officers pulled themselves together and set about rallying the men. As fortune would have it, there was one officer more senior than the rest, Brigadier Shapiro Markel, who could take control, circumventing any possible power struggles that might otherwise have occurred between several equally ranked officers.

Shapiro stared at the old gnarled trees that surrounded them on two sides and the field that stretched away into the distance to his rear and right. There was no sign of the other army but for all he knew, they could be ready to ambush them from behind the rolling hills in the pastures or from within the dark, twisted forest. Firstly, Shapiro posted one full squadron to guard the army's perimeter before sending out eight pairs of scouts; the first pair due north according to the sun, the second northwest and the rest at forty five degrees to the pair before so that all directions were covered. The other officers organised the rest of the men into squadrons, some of them a blend of the remains of two or three smaller ones, each with a sergeant assigned to them. Only once a clear chain of command had been established, did he take stock of the immediate surroundings.

It was then that the Brigadier noticed two people standing in the shade of a great oak, watching them. Shapiro frowned. Surely he would have noticed them earlier, no matter how preoccupied he was. As he watched, the two people stepped out from the tree's deep shadow, protected within a haze of aqua.

His eyes widened as he recognised Lord Danton, one of his erstwhile guards, escorting a young woman with the black hair and bright amber eyes of Prince Tarkyn, dressed in a formal deep blue gown. Although Danton was now a fugitive because of his association with the Renegade Prince, the circumstances were too strange for Shapiro to move against him. He needed any information he could glean. So he simply moved forward, away from the listening ears of his men, as they approached.

Navira walked with a stately lack of haste to stand before the Brigadier. Only the faint trembling of her hand on Danton's arm, imperceptible to anyone else, betrayed her tension.

Once they had reached Shapiro, Danton turned to his companion. "Your Highness, may I introduce Brigadier Shapiro Markel, Lord of Cornelthan?" said Danton. "My Lord, this is the Princess Navira, younger sister of the king and Prince Jarand, and older sister of Prince Tarkyn."

The Brigadier frowned in surprise but one look at Navira's haughty expression had him bowing deeply, hand on heart.

The princess waved her hand to indicate that he could rise. "Good afternoon, Brigadier," she said in her low melodious voice. "Welcome to the Forest of Yesterday, Today and Tomorrow; known by its residents, as the Lost Forest. Here, I am known as the Wizardess Stillwaters Pathfinder."

"Your Highness. It is an honour…and a surprise, I must say, to meet you."

At a nod from Navira, Danton waved away his shield.

"You have done well to get your men in order so promptly," she said graciously, not deigning to answer his unspoken query. "No doubt you would like to know what has happened to you."

The Brigadier frowned as he tried to remember everything he had ever heard of the Forest of Yesterday, Today and Tomorrow. Finally he shook his head. "I thought only individuals disappeared into this forest either through the agency of a wizard or by some whimsical chance. Didn't the king's knights come here, centuries ago, to prove themselves?… but still only on lone quests."

The wizardess smiled. "Yes. You remember your folklore well. And they had to face their fears to be released back into the true forests of Eskuzor."

Shapiro waved his hand at his troops arrayed behind him. "Am I to understand that you have transported us here wholesale? And if so, to what purpose? Must we all face our fears, whatever that means, to return?" The Brigadier's voice sharpened with anger. "Surely you are aware that we are in the middle of a major confrontation. It is imperative that we return immediately to support the king." He suddenly transferred his gaze to Danton. "And what are you doing here?"

Danton gave his warm, gentle smile, knowing and accepting that he was the butt of many jokes, even among sorcerers, for his devotion. "As ever, I am here in support of my liege, Prince Tarkyn… and also of Princess Navira."

"So, is this all his doing?" Shapiro jumped acutely to the wrong conclusion. "Does this mean he has decided to support Prince Jarand?"

"Yes, your removal from the battlefield is in accordance with Prince Tarkyn's wishes but no, he is not supporting Jarand any more than he is supporting the king," replied Danton.

Navira smiled disarmingly. "We are working with my brother to protect you and your men from death and mutilation. It may ease your mind to know that Prince Jarand's army has suffered a similar experience to yours."

Alarmed, the Brigadier threw a searching glance around him.

Navira gave a tinkling laugh. "No. We have made sure that they are nowhere near you, even though they too are here in the Lost Forest. And it will do you no good to look for them. Our forest is rife with illusion and we will not allow you to meet up. You will find that the scouts you sent out will return shortly, empty handed and a little confused, each pair having been led in a wide circle when they thought they were moving away from you in a straight line."

Shapiro drew himself up, "So, are we are being held prisoner while Prince Tarkyn disposes of his brothers and usurps the throne?"

"There is no intention of usurping the throne by either of us," said Navira coldly. "Kosar is the rightful king and will be for years to come, followed by his progeny. Prince Tarkyn and I are working together to protect the people of Eskuzor by forcing our brothers to negotiate."

Danton glanced sharply at her, hearing more in her words than she was saying, but questions could wait. The Brigadier was speaking again.

"You both take a great deal upon yourselves, assuming you know the wishes of the people of Eskuzor. We feel honoured to serve the king to resolve his differences."

Navira raised supercilious eyebrows. "Of course you do. I do not know what makes you think we are second-guessing the wishes of the people. We are protecting them, regardless of their wishes."

"You certainly speak like a Tamadil, Madam Wizardess," said the Brigadier wryly. He hesitated then took the plunge of risking her displeasure. "However, I must confess I am perplexed by your sudden appearance. I do not wish to offend you, Ma'am, but how do I know that you are who you say you are? I have already seen that you can change your colouring. How do I know your present colouring is true?"

Navira's cheeks reddened and her grip on Danton's arm tightened. She glanced at him before replying stiffly. "I can give you two reasons; I am accepted by my brother's staunchest ally, Danton Patronell…"

"He could be entranced," interrupted the Brigadier.

"Have the courtesy to wait until I am finished," snapped Navira. She waved her hand and a bronze shield blossomed around her. "You may ask any of your wizards. A wizard can change his or her colouring but no one can change the colour of their magic…and bronze magic has only ever occurred within the Tamadil line."

"Princess Navira can bring forth witnesses to testify to the authenticity of her claim," said Danton, "one of whom is Stormaway Treemaster, Prince Tarkyn's personal wizard and previously wizard to King Markazon."

They spent the next half hour explaining Navira's story to the Brigadier, while ten thousand men waited patiently behind them, their minds raging with conjecture.

Finally when Shapiro was totally clear, he turned and addressed his men. To ensure that everyone could hear, Navira provided him with a resonance spell. This startled him when he first spoke but he smiled his thanks when he realised what she was doing. "I know you felt honoured to have the opportunity to fight for your king," he said to his men, "and that this turn of events will be a blow to you. But we have been left with no choices." Shapiro explained their predicament, the reason for it and finally, the identity of the people standing with him.

"Be assured that the Princess Navira is who she says she is. Show your respect."

With that, every man in the army snapped to attention, hand on heart and dropped to one knee.

Using her own resonance spell, Navira bade them stand at ease. "Lord Shapiro will explain to your officers the reasons for my long absence from public life; they in turn will pass it on to you. We must leave you now." She gave a little laugh, "We have another army to address." She waited for the ripple of laughter, some sycophantic, some genuine, to subside before continuing, "Be assured you will be supplied with food and drink for the short time you are within these forests. Since lining up to face the slaughter of battle is proof enough of your courage, you will not have to face your fears, as people in the past have done, to be released from this forest. When my brothers have resolved their differences, you will be returned to Eskuzor." She nodded at Danton. "Are you ready?"

With that, they both intoned, "*Maya Mureva Araya.*" and disappeared from sight to address Jarand's army in a similar fashion.

CHAPTER 82

Kosar sat himself at one end of the table and expanded his shield so that he could safely reach the wine and food at his end. He calmly poured golden wine into a silver goblet and took a slow sip. He swirled it in his mouth before remarking, "Yes, a fine wine, this one, Jarand. I think you may enjoy it."

Jarand copied his brother and replied urbanely, "Indeed, quite pleasant. From the mountain regions, I believe."

Kosar took another sip, then without looking at Tarkyn, said, "Tarkyn, have the courtesy to withdraw out of ear shot… and take that strange little boy with you."

Tarkyn felt a surge of anger but accepted that Kosar needed a petty revenge. He inclined his head, "I would be happy to oblige, but I don't think Midnight can increase his shield to that extent." In fact, Tarkyn was beginning to worry that Midnight might not be able to maintain concentration for much longer at all and he himself would find it too taxing to hold two shields on his own for an extended period. "Perhaps I might ask Borovar, a sorcerer from the Forest of Yesterday, Today and Tomorrow, to join us, if you will allow his unimpeded passage."

Kosar waved his hand magnanimously while Jarand gave a tight nod, both aware that there was little point in making things difficult.

After an image from Midnight reached Waterstone, Borovar was sent forth. When he arrived in the middle of the battlefield enclosed within his peacock blue dome, he gave a low bow to the king, a slightly shallower bow to Prince Jarand and, so as not to fuel their indignation even further, an even shallower bow to Tarkyn before extending his peacock blue dome up and over the outside of Midnight's.

At a gesture from Tarkyn, Midnight dropped his shield, almost sagging with relief as he was released from the pressure of concentration. Tarkyn scooped him into his arms before the little boy's legs gave way. "Make your shield large enough, Borovar, to give them a semblance of privacy." Once they had moved away from his brothers, he looked hopefully at the pack on Borovar's broad back and murmured, "I don't suppose you happened to bring any food with you. This could be a long wait."

Borovar swung the pack from his back. "Yes, I did happen to, Sire. We could see that you had set up food for your brothers, but not for Midnight or yourself." He glanced around at Journeyman, Colonel Argyve, and the soldiers that surrounded them. "Saying that, I'm sure these people would heed any request you might make."

"I am sure they would," agreed Tarkyn quietly, "But could we trust that the food was not poisoned?"

"Oh. Good point. I should have thought of that."

"If you had been the focus of my brothers' ill will as I am, you would have taken it for granted." He sat himself down with Midnight in his lap against the wall of Borovar's peacock blue shield. "Let's leave them to it."

As soon as Tarkyn had moved away, Kosar leaned forward and spoke with quiet intensity, "Jarand, we can come to no compromise. Clearly you want to be king. Just as clearly, I am king and have no intention of giving up my birth right. And it is my birth right. Even if it is only by twenty minutes, I am still our father's oldest son."

Jarand simmered, just as Kosar intended. "I hardly think I need you to tell me that. It has been rammed down my throat my whole life."

Suddenly Kosar laughed, "I suppose it has." There was too much delight in his laughter for this to be construed as a gesture of fellow feeling. He glanced at Tarkyn before helping himself to an oaten biscuit. With great deliberation, Kosar spread the biscuit with rich chicken pate before returning his gaze to his twin's face. "I don't know what we can do. Our bloody younger brother refuses to take sides, even his own, as far as I can see."

"Not quite true, Kosar. He supports the common man…including his forest dwellers."

"Apparently. But not to the point of disrupting the natural line of succession, I see."

"Unless you force him into it. Didn't he say he would rule the men of our armies if he must?"

Kosar gave a growl of frustration deep in his throat. "By rights, I should hang him… and you for plotting against the crown… but clearly our younger brother doesn't agree with either of those courses of action. If he did, presumably he would have given you into my hands."

For a while Jarand said nothing, watching his long fingers running round and round the rim of his goblet. Finally, he looked up and spoke softly, "I was trying to support you, you know, but you never gave me any credit or any say in the nation's affairs."

The king gave a snort of disbelief. "What? With your recruitment agency at the encampment?"

"Yes," replied Jarand emphatically. "I was trying to enlist enough men to fight against the rising tide of lawlessness that was sweeping through the west of Eskuzor and along the Great West Road." He drew in an impatient breath and with an irritated wave, flicked his shield out of existence. "Oh, this is ridiculous. How can we talk properly through two layers of red mist?"

Kosar ignored his brother's gesture, focused purely on what Jarand was saying to defend himself. "And yet here they all are...or were, your carefully recruited men; arrayed in an army against me."

Jarand scowled. "Well, what did you expect after bringing a full battalion to publicly wrest control of the encampment from me, after all I had done to support you? You do not repay loyal service very well, Kosar. Look at Tarkyn."

"Don't lay that at my door, Jarand. You know perfectly well we both made that error."

"Perhaps." Jarand's gaze wandered casually along the curve of the dark red dome of Kosar's shield. He poured himself some wine and took a slow sip.

For the next half an hour, each of them raked up old scores that had rankled with him while the other deflected them. Neither ever reached the point where he acknowledged or apologized for the ill intent of his actions, but finally Jarand seemed content to let past conflicts lie and instead asked matter-of-factly, "What has happened to the encampment since I left? I put a lot of work into making that encampment a safe refuge for travellers, especially for those people who had been rescued from marauder attacks. In fact, I thought perhaps a small village might be established there eventually."

"Our interfering younger brother stipulated that only two companies of men and five houses for refreshments, stores and accommodation could remain."

"What! How dare he dictate to you?" Jarand glared in Tarkyn's direction.

Tarkyn, who had been filling a roll with cheese for Midnight, felt his brother's eyes on him and looked around. He gave an inward shrug at the venom he saw in them. Perhaps his brothers' shared antipathy towards him might provide the basis for their reconciliation. Judging by the absence of Jarand's shield, they seemed to be making at least a little progress.

Jarand looked deliberately away from him and leant forward to focus Kosar's attention on him. "Well?"

Kosar let out a long breath. "What you don't know is that our father bequeathed sovereignty of the forest to Tarkyn."

"*What?*" Jarand's eyes nearly bugged out of his head. "As *well* as that sorcerous oath?"

"What do you know about the sorcerous oath?" demanded Kosar.

"As much as you do, I should imagine." Jarand gave a slow smile. "Journeyman and I used to eavesdrop on Stormaway Treemaster. It was very illuminating, especially when he consulted with the king."

Kosar nodded dismissively, "I expect you used that hidden passageway too, but clearly you didn't hear them discuss the legacy of the forest, as I did." He scowled, "If not for that bloody sorcerous oath, I could have overridden our father's behest. I thought I could dispose of Tarkyn before he found out. But now, with the woodfolk behind him, Tarkyn and the forest are virtually unassailable."

"Stars above! Those forests cover nearly a third of Eskuzor, even more after their recent increase." Jarand's voice was raw with consternation. "And it's right in the middle of Eskuzor. How can you countenance that, Kosar?"

Kosar drummed his fingers on the table top, thinking hard. "You see what I am dealing with. Instead of fighting each other, we should be combining against him."

Tarkyn watched with some satisfaction as Kosar, in response to Jarand's nod of brotherly sympathy, slowly waved away his shield.

In an instant, Jarand's face transformed from brotherly concern into a victorious rictus as he sent a blast of dark red power, not at Kosar but at the wall of Tarkyn's shield halfway between them. The deadly beam bounced off the inside wall of Tarkyn's shield which, in response to Tarkyn's shock, redoubled and reflected the beam's strength before it slammed into Kosar's chest.

But the movement of Kosar's hand as he waved his shield away had altered his position just enough for the shaft of power to hit him slightly to one side instead of directly over his heart. Even as he jolted backwards, Kosar thrust his hand forward and sent everything he had into his own ferocious jet of dark red power. Jarand, realising his shaft had gone awry, had already adjusted his aim. He sent a second shaft ricocheting after the first, just as Kosar's final desperate effort hit Tarkyn's shield above, then behind Jarand before rebounding with massive force against the back of his head.

Jarand's second shaft hit Kosar directly over his heart and threw him crashing to the ground. Kosar's shaft drove Jarand forward to sprawl face down on the table, killing him instantly.

"Nooo!!!" screamed Tarkyn as he flicked his shield away, all thought for his own safety gone. The eagle shrieked as her perch disappeared, dropping her onto the table in a ruffled heap between the two princes.

But it was all too late.

As he rushed to his brothers' inert forms, he yelled to Borovar. "Let in Stargazer, Journeyman and Argyve… who else? Guerion, Harmon, if they're still here. And healers. Lots of healers."

By the time Tarkyn reached him, Kosar was lying on his back, his eyes staring blindly through Borovar's peacock blue shield to the sky beyond. Tarkyn felt frantically for a pulse but could find nothing. Stargazer, Argyve and a healer he didn't know clustered around him.

Tarkyn screamed *Stormaway* with his mind but his message was blocked by Borovar's shield. "Remove your shield, Borovar," he snapped.

As Boravar obeyed, the eagle spread her great wings and thrust herself skywards out of the chaos. Tarkyn didn't even notice. He called once more for Stormaway as he placed his hand on Kosar's shoulder and drew desperately on his *esse*, pouring his life force into his brother. Beside him, the healer, a tough flea-bitten soldier pumped Kosar's chest and tried to rekindle the spark of life.

As a last resort, Tarkyn followed his *esse* into Kosar but found himself in a deep dark hole, no flicker of light or life anywhere. The emptiness of it horrified him and he threw himself back out into his own body.

"He's gone," Tarkyn said to the healer. "By all means keep trying, but he has gone."

The healer, intent on his work, had no reason to think that Tarkyn knew what he was talking about, so merely glanced at him and ignored what he said.

Tarkyn rushed to the other end of the table but was stopped by Journeyman, who put his arm out and said firmly, "Stop Sire, there is nothing you can do."

"But I can give him my *esse*, my life force."

"I know of this, Sire, but even you cannot raise the dead, I think."

Tarkyn remembered the time he had drawn the remains of Pipeless' body from within the ground and had brought him back to life; but it had lasted only for minutes. He could not do it permanently. He shook his head. "No, I can't." His head kept shaking from side to side as his whole body tried to deny what had just happened.

Colonel Argyve came to stand in front of Tarkyn and took him by both shoulders, risking retribution for laying hands on him in order to gain his attention. "Stop. Look at me." The inherent strength and kindness of the older man steadied Tarkyn. "Hundreds of men witnessed this. The king and crown prince inflicted their deaths on each other. You are not to blame. You did everything you could to resolve their conflict." Tarkyn's head had stopped moving but his eyes were still glazed with shock. "Look at me, Sire."

With a struggle, Tarkyn gathered his scattered wits to focus in on the colonel. He frowned, wondering what Argyve wanted. As soon as Argyve was sure that he had Tarkyn's full attention, he let go of his shoulders, sank to one knee and placed his hand over his heart. "Your Majesty, I pledge you my service. I am overjoyed to have you as my king."

"Oh no, no. I can't be," murmured Tarkyn vaguely. Then, more loudly and firmly, he repeated, "No! No! I can't be your king."

But his words were drowned out by a rising tide of shouting as the cry went up from every man left on the battlefield, "The king is dead! Long live the king! Long live King Tarkyn."

Part 10: The Settling Dust

CHAPTER 83

Within the tree line, Waterstone, Rainstorm, Ancient Oak and every member of Tarkyn's home guard watched in horror as events dragged their friend and forest guardian away from them.

"He said he could never leave us," said Ancient Oak more creakily than ever, "but how can he turn his back on his sorcerers now? They're not like us. They *need* a leader."

"Blast his stupid brothers!" exclaimed Rainstorm, throwing a wad of bark savagely against the trunk of an old beech tree. "We never saw this coming, did we? Not in a million years. What are we going to do?"

Waterstone grunted. "There's nothing we can do. Sorcerer business is not our business. It doesn't look as though Tarkyn is in danger and he hasn't called for any of us except Stormaway who is, after all, half sorcerer and couldn't hear him anyway from the Lost Forest."

Ancient Oak eyed him, sensing the hurt beneath his words.

Rainstorm glanced from one to the other and said kindly, "Give him time, Waterstone. He has just lost his brothers... and gained thousands of sycophantic sorcerers. He must be feeling pretty overwhelmed at the moment." Suddenly he grinned, "Oh well. At least he will have all that adulation he's apparently used to." Then his smile faded and he demanded, "And what about his betrothal to Lapping Water? What's going to happen about that?"

At which point, they realised that Lapping Water was missing. Immediately, they sent out mind messages to her but received no response.

"She's shielding her mind," said Waterstone shortly. "She must want to be alone."

Rainstorm looked unhappily at the older woodfolk around him. "I don't want her to be on her own though." He frowned, for once unsure of himself. "Should we just respect her wishes… or should I go and find her?"

Waterstone unbent enough to smile at him. "Rainstorm, follow your instincts. Out of all of us, your instincts lead you most truly. What do you think you should do?"

The young woodman's cheeks reddened at the compliment. He gave an unusually shy smile, which broadened as his normal confidence reasserted itself. "Find her, of course. Can't have her being miserable on her own."

Even as Waterstone said, "Off you go then," Rainstorm flicked out of sight.

It took him nearly half an hour to track her down.

Lapping Water was seated high in an old oak, where she could look out over the battlefield. She turned her head but made no attempt to leave, as Rainstorm climbed around the trunk and across two large branches before lowering himself onto the branch next to her. Her face was streaked with tears but she attempted a welcoming smile which was wan at best and wavered into a sniff. Rainstorm didn't say a word but just reached over and enveloped her in his arms. She gave up any pretence and sobbed into his shoulder until, sometime later, his stroking of her hair soothed her enough to sit up.

She gave him a watery smile and said between sniffs, "Oh well. I guess that's what happens when you fall in love with a legend. One day you wake up and realise it was all just a dream." She waved her hand towards the battlefield. "Look. He's only five hundred yards away and he could be on the moon, for all I can reach him."

Even as they watched, the large knot of people around him ushered Tarkyn into the command tent and out of their view. For a moment Lapping Water looked as though she would dissolve into tears again but she took a deep shuddering breath and said, "Well, that's that then. I can't even see him any more…Thanks for coming, Rainstorm."

He gave her a squeeze and mumbled something unintelligible.

Lapping Water concentrated on folding and unfolding a sodden handkerchief as she spoke. "I suppose everyone thinks I'm an idiot now, do they?"

Rainstorm was so surprised, he laughed. "No. Of course they don't. We're all upset, not just you. But none of us, least of all Tarkyn, predicted this. Don't look at it as a betrayal. Tarkyn has just been swept up by events. How can that make a fool of you?"

"Because I was dewy-eyed enough to think that a woodwoman who can't leave the woods could partner a person of such signal importance to the world of sorcerers." She snorted contemptuously. "I usually have more sense than that."

"You knew it was risky and took the chance. Some risks are worth taking, whether you succeed or not." Rainstorm smiled at her, "And I personally think that Tarkyn is worth taking risks for."

"You mean, was worth taking risks for."

"No. I hope I mean is."

Suddenly Lapping Water's attention was diverted by the sight of Boravar, hand in hand with Midnight, emerging from the command tent and walking back towards the woods.

"Oh!" she squeaked. "He'll have news of Tarkyn."

Much to his bemusement, Rainstorm found himself alone as Lapping Water flicked her way to the bottom of the tree and then as close to the edge of the forest as safety would allow. He shook his head, "So much for having sense."

Rainstorm followed at a more decorous pace, arriving just as Boravar was finishing the description of Tarkyn's brothers' demise. Waterstone was sitting against a tree a little away from the main throng but still within hearing. Midnight, pale-faced and eyes big with strain, huddled on the woodman's knee within the circle of his arm, Sparrow seated beside him.

"And why have you come back now?" asked Rainstorm, butting in as soon as Boravar drew breath. "And how is Tarkyn? And what is he doing?"

The big sorcerer raised his hand to stop the deluge. "Tarkyn is… Tarkyn is less in control than I have ever seen him. I think he's in shock. He looks stunned." He held up a folded piece of parchment. "But amidst all the demands and questions and requests that were being thrown at him, he sat down at that cedar table you saw, which is now back in the command tent, and asked for parchment and ink. For a good minute, no one took any notice. And to do him credit, he didn't lose his temper. He just ignored everything anybody said and kept re-iterating his request until it was heeded…" He shrugged unhappily. "They're calling him Your Majesty now, you know."

Rainstorm snorted, "Doesn't sound like they're treating him like 'Your Majesty.'"

"Oh they are. Their whole world now revolves around him. They are all trying to get close to him as the power shifts from his brothers to him."

"So come on, Boravar," prompted Autumn Leaves. "What's in the letter?"

Boravar harrumphed. "Perhaps String or Bean might like to read it."

Bean sent him a shrewd glance and accepted the parchment without demur.

To all of you,

I will not use names in order to protect your identities. My every move is watched by a hundred eyes. But to my family, all my friends and especially my betrothed, I send my love. I have not forgotten you. I will never forget you. But I do not know when I will be able to extricate myself long enough to see you.

Would you please send Danton, Harkell and those of his family who wish to accompany him, Stormaway, Caroman and of course Navira, to me. Boravar will act as go-between until they arrive, but his place is in the woods with his betrothed. String and Bean may come or not as they and you choose, but I would value their advice.

I also need Lord Tolward and his wife, Juny, Trey, Vaska and Varga to attend me.

Since there is no longer any danger of a battle, my brothers' armies should be returned to this valley. Stormaway, Caroman and Navira will be able to effect this before joining me.

Look after my little Midnight. The turmoil that currently surrounds me is no place for a little boy but I will send for him when things are calmer.

All my love

Tarkyn.

"Reassuring to hear that Tarkyn is at his peremptory best," said Waterstone dryly.

"Yes, it is," agreed Boravar firmly. "I am pleasantly surprised that he has enough presence of mind to have been able to write that. That Colonel Argyve… remember the one who was commanding Kosar's secret battalion?… pulled him together when he was reeling in shock at his brothers' deaths, but Tarkyn is still dazed. And he had no time to come to terms with their deaths or his role before he was beset on all sides."

"It is a very unofficial official letter, isn't it?" Harkell smiled, "It may be full of instructions but not many monarchs sign their official letters with 'all my love.'"

"Tarkyn is reaching out to us, as well as he can," said Summer Rain. "That boy of ours is in trouble. He's just been cut off from everyone he trusts. So go on, you sorcerers. Get out there and look after him."

"Yes ma'am." Harkell grinned and gave a little bow. "We will do our best."

After a short discussion, it was decided that Harkell, Drakell, Rena, String and Bean would not wait for those in the Lost Forest but would accompany Boravar immediately.

As soon as they broke cover, Boravar raised his peacock blue shield around them. As they approached the scattered groups of soldiers, they could see messages being passed through the ranks. Long before they reached the command tent, their way was blocked by a line of soldiers, swords drawn.

Harkell scanned their faces and realised he knew a few of them, but by sight only. Nevertheless, he spoke with quiet command, "Prince Tarkyn has requested our presence. Let us pass."

"He's King Tarkyn now. And we have orders from Colonel Carrioll not to let anyone through."

Boravar waved Tarkyn's letter, "And we have orders from the king to attend him."

The soldier just set his mouth and stood his ground.

"Boravar, expand your shield so that you include that campfire to our right." Bean turned to Rena. "You can send strong shafts of power, can't you?" When Rena nodded, he pointed to a large frying pan that was lying next to the fire. "Hit that frying pan with it."

Watched by twenty aggressive soldiers, Rena sent a harsh stream of orange light at it which made it glow with heat but did little else.

String gave a snort of disgust, "Bean, stop trying to be tricky. If you want to make a loud noise, just pick the bloody thing up and belt it with a stick. Mind you, now you'll have to put a rag around your hand to make sure the handle doesn't burn you."

"Knife hilt might be better," suggested Harkell, "or a metal cup." He grinned. "And a few bloodcurdling screams from you, Rena, would be very helpful. They will carry better than us shouting."

Just as String took his arm back to swing and Rena drew breath to scream, the sounds of agitated voices reached them bare moments before the flap of the tent door was thrust aside and Tarkyn strode out, surrounded by a gaggle of protesting men. Tarkyn spun himself through a full circle and snapped, "*Shturrum!*"

Immediately, the voices fell silent as every man surrounding him was immobilised. Tarkyn didn't even look at them. He stormed straight up to the soldiers barring his friends' egress and demanded, "Under whose orders are you acting?"

The soldiers bowed low but Tarkyn was in no mood for niceties, "Get up and answer my question."

Their spokesman swallowed. "Colonel Carrioll's, Sire."

"And were you shown the summons that I sent to these people?"

The soldier nodded miserably. He threw a glance at the stationary Carrioll. "He…we… that is…"

"You need fear no retribution from Colonel Carrioll. He will not be in a position to mete it out." Tarkyn stood tall, strong and angry, all sign of bewilderment banished. His fierce amber eyes glared down at the man. "I am sure you know that my orders far outweigh the orders of a mere colonel. Explain yourself."

"Colonel… Lord Carrioll believes that you already have more than enough advisors, Sire." The soldier swallowed again, "And he said the calibre of person that an exiled prince mixes with, is not the calibre of person fit for a king… He thought that if these people were denied access, they would simply go away and you would think that they had failed to respond to your summons."

"I didn't ask you to explain Carrioll. I said, 'Explain *yourself.*'"

The soldier's eyes widened in horror. He just stared at Tarkyn, his mouth opening and closing but with no sound coming out. Suddenly he went down on one knee and bowed his head, "I most humbly beg your pardon, Your Majesty."

Tarkyn frowned in irritation and left the man kneeling. He turned around to face the motionless men clustered around the doorway of the command tent. "When I wave my spell away, I want no comments, no advice. Is that clear? You do not address me unless I give you my permission." He waved his hand, releasing the spell. "Carrioll, come here."

Colonel Carrioll, although clearly frightened, raised his head proudly and marched over to join Tarkyn. He bowed deeply but remained silent when he straightened.

Tarkyn's voice was low, but carried clearly to everyone present. "Carrioll, I have no doubt that it was your interests, not mine, that motivated your treasonous behaviour. But even were it in pursuit of my interests, neither you nor anyone else has the right to make my decisions for me." He turned to Boravar. "Remove your shield, if you will. You are quite safe now." He turned back to Carrioll. "I hereby relieve you of your command. Return to your estates. You will send me, in gold, the equivalent of a colonel's annual salary. You will not exact this from your tenants but will provide it from your own wealth. As you must realise by now, I have eyes everywhere. If I hear even one hint of resentment against these people or further sedition against the monarchy, you will be arrested and summarily executed. In one year's time, depending on your actions during the intervening period, your case will be reviewed."

Carrioll bowed low as a gesture of acceptance since he was still not permitted to speak.

"And now, Carrioll, you may apologise to *General* Harkell and his companions."

Carrioll turned to Harkell, his face stiff with distaste. "I apologise for impeding your access."

"Lord Carrioll, I may not have liked your attitude towards me but you were always a dedicated, loyal officer." With a struggle, Harkell did not use the moment to justify himself. "You will find that straightforward service rather than manoeuvring works best with this Tamadil. I believe Eskuzor may be in for a long overdue change in culture."

"Ah laddie," put in Bean, dressed head to foot in tatty grubby furs and speaking to Carrioll in the most atrocious accent Tarkyn had ever heard him use. "I can see it sticks in your craw to apologise to the likes of us… But don't be deceived by our good looks. We and others like us prevented a civil war and wholesale slaughter on these fields today."

"Yes, but…" began Carrioll.

Bean shook his head, an absolute picture of bovine ignorance. "No 'yes but', laddie. We did not kill or even threaten the previous king and crown prince. You know perfectly well they brought that upon themselves… You may have blotted your copy book…in fact, you certainly have. But if you ever return to command, you will have this lad here," he jerked a grubby thumb at Harkell, "among others, to thank for the fact that there will actually be soldiers left to command."

Carrioll turned to Tarkyn, "May I speak, Sire?" When Tarkyn nodded, he said, "I thank General Harkell for his words. I am dedicated and loyal. It was misjudgement, not a manoeuvre to secure my position in your new court that motivated me. As everyone knows, I have always strongly maintained that all people should work to the best of their ability in the roles they are born to. I beg your pardon if, by my actions, I tried to force my opinions on you. Thank you for your clemency."

Tarkyn gave a grim smile, "You are very lucky that I have kept the company I have, for these past months. Many of them, particularly Harkell, have been teaching me to control my temper. Had I given rein to my immediate outrage, I doubt that you would have survived. You may withdraw."

Visibly shaken, Carrioll bowed and backed away a few steps before turning to collect his horse and belongings, and begin his long journey into ignominy.

Finally Tarkyn looked down at the soldier still kneeling at his feet.

"Today, I will pardon you. Tomorrow or in the future, if you ever take anyone's orders over those of the reigning monarch, you will be hanged for treason. Clear?"

The soldier nodded without looking up.

"Now, line your men up into an honour guard for these members of my home guard."

Chapter 84

Danton stood in the shade of three old gnarled oaks, idly watching Jarand's army while some distance deeper in the woods behind him, Navira conferred with Caroman and Stormaway, waiting to hear that Kosar and Jarand had reached a resolution.

A faint thrumming in the air signalled the arrival of Singing Bird and Ancient Oak into the Lost Forest. Danton breathed a sigh of relief. At last the waiting was over. He walked over to join the three wizards, but well before he reached them he could see they were agitated. Then a cry of outrage issuing from his beloved stopped him in his tracks. Alarmed, Danton picked up his pace as all three wizards started speaking at once.

Perhaps most shocking of all, the three fell silent as Danton reached them.

"What? What has happened?" Danton demanded.

The three wizards exchanged glances before Stormaway answered. "Jarand attacked Kosar using Tarkyn's shield to reflect and intensify his power. Kosar retaliated just before Jarand struck for the second time."

Danton was aghast. "How could Jarand break parley like that? Now they will take ages to come to an agreement. Were either of them hurt?"

"Yes Danton," said Stormaway gently. "They are both dead. They killed each other."

"They *what*!" After a stunned moment, Danton's brain started working again. He turned to stare at Navira. "Oh my stars! The Tamadil succession is determined by absolute primogeniture. That makes you queen!"

"Well, I'm glad *you* recognise that," said Navira at her iciest. "Your two-faced liege has been proclaimed king in my absence."

Danton surveyed the set faces of the two wizards standing on either side of Navira. "And you two," he said slowly, "even you, Stormaway, will back Navira against Tarkyn, won't you?"

"It is her right," said Stormaway quietly.

Knowing he was risking his betrothed's ire, Danton replied, "It is only her right if Tarkyn acknowledges her as his legitimate older sister and overturns the sentence passed upon her all those years ago. Otherwise, she has effectively been struck from the line of succession."

"Tarkyn has also been sentenced to hang. Why then is his claim any better than mine?" demanded Navira imperiously.

"Because Tarkyn's sentence wasn't carried out whereas, officially, yours was. In fact, according to public records, you weren't even born." Danton shrugged. "So, no matter what colour your magic, no one will believe your claim if Tarkyn does not accept it. They know and trust Tarkyn. They don't know you."

Navira drew herself up. "You realise that you become king if I become queen?"

"Prince Consort," muttered Caroman.

"King, equal in rule with me." reitereated Navira firmly. "Danton, we have both armies here. Tarkyn has very few men left under his command…"

Danton turned to look her straight in the face. She flinched before the fury blazing in his purple eyes. When he spoke, his voice shook with anger. "How little you must think of me, if you believe I would forsake my lifelong friend and liege for the hope of reward." He heaved a couple of breaths, visibly straining to keep control. "We have worked for months to prevent a civil war. I am not about to help you start another one."

Danton took a few paces back and forth before turning and confronting the three of them. When he spoke it was evident that he had managed to rein in his anger. In a tone of quiet reasoning, he said, "Have faith in Tarkyn. You said you would never work against the Guardian of Eskuzor and in this situation, it is his right to determine her future. Return these armies and place them under Tarkyn's command while you talk to him. Unlike his brothers, he is open to negotiation."

When she hesitated, Danton turned to Singing Bird and asked conversationally, "How do you think the woodfolk would respond if Navira brought these armies against your forest guardian?"

Singing Bird glanced at Navira before answering, "The Wizardess of the Lost Forest has always acknowledged and respected the forest guardians. The Guardians of the Past helped to raise her. I have no doubt that she spoke in haste at this fraught time, just as I am sure that she would not want the might of the woodfolk nation turned against her." As though she had not just threatened her, the slight woodwoman turned to Navira and said in a perfectly friendly tone, "Stillwaters, besides the news of the twins' deaths, I also bear an urgent request from Tarkyn for the four of you and the armies to return to the Dry Mile."

Navira raised her eyebrows. "Request or summons?"

Singing Bird thought for a minute, recalling Tarkyn's letter. "It was phrased courteously. His letter conveyed that he was beset on all sides by would-be advisors and wants people he can trust around him."

"Obviously he has erred in counting you three amongst those he could trust," said Ancient Oak scathingly.

"Ancient Oak, you of all people should know that Tarkyn has never wanted to be king," protested Stormaway. "I am not acting against any wishes he has ever expressed, by supporting Navira's legitimate claim."

"Do you really think he wants two armies lined up against him with Eskuzor divided again along new battle lines?"

Stormaway gave a short laugh. "No, of course I don't. And I have no intention of supporting Navira's claim with force."

"And you, Caroman?" asked Navira. "Would you follow me into battle against my brother?"

Caroman bowed. "I am your sworn man, my lady. I would." He gave a slight smile. "But I would try everything first to dissuade you."

Navira huffed. After a moment she resolutely met Danton's eyes. "I do not think little of you. In fact, I think the world of you. Singing Bird is right. I was angry and did speak in haste. I am sorry that I cast such a slur on your honour." Her eyes shone with unshed tears but she did not acknowledge them. "I know you are Tarkyn's liegeman, but I really wish I could have you by my side when I put my case to Tarkyn. I need you, Danton."

Danton returned her gaze silently for several long seconds. "I accept your apology," he said, but his tone said only just. Then he relented, stepping forward to wrap her in his arms. "You shall have me by your side, every step of the way. I may not always agree and I will state my views, but as long as you are straight forward with Tarkyn, I will be there." He stroked her hair, smiling down at her. "Besides, how could you manage on your own? You need me to keep you in check when your emotions run away with you." He felt her hands ball into fists against his chest, ready to push him away. He laughed as he released her. "Come on. Let's get ourselves and these armies back to the Dry Mile."

Chapter 85

"How did you know to come outside just then, or was it mere coincidence?" asked Harkell as he accepted a cup of tea and plate of cakes from one of the many men who hovered around them, anxious to please Tarkyn.

"Waterstone," answered Tarkyn briefly, knowing the name alone was not enough to betray either the woodfolks' existence or the extent of his mental powers.

The six sorcerers from his home guard sat with him around the cedar table, now lengthened by several leaves, in company with Stargazer Bookbinder, Journeyman Cloudmaker, Colonel Argyve and Colonel Charford, who had been the man to hang Andoran and Sargon. Tarkyn was fully aware that the colonels were not the most senior representatives from each side but he knew and respected each of them. From all accounts, Stargazer was a gentle, scholarly wizard while Journeyman was a devious force whom Tarkyn wished to have aligned with him, not against him.

Journeyman's eyes met his and Tarkyn remembered that the wizard knew of woodfolk. But Journeyman was no fool and gave no other sign that he knew what Tarkyn was talking about. Instead he said, "And have you formed any clear intention yet of your next moves, Sire?"

"I will make no move until everyone is returned from the Lost Forest." Remembering that was the woodfolk term, Tarkyn corrected himself, "…the Forest of Yesterday, Today and Tomorrow. I assume that Navira and Danton will have informed our armies of the current state of play. However, I think it would be wise to have officers standing by to provide eye witness accounts to the men as soon as they return. This tragedy is great enough without uninformed rumours exaggerating it. I want any hints that this may have been a deliberate coup listened to, but then unequivocally quashed. I do not want the people of Eskuzor believing that their new monarch would have sanctioned Kosar and Jarand's deaths. Colonel Charford, Colonel Argyve, will you arrange this please? Stargazer and Journeyman, will you explain the translocation of the armies to the Lost Forest and the events that occurred here to your magic makers? Perhaps at some future time, Stormaway and Caroman will explain the machinations of their spell more fully to you all."

The four of them stood up and bowed. As Argyve straightened, he said, "Sire, may I say what a pleasure it is to be commanded with such courtesy?"

Tarkyn shook his head, smiling, and wished he could transmit the words of the scene to Waterstone. "Thank you, Colonel. I will see you shortly."

As soon as they had left, Tarkyn raised his voice, "Now, other than the people seated around the table, I would like everyone to leave this tent... immediately. Do not return until I call for you or until Princess Navira arrives."

In a flurry of activity, men bowed and withdrew. The last to leave was old Farlowe, Kosar's manservant, who hesitated at the doorway of the tent, "Are you sure there is nothing else you need, Sire, before I leave?"

Suddenly Tarkyn focused on him and, with his newly-developed recognition of people's value beyond their functions, realized that the old man would be even more grief-stricken than he was. "No, there is nothing else, Farlowe, but you may stay with us. Even though Kosar did not always treat you well, I know you will miss my brother dreadfully. You served him faithfully for as long as I can remember. You do not deserve to be tossed into the cold with everyone else."

Tears sprang to the old man's eyes. He stood wringing his hands. "Thank you, Sire. I was sorry for what my master did to you, but even so, I was always fond of him, ever since he was a lad. I can't imagine a world without him in it." Farlowe choked down a sob.

Knowing the manservant would not feel comfortable seated at the table, Tarkyn said, "Could one of you get Farlowe a cup of tea please? Then Farlowe, you may stand behind me while you drink it and remain with us afterwards. I will assume that the discretion with which you served Kosar now extends to me."

Farlowe nodded, still unable to speak, and moved quietly to take his place behind his new liege. From then on, Tarkyn ignored him and conversed freely with the others as though he wasn't there.

Tarkyn had just finished hearing about the reactions of Lapping Water, Waterstone and the other woodfolk when the air thwanged with such force that their chests felt momentarily crushed. A commotion outside heralded the arrival of the people from the Lost Forest. Then a muted chant started up that gradually ascended into a roar from the newly arrived armies. "Long live the King! Long live the King! Long live King Tarkyn! Long live the King!"

Tarkyn shook his head and sighed. "This is all wrong. But I will have to go out and acknowledge them. Harkell, Boravar, come with me."

As he appeared outside, a huge roar went up and the volume of the chanting redoubled. The men and women who followed the armies had swelled their numbers, pressing in to gain sight of their new monarch and to greet the returning armies. News had spread fast and people from the surrounding villages and countryside had also gathered within the Dry Mile so that the crowd Tarkyn faced numbered nearly forty thousand.

"Navira and Danton appear to have explained the deaths of my brothers accurately to their armies, for me to be greeted with such enthusiasm." Tarkyn murmured.

"No, Tarkyn," said Harkell. "All they could do is allay suspicion. Your actions and your integrity have earned you this reaction."

Even as he raised his arm to acknowledge the greeting of forty thousand people, Tarkyn could see the angry glitter in Navira's eyes as she approached, and Danton's calming arm placed strategically across her back. For the moment, he merely nodded at them as he kept his attention on the vast masses that surrounded him. As the shouting began to die down, he said quietly to Navira, "I know this may take a huge leap of faith, but could you please provide me with your reverberation spell? I don't know it and I wish to address these people."

Navira's eyes narrowed but as Danton gave her shoulder a subtle squeeze, she nodded curtly and murmured a few potent words.

When all were finally quiet, Tarkyn began. "Soldiers of Eskuzor, I thank you for answering the call of your liege lords and coming forth to do battle on their behalf. I acknowledge your honour and courage for doing so. As you must now realise, I was opposed to civil war. I intended to prevent it by setting my brothers up to negotiate. To my great sorrow, they chose instead to destroy each other."

He paused. "For the last ten years, all of us in Eskuzor have lived under King Kosar's reign and many of you have faithfully served Prince Jarand. This should never have presented a dilemma for you. To serve one Tamadil should be to serve all of us and thus it will be in the future." He turned and gestured towards Navira. "For those of you who are not yet aware of her, may I present my older sister, Her Royal Highness, Princess Navira?" A cheer went up but it held less vigour than the shouts for Tarkyn had. "Just as I have, she has fought to spare you from the trials of civil war. You may have forgotten, since the oldest child in our line for several generations has been male, but the Tamadil succession is determined by absolute primogeniture, not by male primogeniture. So it is Navira not I, who should be your next monarch."

There was a shocked silence. Then mutters of discontent rumbled through the audience.

Before they could gain momentum, Tarkyn held up his hand. "You have greeted me as your king and it would be churlish of me indeed, to turn away from you at our most uncertain hour. I have no intention of doing so. You people of Eskuzor have endured ten years of division, uncertainty and neglect." He put his hand out, inviting Navira to take it and to stand beside him. With their striking amber eyes and long black hair, no one could doubt their kinship. "Be assured, Navira and I will always work together. If you serve me, you also serve her. To honour her is to honour me."

For a moment there was silence. Then murmuring rippled through the ranks, which crescendoed into the chaos of a thousand conversations.

Tarkyn glanced at Navira and muttered, "I don't know what it is about me that has changed but I do not seem to incite the same reverence in people that I once did. You'll get used to this; being talked about, even in front of you."

As the volume of conversation threatened to become deafening, someone started a slow clap which others took up, until forty thousand men and women were clapping and roaring their approval.

Tarkyn smiled down at his sister as he raised their linked hands high in acknowledgement. "Thank you for trusting me," he whispered.

Chapter 86

An hour later, Tarkyn sat at the table in the command tent with a select group; Navira, Danton, Stormaway, Caroman and Harkell. Farlowe stood discreetly in the background while the others had been dispatched to wander through the troops, to pick up the feeling among the men and the thousands of camp followers who were camped in wagons and tents at the edges of the armies. Much to Twig Snap's displeasure, watching her beloved from afar, Boravar had been paired with Rena to ensure her safety as the only woman in a battlefield of men.

Despite Danton's best efforts, Navira's mood was icy.

"I did warn you, Navira," said Danton patiently. "You can't expect to be popular if they don't know anything about you. They have watched Tarkyn all his life."

"Navira," said Caroman sternly, "Tarkyn has given you the best possible start. He has managed to share his popularity with you."

Navira ironed out a crease on her skirt before looking up. "That is all very well, but…" Suddenly she rounded on Tarkyn, "But what did you mean when you said you had no intention of abandoning them? Does that mean you intend to keep my throne?"

Tarkyn considered her for so long that her colour heightened under his scrutiny. "It might," he said eventually.

Three people jerked forward in consternation; Navira, Stormaway and Caroman. Tarkyn's eyes narrowed. "So. We see where loyalties lie, don't we? I am disappointed in you, Stormaway."

Once more, Stormaway stated his case. "I am merely concerned for you, Sire. I know that you have never wanted to be king… and I admit some surprise. I had expected you to honour the true line of succession."

Tarkyn's eyes lingered on him a moment longer, making Stormaway shift uncomfortably, before Navira drew his attention.

"What do you mean, 'It might'?" she asked coldly.

"You saw them out there. How can I just walk away from that passionate avowal of faith? Stormaway is right. I have no wish to be king. You may not have noticed, but once I had gathered my wits, I forbade anyone to address me as Your Majesty, knowing that title belongs to you. So at the moment, none of the courtiers out there clamouring to get in knows what to call me. Everyone is just addressing me as Sire."

A little smile appeared on Navira's face. "So they are."

Tarkyn shrugged, "It doesn't seem to have helped much. If everyone had known of you earlier, this would have been much easier, but as it is…" He leaned across the table. "Listen Navira, I want nothing more than to walk out that door, back into the woods. But I am the Guardian of Eskuzor and her welfare comes before mine."

Navira studied him silently for a full minute, clearly gauging the truth of his words before deciding on her response. She took a sip of wine, holding his gaze over the glass's rim. Finally, she drew breath and released it. "I agree, Tarkyn, you cannot turn away from the faith these people have in you. But equally, you need not be king to guide them into the future. The choice is yours. You hold the kingdom in the palm of your hand and it will only be by your grace that I assume my birthright." She leaned across the table and took his hand in both of hers. "No wonder Kosar and Jarand saw you as a threat. I too would see you as a threat if I didn't have Danton reassuring me at every turn. I envy you."

The artfulness of this little speech was not lost on Tarquin, but he appreciated the effort it had cost her to place her fate in his hands. "Don't be too impressed," he said wryly. "Those same people were crying out for my blood a few months ago."

His sister gave a friendly smile. "We will have to make sure that doesn't happen again, won't we?"

For a moment, it crossed Tarkyn's mind that this was a veiled threat but her smile seemed relaxed and genuine. He glanced at Danton, his expert on guile, who gave a faint nod. Reassured but wishing to be more formal, Tarkyn removed his hand from Navira's grasp on the pretext of helping himself to more wine. "Navira, I was impressed by what I saw of you during the fire and during our efforts to avert the battle. But from Danton's account, your attitude to people in the Lost Forest may have befitted Kosar and Jarand's courts, but will not suit the future I envisage for Eskuzor."

"I may intend to be more formal than perhaps you would be," said Navira, "but I do not intend to be cruel or excessively intimidating. You and your people have made it all too clear that I might discourage valuable ideas and skills, if I were." She glanced at Danton sitting beside her. "And I have Danton, who can guide me through intrigue and protocols, who will call me to account and who will be king by my side… " She gave a short laugh, "…provided you sanction it." She sent a whimsical smile to the wizard who had raised her. "And you may not realize this, but Caroman has trained me all my life in the expected behaviour of a queen so that I would be ready when I ascended the throne."

The air of congenial negotiation evaporated. Tarkyn's eyebrows snapped together. "*When* you ascended the throne? You *knew* Kosar and Jarand would die?"

Navira nodded uncertainly, suddenly aware that she was on dangerous ground.

"And you did nothing to prevent it?"

She looked in appeal at the older wizards.

In response, Stormaway drew Tarkyn's fire. "We did not know that it would end here and now, but we did know that these brothers would never come to a resolution… and that the only way the conflict would ever end was for one or both of them to die." He gave an apologetic shrug. "And just as I knew you to be the hope for Eskuzor's future, I also knew that the brothers would die together."

"So you let us set them up to negotiate, knowing that it wouldn't work?"

"Knowing that at best, it would only work temporarily and knowing that one day they would die together." Stormaway smiled. "Tarkyn, you are a true idealist, but the world does not always march to your tune. Remember I said to you, 'Sometimes there is no right decision; only the lesser of two evils'?" The wizard could no longer hold Tarkyn's ferocious glare. He dropped his eyes to his plate and concentrated on crumbling a piece of bread as he talked. "Forcing them to negotiate increased the chance of them killing each other sooner, rather than later. By doing this, you have saved Eskuzor from a protracted civil war, which would only have ended in their joint demise anyway."

Tarkyn did not move his gaze. "I remember now… When I asked you whether I would fail to protect Eskuzor, you said, 'No, but you might not like how you succeed.'" Tarkyn stood up suddenly and swiped his arm across the table, sending plates and glasses flying everywhere. The whole floor rocked beneath them and the sides of the tent billowed as Tarkyn's anger blasted outward. "You bastard! You set me up to kill my own brothers. How could you, Stormaway? How could the Guardians of the Past ever say that I could trust you?"

Stormaway cowered but managed to say in a small voice, "Because they are Guardians of Eskuzor so her welfare is paramount to them… as it is to you… and to me."

Tarkyn strode up and down the confines of the tent a few times before coming to a halt, hands on hips, before Stormaway. "Straighten yourself up, Stormaway. I am not going to hit you. When have I ever hit anyone?" Suddenly he turned on Danton and Harkell. "So were you two in on this conspiracy? Have I anyone left I can trust?"

They both started speaking at once then stopped. Harkell gestured to Danton. "Go on. You first."

"Tarkyn, I never understood why it was so urgent for Stillwaters… Navira, to secure my troth. You know how enigmatic she can be."

He glanced at her and shrugged. "She just said that events outside the forest were rushing towards a resolution. I had no idea it was this resolution. I was horrified when I heard of your brothers' deaths, despite what they'd done to you."

The older wizards nodded in agreement. "He was," corroborated Caroman.

Tarkyn nodded and transferred his glare to Harkell. "And you?"

"I have hidden nothing from you," Harkell shrugged, "but perhaps my judgement has been faulty. Maybe I should have listened more when String and Bean described your brothers as pathologically jealous. Maybe we should have realised that if Kosar and Jarand were prepared to kill one brother, you, then they would be prepared to kill another brother. Maybe we overestimated the twin connection." He ran his hands through his hair and sighed. "I don't know. I feel that we have all failed you and left you in a situation you never wanted to be in. I can only say I'm sorry."

Inevitably, Tarkyn's care for his liegeman overrode all else. "No Harkell. You are not at fault." He gave a wry smile. "I doubt that you could have convinced me, even if you had worked it out. Waterstone has often been sceptical about my optimism but he never came close to deterring me."

"Tarkyn," said Stormaway, seeing a chance to redeem himself. "What would it have done to your resolve, had you known that the end to Esukor's strife would only be achieved by the death of your brothers? If you feel bad now, imagine how you would have felt, had you knowingly set up a circumstance in which they might kill each other?"

"Don't bother trying to justify yourself. You may or may not be right, but I am not yet ready to forgive you... or myself." Tarkyn's head ached, overloaded with the horror of his brothers' deaths, the duplicity of the wizards and the enormity of sorting out Eskuzor's future. "I have had enough of the straight lines and right angles inside this tent. I'm going outside for some air."

Chapter 87

Tarkyn's exit left an uncomfortable silence within the command tent. Both Danton and Harkell would have preferred to go with him but Tarkyn had made it clear that he needed time alone. Quietly in the background, Farlowe picked up the fallen plates and cutlery, righted glasses and bottles, and wiped up the spillages that had resulted from Tarkyn's ire.

Looking at the destruction wrought by a moment's lapse, Harkell reflected on the Tamadil volatility that he had trained over the last few months. At least the prince hadn't lashed out with magic. Harkell's soft brown eyes flitted back and forth between the wizards and Danton. Poor Danton was in the unenviable position of having a foot in each camp. No wonder he was looking so dismal.

"Excuse me, General," murmured Farlowe, as he wiped a damp patch at Harkell's elbow.

Harkell obligingly lifted his arm, inwardly wincing at being addressed by a title that everyone else in the tent knew was merely a ruse. *I must put an end to this,* he thought.

His attention was caught by Danton, who heaved a sigh and said, "Well, my Lady and my Lord Wizards, you have certainly made fools of us all. And here we were, mistakenly thinking that we were all working together for the same cause."

"We *are* working for the same cause," said Navira, "Eskuzor's welfare."

Danton pointedly moved his chair away from her. "Eskuzor's welfare or your own? It seems to me that the throne is all you care about."

"No, Danton. That is not true. I may have had prior knowledge that the twins would die together but I did everything that was asked of me to promote a peaceful outcome. I did not conspire to kill either of them, any more than you did. Tell me, what should I have done differently?"

"You wizards should have shared your knowledge," said Harkell quietly. "Despite your years of learning, you have not cornered the market on wisdom. Had we realised the risk, we could, for instance, have placed Kosar within Tarkyn's shield and Jarand within Boravar's to negotiate."

"Perhaps," said Caroman. "But what would you have done, had they failed to reach an agreement? And how, after all their duplicity, could you have had any faith in a pact made between them? We all know they would have double-crossed each other as soon as practicable."

Stormaway leaned over the table to reach a bottle of mountainfolk white wine. "Harkell, Tarkyn knew I was keeping information back," the wizard gave a quirk of a smile, "…and decided to put his faith in me. Have I betrayed him? I don't think so." He took a long draught of wine. "I took too great a burden from a young man's shoulders. In all else but this, I would trust Tarkyn's judgement. But no man should have to decide between the lives of his brothers and the lives of hundreds, perhaps thousands, of people." He put up his hand to forestall their protests. "Don't mistake me. None of us knew this would be the immediate outcome, least of all Navira, but I admit Caroman and I did hope it would be."

"But above all," said Caroman, "like you, we strove most sincerely to prevent civil war."

Harkell conceded the truth of this. When he thought about it, all three wizards were showing signs of strain. They had indeed performed great deeds of magic and without them, it would have been almost impossible to prevent the fighting.

But clearly, Danton still had a bone to pick. "Very well. Let us say for the moment that I accept your argument." He folded his arms and turned to Navira. "So, do you have any more surprises in store for me? For I can tell you right now that if you ever wrong-foot me like this in public, that will be the end of it. It is bad enough that I am made to look an ignorant fool in front of Tarkyn… and Harkell for that matter, when as your partner, I should know what is going on. But in public, it would be unconscionable."

Harkell felt absurdly flattered that Danton would still care about his opinion, now that they were back within the hierarchical society of sorcerers.

Navira eyed her angry betrothed. Then she broke into a smile filled with contrition. "No Danton. There is nothing else. And I do ask your pardon but had I told you, you would have felt obliged to force the burden of foreknowledge on Tarkyn. It has not been easy for either of us, but you have my word that from now on, I will not knowingly withhold important information from you." She glanced around at the other three before returning her gaze to Danton. Abruptly, her voice became cooler. "But in future, I would consider it a kindness if our disagreements could be aired when we are alone."

Oh, she will lead him on a merry dance, thought Harkell with an inward *chuckle. But I think Danton has her measure.*

CHAPTER 88

Tarkyn ducked out though the doorway of the command tent into the cool of early evening. Guards on either side of the door snapped to attention. Above him, thousands of stars studded the soft black sky and his breath produced puffs of white steam.

He glanced uneasily at the white tent some fifty yards to his left, which he knew housed the laid out bodies of his brothers. But his attention was distracted by ragged cheers rising from the nearby campfires. Just as three people converged on him, a raucous cry heralded the arrival of his great mountain eagle from somewhere beyond the hundreds of campfires that dotted the valley. Moments later, Bird landed on his shoulder in a flurry of enormous wings. Despite his preoccupations, Tarkyn grinned as a space cleared miraculously around him.

"Hello, Bird." Tarkyn reached up to stroke her. "I'm glad you're back."

Ignoring the guards who fell in behind him and the people wishing to confer with him but held at bay by Bird's presence, Tarkyn walked slowly among the camp fires, nodding at the soldiers who scrambled to their feet and bowed. He studied their clothing, the tell-tale signs of kit thrown hurriedly together to answer their lieges' call contrasting the smarter uniforms of the career soldiers. Around outlying campfires, men and women sat together, laughing, talking and drinking, some close to their wagons. All through the Valley of the Dry Mile, he could hear scattered pockets of revelry as people celebrated the end of the civil war and the beginning of a new era. He watched their faces, young and old, change as he approached, their expressions ranging from adulation to grim approval and occasionally scepticism.

Out of all of these thousands of sorcerers and all the woodfolk in the forest, who could he talk to, who wouldn't have a vested interest in what he chose for the future? Normally, he would talk to Waterstone but the woodman's care for Tarkyn's welfare far outweighed his care for the welfare of Eskuzor's sorcerers. A group of soldiers felt honoured to receive a smile from Tarkyn as he passed, not realising it was actually elicited by the irony of the woodfolk wanting him to stay with them.

His thoughts moved on, to consider the sorcerers. He could not confer with Harkell and Danton because both would be too closely affected by his decisions. The same applied to his sister and her two wizards. With a jolt he realised that he no longer thought of Stormaway as his. He felt a surge of anger when he thought about the twenty-two year old plan that Stormaway and Caroman had carried out, to protect Navira and eventually place her on the throne. It was her right, he conceded, but he was disappointed to realise that Stormaway had never thought of him as a potential future king. Not that he had wanted to be, but that was not the point… Yet surely he remembered Stormaway looking unconvinced when Tarkyn had stated that he was too gullible ever to be king? Hmph. Maybe Stormaway did think he was capable enough, just not next in line.

Tarkyn shook his head a little; so many new perspectives to think about and no time. He came to such a sudden halt that the guards behind him nearly cannoned into him. He seemed to have collected people as he passed through the campsites so that now, more than a dozen people were waiting to speak to him. He realised that he could not continue to give himself the indulgence of self-reflection. "Your pardon for ignoring you. I have much on my mind. But I am sure you also have many pressing matters which require my attention. Let me hear your concerns and we shall try to resolve them as we walk."

The next hour was spent discussing the logistics of maintaining twenty thousand soldiers, the timing of the troops' withdrawal and the disbandment of the conscripted soldiers. Tarkyn made it clear that, at the moment, he would only address the more immediate pragmatic issues. All troops were to remain stationed within the Valley of the Dry Mile until the future governance of Eskuzor had been determined.

Well before the full gamut of requests had been dealt with, Tarkyn spotted a smaller, out of the way campfire, which seemed to have attracted a group of the more ragged soldiers and several roughly dressed women. And right in their midst were the scruffy figures of String and Bean. Suddenly Tarkyn realised that they, out of everyone, would give him an honest, objective sounding board. They wanted nothing that sorcerer society could give them and beyond each other's, had no need for other people's company or favour. Their interest in other people and events was largely academic.

As the prince bore down on them, the ragged soldiers scrambled to their feet and bowed, followed more slowly by String and Bean. These soldiers stared fearfully at him, their hard lives making them expect the worst from those in authority.

The prince turned to Colonel Charford. "These men's clothes are a disgrace to the army. Please see to it that they are better clothed before the cold of the night sets in. See Stormaway tomorrow for funds to procure them new civilian clothes from that local village, West Wandering." He smiled at the soldiers who had watched this interchange with set faces. "Your pardon. I did not mean to cast aspersions on you, but the rigours of the army's long march and rough living have worn out your clothes and you need replacements. " Not feeling it was within his gift to address the women's attire, he merely smiled at them and nodded, no better at speaking to unfamiliar women sorcerers now than he ever had been.

Both the soldiers and he knew that their clothes had been worn out long before they were conscripted, but his words preserved their dignity enough for them to nod their thanks and accept his largesse.

"And now, gentlemen," Tarkyn indicated the officers and courtiers around him as well as the ragged soldiers and their companions, "would you please find yourselves other campfires for the next hour so that I may converse privately with these trappers? Set guards around this campfire at a distance of twenty five yards to guarantee the privacy of our discussion."

String and Bean, far from seeming gratified at this signal honour, merely looked speculatively at Tarkyn, waiting for the others to withdraw and Tarkyn to sit down, before reseating themselves. Bird nonchalantly rode Tarkyn's shoulder to the ground but hopped off once he was settled. She then strutted back and forth between the guards and him, before finding a perch on an unburned piece of firewood.

Keeping a weather eye on the eagle, Bean asked, "What's up, Tarkyn? Have we done something wrong? You look grim."

Tarkyn forced a smile. "No. You are, as ever, in my good books. In fact, out of everyone in Eskuzor, I am turning to you to talk me through this situation into the future."

Now they did look gratified. "Wow," breathed String. "That is some honour."

Bean grunted, "Yeah, though I can see why. We're honest and uninvolved, aren't we? Hmm. Not too many people around here who aren't waiting with baited breath for the outcome."

"So come on Tarkyn. Tell us the story so far and we'll go from there."

It actually took very little time to fill in the two trappers. Most of it they knew. Only the fore-knowledge of the wizards surprised them, as much as it had Tarkyn.

"So now you've gone from the most hated to the most loved among both woodfolk and sorcerers in the space of a few months," said String. "Huh. Quite an achievement."

Bean took a slug from a flagon of mountain whiskey before handing it to Tarkyn. "I know you're mad at him, but you have Stormaway to thank for most of the sorcerers' change in attitude, you know. He spread the news about you saving the family on the Great West Road and broadcast the anomaly of you having won that tournament you were supposed to have destroyed so that people began to question Kosar's indictment of you."

"Hmph." Tarkyn took a gulp of whiskey and waited until the shudders subsided. "Everything Stormaway did was aimed at bringing the confrontation between Jarand and Kosar to a head… so that Navira could take the throne."

Bean gave a wry smile. "It's not quite that simple, but I won't argue. Let's just acknowledge that you're mad at Stormaway and leave it at that. What do you want to do?"

"About Stormaway?"

String shook his head impatiently. "No. About the future."

Tarkyn shrugged. "What I personally want doesn't come into it. What matters is Eskuzor's future."

Bean wrinkled his nose. "Phew! Smell of burning martyr is getting a bit strong around here."

Tarkyn gave a reluctant smile. "Very funny. Actually the reason I need you two is to make sure that my personal wishes don't influence my decision one way or the other."

"I may have missed something here, but isn't this supposed to be a negotiation between you and Navira?" asked String.

"Publicly, yes. But in reality, I have the backing of both armies and Danton, who is Navira's partner." Tarkyn took a smaller sip and handed the flagon on to String. "…and I am worried about handing Eskuzor over to an untried monarch."

String took a slug and wiped his mouth. "Someone like you, you mean?" he quipped then encountered a glare that made him wish he had not been so flippant.

"I may be untried, but at least I have always lived in Eskuzor as a member of the ruling family, while Navira only has theoretical knowledge of us… And we have so little knowledge of her."

Bean pushed the end of a burning branch further into the fire. "Tarkyn, the succession is not based on merit. It is her birth right. If you cut Navira out, sooner or later some factions will take her part… unless you were planning to kill her." As Tarkyn's eyes widened in shock, Bean hurried on. "No. I didn't think so." He reached for the flagon. "Banishment or imprisonment are other options, I suppose."

"I could give her the north or the south of Eskuzor to hold in trust, as Jarand did."

String snorted. "That didn't work out too well for Kosar, did it? That would only work if she wholeheartedly supported your decision… If she didn't agree, I suppose you could declare her to be a rogue sorcerer still and therefore unfit to rule. That would probably be the safest bet," continued the trapper blandly, as he relinquished the whiskey to Bean.

He eyed Tarkyn for a moment before adding, "It must be heady to be on the receiving end of all that adulation. Maybe it is too hard to walk away from?"

Tarkyn gave a slight smile, fully aware that String was playing devil's advocate. "No, String. I am not my brothers. If Jarand had won this war, he would be revelling in the adulation of the extra thousands. Kosar would be pleased but take it as his due, which it should have been. And I? I have had it for most of my life in varying degrees. I expect it, but don't need it. Had I needed it, I wouldn't have been able to cope with living amongst woodfolk, would I?" He held his hand out for the flagon. "In fact, it is quite the opposite. At the moment it feels fraudulent to be the focus of all that approbation. How would you like it, if crowds were cheering you for killing Bean? And they are hailing me as king, when it is not my right. And I know that if I am true to the succession, I will have to disappoint thousands of people." Suddenly he gave a shudder that was not all due to the whiskey.

String and Bean glanced at each other and let the silence linger.

Eventually Tarkyn took another swig of whiskey and sighed as he passed it on to String. "No. It is not the adulation. It is the power that is hard to relinquish." Their shocked faces pulled him out of his downward spiral and made him grin. "It's true! I feel a great reluctance to give away control of Eskuzor now that I have it in my grasp; to entrust her people's welfare to someone else."

String shook his head. "This is heady stuff… and I'm not sure whether I mean the whiskey or the conversation."

"I can see why you mightn't want to let the power go," said Bean, ignoring String's frivolity as he accepted the flagon. "We have had to work so hard to manoeuvre events without it, haven't we, and now it could be so much easier. You could use it to change so much for the better."

Tarkyn glanced at them and then into the fire, "… and I have become accustomed to being the highest authority within my sphere of influence."

"And yet, I know you. You could never act dishonourably," said Bean firmly.

Tarkyn looked up and gave a reluctant smile. "No, I couldn't. But my highest duty has always been and always will be to Eskuzor, not to any one individual."

"Perhaps so. But the woodfolk are also part of Eskuzor. Surely you must also consider them… Lapping Water, who is currently devastated, Midnight, who was looking like a stressed ghost last time we saw him, Waterstone, Sparrow, Ancient Oak… All of these people matter too.

Besides which, you and they are bound by oath to each other, as I understand it."

"Yes, of course they matter." Tarkyn rubbed his eyes with the heels of his hands then let out a great sigh. "But I worry that my concern for them might be a rationalisation for my own natural inclination to return to the woodlands."

String rolled his eyes. "You were right. You did need someone to talk to."

"Be kind, String," said Bean. "He's only young. Of course he needs someone to talk to. He holds the welfare of two nations in his hands."

String placed his hand on Tarkyn's arm in an unusually avuncular gesture, all joking aside. "Tarkyn, as Guardian of Eskuzor, your role is far more important and enduring than a king's. How could you stand back and guide her welfare for the next three or four hundred years if you're enmeshed in her politics?"

"True, String," said Bean. "Good point."

Tarkyn glanced at him but instead of replying, lifted the flagon to his lips. He lowered it without drinking. "Hmm. This flagon is almost finished. I think we'd better have something to eat." He snapped his fingers and a guard came running. When he had delivered orders for food and another flagon, he forced a smile, "Couldn't get away with doing that among the woodfolk, could I? Ah well, nothing is perfect."

CHAPTER 89

Harkell made his way between the campfires, acutely aware that many of Jarand's soldiers would see him as a traitor. With a conscious effort, he held his head high and met the gaze of anyone he saw watching him. Some of them waited until he met their eyes and then looked deliberately away. Others waited until he had passed, then spat on the ground. Others still watched him thoughtfully, reserving their judgement. No one gave him a smile or word of welcome.

After what seemed an eternity, Harkell reached the tent he had been assigned and slipped past two stony-faced guards into the softly lit interior. He wondered vaguely who had posted the guards. A lantern hanging in the centre of the tent threw enough light to show him two stretchers, a sleeping mat, two chairs set up on either side of a small folding table in the corner. Another officer's kit was propped against one of the stretchers but he had none of his own. He recognised Nyrus' pack lying at the end of the mat.

Harkell threw himself down on his stretcher and let out a long breath, relieved to be shielded from the condemnation he had read on so many faces. He put his hands behind his head and tried to contemplate his future. *Strange,* he thought. *I have fought on the winning side and lost everything.*

I have an embarrassing rank which I will eschew as soon as I am able. Tarkyn must return to the world of sorcerers where princes do not consort with commoners. And I? I cannot return to my role as captain in the southern army after so patently deserting them, especially now that I have held the rank of general. It is hard enough to walk between them, let alone work with them. Blast Tarkyn's brothers! Why did they have to kill each other?

The sound of the tent flap opening distracted him. He saw Nyrus enter, his face lighting up when he first saw Harkell. Then the expression was replaced with an uncertain wariness.

Harkell swung his legs around to sit on the edge of the stretcher. "Good evening Nyrus. I am pleased to see you."

"General." Nyrus snapped a smart salute and stood rigidly at attention.

"At ease, Nyrus. See if you can find me some shaving gear, water, parchment and a pen."

"Yes sir." Nyrus rummaged through his own rucksack and produced writing materials. "These are yours, sir, but I will have to scout about to find some shaving gear."

"Just wait while I write this then." Harkell thought for a minute then wrote a brief missive and handed it to Nyrus with instructions for delivery.

As the young batman turned towards the door, he hesitated.

"Yes?"

"I just wondered…" He shrugged. "Nothing sir. Don't worry."

"Go on. At least you are speaking to me. That is better than everyone else."

"How did Prince Tarkyn force you to betray us? I know you wouldn't have unless you had no choice."

"Oh Nyrus. Thank you for your faith. I hate to disappoint you but I worked willingly with Prince Tarkyn."

Just as he spoke, the tent flap opened again. Captain Guerion walked in and spun his cap across the tent to land neatly on the end of his stretcher. He gave an almost insolent salute and drawled, "General."

When Harkell had nodded his acknowledgement, Guerion continued dryly, "My felicitations. You have certainly benefited from your change of sides. Never have I known such a mercurial rise through the ranks. I had, however, expected better of you."

Harkell eyed his erstwhile friend who was standing over him, his mouth set in a severe line, "Will you let me explain?"

Guerion gave a short nod and sat down on the opposite stretcher. "It is to give you that opportunity that I agreed to share a tent with you and to act as your temporary aide de camp…That and the fact that no one else would have a bar of you."

"Nyrus, you too are owed an explanation. So you may stay and listen for a few minutes before following my orders." Harkell returned his attention to the captain. "You remember when I was flogged and left hanging in that tree? As I told you, Prince Tarkyn's forces rescued me."

"I remember. We all do."

"Prince Tarkyn healed me with the magic he possesses as a forest guardian. He then offered me the opportunity to swear allegiance to him. I did not jump at it so he gave me two hours to decide."

"What? And then he was going to kill you if you didn't?"

Harkell smiled and shook his head. "No. Then he was going to leave me behind as he set off with his people on his journey north across the mountains. From what I know of him now, I am sure Tarkyn would have left me provisions, had I decided to stay."

"So why didn't you?"

"I walked back to the tree where I was flogged. No one was around for miles in any direction. I would have died hanging there. Prince Jarand had completely forsaken me. I had nothing to go back to. So I decided that the bond between liegeman and liege had been broken. I gave my oath to Prince Tarkyn and have been loyal to him ever since."

For a full minute, no one spoke. Then Guerion drew a breath. "So when you resumed your command at the encampment, you were already Prince Tarkyn's man?"

"I was, and I had no intention of rejoining Prince Jarand's forces. I did not even think it was an option. But Saker and Biggin spotted me and kindly but mistakenly worked to have me reinstated," Harkell's mouth quirked, "which left me in the invidious position of being mistrusted by both princes for a while."

"So what was your intention in coming to the encampment?" The captain's voice was hard.

"Simply to gather information. Tarkyn was trying to protect the people of Eskuzor against the effects of his brothers' rivalry." Harkell looked at Guerion appraisingly, "You probably don't realise this, but the king sent well over a thousand men to wrest control of the encampment from Prince Jarand. Tarkyn's people held them up long enough for Jarand to get clean away and avoid an embarrassing confrontation with Kosar. Not only was a pitched battle avoided, but all of those in Jarand's service were saved from the fallout of his wrath."

Guerion stared at him. "So all the time you joked and ate and laughed with us, you saw us as the enemy."

Harkell shifted, uncomfortable beneath his gaze. "Danton never regarded the king's soldiers as his enemies and I never regarded any of you as my enemies. I did wish that I could be open with you but I have never worked against your welfare or even that of Prince Jarand… although I did work against his wishes. Everything I have done with Tarkyn was aimed at preventing civil war and saving the lives and limbs of countless soldiers and conscripts… right up until today." He heaved a sigh. "We succeeded in preventing the war, but at such a cost. None of us expected this. Tarkyn was just trying to force his brothers to negotiate."

"Hmph." Guerion looked at Nyrus. "What? Are you still here? Off you go and do the general's bidding."

Nyrus bobbed his head and fled.

"So where is your army, General? Why haven't they joined us on the battlefield?"

Harkell could not betray Tarkyn's ruse without talking to him first. So he said, "My army is stationed deep within the forest and will remain there. It was never Tarkyn's intention to stage a three-way civil war. They would only have been deployed to rescue Tarkyn if the need arose."

"Now, don't take this the wrong way, Harkell. I don't mean to snipe at you, but I would have thought that the vast majority of Eskuzor's trained soldiers were camped around us."

Recognising that with the use of his name Guerion had reinstated their friendship, Harkell let out a long breath and ran his hands through his hair. "Ah Guerion, of course you are right. I will admit I lead a very unusual army but sadly, without the prince's permission, I cannot tell you much more at the moment."

"Fair enough." Guerion rummaged in his bag and produced two rather warm beers. He knocked the tops off and handed one bottle to Harkell. "Here. I hope, as general, you can get us some more. Supplies are scarce."

Harkell smiled. "Thank you, my friend."

"How's your family? I met your brother Drakell in an inn, a day's ride north of Montraya. He looks just like you. Soon after he left, we received orders to bring them in." He glanced at Harkell, "I didn't know you had changed sides then. I just thought Jarand was getting himself some insurance because you had associated with Tarkyn. I didn't like the idea of your family being detained. So I did my best to hold the search up as long as I could, giving confusing orders that needed clarification. Then I sent soldiers off in small groups to give your family a better chance of getting away." He shrugged and gave a shy smile. "Seems to have worked. One group came very close but their way was blocked by huge trees that fell fortuitously across the road…"

Harkell answered the question in the statement with a grin. "Yes. Moving heavy objects is a blacksmith talent that I too possess. Thank you for doing the best you could under the circumstances. My family arrived safely." He went on to explain the part Jarand had made him play in his devious efforts to force Tarkyn's allegiance. "We all knew that I was living on borrowed time with Jarand. So Tarkyn organised my family's rescue. Otherwise I would have had to return to face Jarand's punishment to save my family."

Guerion raised his eyebrows. "Impressive. Still, I think we all recognise that Prince Tarkyn possesses a greater humanity then his brothers did. I have never seen a nation change its allegiance so willingly or so fast."

At this point, sounds of shouting interrupted them. The shouting drew closer, converging on the tent from all sides. Nyrus scooted in, clutching the required items, his eyes wide with fear and his chest heaving.

"What's going on?" demanded Guerion.

Between breaths, Nyrus gasped out, "Some soldiers asked me about General Harkell, sir, and I only had time to say he willingly changed sides before they started growling and yelling and picking up weapons."

He sobbed, "I ran as fast as I could to warn you. I didn't mean to cause trouble, sir. I didn't get the chance to finish the story."

Harkell sprang to his feet "Right. I'd better go out there and face them."

"I'm coming with you," said Guerion firmly.

"Don't suppose you can raise a shield?"

Guerion grimaced, "Not for long. Maybe five minutes?"

"We won't use it unless we have to. Come on."

Harkell took a deep breath, squared his shoulders, belted on his sword and loosened it in its scabbard before stepping out into the night. The guards standing at the door were tense, ready to spring into action, but they, at least, had not turned on him. Blocking his path stood an angry mob brandishing swords, spears and axes. Hoots of derision went up at his appearance.

"Traitor!"

"Turncoat!"

"Blackguard!"

Harkell met their eyes with well-feigned confidence but no defiance, and held up his hand. He wished he was wearing something more impressive than soft, un-emphatic woodfolk brown, but slowly his lack of reaction quietened them.

"I have two things to say to you. I am pleased you have come because it gives me the chance to explain my position. Secondly, I am pleased that you have not attacked me since the consequences to you would be harsh indeed. Whether you like it or not, my liege is now also yours."

"It's not the king we're worried about," yelled someone from the back. "It's you."

This caused another flurry of shouting. When it died down, Harkell spoke with the authority that he had brought to his role as captain, "I expect better from Prince Jarand's soldiers than this. I do not like to think what impression King Kosar's forces are forming of you. You are not hooligans. You are soldiers of the south. Act like it. Put away your weapons and show the respect due to my rank. Then, and only then, will I provide the explanation you seek."

Harkell's words and demeanour quietened them. But just as weapons were being lowered and the men were straightening themselves up to stand at attention, a raucous outcry sounded behind them.

"Look. They've cornered the bastard!

Rowdy soldiers converged to swell the numbers. Many had clearly been drinking.

Suddenly a spear came hurtling towards Harkell.

As Harkell threw himself to one side, a brilliant ray of peacock blue power intercepted the incoming spear in mid-air. Ash and spatters of molten metal sprayed out, burning some of the nearby soldiers. Guerion slammed his lilac shield down over Harkell and himself, in the same split second that Rena sent forth a shaft of orange magic to strike down the spear thrower.

The rabble was shocked into silence. They stared at the massive, bearded man and the magic-wielding woman, both clad in the soft brown of the woodfolk, who had moved to stand stoically beside their general, just outside the lilac dome of Guerion's shield. Many frowned in distaste at the sight of a woman wearing leggings and using power.

Without any haste, Harkell picked himself and dusted himself off. "Thank you for your intercession, Boravar and Rena. And you, Guerion. But please remove your shield now. There are barriers enough between these soldiers and me."

In the back row, the spear-throwing soldier groaned and sat up rubbing his head.

Hearing mutters of derision aimed at Rena, Harkell said loudly, "Well done, Rena. You were able to stun him without killing him. It is not, after all, your role to be judge and executioner. But very few sorcerers are so adept with their power."

"Thank you, sir," said Rena with a complicit smile.

Guerion raised his eyebrows and murmured so that only Harkell could hear him, "I see what you mean about an unusual army." He turned to the men assembled before them. "I want that man restrained before he recovers. You two, tie his hands and guard him. He will face court martial in due course." He took a step back and nodded, as he handed back to Harkell.

Harkell was just drawing breath to speak when he lost eye contact with his audience as they unexpectedly bowed low. Accurately assuming that this was not directed towards him, Harkell turned to see whose arrival had caused their obeisance. He did a double take as he saw Danton striding towards him, his blond hair bouncing gently on his shoulders with every springy step, garbed in a magnificent deep blue surcoat richly decorated with pearls and silver embroidery, white lace at the neck and wrists. Two guards trailed in his wake. Suddenly, Harkell realised that these soldiers regarded Danton, by virtue of his future marriage to Navira, as one of the most powerful, highly-ranked men in the land. Harkell's mouth quirked, as he also sketched a shallow bow.

Danton nodded to the troops in acknowledgement, not a vestige of a smile on his face and lifted his hand to indicate that they could rise before turning to the officers. "General. Captain. Excuse me for interrupting, but I have need of General Harkell. Guerion, I assume you can take over this briefing. I have heard excellent reports of the southern army's professionalism, both officers and troops, from many sources but particularly from General Harkell. So I look forward to working with you all in the future."

The men of the rabble straightened their shoulders at the compliment but puzzled frowns passed between them.

Danton's mouth became less severe but did not stretch to a smile. "Don't look so surprised. General Harkell and I have worked side by side with Prince Tarkyn for your welfare. You may not have had the opportunity to win booty in battle but at least you return whole to your families. Now attend to Captain Guerion. If you would come with me, General?" He turned on his heel and walked back the way he had come, Harkell at his side. His gait seemed leisurely but Harkell, who knew how he moved, could tell that Danton was deliberately conveying the impression that he was unconcerned.

Once their steps had taken them out of sight of the rabble, Danton signed to the guards to drop back and grinned. "So was that helpful or are you angry with me for interfering?"

Harkell gave a surprised laugh. "I didn't even think about it in those terms. I was just following your orders. You are a consummate actor, my lord."

Danton scowled, "Don't you "my lord" me… at least not in private." He cocked his head while he thought. "Hmm. This must be as confusing for you as it was for me when I first entered the forest. All the rules have changed, haven't they? And you don't know where you stand." He clapped Harkell on the back. "Come on, my friend. We need to talk. Let's go to my tent and down a few beers. I am not sharing with anyone, so we will have it to ourselves."

Once they were settled with a supply of beer, Danton asked his question again. "So, was it helpful?"

Harkell considered. "Yes, I think so. I am certainly not angry at your intervention. I think my story will come better from Guerion's lips than from mine. It is not an ideal situation for a senior officer to have to justify himself to his men… not that they are my men, but you know what I mean. So thank you."

"It occurred to me a few hours ago that you would be in an invidious position, walking amongst your former colleagues. So I had a couple of people keeping an eye out for any rumblings. Boravar and Rena did an excellent job."

"Thanks. They did." Harkell fiddled with his beer bottle, spinning it slowly round and round. After a few moments, he sighed. "This will not be the end of it, of course. I had trouble enough making the decision to change allegiance. So I'm sure many will not agree with my actions." He glanced at Danton as though he were about to say something further but instead dropped his eyes to his bottle of beer and watched the light catch flashes of amber as he swirled it between his fingers. Suddenly he laughed. "I wonder at what point Tarkyn will realise that he has to tell me that I am no longer a general. I would love to see his face." He waved his hand as he saw Danton's look of consternation. "No, don't worry. I won't force him into that dilemma. I have already sent him a letter resigning my so-called commission."

This did nothing to ameliorate Danton's expression. "For once I am not concerned for my liege. I am concerned for you. Surely this must come as a harsh disappointment for you."

Harkell thumped his beer down so hard on the table that some of it slopped up out of the neck. "When will you ever stop underestimating me? A rank bestowed on me for the sole purpose of creating the impression that we had a large army is not worth the snap of my fingers. I have never thought of myself as a general. You and I both know it was purely play-acting. How then could I be disappointed to lose it?"

"I beg your pardon," said Danton stiffly. After a few moments the tension went out of him and he added, "I really do. The more I think about it, the more I realise that sometimes," he grimaced, "maybe often, I fall into the trap of underestimating you." He frowned. "And yet I know you are no fool. I don't know why I do it."

"Blind prejudice, Danton. Stormaway does it too. Never mind. I know you don't do it intentionally. I may get exasperated sometimes, but that's only because I overestimate you and am disappointed when you fall short of my unrealistically high expectations of you." Harkell grinned. "You are, after all, only nobility and don't know any better."

For a moment, Danton looked deeply offended. Then slowly, a little smile appeared on his face that gradually spread into a broad grin. "I remember Tarkyn telling me how salutary your company was. It certainly is." He took a swig of beer and banged the bottle down on the table, mimicking Harkell's actions. "Now, the question is, how can I avoid disappointing you in future? I do like to live up to high expectations, you know. Hmm." He drummed his fingers on the table as he thought. "I know. I will work out how I would react in a situation and then assume that you would react a similar way."

Harkell smiled. "I think that would be a good starting point. We are both intelligent men with a strong sense of honour and a broad knowledge of the issues facing Eskuzor. Even though our roles are different, and will be more so in the future, we are similar in many ways."

A wave of unease swept across Danton's face. "This has been a long day, hasn't it? Everything has changed. Suddenly, no matter which of them takes the throne, I will be thrust out of the forest, back into the intricacies of court life. I used to manoeuvre events from the sidelines but this time, the manipulation and fawning will be aimed more directly at me, as a member of the royal family. That will make it harder for me to protect them. People will not be so forthcoming with me as they once were and I will not be privy to the plotting and scheming that goes on in the salons and behind the scenes."

"Do you not fear also for yourself?"

Danton's eyes twinkled. "No, my friend. I am as I always was. My first care will always be for Tarkyn and Navira. The only advantage of a foot in each camp is that I, more than anyone, can be sure of my new role; I will be supporting the next monarch as his or her right hand man." He gave a little grimace. "I will miss the woodfolk though, especially Rainstorm and Waterstone. I will have to find a way to visit them from time to time. After all, I cannot just reject my bloodbrother out of hand, can I? And they too are my people now."

"You should be able to visit them when you are travelling the forest road between Tormadell and Montraya, especially since you are able to translocate."

"True." Danton smiled. "And although I shall miss the woodfolk, I will enjoy the colour, fashion and intrigue of court. I always have." His smile faded. "But what about you?"

Harkell shrugged self-consciously. "I don't know yet. It will depend on Tarkyn: what he decides to do himself, what his attitude is to me if he chooses to return to sorcerer society."

Danton frowned. "Whatever happens, you and I must make every effort to maintain our friendship."

Harkell gave a whimsical smile. "I am willing but I think it must be you who makes the effort. I doubt I will be allowed anywhere near you without an invitation, once the old protocols kick in."

CHAPTER 90

Bean bit into a doughy roll filled with soft cheese and thinly sliced chicken. "Hmm. This is better food than these poor buggers around us can afford. Some of these men were forced from their homes with just the clothes on their backs. No time to pack or even say goodbye."

"Bloody thugs, Jarand's soldiers," muttered String.

"Be fair. Not all of them, String."

Tarkyn grimaced. "Yet another problem to sort out. Jarand has gone but I'll have to find a replacement for Jarand's general. He has bred a culture of brutality and disrespect for the people of the south. How will I find someone with integrity to replace him?" Without waiting for a reply, Tarkyn followed his own train of thought aloud. "In my opinion, it should be someone from the southwest. Possibilities I have considered: Colonel Charford, but really I don't know much about him except that he had Andoran and Sargon hanged which means that, at least in that instance, he meted out justice. Lord Davorad, who financed Jarand's recruitment encampment and was almost certainly involved in nefarious practices with Sargon and Andoran. Besides, I never liked what I saw of him at court. Lord Tolward from the Grasslands. He would be very good except that I gather his health is failing. Besides, neither of them is a military man, I think." He shrugged. "I don't really personally know any other noblemen from the southwest. Anyone you know of?"

"Harkell," chorused the trappers.

"No," said Tarkyn firmly. "Harkell is not a nobleman. He is only a captain and his family are blacksmiths, for goodness sakes. He's done well to rise as high as he has."

"But surely I heard you introduce him as a general," objected String.

"You know perfectly well that I gave him that rank purely to give our opposition the impression that our numbers in the forest were larger than they are," Tarkyn protested.

"I see," said String slowly. "So now you are back in the real world of sorcerers, you are going to strip him of his rank, are you?"

Bean shook his head. "I had thought better of you than that."

"But let's face it, Bean," said String spuriously, "Tarkyn has generations of ingrained class consciousness to overcome. He's done well to get as far as he has."

This deliberate parody of his own patronizing words was not lost on Tarkyn. He scowled. "Any other suggestions?"

"Hmm. There's always Colonel Carrioll," suggested String provocatively. "You seem to share his values, Your Highness."

Tarkyn's eyes narrowed. String drew back, worried that this time, he had pushed too hard. For two long minutes, the prince stared at him, unaware or unconcerned that he was making String feel uncomfortable. Finally, he said, "I was brought up with the same values as Colonel Carrioll. My acquaintance with Harkell and the woodfolk has led me to reconsider those values, but I am not sure to what extent. The adjustments I have made during my tenure among the woodfolk do not transfer wholesale into sorcerer society. I will have to think about it."

He stood up, unwinding his long frame to tower over them. In the public glare of the surrounding soldiers and camp followers, the trappers hastened to stand also, as Tarkyn added, "You are right about one aspect though. I have, almost light-heartedly, given Harkell an empty rank that probably matters a great deal to him. And really, he was never in charge of anyone within the forest, was he? He organised the refugees during the fire but few of them are true soldiers. And my supposed army is the woodfolk, who would not answer to anyone but me and each other." He ran his hand through his hair. "Oh dear." He pulled himself together to raise a smile. "Thank you for your help, you two, even though you have presented me with new conundrums. Good night."

Bird's huge wings made String and Bean duck, as she launched herself into the air to grab hold of Tarkyn's shoulder, digging in her sharp talons and hitting Tarkyn around the head with her wings as she strove to get her balance. Tarkyn rolled his eyes at the trappers' grinning faces, "Hilarious. She weighs a ton and I have to wear shoulder protection all the time." He gave a vague wave and strode off, with Bird bobbing up and down on his shoulder, gathering his guardsmen around him.

Tarkyn did not return to continue discussions with Navira but instead headed to Kosar's sleeping quarters, which had been prepared for his own use.

Farlowe had anticipated him and was waiting for him as he entered. "Your Highness, two missives await your attention."

The first was from Danton reiterating his loyalty and his innocence of any part of the wizard's planning. The second was from Harkell:

Dear Tarkyn,

Sooner or later you will realise that I cannot continue to act as a general when in fact, there is no army to command. At the time, we used the rank to impress outsiders with the size of your supposed force within the forest, but that time has passed.

Sitting with the Princess Navira, Lord Danton, the wizards and you, I suddenly realised that, as a general with no army, I was living more than a lie, I was living a farce.

To save us both further embarrassment, I am resigning my commission, such as it is. You may tell people it was for family reasons, if you wish, and time the announcement to suit your need.

Be assured you have my complete support, particularly through this time of transition.

Beyond that, if you still wish for an ex-Captain, blacksmith's son, to advise and support you, I am your man. However, I fully appreciate, none better, the pressures of sorcerer society and will completely understand if my time at your side has passed.

Although the ending was not what we envisaged, we did achieve what we set out to do, which was to avert a civil war.

I am always yours to command.

Your friend and liegeman,

Harkell

"Blast! Blast! Blast! Blast!" fumed Tarkyn. "What have I done?" He stormed back and forth within the tent, waving the letter. Farlowe, used to Kosar, stood quietly to one side and kept as much out of the way as he could. When he had calmed down, Tarkyn sat on the edge of the bed and re-read the letter. "He's well educated for a blacksmith's son," he mused before throwing the letter down on the bed beside him. "Oh blast him! He has worked so hard to get where he is… or was. And then my bloody brother destroyed all his hard work and hopes in an afternoon. And now I have done the same."

Seeing Farlowe standing there with carefully schooled, polite disinterest on his face, he explained, "I am talking about Harkell. What is your impression of him?"

Farlowe's face lit up at being addressed, "Oh, General Harkell, Sire? He is a fine man, a true gentleman."

Tarkyn nodded curtly. "Go on."

"Well Sire, I heard some soldiers saying they were relieved he had survived. They thought Prince Jarand must have ordered him killed when he disappeared so suddenly. I heard one soldier jest that General Harkell would go to any lengths to protect his men, even if it meant deserting."

"From what I know of him, I am sure that he was an excellent officer, even under my brother."

"I believe so, Sire. Of course some people are calling him a turncoat and resent that he has gained so much from changing sides… and I heard one officer say how glad he was that General Harkell wasn't *their* commander."

"Did he say why?"

Farlowe shook his head. "Not in my hearing, Sire." He hesitated then added, "However, I believe this particular officer has a reputation for his ruthless quelling of unrest and his particularly high conscription rate."

Tarkyn picked up Harkell's letter and read it through once more. When he had finished, he folded it and put it in an inner pocket before looking up. "You are an unexpected wealth of information, Farlowe. My brother was lucky to have you." Suddenly he remembered the previous time he had seen Farlowe when Kosar had ordered him to be strung up mistakenly as a traitor. "How are your shoulders?"

Farlowe glanced at him as he put aside the cloak and picked up Tarkyn's soft leather boots, ready to clean them. "I would not presume to complain, Sire."

"You are not complaining. You are answering a direct question, to which I require an answer."

"Very painful, Sire, especially on cold mornings, but," he added hastily, "I am still able to perform my duties."

"I am sure you are," said Tarkyn reassuringly. "Now sit down beside me on the bed."

Farlowe gave Tarkyn a strange look but put down the boots and complied.

"Farlowe, perhaps you have heard that I am a guardian of the forest?" When the manservant nodded, he continued, "I have a healing power, which I am about to use on you. After all, it was our efforts to intimidate Kosar and Jarand that caused you to be falsely accused and punished. So I believe I owe you reparation."

The old man merely looked frightened but did not move.

Tarkyn smiled. "It doesn't hurt. I will place my hands on your shoulders and send my into you. Ready?"

A few minutes later, Farlowe was blinking in surprise. "My word. That is so much better. Thank you… But a word of warning, Sire, if I may. Do not advertise your power too widely. You will be inundated with people who need healing."

"Hmm. Yet, if I have power, surely I should use it for the good of people? Still, I can see your point. I could not minister to the needs of thousands." Tarkyn gave a little smile. "Nothing is easy, is it?"

CHAPTER 91

Tarkyn sent Farlowe away to give himself breathing space to think. He sat on the edge of the bed for some minutes, mulling over the events of the past day. He had changed. The world had changed around him and he had responded. Now he held Eskuzor in the palm of his hand and he wasn't at all sure that he wanted to let her go. He gave his head a little shake as he remembered that the bodies of his brothers lay not one hundred yards away from him.

He knew he had to settle things with Navira but realised he would deal better with her if he rested first and met her with a clear head. But as soon as he lay down, his mind was beset by dreams of cheering crowds, conniving courtiers, woodfolk fading into the woods and his sister's angry amber eyes; all swirling around him as he issued strings of orders that swept like rays of magic transforming everything in their path.

Yet from the chaos of his dreams, he awoke an hour later, resolved upon a course of action.

He ordered warm water to refresh himself and while he waited for its arrival, crossed to the small desk in the corner and scribbled a note. As soon as Farlowe had laid out towels and the basin of water, Tarkyn gave him the note. "Take this to my sister. I will need a second chair. Invite her to share supper with me."

Farlowe returned shortly, bearing a brief missive from Navira:

Tarkyn,

A queen does not respond to summonses. She issues them. You may attend me when you are ready.

Navira.

Tarkyn gave a crack of laughter. "She has been schooled in the behaviour of a queen, hasn't she? But she has missed her mark this time… Now, shall I simply outwait her or shall I increase the stakes?"

Farlowe looked faintly alarmed. "I couldn't say, Sire."

"Hmm. I don't think I have the patience to outwait her. So…" Once more the prince scribbled a note and handed it to his manservant. "Take this to Stormaway please."

Ten minutes later, Stormaway presented himself at the door of the tent, looking rather flustered, with Journeyman in tow. Both wizards bowed before entering.

Tarkyn gave a curt nod. "I am pleasantly surprised to see that you are holding true to your oath to me, Stormaway. Do I gather from your demeanour that you met with some opposition in responding to my summons?"

"A little, Sire." Knowing he was still on rocky ground, Stormaway hesitated before adding, "I sincerely hope, Sire, that we have not exchanged one destructive sibling rivalry for another."

"No Stormaway. This is merely a temporary jostling for position." He turned to the younger wizard. "Now Journeyman, having been on the receiving end of your contrivances, I know you to be a wizard of great cunning and an impressive degree of skill, but also that you possess uncertain morals. This may or may not be because you have been in my brother's service. However, I now wish you to enter my service. Are you willing?"

Journeyman knelt and placed his hand on his heart. "Yes, my lord."

"Stormaway, this time I do require a binding spell. And Journeyman, in giving me your fealty, you are guaranteeing to act according to my values. Do you understand? You may not use the ends to justify immoral means; devious yes, blatantly immoral, no. Stormaway will instruct you on my view of the world." Tarkyn nodded. "You may begin."

Stormaway eyed Tarkyn, clearly wanting to protest, but the prince's implacable expression deterred him. So instead, he muttered a series of unintelligible words that made Journeyman blanch. A green haze enveloped the young wizard as he knelt before Tarkyn.

"Now," ordered Stormaway.

"Tarkyn Tamadil, I give you my pledge that I will honour and serve you, body and soul, to the end of my days, on pain of death."

"Journeyman, I give you my vow that I will protect and support you, as your liege lord."

The green haze swirled around the head of the kneeling wizard then slowly spiralled into him. Journeyman's eyes widened and his whole body shuddered.

At a nod from Stormaway, Tarkyn bade him rise. Journeyman rose shakily to his feet. He looked close to tears. "You didn't have to do that, you know. I was never disloyal to Prince Jarand and I would never now betray you, Your Highness. I accept without question your decision to bind my compliance, but it was not needed."

"I'm sorry, Journeyman. You may have been true to Jarand but you worked against your master, Stormaway, while you were still his apprentice. Consider it a mark of respect for your power. Over and over, Stormaway and I have had to counteract your spells and I want to be absolutely sure that I now have you on my side." Tarkyn smiled and placed his hand on the young wizard's shoulder. "And I think you may still have a bit to learn from Stormaway, as do I. Welcome to my service." His smile broadened. "Thank you for your assistance, Stormaway. You may both leave."

The wizards glanced at each other in confusion, then back at Tarkyn. But for all his apparent friendliness, Tarkyn was clearly awaiting their departure.

As they bowed and turned away, Tarkyn called Journeyman back.

Stormaway hesitated but reluctantly continued on his way as Journeyman, left alone with Tarkyn, eyed him nervously. "Yes, my lord?"

"What do you know of Prince Jarand's general? Lord Maltran, as I remember."

The young wizard thought for a minute, clearly anxious to impress with his answer. "As I gather Your Highness knows, Prince Jarand's soldiers are feared for their brutality. Lord Maltran cares deeply for results, but less about the means. Your meeting with Prince Jarand prompted a few reforms, Sire, but neither General Maltran nor the prince was particularly committed to anything beyond a few cosmetic changes. In fact I heard the general mutter something about… hmm…" Journeyman gave a little cough and faltered to a stop.

"Yes Journeyman? Continue what you were saying."

"…idealistic youth, Sire." Journeyman winced and made a small convulsive ducking movement.

"Journeyman," said Tarkyn quietly, "I will never hit you, you have my word."

The young wizard straightened and considered the prince for several long seconds. Then a slow smile dawned. "Why, Sire, I believe you wouldn't."

Tarkyn laughed. "As an idealistic youth, how could I?" He nodded to the other chair. "Take a seat. Now, tell me, who would you recommend to replace Lord Maltram in order to clean up the attitudes and behaviour of the Southern Army?" Seeing Journeyman's frown, he held up his hand, "I am aware that many men and officers are honourable but I do not know my brother's army well enough to discern which ones."

"The higher ranked officers were handpicked by General Maltram but Colonel Carrioll is… was good, Sire. Colonel Charford, Captain Guerion. …" He listed a few other possibilities before saying, "and I believe you know Captain, pardon me, General Harkell." He paused. "Captain Harkell was exemplary, Sire. The prince tried for years to break him. He constantly belittled him in front of his men, courtiers and the public, and always gave him the tasks with the least chance of success. Most recently, he and his company were assigned the unruliest area of Montraya where they succeeded in maintaining order without inflaming the community's resentment. No mean feat, Sire."

"If Jarand did not like having a commoner as captain in his forces, why did he allow it?"

"I believe he was fascinated by the anomaly of it. He enjoyed testing Harkell's limits. In fact, I suspect Prince Jarand had formed a grudging respect for Captain Harkell and took his failure against your forces as a personal slight. Certainly, the punishment meted out by the prince seemed harsher than usual… and he regretted it later."

Tarkyn frowned. "You are not just saying this because you know that Harkell is a friend of mine, are you?"

Journeyman cast his eyes down, shook his head and mumbled something that Tarkyn did not catch. At Tarkyn's request, the wizard raised his head, looked him reluctantly in the eye and repeated what he had said. His face was flushed with embarrassment. "I said, 'I couldn't lie to you if I wanted to.' The binding spell would not let me."

"I see. I beg your pardon then."

Journeyman just looked at him, unable to think of a rejoinder that wouldn't sound disrespectful.

Tarkyn nodded slowly, understanding. "It is the binding spell that distresses you, isn't it?"

"I am sorry, my lord. If it is your wish, it should also be my desire. I will do my utmost to come to terms with it." He shrugged. "But without my own will, I will never be able to prove my dedication to you."

"I am fairly sure that you could get away with a minimal level of service to satisfy the binding spell. So I will recognise when you are working above and beyond its expectations. But with or without the binding spell, only time and knowledge of you will convince me of your true, unbound loyalty to me." The prince smiled sympathetically. "If it is any consolation, you are well on your way to convincing me. Don't try too hard. It will come in time."

"You are kind to be concerned for me, my lord, even if you are the source of my discontent. And despite the fact that I have regarded you as Prince Jarand's adversary for many years, I find I am coming to like you." Suddenly Journeyman grinned, making him look younger and more vulnerable. "And you can tell I am not just flattering you because I can't lie to you."

Tarkyn laughed. "Thank you Journeyman. Now you had better leave. I am expecting a visitor."

Not ten minutes later, Navira stormed into his tent, in a flurry of blue skirts, her cheeks red with anger. "Just what do you think you're doing, swearing people into your service?"

"Good evening, Navira. So pleased you could find time, amid the myriad demands on your attention, to see me."

"Stop toying with me, Tarkyn."

Tarkyn raised his eyebrows. "I cannot see what possible objection you could have. I announced that if people served me, they would also serve you," he shrugged, "… always assuming we can reach an accord." He waved his hand, "Farlowe, some tea for my sister and myself and perhaps a teacake if you can find one." As soon as he was gone, the prince sat down and indicated the other seat. "So far, I feel that I have been manipulated to achieve your ends… and I gather you even briefly considered bringing the two armies against me."

"Who told you that?" demanded Navira.

"Ancient Oak, using images. So we had better sort out our differences before we have another civil war on our hands. After all, I gave my word to those people out there that we would stand united." Tarkyn leant forward. "Navira, as you so rightly pointed out, I hold the balance of power. But more than that, I am Guardian of Eskuzor. I remember clearly you saying that no power is as great as that of the forests of Eskuzor and no authority higher than its Guardian. You said you would work in alliance with me and yet you considered sending the armies of Eskuzor against me. That is no type of alliance that I know of."

Navira's cheeks reddened with embarrassment. "I beg your pardon, Tarkyn. That was poorly done. I'm afraid I panicked when I thought you had knowingly usurped me. The intention died within minutes."

Tarkyn did not relent. "Only because no one supported you. What if they had egged you on? When your temper had cooled, would you have had the courage to admit you had been hasty or would you have been irrevocably committed to fighting me?"

Navira's cheeks burned. For a full minute, she sat looking steadfastly down. Finally she raised her eyes. When she spoke, her voice was so low Tarkyn could barely hear it. "Perhaps you are right. Perhaps, despite all the work I have done to master my power and my emotions, I am still no fit person to rule Eskuzor." But just as Tarkyn was strong, so too was she. The martial spark returned to her eye as she added, "But I did insure against my volatility by asking Danton to marry me. I knew he would be able to rein me in… and he did."

"I hope he means more to you than that."

Navira gave a quirky smile. "I am glad you care so much for him. Danton asked me much the same question and I will tell you what I told him: I love him and believe that in him, I have found my soul mate." She took a breath, "…And I will trust you with one thing more that I didn't tell him; I don't think I could live without him."

"That places you in a weak position."

Navira shrugged. "So be it."

"Before we go any further, Navira, you must swear an oath of alliance with me. You offered to before, but never did."

Tarkyn found himself looking at his own haughty expression on his sister's face.

"Must?"

He smiled as he recognised the expression. "Must," he said calmly.

Tarkyn waited while Farlowe re-entered the tent and set out a teapot, fine china cups, plates and silver knives. With the magic of a highly-trained, well-connected manservant, he had managed to procure the requested teacake, which he set down with the hint of a victorious flourish.

Tarkyn smiled. "Well done Farlowe. You are a genius. Leave the rest. We will serve ourselves. I will call you if I need anything else."

Farlowe bowed, nodded to Navira and withdrew.

As he set about pouring the tea, Tarkyn said, "And you must publicly acknowledge my authority as Guardian of Eskuzor."

She accepted a cup of tea and after blowing on it, took a careful sip. "And if I do, what do I gain from it?"

"All you have worked towards and yet none of it."

Navira gave a sigh of exasperation. "You speak in riddles. I have already acknowledged that you hold the balance of power. Is that not enough for you?"

"No. I do not want my authority to rely on the threat of brute force. I want it built into Eskuzor's constitution and sorcerers' lore. I want all children, including your children, to learn the legends of forest guardians so that as I live through generations of kings and queens, people will recognize my right to guide Eskuzor's future." He gave her a smile of genuine warmth. "You will be Queen, Navira, but I will be the highest authority in the land."

To his surprise, Navira laughed with delight. "Oh thank you, Tarkyn. I give you my oath that I will work in alliance with you from henceforward, just as I have until now except for that one unfortunate moment of weakness. I will heed your advice, knowing you will glean your knowledge from a wider perspective." Her eyes twinkled provocatively. "But I do not promise always to agree with you."

Tarkyn laughed. "I can cope with that. Even Danton, my most devoted liegeman, does not always agree with me." His smile faded. "However, I will retain the right to override the reigning monarch's decisions… even though I hope never to use it."

Navira put her hand over Tarkyn's. "As long as you remember that even forest guardians are fallible. Remember the injustice of the Lost Forest? The forest guardians of yore allowed it to continue for centuries until your friend Harkell challenged the premise and you outfaced the guardians."

"I will remember." He grinned. "And if I don't, I am sure the woodfolk will remind me."

Chapter 92

For some time after Navira left, Tarkyn sat quietly, finishing off the tea in the pot, even though it had become over-stewed. He was just about to prepare for bed, when an image appeared in his mind of Lapping Water, Waterstone, Rainstorm and Autumn Leaves standing together beckoning him emphatically. Midnight was in Lapping Waters' arms, with his head on her shoulder looking, just as Bean had said, like a stressed ghost. In that moment, the little boy must have tuned in to what the woodfolk around him were doing, because Tarkyn was assailed by a jumbled wave of confusion, fear and, threading through it all, longing.

Assuming that they had good reason, Tarkyn took no offence at their dictatorial style, merely sending an image of himself giving a tired smile and nodding.

He checked that he still had the leaf in his pocket that he had placed there before the confrontation with his brothers and their armies, what seemed a lifetime ago. Then he felt around on the ground and plucked a few strong pieces of grass from the periphery of the tent's floor where the carpet did not quite reach the wall.

To Farlowe, he said, "Inform the guards not to admit anyone until I return. I am off into the woods for a while. Do not wait up for me. I will not require your service until the morning." Taking the leaf from his pocket, he murmured, "*Maya Mureva Araya....*"

He arrived with a thud as he dropped the last foot onto the ground from the leaf's place of origin on a low branch. He lay on his right side under the bush, taking long slow breaths to counteract the nausea of translocation.

When he opened his eyes, he looked straight into the brilliant green of Midnight's eyes. The little boy was squatting next to him, waiting patiently for him to recover.

Tarkyn smiled in the darkness, "You are something special, aren't you, little one?" He lifted his left arm and Midnight crawled under to snuggle up against his chest. Tarkyn closed his arm around him and kissed the top of his head as the little boy heaved a huge sigh of relief. For a while, they just lay in the dark, exchanging images about the way they had worked together to capture the king and his twin, followed by the shock of the twins' unexpected deaths, the disappearing armies and the roaring crowds.

Eventually, a voice came out of the darkness. "There are others of us who would like to talk to you, you know."

Tarkyn grinned. "Hello Rainstorm." He gave Midnight a final squeeze.

"Come on little one. Enough of this nonsense." He sprang to his feet and took Midnight's hand before emerging from among the bushes into the light of a newly stoked firesite.

Most of the home guard were standing around the fire, waiting for him. None of the sorcerers was there. Presumably the woodfolk hadn't woken them. Many were rubbing sleep from their eyes or tousling their hair to wake themselves up. Unsure of the effect on Tarkyn of the day's events, there was an air of constraint.

From within their midst, Waterstone strode forward and threw his arms around Tarkyn. "Well my brother, whatever the outcome, you must have been through fire and rapids today. I am glad you have returned to us, even if it is only for a short time."

Waterstone's kindness felt like coming home. Tarkyn's whole body relaxed as he finally felt safe enough to give way to his grief for his brothers and slough off the strain of the whole complicated mess he had had to manage. He felt other arms across his back, and hands laid on any part of him they could reach, as his home guard crowded around him. Then something scrabbled against his thigh. He looked down into Sparrow's upturned face.

He grinned. "Hello Sparrow." As he extricated an arm to tousle her hair, the people around him pulled away, giving the odd final pat as they withdrew.

"Come on, Tarkyn. Come and sit by the fire while I make us all some tea," said Autumn Leaves.

Tarkyn nodded and did as he was told.

As he moved towards the fire, Lapping Water walked beside him, tucking her arm into his. "I am sorry to hear about your brothers. I am sure that despite their shortcomings, there would have been memories of them that you cherished. No one is all bad." Nothing in her demeanour gave away that she had been a devastated wreck a few hours before. She stayed with him as he found a seat beside the fire and kept her hand on his knee.

Ancient Oak sat down on the other side of him, holding two soft doughy rolls filled with creamy cheese, chunks of venison and an assortment of green leaves. He handed one to Tarkyn and kept one for himself. "Good to see you, little brother."

"Good to see you too." Tarkyn leant back against a log and let out a gusty sigh. "You have no idea…"

Summer Rain appeared with the inevitable disgusting tonic. So glad was he to be back, that he merely smiled his thanks and drank it without demur, managing to hide his shudders at its bitterness. Nevertheless he thanked Autumn Leaves fervently for his cup of tea when it arrived, relieved to be able to wash away the taste.

For a while no one spoke to him, giving him time to recover. Tarkyn bit into the roll, thinking he had eaten a great deal that evening. "Well, with forty thousand sorcerers vying for my attention, here I am. Why did you summon me?"

"Avid curiosity," said Rainstorm promptly. "We have no idea what is going on and although once we couldn't care less what was happening in the sorcerer world, now it is pivotal to your wellbeing, so now we do."

"Don't listen to this young pup," said Autumn Leaves. "We called you back because we knew you needed us." He laughed as a puzzled frown appeared on Tarkyn's brow. "You may not have known it, but we did."

Tarkyn stared at him for a few moments as he took another bite of his roll and chewed while he thought. Slowly a small smile began to play around his mouth. "I have always considered it a weakness to need anyone." He held up a forestalling hand as he saw several people preparing to take issue. "But I now realise that you people take it for granted that you need and are needed by each other… and because it is two-way, it is not a weakness… You're right. I do need you. It has been very hard, getting through today without you all around me."

"I bet it has," said Rainstorm. "And we miss you already."

Tarkyn laughed. "Thanks. So you may be pleased to know that it will not be forever. I have acceded to Navira her right to be the next monarch." The carefully quiet woodfolk forgot themselves enough to raise a muted cheer. Amidst a sea of smiling faces, he added, "… on the condition that my authority as forest guardian is recognised far and wide as the highest in the land."

A babble of voices broke out as the woodfolk simultaneously shared their views. Finally Thunder Storm's deep voice made itself heard. "Wise move Tarkyn. That should make it easier to look after Eskuzor, especially down the generations. We won't have to connive and plot to make your voice heard."

"And despite her moment of perfidy," said Ancient Oak, "I think Navira will do well. She's a little passionate and haughty at times, perhaps more so than you, but with Danton by her side, she will mellow."

Creaking Bough nodded. "She is strong, brave and decisive, but also kind when she needs to be and open to Danton's censure. I think she will make a fine queen."

"I am glad you approve," said Tarkyn, with a touch of dryness in his voice. "I will, however, have to live in Tormadell for at least six months, maybe a year, to sort out the legalities, to make sure everyone can see that

Navira has my seal of approval … and to support her. Even Danton does not know everything there is to know about being a Tamadil. After that, I will return to live here in the forests."

Waterstone nodded his approval. "Pleased to hear it, both for you and us. Besides, Navira and Danton should be left to rule unhampered and you will make a better watchdog observing from afar."

"True." Tarkyn smiled privately at the assurance in the voice of one who knew so little of royalty. He sipped his tea, enjoying his time with them but knowing it would soon end. He took a breath. "But until then, I'm afraid I will have to manage without you all, much as it grieves me."

"No, you won't." Lapping Water squeezed his knee. "Just because this disaster has befallen you, we will not forsake you. You forget. Wherever you are, we are sworn to you. Besides, we care for you. You are one of us."

Tarkyn frowned in confusion. "But you can't come to court. You would be betraying your woodfolk oath of concealment."

"No, we can't come to court. You will have to rely on your guards and Danton to protect you there. Although even there, if your need were dire, we would come." She smiled provocatively at him. "But we have a plan that requires just a bit of work from you…"

"Really?" Tarkyn raised his eyebrows. "And just what are you suggesting?"

Ancient Oak laughed at Tarkyn's emphasis. "Don't get up on your high horse. This is for your own good. We want you to finish what you started and grow corridors of bushland between the forest and your two cities, Tormadell and Montraya. After all, there are already new copses everywhere across western Eskuzor. So now is the time to do it before people start to clear the new growth away."

"Then we can travel undetected across the breadth of Eskuzor," said Autumn Leaves triumphantly. "We wanderers could even organise to convey messages about the kingdom while we are on our travels. I'm sure you could set up drop-off places where they would be safe from prying eyes." He grinned at Tarkyn's stunned expression. "Are there any woods close to this palace of yours where we could set up a firesite? If not, you'll have to plant some."

"Are you telling me that you would come so close to sorcerers' dwellings? Right into the middle of the city?" Tarkyn shook his head in amazement. "Are you sure? I would never ask it of you… The palace forecourts are formal, containing only a few ornamental trees but there are wooded grounds at the rear, out of sight of the public. Montraya is basically the same. I cannot yet draw on the forest's power but it will come and perhaps Midnight can help." He gave a dazed smile. "I can't believe you'd do this for me."

"Well, we would," said Rainstorm shortly. He shrugged. "Anyway, it's not just for you. We had to think of something to cheer up Lapping Water." He grinned mischievously. "And she was very upset, so it took something quite radical."

"*Rainstorm. Shut up.*"

Tarkyn put his arm around her and kissed the top of her head. "Were you upset? So was I. I thought I had lost you, lost all of you. My whole world has been turned upside down twice today and now you've overset my assumptions again. But at least this time, it is something I am pleased about." He went on to tell them of the wizards' foreknowledge of his brothers' deaths.

"I'm glad we didn't know," muttered Waterstone. He gave a grim smile, "I'll have to thank Stormaway when I see him, for keeping that particular weight from your shoulders."

"Hmph. He will not be receiving my thanks for it."

"Of course not," replied Waterstone. "You could hardly thank him for not preventing the early demise of your brothers, but I can. He has served you truly, in the full knowledge that you would not be pleased."

"Stormaway and Caroman have acted independently and high-handedly for too long. This must be the end of it. I want no more secrets kept from me."

"Of course you don't, you dear boy. You have every right to feel angry." Summer Rain's eyes shone with unshed tears. "I was so worried for you when you were swept off by all those sorcerers after your brothers died. You were too dazed to know what you were doing. I thought you might drown in their demands."

As Tarkyn blinked in surprise at her unusual display of emotion, Waterstone chuckled. "You should have seen Summer Rain herding your sorcerers out of here to go to your aid. They hardly had time to catch their breath."

Summer Rain coloured and became very busy with stoking the fire.

"Thank you, Summer Rain. I was indeed beset on all sides, stunned by my brothers' deaths… and there was a sea of sorcerers between all of you and me. And thank you, Waterstone, for sending me that image of the soldiers barring Boravar and our sorcerers from reaching me." Tarkyn shook his head and scowled. "Trying to control my choice of associates from the moment they thought I was king."

"Is that why they did it? We thought the soldiers must have considered them a threat," said Rainstorm. "But I remember now. When you lived among sorcerers, you only associated with particular types of people, didn't you? Hmm. So, in your sorcerer society, Navira of course, Danton and the wizards would be the only sorcerers from our lot to be considered qualified, or whatever you call it, to stay with you. Correct?"

"According to protocol, yes."

Rainstorm grinned. "Just as well really. Boravar, the trappers, Harkell and his lot are all rubbish anyway, aren't they?"

Tarkyn's mouth thinned. "For your information, I have had Harkell with me during all the discussions so far."

"Yeah. That's now, when things are unsettled. What about when you return to court and your precious protocol reasserts itself?"

Tarkyn glared at him for several seconds. Then he gave a deep sigh. "That's just what I have been asking myself."

When everyone did nothing but wait expectantly, he continued, "Not only would it outrage some… many… most of the highborn families if I brought the sorcerers of my home guard to court, but my sorcerers would probably feel overawed and uncomfortable. Most commoners do, for the short time they attend court to present grievances. And some of those nobles wanting influence would scheme against them to ridicule and undermine them. Just because I might wish it, and I'm not sure that I do, it doesn't make it achievable."

There was a stunned silence.

"Wow," breathed Rainstorm. "At least you're honest."

Tarkyn's mouth quirked. "I will take that as meaning there is nothing else you approve of in what I just said. Even if I believed in complete equality, I could no more change sorcerer society, than I was able to change your egalitarian society. Admittedly, I will have significant influence. But if you remember, I had absolute sorcery-driven power over all of you when I first arrived, and even that was not enough to change your basic tenets."

"It might have been, over time, had you set up a hierarchy and enforced it," said Waterstone.

Tarkyn raised his eyebrows. "I doubt it. You are far stronger than that. But even so, I am still the same person I was then. I didn't force then and I won't force now."

"But it is so wrong, Tarkyn," exclaimed Lapping Water, her soft green eyes shining with indignation. "What about all those people in your prisons, just there for displeasing your brothers? What about all those people like Harkell, who want to choose what they do?"

Tarkyn removed his arm from around Lapping Water and stood up. For a moment he stood hands on hips, looking down at the seated woodfolk.

"I have never passed judgement on woodfolk society."

Without another word, he walked beyond the circle of light to the woodpile and spent some time selecting suitable branches before returning to feed them onto the fire.

As he straightened, Lapping Water took a deep breath. "Sorry, Tarkyn."

Tarkyn smiled wryly down at her. "Hmm. Sorry for upsetting me but not sorry for what you said. Anyway, I agree that the cases of those in prisons should be reviewed. My brothers were far too harsh." He sat down again and brushed the wood dust off his hands. "But our society has developed over centuries and cannot be so easily undone. Perhaps, sometime in the future, we could provide more opportunity for advancement through the classes for exceptional individuals, but I could not imagine dismantling, or even wishing to dismantle, our entire social system."

"Especially since you are at the top of it," said Rainstorm flippantly.

"Precisely." Tarkyn did not look amused. He looked around the firesite at the closed faces surrounding him. "I begin to wonder if I have erred in returning to you. Perhaps, after all, our values are too disparate."

Consternation flooded Rainstorm's face. He rushed to Tarkyn and grabbed his arm. "No, no, no. Don't think that. I was only joking. I know you wouldn't decide something based on self-interest. You know that, don't you? Sorry, sorry, sorry. I can see now that you're trying to talk your way through a dilemma and we are not being helpful, are we?"

Tarkyn couldn't help smiling. "No, you're not. You are badgering me and judging me, and judging my heritage. I'm telling you the reality of the situation. Whether it's right or wrong, it is what it is."

"Sorry, Tarkyn," said Waterstone, speaking for them all.

After a short silence, Rainstorm said, "Now don't take this as badgering. I'm just asking; how did lords become lords in the first place…or are they a different race? They don't look different, as far as I can see. And what about Stormaway? He seems to be some sort of lord but his father was a woodman."

"His mother was a noblewoman. Most wizards are." Tarkyn poured himself a new cup of tea before sitting down again. "Lords were granted their titles and lands generations ago, mostly during the wars against the Granthian invaders. Since then, in the years of peace, new titles have only been granted to members of those families."

There was a sudden stir as a message was received from the lookouts. Tarkyn was warned into silence.

Moments later, Harkell walked quietly into the firesite. He looked in surprise at the number of people gathered around the fire. "Hello. I didn't expect to see all of you up so late." He gave a rueful grimace.

"I've just had it up to the eyebrows with snide remarks and stony stares. So I thought I'd sneak back for a while to..." It was then he noticed Tarkyn sitting amongst them. "Oh." He sketched a bow, the picture of confusion. "I beg your pardon, Sire. I really did not mean to dog your footsteps. Please excuse me." He bowed again, turned on his heel and set off the way he had come.

"Not so quickly, Harkell."

Harkell stopped, turned and waited.

"Your letter has placed me on the horns of a dilemma."

Harkell smiled. "It was not intended to, Sire. It was intended to pave the way for my dismissal in the changed circumstances. I will always be your man but be assured, Sire, that I can find another path to follow. I will miss you, of course, but..."

"Harkell, stop. You realise that knowing you has made me question the very foundations of my beliefs. You are strong, true, courageous, clever... more so than many noblemen I could name and yet..."

"And yet I am a blacksmith's son." Years of hidden bitterness surfaced in Harkell's voice. "I understand, Sire. Believe me, I do. I don't like it but I understand. Please don't insult me by pandering to my vanity. Just as you know yours, I know my own worth and it has nothing to do with titles or nobility or birth. Let us just..."

"HARKELL. Be quiet... before you start to lose my goodwill." The prince stood up and waved Harkell to stand before him. "You will accompany me to Tormadell and remain with me until the investitures and celebrations are over. Then I will stay in Tormadell and our ways will part."

"Yes, Sire," said Harkell woodenly. "I am honoured to be included in such an occasion."

"*Harkell.* Don't be so bad tempered." Tarkyn took a deep breath as he reached an irrevocable decision. "And then Harkell, I want you to take up commission as General of the Montrayan army."

Harkell blinked. "I beg your pardon?"

"You heard me, you bad-tempered bastard. I want you to command the troops of Eskuzor's south."

For a full minute, Harkell stood dazed. Then he passed his hand across his forehead. "Really?"

"Really."

"What about General Maltran?"

"Retiring."

"And what about all those officers more senior than I?

"Are they better than you?"

"Well no, in fact many of them are younger and less experienced, just better connected. But they do have experience in commanding larger numbers."

"Are you saying you can't do it?"

For a moment, Harkell didn't answer. His soft brown eyes moved slowly from Tarkyn to the trees above him, to Autumn Leaves standing a little distance to his left, then around the full circle of woodfolk watching intently.

"Well?" pressed Tarkyn.

"Just thinking it through. I wouldn't want to give you an answer with no basis to it." Suddenly Harkell grinned. "Yes, I can do it. There will be some resistance to overcome, quite a lot actually. But yes, I can do it."

Tarkyn grunted. "It will not be easy. I will expect you to root out all practice of bullying and brutality. I want a disciplined army, proud to serve and protect the people of southern Eskuzor… and you."

Harkell's eyes shone with excitement. "We are of one accord."

"Now, give me your sword. On your knees."

Harkell's eyebrows twitched but he complied without question.

"You cannot win all the battles, Harkell. I will not have a commoner as the General of the South." Tarkyn smote him gently with the flat of his sword on each shoulder then on the crown of his head. "By the power invested in me as Guardian of the Forests and Prince of Eskuzor, I dub thee lord. Arise Harkell, Lord of… hmm…I'm not sure where. We will have to sort that out later. You can't have Montraya. Danton will have to hold that in trust for their firstborn. For now, arise Lord Harkell. We will do this publicly…and better, later." As Harkell rose and stood before him, Tarkyn grinned and handed him back his sword. "Besides Lady Kayama will want to see your investiture. So too will your children and the rest of your family."

"Well, that was interesting," said Rainstorm from the sidelines.

Waterstone laughed. "I have never seen you do anything so formal so casually, Tarkyn. I think you may have to sharpen up for your sorcerers." He strode over and slapped Harkell on the back. "Congratulations, Harkell. Titles may mean nothing to us but I know they mean a great deal to you."

Lord Harkell's soft brown eyes twinkled in the firelight. "My belief in the equality of all men makes me wish that this did not matter to me. But it does. Even the wildest dreams that I dared not contemplate, did not take me this far. I thank you, Tarkyn, for your willingness to change, without which this would never have been possible."

Tarkyn placed his hands on Harkell's shoulders. "Do not underrate yourself. I think several people can attest to the fact that I had no intention of breaking with sorcerer tradition. Take credit for the fact that I have. Everyone I spoke to considered you above and beyond, even Journeyman, until all I had left to argue against your appointment was my inbred prejudice."

"But, Sire, you *listened* to them." Harkell shook his head, laughing. On impulse, he stepped forward and to everyone's surprise, dragged Tarkyn into a huge bear hug. When he let go, Harkell grinned up at Tarkyn, who was looking a little stunned. "You too underestimate yourself. You *listen* and because of that, you will be the greatest Guardian that Eskuzor has ever known."

Jennifer Jane Ealey was born in outback Western Australia where her father was studying kangaroos on a research station, one hundred miles from the nearest town. Her arrival into the world was watched, unexpectedly, by their pet kangaroo who had hopped into the hospital. Having survived the excitement of her birth, she moved firstly to Perth and then Melbourne where she spent most of her formative years. She took a year off from studying to ride a motorbike around Australia before working as a mathematics teacher and school psychologist in England and Australia, a bicycle courier in London and running a pub in outback New South Wales.

She now lives in Melton, a country town just outside Melbourne, working by day as a psychologist and beavering away by night as a novelist. She has written two detective novels and has just completed *The Sorcerer's Oath*, a series of fantasy novels:

Bronze Magic, *Wizard's Curse*, *The Lost Forest*, and this final book *The Wizardess*.

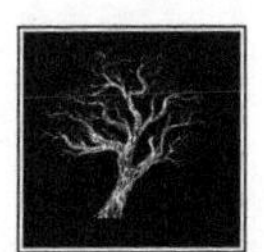

ESKUZOR PUBLISHING